P. G. Wodehouse

PSMITH - Complete Series

e-artnow 2022

P. G. Wodehouse
PSMITH - Complete Series

Mike, Mike and Psmith, Psmith in the City, The Prince and Betty and Psmith, Journalist

e-artnow, 2022
Contact: info@e-artnow.org

ISBN 978-80-273-4508-3

Contents

Mike	15
CHAPTER I: MIKE	16
CHAPTER II: THE JOURNEY DOWN	19
CHAPTER III: MIKE FINDS A FRIENDLY NATIVE	22
CHAPTER IV: AT THE NETS	25
CHAPTER V: REVELRY BY NIGHT	28
CHAPTER VI: IN WHICH A TIGHT CORNER IS EVADED	33
CHAPTER VII: IN WHICH MIKE IS DISCUSSED	36
CHAPTER VIII: A ROW WITH THE TOWN	40
CHAPTER IX: BEFORE THE STORM	44
CHAPTER X: THE GREAT PICNIC	48
CHAPTER XI: THE CONCLUSION OF THE PICNIC	51
CHAPTER XII: MIKE GETS HIS CHANCE	54
CHAPTER XIII: THE M.C.C. MATCH	58
CHAPTER XIV: A SLIGHT IMBROGLIO	63
CHAPTER XV: MIKE CREATES A VACANCY	66
CHAPTER XVI: AN EXPERT EXAMINATION	70
CHAPTER XVII: ANOTHER VACANCY	73
CHAPTER XVIII: BOB HAS NEWS TO IMPART	76
CHAPTER XIX: MIKE GOES TO SLEEP AGAIN	79
CHAPTER XX: THE TEAM IS FILLED UP	84
CHAPTER XXI: MARJORY THE FRANK	87
CHAPTER XXII: WYATT IS REMINDED OF AN ENGAGEMENT	91
CHAPTER XXIII: A SURPRISE FOR MR. APPLEBY	94
CHAPTER XXIV: CAUGHT	97
CHAPTER XXV: MARCHING ORDERS	100
CHAPTER XXVI: THE AFTERMATH	103
CHAPTER XXVII: THE RIPTON MATCH	107
CHAPTER XXVIII: MIKE WINS HOME	111
CHAPTER XXIX: WYATT AGAIN	117
CHAPTER XXX: MR. JACKSON MAKES UP HIS MIND	119
CHAPTER XXXI: SEDLEIGH	122
CHAPTER XXXII: PSMITH	125
CHAPTER XXXIII: STAKING OUT A CLAIM	128
CHAPTER XXXIV: :GUERRILLA WARFARE	133
CHAPTER XXXV: UNPLEASANTNESS IN THE SMALL HOURS	137
CHAPTER XXXVI: ADAIR	141
CHAPTER XXXVII: MIKE FINDS OCCUPATION	144

CHAPTER XXXVIII: THE FIRE BRIGADE MEETING	147
CHAPTER XXXIX: ACHILLES LEAVES HIS TENT	151
CHAPTER XL: THE MATCH WITH DOWNING'S	155
CHAPTER XLI: THE SINGULAR BEHAVIOUR OF JELLICOE	161
CHAPTER XLII: JELLICOE GOES ON THE SICK-LIST	164
CHAPTER XLIII: MIKE RECEIVES A COMMISSION	166
CHAPTER XLIV: AND FULFILS IT	169
CHAPTER XLV: PURSUIT	172
CHAPTER XLVI: THE DECORATION OF SAMMY	176
CHAPTER XLVII: MR. DOWNING ON THE SCENT	178
CHAPTER XLVIII: THE SLEUTH-HOUND	182
CHAPTER XLIX: A CHECK	185
CHAPTER L: THE DESTROYER OF EVIDENCE	189
CHAPTER LI: MAINLY ABOUT BOOTS	193
CHAPTER LII: ON THE TRAIL AGAIN	198
CHAPTER LIII: THE KETTLE METHOD	200
CHAPTER LIV: ADAIR HAS A WORD WITH MIKE	204
CHAPTER LV: CLEARING THE AIR	207
CHAPTER LVI: IN WHICH PEACE IS DECLARED	210
CHAPTER LVII: MR. DOWNING MOVES	214
CHAPTER LVIII: THE ARTIST CLAIMS HIS WORK	219
CHAPTER LIX: SEDLEIGH v. WRYKYN	224

Mike and Psmith		227
1	: MR. JACKSON MAKES UP HIS MIND	228
2	: SEDLEIGH	231
3	: PSMITH	234
4	: STAKING OUT A CLAIM	237
5	: GUERRILLA WARFARE	241
6	: UNPLEASANTNESS IN THE SMALL HOURS	245
7	: ADAIR	248
8	: MIKE FINDS OCCUPATION	251
9	: THE FIRE BRIGADE MEETING	255
10	: ACHILLES LEAVES HIS TENT	259
11	: THE MATCH WITH DOWNING'S	262
12	: THE SINGULAR BEHAVIOR OF JELLICOE	267
13	: JELLICOE GOES ON THE SICK LIST	270
14	: MIKE RECEIVES A COMMISSION	272
15	: ... AND FULFILLS IT	275
16	: PURSUIT	278
17	: THE DECORATION OF SAMMY	282

18	: MR. DOWNING ON THE SCENT	284
19	: THE SLEUTH-HOUND	287
20	: A CHECK	291
21	: THE DESTROYER OF EVIDENCE	295
22	: MAINLY ABOUT SHOES	299
23	: ON THE TRAIL AGAIN	303
24	: THE ADAIR METHOD	305
25	: ADAIR HAS A WORD WITH MIKE	309
26	: CLEARING THE AIR	312
27	: IN WHICH PEACE IS DECLARED	315
28	: MR. DOWNING MOVEs	319
29	: THE ARTIST CLAIMS HIS WORK	323
30	: SEDLEIGH V. WRYKYN	328

Psmith in the City — 331

1.	Mr Bickersdyke Walks behind the Bowler's Arm	332
2.	Mike Hears Bad News	336
3.	The New Era Begins	338
4.	First Steps in a Business Career	341
5.	The Other Man	344
6.	Psmith Explains	346
7.	Going into Winter Quarters	349
8.	The Friendly Native	352
9.	The Haunting of Mr Bickersdyke	356
10.	Mr Bickersdyke Addresses His Constituents	359
11.	Misunderstood	362
12.	In a Nutshell	365
13.	Mike is Moved On	368
14.	Mr Waller Appears in a New Light	370
15.	Stirring Times on the Common	373
16.	Further Developments	377
17.	Sunday Supper	380
18.	Psmith Makes a Discovery	384
19.	The Illness of Edward	387
20.	Concerning a Cheque	390
21.	Psmith Makes Inquiries	393
22.	And Take Steps	396
23.	Mr Bickersdyke Makes a Concession	398
24.	The Spirit of Unrest	402

25. At the Telephone	405
26. Breaking The News	407
27. At Lord's	410
28. Psmith Arranges his Future	414
29. And Mike's	417
30. The Last Sad Farewells	420
The Prince and Betty	423
CHAPTER I: THE CABLE PROM MERVO	424
CHAPTER II: MERVO AND ITS OWNER	427
CHAPTER III: JOHN	432
CHAPTER IV: VIVE LE ROI!	436
CHAPTER V: MR. SCOBELL HAS ANOTHER IDEA	440
CHAPTER VI: YOUNG ADAM CUPID	444
CHAPTER VII: MR. SCOBELL IS FRANK	447
CHAPTER VIII: AN ULTIMATUM FROM THE THRONE	451
CHAPTER IX: MERVO CHANGES ITS CONSTITUTION	455
CHAPTER X: MRS. OAKLEY	460
CHAPTER XI: A LETTER OF INTRODUCTION	463
CHAPTER XII "PEACEFUL MOMENTS"	467
CHAPTER XIII: BETTY MAKES A FRIEND	471
CHAPTER XIV: A CHANGE OF POLICY	475
CHAPTER XV: THE HONEYED WORD	479
CHAPTER XVI: TWO VISITORS TO THE OFFICE	482
CHAPTER XVII: THE MAN AT THE ASTOR	487
CHAPTER XVIII: THE HIGHFIELD	492
CHAPTER XIX: THE FIRST BATTLE	497
CHAPTER XX: BETTY AT LARGE	501
CHAPTER XXI: CHANGES IN THE STAFF	505
CHAPTER XXII: A GATHERING OF CAT SPECIALISTS	508
CHAPTER XXIII: THE RETIREMENT OF SMITH	511
CHAPTER XXIV: THE CAMPAIGN QUICKENS	514
CHAPTER XXV: CORNERED	518
CHAPTER XXVI: JOURNEY'S END	521
CHAPTER XXVII: A LEMON	525
CHAPTER XXVIII: THE FINAL ATTEMPT	530
CHAPTER XXIX: A REPRESENTATIVE GATHERING	534
CHAPTER XXX: CONCLUSION	539
Psmith, Journalist	541
CHAPTER I: "COSY MOMENTS"	542

CHAPTER II: BILLY WINDSOR	545
CHAPTER III: AT "THE GARDENIA"	547
CHAPTER IV: BAT JARVIS	550
CHAPTER V: PLANNING IMPROVEMENTS	553
CHAPTER VI: THE TENEMENTS	556
CHAPTER VII: VISITORS AT THE OFFICE	559
CHAPTER VIII: THE HONEYED WORD	561
CHAPTER IX: FULL STEAM AHEAD	565
CHAPTER X: GOING SOME	568
CHAPTER XI: THE MAN AT THE ASTOR	573
CHAPTER XII: A RED TAXIMETER	577
CHAPTER XIII: REVIEWING THE SITUATION	580
CHAPTER XIV: THE HIGHFIELD	583
CHAPTER XV: AN ADDITION TO THE STAFF	587
CHAPTER XVI: THE FIRST BATTLE	590
CHAPTER XVII: GUERILLA WARFARE	595
CHAPTER XVIII: AN EPISODE BY THE WAY	598
CHAPTER XIX: IN PLEASANT STREET	601
CHAPTER XX: CORNERED	604
CHAPTER XXI: THE BATTLE OF PLEASANT STREET	608
CHAPTER XXII: CONCERNING MR. WARING	612
CHAPTER XXIII: REDUCTIONS IN THE STAFF	615
CHAPTER XXIV: A GATHERING OF CAT-SPECIALISTS	620
CHAPTER XXV: TRAPPED	625
CHAPTER XXVI: A FRIEND IN NEED	630
CHAPTER XXVII: PSMITH CONCLUDES HIS RIDE	633
CHAPTER XXVIII: STANDING ROOM ONLY	636
CHAPTER XXIX: THE KNOCK-OUT FOR MR. WARING	640
CONCLUSION	644

Mike

CHAPTER I

MIKE

It was a morning in the middle of April, and the Jackson family were consequently breakfasting in comparative silence.; The cricket season had not begun, and except during the cricket season they were in the habit of devoting their powerful minds at breakfast almost exclusively to the task of victualling against the labours of the day.; In May, June, July, and August the silence was broken.; The three grown-up Jacksons played regularly in first-class cricket, and there was always keen competition among their brothers and sisters for the copy of the *Sportsman* which was to be found on the hall table with the letters.; Whoever got it usually gloated over it in silence till urged wrathfully by the multitude to let them know what had happened; when it would appear that Joe had notched his seventh century, or that Reggie had been run out when he was just getting set, or, as sometimes occurred, that that ass Frank had dropped Fry or Hayward in the slips before he had scored, with the result that the spared expert had made a couple of hundred and was still going strong.

In such a case the criticisms of the family circle, particularly of the smaller Jackson sisters, were so breezy and unrestrained that Mrs. Jackson generally felt it necessary to apply the closure.; Indeed, Marjory Jackson, aged fourteen, had on three several occasions been fined pudding at lunch for her caustic comments on the batting of her brother Reggie in important fixtures.; Cricket was a tradition in the family, and the ladies, unable to their sorrow to play the game themselves, were resolved that it should not be their fault if the standard was not kept up.

On this particular morning silence reigned.; A deep gasp from some small Jackson, wrestling with bread-and-milk, and an occasional remark from Mr. Jackson on the letters he was reading, alone broke it.

"Mike's late again," said Mrs. Jackson plaintively, at last.

"He's getting up," said Marjory.; "I went in to see what he was doing, and he was asleep.; So," she added with a satanic chuckle, "I squeezed a sponge over him.; He swallowed an awful lot, and then he woke up, and tried to catch me, so he's certain to be down soon."

"Marjory!"

"Well, he was on his back with his mouth wide open.; I had to.; He was snoring like anything."

"You might have choked him."

"I did," said Marjory with satisfaction.; "Jam, please, Phyllis, you pig."

Mr. Jackson looked up.

"Mike will have to be more punctual when he goes to Wrykyn," he said.

"Oh, father, is Mike going to Wrykyn?" asked Marjory.; "When?"

"Next term," said Mr. Jackson.; "I've just heard from Mr. Wain," he added across the table to Mrs. Jackson.; "The house is full, but he is turning a small room into an extra dormitory, so he can take Mike after all."

The first comment on this momentous piece of news came from Bob Jackson.; Bob was eighteen.; The following term would be his last at Wrykyn, and, having won through so far without the infliction of a small brother, he disliked the prospect of not being allowed to finish as he had begun.

"I say!" he said.; "What?"

"He ought to have gone before," said Mr. Jackson.; "He's fifteen.; Much too old for that private school.; He has had it all his own way there, and it isn't good for him."

"He's got cheek enough for ten," agreed Bob.

"Wrykyn will do him a world of good."

"We aren't in the same house.; That's one comfort."

Bob was in Donaldson's.; It softened the blow to a certain extent that Mike should be going to Wain's.; He had the same feeling for Mike that most boys of eighteen have for their fifteen-year-old brothers.; He was fond of him in the abstract, but preferred him at a distance.

Marjory gave tongue again.; She had rescued the jam from Phyllis, who had shown signs of finishing it, and was now at liberty to turn her mind to less pressing matters.; Mike was her special ally, and anything that affected his fortunes affected her.

"Hooray!; Mike's going to Wrykyn.; I bet he gets into the first eleven his first term."

"Considering there are eight old colours left," said Bob loftily, "besides heaps of last year's seconds, it's hardly likely that a kid like Mike'll get a look in.; He might get his third, if he sweats."

The aspersion stung Marjory.

"I bet he gets in before you, anyway," she said.

Bob disdained to reply.; He was among those heaps of last year's seconds to whom he had referred.; He was a sound bat, though lacking the brilliance of his elder brothers, and he fancied that his cap was a certainty this season.; Last year he had been tried once or twice.; This year it should be all right.

Mrs. Jackson intervened.

"Go on with your breakfast, Marjory," she said.; "You mustn't say 'I bet' so much."

Marjory bit off a section of her slice of bread-and-jam.

"Anyhow, I bet he does," she muttered truculently through it.

There was a sound of footsteps in the passage outside.; The door opened, and the missing member of the family appeared.; Mike Jackson was tall for his age.; His figure was thin and wiry.; His arms and legs looked a shade too long for his body.; He was evidently going to be very tall some day.; In face, he was curiously like his brother Joe, whose appearance is familiar to every one who takes an interest in first-class cricket.; The resemblance was even more marked on the cricket field.; Mike had Joe's batting style to the last detail.; He was a pocket edition of his century-making brother.; "Hullo," he said, "sorry I'm late."

This was mere stereo.; He had made the same remark nearly every morning since the beginning of the holidays.

"All right, Marjory, you little beast," was his reference to the sponge incident.

His third remark was of a practical nature.

"I say, what's under that dish?"

"Mike," began Mr. Jackson —this again was stereo —"you really must learn to be more punctual — —"

He was interrupted by a chorus.

"Mike, you're going to Wrykyn next term," shouted Marjory.

"Mike, father's just had a letter to say you're going to Wrykyn next term."; From Phyllis.

"Mike, you're going to Wrykyn."; From Ella.

Gladys Maud Evangeline, aged three, obliged with a solo of her own composition, in six-eight time, as follows:; "Mike Wryky.; Mike Wryky.; Mike Wryke Wryke Wryke Mike Wryke Wryke Mike Wryke Mike Wryke."

"Oh, put a green baize cloth over that kid, somebody," groaned Bob.

Whereat Gladys Maud, having fixed him with a chilly stare for some seconds, suddenly drew a long breath, and squealed deafeningly for more milk.

Mike looked round the table.; It was a great moment.; He rose to it with the utmost dignity.

"Good," he said.; "I say, what's under that dish?"

* * * * *

After breakfast, Mike and Marjory went off together to the meadow at the end of the garden.; Saunders, the professional, assisted by the gardener's boy, was engaged in putting up the net.; Mr. Jackson believed in private coaching; and every spring since Joe, the eldest of the family, had been able to use a bat a man had come down from the Oval to teach him the best way to do so.; Each of the boys in turn had passed from spectators to active participants in the net practice in the meadow.; For several years now Saunders had been the chosen man, and his attitude towards the Jacksons was that of the Faithful Old Retainer in melodrama.; Mike was his special favourite.; He felt that in him he had material of the finest order to work upon.; There was nothing the matter about Bob.; In Bob he would turn out a good, sound article.; Bob would be a Blue in his third or fourth year, and probably a creditable performer among the rank and file of a county team later on.; But he was not a cricket genius, like Mike.; Saunders would lie awake at night sometimes thinking of the possibilities that were in Mike.; The strength could only come with years, but the style was there already.; Joe's style, with improvements.

Mike put on his pads; and Marjory walked with the professional to the bowling crease.

"Mike's going to Wrykyn next term, Saunders," she said.; "All the boys were there, you know.; So was father, ages ago."

"Is he, miss?; I was thinking he would be soon."

"Do you think he'll get into the school team?"

"School team, miss!; Master Mike get into a school team!; He'll be playing for England in another eight years.; That's what he'll be playing for."

"Yes, but I meant next term.; It would be a record if he did.; Even Joe only got in after he'd been at school two years.; Don't you think he might, Saunders?; He's awfully good, isn't he?; He's better than Bob, isn't he?; And Bob's almost certain to get in this term."

Saunders looked a little doubtful.

"Next term!" he said.; "Well, you see, miss, it's this way.; It's all there, in a manner of speaking, with Master Mike.; He's got as much style as Mr. Joe's got, every bit.; The whole thing is, you see, miss, you get these young gentlemen of eighteen, and nineteen perhaps, and it stands to reason they're stronger.; There's a young gentleman, perhaps, doesn't know as much about what I call real playing as Master Mike's forgotten; but then he can hit 'em harder when he does hit 'em, and that's where the runs come in.; They aren't going to play Master Mike because he'll be in the England team when he leaves school.; They'll give the cap to somebody that can make a few then and there."

"But Mike's jolly strong."

"Ah, I'm not saying it mightn't be, miss.; I was only saying don't count on it, so you won't be disappointed if it doesn't happen.; It's quite likely that it will, only all I say is don't count on it.; I only hope that they won't knock all the style out of him before they're done with him.; You know these school professionals, miss."

"No, I don't, Saunders.; What are they like?"

"Well, there's too much of the come-right-out-at-everything about 'em for my taste.; Seem to think playing forward the alpha and omugger of batting.; They'll make him pat balls back to the bowler which he'd cut for twos and threes if he was left to himself.; Still, we'll hope for the best, miss.; Ready, Master Mike?; Play."

As Saunders had said, it was all there.; Of Mike's style there could be no doubt.; To-day, too, he was playing more strongly than usual.; Marjory had to run to the end of the meadow to fetch one straight drive.; "He hit that hard enough, didn't he, Saunders?" she asked, as she returned the ball.

"If he could keep on doing ones like that, miss," said the professional, "they'd have him in the team before you could say knife."

Marjory sat down again beside the net, and watched more hopefully.

CHAPTER II

THE JOURNEY DOWN

The seeing off of Mike on the last day of the holidays was an imposing spectacle, a sort of pageant.; Going to a public school, especially at the beginning of the summer term, is no great hardship, more particularly when the departing hero has a brother on the verge of the school eleven and three other brothers playing for counties; and Mike seemed in no way disturbed by the prospect.; Mothers, however, to the end of time will foster a secret fear that their sons will be bullied at a big school, and Mrs. Jackson's anxious look lent a fine solemnity to the proceedings.

And as Marjory, Phyllis, and Ella invariably broke down when the time of separation arrived, and made no exception to their rule on the present occasion, a suitable gloom was the keynote of the gathering.; Mr. Jackson seemed to bear the parting with fortitude, as did Mike's Uncle John (providentially roped in at the eleventh hour on his way to Scotland, in time to come down with a handsome tip).; To their coarse-fibred minds there was nothing pathetic or tragic about the affair at all. (At the very moment when the train began to glide out of the station Uncle John was heard to remark that, in his opinion, these Bocks weren't a patch on the old shaped Larranaga.) Among others present might have been noticed Saunders, practising late cuts rather coyly with a walking-stick in the background; the village idiot, who had rolled up on the chance of a dole; Gladys Maud Evangeline's nurse, smiling vaguely; and Gladys Maud Evangeline herself, frankly bored with the whole business.

The train gathered speed.; The air was full of last messages.; Uncle John said on second thoughts he wasn't sure these Bocks weren't half a bad smoke after all.; Gladys Maud cried, because she had taken a sudden dislike to the village idiot; and Mike settled himself in the corner and opened a magazine.

He was alone in the carriage.; Bob, who had been spending the last week of the holidays with an aunt further down the line, was to board the train at East Wobsley, and the brothers were to make a state entry into Wrykyn together.; Meanwhile, Mike was left to his milk chocolate, his magazines, and his reflections.

The latter were not numerous, nor profound.; He was excited.; He had been petitioning the home authorities for the past year to be allowed to leave his private school and go to Wrykyn, and now the thing had come about.; He wondered what sort of a house Wain's was, and whether they had any chance of the cricket cup.; According to Bob they had no earthly; but then Bob only recognised one house, Donaldson's.; He wondered if Bob would get his first eleven cap this year, and if he himself were likely to do anything at cricket.; Marjory had faithfully reported every word Saunders had said on the subject, but Bob had been so careful to point out his insignificance when compared with the humblest Wrykynian that the professional's glowing prophecies had not had much effect.; It might be true that some day he would play for England, but just at present he felt he would exchange his place in the team for one in the Wrykyn third eleven.; A sort of mist enveloped everything Wrykynian.; It seemed almost hopeless to try and compete with these unknown experts.; On the other hand, there was Bob.; Bob, by all accounts, was on the verge of the first eleven, and he was nothing special.

While he was engaged on these reflections, the train drew up at a small station.; Opposite the door of Mike's compartment was standing a boy of about Mike's size, though evidently some years older.; He had a sharp face, with rather a prominent nose; and a pair of pince-nez gave him a supercilious look.; He wore a bowler hat, and carried a small portmanteau.

He opened the door, and took the seat opposite to Mike, whom he scrutinised for a moment rather after the fashion of a naturalist examining some new and unpleasant variety of beetle.; He seemed about to make some remark, but, instead, got up and looked through the open window.

"Where's that porter?" Mike heard him say.

The porter came skimming down the platform at that moment.

"Porter."

"Sir?"

"Are those frightful boxes of mine in all right?"

"Yes, sir."

"Because, you know, there'll be a frightful row if any of them get lost."

"No chance of that, sir."

"Here you are, then."

"Thank you, sir."

The youth drew his head and shoulders in, stared at Mike again, and finally sat down.; Mike noticed that he had nothing to read, and wondered if he wanted anything; but he did not feel equal to offering him one of his magazines.; He did not like the looks of him particularly.; Judging by appearances, he seemed to carry enough side for three.; If he wanted a magazine, thought Mike, let him ask for it.

The other made no overtures, and at the next stop got out.; That explained his magazineless condition.; He was only travelling a short way.

"Good business," said Mike to himself.; He had all the Englishman's love of a carriage to himself.

The train was just moving out of the station when his eye was suddenly caught by the stranger's bag, lying snugly in the rack.

And here, I regret to say, Mike acted from the best motives, which is always fatal.

He realised in an instant what had happened.; The fellow had forgotten his bag.

Mike had not been greatly fascinated by the stranger's looks; but, after all, the most supercilious person on earth has a right to his own property.; Besides, he might have been quite a nice fellow when you got to know him.; Anyhow, the bag had better be returned at once.; The train was already moving quite fast, and Mike's compartment was nearing the end of the platform.

He snatched the bag from the rack and hurled it out of the window.; (Porter Robinson, who happened to be in the line of fire, escaped with a flesh wound.) Then he sat down again with the inward glow of satisfaction which comes to one when one has risen successfully to a sudden emergency.

* * * * *

The glow lasted till the next stoppage, which did not occur for a good many miles.; Then it ceased abruptly, for the train had scarcely come to a standstill when the opening above the door was darkened by a head and shoulders.; The head was surmounted by a bowler, and a pair of pince-nez gleamed from the shadow.

"Hullo, I say," said the stranger.; "Have you changed carriages, or what?"

"No," said Mike.

"Then, dash it, where's my frightful bag?"

Life teems with embarrassing situations.; This was one of them.

"The fact is," said Mike, "I chucked it out."

"Chucked it out! what do you mean?; When?"

"At the last station."

The guard blew his whistle, and the other jumped into the carriage.

"I thought you'd got out there for good," explained Mike.; "I'm awfully sorry."

"Where *is* the bag?"

"On the platform at the last station.; It hit a porter."

Against his will, for he wished to treat the matter with fitting solemnity, Mike grinned at the recollection.; The look on Porter Robinson's face as the bag took him in the small of the back had been funny, though not intentionally so.

The bereaved owner disapproved of this levity; and said as much.

"Don't *grin*, you little beast," he shouted.; "There's nothing to laugh at.; You go chucking bags that don't belong to you out of the window, and then you have the frightful cheek to grin about it."

"It wasn't that," said Mike hurriedly.; "Only the porter looked awfully funny when it hit him."

"Dash the porter!; What's going to happen about my bag?; I can't get out for half a second to buy a magazine without your flinging my things about the platform.; What you want is a frightful kicking."

The situation was becoming difficult.; But fortunately at this moment the train stopped once again; and, looking out of the window, Mike saw a board with East Wobsley upon it in large letters.; A moment later Bob's head appeared in the doorway.

"Hullo, there you are," said Bob.

His eye fell upon Mike's companion.

"Hullo, Gazeka!" he exclaimed.; "Where did you spring from?; Do you know my brother?; He's coming to Wrykyn this term.; By the way, rather lucky you've met.; He's in your house.; Firby-Smith's head of Wain's, Mike."

Mike gathered that Gazeka and Firby-Smith were one and the same person.; He grinned again.; Firby-Smith continued to look ruffled, though not aggressive.

"Oh, are you in Wain's?" he said.

"I say, Bob," said Mike, "I've made rather an ass of myself."

"Naturally."

"I mean, what happened was this.; I chucked Firby-Smith's portmanteau out of the window, thinking he'd got out, only he hadn't really, and it's at a station miles back."

"You're a bit of a rotter, aren't you?; Had it got your name and address on it, Gazeka?"

"Yes."

"Oh, then it's certain to be all right.; It's bound to turn up some time.; They'll send it on by the next train, and you'll get it either to-night or to-morrow."

"Frightful nuisance, all the same.; Lots of things in it I wanted."

"Oh, never mind, it's all right.; I say, what have you been doing in the holidays?; I didn't know you lived on this line at all."

From this point onwards Mike was out of the conversation altogether.; Bob and Firby-Smith talked of Wrykyn, discussing events of the previous term of which Mike had never heard.; Names came into their conversation which were entirely new to him.; He realised that school politics were being talked, and that contributions from him to the dialogue were not required.; He took up his magazine again, listening the while.; They were discussing Wain's now.; The name Wyatt cropped up with some frequency.; Wyatt was apparently something of a character.; Mention was made of rows in which he had played a part in the past.

"It must be pretty rotten for him," said Bob.; "He and Wain never get on very well, and yet they have to be together, holidays as well as term.; Pretty bad having a step-father at all—I shouldn't care to—and when your house-master and your step-father are the same man, it's a bit thick."

"Frightful," agreed Firby-Smith.

"I swear, if I were in Wyatt's place, I should rot about like anything.; It isn't as if he'd anything to look forward to when he leaves.; He told me last term that Wain had got a nomination for him in some beastly bank, and that he was going into it directly after the end of this term.; Rather rough on a chap like Wyatt.; Good cricketer and footballer, I mean, and all that sort of thing.; It's just the sort of life he'll hate most.; Hullo, here we are."

Mike looked out of the window.; It was Wrykyn at last.

CHAPTER III

MIKE FINDS A FRIENDLY NATIVE

Mike was surprised to find, on alighting, that the platform was entirely free from Wrykynians.; In all the stories he had read the whole school came back by the same train, and, having smashed in one another's hats and chaffed the porters, made their way to the school buildings in a solid column.; But here they were alone.

A remark of Bob's to Firby-Smith explained this.; "Can't make out why none of the fellows came back by this train," he said.; "Heaps of them must come by this line, and it's the only Christian train they run,"

"Don't want to get here before the last minute they can possibly manage.; Silly idea.; I suppose they think there'd be nothing to do."

"What shall *we* do?" said Bob.; "Come and have some tea at Cook's?"

"All right."

Bob looked at Mike.; There was no disguising the fact that he would be in the way; but how convey this fact delicately to him?

"Look here, Mike," he said, with a happy inspiration, "Firby-Smith and I are just going to get some tea.; I think you'd better nip up to the school.; Probably Wain will want to see you, and tell you all about things, which is your dorm. and so on.; See you later," he concluded airily.; "Any one'll tell you the way to the school.; Go straight on.; They'll send your luggage on later.; So long."; And his sole prop in this world of strangers departed, leaving him to find his way for himself.

There is no subject on which opinions differ so widely as this matter of finding the way to a place.; To the man who knows, it is simplicity itself.; Probably he really does imagine that he goes straight on, ignoring the fact that for him the choice of three roads, all more or less straight, has no perplexities.; The man who does not know feels as if he were in a maze.

Mike started out boldly, and lost his way.; Go in which direction he would, he always seemed to arrive at a square with a fountain and an equestrian statue in its centre.; On the fourth repetition of this feat he stopped in a disheartened way, and looked about him.; He was beginning to feel bitter towards Bob.; The man might at least have shown him where to get some tea.

At this moment a ray of hope shone through the gloom.; Crossing the square was a short, thick-set figure clad in grey flannel trousers, a blue blazer, and a straw hat with a coloured band.; Plainly a Wrykynian.; Mike made for him.

"Can you tell me the way to the school, please," he said.

"Oh, you're going to the school," said the other.; He had a pleasant, square-jawed face, reminiscent of a good-tempered bull-dog, and a pair of very deep-set grey eyes which somehow put Mike at his ease.; There was something singularly cool and genial about them.; He felt that they saw the humour in things, and that their owner was a person who liked most people and whom most people liked.

"You look rather lost," said the stranger.; "Been hunting for it long?"

"Yes," said Mike.

"Which house do you want?"

"Wain's."

"Wain's?; Then you've come to the right man this time.; What I don't know about Wain's isn't worth knowing."

"Are you there, too?"

"Am I not!; Term *and* holidays.; There's no close season for me."

"Oh, are you Wyatt, then?" asked Mike.

"Hullo, this is fame.; How did you know my name, as the ass in the detective story always says to the detective, who's seen it in the lining of his hat?; Who's been talking about me?"

"I heard my brother saying something about you in the train."

"Who's your brother?"

"Jackson.; He's in Donaldson's."

"I know.; A stout fellow.; So you're the newest make of Jackson, latest model, with all the modern improvements?; Are there any more of you?"

"Not brothers," said Mike.

"Pity.; You can't quite raise a team, then?; Are you a sort of young Tyldesley, too?"

"I played a bit at my last school.; Only a private school, you know," added Mike modestly.

"Make any runs?; What was your best score?"

"Hundred and twenty-three," said Mike awkwardly.; "It was only against kids, you know."; He was in terror lest he should seem to be bragging.

"That's pretty useful.; Any more centuries?"

"Yes," said Mike, shuffling.

"How many?"

"Seven altogether.; You know, it was really awfully rotten bowling.; And I was a good bit bigger than most of the chaps there.; And my pater always has a pro. down in the Easter holidays, which gave me a bit of an advantage."

"All the same, seven centuries isn't so dusty against any bowling.; We shall want some batting in the house this term.; Look here, I was just going to have some tea.; You come along, too."

"Oh, thanks awfully," said Mike.; "My brother and Firby-Smith have gone to a place called Cook's."

"The old Gazeka?; I didn't know he lived in your part of the world.; He's head of Wain's."

"Yes, I know," said Mike.; "Why is he called Gazeka?" he asked after a pause.

"Don't you think he looks like one?; What did you think of him?"

"I didn't speak to him much," said Mike cautiously.; It is always delicate work answering a question like this unless one has some sort of an inkling as to the views of the questioner.

"He's all right," said Wyatt, answering for himself.; "He's got a habit of talking to one as if he were a prince of the blood dropping a gracious word to one of the three Small-Heads at the Hippodrome, but that's his misfortune.; We all have our troubles.; That's his.; Let's go in here.; It's too far to sweat to Cook's."

It was about a mile from the tea-shop to the school.; Mike's first impression on arriving at the school grounds was of his smallness and insignificance.; Everything looked so big—the buildings, the grounds, everything.; He felt out of the picture.; He was glad that he had met Wyatt.; To make his entrance into this strange land alone would have been more of an ordeal than he would have cared to face.

"That's Wain's," said Wyatt, pointing to one of half a dozen large houses which lined the road on the south side of the cricket field.; Mike followed his finger, and took in the size of his new home.

"I say, it's jolly big," he said.; "How many fellows are there in it?"

"Thirty-one this term, I believe."

"That's more than there were at King-Hall's."

"What's King-Hall's?"

"The private school I was at.; At Emsworth."

Emsworth seemed very remote and unreal to him as he spoke.

They skirted the cricket field, walking along the path that divided the two terraces.; The Wrykyn playing-fields were formed of a series of huge steps, cut out of the hill.; At the top of the hill came the school.; On the first terrace was a sort of informal practice ground, where, though no games were played on it, there was a good deal of punting and drop-kicking in the winter and fielding-practice in the summer.; The next terrace was the biggest of all, and formed the first eleven cricket ground, a beautiful piece of turf, a shade too narrow for its length, bounded on the terrace side by a sharply sloping bank, some fifteen feet deep, and on the other by the precipice leading to the next terrace.; At the far end of the ground stood the pavilion,

23

and beside it a little ivy-covered rabbit-hutch for the scorers.; Old Wrykynians always claimed that it was the prettiest school ground in England.; It certainly had the finest view.; From the verandah of the pavilion you could look over three counties.

Wain's house wore an empty and desolate appearance.; There were signs of activity, however, inside; and a smell of soap and warm water told of preparations recently completed.

Wyatt took Mike into the matron's room, a small room opening out of the main passage.

"This is Jackson," he said.; "Which dormitory is he in, Miss Payne?"

The matron consulted a paper.

"He's in yours, Wyatt."

"Good business.; Who's in the other bed?; There are going to be three of us, aren't there?"

"Fereira was to have slept there, but we have just heard that he is not coming back this term.; He has had to go on a sea-voyage for his health."

"Seems queer any one actually taking the trouble to keep Fereira in the world," said Wyatt.; "I've often thought of giving him Rough On Rats myself.; Come along, Jackson, and I'll show you the room."

They went along the passage, and up a flight of stairs.

"Here you are," said Wyatt.

It was a fair-sized room.; The window, heavily barred, looked out over a large garden.

"I used to sleep here alone last term," said Wyatt, "but the house is so full now they've turned it into a dormitory."

"I say, I wish these bars weren't here.; It would be rather a rag to get out of the window on to that wall at night, and hop down into the garden and explore," said Mike.

Wyatt looked at him curiously, and moved to the window.

"I'm not going to let you do it, of course," he said, "because you'd go getting caught, and dropped on, which isn't good for one in one's first term; but just to amuse you ———"

He jerked at the middle bar, and the next moment he was standing with it in his hand, and the way to the garden was clear.

"By Jove!" said Mike.

"That's simply an object-lesson, you know," said Wyatt, replacing the bar, and pushing the screws back into their putty.; "I get out at night myself because I think my health needs it.; Besides, it's my last term, anyhow, so it doesn't matter what I do.; But if I find you trying to cut out in the small hours, there'll be trouble.; See?"

"All right," said Mike, reluctantly.; "But I wish you'd let me."

"Not if I know it.; Promise you won't try it on."

"All right.; But, I say, what do you do out there?"

"I shoot at cats with an air-pistol, the beauty of which is that even if you hit them it doesn't hurt—simply keeps them bright and interested in life; and if you miss you've had all the fun anyhow.; Have you ever shot at a rocketing cat?; Finest mark you can have.; Society's latest craze.; Buy a pistol and see life."

"I wish you'd let me come."

"I daresay you do.; Not much, however.; Now, if you like, I'll take you over the rest of the school.; You'll have to see it sooner or later, so you may as well get it over at once."

CHAPTER IV

AT THE NETS

There are few better things in life than a public school summer term.; The winter term is good, especially towards the end, and there are points, though not many, about the Easter term:; but it is in the summer that one really appreciates public school life.; The freedom of it, after the restrictions of even the most easy-going private school, is intoxicating.; The change is almost as great as that from public school to 'Varsity.

For Mike the path was made particularly easy.; The only drawback to going to a big school for the first time is the fact that one is made to feel so very small and inconspicuous.; New boys who have been leading lights at their private schools feel it acutely for the first week.; At one time it was the custom, if we may believe writers of a generation or so back, for boys to take quite an embarrassing interest in the newcomer.; He was asked a rain of questions, and was, generally, in the very centre of the stage.; Nowadays an absolute lack of interest is the fashion.; A new boy arrives, and there he is, one of a crowd.

Mike was saved this salutary treatment to a large extent, at first by virtue of the greatness of his family, and, later, by his own performances on the cricket field.; His three elder brothers were objects of veneration to most Wrykynians, and Mike got a certain amount of reflected glory from them.; The brother of first-class cricketers has a dignity of his own.; Then Bob was a help.; He was on the verge of the cricket team and had been the school full-back for two seasons.; Mike found that people came up and spoke to him, anxious to know if he were Jackson's brother; and became friendly when he replied in the affirmative.; Influential relations are a help in every stage of life.

It was Wyatt who gave him his first chance at cricket.; There were nets on the first afternoon of term for all old colours of the three teams and a dozen or so of those most likely to fill the vacant places.; Wyatt was there, of course.; He had got his first eleven cap in the previous season as a mighty hitter and a fair slow bowler.; Mike met him crossing the field with his cricket bag.

"Hullo, where are you off to?" asked Wyatt.; "Coming to watch the nets?"

Mike had no particular programme for the afternoon.; Junior cricket had not begun, and it was a little difficult to know how to fill in the time.

"I tell you what," said Wyatt, "nip into the house and shove on some things, and I'll try and get Burgess to let you have a knock later on."

This suited Mike admirably.; A quarter of an hour later he was sitting at the back of the first eleven net, watching the practice.

Burgess, the captain of the Wrykyn team, made no pretence of being a bat.; He was the school fast bowler and concentrated his energies on that department of the game.; He sometimes took ten minutes at the wicket after everybody else had had an innings, but it was to bowl that he came to the nets.

He was bowling now to one of the old colours whose name Mike did not know.; Wyatt and one of the professionals were the other two bowlers.; Two nets away Firby-Smith, who had changed his pince-nez for a pair of huge spectacles, was performing rather ineffectively against some very bad bowling.; Mike fixed his attention on the first eleven man.

He was evidently a good bat.; There was style and power in his batting.; He had a way of gliding Burgess's fastest to leg which Mike admired greatly.; He was succeeded at the end of a quarter of an hour by another eleven man, and then Bob appeared.

It was soon made evident that this was not Bob's day.; Nobody is at his best on the first day of term; but Bob was worse than he had any right to be.; He scratched forward at nearly everything, and when Burgess, who had been resting, took up the ball again, he had each stump uprooted in a regular series in seven balls.; Once he skied one of Wyatt's slows over the net behind the wicket; and Mike, jumping up, caught him neatly.

"Thanks," said Bob austerely, as Mike returned the ball to him.; He seemed depressed.

Towards the end of the afternoon, Wyatt went up to Burgess.

"Burgess," he said, "see that kid sitting behind the net?"

"With the naked eye," said Burgess.; "Why?"

"He's just come to Wain's.; He's Bob Jackson's brother, and I've a sort of idea that he's a bit of a bat.; I told him I'd ask you if he could have a knock.; Why not send him in at the end net?; There's nobody there now."

Burgess's amiability off the field equalled his ruthlessness when bowling.

"All right," he said.; "Only if you think that I'm going to sweat to bowl to him, you're making a fatal error."

"You needn't do a thing.; Just sit and watch.; I rather fancy this kid's something special."

* * * * *

Mike put on Wyatt's pads and gloves, borrowed his bat, and walked round into the net.

"Not in a funk, are you?" asked Wyatt, as he passed.

Mike grinned.; The fact was that he had far too good an opinion of himself to be nervous.; An entirely modest person seldom makes a good batsman.; Batting is one of those things which demand first and foremost a thorough belief in oneself.; It need not be aggressive, but it must be there.

Wyatt and the professional were the bowlers.; Mike had seen enough of Wyatt's bowling to know that it was merely ordinary "slow tosh," and the professional did not look as difficult as Saunders.; The first half-dozen balls he played carefully.; He was on trial, and he meant to take no risks.; Then the professional over-pitched one slightly on the off.; Mike jumped out, and got the full face of the bat on to it.; The ball hit one of the ropes of the net, and nearly broke it.

"How's that?" said Wyatt, with the smile of an impresario on the first night of a successful piece.

"Not bad," admitted Burgess.

A few moments later he was still more complimentary.; He got up and took a ball himself.

Mike braced himself up as Burgess began his run.; This time he was more than a trifle nervous.; The bowling he had had so far had been tame.; This would be the real ordeal.

As the ball left Burgess's hand he began instinctively to shape for a forward stroke.; Then suddenly he realised that the thing was going to be a yorker, and banged his bat down in the block just as the ball arrived.; An unpleasant sensation as of having been struck by a thunderbolt was succeeded by a feeling of relief that he had kept the ball out of his wicket.; There are easier things in the world than stopping a fast yorker.

"Well played," said Burgess.

Mike felt like a successful general receiving the thanks of the nation.

The fact that Burgess's next ball knocked middle and off stumps out of the ground saddened him somewhat; but this was the last tragedy that occurred.; He could not do much with the bowling beyond stopping it and feeling repetitions of the thunderbolt experience, but he kept up his end; and a short conversation which he had with Burgess at the end of his innings was full of encouragement to one skilled in reading between the lines.

"Thanks awfully," said Mike, referring to the square manner in which the captain had behaved in letting him bat.

"What school were you at before you came here?" asked Burgess.

"A private school in Hampshire," said Mike.; "King-Hall's.; At a place called Emsworth."

"Get much cricket there?"

"Yes, a good lot.; One of the masters, a chap called Westbrook, was an awfully good slow bowler."

Burgess nodded.

"You don't run away, which is something," he said.

Mike turned purple with pleasure at this stately compliment.; Then, having waited for further remarks, but gathering from the captain's silence that the audience was at an end, he proceeded to unbuckle his pads.; Wyatt overtook him on his way to the house.

"Well played," he said.; "I'd no idea you were such hot stuff.; You're a regular pro."

"I say," said Mike gratefully, "it was most awfully decent of you getting Burgess to let me go in.; It was simply ripping of you."

"Oh, that's all right.; If you don't get pushed a bit here you stay for ages in the hundredth game with the cripples and the kids.; Now you've shown them what you can do you ought to get into the Under Sixteen team straight away.; Probably into the third, too."

"By Jove, that would be all right."

"I asked Burgess afterwards what he thought of your batting, and he said, 'Not bad.'; But he says that about everything.; It's his highest form of praise.; He says it when he wants to let himself go and simply butter up a thing.; If you took him to see N. A. Knox bowl, he'd say he wasn't bad.; What he meant was that he was jolly struck with your batting, and is going to play you for the Under Sixteen."

"I hope so," said Mike.

The prophecy was fulfilled.; On the following Wednesday there was a match between the Under Sixteen and a scratch side.; Mike's name was among the Under Sixteen.; And on the Saturday he was playing for the third eleven in a trial game.

"This place is ripping," he said to himself, as he saw his name on the list.; "Thought I should like it."

And that night he wrote a letter to his father, notifying him of the fact.

CHAPTER V

REVELRY BY NIGHT

A succession of events combined to upset Mike during his first fortnight at school.; He was far more successful than he had any right to be at his age.; There is nothing more heady than success, and if it comes before we are prepared for it, it is apt to throw us off our balance.; As a rule, at school, years of wholesome obscurity make us ready for any small triumphs we may achieve at the end of our time there.; Mike had skipped these years.; He was older than the average new boy, and his batting was undeniable.; He knew quite well that he was regarded as a find by the cricket authorities; and the knowledge was not particularly good for him.; It did not make him conceited, for his was not a nature at all addicted to conceit.; The effect it had on him was to make him excessively pleased with life.; And when Mike was pleased with life he always found a difficulty in obeying Authority and its rules.; His state of mind was not improved by an interview with Bob.

Some evil genius put it into Bob's mind that it was his duty to be, if only for one performance, the Heavy Elder Brother to Mike; to give him good advice.; It is never the smallest use for an elder brother to attempt to do anything for the good of a younger brother at school, for the latter rebels automatically against such interference in his concerns; but Bob did not know this.; He only knew that he had received a letter from home, in which his mother had assumed without evidence that he was leading Mike by the hand round the pitfalls of life at Wrykyn; and his conscience smote him.; Beyond asking him occasionally, when they met, how he was getting on (a question to which Mike invariably replied, "Oh, all right"), he was not aware of having done anything brotherly towards the youngster.; So he asked Mike to tea in his study one afternoon before going to the nets.

Mike arrived, sidling into the study in the half-sheepish, half-defiant manner peculiar to small brothers in the presence of their elders, and stared in silence at the photographs on the walls.; Bob was changing into his cricket things.; The atmosphere was one of constraint and awkwardness.

The arrival of tea was the cue for conversation.

"Well, how are you getting on?" asked Bob.

"Oh, all right," said Mike.

Silence.

"Sugar?" asked Bob.

"Thanks," said Mike.

"How many lumps?"

"Two, please."

"Cake?"

"Thanks."

Silence.

Bob pulled himself together.

"Like Wain's?"

"Ripping."

"I asked Firby-Smith to keep an eye on you," said Bob.

"What!" said Mike.

The mere idea of a worm like the Gazeka being told to keep an eye on *him* was degrading.

"He said he'd look after you," added Bob, making things worse.

Look after him!; Him!!; M. Jackson, of the third eleven!!!

Mike helped himself to another chunk of cake, and spoke crushingly.

"He needn't trouble," he said.; "I can look after myself all right, thanks."

Bob saw an opening for the entry of the Heavy Elder Brother.

"Look here, Mike," he said, "I'm only saying it for your good——"

I should like to state here that it was not Bob's habit to go about the world telling people things solely for their good.; He was only doing it now to ease his conscience.

"Yes?" said Mike coldly.

"It's only this.; You know, I should keep an eye on myself if I were you.; There's nothing that gets a chap so barred here as side."

"What do you mean?" said Mike, outraged.

"Oh, I'm not saying anything against you so far," said Bob.; "You've been all right up to now.; What I mean to say is, you've got on so well at cricket, in the third and so on, there's just a chance you might start to side about a bit soon, if you don't watch yourself.; I'm not saying a word against you so far, of course.; Only you see what I mean."

Mike's feelings were too deep for words.; In sombre silence he reached out for the jam; while Bob, satisfied that he had delivered his message in a pleasant and tactful manner, filled his cup, and cast about him for further words of wisdom.

"Seen you about with Wyatt a good deal," he said at length.

"Yes," said Mike.

"Like him?"

"Yes," said Mike cautiously.

"You know," said Bob, "I shouldn't—I mean, I should take care what you're doing with Wyatt."

"What do you mean?"

"Well, he's an awfully good chap, of course, but still——"

"Still what?"

"Well, I mean, he's the sort of chap who'll probably get into some thundering row before he leaves.; He doesn't care a hang what he does.; He's that sort of chap.; He's never been dropped on yet, but if you go on breaking rules you're bound to be sooner or later.; Thing is, it doesn't matter much for him, because he's leaving at the end of the term.; But don't let him drag you into anything.; Not that he would try to.; But you might think it was the blood thing to do to imitate him, and the first thing you knew you'd be dropped on by Wain or somebody.; See what I mean?"

Bob was well-intentioned, but tact did not enter greatly into his composition.

"What rot!" said Mike.

"All right.; But don't you go doing it.; I'm going over to the nets.; I see Burgess has shoved you down for them.; You'd better be going and changing.; Stick on here a bit, though, if you want any more tea.; I've got to be off myself."

Mike changed for net-practice in a ferment of spiritual injury.; It was maddening to be treated as an infant who had to be looked after.; He felt very sore against Bob.

A good innings at the third eleven net, followed by some strenuous fielding in the deep, soothed his ruffled feelings to a large extent; and all might have been well but for the intervention of Firby-Smith.

That youth, all spectacles and front teeth, met Mike at the door of Wain's.

"Ah, I wanted to see you, young man," he said. (Mike disliked being called "young man.") "Come up to my study."

Mike followed him in silence to his study, and preserved his silence till Firby-Smith, having deposited his cricket-bag in a corner of the room and examined himself carefully in a looking-glass that hung over the mantelpiece, spoke again.

"I've been hearing all about you, young man."; Mike shuffled.

"You're a frightful character from all accounts."; Mike could not think of anything to say that was not rude, so said nothing.

"Your brother has asked me to keep an eye on you."

Mike's soul began to tie itself into knots again.; He was just at the age when one is most sensitive to patronage and most resentful of it.

29

"I promised I would," said the Gazeka, turning round and examining himself in the mirror again.; "You'll get on all right if you behave yourself.; Don't make a frightful row in the house.; Don't cheek your elders and betters.; Wash.; That's all.; Cut along."

Mike had a vague idea of sacrificing his career to the momentary pleasure of flinging a chair at the head of the house.; Overcoming this feeling, he walked out of the room, and up to his dormitory to change.

* * * * *

In the dormitory that night the feeling of revolt, of wanting to do something actively illegal, increased.; Like Eric, he burned, not with shame and remorse, but with rage and all that sort of thing.; He dropped off to sleep full of half-formed plans for asserting himself.; He was awakened from a dream in which he was batting against Firby-Smith's bowling, and hitting it into space every time, by a slight sound.; He opened his eyes, and saw a dark figure silhouetted against the light of the window.; He sat up in bed.

"Hullo," he said.; "Is that you, Wyatt?"

"Are you awake?" said Wyatt.; "Sorry if I've spoiled your beauty sleep."

"Are you going out?"

"I am," said Wyatt.; "The cats are particularly strong on the wing just now.; Mustn't miss a chance like this.; Specially as there's a good moon, too.; I shall be deadly."

"I say, can't I come too?"

A moonlight prowl, with or without an air-pistol, would just have suited Mike's mood.

"No, you can't," said Wyatt.; "When I'm caught, as I'm morally certain to be some day, or night rather, they're bound to ask if you've ever been out as well as me.; Then you'll be able to put your hand on your little heart and do a big George Washington act.; You'll find that useful when the time comes."

"Do you think you will be caught?"

"Shouldn't be surprised.; Anyhow, you stay where you are.; Go to sleep and dream that you're playing for the school against Ripton.; So long."

And Wyatt, laying the bar he had extracted on the window-sill, wriggled out.; Mike saw him disappearing along the wall.

* * * * *

It was all very well for Wyatt to tell him to go to sleep, but it was not so easy to do it.; The room was almost light; and Mike always found it difficult to sleep unless it was dark.; He turned over on his side and shut his eyes, but he had never felt wider awake.; Twice he heard the quarters chime from the school clock; and the second time he gave up the struggle.; He got out of bed and went to the window.; It was a lovely night, just the sort of night on which, if he had been at home, he would have been out after moths with a lantern.

A sharp yowl from an unseen cat told of Wyatt's presence somewhere in the big garden.; He would have given much to be with him, but he realised that he was on parole.; He had promised not to leave the house, and there was an end of it.

He turned away from the window and sat down on his bed.; Then a beautiful, consoling thought came to him.; He had given his word that he would not go into the garden, but nothing had been said about exploring inside the house.; It was quite late now.; Everybody would be in bed.; It would be quite safe.; And there must be all sorts of things to interest the visitor in Wain's part of the house.; Food, perhaps.; Mike felt that he could just do with a biscuit.; And there were bound to be biscuits on the sideboard in Wain's dining-room.

He crept quietly out of the dormitory.

He had been long enough in the house to know the way, in spite of the fact that all was darkness.; Down the stairs, along the passage to the left, and up a few more stairs at the end.

The beauty of the position was that the dining-room had two doors, one leading into Wain's part of the house, the other into the boys' section.; Any interruption that there might be would come from the further door.

To make himself more secure he locked that door; then, turning up the incandescent light, he proceeded to look about him.

Mr. Wain's dining-room repaid inspection.; There were the remains of supper on the table.; Mike cut himself some cheese and took some biscuits from the box, feeling that he was doing himself well.; This was Life.; There was a little soda-water in the syphon.; He finished it.; As it swished into the glass, it made a noise that seemed to him like three hundred Niagaras; but nobody else in the house appeared to have noticed it.

He took some more biscuits, and an apple.

After which, feeling a new man, he examined the room.

And this was where the trouble began.

On a table in one corner stood a small gramophone.; And gramophones happened to be Mike's particular craze.

All thought of risk left him.; The soda-water may have got into his head, or he may have been in a particularly reckless mood, as indeed he was.; The fact remains that *he* inserted the first record that came to hand, wound the machine up, and set it going.

The next moment, very loud and nasal, a voice from the machine announced that Mr. Godfrey Field would sing "The Quaint Old Bird."; And, after a few preliminary chords, Mr. Field actually did so.

"Auntie went to Aldershot in a Paris pom-pom hat."

Mike stood and drained it in.

"...; *Good gracious* (sang Mr. Field), *what was that?*"

It was a rattling at the handle of the door.; A rattling that turned almost immediately into a spirited banging.; A voice accompanied the banging.; "Who is there?" inquired the voice.; Mike recognised it as Mr. Wain's.; He was not alarmed.; The man who holds the ace of trumps has no need to be alarmed.; His position was impregnable.; The enemy was held in check by the locked door, while the other door offered an admirable and instantaneous way of escape.

Mike crept across the room on tip-toe and opened the window.; It had occurred to him, just in time, that if Mr. Wain, on entering the room, found that the occupant had retired by way of the boys' part of the house, he might possibly obtain a clue to his identity.; If, on the other hand, he opened the window, suspicion would be diverted.; Mike had not read his "Raffles" for nothing.

The handle-rattling was resumed.; This was good.; So long as the frontal attack was kept up, there was no chance of his being taken in the rear—his only danger.

He stopped the gramophone, which had been pegging away patiently at "The Quaint Old Bird" all the time, and reflected.; It seemed a pity to evacuate the position and ring down the curtain on what was, to date, the most exciting episode of his life; but he must not overdo the thing, and get caught.; At any moment the noise might bring reinforcements to the besieging force, though it was not likely, for the dining-room was a long way from the dormitories; and it might flash upon their minds that there were two entrances to the room.; Or the same bright thought might come to Wain himself.

"Now what," pondered Mike, "would A. J. Raffles have done in a case like this?; Suppose he'd been after somebody's jewels, and found that they were after him, and he'd locked one door, and could get away by the other."

The answer was simple.

"He'd clear out," thought Mike.

Two minutes later he was in bed.

He lay there, tingling all over with the consciousness of having played a masterly game, when suddenly a gruesome idea came to him, and he sat up, breathless.; Suppose Wain took it into his head to make a tour of the dormitories, to see that all was well!; Wyatt was still in the garden somewhere, blissfully unconscious of what was going on indoors.; He would be caught for a certainty!

CHAPTER VI

IN WHICH A TIGHT CORNER IS EVADED

For a moment the situation paralysed Mike. Then he began to be equal to it. In times of excitement one thinks rapidly and clearly. The main point, the kernel of the whole thing, was that he must get into the garden somehow, and warn Wyatt. And at the same time, he must keep Mr. Wain from coming to the dormitory. He jumped out of bed, and dashed down the dark stairs.

He had taken care to close the dining-room door after him. It was open now, and he could hear somebody moving inside the room. Evidently his retreat had been made just in time.

He knocked at the door, and went in.

Mr. Wain was standing at the window, looking out. He spun round at the knock, and stared in astonishment at Mike's pyjama-clad figure. Mike, in spite of his anxiety, could barely check a laugh. Mr. Wain was a tall, thin man, with a serious face partially obscured by a grizzled beard. He wore spectacles, through which he peered owlishly at Mike. His body was wrapped in a brown dressing-gown. His hair was ruffled. He looked like some weird bird.

"Please, sir, I thought I heard a noise," said Mike.

Mr. Wain continued to stare.

"What are you doing here?" said he at last.

"Thought I heard a noise, please, sir."

"A noise?"

"Please, sir, a row."

"You thought you heard — —!"

The thing seemed to be worrying Mr. Wain.

"So I came down, sir," said Mike.

The house-master's giant brain still appeared to be somewhat clouded. He looked about him, and, catching sight of the gramophone, drew inspiration from it.

"Did you turn on the gramophone?" he asked.

"*Me*, sir!" said Mike, with the air of a bishop accused of contributing to the *Police News*.

"Of course not, of course not," said Mr. Wain hurriedly. "Of course not. I don't know why I asked. All this is very unsettling. What are you doing here?"

"Thought I heard a noise, please, sir."

"A noise?"

"A row, sir."

If it was Mr. Wain's wish that he should spend the night playing Massa Tambo to his Massa Bones, it was not for him to baulk the house-master's innocent pleasure. He was prepared to continue the snappy dialogue till breakfast time.

"I think there must have been a burglar in here, Jackson."

"Looks like it, sir."

"I found the window open."

"He's probably in the garden, sir."

Mr. Wain looked out into the garden with an annoyed expression, as if its behaviour in letting burglars be in it struck him as unworthy of a respectable garden.

"He might be still in the house," said Mr. Wain, ruminatively.

"Not likely, sir."

"You think not?"

"Wouldn't be such a fool, sir. I mean, such an ass, sir."

"Perhaps you are right, Jackson."

"I shouldn't wonder if he was hiding in the shrubbery, sir."

Mr. Wain looked at the shrubbery, as who should say, *"Et tu, Brute!"*

33

"By Jove!; I think I see him," cried Mike.; He ran to the window, and vaulted through it on to the lawn.; An inarticulate protest from Mr. Wain, rendered speechless by this move just as he had been beginning to recover his faculties, and he was running across the lawn into the shrubbery.; He felt that all was well.; There might be a bit of a row on his return, but he could always plead overwhelming excitement.

Wyatt was round at the back somewhere, and the problem was how to get back without being seen from the dining-room window.; Fortunately a belt of evergreens ran along the path right up to the house.; Mike worked his way cautiously through these till he was out of sight, then tore for the regions at the back.

The moon had gone behind the clouds, and it was not easy to find a way through the bushes.; Twice branches sprang out from nowhere, and hit Mike smartly over the shins, eliciting sharp howls of pain.

On the second of these occasions a low voice spoke from somewhere on his right.

"Who on earth's that?" it said.

Mike stopped.

"Is that you, Wyatt?; I say ——"

"Jackson!"

The moon came out again, and Mike saw Wyatt clearly.; His knees were covered with mould.; He had evidently been crouching in the bushes on all fours.

"You young ass," said Wyatt.; "You promised me that you wouldn't get out."

"Yes, I know, but ——"

"I heard you crashing through the shrubbery like a hundred elephants.; If you *must* get out at night and chance being sacked, you might at least have the sense to walk quietly."

"Yes, but you don't understand."

And Mike rapidly explained the situation.

"But how the dickens did he hear you, if you were in the dining-room?" asked Wyatt.; "It's miles from his bedroom.; You must tread like a policeman."

"It wasn't that.; The thing was, you see, it was rather a rotten thing to do, I suppose, but I turned on the gramophone."

"You —*what?*"

"The gramophone.; It started playing 'The Quaint Old Bird.'; Ripping it was, till Wain came along."

Wyatt doubled up with noiseless laughter.

"You're a genius," he said.; "I never saw such a man.; Well, what's the game now?; What's the idea?"

"I think you'd better nip back along the wall and in through the window, and I'll go back to the dining-room.; Then it'll be all right if Wain comes and looks into the dorm.; Or, if you like, you might come down too, as if you'd just woke up and thought you'd heard a row."

"That's not a bad idea.; All right.; You dash along then.; I'll get back."

Mr. Wain was still in the dining-room, drinking in the beauties of the summer night through the open window.; He gibbered slightly when Mike reappeared.

"Jackson!; What do you mean by running about outside the house in this way!; I shall punish you very heavily.; I shall certainly report the matter to the headmaster.; I will not have boys rushing about the garden in their pyjamas.; You will catch an exceedingly bad cold.; You will do me two hundred lines, Latin and English.; Exceedingly so.; I will not have it.; Did you not hear me call to you?"

"Please, sir, so excited," said Mike, standing outside with his hands on the sill.

"You have no business to be excited.; I will not have it.; It is exceedingly impertinent of you."

"Please, sir, may I come in?"

"Come in!; Of course, come in.; Have you no sense, boy?; You are laying the seeds of a bad cold.; Come in at once."

Mike clambered through the window.

"I couldn't find him, sir.; He must have got out of the garden."

"Undoubtedly," said Mr. Wain.; "Undoubtedly so.; It was very wrong of you to search for him.; You have been seriously injured.; Exceedingly so."

He was about to say more on the subject when Wyatt strolled into the room.; Wyatt wore the rather dazed expression of one who has been aroused from deep sleep.; He yawned before he spoke.

"I thought I heard a noise, sir," he said.

He called Mr. Wain "father" in private, "sir" in public.; The presence of Mike made this a public occasion.

"Has there been a burglary?"

"Yes," said Mike, "only he has got away."

"Shall I go out into the garden, and have a look round, sir?" asked Wyatt helpfully.

The question stung Mr. Wain into active eruption once more.

"Under no circumstances whatever," he said excitedly.; "Stay where you are, James.; I will not have boys running about my garden at night.; It is preposterous.; Inordinately so.; Both of you go to bed immediately.; I shall not speak to you again on this subject.; I must be obeyed instantly.; You hear me, Jackson?; James, you understand me?; To bed at once.; And, if I find you outside your dormitory again to-night, you will both be punished with extreme severity.; I will not have this lax and reckless behaviour."

"But the burglar, sir?" said Wyatt.

"We might catch him, sir," said Mike.

Mr. Wain's manner changed to a slow and stately sarcasm, in much the same way as a motor-car changes from the top speed to its first.

"I was under the impression," he said, in the heavy way almost invariably affected by weak masters in their dealings with the obstreperous, "I was distinctly under the impression that I had ordered you to retire immediately to your dormitory.; It is possible that you mistook my meaning.; In that case I shall be happy to repeat what I said.; It is also in my mind that I threatened to punish you with the utmost severity if you did not retire at once.; In these circumstances, James —and you, Jackson— you will doubtless see the necessity of complying with my wishes."

They made it so.

CHAPTER VII

IN WHICH MIKE IS DISCUSSED

Trevor and Clowes, of Donaldson's, were sitting in their study a week after the gramophone incident, preparatory to going on the river. At least Trevor was in the study, getting tea ready. Clowes was on the window-sill, one leg in the room, the other outside, hanging over space. He loved to sit in this attitude, watching some one else work, and giving his views on life to whoever would listen to them. Clowes was tall, and looked sad, which he was not. Trevor was shorter, and very much in earnest over all that he did. On the present occasion he was measuring out tea with a concentration worthy of a general planning a campaign.

"One for the pot," said Clowes.

"All right," breathed Trevor; "Come and help, you slacker."

"Too busy."

"You aren't doing a stroke."

"My lad, I'm thinking of Life. That's a thing you couldn't do. I often say to people, 'Good chap, Trevor, but can't think of Life. Give him a tea-pot and half a pound of butter to mess about with,' I say, 'and he's all right. But when it comes to deep thought, where is he? Among the also-rans.' That's what I say."

"Silly ass," said Trevor, slicing bread. "What particular rot were you thinking about just then? What fun it was sitting back and watching other fellows work, I should think."

"My mind at the moment," said Clowes, "was tensely occupied with the problem of brothers at school. Have you got any brothers, Trevor?"

"One. Couple of years younger than me. I say, we shall want some more jam to-morrow. Better order it to-day."

"See it done, Tigellinus, as our old pal Nero used to remark. Where is he? Your brother, I mean."

"Marlborough."

"That shows your sense. I have always had a high opinion of your sense, Trevor. If you'd been a silly ass, you'd have let your people send him here."

"Why not? Shouldn't have minded."

"I withdraw what I said about your sense. Consider it unsaid. I have a brother myself. Aged fifteen. Not a bad chap in his way. Like the heroes of the school stories. 'Big blue eyes literally bubbling over with fun.' At least, I suppose it's fun to him. Cheek's what I call it. My people wanted to send him here. I lodged a protest. I said, 'One Clowes is ample for any public school.'"

"You were right there," said Trevor.

"I said, 'One Clowes is luxury, two excess.' I pointed out that I was just on the verge of becoming rather a blood at Wrykyn, and that I didn't want the work of years spoiled by a brother who would think it a rag to tell fellows who respected and admired me ——"

"Such as who?"

"——Anecdotes of a chequered infancy. There are stories about me which only my brother knows. Did I want them spread about the school? No, laddie, I did not. Hence, we see my brother two terms ago, packing up his little box, and tooling off to Rugby. And here am I at Wrykyn, with an unstained reputation, loved by all who know me, revered by all who don't; courted by boys, fawned upon by masters. People's faces brighten when I throw them a nod. If I frown ——"

"Oh, come on," said Trevor.

Bread and jam and cake monopolised Clowes's attention for the next quarter of an hour. At the end of that period, however, he returned to his subject.

"After the serious business of the meal was concluded, and a simple hymn had been sung by those present," he said, "Mr. Clowes resumed his very interesting remarks.; We were on the subject of brothers at school.; Now, take the melancholy case of Jackson Brothers.; My heart bleeds for Bob."

"Jackson's all right.; What's wrong with him?; Besides, naturally, young Jackson came to Wrykyn when all his brothers had been here."

"What a rotten argument.; It's just the one used by chaps' people, too.; They think how nice it will be for all the sons to have been at the same school.; It may be all right after they're left, but while they're there, it's the limit.; You say Jackson's all right.; At present, perhaps, he is.; But the term's hardly started yet."

"Well?"

"Look here, what's at the bottom of this sending young brothers to the same school as elder brothers?"

"Elder brother can keep an eye on him, I suppose."

"That's just it.; For once in your life you've touched the spot.; In other words, Bob Jackson is practically responsible for the kid.; That's where the whole rotten trouble starts."

"Why?"

"Well, what happens?; He either lets the kid rip, in which case he may find himself any morning in the pleasant position of having to explain to his people exactly why it is that little Willie has just received the boot, and why he didn't look after him better:; or he spends all his spare time shadowing him to see that he doesn't get into trouble.; He feels that his reputation hangs on the kid's conduct, so he broods over him like a policeman, which is pretty rotten for him and maddens the kid, who looks on him as no sportsman.; Bob seems to be trying the first way, which is what I should do myself.; It's all right, so far, but, as I said, the term's only just started."

"Young Jackson seems all right.; What's wrong with him?; He doesn't stick on side any way, which he might easily do, considering his cricket."

"There's nothing wrong with him in that way.; I've talked to him several times at the nets, and he's very decent.; But his getting into trouble hasn't anything to do with us.; It's the masters you've got to consider."

"What's up?; Does he rag?"

"From what I gather from fellows in his form he's got a genius for ragging.; Thinks of things that don't occur to anybody else, and does them, too."

"He never seems to be in extra.; One always sees him about on half-holidays."

"That's always the way with that sort of chap.; He keeps on wriggling out of small rows till he thinks he can do anything he likes without being dropped on, and then all of a sudden he finds himself up to the eyebrows in a record smash.; I don't say young Jackson will land himself like that.; All I say is that he's just the sort who does.; He's asking for trouble.; Besides, who do you see him about with all the time?"

"He's generally with Wyatt when I meet him."

"Yes.; Well, then!"

"What's wrong with Wyatt?; He's one of the decentest men in the school."

"I know.; But he's working up for a tremendous row one of these days, unless he leaves before it comes off.; The odds are, if Jackson's so thick with him, that he'll be roped into it too.; Wyatt wouldn't land him if he could help it, but he probably wouldn't realise what he was letting the kid in for.; For instance, I happen to know that Wyatt breaks out of his dorm. every other night.; I don't know if he takes Jackson with him.; I shouldn't think so.; But there's nothing to prevent Jackson following him on his own.; And if you're caught at that game, it's the boot every time."

Trevor looked disturbed.

"Somebody ought to speak to Bob."

"What's the good?; Why worry him?; Bob couldn't do anything.; You'd only make him do the policeman business, which he hasn't time for, and which is bound to make rows between them.; Better leave him alone."

"I don't know.; It would be a beastly thing for Bob if the kid did get into a really bad row."

"If you must tell anybody, tell the Gazeka.; He's head of Wain's, and has got far more chance of keeping an eye on Jackson than Bob has."

"The Gazeka is a fool."

"All front teeth and side.; Still, he's on the spot.; But what's the good of worrying.; It's nothing to do with us, anyhow.; Let's stagger out, shall we?"

* * * * *

Trevor's conscientious nature, however, made it impossible for him to drop the matter.; It disturbed him all the time that he and Clowes were on the river; and, walking back to the house, he resolved to see Bob about it during preparation.

He found him in his study, oiling a bat.

"I say, Bob," he said, "look here.; Are you busy?"

"No.; Why?"

"It's this way.; Clowes and I were talking — —"

"If Clowes was there he was probably talking.; Well?"

"About your brother."

"Oh, by Jove," said Bob, sitting up.; "That reminds me.; I forgot to get the evening paper.; Did he get his century all right?"

"Who?" asked Trevor, bewildered.

"My brother, J. W. He'd made sixty-three not out against Kent in this morning's paper.; What happened?"

"I didn't get a paper either.; I didn't mean that brother.; I meant the one here."

"Oh, Mike?; What's Mike been up to?"

"Nothing as yet, that I know of; but, I say, you know, he seems a great pal of Wyatt's."

"I know.; I spoke to him about it."

"Oh, you did?; That's all right, then."

"Not that there's anything wrong with Wyatt."

"Not a bit.; Only he is rather mucking about this term, I hear.; It's his last, so I suppose he wants to have a rag."

"Don't blame him."

"Nor do I. Rather rot, though, if he lugged your brother into a row by accident."

"I should get blamed.; I think I'll speak to him again."

"I should, I think."

"I hope he isn't idiot enough to go out at night with Wyatt.; If Wyatt likes to risk it, all right.; That's his look out.; But it won't do for Mike to go playing the goat too."

"Clowes suggested putting Firby-Smith on to him.; He'd have more chance, being in the same house, of seeing that he didn't come a mucker than you would."

"I've done that.; Smith said he'd speak to him."

"That's all right then.; Is that a new bat?"

"Got it to-day.; Smashed my other yesterday —against the school house."

Donaldson's had played a friendly with the school house during the last two days, and had beaten them.

"I thought I heard it go.; You were rather in form."

"Better than at the beginning of the term, anyhow.; I simply couldn't do a thing then.; But my last three innings have been 33 not out, 18, and 51.

"I should think you're bound to get your first all right."

"Hope so.; I see Mike's playing for the second against the O.W.s."

"Yes.; Pretty good for his first term.; You have a pro. to coach you in the holidays, don't you?"

"Yes.; I didn't go to him much this last time.; I was away a lot.; But Mike fairly lived inside the net."

"Well, it's not been chucked away.; I suppose he'll get his first next year.; There'll be a big clearing-out of colours at the end of this term.; Nearly all the first are leaving.; Henfrey'll be captain, I expect."

"Saunders, the pro. at home, always says that Mike's going to be the star cricketer of the family.; Better than J. W. even, he thinks.; I asked him what he thought of me, and he said, 'You'll be making a lot of runs some day, Mr. Bob.'; There's a subtle difference, isn't there?; I shall have Mike cutting me out before I leave school if I'm not careful."

"Sort of infant prodigy," said Trevor.; "Don't think he's quite up to it yet, though."

He went back to his study, and Bob, having finished his oiling and washed his hands, started on his Thucydides.; And, in the stress of wrestling with the speech of an apparently delirious Athenian general, whose remarks seemed to contain nothing even remotely resembling sense and coherence, he allowed the question of Mike's welfare to fade from his mind like a dissolving view.

CHAPTER VIII

A ROW WITH THE TOWN

The beginning of a big row, one of those rows which turn a school upside down like a volcanic eruption and provide old boys with something to talk about, when they meet, for years, is not unlike the beginning of a thunderstorm.

You are walking along one seemingly fine day, when suddenly there is a hush, and there falls on you from space one big drop.; The next moment the thing has begun, and you are standing in a shower-bath.; It is just the same with a row.; Some trivial episode occurs, and in an instant the place is in a ferment.; It was so with the great picnic at Wrykyn.

The bare outlines of the beginning of this affair are included in a letter which Mike wrote to his father on the Sunday following the Old Wrykynian matches.

This was the letter:;

> "DEAR FATHER, —Thanks awfully for your letter.; I hope you are quite well.; I have been getting on all right at cricket lately.; My scores since I wrote last have been 0 in a scratch game (the sun got in my eyes just as I played, and I got bowled); 15 for the third against an eleven of masters (without G. B. Jones, the Surrey man, and Spence); 28 not out in the Under Sixteen game; and 30 in a form match.; Rather decent.; Yesterday one of the men put down for the second against the O.W.'s second couldn't play because his father was very ill, so I played.; Wasn't it luck?; It's the first time I've played for the second.; I didn't do much, because I didn't get an innings.; They stop the cricket on O.W. matches day because they have a lot of rotten Greek plays and things which take up a frightful time, and half the chaps are acting, so we stop from lunch to four.; Rot I call it.; So I didn't go in, because they won the toss and made 215, and by the time we'd made 140 for 6 it was close of play.; They'd stuck me in eighth wicket.; Rather rot.; Still, I may get another shot.; And I made rather a decent catch at mid-on.; Low down.; I had to dive for it.; Bob played for the first, but didn't do much.; He was run out after he'd got ten.; I believe he's rather sick about it.
>
> "Rather a rummy thing happened after lock-up.; I wasn't in it, but a fellow called Wyatt (awfully decent chap.; He's Wain's step-son, only they bar one another) told me about it.; He was in it all right.; There's a dinner after the matches on O.W. day, and some of the chaps were going back to their houses after it when they got into a row with a lot of brickies from the town, and there was rather a row.; There was a policeman mixed up in it somehow, only I don't quite know where he comes in.; I'll find out and tell you next time I write.; Love to everybody.; Tell Marjory I'll write to her in a day or two.
>
> "Your loving son,
>
> "MIKE.
>
> "P.S. —I say, I suppose you couldn't send me five bob, could you?; I'm rather broke.
> "P.P.S. —Half-a-crown would do, only I'd rather it was five bob."

And, on the back of the envelope, these words:; "Or a bob would be better than nothing."

* * * * *

The outline of the case was as Mike had stated.; But there were certain details of some importance which had not come to his notice when he sent the letter.; On the Monday they were public property.

The thing had happened after this fashion.; At the conclusion of the day's cricket, all those who had been playing in the four elevens which the school put into the field against the old boys, together with the school choir, were entertained by the headmaster to supper in the Great Hall.; The banquet, lengthened by speeches, songs, and recitations which the reciters imagined to be songs, lasted, as a rule, till about ten o'clock, when the revellers were supposed to go back to their houses by the nearest route, and turn in.; This was the official programme.; The school usually performed it with certain modifications and improvements.

About midway between Wrykyn, the school, and Wrykyn, the town, there stands on an island in the centre of the road a solitary lamp-post.; It was the custom, and had been the custom for generations back, for the diners to trudge off to this lamp-post, dance round it for some minutes singing the school song or whatever happened to be the popular song of the moment, and then race back to their houses.; Antiquity had given the custom a sort of sanctity, and the authorities, if they knew —which they must have done —never interfered.

But there were others.

Wrykyn, the town, was peculiarly rich in "gangs of youths.".; Like the vast majority of the inhabitants of the place, they seemed to have no work of any kind whatsoever to occupy their time, which they used, accordingly, to spend prowling about and indulging in a mild, brainless, rural type of hooliganism.; They seldom proceeded to practical rowdyism and never except with the school.; As a rule, they amused themselves by shouting rude chaff.; The school regarded them with a lofty contempt, much as an Oxford man regards the townee.; The school was always anxious for a row, but it was the unwritten law that only in special circumstances should they proceed to active measures.; A curious dislike for school-and-town rows and most misplaced severity in dealing with the offenders when they took place, were among the few flaws in the otherwise admirable character of the headmaster of Wrykyn.; It was understood that one scragged bargees at one's own risk, and, as a rule, it was not considered worth it.

But after an excellent supper and much singing and joviality, one's views are apt to alter.; Risks which before supper seemed great, show a tendency to dwindle.

When, therefore, the twenty or so Wrykynians who were dancing round the lamp-post were aware, in the midst of their festivities, that they were being observed and criticised by an equal number of townees, and that the criticisms were, as usual, essentially candid and personal, they found themselves forgetting the headmaster's prejudices and feeling only that these outsiders must be put to the sword as speedily as possible, for the honour of the school.

Possibly, if the town brigade had stuck to a purely verbal form of attack, all might yet have been peace.; Words can be overlooked.

But tomatoes cannot.

No man of spirit can bear to be pelted with over-ripe tomatoes for any length of time without feeling that if the thing goes on much longer he will be reluctantly compelled to take steps.

In the present crisis, the first tomato was enough to set matters moving.

As the two armies stood facing each other in silence under the dim and mysterious rays of the lamp, it suddenly whizzed out from the enemy's ranks, and hit Wyatt on the right ear.

There was a moment of suspense.; Wyatt took out his handkerchief and wiped his face, over which the succulent vegetable had spread itself.

"I don't know how you fellows are going to pass the evening," he said quietly.; "My idea of a good after-dinner game is to try and find the chap who threw that.; Anybody coming?"

For the first five minutes it was as even a fight as one could have wished to see.; It raged up and down the road without a pause, now in a solid mass, now splitting up into little groups.; The science was on the side of the school.; Most Wrykynians knew how to box to a certain extent.; But, at any rate at first, it was no time for science.; To be scientific one must have an opponent who observes at least the more important rules of the ring.; It is impossible to do the latest ducks and hooks taught you by the instructor if your antagonist butts you in the chest, and then kicks your shins, while some dear friend of his, of whose presence you had no idea, hits you at the same time on the back of the head.; The greatest expert would lose his science in such circumstances.

Probably what gave the school the victory in the end was the righteousness of their cause.; They were smarting under a sense of injury, and there is nothing that adds a force to one's blows and a recklessness to one's style of delivering them more than a sense of injury.

Wyatt, one side of his face still showing traces of the tomato, led the school with a vigour that could not be resisted.; He very seldom lost his temper, but he did draw the line at bad tomatoes.

Presently the school noticed that the enemy were vanishing little by little into the darkness which concealed the town.; Barely a dozen remained.; And their lonely condition seemed to be borne in upon these by a simultaneous brain-wave, for they suddenly gave the fight up, and stampeded as one man.

The leaders were beyond recall, but two remained, tackled low by Wyatt and Clowes after the fashion of the football-field.

* * * * *

The school gathered round its prisoners, panting.; The scene of the conflict had shifted little by little to a spot some fifty yards from where it had started.; By the side of the road at this point was a green, depressed looking pond.; Gloomy in the daytime, it looked unspeakable at night.; It struck Wyatt, whose finer feelings had been entirely blotted out by tomato, as an ideal place in which to bestow the captives.

"Let's chuck 'em in there," he said.

The idea was welcomed gladly by all, except the prisoners.; A move was made towards the pond, and the procession had halted on the brink, when a new voice made itself heard.

"Now then," it said, "what's all this?"

A stout figure in policeman's uniform was standing surveying them with the aid of a small bull's-eye lantern.

"What's all this?"

"It's all right," said Wyatt.

"All right, is it?; What's on?"

One of the prisoners spoke.

"Make 'em leave hold of us, Mr. Butt.; They're a-going to chuck us in the pond."

"Ho!" said the policeman, with a change in his voice.; "Ho, are they?; Come now, young gentleman, a lark's a lark, but you ought to know where to stop."

"It's anything but a lark," said Wyatt in the creamy voice he used when feeling particularly savage.; "We're the Strong Right Arm of Justice.; That's what we are.; This isn't a lark, it's an execution."

"I don't want none of your lip, whoever you are," said Mr. Butt, understanding but dimly, and suspecting impudence by instinct.

"This is quite a private matter," said Wyatt.; "You run along on your beat.; You can't do anything here."

"Ho!"

"Shove 'em in, you chaps."

"Stop!" From Mr. Butt.

"Oo-er!" From prisoner number one.

There was a sounding splash as willing hands urged the first of the captives into the depths.; He ploughed his way to the bank, scrambled out, and vanished.

Wyatt turned to the other prisoner.

"You'll have the worst of it, going in second.; He'll have churned up the mud a bit.; Don't swallow more than you can help, or you'll go getting typhoid.; I expect there are leeches and things there, but if you nip out quick they may not get on to you.; Carry on, you chaps."

It was here that the regrettable incident occurred.; Just as the second prisoner was being launched, Constable Butt, determined to assert himself even at the eleventh hour, sprang forward, and seized the captive by the arm.; A drowning man will clutch at a straw.; A man about to be hurled into an excessively dirty pond will clutch at a stout policeman.; The prisoner did.

Constable Butt represented his one link with dry land.; As he came within reach he attached himself to his tunic with the vigour and concentration of a limpet.

At the same moment the executioners gave their man the final heave.; The policeman realised his peril too late.; A medley of noises made the peaceful night hideous.; A howl from the townee, a yell from the policeman, a cheer from the launching party, a frightened squawk from some birds in a neighbouring tree, and a splash compared with which the first had been as nothing, and all was over.

The dark waters were lashed into a maelstrom; and then two streaming figures squelched up the further bank.

THE DARK WATERS WERE LASHED INTO A MAELSTROM

The school stood in silent consternation.; It was no occasion for light apologies.

"Do you know," said Wyatt, as he watched the Law shaking the water from itself on the other side of the pond, "I'm not half sure that we hadn't better be moving!"

CHAPTER IX

BEFORE THE STORM

Your real, devastating row has many points of resemblance with a prairie fire.; A man on a prairie lights his pipe, and throws away the match.; The flame catches a bunch of dry grass, and, before any one can realise what is happening, sheets of fire are racing over the country; and the interested neighbours are following their example. (I have already compared a row with a thunderstorm; but both comparisons may stand.; In dealing with so vast a matter as a row there must be no stint.)

The tomato which hit Wyatt in the face was the thrown-away match.; But for the unerring aim of the town marksman great events would never have happened.; A tomato is a trivial thing (though it is possible that the man whom it hits may not think so), but in the present case, it was the direct cause of epoch-making trouble.

The tomato hit Wyatt.; Wyatt, with others, went to look for the thrower.; The remnants of the thrower's friends were placed in the pond, and "with them," as they say in the courts of law, Police Constable Alfred Butt.

Following the chain of events, we find Mr. Butt, having prudently changed his clothes, calling upon the headmaster.

The headmaster was grave and sympathetic; Mr. Butt fierce and revengeful.

The imagination of the force is proverbial.; Nurtured on motor-cars and fed with stop-watches, it has become world-famous.; Mr. Butt gave free rein to it.

"Threw me in, they did, sir.; Yes, sir."

"Threw you in!"

"Yes, sir. *Plop!*" said Mr. Butt, with a certain sad relish.

"Really, really!" said the headmaster.; "Indeed!; This is —dear me!; I shall certainly —They threw you in! —Yes, I shall —certainly — —"

Encouraged by this appreciative reception of his story, Mr. Butt started it again, right from the beginning.

"I was on my beat, sir, and I thought I heard a disturbance.; I says to myself, ''Allo,' I says, 'a frakkus.; Lots of them all gathered together, and fighting.'; I says, beginning to suspect something, 'Wot's this all about, I wonder?' I says.; 'Blow me if I don't think it's a frakkus.'; And," concluded Mr. Butt, with the air of one confiding a secret, "and it *was* a frakkus!"

"And these boys actually threw you into the pond?"

"*Plop*, sir!; Mrs. Butt is drying my uniform at home at this very moment as we sit talking here, sir.; She says to me, 'Why, whatever 'ave you been a-doing?; You're all wet.'; And," he added, again with the confidential air, "I *was* wet, too.; Wringin' wet."

The headmaster's frown deepened.

"And you are certain that your assailants were boys from the school?"

"Sure as I am that I'm sitting here, sir.; They all 'ad their caps on their heads, sir."

"I have never heard of such a thing.; I can hardly believe that it is possible.; They actually seized you, and threw you into the water — —"

"*Splish*, sir!" said the policeman, with a vividness of imagery both surprising and gratifying.

The headmaster tapped restlessly on the floor with his foot.

"How many boys were there?" he asked.

"Couple of 'undred, sir," said Mr. Butt promptly.

"Two hundred!"

"It was dark, sir, and I couldn't see not to say properly; but if you ask me my frank and private opinion I should say couple of 'undred."

"H'm —Well, I will look into the matter at once.; They shall be punished."

"Yes, sir."

"Ye-e-s —H'm —Yes —Most severely."

"Yes, sir."

"Yes —Thank you, constable.; Good-night."

"Good-night, sir."

The headmaster of Wrykyn was not a motorist.; Owing to this disadvantage he made a mistake.; Had he been a motorist, he would have known that statements by the police in the matter of figures must be divided by any number from two to ten, according to discretion.; As it was, he accepted Constable Butt's report almost as it stood.; He thought that he might possibly have been mistaken as to the exact numbers of those concerned in his immersion; but he accepted the statement in so far as it indicated that the thing had been the work of a considerable section of the school, and not of only one or two individuals.; And this made all the difference to his method of dealing with the affair.; Had he known how few were the numbers of those responsible for the cold in the head which subsequently attacked Constable Butt, he would have asked for their names, and an extra lesson would have settled the entire matter.

As it was, however, he got the impression that the school, as a whole, was culpable, and he proceeded to punish the school as a whole.

It happened that, about a week before the pond episode, a certain member of the Royal Family had recovered from a dangerous illness, which at one time had looked like being fatal.; No official holiday had been given to the schools in honour of the recovery, but Eton and Harrow had set the example, which was followed throughout the kingdom, and Wrykyn had come into line with the rest.; Only two days before the O.W.'s matches the headmaster had given out a notice in the hall that the following Friday would be a whole holiday; and the school, always ready to stop work, had approved of the announcement exceedingly.

The step which the headmaster decided to take by way of avenging Mr. Butt's wrongs was to stop this holiday.

He gave out a notice to that effect on the Monday.

The school was thunderstruck.; It could not understand it.; The pond affair had, of course, become public property; and those who had had nothing to do with it had been much amused.; "There'll be a frightful row about it," they had said, thrilled with the pleasant excitement of those who see trouble approaching and themselves looking on from a comfortable distance without risk or uneasiness.; They were not malicious.; They did not want to see their friends in difficulties.; But there is no denying that a row does break the monotony of a school term.; The thrilling feeling that something is going to happen is the salt of life....

And here they were, right in it after all.; The blow had fallen, and crushed guilty and innocent alike.

* * * * *

The school's attitude can be summed up in three words.; It was one vast, blank, astounded "Here, I say!"

Everybody was saying it, though not always in those words.; When condensed, everybody's comment on the situation came to that.

* * * * *

There is something rather pathetic in the indignation of a school.; It must always, or nearly always, expend itself in words, and in private at that.; Even the consolation of getting on to platforms and shouting at itself is denied to it.; A public school has no Hyde Park.

There is every probability —in fact, it is certain —that, but for one malcontent, the school's indignation would have been allowed to simmer down in the usual way, and finally become a mere vague memory.

The malcontent was Wyatt. He had been responsible for the starting of the matter, and he proceeded now to carry it on till it blazed up into the biggest thing of its kind ever known at Wrykyn—the Great Picnic.

* * * * *

Any one who knows the public schools, their ironbound conservatism, and, as a whole, intense respect for order and authority, will appreciate the magnitude of his feat, even though he may not approve of it. Leaders of men are rare. Leaders of boys are almost unknown. It requires genius to sway a school.

It would be an absorbing task for a psychologist to trace the various stages by which an impossibility was changed into a reality. Wyatt's coolness and matter-of-fact determination were his chief weapons. His popularity and reputation for lawlessness helped him. A conversation which he had with Neville-Smith, a day-boy, is typical of the way in which he forced his point of view on the school.

Neville-Smith was thoroughly representative of the average Wrykynian. He could play his part in any minor "rag" which interested him, and probably considered himself, on the whole, a daring sort of person. But at heart he had an enormous respect for authority. Before he came to Wyatt, he would not have dreamed of proceeding beyond words in his revolt. Wyatt acted on him like some drug.

Neville-Smith came upon Wyatt on his way to the nets. The notice concerning the holiday had only been given out that morning, and he was full of it. He expressed his opinion of the headmaster freely and in well-chosen words. He said it was a swindle, that it was all rot, and that it was a beastly shame. He added that something ought to be done about it.

"What are you going to do?" asked Wyatt.

"Well," said Neville-Smith a little awkwardly, guiltily conscious that he had been frothing, and scenting sarcasm, "I don't suppose one can actually *do* anything."

"Why not?" said Wyatt.

"What do you mean?"

"Why don't you take the holiday?"

"What? Not turn up on Friday!"

"Yes. I'm not going to."

Neville-Smith stopped and stared. Wyatt was unmoved.

"You're what?"

"I simply sha'n't go to school."

"You're rotting."

"All right."

"No, but, I say, ragging barred. Are you just going to cut off, though the holiday's been stopped?"

"That's the idea."

"You'll get sacked."

"I suppose so. But only because I shall be the only one to do it. If the whole school took Friday off, they couldn't do much. They couldn't sack the whole school."

"By Jove, nor could they! I say!"

They walked on, Neville-Smith's mind in a whirl, Wyatt whistling.

"I say," said Neville-Smith after a pause. "It would be a bit of a rag."

"Not bad."

"Do you think the chaps would do it?"

"If they understood they wouldn't be alone."

Another pause.

"Shall I ask some of them?" said Neville-Smith.

"Do."

"I could get quite a lot, I believe."

"That would be a start, wouldn't it?; I could get a couple of dozen from Wain's.; We should be forty or fifty strong to start with."

"I say, what a score, wouldn't it be?"

"Yes."

"I'll speak to the chaps to-night, and let you know."

"All right," said Wyatt.; "Tell them that I shall be going anyhow.; I should be glad of a little company."

* * * * *

The school turned in on the Thursday night in a restless, excited way.; There were mysterious whisperings and gigglings.; Groups kept forming in corners apart, to disperse casually and innocently on the approach of some person in authority.

An air of expectancy permeated each of the houses.

CHAPTER X

THE GREAT PICNIC

Morning school at Wrykyn started at nine o'clock.; At that hour there was a call-over in each of the form-rooms.; After call-over the forms proceeded to the Great Hall for prayers.

A strangely desolate feeling was in the air at nine o'clock on the Friday morning.; Sit in the grounds of a public school any afternoon in the summer holidays, and you will get exactly the same sensation of being alone in the world as came to the dozen or so day-boys who bicycled through the gates that morning.; Wrykyn was a boarding-school for the most part, but it had its leaven of day-boys.; The majority of these lived in the town, and walked to school.; A few, however, whose homes were farther away, came on bicycles.; One plutocrat did the journey in a motor-car, rather to the scandal of the authorities, who, though unable to interfere, looked askance when compelled by the warning toot of the horn to skip from road to pavement.; A form-master has the strongest objection to being made to skip like a young ram by a boy to whom he has only the day before given a hundred lines for shuffling his feet in form.

It seemed curious to these cyclists that there should be nobody about.; Punctuality is the politeness of princes, but it was not a leading characteristic of the school; and at three minutes to nine, as a general rule, you might see the gravel in front of the buildings freely dotted with sprinters, trying to get in in time to answer their names.

It was curious that there should be nobody about to-day.; A wave of reform could scarcely have swept through the houses during the night.

And yet —where was everybody?

Time only deepened the mystery.; The form-rooms, like the gravel, were empty.

The cyclists looked at one another in astonishment.; What could it mean?

It was an occasion on which sane people wonder if their brains are not playing them some unaccountable trick.

"I say," said Willoughby, of the Lower Fifth, to Brown, the only other occupant of the form-room, "the old man *did* stop the holiday to-day, didn't he?"

"Just what I was going to ask you," said Brown.; "It's jolly rum.; I distinctly remember him giving it out in hall that it was going to be stopped because of the O.W.'s day row."

"So do I. I can't make it out.; Where *is* everybody?"

"They can't *all* be late."

"Somebody would have turned up by now.; Why, it's just striking."

"Perhaps he sent another notice round the houses late last night, saying it was on again all right.; I say, what a swindle if he did.; Some one might have let us know.; I should have got up an hour later."

"So should I."

"Hullo, here *is* somebody."

It was the master of the Lower Fifth, Mr. Spence.; He walked briskly into the room, as was his habit.; Seeing the obvious void, he stopped in his stride, and looked puzzled.

"Willoughby.; Brown.; Are you the only two here?; Where is everybody?"

"Please, sir, we don't know.; We were just wondering."

"Have you seen nobody?"

"No, sir."

"We were just wondering, sir, if the holiday had been put on again, after all."

"I've heard nothing about it.; I should have received some sort of intimation if it had been."

"Yes, sir."

"Do you mean to say that you have seen *nobody*, Brown?"

"Only about a dozen fellows, sir.; The usual lot who come on bikes, sir."

"None of the boarders?"

"No, sir.; Not a single one."

"This is extraordinary."

Mr. Spence pondered.

"Well," he said, "you two fellows had better go along up to Hall.; I shall go to the Common Room and make inquiries.; Perhaps, as you say, there is a holiday to-day, and the notice was not brought to me."

Mr. Spence told himself, as he walked to the Common Room, that this might be a possible solution of the difficulty.; He was not a house-master, and lived by himself in rooms in the town.; It was just conceivable that they might have forgotten to tell him of the change in the arrangements.

But in the Common Room the same perplexity reigned.; Half a dozen masters were seated round the room, and a few more were standing.; And they were all very puzzled.

A brisk conversation was going on.; Several voices hailed Mr. Spence as he entered.

"Hullo, Spence.; Are you alone in the world too?"

"Any of your boys turned up, Spence?"

"You in the same condition as we are, Spence?"

Mr. Spence seated himself on the table.

"Haven't any of your fellows turned up, either?" he said.

"When I accepted the honourable post of Lower Fourth master in this abode of sin," said Mr. Seymour, "it was on the distinct understanding that there was going to *be* a Lower Fourth.; Yet I go into my form-room this morning, and what do I find?; Simply Emptiness, and Pickersgill II. whistling 'The Church Parade,' all flat.; I consider I have been hardly treated."

"I have no complaint to make against Brown and Willoughby, as individuals," said Mr. Spence; "but, considered as a form, I call them short measure."

"I confess that I am entirely at a loss," said Mr. Shields precisely.; "I have never been confronted with a situation like this since I became a schoolmaster."

"It is most mysterious," agreed Mr. Wain, plucking at his beard.; "Exceedingly so."

The younger masters, notably Mr. Spence and Mr. Seymour, had begun to look on the thing as a huge jest.

"We had better teach ourselves," said Mr. Seymour.; "Spence, do a hundred lines for laughing in form."

The door burst open.

"Hullo, here's another scholastic Little Bo-Peep," said Mr. Seymour.; "Well, Appleby, have you lost your sheep, too?"

"You don't mean to tell me — —" began Mr. Appleby.

"I do," said Mr. Seymour.; "Here we are, fifteen of us, all good men and true, graduates of our Universities, and, as far as I can see, if we divide up the boys who have come to school this morning on fair share-and-share-alike lines, it will work out at about two-thirds of a boy each.; Spence, will you take a third of Pickersgill II.?"

"I want none of your charity," said Mr. Spence loftily.; "You don't seem to realise that I'm the best off of you all.; I've got two in my form.; It's no good offering me your Pickersgills.; I simply haven't room for them."

"What does it all mean?" exclaimed Mr. Appleby.

"If you ask me," said Mr. Seymour, "I should say that it meant that the school, holding the sensible view that first thoughts are best, have ignored the head's change of mind, and are taking their holiday as per original programme."

"They surely cannot — —!"

"Well, where are they then?"

"Do you seriously mean that the entire school has —has *rebelled*?"

"'Nay, sire,'" quoted Mr. Spence, "'a revolution!'"

"I never heard of such a thing!"

"We're making history," said Mr. Seymour.

"It will be rather interesting," said Mr. Spence, "to see how the head will deal with a situation like this.; One can rely on him to do the statesman-like thing, but I'm bound to say I shouldn't care to be in his place.; It seems to me these boys hold all the cards.; You can't expel a whole school.; There's safety in numbers.; The thing is colossal."

"It is deplorable," said Mr. Wain, with austerity.; "Exceedingly so."

"I try to think so," said Mr. Spence, "but it's a struggle.; There's a Napoleonic touch about the business that appeals to one.; Disorder on a small scale is bad, but this is immense.; I've never heard of anything like it at any public school.; When I was at Winchester, my last year there, there was pretty nearly a revolution because the captain of cricket was expelled on the eve of the Eton match.; I remember making inflammatory speeches myself on that occasion.; But we stopped on the right side of the line.; We were satisfied with growling.; But this — —!"

Mr. Seymour got up.

"It's an ill wind," he said.; "With any luck we ought to get the day off, and it's ideal weather for a holiday.; The head can hardly ask us to sit indoors, teaching nobody.; If I have to stew in my form-room all day, instructing Pickersgill II., I shall make things exceedingly sultry for that youth.; He will wish that the Pickersgill progeny had stopped short at his elder brother.; He will not value life.; In the meantime, as it's already ten past, hadn't we better be going up to Hall to see what the orders of the day *are*?"

"Look at Shields," said Mr. Spence.; "He might be posing for a statue to be called 'Despair!' He reminds me of Macduff. *Macbeth*, Act iv., somewhere near the end.; 'What, all my pretty chickens, at one fell swoop?' That's what Shields is saying to himself."

"It's all very well to make a joke of it, Spence," said Mr. Shields querulously, "but it is most disturbing.; Most."

"Exceedingly," agreed Mr. Wain.

The bereaved company of masters walked on up the stairs that led to the Great Hall.

CHAPTER XI

THE CONCLUSION OF THE PICNIC

If the form-rooms had been lonely, the Great Hall was doubly, trebly, so.; It was a vast room, stretching from side to side of the middle block, and its ceiling soared up into a distant dome.; At one end was a dais and an organ, and at intervals down the room stood long tables.; The panels were covered with the names of Wrykynians who had won scholarships at Oxford and Cambridge, and of Old Wrykynians who had taken first in Mods or Greats, or achieved any other recognised success, such as a place in the Indian Civil Service list.; A silent testimony, these panels, to the work the school had done in the world.

Nobody knew exactly how many the Hall could hold, when packed to its fullest capacity.; The six hundred odd boys at the school seemed to leave large gaps unfilled.

This morning there was a mere handful, and the place looked worse than empty.

The Sixth Form were there, and the school prefects.; The Great Picnic had not affected their numbers.; The Sixth stood by their table in a solid group.; The other tables were occupied by ones and twos.; A buzz of conversation was going on, which did not cease when the masters filed into the room and took their places.; Every one realised by this time that the biggest row in Wrykyn history was well under way; and the thing had to be discussed.

In the Masters' library Mr. Wain and Mr. Shields, the spokesmen of the Common Room, were breaking the news to the headmaster.

The headmaster was a man who rarely betrayed emotion in his public capacity.; He heard Mr. Shields's rambling remarks, punctuated by Mr. Wain's "Exceedinglys," to an end.; Then he gathered up his cap and gown.

"You say that the whole school is absent?" he remarked quietly.

Mr. Shields, in a long-winded flow of words, replied that that was what he did say.

"Ah!" said the headmaster.

There was a silence.

"M!" said the headmaster.

There was another silence.

"Ye —e —s!" said the headmaster.

He then led the way into the Hall.

Conversation ceased abruptly as he entered.; The school, like an audience at a theatre when the hero has just appeared on the stage, felt that the serious interest of the drama had begun.; There was a dead silence at every table as he strode up the room and on to the dais.

There was something Titanic in his calmness.; Every eye was on his face as he passed up the Hall, but not a sign of perturbation could the school read.; To judge from his expression, he might have been unaware of the emptiness around him.

The master who looked after the music of the school, and incidentally accompanied the hymn with which prayers at Wrykyn opened, was waiting, puzzled, at the foot of the dais.; It seemed improbable that things would go on as usual, and he did not know whether he was expected to be at the organ, or not.; The headmaster's placid face reassured him.; He went to his post.

The hymn began.; It was a long hymn, and one which the school liked for its swing and noise.; As a rule, when it was sung, the Hall re-echoed.; To-day, the thin sound of the voices had quite an uncanny effect.; The organ boomed through the deserted room.

The school, or the remnants of it, waited impatiently while the prefect whose turn it was to read stammered nervously through the lesson.; They were anxious to get on to what the Head was going to say at the end of prayers.; At last it was over.; The school waited, all ears.

The headmaster bent down from the dais and called to Firby-Smith, who was standing in his place with the Sixth.

The Gazeka, blushing warmly, stepped forward.

"Bring me a school list, Firby-Smith," said the headmaster.

The Gazeka was wearing a pair of very squeaky boots that morning.; They sounded deafening as he walked out of the room.

The school waited.

Presently a distant squeaking was heard, and Firby-Smith returned, bearing a large sheet of paper.

The headmaster thanked him, and spread it out on the reading-desk.

Then, calmly, as if it were an occurrence of every day, he began to call the roll.

"Abney."

No answer.

"Adams."

No answer.

"Allenby."

"Here, sir," from a table at the end of the room.; Allenby was a prefect, in the Science Sixth.

The headmaster made a mark against his name with a pencil.

"Arkwright."

No answer.

He began to call the names more rapidly.

"Arlington.; Arthur.; Ashe.; Aston."

"Here, sir," in a shrill treble from the rider in motorcars.

The headmaster made another tick.

The list came to an end after what seemed to the school an unconscionable time, and he rolled up the paper again, and stepped to the edge of the dais.

"All boys not in the Sixth Form," he said, "will go to their form-rooms and get their books and writing-materials, and return to the Hall."

("Good work," murmured Mr. Seymour to himself.; "Looks as if we should get that holiday after all.")

"The Sixth Form will go to their form-room as usual.; I should like to speak to the masters for a moment."

He nodded dismissal to the school.

The masters collected on the daïs.

"I find that I shall not require your services to-day," said the headmaster.; "If you will kindly set the boys in your forms some work that will keep them occupied, I will look after them here.; It is a lovely day," he added, with a smile, "and I am sure you will all enjoy yourselves a great deal more in the open air."

"That," said Mr. Seymour to Mr. Spence, as they went downstairs, "is what I call a genuine sportsman."

"My opinion neatly expressed," said Mr. Spence.; "Come on the river.; Or shall we put up a net, and have a knock?"

"River, I think.; Meet you at the boat-house."

"All right.; Don't be long."

"If every day were run on these lines, school-mastering wouldn't be such a bad profession.; I wonder if one could persuade one's form to run amuck as a regular thing."

"Pity one can't.; It seems to me the ideal state of things.; Ensures the greatest happiness of the greatest number."

"I say!; Suppose the school has gone up the river, too, and we meet them!; What shall we do?"

"Thank them," said Mr. Spence, "most kindly.; They've done us well."

The school had not gone up the river.; They had marched in a solid body, with the school band at their head playing Sousa, in the direction of Worfield, a market town of some importance, distant about five miles.; Of what they did and what the natives thought of it all, no very distinct records remain.; The thing is a tradition on the countryside now, an event colossal and heroic, to be talked about in the tap-room of the village inn during the long winter evenings.;

The papers got hold of it, but were curiously misled as to the nature of the demonstration.; This was the fault of the reporter on the staff of the *Worfield Intelligencer and Farmers' Guide*, who saw in the thing a legitimate "march-out," and, questioning a straggler as to the reason for the expedition and gathering foggily that the restoration to health of the Eminent Person was at the bottom of it, said so in his paper.; And two days later, at about the time when Retribution had got seriously to work, the *Daily Mail* reprinted the account, with comments and elaborations, and headed it "Loyal Schoolboys."; The writer said that great credit was due to the headmaster of Wrykyn for his ingenuity in devising and organising so novel a thanksgiving celebration.; And there was the usual conversation between "a rosy-cheeked lad of some sixteen summers" and "our representative," in which the rosy-cheeked one spoke most kindly of the head-master, who seemed to be a warm personal friend of his.

The remarkable thing about the Great Picnic was its orderliness.; Considering that five hundred and fifty boys were ranging the country in a compact mass, there was wonderfully little damage done to property.; Wyatt's genius did not stop short at organising the march.; In addition, he arranged a system of officers which effectually controlled the animal spirits of the rank and file.; The prompt and decisive way in which rioters were dealt with during the earlier stages of the business proved a wholesome lesson to others who would have wished to have gone and done likewise.; A spirit of martial law reigned over the Great Picnic.; And towards the end of the day fatigue kept the rowdy-minded quiet.

At Worfield the expedition lunched.; It was not a market-day, fortunately, or the confusion in the narrow streets would have been hopeless.; On ordinary days Worfield was more or less deserted.; It is astonishing that the resources of the little town were equal to satisfying the needs of the picnickers.; They descended on the place like an army of locusts.

Wyatt, as generalissimo of the expedition, walked into the "Grasshopper and Ant," the leading inn of the town.

"Anything I can do for you, sir?" inquired the landlord politely.

"Yes, please," said Wyatt, "I want lunch for five hundred and fifty."

That was the supreme moment in mine host's life.; It was his big subject of conversation ever afterwards.; He always told that as his best story, and he always ended with the words, "You could ha' knocked me down with a feather!"

The first shock over, the staff of the "Grasshopper and Ant" bustled about.; Other inns were called upon for help.; Private citizens rallied round with bread, jam, and apples.; And the army lunched sumptuously.

In the early afternoon they rested, and as evening began to fall, the march home was started.

* * * * *

At the school, net practice was just coming to an end when, faintly, as the garrison of Lucknow heard the first skirl of the pipes of the relieving force, those on the grounds heard the strains of the school band and a murmur of many voices.; Presently the sounds grew more distinct, and up the Wrykyn road came marching the vanguard of the column, singing the school song.; They looked weary but cheerful.

As the army drew near to the school, it melted away little by little, each house claiming its representatives.; At the school gates only a handful were left.

Bob Jackson, walking back to Donaldson's, met Wyatt at the gate, and gazed at him, speechless.

"Hullo," said Wyatt, "been to the nets?; I wonder if there's time for a ginger-beer before the shop shuts."

CHAPTER XII

MIKE GETS HIS CHANCE

The headmaster was quite bland and business-like about it all. There were no impassioned addresses from the dais. He did not tell the school that it ought to be ashamed of itself. Nor did he say that he should never have thought it of them. Prayers on the Saturday morning were marked by no unusual features. There was, indeed, a stir of excitement when he came to the edge of the dais, and cleared his throat as a preliminary to making an announcement. Now for it, thought the school.

This was the announcement.

"There has been an outbreak of chicken-pox in the town. All streets except the High Street will in consequence be out of bounds till further notice."

He then gave the nod of dismissal.

The school streamed downstairs, marvelling.

The less astute of the picnickers, unmindful of the homely proverb about hallooing before leaving the wood, were openly exulting. It seemed plain to them that the headmaster, baffled by the magnitude of the thing, had resolved to pursue the safe course of ignoring it altogether. To lie low is always a shrewd piece of tactics, and there seemed no reason why the Head should not have decided on it in the present instance.

Neville-Smith was among these premature rejoicers.

"I say," he chuckled, overtaking Wyatt in the cloisters, "this is all right, isn't it! He's funked it. I thought he would. Finds the job too big to tackle."

Wyatt was damping.

"My dear chap," he said, "it's not over yet by a long chalk. It hasn't started yet."

"What do you mean? Why didn't he say anything about it in Hall, then?"

"Why should he? Have you ever had tick at a shop?"

"Of course I have. What do you mean? Why?"

"Well, they didn't send in the bill right away. But it came all right."

"Do you think he's going to do something, then?"

"Rather. You wait."

Wyatt was right.

Between ten and eleven on Wednesdays and Saturdays old Bates, the school sergeant, used to copy out the names of those who were in extra lesson, and post them outside the school shop. The school inspected the list during the quarter to eleven interval.

To-day, rushing to the shop for its midday bun, the school was aware of a vast sheet of paper where usually there was but a small one. They surged round it. Buns were forgotten. What was it?

Then the meaning of the notice flashed upon them. The headmaster had acted. This bloated document was the extra lesson list, swollen with names as a stream swells with rain. It was a comprehensive document. It left out little.

"The following boys will go in to extra lesson this afternoon and next Wednesday," it began. And "the following boys" numbered four hundred.

"Bates must have got writer's cramp," said Clowes, as he read the huge scroll.

* * * * *

Wyatt met Mike after school, as they went back to the house.

"Seen the 'extra' list?" he remarked. "None of the kids are in it, I notice. Only the bigger fellows. Rather a good thing. I'm glad you got off."

"Thanks," said Mike, who was walking a little stiffly.; "I don't know what you call getting off.; It seems to me you're the chaps who got off."

"How do you mean?"

"We got tanned," said Mike ruefully.

"What!"

"Yes.; Everybody below the Upper Fourth."

Wyatt roared with laughter.

"By Gad," he said, "he is an old sportsman.; I never saw such a man.; He lowers all records."

"Glad you think it funny.; You wouldn't have if you'd been me.; I was one of the first to get it.; He was quite fresh."

"Sting?"

"Should think it did."

"Well, buck up.; Don't break down."

"I'm not breaking down," said Mike indignantly.

"All right, I thought you weren't.; Anyhow, you're better off than I am."

"An extra's nothing much," said Mike.

"It is when it happens to come on the same day as the M.C.C. match."

"Oh, by Jove!; I forgot.; That's next Wednesday, isn't it?; You won't be able to play!"

"No."

"I say, what rot!"

"It is, rather.; Still, nobody can say I didn't ask for it.; If one goes out of one's way to beg and beseech the Old Man to put one in extra, it would be a little rough on him to curse him when he does it."

"I should be awfully sick, if it were me."

"Well, it isn't you, so you're all right.; You'll probably get my place in the team."

Mike smiled dutifully at what he supposed to be a humorous sally.

"Or, rather, one of the places," continued Wyatt, who seemed to be sufficiently in earnest.; "They'll put a bowler in instead of me.; Probably Druce.; But there'll be several vacancies.; Let's see.; Me.; Adams.; Ashe.; Any more?; No, that's the lot.; I should think they'd give you a chance."

"You needn't rot," said Mike uncomfortably.; He had his day-dreams, like everybody else, and they always took the form of playing for the first eleven (and, incidentally, making a century in record time).; To have to listen while the subject was talked about lightly made him hot and prickly all over.

"I'm not rotting," said Wyatt seriously, "I'll suggest it to Burgess to-night."

"You don't think there's any chance of it, really, do you?" said Mike awkwardly.

"I don't see why not?; Buck up in the scratch game this afternoon.; Fielding especially.; Burgess is simply mad on fielding.; I don't blame him either, especially as he's a bowler himself.; He'd shove a man into the team like a shot, whatever his batting was like, if his fielding was something extra special.; So you field like a demon this afternoon, and I'll carry on the good work in the evening."

"I say," said Mike, overcome, "it's awfully decent of you, Wyatt."

* * * * *

Billy Burgess, captain of Wrykyn cricket, was a genial giant, who seldom allowed himself to be ruffled.; The present was one of the rare occasions on which he permitted himself that luxury.; Wyatt found him in his study, shortly before lock-up, full of strange oaths, like the soldier in Shakespeare.

"You rotter!; You rotter!; You *worm*!" he observed crisply, as Wyatt appeared.

"Dear old Billy!" said Wyatt.; "Come on, give me a kiss, and let's be friends."

"You ——!"

"William!; William!"

"If it wasn't illegal, I'd like to tie you and Ashe and that blackguard Adams up in a big sack, and drop you into the river.; And I'd jump on the sack first.; What do you mean by letting the team down like this?; I know you were at the bottom of it all."

He struggled into his shirt —he was changing after a bath —and his face popped wrathfully out at the other end.

"I'm awfully sorry, Bill," said Wyatt.; "The fact is, in the excitement of the moment the M.C.C. match went clean out of my mind."

"You haven't got a mind," grumbled Burgess.; "You've got a cheap brown paper substitute.; That's your trouble."

Wyatt turned the conversation tactfully.

"How many wickets did you get to-day?" he asked.

"Eight.; For a hundred and three.; I was on the spot.; Young Jackson caught a hot one off me at third man.; That kid's good."

"Why don't you play him against the M.C.C. on Wednesday?" said Wyatt, jumping at his opportunity.

"What?; Are you sitting on my left shoe?"

"No.; There it is in the corner."

"Right ho!...; What were you saying?"

"Why not play young Jackson for the first?"

"Too small."

"Rot.; What does size matter?; Cricket isn't footer.; Besides, he isn't small.; He's as tall as I am."

"I suppose he is.; Dash, I've dropped my stud."

Wyatt waited patiently till he had retrieved it.; Then he returned to the attack.

"He's as good a bat as his brother, and a better field."

"Old Bob can't field for toffee.; I will say that for him.; Dropped a sitter off me to-day.; Why the deuce fellows can't hold catches when they drop slowly into their mouths I'm hanged if I can see."

"You play him," said Wyatt.; "Just give him a trial.; That kid's a genius at cricket.; He's going to be better than any of his brothers, even Joe.; Give him a shot."

Burgess hesitated.

"You know, it's a bit risky," he said.; "With you three lunatics out of the team we can't afford to try many experiments.; Better stick to the men at the top of the second."

Wyatt got up, and kicked the wall as a vent for his feelings.

"You rotter," he said.; "Can't you *see* when you've got a good man?; Here's this kid waiting for you ready made with a style like Trumper's, and you rave about top men in the second, chaps who play forward at everything, and pat half-volleys back to the bowler!; Do you realise that your only chance of being known to Posterity is as the man who gave M. Jackson his colours at Wrykyn?; In a few years he'll be playing for England, and you'll think it a favour if he nods to you in the pav. at Lord's.; When you're a white-haired old man you'll go doddering about, gassing to your grandchildren, poor kids, how you 'discovered' M. Jackson.; It'll be the only thing they'll respect you for."

Wyatt stopped for breath.

"All right," said Burgess, "I'll think it over.; Frightful gift of the gab you've got, Wyatt."

"Good," said Wyatt; "Think it over.; And don't forget what I said about the grandchildren.; You would like little Wyatt Burgess and the other little Burgesses to respect you in your old age, wouldn't you?; Very well, then.; So long.; The bell went ages ago.; I shall be locked out."

* * * * *

On the Monday morning Mike passed the notice-board just as Burgess turned away from pinning up the list of the team to play the M.C.C.; He read it, and his heart missed a beat.; For, bottom but one, just above the W. B. Burgess, was a name that leaped from the paper at him.; His own name.

CHAPTER XIII

THE M.C.C. MATCH

If the day happens to be fine, there is a curious, dream-like atmosphere about the opening stages of a first eleven match. Everything seems hushed and expectant. The rest of the school have gone in after the interval at eleven o'clock, and you are alone on the grounds with a cricket-bag. The only signs of life are a few pedestrians on the road beyond the railings and one or two blazer and flannel-clad forms in the pavilion. The sense of isolation is trying to the nerves, and a school team usually bats 25 per cent. better after lunch, when the strangeness has worn off.

Mike walked across from Wain's, where he had changed, feeling quite hollow. He could almost have cried with pure fright. Bob had shouted after him from a window as he passed Donaldson's, to wait, so that they could walk over together; but conversation was the last thing Mike desired at that moment.

He had almost reached the pavilion when one of the M.C.C. team came down the steps, saw him, and stopped dead.

"By Jove, Saunders!" cried Mike.

"Why, Master Mike!"

The professional beamed, and quite suddenly, the lost, hopeless feeling left Mike. He felt as cheerful as if he and Saunders had met in the meadow at home, and were just going to begin a little quiet net-practice.

"Why, Master Mike, you don't mean to say you're playing for the school already?"

Mike nodded happily.

"Isn't it ripping," he said.

Saunders slapped his leg in a sort of ecstasy.

"Didn't I always say it, sir," he chuckled. "Wasn't I right? I used to say to myself it 'ud be a pretty good school team that 'ud leave you out."

"Of course, I'm only playing as a sub., you know. Three chaps are in extra, and I got one of the places."

"Well, you'll make a hundred to-day, Master Mike, and then they'll have to put you in."

"Wish I could!"

"Master Joe's come down with the Club," said Saunders.

"Joe! Has he really? How ripping! Hullo, here he is. Hullo, Joe?"

The greatest of all the Jacksons was descending the pavilion steps with the gravity befitting an All England batsman. He stopped short, as Saunders had done.

"Mike! You aren't playing!"

"Yes."

"Well, I'm hanged! Young marvel, isn't he, Saunders?"

"He is, sir," said Saunders. "Got all the strokes. I always said it, Master Joe. Only wants the strength."

Joe took Mike by the shoulder, and walked him off in the direction of a man in a Zingari blazer who was bowling slows to another of the M.C.C. team. Mike recognised him with awe as one of the three best amateur wicket-keepers in the country.

"What do you think of this?" said Joe, exhibiting Mike, who grinned bashfully. "Aged ten last birthday, and playing for the school. You are only ten, aren't you, Mike?"

"Brother of yours?" asked the wicket-keeper.

"Probably too proud to own the relationship, but he is."

"Isn't there any end to you Jacksons?" demanded the wicket-keeper in an aggrieved tone. "I never saw such a family."

"This is our star. You wait till he gets at us to-day. Saunders is our only bowler, and Mike's been brought up on Saunders. You'd better win the toss if you want a chance of getting a knock and lifting your average out of the minuses."

"I *have* won the toss," said the other with dignity. "Do you think I don't know the elementary duties of a captain?"

* * * * *

The school went out to field with mixed feelings. The wicket was hard and true, which would have made it pleasant to be going in first. On the other hand, they would feel decidedly better and fitter for centuries after the game had been in progress an hour or so. Burgess was glad as a private individual, sorry as a captain. For himself, the sooner he got hold of the ball and began to bowl the better he liked it. As a captain, he realised that a side with Joe Jackson on it, not to mention the other first-class men, was not a side to which he would have preferred to give away an advantage. Mike was feeling that by no possibility could he hold the simplest catch, and hoping that nothing would come his way. Bob, conscious of being an uncertain field, was feeling just the same.

The M.C.C. opened with Joe and a man in an Oxford Authentic cap. The beginning of the game was quiet. Burgess's yorker was nearly too much for the latter in the first over, but he contrived to chop it away, and the pair gradually settled down. At twenty, Joe began to open his shoulders. Twenty became forty with disturbing swiftness, and Burgess tried a change of bowling.

It seemed for one instant as if the move had been a success, for Joe, still taking risks, tried to late-cut a rising ball, and snicked it straight into Bob's hands at second slip. It was the easiest of slip-catches, but Bob fumbled it, dropped it, almost held it a second time, and finally let it fall miserably to the ground. It was a moment too painful for words. He rolled the ball back to the bowler in silence.

One of those weary periods followed when the batsman's defence seems to the fieldsmen absolutely impregnable. There was a sickening inevitableness in the way in which every ball was played with the very centre of the bat. And, as usual, just when things seemed most hopeless, relief came. The Authentic, getting in front of his wicket, to pull one of the simplest long-hops ever seen on a cricket field, missed it, and was l.b.w. And the next ball upset the newcomer's leg stump.

The school revived. Bowlers and field were infused with a new life. Another wicket —two stumps knocked out of the ground by Burgess —helped the thing on. When the bell rang for the end of morning school, five wickets were down for a hundred and thirteen.

But from the end of school till lunch things went very wrong indeed. Joe was still in at one end, invincible; and at the other was the great wicket-keeper. And the pair of them suddenly began to force the pace till the bowling was in a tangled knot. Four after four, all round the wicket, with never a chance or a mishit to vary the monotony. Two hundred went up, and two hundred and fifty. Then Joe reached his century, and was stumped next ball. Then came lunch.

The rest of the innings was like the gentle rain after the thunderstorm. Runs came with fair regularity, but wickets fell at intervals, and when the wicket-keeper was run out at length for a lively sixty-three, the end was very near. Saunders, coming in last, hit two boundaries, and was then caught by Mike. His second hit had just lifted the M.C.C. total over the three hundred.

* * * * *

Three hundred is a score that takes some making on any ground, but on a fine day it was not an unusual total for the Wrykyn eleven. Some years before, against Ripton, they had run up four hundred and sixteen; and only last season had massacred a very weak team of Old Wrykynians with a score that only just missed the fourth hundred.

Unfortunately, on the present occasion, there was scarcely time, unless the bowling happened to get completely collared, to make the runs. It was a quarter to four when the innings began, and stumps were to be drawn at a quarter to seven. A hundred an hour is quick work.

Burgess, however, was optimistic, as usual. "Better have a go for them," he said to Berridge and Marsh, the school first pair.

Following out this courageous advice, Berridge, after hitting three boundaries in his first two overs, was stumped half-way through the third.

After this, things settled down. Morris, the first-wicket man, was a thoroughly sound bat, a little on the slow side, but exceedingly hard to shift. He and Marsh proceeded to play themselves in, until it looked as if they were likely to stay till the drawing of stumps.

A comfortable, rather somnolent feeling settled upon the school. A long stand at cricket is a soothing sight to watch. There was an absence of hurry about the batsmen which harmonised well with the drowsy summer afternoon. And yet runs were coming at a fair pace. The hundred went up at five o'clock, the hundred and fifty at half-past. Both batsmen were completely at home, and the M.C.C. third-change bowlers had been put on.

Then the great wicket-keeper took off the pads and gloves, and the fieldsmen retired to posts at the extreme edge of the ground.

"Lobs," said Burgess. "By Jove, I wish I was in."

It seemed to be the general opinion among the members of the Wrykyn eleven on the pavilion balcony that Morris and Marsh were in luck. The team did not grudge them their good fortune, because they had earned it; but they were distinctly envious.

Lobs are the most dangerous, insinuating things in the world. Everybody knows in theory the right way to treat them. Everybody knows that the man who is content not to try to score more than a single cannot get out to them. Yet nearly everybody does get out to them.

It was the same story to-day. The first over yielded six runs, all through gentle taps along the ground. In the second, Marsh hit an over-pitched one along the ground to the terrace bank. The next ball he swept round to the leg boundary. And that was the end of Marsh. He saw himself scoring at the rate of twenty-four an over. Off the last ball he was stumped by several feet, having done himself credit by scoring seventy.

The long stand was followed, as usual, by a series of disasters. Marsh's wicket had fallen at a hundred and eighty. Ellerby left at a hundred and eighty-six. By the time the scoring-board registered two hundred, five wickets were down, three of them victims to the lobs. Morris was still in at one end. He had refused to be tempted. He was jogging on steadily to his century.

Bob Jackson went in next, with instructions to keep his eye on the lob-man.

For a time things went well. Saunders, who had gone on to bowl again after a rest, seemed to give Morris no trouble, and Bob put him through the slips with apparent ease. Twenty runs were added, when the lob-bowler once more got in his deadly work. Bob, letting alone a ball wide of the off-stump under the impression that it was going to break away, was disagreeably surprised to find it break in instead, and hit the wicket. The bowler smiled sadly, as if he hated to have to do these things.

Mike's heart jumped as he saw the bails go. It was his turn next.

"Two hundred and twenty-nine," said Burgess, "and it's ten past six. No good trying for the runs now. Stick in," he added to Mike. "That's all you've got to do."

All!... Mike felt as if he was being strangled. His heart was racing like the engines of a motor. He knew his teeth were chattering. He wished he could stop them. What a time Bob was taking to get back to the pavilion! He wanted to rush out, and get the thing over.

At last he arrived, and Mike, fumbling at a glove, tottered out into the sunshine. He heard miles and miles away a sound of clapping, and a thin, shrill noise as if somebody were screaming in the distance. As a matter of fact, several members of his form and of the junior day-room at Wain's nearly burst themselves at that moment.

At the wickets, he felt better. Bob had fallen to the last ball of the over, and Morris, standing ready for Saunders's delivery, looked so calm and certain of himself that it was impossible to feel entirely without hope and self-confidence. Mike knew that Morris had made ninety-eight, and he supposed that Morris knew that he was very near his century; yet he seemed to be absolutely undisturbed. Mike drew courage from his attitude.

Morris pushed the first ball away to leg. Mike would have liked to have run two, but short leg had retrieved the ball as he reached the crease.

The moment had come, the moment which he had experienced only in dreams. And in the dreams he was always full of confidence, and invariably hit a boundary. Sometimes a drive, sometimes a cut, but always a boundary.

"To leg, sir," said the umpire.

"Don't be in a funk," said a voice. "Play straight, and you can't get out."

It was Joe, who had taken the gloves when the wicket-keeper went on to bowl.

Mike grinned, wryly but gratefully.

Saunders was beginning his run. It was all so home-like that for a moment Mike felt himself again. How often he had seen those two little skips and the jump. It was like being in the paddock again, with Marjory and the dogs waiting by the railings to fetch the ball if he made a drive.

Saunders ran to the crease, and bowled.

Now, Saunders was a conscientious man, and, doubtless, bowled the very best ball that he possibly could. On the other hand, it was Mike's first appearance for the school, and Saunders, besides being conscientious, was undoubtedly kind-hearted. It is useless to speculate as to whether he was trying to bowl his best that ball. If so, he failed signally. It was a half-volley, just the right distance away from the off-stump; the sort of ball Mike was wont to send nearly through the net at home....

The next moment the dreams had come true. The umpire was signalling to the scoring-box, the school was shouting, extra-cover was trotting to the boundary to fetch the ball, and Mike was blushing and wondering whether it was bad form to grin.

From that ball onwards all was for the best in this best of all possible worlds. Saunders bowled no more half-volleys; but Mike played everything that he did bowl. He met the lobs with a bat like a barn-door. Even the departure of Morris, caught in the slips off Saunders's next over for a chanceless hundred and five, did not disturb him. All nervousness had left him. He felt equal to the situation. Burgess came in, and began to hit out as if he meant to knock off the runs. The bowling became a shade loose. Twice he was given full tosses to leg, which he hit to the terrace bank. Half-past six chimed, and two hundred and fifty went up on the telegraph board. Burgess continued to hit. Mike's whole soul was concentrated on keeping up his wicket. There was only Reeves to follow him, and Reeves was a victim to the first straight ball. Burgess had to hit because it was the only game he knew; but he himself must simply stay in.

The hands of the clock seemed to have stopped. Then suddenly he heard the umpire say "Last over," and he settled down to keep those six balls out of his wicket.

The lob bowler had taken himself off, and the Oxford Authentic had gone on, fast left-hand.

The first ball was short and wide of the off-stump. Mike let it alone. Number two: yorker. Got him! Three: straight half-volley. Mike played it back to the bowler. Four: beat him, and missed the wicket by an inch. Five: another yorker. Down on it again in the old familiar way.

All was well. The match was a draw now whatever happened to him. He hit out, almost at a venture, at the last ball, and mid-off, jumping, just failed to reach it. It hummed over his head, and ran like a streak along the turf and up the bank, and a great howl of delight went up from the school as the umpire took off the bails.

Mike walked away from the wickets with Joe and the wicket-keeper.

"I'm sorry about your nose, Joe," said the wicket-keeper in tones of grave solicitude.

"What's wrong with it?"

"At present," said the wicket-keeper, "nothing. But in a few years I'm afraid it's going to be put badly out of joint."

CHAPTER XIV

A SLIGHT IMBROGLIO

Mike got his third eleven colours after the M.C.C. match.; As he had made twenty-three not out in a crisis in a first eleven match, this may not seem an excessive reward.; But it was all that he expected.; One had to take the rungs of the ladder singly at Wrykyn.; First one was given one's third eleven cap.; That meant, "You are a promising man, and we have our eye on you."; Then came the second colours.; They might mean anything from "Well, here you *are*.; You won't get any higher, so you may as well have the thing now," to "This is just to show that we still have our eye on you."

Mike was a certainty now for the second.; But it needed more than one performance to secure the first cap.

"I told you so," said Wyatt, naturally, to Burgess after the match.

"He's not bad," said Burgess.; "I'll give him another shot."

But Burgess, as has been pointed out, was not a person who ever became gushing with enthusiasm.

* * * * *

So Wilkins, of the School House, who had played twice for the first eleven, dropped down into the second, as many a good man had done before him, and Mike got his place in the next match, against the Gentlemen of the County.; Unfortunately for him, the visiting team, however gentlemanly, were not brilliant cricketers, at any rate as far as bowling was concerned.; The school won the toss, went in first, and made three hundred and sixteen for five wickets, Morris making another placid century.; The innings was declared closed before Mike had a chance of distinguishing himself.; In an innings which lasted for one over he made two runs, not out; and had to console himself for the cutting short of his performance by the fact that his average for the school was still infinity.; Bob, who was one of those lucky enough to have an unabridged innings, did better in this match, making twenty-five.; But with Morris making a hundred and seventeen, and Berridge, Ellerby, and Marsh all passing the half-century, this score did not show up excessively.

We now come to what was practically a turning-point in Mike's career at Wrykyn.; There is no doubt that his meteor-like flights at cricket had an unsettling effect on him.; He was enjoying life amazingly, and, as is not uncommon with the prosperous, he waxed fat and kicked.; Fortunately for him —though he did not look upon it in that light at the time —he kicked the one person it was most imprudent to kick.; The person he selected was Firby-Smith.; With anybody else the thing might have blown over, to the detriment of Mike's character; but Firby-Smith, having the most tender affection for his dignity, made a fuss.

It happened in this way.; The immediate cause of the disturbance was a remark of Mike's, but the indirect cause was the unbearably patronising manner which the head of Wain's chose to adopt towards him.; The fact that he was playing for the school seemed to make no difference at all.; Firby-Smith continued to address Mike merely as the small boy.

The following, *verbatim*, was the tactful speech which he addressed to him on the evening of the M.C.C. match, having summoned him to his study for the purpose.

"Well," he said, "you played a very decent innings this afternoon, and I suppose you're frightfully pleased with yourself, eh?; Well, mind you don't go getting swelled head.; See?; That's all.; Run along."

Mike departed, bursting with fury.

The next link in the chain was forged a week after the Gentlemen of the County match.; House matches had begun, and Wain's were playing Appleby's.; Appleby's made a hundred and fifty odd, shaping badly for the most part against Wyatt's slows.; Then Wain's opened their innings.; The Gazeka, as head of the house, was captain of the side, and he and Wyatt went in first.; Wyatt made a few mighty hits, and was then caught at cover.; Mike went in first wicket.

For some ten minutes all was peace.; Firby-Smith scratched away at his end, getting here and there a single and now and then a two, and Mike settled down at once to play what he felt was going to be the innings of a lifetime.; Appleby's bowling was on the feeble side, with Raikes, of the third eleven, as the star, supported by some small change.; Mike pounded it vigorously.; To one who had been brought up on Saunders, Raikes possessed few subtleties.; He had made seventeen, and was thoroughly set, when the Gazeka, who had the bowling, hit one in the direction of cover-point.; With a certain type of batsman a single is a thing to take big risks for.; And the Gazeka badly wanted that single.

"Come on," he shouted, prancing down the pitch.

Mike, who had remained in his crease with the idea that nobody even moderately sane would attempt a run for a hit like that, moved forward in a startled and irresolute manner.; Firby-Smith arrived, shouting "Run!" and, cover having thrown the ball in, the wicket-keeper removed the bails.

These are solemn moments.

The only possible way of smoothing over an episode of this kind is for the guilty man to grovel.

Firby-Smith did not grovel.

"Easy run there, you know," he said reprovingly.

The world swam before Mike's eyes.; Through the red mist he could see Firby-Smith's face.; The sun glinted on his rather prominent teeth.; To Mike's distorted vision it seemed that the criminal was amused.

"Don't *laugh*, you grinning ape!" he cried.; "It isn't funny."

"DON'T *LAUGH*, YOU GRINNING APE!"

He then made for the trees where the rest of the team were sitting.

Now Firby-Smith not only possessed rather prominent teeth; he was also sensitive on the subject.; Mike's shaft sank in deeply.; The fact that emotion caused him to swipe at a straight half-volley, miss it, and be bowled next ball made the wound rankle.

He avoided Mike on his return to the trees.; And Mike, feeling now a little apprehensive, avoided him.

The Gazeka brooded apart for the rest of the afternoon, chewing the insult.; At close of play he sought Burgess.

Burgess, besides being captain of the eleven, was also head of the school.; He was the man who arranged prefects' meetings.; And only a prefects' meeting, thought Firby-Smith, could adequately avenge his lacerated dignity.

"I want to speak to you, Burgess," he said.

"What's up?" said Burgess.

"You know young Jackson in our house."

"What about him?"

"He's been frightfully insolent."

"Cheeked you?" said Burgess, a man of simple speech.

"I want you to call a prefects' meeting, and lick him."

Burgess looked incredulous.

"Rather a large order, a prefects' meeting," he said.; "It has to be a pretty serious sort of thing for that."

"Frightful cheek to a school prefect is a serious thing," said Firby-Smith, with the air of one uttering an epigram.

"Well, I suppose —What did he say to you?"

Firby-Smith related the painful details.

Burgess started to laugh, but turned the laugh into a cough.

"Yes," he said meditatively.; "Rather thick.; Still, I mean —A prefects' meeting.; Rather like crushing a thingummy with a what-d'you-call-it.; Besides, he's a decent kid."

"He's frightfully conceited."

"Oh, well —Well, anyhow, look here, I'll think it over, and let you know to-morrow.; It's not the sort of thing to rush through without thinking about it."

And the matter was left temporarily at that.

CHAPTER XV

MIKE CREATES A VACANCY

Burgess walked off the ground feeling that fate was not using him well.

Here was he, a well-meaning youth who wanted to be on good terms with all the world, being jockeyed into slaughtering a kid whose batting he admired and whom personally he liked.; And the worst of it was that he sympathised with Mike.; He knew what it felt like to be run out just when one had got set, and he knew exactly how maddening the Gazeka's manner would be on such an occasion.; On the other hand, officially he was bound to support the head of Wain's.; Prefects must stand together or chaos will come.

He thought he would talk it over with somebody.; Bob occurred to him.; It was only fair that Bob should be told, as the nearest of kin.

And here was another grievance against fate.; Bob was a person he did not particularly wish to see just then.; For that morning he had posted up the list of the team to play for the school against Geddington, one of the four schools which Wrykyn met at cricket; and Bob's name did not appear on that list.; Several things had contributed to that melancholy omission.; In the first place, Geddington, to judge from the weekly reports in the *Sportsman* and *Field*, were strong this year at batting.; In the second place, the results of the last few matches, and particularly the M.C.C. match, had given Burgess the idea that Wrykyn was weak at bowling.; It became necessary, therefore, to drop a batsman out of the team in favour of a bowler.; And either Mike or Bob must be the man.

Burgess was as rigidly conscientious as the captain of a school eleven should be.; Bob was one of his best friends, and he would have given much to be able to put him in the team; but he thought the thing over, and put the temptation sturdily behind him.; At batting there was not much to choose between the two, but in fielding there was a great deal.; Mike was good.; Bob was bad.; So out Bob had gone, and Neville-Smith, a fair fast bowler at all times and on his day dangerous, took his place.

These clashings of public duty with private inclination are the drawbacks to the despotic position of captain of cricket at a public school.; It is awkward having to meet your best friend after you have dropped him from the team, and it is difficult to talk to him as if nothing had happened.

Burgess felt very self-conscious as he entered Bob's study, and was rather glad that he had a topic of conversation ready to hand.

"Busy, Bob?" he asked.

"Hullo," said Bob, with a cheerfulness rather over-done in his anxiety to show Burgess, the man, that he did not hold him responsible in any way for the distressing acts of Burgess, the captain.; "Take a pew.; Don't these studies get beastly hot this weather.; There's some ginger-beer in the cupboard.; Have some?"

"No, thanks.; I say, Bob, look here, I want to see you."

"Well, you can, can't you?; This is me, sitting over here.; The tall, dark, handsome chap."

"It's awfully awkward, you know," continued Burgess gloomily; "that ass of a young brother of yours — Sorry, but he *is* an ass, though he's your brother — —"

"Thanks for the 'though,' Billy.; You know how to put a thing nicely.; What's Mike been up to?"

"It's that old fool the Gazeka.; He came to me frothing with rage, and wanted me to call a prefects' meeting and touch young Mike up."

Bob displayed interest and excitement for the first time.

"Prefects' meeting!; What the dickens is up?; What's he been doing?; Smith must be drunk.; What's all the row about?"

Burgess repeated the main facts of the case as he had them from Firby-Smith.

"Personally, I sympathise with the kid," he added, "Still, the Gazeka *is* a prefect — —"

Bob gnawed a pen-holder morosely.

"Silly young idiot," he said.

"Sickening thing being run out," suggested Burgess.

"Still — —"

"I know.; It's rather hard to see what to do.; I suppose if the Gazeka insists, one's bound to support him."

"I suppose so."

"Awful rot.; Prefects' lickings aren't meant for that sort of thing.; They're supposed to be for kids who steal buns at the shop or muck about generally.; Not for a chap who curses a fellow who runs him out.; I tell you what, there's just a chance Firby-Smith won't press the thing.; He hadn't had time to get over it when he saw me.; By now he'll have simmered down a bit.; Look here, you're a pal of his, aren't you?; Well, go and ask him to drop the business.; Say you'll curse your brother and make him apologise, and that I'll kick him out of the team for the Geddington match."

It was a difficult moment for Bob.; One cannot help one's thoughts, and for an instant the idea of going to Geddington with the team, as he would certainly do if Mike did not play, made him waver.; But he recovered himself.

"Don't do that," he said.; "I don't see there's a need for anything of that sort.; You must play the best side you've got.; I can easily talk the old Gazeka over.; He gets all right in a second if he's treated the right way.; I'll go and do it now."

Burgess looked miserable.

"I say, Bob," he said.

"Yes?"

"Oh, nothing —I mean, you're not a bad sort.".; With which glowing eulogy he dashed out of the room, thanking his stars that he had won through a confoundedly awkward business.

Bob went across to Wain's to interview and soothe Firby-Smith.

He found that outraged hero sitting moodily in his study like Achilles in his tent.

Seeing Bob, he became all animation.

"Look here," he said, "I wanted to see you.; You know, that frightful young brother of yours — —"

"I know, I know," said Bob.; "Burgess was telling me.; He wants kicking."

"He wants a frightful licking from the prefects," emended the aggrieved party.

"Well, I don't know, you know.; Not much good lugging the prefects into it, is there?; I mean, apart from everything else, not much of a catch for me, would it be, having to sit there and look on.; I'm a prefect, too, you know."

Firby-Smith looked a little blank at this.; He had a great admiration for Bob.

"I didn't think of you," he said.

"I thought you hadn't," said Bob.; "You see it now, though, don't you?"

Firby-Smith returned to the original grievance.

"Well, you know, it was frightful cheek."

"Of course it was.; Still, I think if I saw him and cursed him, and sent him up to you to apologise —How would that do?"

"All right.; After all, I did run him out."

"Yes, there's that, of course.; Mike's all right, really.; It isn't as if he did that sort of thing as a habit."

"No.; All right then."

"Thanks," said Bob, and went to find Mike.

* * * * *

The lecture on deportment which he read that future All-England batsman in a secluded passage near the junior day-room left the latter rather limp and exceedingly meek.; For the moment all the jauntiness and exuberance had been drained out of him.; He was a punctured balloon.; Reflection, and the distinctly discouraging replies of those experts in school law to whom he had put the question, "What d'you think he'll do?" had induced a very chastened frame of mind.

He perceived that he had walked very nearly into a hornets' nest, and the realisation of his escape made him agree readily to all the conditions imposed.; The apology to the Gazeka was made without reserve, and the offensively forgiving, say-no-more-about-it-but-take-care-in-future air of the head of the house roused no spark of resentment in him, so subdued was his fighting spirit.; All he wanted was to get the thing done with.; He was not inclined to be critical.

And, most of all, he felt grateful to Bob.; Firby-Smith, in the course of his address, had not omitted to lay stress on the importance of Bob's intervention.; But for Bob, he gave him to understand, he, Mike, would have been prosecuted with the utmost rigour of the law.; Mike came away with a confused picture in his mind of a horde of furious prefects bent on his slaughter, after the manner of a stage "excited crowd," and Bob waving them back.; He realised that Bob had done him a good turn.; He wished he could find some way of repaying him.

Curiously enough, it was an enemy of Bob's who suggested the way —Burton, of Donaldson's.; Burton was a slippery young gentleman, fourteen years of age, who had frequently come into contact with Bob in the house, and owed him many grudges.; With Mike he had always tried to form an alliance, though without success.

He happened to meet Mike going to school next morning, and unburdened his soul to him.; It chanced that Bob and he had had another small encounter immediately after breakfast, and Burton felt revengeful.

"I say," said Burton, "I'm jolly glad you're playing for the first against Geddington."

"Thanks," said Mike.

"I'm specially glad for one reason."

"What's that?" inquired Mike, without interest.

"Because your beast of a brother has been chucked out.; He'd have been playing but for you."

At any other time Mike would have heard Bob called a beast without active protest.; He would have felt that it was no business of his to fight his brother's battles for him.; But on this occasion he deviated from his rule.

He kicked Burton.; Not once or twice, but several times, so that Burton, retiring hurriedly, came to the conclusion that it must be something in the Jackson blood, some taint, as it were.; They were *all* beasts.

* * * * *

Mike walked on, weighing this remark, and gradually made up his mind.; It must be remembered that he was in a confused mental condition, and that the only thing he realised clearly was that Bob had pulled him out of an uncommonly nasty hole.; It seemed to him that it was necessary to repay Bob.; He thought the thing over more fully during school, and his decision remained unaltered.

On the evening before the Geddington match, just before lock-up, Mike tapped at Burgess's study door.; He tapped with his right hand, for his left was in a sling.

"Come in!" yelled the captain.; "Hullo!"

"I'm awfully sorry, Burgess," said Mike.; "I've crocked my wrist a bit."

"How did you do that?; You were all right at the nets?"

"Slipped as I was changing," said Mike stolidly.

"Is it bad?"

"Nothing much.; I'm afraid I shan't be able to play to-morrow."

"I say, that's bad luck.; Beastly bad luck.; We wanted your batting, too.; Be all right, though, in a day or two, I suppose?"

"Oh, yes, rather."

"Hope so, anyway."

"Thanks.; Good-night."

"Good-night."

And Burgess, with the comfortable feeling that he had managed to combine duty and pleasure after all, wrote a note to Bob at Donaldson's, telling him to be ready to start with the team for Geddington by the 8.54 next morning.

CHAPTER XVI

AN EXPERT EXAMINATION

Mike's Uncle John was a wanderer on the face of the earth.; He had been an army surgeon in the days of his youth, and, after an adventurous career, mainly in Afghanistan, had inherited enough money to keep him in comfort for the rest of his life.; He had thereupon left the service, and now spent most of his time flitting from one spot of Europe to another.; He had been dashing up to Scotland on the day when Mike first became a Wrykynian, but a few weeks in an uncomfortable hotel in Skye and a few days in a comfortable one in Edinburgh had left him with the impression that he had now seen all that there was to be seen in North Britain and might reasonably shift his camp again.

Coming south, he had looked in on Mike's people for a brief space, and, at the request of Mike's mother, took the early express to Wrykyn in order to pay a visit of inspection.

His telegram arrived during morning school.; Mike went down to the station to meet him after lunch.

Uncle John took command of the situation at once.

"School playing anybody to-day, Mike?; I want to see a match."

"They're playing Geddington.; Only it's away.; There's a second match on."

"Why aren't you —Hullo, I didn't see.; What have you been doing to yourself?"

"Crocked my wrist a bit.; It's nothing much."

"How did you do that?"

"Slipped while I was changing after cricket."

"Hurt?"

"Not much, thanks."

"Doctor seen it?"

"No.; But it's really nothing.; Be all right by Monday."

"H'm.; Somebody ought to look at it.; I'll have a look later on."

Mike did not appear to relish this prospect.

"It isn't anything, Uncle John, really.; It doesn't matter a bit."

"Never mind.; It won't do any harm having somebody examine it who knows a bit about these things.; Now, what shall we do.; Go on the river?"

"I shouldn't be able to steer."

"I could manage about that.; Still, I think I should like to see the place first.; Your mother's sure to ask me if you showed me round.; It's like going over the stables when you're stopping at a country-house.; Got to be done, and better do it as soon as possible."

It is never very interesting playing the part of showman at school.; Both Mike and his uncle were inclined to scamp the business.; Mike pointed out the various landmarks without much enthusiasm —it is only after one has left a few years that the school buildings take to themselves romance —and Uncle John said, "Ah yes, I see.; Very nice," two or three times in an absent voice; and they passed on to the cricket field, where the second eleven were playing a neighbouring engineering school.; It was a glorious day.; The sun had never seemed to Mike so bright or the grass so green.; It was one of those days when the ball looks like a large vermilion-coloured football as it leaves the bowler's hand.; If ever there was a day when it seemed to Mike that a century would have been a certainty, it was this Saturday.; A sudden, bitter realisation of all he had given up swept over him, but he choked the feeling down.; The thing was done, and it was no good brooding over the might-have-beens now.; Still —And the Geddington ground was supposed to be one of the easiest scoring grounds of all the public schools!

"Well hit, by George!" remarked Uncle John, as Trevor, who had gone in first wicket for the second eleven, swept a half-volley to leg round to the bank where they were sitting.

"That's Trevor," said Mike.; "Chap in Donaldson's.; The fellow at the other end is Wilkins.; He's in the School House.; They look as if they were getting set.; By Jove," he said enviously, "pretty good fun batting on a day like this."

Uncle John detected the envious note.

"I suppose you would have been playing here but for your wrist?"

"No, I was playing for the first."

"For the first?; For the school!; My word, Mike, I didn't know that.; No wonder you're feeling badly treated.; Of course, I remember your father saying you had played once for the school, and done well; but I thought that was only as a substitute.; I didn't know you were a regular member of the team.; What bad luck.; Will you get another chance?"

"Depends on Bob."

"Has Bob got your place?"

Mike nodded.

"If he does well to-day, they'll probably keep him in."

"Isn't there room for both of you?"

"Such a lot of old colours.; There are only three vacancies, and Henfrey got one of those a week ago.; I expect they'll give one of the other two to a bowler, Neville-Smith, I should think, if he does well against Geddington.; Then there'll be only the last place left."

"Rather awkward, that."

"Still, it's Bob's last year.; I've got plenty of time.; But I wish I could get in this year."

After they had watched the match for an hour, Uncle John's restless nature asserted itself.

"Suppose we go for a pull on the river now?" he suggested.

They got up.

"Let's just call at the shop," said Mike.; "There ought to be a telegram from Geddington by this time.; I wonder how Bob's got on."

Apparently Bob had not had a chance yet of distinguishing himself.; The telegram read, "Geddington 151 for four.; Lunch."

"Not bad that," said Mike.; "But I believe they're weak in bowling."

They walked down the road towards the school landing-stage.

"The worst of a school," said Uncle John, as he pulled up-stream with strong, unskilful stroke, "is that one isn't allowed to smoke on the grounds.; I badly want a pipe.; The next piece of shade that you see, sing out, and we'll put in there."

"Pull your left," said Mike.; "That willow's what you want."

Uncle John looked over his shoulder, caught a crab, recovered himself, and steered the boat in under the shade of the branches.

"Put the rope over that stump.; Can you manage with one hand?; Here, let me —Done it?; Good.; A-ah!"

He blew a great cloud of smoke into the air, and sighed contentedly.

"I hope you don't smoke, Mike?"

"No."

"Rotten trick for a boy.; When you get to my age you need it.; Boys ought to be thinking about keeping themselves fit and being good at games.; Which reminds me.; Let's have a look at the wrist."

A hunted expression came into Mike's eyes.

"It's really nothing," he began, but his uncle had already removed the sling, and was examining the arm with the neat rapidity of one who has been brought up to such things.

To Mike it seemed as if everything in the world was standing still and waiting.; He could hear nothing but his own breathing.

His uncle pressed the wrist gingerly once or twice, then gave it a little twist.

"That hurt?" he asked.

"Ye —no," stammered Mike.

Uncle John looked up sharply.; Mike was crimson.

"What's the game?" inquired Uncle John.

Mike said nothing.

There was a twinkle in his uncle's eyes.

"May as well tell me.; I won't give you away.; Why this wounded warrior business when you've no more the matter with you than I have?"

Mike hesitated.

"I only wanted to get out of having to write this morning.; There was an exam. on."

The idea had occurred to him just before he spoke.; It had struck him as neat and plausible. To Uncle John it did not appear in the same light.

"Do you always write with your left hand?; And if you had gone with the first eleven to Geddington, wouldn't that have got you out of your exam?; Try again."

When in doubt, one may as well tell the truth.; Mike told it.

"I know.; It wasn't that, really.; Only ——"

"Well?"

"Oh, well, dash it all then.; Old Bob got me out of an awful row the day before yesterday, and he seemed a bit sick at not playing for the first, so I thought I might as well let him.; That's how it was.; Look here, swear you won't tell him."

Uncle John was silent.; Inwardly he was deciding that the five shillings which he had intended to bestow on Mike on his departure should become a sovereign. (This, it may be mentioned as an interesting biographical fact, was the only occasion in his life on which Mike earned money at the rate of fifteen shillings a half-minute.)

"Swear you won't tell him.; He'd be most frightfully sick if he knew."

"I won't tell him."

Conversation dwindled to vanishing-point.; Uncle John smoked on in weighty silence, while Mike, staring up at the blue sky through the branches of the willow, let his mind wander to Geddington, where his fate was even now being sealed.; How had the school got on?; What had Bob done?; If he made about twenty, would they give him his cap?; Supposing....

A faint snore from Uncle John broke in on his meditations.; Then there was a clatter as a briar pipe dropped on to the floor of the boat, and his uncle sat up, gaping.

"Jove, I was nearly asleep.; What's the time?; Just on six?; Didn't know it was so late."

"I ought to be getting back soon, I think.; Lock-up's at half-past."

"Up with the anchor, then.; You can tackle that rope with two hands now, eh?; We are not observed.; Don't fall overboard.; I'm going to shove her off."

"There'll be another telegram, I should think," said Mike, as they reached the school gates.

"Shall we go and look?"

They walked to the shop.

A second piece of grey paper had been pinned up under the first.; Mike pushed his way through the crowd.; It was a longer message this time.

It ran as follows:;

;;;"Geddington 247 (Burgess six wickets, Neville-Smith four).;

;;;Wrykyn 270 for nine (Berridge 86, Marsh 58, Jackson 48)."

Mike worked his way back through the throng, and rejoined his uncle.

"Well?" said Uncle John.

"We won."

He paused for a moment.

"Bob made forty-eight," he added carelessly.

Uncle John felt in his pocket, and silently slid a sovereign into Mike's hand.

It was the only possible reply.

CHAPTER XVII

ANOTHER VACANCY

Wyatt got back late that night, arriving at the dormitory as Mike was going to bed.

"By Jove, I'm done," he said.; "It was simply baking at Geddington.; And I came back in a carriage with Neville-Smith and Ellerby, and they ragged the whole time.; I wanted to go to sleep, only they wouldn't let me.; Old Smith was awfully bucked because he'd taken four wickets.; I should think he'd go off his nut if he took eight ever.; He was singing comic songs when he wasn't trying to put Ellerby under the seat.; How's your wrist?"

"Oh, better, thanks."

Wyatt began to undress.

"Any colours?" asked Mike after a pause.; First eleven colours were generally given in the pavilion after a match or on the journey home.

"No.; Only one or two thirds.; Jenkins and Clephane, and another chap, can't remember who.; No first, though."

"What was Bob's innings like?"

"Not bad.; A bit lucky.; He ought to have been out before he'd scored, and he was out when he'd made about sixteen, only the umpire didn't seem to know that it's l-b-w when you get your leg right in front of the wicket and the ball hits it.; Never saw a clearer case in my life.; I was in at the other end.; Bit rotten for the Geddington chaps.; Just lost them the match.; Their umpire, too.; Bit of luck for Bob.; He didn't give the ghost of a chance after that."

"I should have thought they'd have given him his colours."

"Most captains would have done, only Burgess is so keen on fielding that he rather keeps off it."

"Why, did he field badly?"

"Rottenly.; And the man always will choose Billy's bowling to drop catches off.; And Billy would cut his rich uncle from Australia if he kept on dropping them off him.; Bob's fielding's perfectly sinful.; He was pretty bad at the beginning of the season, but now he's got so nervous that he's a dozen times worse.; He turns a delicate green when he sees a catch coming.; He let their best man off twice in one over, off Billy, to-day; and the chap went on and made a hundred odd.; Ripping innings bar those two chances.; I hear he's got an average of eighty in school matches this season.; Beastly man to bowl to.; Knocked me off in half a dozen overs.; And, when he does give a couple of easy chances, Bob puts them both on the floor.; Billy wouldn't have given him his cap after the match if he'd made a hundred.; Bob's the sort of man who wouldn't catch a ball if you handed it to him on a plate, with watercress round it."

Burgess, reviewing the match that night, as he lay awake in his cubicle, had come to much the same conclusion.; He was very fond of Bob, but two missed catches in one over was straining the bonds of human affection too far.; There would have been serious trouble between David and Jonathan if either had persisted in dropping catches off the other's bowling.; He writhed in bed as he remembered the second of the two chances which the wretched Bob had refused.; The scene was indelibly printed on his mind.; Chap had got a late cut which he fancied rather.; With great guile he had fed this late cut.; Sent down a couple which he put to the boundary.; Then fired a third much faster and a bit shorter.; Chap had a go at it, just as he had expected:; and he felt that life was a good thing after all when the ball just touched the corner of the bat and flew into Bob's hands.; And Bob dropped it!

The memory was too bitter.; If he dwelt on it, he felt, he would get insomnia.; So he turned to pleasanter reflections:; the yorker which had shattered the second-wicket man, and the slow head-ball which had led to a big hitter being caught on the boundary.; Soothed by these memories, he fell asleep.

Next morning he found himself in a softened frame of mind.; He thought of Bob's iniquities with sorrow rather than wrath.; He felt towards him much as a father feels towards a prodigal son whom there is still a chance of reforming.; He overtook Bob on his way to chapel.

Directness was always one of Burgess's leading qualities.

"Look here, Bob.; About your fielding.; It's simply awful."

Bob was all remorse.

"It's those beastly slip catches.; I can't time them."

"That one yesterday was right into your hands.; Both of them were."

"I know.; I'm frightfully sorry."

"Well, but I mean, why *can't* you hold them?; It's no good being a good bat —you're that all right —if you're going to give away runs in the field."

"Do you know, I believe I should do better in the deep.; I could get time to watch them there.; I wish you'd give me a shot in the deep —for the second."

"Second be blowed!; I want your batting in the first.; Do you think you'd really do better in the deep?"

"I'm almost certain I should.; I'll practise like mad.; Trevor'll hit me up catches.; I hate the slips.; I get in the dickens of a funk directly the bowler starts his run now.; I know that if a catch does come, I shall miss it.; I'm certain the deep would be much better."

"All right then.; Try it."

The conversation turned to less pressing topics.

* * * * *

In the next two matches, accordingly, Bob figured on the boundary, where he had not much to do except throw the ball back to the bowler, and stop an occasional drive along the carpet.; The beauty of fielding in the deep is that no unpleasant surprises can be sprung upon one.; There is just that moment or two for collecting one's thoughts which makes the whole difference.; Bob, as he stood regarding the game from afar, found his self-confidence returning slowly, drop by drop.

As for Mike, he played for the second, and hoped for the day.

* * * * *

His opportunity came at last.; It will be remembered that on the morning after the Great Picnic the headmaster made an announcement in Hall to the effect that, owing to an outbreak of chicken-pox in the town, all streets except the High Street would be out of bounds.; This did not affect the bulk of the school, for most of the shops to which any one ever thought of going were in the High Street.; But there were certain inquiring minds who liked to ferret about in odd corners.

Among these was one Leather-Twigg, of Seymour's, better known in criminal circles as Shoeblossom.

Shoeblossom was a curious mixture of the Energetic Ragger and the Quiet Student.; On a Monday evening you would hear a hideous uproar proceeding from Seymour's junior day-room; and, going down with a swagger-stick to investigate, you would find a tangled heap of squealing humanity on the floor, and at the bottom of the heap, squealing louder than any two others, would be Shoeblossom, his collar burst and blackened and his face apoplectically crimson.; On the Tuesday afternoon, strolling in some shady corner of the grounds you would come upon him lying on his chest, deep in some work of fiction and resentful of interruption.; On the Wednesday morning he would be in receipt of four hundred lines from his housemaster for breaking three windows and a gas-globe.; Essentially a man of moods, Shoeblossom.

It happened about the date of the Geddington match that he took out from the school library a copy of "The Iron Pirate," and for the next day or two he wandered about like a lost spirit trying to find a sequestered spot in which to read it.; His inability to hit on such a spot was rendered more irritating by the fact that, to judge from the first few chapters (which he had managed to get through during prep. one night under the eye of a short-sighted master), the book was obviously the last word in hot stuff.; He tried the junior day-room, but people threw cushions at him.; He tried out of doors, and a ball hit from a neighbouring net nearly scalped him.; Anything in the nature of concentration became impossible in these circumstances.

Then he recollected that in a quiet backwater off the High Street there was a little confectioner's shop, where tea might be had at a reasonable sum, and also, what was more important, peace.

He made his way there, and in the dingy back shop, all amongst the dust and bluebottles, settled down to a thoughtful perusal of chapter six.

Upstairs, at the same moment, the doctor was recommending that Master John George, the son of the house, be kept warm and out of draughts and not permitted to scratch himself, however necessary such an action might seem to him.; In brief, he was attending J. G. for chicken-pox.

Shoeblossom came away, entering the High Street furtively, lest Authority should see him out of bounds, and returned to the school, where he went about his lawful occasions as if there were no such thing as chicken-pox in the world.

But all the while the microbe was getting in some unostentatious but clever work.; A week later Shoeblossom began to feel queer.; He had occasional headaches, and found himself oppressed by a queer distaste for food.; The professional advice of Dr. Oakes, the school doctor, was called for, and Shoeblossom took up his abode in the Infirmary, where he read *Punch*, sucked oranges, and thought of Life.

Two days later Barry felt queer.; He, too, disappeared from Society.

Chicken-pox is no respecter of persons.; The next victim was Marsh, of the first eleven.; Marsh, who was top of the school averages.; Where were his drives now, his late cuts that were wont to set the pavilion in a roar.; Wrapped in a blanket, and looking like the spotted marvel of a travelling circus, he was driven across to the Infirmary in a four-wheeler, and it became incumbent upon Burgess to select a substitute for him.

And so it came about that Mike soared once again into the ranks of the elect, and found his name down in the team to play against the Incogniti.

CHAPTER XVIII

BOB HAS NEWS TO IMPART

Wrykyn went down badly before the Incogs.; It generally happens at least once in a school cricket season that the team collapses hopelessly, for no apparent reason.; Some schools do it in nearly every match, but Wrykyn so far had been particularly fortunate this year.; They had only been beaten once, and that by a mere twenty odd runs in a hard-fought game.; But on this particular day, against a not overwhelmingly strong side, they failed miserably.; The weather may have had something to do with it, for rain fell early in the morning, and the school, batting first on the drying wicket, found themselves considerably puzzled by a slow left-hander.; Morris and Berridge left with the score still short of ten, and after that the rout began.; Bob, going in fourth wicket, made a dozen, and Mike kept his end up, and was not out eleven; but nobody except Wyatt, who hit out at everything and knocked up thirty before he was stumped, did anything to distinguish himself.; The total was a hundred and seven, and the Incogniti, batting when the wicket was easier, doubled this.

The general opinion of the school after this match was that either Mike or Bob would have to stand down from the team when it was definitely filled up, for Neville-Smith, by showing up well with the ball against the Incogniti when the others failed with the bat, made it practically certain that he would get one of the two vacancies.

"If I do" he said to Wyatt, "there will be the biggest bust of modern times at my place.; My pater is away for a holiday in Norway, and I'm alone, bar the servants.; And I can square them.; Will you come?"

"Tea?"

"Tea!" said Neville-Smith scornfully.

"Well, what then?"

"Don't you ever have feeds in the dorms. after lights-out in the houses?"

"Used to when I was a kid.; Too old now.; Have to look after my digestion.; I remember, three years ago, when Wain's won the footer cup, we got up and fed at about two in the morning.; All sorts of luxuries.; Sardines on sugar-biscuits.; I've got the taste in my mouth still.; Do you remember Macpherson?; Left a couple of years ago.; His food ran out, so he spread brown-boot polish on bread, and ate that.; Got through a slice, too.; Wonderful chap!; But what about this thing of yours?; What time's it going to be?"

"Eleven suit you?"

"All right."

"How about getting out?"

"I'll do it as quickly as the team did to-day.; I can't say more than that."

"You were all right."

"I'm an exceptional sort of chap."

"What about the Jacksons?"

"It's going to be a close thing.; If Bob's fielding were to improve suddenly, he would just do it.; But young Mike's all over him as a bat.; In a year or two that kid'll be a marvel.; He's bound to get in next year, of course, so perhaps it would be better if Bob got the place as it's his last season.; Still, one wants the best man, of course."

* * * * *

Mike avoided Bob as much as possible during this anxious period; and he privately thought it rather tactless of the latter when, meeting him one day outside Donaldson's, he insisted on his coming in and having some tea.

Mike shuffled uncomfortably as his brother filled the kettle and lit the Etna. It required more tact than he had at his disposal to carry off a situation like this.

Bob, being older, was more at his ease. He got tea ready, making desultory conversation the while, as if there were no particular reason why either of them should feel uncomfortable in the other's presence. When he had finished, he poured Mike out a cup, passed him the bread, and sat down.

"Not seen much of each other lately, Mike, what?"

Mike murmured unintelligibly through a mouthful of bread-and-jam.

"It's no good pretending it isn't an awkward situation," continued Bob, "because it is. Beastly awkward."

"Awful rot the pater sending us to the same school."

"Oh, I don't know. We've all been at Wrykyn. Pity to spoil the record. It's your fault for being such a young Infant Prodigy, and mine for not being able to field like an ordinary human being."

"You get on much better in the deep."

"Bit better, yes. Liable at any moment to miss a sitter, though. Not that it matters much really whether I do now."

Mike stared.

"What! Why?"

"That's what I wanted to see you about. Has Burgess said anything to you yet?"

"No. Why? What about?"

"Well, I've a sort of idea our little race is over. I fancy you've won."

"I've not heard a word — —"

"I have. I'll tell you what makes me think the thing's settled. I was in the pav. just now, in the First room, trying to find a batting-glove I'd mislaid. There was a copy of the *Wrykynian* lying on the mantelpiece, and I picked it up and started reading it. So there wasn't any noise to show anybody outside that there was some one in the room. And then I heard Burgess and Spence jawing on the steps. They thought the place was empty, of course. I couldn't help hearing what they said. The pav.'s like a sounding-board. I heard every word. Spence said, 'Well, it's about as difficult a problem as any captain of cricket at Wrykyn has ever had to tackle.' I had a sort of idea that old Billy liked to boss things all on his own, but apparently he does consult Spence sometimes. After all, he's cricket-master, and that's what he's there for. Well, Billy said, 'I don't know what to do. What do you think, sir?' Spence said, 'Well, I'll give you my opinion, Burgess, but don't feel bound to act on it. I'm simply saying what I think.'; 'Yes, sir,' said old Bill, doing a big Young Disciple with Wise Master act. '*I* think M.,' said Spence. 'Decidedly M. He's a shade better than R. now, and in a year or two, of course, there'll be no comparison.'"

"Oh, rot," muttered Mike, wiping the sweat off his forehead. This was one of the most harrowing interviews he had ever been through.

"Not at all. Billy agreed with him. 'That's just what I think, sir,' he said. 'It's rough on Bob, but still — —' And then they walked down the steps. I waited a bit to give them a good start, and then sheered off myself. And so home."

Mike looked at the floor, and said nothing.

There was nothing much to *be* said.

"Well, what I wanted to see you about was this," resumed Bob. "I don't propose to kiss you or anything; but, on the other hand, don't let's go to the other extreme. I'm not saying that it isn't a bit of a brick just missing my cap like this, but it would have been just as bad for you if you'd been the one dropped. It's the fortune of war. I don't want you to go about feeling that you've blighted my life, and so on, and dashing up side-streets to avoid me because you think the sight of you will be painful. As it isn't me, I'm jolly glad it's you; and I shall cadge a seat in the pavilion from you when you're playing for England at the Oval. Congratulate you."

It was the custom at Wrykyn, when you congratulated a man on getting colours, to shake his hand. They shook hands.

"Thanks, awfully, Bob," said Mike. And after that there seemed to be nothing much to talk about. So Mike edged out of the room, and tore across to Wain's.

He was sorry for Bob, but he would not have been human (which he certainly was) if the triumph of having won through at last into the first eleven had not dwarfed commiseration. It had been his one ambition, and now he had achieved it.

The annoying part of the thing was that he had nobody to talk to about it. Until the news was official he could not mention it to the common herd. It wouldn't do. The only possible confidant was Wyatt. And Wyatt was at Bisley, shooting with the School Eight for the Ashburton. For bull's-eyes as well as cats came within Wyatt's range as a marksman. Cricket took up too much of his time for him to be captain of the Eight and the man chosen to shoot for the Spencer, as he would otherwise almost certainly have been; but even though short of practice he was well up in the team.

Until he returned, Mike could tell nobody. And by the time he returned the notice would probably be up in the Senior Block with the other cricket notices.

In this fermenting state Mike went into the house.

The list of the team to play for Wain's *v.* Seymour's on the following Monday was on the board. As he passed it, a few words scrawled in pencil at the bottom caught his eye.

"All the above will turn out for house-fielding at 6.30 to-morrow morning. —W. F.-S."

"Oh, dash it," said Mike, "what rot! Why on earth can't he leave us alone!"

For getting up an hour before his customary time for rising was not among Mike's favourite pastimes. Still, orders were orders, he felt. It would have to be done.

CHAPTER XIX

MIKE GOES TO SLEEP AGAIN

Mike was a stout supporter of the view that sleep in large quantities is good for one.; He belonged to the school of thought which holds that a man becomes plain and pasty if deprived of his full spell in bed.; He aimed at the peach-bloom complexion.

To be routed out of bed a clear hour before the proper time, even on a summer morning, was not, therefore, a prospect that appealed to him.

When he woke it seemed even less attractive than it had done when he went to sleep.; He had banged his head on the pillow six times over-night, and this silent alarm proved effective, as it always does.; Reaching out a hand for his watch, he found that it was five minutes past six.

This was to the good.; He could manage another quarter of an hour between the sheets.; It would only take him ten minutes to wash and get into his flannels.

He took his quarter of an hour, and a little more.; He woke from a sort of doze to find that it was twenty-five past.

Man's inability to get out of bed in the morning is a curious thing.; One may reason with oneself clearly and forcibly without the slightest effect.; One knows that delay means inconvenience.; Perhaps it may spoil one's whole day.; And one also knows that a single resolute heave will do the trick.; But logic is of no use.; One simply lies there.

Mike thought he would take another minute.

And during that minute there floated into his mind the question, Who *was* Firby-Smith?; That was the point.; Who *was* he, after all?

This started quite a new train of thought.; Previously Mike had firmly intended to get up — some time.; Now he began to waver.

The more he considered the Gazeka's insignificance and futility and his own magnificence, the more outrageous did it seem that he should be dragged out of bed to please Firby-Smith's vapid mind.; Here was he, about to receive his first eleven colours on this very day probably, being ordered about, inconvenienced —in short, put upon by a worm who had only just scraped into the third.

Was this right, he asked himself.; Was this proper?

And the hands of the watch moved round to twenty to.

What was the matter with his fielding? *It* was all right.; Make the rest of the team fag about, yes.; But not a chap who, dash it all, had got his first *for* fielding!

It was with almost a feeling of self-righteousness that Mike turned over on his side and went to sleep again.

And outside in the cricket-field, the massive mind of the Gazeka was filled with rage, as it was gradually borne in upon him that this was not a question of mere lateness —which, he felt, would be bad enough, for when he said six-thirty he meant six-thirty —but of actual desertion.; It was time, he said to himself, that the foot of Authority was set firmly down, and the strong right hand of Justice allowed to put in some energetic work.; His comments on the team's fielding that morning were bitter and sarcastic.; His eyes gleamed behind their pince-nez.

The painful interview took place after breakfast.; The head of the house despatched his fag in search of Mike, and waited.; He paced up and down the room like a hungry lion, adjusting his pince-nez (a thing, by the way, which lions seldom do) and behaving in other respects like a monarch of the desert.; One would have felt, looking at him, that Mike, in coming to his den, was doing a deed which would make the achievement of Daniel seem in comparison like the tentative effort of some timid novice.

And certainly Mike was not without qualms as he knocked at the door, and went in in response to the hoarse roar from the other side of it.

Firby-Smith straightened his tie, and glared.

"Young Jackson," he said, "look here, I want to know what it all means, and jolly quick.; You weren't at house-fielding this morning.; Didn't you see the notice?"

Mike admitted that he had seen the notice.

"Then you frightful kid, what do you mean by it?; What?"

Mike hesitated.; Awfully embarrassing, this.; His real reason for not turning up to house-fielding was that he considered himself above such things, and Firby-Smith a toothy weed.; Could he give this excuse?; He had not his Book of Etiquette by him at the moment, but he rather fancied not.; There was no arguing against the fact that the head of the house *was* a toothy weed; but he felt a firm conviction that it would not be politic to say so.

Happy thought:; over-slept himself.

He mentioned this.

"Over-slept yourself!; You must jolly well not over-sleep yourself.; What do you mean by over-sleeping yourself?"

Very trying this sort of thing.

"What time did you wake up?"

"Six," said Mike.

It was not according to his complicated, yet intelligible code of morality to tell lies to save himself.; When others were concerned he could suppress the true and suggest the false with a face of brass.

"Six!"

"Five past."

"Why didn't you get up then?"

"I went to sleep again."

"Oh, you went to sleep again, did you?; Well, just listen to me.; I've had my eye on you for some time, and I've seen it coming on.; You've got swelled head, young man.; That's what you've got.; Frightful swelled head.; You think the place belongs to you."

"I don't," said Mike indignantly.

"Yes, you do," said the Gazeka shrilly.; "You think the whole frightful place belongs to you.; You go siding about as if you'd bought it.; Just because you've got your second, you think you can do what you like; turn up or not, as you please.; It doesn't matter whether I'm only in the third and you're in the first.; That's got nothing to do with it.; The point is that you're one of the house team, and I'm captain of it, so you've jolly well got to turn out for fielding with the others when I think it necessary.; See?"

Mike said nothing.

"Do —you —see, you frightful kid?"

"DO—YOU—SEE, YOU FRIGHTFUL KID?"

Mike remained stonily silent.; The rather large grain of truth in what Firby-Smith had said had gone home, as the unpleasant truth about ourselves is apt to do; and his feelings were hurt.; He was determined not to give in and say that he saw even if the head of the house invoked all the majesty of the prefects' room to help him, as he had nearly done once before.; He set his teeth, and stared at a photograph on the wall.

Firby-Smith's manner became ominously calm.; He produced a swagger-stick from a corner. "Do you see?" he asked again.

81

Mike's jaw set more tightly.

What one really wants here is a row of stars.

*;;;;; *;;;;; *;;;;; *;;;;; *

Mike was still full of his injuries when Wyatt came back.; Wyatt was worn out, but cheerful.; The school had finished sixth for the Ashburton, which was an improvement of eight places on their last year's form, and he himself had scored thirty at the two hundred and twenty-seven at the five hundred totals, which had put him in a very good humour with the world.

"Me ancient skill has not deserted me," he said, "That's the cats.; The man who can wing a cat by moonlight can put a bullet where he likes on a target.; I didn't hit the bull every time, but that was to give the other fellows a chance.; My fatal modesty has always been a hindrance to me in life, and I suppose it always will be.; Well, well!; And what of the old homestead?; Anything happened since I went away?; Me old father, is he well?; Has the lost will been discovered, or is there a mortgage on the family estates?; By Jove, I could do with a stoup of Malvoisie.; I wonder if the moke's gone to bed yet.; I'll go down and look.; A jug of water drawn from the well in the old courtyard where my ancestors have played as children for centuries back would just about save my life."

He left the dormitory, and Mike began to brood over his wrongs once more.

Wyatt came back, brandishing a jug of water and a glass.

"Oh, for a beaker full of the warm south, full of the true, the blushful Hippocrene!; Have you ever tasted Hippocrene, young Jackson?; Rather like ginger-beer, with a dash of raspberry-vinegar.; Very heady.; Failing that, water will do.; A-ah!"

He put down the glass, and surveyed Mike, who had maintained a moody silence throughout this speech.

"What's your trouble?" he asked.; "For pains in the back try Ju-jar.; If it's a broken heart, Zam-buk's what you want.; Who's been quarrelling with you?"

"It's only that ass Firby-Smith."

"Again!; I never saw such chaps as you two.; Always at it.; What was the trouble this time?; Call him a grinning ape again?; Your passion for the truth'll be getting you into trouble one of these days."

"He said I stuck on side."

"Why?"

"I don't know."

"I mean, did he buttonhole you on your way to school, and say, 'Jackson, a word in your ear.; You stick on side.'; Or did he lead up to it in any way?; Did he say, 'Talking of side, you stick it on.'; What had you been doing to him?"

"It was the house-fielding."

"But you can't stick on side at house-fielding.; I defy any one to.; It's too early in the morning."

"I didn't turn up."

"What!; Why?"

"Oh, I don't know."

"No, but, look here, really.; Did you simply bunk it?"

"Yes."

Wyatt leaned on the end of Mike's bed, and, having observed its occupant thoughtfully for a moment, proceeded to speak wisdom for the good of his soul.

"I say, I don't want to jaw — I'm one of those quiet chaps with strong, silent natures; you may have noticed it — but I must put in a well-chosen word at this juncture.; Don't pretend to be dropping off to sleep.; Sit up and listen to what your kind old uncle's got to say to you about manners and deportment.; Otherwise, blood as you are at cricket, you'll have a rotten time here.;

There are some things you simply can't do; and one of them is bunking a thing when you're put down for it.; It doesn't matter who it is puts you down.; If he's captain, you've got to obey him.; That's discipline, that 'ere is.; The speaker then paused, and took a sip of water from the carafe which stood at his elbow.; Cheers from the audience, and a voice 'Hear!; Hear!'"

Mike rolled over in bed and glared up at the orator.; Most of his face was covered by the water-jug, but his eyes stared fixedly from above it.; He winked in a friendly way, and, putting down the jug, drew a deep breath.

"Nothing like this old '87 water," he said.; "Such body."

"I like you jawing about discipline," said Mike morosely.

"And why, my gentle che-ild, should I not talk about discipline?"

"Considering you break out of the house nearly every night."

"In passing, rather rum when you think that a burglar would get it hot for breaking in, while I get dropped on if I break out.; Why should there be one law for the burglar and one for me?; But you were saying —just so.; I thank you.; About my breaking out.; When you're a white-haired old man like me, young Jackson, you'll see that there are two sorts of discipline at school.; One you can break if you feel like taking the risks; the other you mustn't ever break.; I don't know why, but it isn't done.; Until you learn that, you can never hope to become the Perfect Wrykynian like," he concluded modestly, "me."

Mike made no reply.; He would have perished rather than admit it, but Wyatt's words had sunk in.; That moment marked a distinct epoch in his career.; His feelings were curiously mixed.; He was still furious with Firby-Smith, yet at the same time he could not help acknowledging to himself that the latter had had the right on his side.; He saw and approved of Wyatt's point of view, which was the more impressive to him from his knowledge of his friend's contempt for, or, rather, cheerful disregard of, most forms of law and order.; If Wyatt, reckless though he was as regarded written school rules, held so rigid a respect for those that were unwritten, these last must be things which could not be treated lightly.; That night, for the first time in his life, Mike went to sleep with a clear idea of what the public school spirit, of which so much is talked and written, really meant.

CHAPTER XX

THE TEAM IS FILLED UP

When Burgess, at the end of the conversation in the pavilion with Mr. Spence which Bob Jackson had overheard, accompanied the cricket-master across the field to the boarding-houses, he had distinctly made up his mind to give Mike his first eleven colours next day.; There was only one more match to be played before the school fixture-list was finished.; That was the match with Ripton.; Both at cricket and football Ripton was the school that mattered most.; Wrykyn did not always win its other school matches; but it generally did.; The public schools of England divide themselves naturally into little groups, as far as games are concerned.; Harrow, Eton, and Winchester are one group:; Westminster and Charterhouse another:; Bedford, Tonbridge, Dulwich, Haileybury, and St. Paul's are a third.; In this way, Wrykyn, Ripton, Geddington, and Wilborough formed a group.; There was no actual championship competition, but each played each, and by the end of the season it was easy to see which was entitled to first place.; This nearly always lay between Ripton and Wrykyn.; Sometimes an exceptional Geddington team would sweep the board, or Wrykyn, having beaten Ripton, would go down before Wilborough.; But this did not happen often.; Usually Wilborough and Geddington were left to scramble for the wooden spoon.

Secretaries of cricket at Ripton and Wrykyn always liked to arrange the date of the match towards the end of the term, so that they might take the field with representative and not experimental teams.; By July the weeding-out process had generally finished.; Besides which the members of the teams had had time to get into form.

At Wrykyn it was the custom to fill up the team, if possible, before the Ripton match.; A player is likely to show better form if he has got his colours than if his fate depends on what he does in that particular match.

Burgess, accordingly, had resolved to fill up the first eleven just a week before Ripton visited Wrykyn.; There were two vacancies.; One gave him no trouble.; Neville-Smith was not a great bowler, but he was steady, and he had done well in the earlier matches.; He had fairly earned his place.; But the choice between Bob and Mike had kept him awake into the small hours two nights in succession.; Finally he had consulted Mr. Spence, and Mr. Spence had voted for Mike.

Burgess was glad the thing was settled.; The temptation to allow sentiment to interfere with business might have become too strong if he had waited much longer.; He knew that it would be a wrench definitely excluding Bob from the team, and he hated to have to do it.; The more he thought of it, the sorrier he was for him.; If he could have pleased himself, he would have kept Bob In.; But, as the poet has it, "Pleasure is pleasure, and biz is biz, and kep' in a sepyrit jug."; The first duty of a captain is to have no friends.

From small causes great events do spring.; If Burgess had not picked up a particularly interesting novel after breakfast on the morning of Mike's interview with Firby-Smith in the study, the list would have gone up on the notice-board after prayers.; As it was, engrossed in his book, he let the moments go by till the sound on the bell startled him into movement.; And then there was only time to gather up his cap, and sprint.; The paper on which he had intended to write the list and the pen he had laid out to write it with lay untouched on the table.

And, as it was not his habit to put up notices except during the morning, he postponed the thing.; He could write it after tea.; After all, there was a week before the match.

* * * * *

When school was over, he went across to the Infirmary to inquire about Marsh.; The report was more than favourable.; Marsh had better not see any one just yet, In case of accident, but he was certain to be out in time to play against Ripton.

"Doctor Oakes thinks he will be back in school on Tuesday."

"Banzai!" said Burgess, feeling that life was good. To take the field against Ripton without Marsh would have been to court disaster. Marsh's fielding alone was worth the money. With him at short slip, Burgess felt safe when he bowled.

The uncomfortable burden of the knowledge that he was about temporarily to sour Bob Jackson's life ceased for the moment to trouble him. He crooned extracts from musical comedy as he walked towards the nets.

Recollection of Bob's hard case was brought to him by the sight of that about-to-be-soured sportsman tearing across the ground in the middle distance in an effort to get to a high catch which Trevor had hit up to him. It was a difficult catch, and Burgess waited to see if he would bring it off.

Bob got to it with one hand, and held it. His impetus carried him on almost to where Burgess was standing.

"Well held," said Burgess.

"Hullo," said Bob awkwardly. A gruesome thought had flashed across his mind that the captain might think that this gallery-work was an organised advertisement.

"I couldn't get both hands to it," he explained.

"You're hot stuff in the deep."

"Easy when you're only practising."

"I've just been to the Infirmary."

"Oh. How's Marsh?"

"They wouldn't let me see him, but it's all right. He'll be able to play on Saturday."

"Good," said Bob, hoping he had said it as if he meant it. It was decidedly a blow. He was glad for the sake of the school, of course, but one has one's personal ambitions. To the fact that Mike and not himself was the eleventh cap he had become partially resigned:; but he had wanted rather badly to play against Ripton.

Burgess passed on, his mind full of Bob once more. What hard luck it was!; There was he, dashing about in the sun to improve his fielding, and all the time the team was filled up. He felt as if he were playing some low trick on a pal.

Then the Jekyll and Hyde business completed itself. He suppressed his personal feelings, and became the cricket captain again.

It was the cricket captain who, towards the end of the evening, came upon Firby-Smith and Mike parting at the conclusion of a conversation. That it had not been a friendly conversation would have been evident to the most casual observer from the manner in which Mike stumped off, swinging his cricket-bag as if it were a weapon of offence. There are many kinds of walk. Mike's was the walk of the Overwrought Soul.

"What's up?" inquired Burgess.

"Young Jackson, do you mean?; Oh, nothing. I was only telling him that there was going to be house-fielding to-morrow before breakfast."

"Didn't he like the idea?"

"He's jolly well got to like it," said the Gazeka, as who should say, "This way for Iron Wills."; "The frightful kid cut it this morning. There'll be worse trouble if he does it again."

There was, it may be mentioned, not an ounce of malice in the head of Wain's house. That by telling the captain of cricket that Mike had shirked fielding-practice he might injure the latter's prospects of a first eleven cap simply did not occur to him. That Burgess would feel, on being told of Mike's slackness, much as a bishop might feel if he heard that a favourite curate had become a Mahometan or a Mumbo-Jumboist, did not enter his mind. All he considered was that the story of his dealings with Mike showed him, Firby-Smith, in the favourable and dashing character of the fellow-who-will-stand-no-nonsense, a sort of Captain Kettle on dry land, in fact; and so he proceeded to tell it in detail.

Burgess parted with him with the firm conviction that Mike was a young slacker. Keenness in fielding was a fetish with him; and to cut practice struck him as a crime.

He felt that he had been deceived in Mike.

* * * * *

When, therefore, one takes into consideration his private bias in favour of Bob, and adds to it the reaction caused by this sudden unmasking of Mike, it is not surprising that the list Burgess made out that night before he went to bed differed in an important respect from the one he had intended to write before school.

Mike happened to be near the notice-board when he pinned it up.; It was only the pleasure of seeing his name down in black-and-white that made him trouble to look at the list.; Bob's news of the day before yesterday had made it clear how that list would run.

The crowd that collected the moment Burgess had walked off carried him right up to the board.

He looked at the paper.

"Hard luck!" said somebody.

Mike scarcely heard him.

He felt physically sick with the shock of the disappointment.; For the initial before the name Jackson was R.

There was no possibility of mistake.; Since writing was invented, there had never been an R. that looked less like an M. than the one on that list.

Bob had beaten him on the tape.

CHAPTER XXI

MARJORY THE FRANK

At the door of the senior block Burgess, going out, met Bob coming in, hurrying, as he was rather late.

"Congratulate you, Bob," he said; and passed on.

Bob stared after him.; As he stared, Trevor came out of the block.

"Congratulate you, Bob."

"What's the matter now?"

"Haven't you seen?"

"Seen what?"

"Why the list.; You've got your first."

"My—what? you're rotting."

"No, I'm not.; Go and look."

The thing seemed incredible.; Had he dreamed that conversation between Spence and Burgess on the pavilion steps?; Had he mixed up the names?; He was certain that he had heard Spence give his verdict for Mike, and Burgess agree with him.

Just then, Mike, feeling very ill, came down the steps.; He caught sight of Bob and was passing with a feeble grin, when something told him that this was one of those occasions on which one has to show a Red Indian fortitude and stifle one's private feelings.

"Congratulate you, Bob," he said awkwardly.

"Thanks awfully," said Bob, with equal awkwardness.; Trevor moved on, delicately.; This was no place for him.; Bob's face was looking like a stuffed frog's, which was Bob's way of trying to appear unconcerned and at his ease, while Mike seemed as if at any moment he might burst into tears.; Spectators are not wanted at these awkward interviews.

There was a short silence.

"Jolly glad you've got it," said Mike.

"I believe there's a mistake.; I swear I heard Burgess say to Spence——"

"He changed his mind probably.; No reason why he shouldn't."

"Well, it's jolly rummy."

Bob endeavoured to find consolation.

"Anyhow, you'll have three years in the first.; You're a cert. for next year."

"Hope so," said Mike, with such manifest lack of enthusiasm that Bob abandoned this line of argument.; When one has missed one's colours, next year seems a very, very long way off.

They moved slowly through the cloisters, neither speaking, and up the stairs that led to the Great Hall.; Each was gratefully conscious of the fact that prayers would be beginning in another minute, putting an end to an uncomfortable situation.

"Heard from home lately?" inquired Mike.

Bob snatched gladly at the subject.

"Got a letter from mother this morning.; I showed you the last one, didn't I?; I've only just had time to skim through this one, as the post was late, and I only got it just as I was going to dash across to school.; Not much in it.; Here it is, if you want to read it."

"Thanks.; It'll be something to do during Math."

"Marjory wrote, too, for the first time in her life.; Haven't had time to look at it yet."

"After you.; Sure it isn't meant for me?; She owes me a letter."

"No, it's for me all right.; I'll give it you in the interval."

The arrival of the headmaster put an end to the conversation.

* * * * *

By a quarter to eleven Mike had begun to grow reconciled to his fate. The disappointment was still there, but it was lessened. These things are like kicks on the shin; A brief spell of agony, and then a dull pain of which we are not always conscious unless our attention is directed to it, and which in time disappears altogether. When the bell rang for the interval that morning, Mike was, as it were, sitting up and taking nourishment.

He was doing this in a literal as well as in a figurative sense when Bob entered the school shop.

Bob appeared curiously agitated. He looked round, and, seeing Mike, pushed his way towards him through the crowd. Most of those present congratulated him as he passed; and Mike noticed, with some surprise, that, in place of the blushful grin which custom demands from the man who is being congratulated on receipt of colours, there appeared on his face a worried, even an irritated look. He seemed to have something on his mind.

"Hullo," said Mike amiably. "Got that letter?"

"Yes. I'll show it you outside."

"Why not here?"

"Come on."

Mike resented the tone, but followed. Evidently something had happened to upset Bob seriously. As they went out on the gravel, somebody congratulated Bob again, and again Bob hardly seemed to appreciate it.'

Bob led the way across the gravel and on to the first terrace. When they had left the crowd behind, he stopped.

"What's up?" asked Mike.

"I want you to read ——"

"Jackson!"

They both turned. The headmaster was standing on the edge of the gravel.

Bob pushed the letter into Mike's hands.

"Read that," he said, and went up to the headmaster. Mike heard the words "English Essay," and, seeing that the conversation was apparently going to be one of some length, capped the headmaster and walked off. He was just going to read the letter when the bell rang. He put the missive in his pocket, and went to his form-room wondering what Marjory could have found to say to Bob to touch him on the raw to such an extent. She was a breezy correspondent, with a style of her own, but usually she entertained rather than upset people. No suspicion of the actual contents of the letter crossed his mind.

He read it during school, under the desk; and ceased to wonder. Bob had had cause to look worried. For the thousand and first time in her career of crime Marjory had been and done it! With a strong hand she had shaken the cat out of the bag, and exhibited it plainly to all whom it might concern.

There was a curious absence of construction about the letter. Most authors of sensational matter nurse their bomb-shell, lead up to it, and display it to the best advantage. Marjory dropped hers into the body of the letter, and let it take its chance with the other news-items.

>   "DEAR BOB" (the letter ran), —
>
> "I hope you are quite well. I am quite well. Phyllis has a cold, Ella cheeked Mademoiselle yesterday, and had to write out 'Little Girls must be polite and obedient' a hundred times in French. She was jolly sick about it. I told her it served her right. Joe made eighty-three against Lancashire. Reggie made a duck. Have you got your first?; If you have, it will be all through Mike. Uncle John told Father that Mike pretended to hurt his wrist so that you could play instead of him for the school, and Father said it was very sporting of Mike but nobody must tell you because it wouldn't be fair if you got your first for you to know that you owed it to Mike and I wasn't supposed to hear but I did because I was in the room only they didn't know I was (we were playing hide-and-seek and I was hiding) so I'm writing to tell you,

"From your affectionate sister

"Marjory."

There followed a P.S.

"I'll tell you what you ought to do.; I've been reading a jolly good book called 'The Boys of Dormitory Two,' and the hero's an awfully nice boy named Lionel Tremayne, and his friend Jack Langdale saves his life when a beast of a boatman who's really employed by Lionel's cousin who wants the money that Lionel's going to have when he grows up stuns him and leaves him on the beach to drown.; Well, Lionel is going to play for the school against Loamshire, and it's *the* match of the season, but he goes to the headmaster and says he wants Jack to play instead of him.; Why don't you do that?

;;;"M.

;;;"P.P.S.—This has been a frightful fag to write."

For the life of him Mike could not help giggling as he pictured what Bob's expression must have been when his brother read this document.; But the humorous side of the thing did not appeal to him for long.; What should he say to Bob?; What would Bob say to him?; Dash it all, it made him look such an awful *ass*!; Anyhow, Bob couldn't do much.; In fact he didn't see that he could do anything.; The team was filled up, and Burgess was not likely to alter it.; Besides, why should he alter it?; Probably he would have given Bob his colours anyhow.; Still, it was beastly awkward.; Marjory meant well, but she had put her foot right in it.; Girls oughtn't to meddle with these things.; No girl ought to be taught to write till she came of age.; And Uncle John had behaved in many respects like the Complete Rotter.; If he was going to let out things like that, he might at least have whispered them, or looked behind the curtains to see that the place wasn't chock-full of female kids.; Confound Uncle John!

Throughout the dinner-hour Mike kept out of Bob's way.; But in a small community like a school it is impossible to avoid a man for ever.; They met at the nets.

"Well?" said Bob.

"How do you mean?" said Mike.

"Did you read it?"

"Yes."

"Well, is it all rot, or did you—you know what I mean—sham a crocked wrist?"

"Yes," said Mike, "I did."

Bob stared gloomily at his toes.

"I mean," he said at last, apparently putting the finishing-touch to some train of thought, "I know I ought to be grateful, and all that.; I suppose I am.; I mean it was jolly good of you—Dash it all," he broke off hotly, as if the putting his position into words had suddenly showed him how inglorious it was, "what did you want to do it *for*?; What was the idea?; What right have you got to go about playing Providence over me?; Dash it all, it's like giving a fellow money without consulting him."

"I didn't think you'd ever know.; You wouldn't have if only that ass Uncle John hadn't let it out."

"How did he get to know?; Why did you tell him?"

"He got it out of me.; I couldn't choke him off.; He came down when you were away at Geddington, and would insist on having a look at my arm, and naturally he spotted right away there was nothing the matter with it.; So it came out; that's how it was."

Bob scratched thoughtfully at the turf with a spike of his boot.

"Of course, it was awfully decent——"

Then again the monstrous nature of the affair came home to him.

"But what did you do it *for*?; Why should you rot up your own chances to give me a look in?"

"Oh, I don't know....; You know, you did *me* a jolly good turn."

"I don't remember.; When?"

"That Firby-Smith business."

"What about it?"

"Well, you got me out of a jolly bad hole."

"Oh, rot!; And do you mean to tell me it was simply because of that ——?"

Mike appeared to him in a totally new light.; He stared at him as if he were some strange creature hitherto unknown to the human race.; Mike shuffled uneasily beneath the scrutiny.

"Anyhow, it's all over now," Mike said, "so I don't see what's the point of talking about it."

"I'm hanged if it is.; You don't think I'm going to sit tight and take my first as if nothing had happened?"

"What can you do?; The list's up.; Are you going to the Old Man to ask him if I can play, like Lionel Tremayne?"

The hopelessness of the situation came over Bob like a wave.; He looked helplessly at Mike.

"Besides," added Mike, "I shall get in next year all right.; Half a second, I just want to speak to Wyatt about something."

He sidled off.

"Well, anyhow," said Bob to himself, "I must see Burgess about it."

CHAPTER XXII

WYATT IS REMINDED OF AN ENGAGEMENT

There are situations in life which are beyond one.; The sensible man realises this, and slides out of such situations, admitting himself beaten.; Others try to grapple with them, but it never does any good.; When affairs get into a real tangle, it is best to sit still and let them straighten themselves out.; Or, if one does not do that, simply to think no more about them.; This is Philosophy.; The true philosopher is the man who says "All right," and goes to sleep in his arm-chair.; One's attitude towards Life's Little Difficulties should be that of the gentleman in the fable, who sat down on an acorn one day, and happened to doze.; The warmth of his body caused the acorn to germinate, and it grew so rapidly that, when he awoke, he found himself sitting in the fork of an oak, sixty feet from the ground.; He thought he would go home, but, finding this impossible, he altered his plans.; "Well, well," he said, "if I cannot compel circumstances to my will, I can at least adapt my will to circumstances.; I decide to remain here."; Which he did, and had a not unpleasant time.; The oak lacked some of the comforts of home, but the air was splendid and the view excellent.

To-day's Great Thought for Young Readers.; Imitate this man.

Bob should have done so, but he had not the necessary amount of philosophy.; He still clung to the idea that he and Burgess, in council, might find some way of making things right for everybody.; Though, at the moment, he did not see how eleven caps were to be divided amongst twelve candidates in such a way that each should have one.

And Burgess, consulted on the point, confessed to the same inability to solve the problem.; It took Bob at least a quarter of an hour to get the facts of the case into the captain's head, but at last Burgess grasped the idea of the thing.; At which period he remarked that it was a rum business.

"Very rum," Bob agreed.; "Still, what you say doesn't help us out much, seeing that the point is, what's to be done?"

"Why do anything?"

Burgess was a philosopher, and took the line of least resistance, like the man in the oak-tree.

"But I must do something," said Bob.; "Can't you see how rotten it is for me?"

"I don't see why.; It's not your fault.; Very sporting of your brother and all that, of course, though I'm blowed if I'd have done it myself; but why should you do anything?; You're all right.; Your brother stood out of the team to let you in it, and here you *are*, in it.; What's he got to grumble about?"

"He's not grumbling.; It's me."

"What's the matter with you?; Don't you want your first?"

"Not like this.; Can't you see what a rotten position it is for me?"

"Don't you worry.; You simply keep on saying you're all right.; Besides, what do you want me to do?; Alter the list?"

But for the thought of those unspeakable outsiders, Lionel Tremayne and his headmaster, Bob might have answered this question in the affirmative; but he had the public-school boy's terror of seeming to pose or do anything theatrical.; He would have done a good deal to put matters right, but he could *not* do the self-sacrificing young hero business.; It would not be in the picture.; These things, if they are to be done at school, have to be carried through stealthily, after Mike's fashion.

"I suppose you can't very well, now it's up.; Tell you what, though, I don't see why I shouldn't stand out of the team for the Ripton match.; I could easily fake up some excuse."

"I do.; I don't know if it's occurred to you, but the idea is rather to win the Ripton match, if possible.; So that I'm a lot keen on putting the best team into the field.; Sorry if it upsets your arrangements in any way."

"You know perfectly well Mike's every bit as good as me."

"He isn't so keen."

"What do you mean?"

"Fielding.; He's a young slacker."

When Burgess had once labelled a man as that, he did not readily let the idea out of his mind.

"Slacker?; What rot!; He's as keen as anything."

"Anyhow, his keenness isn't enough to make him turn out for house-fielding.; If you really want to know, that's why you've got your first instead of him.; You sweated away, and improved your fielding twenty per cent.; and I happened to be talking to Firby-Smith and found that young Mike had been shirking his, so out he went.; A bad field's bad enough, but a slack field wants skinning."

"Smith oughtn't to have told you."

"Well, he did tell me.; So you see how it is.; There won't be any changes from the team I've put up on the board."

"Oh, all right," said Bob.; "I was afraid you mightn't be able to do anything.; So long."

"Mind the step," said Burgess.

* * * * *

At about the time when this conversation was in progress, Wyatt, crossing the cricket-field towards the school shop in search of something fizzy that might correct a burning thirst acquired at the nets, espied on the horizon a suit of cricket flannels surmounted by a huge, expansive grin.; As the distance between them lessened, he discovered that inside the flannels was Neville-Smith's body and behind the grin the rest of Neville-Smith's face.; Their visit to the nets not having coincided in point of time, as the Greek exercise books say, Wyatt had not seen his friend since the list of the team had been posted on the board, so he proceeded to congratulate him on his colours.

"Thanks," said Neville-Smith, with a brilliant display of front teeth.

"Feeling good?"

"Not the word for it.; I feel like —I don't know what."

"I'll tell you what you look like, if that's any good to you.; That slight smile of yours will meet behind, if you don't look out, and then the top of your head'll come off."

"I don't care.; I've got my first, whatever happens.; Little Willie's going to buy a nice new cap and a pretty striped jacket all for his own self!; I say, thanks for reminding me.; Not that you did, but supposing you had.; At any rate, I remember what it was I wanted to say to you.; You know what I was saying to you about the bust I meant to have at home in honour of my getting my first, if I did, which I have —well, anyhow it's to-night.; You can roll up, can't you?"

"Delighted.; Anything for a free feed in these hard times.; What time did you say it was?"

"Eleven.; Make it a bit earlier, if you like."

"No, eleven'll do me all right."

"How are you going to get out?"

"'Stone walls do not a prison make, nor iron bars a cage.'; That's what the man said who wrote the libretto for the last set of Latin Verses we had to do.; I shall manage it."

"They ought to allow you a latch-key."

"Yes, I've often thought of asking my pater for one.; Still, I get on very well.; Who are coming besides me?"

"No boarders.; They all funked it."

"The race is degenerating."

"Said it wasn't good enough."

"The school is going to the dogs.; Who did you ask?"

"Clowes was one.; Said he didn't want to miss his beauty-sleep.; And Henfrey backed out because he thought the risk of being sacked wasn't good enough."

92

"That's an aspect of the thing that might occur to some people.; I don't blame him —I might feel like that myself if I'd got another couple of years at school."

"But one or two day-boys are coming.; Clephane is, for one.; And Beverley.; We shall have rather a rag.; I'm going to get the things now."

"When I get to your place —I don't believe I know the way, now I come to think of it —what do I do?; Ring the bell and send in my card? or smash the nearest window and climb in?"

"Don't make too much row, for goodness sake.; All the servants'll have gone to bed.; You'll see the window of my room.; It's just above the porch.; It'll be the only one lighted up.; Heave a pebble at it, and I'll come down."

"So will the glass —with a run, I expect.; Still, I'll try to do as little damage as possible.; After all, I needn't throw a brick."

"You *will* turn up, won't you?"

"Nothing shall stop me."

"Good man."

As Wyatt was turning away, a sudden compunction seized upon Neville-Smith.; He called him back.

"I say, you don't think it's too risky, do you?; I mean, you always are breaking out at night, aren't you?; I don't want to get you into a row."

"Oh, that's all right," said Wyatt.; "Don't you worry about me.; I should have gone out anyhow to-night."

CHAPTER XXIII

A SURPRISE FOR MR. APPLEBY

"You may not know it," said Wyatt to Mike in the dormitory that night, "but this is the maddest, merriest day of all the glad New Year."

Mike could not help thinking that for himself it was the very reverse, but he did not state his view of the case.

"What's up?" he asked.

"Neville-Smith's giving a meal at his place in honour of his getting his first.; I understand the preparations are on a scale of the utmost magnificence.; No expense has been spared.; Ginger-beer will flow like water.; The oldest cask of lemonade has been broached; and a sardine is roasting whole in the market-place."

"Are you going?"

"If I can tear myself away from your delightful society.; The kick-off is fixed for eleven sharp.; I am to stand underneath his window and heave bricks till something happens.; I don't know if he keeps a dog.; If so, I shall probably get bitten to the bone."

"When are you going to start?"

"About five minutes after Wain has been round the dormitories to see that all's well.; That ought to be somewhere about half-past ten."

"Don't go getting caught."

"I shall do my little best not to be.; Rather tricky work, though, getting back.; I've got to climb two garden walls, and I shall probably be so full of Malvoisie that you'll be able to hear it swishing about inside me.; No catch steeple-chasing if you're like that.; They've no thought for people's convenience here.; Now at Bradford they've got studies on the ground floor, the windows looking out over the boundless prairie.; No climbing or steeple-chasing needed at all.; All you have to do is to open the window and step out.; Still, we must make the best of things.; Push us over a pinch of that tooth-powder of yours.; I've used all mine."

Wyatt very seldom penetrated further than his own garden on the occasions when he roamed abroad at night.; For cat-shooting the Wain spinneys were unsurpassed.; There was one particular dustbin where one might be certain of flushing a covey any night; and the wall by the potting-shed was a feline club-house.

But when he did wish to get out into the open country he had a special route which he always took.; He climbed down from the wall that ran beneath the dormitory window into the garden belonging to Mr. Appleby, the master who had the house next to Mr. Wain's.; Crossing this, he climbed another wall, and dropped from it into a small lane which ended in the main road leading to Wrykyn town.

This was the route which he took to-night.; It was a glorious July night, and the scent of the flowers came to him with a curious distinctness as he let himself down from the dormitory window.; At any other time he might have made a lengthy halt, and enjoyed the scents and small summer noises, but now he felt that it would be better not to delay.; There was a full moon, and where he stood he could be seen distinctly from the windows of both houses.; They were all dark, it is true, but on these occasions it was best to take no risks.

He dropped cautiously into Appleby's garden, ran lightly across it, and was in the lane within a minute.

There he paused, dusted his trousers, which had suffered on the two walls, and strolled meditatively in the direction of the town.; Half-past ten had just chimed from the school clock.; He was in plenty of time.

"What a night!" he said to himself, sniffing as he walked.

* * * * *

Now it happened that he was not alone in admiring the beauty of that particular night.; At ten-fifteen it had struck Mr. Appleby, looking out of his study into the moonlit school grounds, that a pipe in the open would make an excellent break in his night's work.; He had acquired a slight headache as the result of correcting a batch of examination papers, and he thought that an interval of an hour in the open air before approaching the half-dozen or so papers which still remained to be looked at might do him good.; The window of his study was open, but the room had got hot and stuffy.; Nothing like a little fresh air for putting him right.

For a few moments he debated the rival claims of a stroll in the cricket-field and a seat in the garden.; Then he decided on the latter.; The little gate in the railings opposite his house might not be open, and it was a long way round to the main entrance.; So he took a deck-chair which leaned against the wall, and let himself out of the back door.

He took up his position in the shadow of a fir-tree with his back to the house.; From here he could see the long garden.; He was fond of his garden, and spent what few moments he could spare from work and games pottering about it.; He had his views as to what the ideal garden should be, and he hoped in time to tinker his own three acres up to the desired standard.; At present there remained much to be done.; Why not, for instance, take away those laurels at the end of the lawn, and have a flower-bed there instead?; Laurels lasted all the year round, true, whereas flowers died and left an empty brown bed in the winter, but then laurels were nothing much to look at at any time, and a garden always had a beastly appearance in winter, whatever you did to it.; Much better have flowers, and get a decent show for one's money in summer at any rate.

The problem of the bed at the end of the lawn occupied his complete attention for more than a quarter of an hour, at the end of which period he discovered that his pipe had gone out.

He was just feeling for his matches to relight it when Wyatt dropped with a slight thud into his favourite herbaceous border.

The surprise, and the agony of feeling that large boots were trampling among his treasures kept him transfixed for just the length of time necessary for Wyatt to cross the garden and climb the opposite wall.; As he dropped into the lane, Mr. Appleby recovered himself sufficiently to emit a sort of strangled croak, but the sound was too slight to reach Wyatt.; That reveller was walking down the Wrykyn road before Mr. Appleby had left his chair.

It is an interesting point that it was the gardener rather than the schoolmaster in Mr. Appleby that first awoke to action.; It was not the idea of a boy breaking out of his house at night that occurred to him first as particularly heinous; it was the fact that the boy had broken out *via* his herbaceous border.; In four strides he was on the scene of the outrage, examining, on hands and knees, with the aid of the moonlight, the extent of the damage done.

As far as he could see, it was not serious.; By a happy accident Wyatt's boots had gone home to right and left of precious plants but not on them.; With a sigh of relief Mr. Appleby smoothed over the cavities, and rose to his feet.

At this point it began to strike him that the episode affected him as a schoolmaster also.

In that startled moment when Wyatt had suddenly crossed his line of vision, he had recognised him.; The moon had shone full on his face as he left the flowerbed.; There was no doubt in his mind as to the identity of the intruder.

He paused, wondering how he should act.; It was not an easy question.; There was nothing of the spy about Mr. Appleby.; He went his way openly, liked and respected by boys and masters.; He always played the game.; The difficulty here was to say exactly what the game was.; Sentiment, of course, bade him forget the episode, treat it as if it had never happened.; That was the simple way out of the difficulty.; There was nothing unsporting about Mr. Appleby.; He knew that there were times when a master might, without blame, close his eyes or look the other way.; If he had met Wyatt out of bounds in the day-time, and it had been possible to convey the impression that he had not seen him, he would have done so.; To be out of bounds is not a particularly deadly sin.; A master must check it if it occurs too frequently, but he may use his discretion.

Breaking out at night, however, was a different thing altogether.; It was on another plane.; There are times when a master must waive sentiment, and remember that he is in a position of trust, and owes a duty directly to his headmaster, and indirectly, through the headmaster, to the parents.; He receives a salary for doing this duty, and, if he feels that sentiment is too strong for him, he should resign in favour of some one of tougher fibre.

This was the conclusion to which Mr. Appleby came over his relighted pipe.; He could not let the matter rest where it was.

In ordinary circumstances it would have been his duty to report the affair to the headmaster but in the present case he thought that a slightly different course might be pursued.; He would lay the whole thing before Mr. Wain, and leave him to deal with it as he thought best.; It was one of the few cases where it was possible for an assistant master to fulfil his duty to a parent directly, instead of through the agency of the headmaster.

* * * * *

Knocking out the ashes of his pipe against a tree, he folded his deck-chair and went into the house.; The examination papers were spread invitingly on the table, but they would have to wait.; He turned down his lamp, and walked round to Wain's.

There was a light in one of the ground-floor windows.; He tapped on the window, and the sound of a chair being pushed back told him that he had been heard.; The blind shot up, and he had a view of a room littered with books and papers, in the middle of which stood Mr. Wain, like a sea-beast among rocks.

Mr. Wain recognised his visitor and opened the window.; Mr. Appleby could not help feeling how like Wain it was to work on a warm summer's night in a hermetically sealed room.; There was always something queer and eccentric about Wyatt's step-father.

"Can I have a word with you, Wain?" he said.

"Appleby!; Is there anything the matter?; I was startled when you tapped.; Exceedingly so."

"Sorry," said Mr. Appleby.; "Wouldn't have disturbed you, only it's something important.; I'll climb in through here, shall I?; No need to unlock the door."; And, greatly to Mr. Wain's surprise and rather to his disapproval, Mr. Appleby vaulted on to the window-sill, and squeezed through into the room.

CHAPTER XXIV

CAUGHT

"Got some rather bad news for you, I'm afraid," began Mr. Appleby.; "I'll smoke, if you don't mind.; About Wyatt."

"James!"

"I was sitting in my garden a few minutes ago, having a pipe before finishing the rest of my papers, and Wyatt dropped from the wall on to my herbaceous border."

Mr. Appleby said this with a tinge of bitterness.; The thing still rankled.

"James!; In your garden!; Impossible.; Why, it is not a quarter of an hour since I left him in his dormitory."

"He's not there now."

"You astound me, Appleby.; I am astonished."

"So was I."

"How is such a thing possible?; His window is heavily barred."

"Bars can be removed."

"You must have been mistaken."

"Possibly," said Mr. Appleby, a little nettled.; Gaping astonishment is always apt to be irritating.; "Let's leave it at that, then.; Sorry to have disturbed you."

"No, sit down, Appleby.; Dear me, this is most extraordinary.; Exceedingly so.; You are certain it was James?"

"Perfectly.; It's like daylight out of doors."

Mr. Wain drummed on the table with his fingers.

"What shall I do?"

Mr. Appleby offered no suggestion.

"I ought to report it to the headmaster.; That is certainly the course I should pursue."

"I don't see why.; It isn't like an ordinary case.; You're the parent.; You can deal with the thing directly.; If you come to think of it, a headmaster's only a sort of middleman between boys and parents.; He plays substitute for the parent in his absence.; I don't see why you should drag in the master at all here."

"There is certainly something in what you say," said Mr. Wain on reflection.

"A good deal.; Tackle the boy when he comes in, and have it out with him.; Remember that it must mean expulsion if you report him to the headmaster.; He would have no choice.; Everybody who has ever broken out of his house here and been caught has been expelled.; I should strongly advise you to deal with the thing yourself."

"I will.; Yes.; You are quite right, Appleby.; That is a very good idea of yours.; You are not going?"

"Must.; Got a pile of examination papers to look over.; Good-night."

"Good-night."

Mr. Appleby made his way out of the window and through the gate into his own territory in a pensive frame of mind.; He was wondering what would happen.; He had taken the only possible course, and, if only Wain kept his head and did not let the matter get through officially to the headmaster, things might not be so bad for Wyatt after all.; He hoped they would not.; He liked Wyatt.; It would be a thousand pities, he felt, if he were to be expelled.; What would Wain do?; What would *he* do in a similar case?; It was difficult to say.; Probably talk violently for as long as he could keep it up, and then consider the episode closed.; He doubted whether Wain would have the common sense to do this.; Altogether it was very painful and disturbing, and he was taking a rather gloomy view of the assistant master's lot as he sat down to finish off the rest of his examination papers.; It was not all roses, the life of an assistant master at a public school.; He had continually to be sinking his own individual sympathies in the claims of his duty.; Mr. Appleby was the last man who would willingly have reported a boy for enjoying a midnight ramble.; But he was the last man to shirk the duty of reporting him, merely because it was one decidedly not to his taste.

Mr. Wain sat on for some minutes after his companion had left, pondering over the news he had heard.; Even now he clung to the idea that Appleby had made some extraordinary mistake.; Gradually he began to convince himself of this.; He had seen Wyatt actually in bed a quarter of an hour before —not asleep, it was true, but apparently on the verge of dropping off.; And the bars across the window had looked so solid....; Could Appleby have been dreaming?; Something of the kind might easily have happened.; He had been working hard, and the night was warm....

Then it occurred to him that he could easily prove or disprove the truth of his colleague's statement by going to the dormitory and seeing if Wyatt were there or not.; If he had gone out, he would hardly have returned yet.

He took a candle, and walked quietly upstairs.

Arrived at his step-son's dormitory, he turned the door-handle softly and went in.; The light of the candle fell on both beds.; Mike was there, asleep.; He grunted, and turned over with his face to the wall as the light shone on his eyes.; But the other bed was empty.; Appleby had been right.

If further proof had been needed, one of the bars was missing from the window.; The moon shone in through the empty space.

The house-master sat down quietly on the vacant bed.; He blew the candle out, and waited there in the semi-darkness, thinking.; For years he and Wyatt had lived in a state of armed neutrality, broken by various small encounters.; Lately, by silent but mutual agreement, they had kept out of each other's way as much as possible, and it had become rare for the house-master to have to find fault officially with his step-son.; But there had never been anything even remotely approaching friendship between them.; Mr. Wain was not a man who inspired affection readily, least of all in those many years younger than himself.; Nor did he easily grow fond of others.; Wyatt he had regarded, from the moment when the threads of their lives became entangled, as a complete nuisance.

It was not, therefore, a sorrowful, so much as an exasperated, vigil that he kept in the dormitory.; There was nothing of the sorrowing father about his frame of mind.; He was the house-master about to deal with a mutineer, and nothing else.

This breaking-out, he reflected wrathfully, was the last straw.; Wyatt's presence had been a nervous inconvenience to him for years.; The time had come to put an end to it.; It was with a comfortable feeling of magnanimity that he resolved not to report the breach of discipline to the headmaster.; Wyatt should not be expelled.; But he should leave, and that immediately.; He would write to the bank before he went to bed, asking them to receive his step-son at once; and the letter should go by the first post next day.; The discipline of the bank would be salutary and steadying.; And —this was a particularly grateful reflection —a fortnight annually was the limit of the holiday allowed by the management to its junior employees.

Mr. Wain had arrived at this conclusion, and was beginning to feel a little cramped, when Mike Jackson suddenly sat up.

"Hullo!" said Mike.

"Go to sleep, Jackson, immediately," snapped the house-master.

Mike had often heard and read of people's hearts leaping to their mouths, but he had never before experienced that sensation of something hot and dry springing in the throat, which is what really happens to us on receipt of a bad shock.; A sickening feeling that the game was up beyond all hope of salvation came to him.; He lay down again without a word.

What a frightful thing to happen!; How on earth had this come about?; What in the world had brought Wain to the dormitory at that hour?; Poor old Wyatt!; If it had upset *him* (Mike) to see the house-master in the room, what would be the effect of such a sight on Wyatt, returning from the revels at Neville-Smith's!

And what could he do?; Nothing.; There was literally no way out.; His mind went back to the night when he had saved Wyatt by a brilliant *coup*.; The most brilliant of *coups* could effect nothing now.; Absolutely and entirely the game was up.

* * * * *

Every minute that passed seemed like an hour to Mike.; Dead silence reigned in the dormitory, broken every now and then by the creak of the other bed, as the house-master shifted his position.; Twelve boomed across the field from the school clock.; Mike could not help thinking what a perfect night it must be for him to be able to hear the strokes so plainly.; He strained his ears for any indication of Wyatt's approach, but could hear nothing.; Then a very faint scraping noise broke the stillness, and presently the patch of moonlight on the floor was darkened.

At that moment Mr. Wain relit his candle.

The unexpected glare took Wyatt momentarily aback.; Mike saw him start.; Then he seemed to recover himself.; In a calm and leisurely manner he climbed into the room.

"James!" said Mr. Wain.; His voice sounded ominously hollow.

Wyatt dusted his knees, and rubbed his hands together.; "Hullo, is that you, father!" he said pleasantly.

CHAPTER XXV

MARCHING ORDERS

A silence followed.; To Mike, lying in bed, holding his breath, it seemed a long silence.; As a matter of fact it lasted for perhaps ten seconds.; Then Mr. Wain spoke.

"You have been out, James?"

It is curious how in the more dramatic moments of life the inane remark is the first that comes to us.

"Yes, sir," said Wyatt.

"I am astonished.; Exceedingly astonished."

"I got a bit of a start myself," said Wyatt.

"I shall talk to you in my study.; Follow me there."

"Yes, sir."

He left the room, and Wyatt suddenly began to chuckle.

"I say, Wyatt!" said Mike, completely thrown off his balance by the events of the night.

Wyatt continued to giggle helplessly.; He flung himself down on his bed, rolling with laughter.; Mike began to get alarmed.

"It's all right," said Wyatt at last, speaking with difficulty.; "But, I say, how long had he been sitting there?"

"It seemed hours.; About an hour, I suppose, really."

"It's the funniest thing I've ever struck.; Me sweating to get in quietly, and all the time him camping out on my bed!"

"But look here, what'll happen?"

Wyatt sat up.

"That reminds me.; Suppose I'd better go down."

"What'll he do, do you think?"

"Ah, now, what!"

"But, I say, it's awful.; What'll happen?"

"That's for him to decide.; Speaking at a venture, I should say — —"

"You don't think — —?"

"The boot.; The swift and sudden boot.; I shall be sorry to part with you, but I'm afraid it's a case of 'Au revoir, my little Hyacinth.'; We shall meet at Philippi.; This is my Moscow.; To-morrow I shall go out into the night with one long, choking sob.; Years hence a white-haired bank-clerk will tap at your door when you're a prosperous professional cricketer with your photograph in *Wisden*.; That'll be me.; Well, I suppose I'd better go down.; We'd better all get to bed *some* time to-night.; Don't go to sleep."

"Not likely."

"I'll tell you all the latest news when I come back.; Where are me slippers?; Ha, 'tis well!; Lead on, then, minions.; I follow."

* * * * *

In the study Mr. Wain was fumbling restlessly with his papers when Wyatt appeared.

"Sit down, James," he said.

Wyatt sat down.; One of his slippers fell off with a clatter.; Mr. Wain jumped nervously.

"Only my slipper," explained Wyatt.; "It slipped."

Mr. Wain took up a pen, and began to tap the table.

"Well, James?"

Wyatt said nothing.

"I should be glad to hear your explanation of this disgraceful matter."

"The fact is — —" said Wyatt.

"Well?"

"I haven't one, sir."

"What were you doing out of your dormitory, out of the house, at that hour?"

"I went for a walk, sir."

"And, may I inquire, are you in the habit of violating the strictest school rules by absenting yourself from the house during the night?"

"Yes, sir."

"What?"

"Yes, sir."

"This is an exceedingly serious matter."

Wyatt nodded agreement with this view.

"Exceedingly."

The pen rose and fell with the rapidity of the cylinder of a motor-car. Wyatt, watching it, became suddenly aware that the thing was hypnotising him. In a minute or two he would be asleep.

"I wish you wouldn't do that, father. Tap like that, I mean. It's sending me to sleep."

"James!"

"It's like a woodpecker."

"Studied impertinence — —"

"I'm very sorry. Only it *was* sending me off."

Mr. Wain suspended tapping operations, and resumed the thread of his discourse.

"I am sorry, exceedingly, to see this attitude in you, James. It is not fitting. It is in keeping with your behaviour throughout. Your conduct has been lax and reckless in the extreme. It is possible that you imagine that the peculiar circumstances of our relationship secure you from the penalties to which the ordinary boy — —"

"No, sir."

"I need hardly say," continued Mr. Wain, ignoring the interruption, "that I shall treat you exactly as I should treat any other member of my house whom I had detected in the same misdemeanour."

"Of course," said Wyatt, approvingly.

"I must ask you not to interrupt me when I am speaking to you, James. I say that your punishment will be no whit less severe than would be that of any other boy. You have repeatedly proved yourself lacking in ballast and a respect for discipline in smaller ways, but this is a far more serious matter. Exceedingly so. It is impossible for me to overlook it, even were I disposed to do so. You are aware of the penalty for such an action as yours?"

"The sack," said Wyatt laconically.

"It is expulsion. You must leave the school. At once."

Wyatt nodded.

"As you know, I have already secured a nomination for you in the London and Oriental Bank. I shall write to-morrow to the manager asking him to receive you at once — —"

"After all, they only gain an extra fortnight of me."

"You will leave directly I receive his letter. I shall arrange with the headmaster that you are withdrawn privately — —"

"*Not* the sack?"

"Withdrawn privately. You will not go to school to-morrow. Do you understand? That is all. Have you anything to say?"

Wyatt reflected.

"No, I don't think — —"

His eye fell on a tray bearing a decanter and a syphon.

"Oh, yes," he said. "Can't I mix you a whisky and soda, father, before I go off to bed?"

* * * * *

"Well?" said Mike.

Wyatt kicked off his slippers, and began to undress.

"What happened?"

"We chatted."

"Has he let you off?"

"Like a gun.; I shoot off almost immediately.; To-morrow I take a well-earned rest away from school, and the day after I become the gay young bank-clerk, all amongst the ink and ledgers."

Mike was miserably silent.

"Buck up," said Wyatt cheerfully.; "It would have happened anyhow in another fortnight.; So why worry?"

Mike was still silent.; The reflection was doubtless philosophic, but it failed to comfort him.

CHAPTER XXVI

THE AFTERMATH

Bad news spreads quickly.; By the quarter to eleven interval next day the facts concerning Wyatt and Mr. Wain were public property.; Mike, as an actual spectator of the drama, was in great request as an informant.; As he told the story to a group of sympathisers outside the school shop, Burgess came up, his eyes rolling in a fine frenzy.

"Anybody seen young—oh, here you are.; What's all this about Jimmy Wyatt?; They're saying he's been sacked, or some rot."

"WHAT'S ALL THIS ABOUT JIMMY WYATT?"

"So he has—at least, he's got to leave."
"What?; When?"

103

"He's left already.; He isn't coming to school again."

Burgess's first thought, as befitted a good cricket captain, was for his team.

"And the Ripton match on Saturday!"

Nobody seemed to have anything except silent sympathy at his command.

"Dash the man!; Silly ass!; What did he want to do it for!; Poor old Jimmy, though!" he added after a pause.; "What rot for him!"

"Beastly," agreed Mike.

"All the same," continued Burgess, with a return to the austere manner of the captain of cricket, "he might have chucked playing the goat till after the Ripton match.; Look here, young Jackson, you'll turn out for fielding with the first this afternoon.; You'll play on Saturday."

"All right," said Mike, without enthusiasm.; The Wyatt disaster was too recent for him to feel much pleasure at playing against Ripton *vice* his friend, withdrawn.

Bob was the next to interview him.; They met in the cloisters.

"Hullo, Mike!" said Bob.; "I say, what's all this about Wyatt?"

"Wain caught him getting back into the dorm. last night after Neville-Smith's, and he's taken him away from the school."

"What's he going to do?; Going into that bank straight away?"

"Yes.; You know, that's the part he bars most.; He'd have been leaving anyhow in a fortnight, you see; only it's awful rot for a chap like Wyatt to have to go and froust in a bank for the rest of his life."

"He'll find it rather a change, I expect.; I suppose you won't be seeing him before he goes?"

"I shouldn't think so.; Not unless he comes to the dorm. during the night.; He's sleeping over in Wain's part of the house, but I shouldn't be surprised if he nipped out after Wain has gone to bed.; Hope he does, anyway."

"I should like to say good-bye.; But I don't suppose it'll be possible."

They separated in the direction of their respective form-rooms.; Mike felt bitter and disappointed at the way the news had been received.; Wyatt was his best friend, his pal; and it offended him that the school should take the tidings of his departure as they had done.; Most of them who had come to him for information had expressed a sort of sympathy with the absent hero of his story, but the chief sensation seemed to be one of pleasurable excitement at the fact that something big had happened to break the monotony of school routine.; They treated the thing much as they would have treated the announcement that a record score had been made in first-class cricket.; The school was not so much regretful as comfortably thrilled.; And Burgess had actually cursed before sympathising.; Mike felt resentful towards Burgess.; As a matter of fact, the cricket captain wrote a letter to Wyatt during preparation that night which would have satisfied even Mike's sense of what was fit.; But Mike had no opportunity of learning this.

There was, however, one exception to the general rule, one member of the school who did not treat the episode as if it were merely an interesting and impersonal item of sensational news.; Neville-Smith heard of what had happened towards the end of the interval, and rushed off instantly in search of Mike.; He was too late to catch him before he went to his form-room, so he waited for him at half-past twelve, when the bell rang for the end of morning school.

"I say, Jackson, is this true about old Wyatt?"

Mike nodded.

"What happened?"

Mike related the story for the sixteenth time.; It was a melancholy pleasure to have found a listener who heard the tale in the right spirit.; There was no doubt about Neville-Smith's interest and sympathy.; He was silent for a moment after Mike had finished.

"It was all my fault," he said at length.; "If it hadn't been for me, this wouldn't have happened.; What a fool I was to ask him to my place!; I might have known he would be caught."

"Oh, I don't know," said Mike.

"It was absolutely my fault."

Mike was not equal to the task of soothing Neville-Smith's wounded conscience. He did not attempt it. They walked on without further conversation till they reached Wain's gate, where Mike left him. Neville-Smith proceeded on his way, plunged in meditation.

The result of which meditation was that Burgess got a second shock before the day was out. Bob, going over to the nets rather late in the afternoon, came upon the captain of cricket standing apart from his fellow men with an expression on his face that spoke of mental upheavals on a vast scale.

"What's up?" asked Bob.

"Nothing much," said Burgess, with a forced and grisly calm. "Only that, as far as I can see, we shall play Ripton on Saturday with a sort of second eleven. You don't happen to have got sacked or anything, by the way, do you?"

"What's happened now?"

"Neville-Smith. In extra on Saturday. That's all. Only our first- and second-change bowlers out of the team for the Ripton match in one day. I suppose by to-morrow half the others'll have gone, and we shall take the field on Saturday with a scratch side of kids from the Junior School."

"Neville-Smith! Why, what's he been doing?"

"Apparently he gave a sort of supper to celebrate his getting his first, and it was while coming back from that that Wyatt got collared. Well, I'm blowed if Neville-Smith doesn't toddle off to the Old Man after school to-day and tell him the whole yarn! Said it was all his fault. What rot! Sort of thing that might have happened to any one. If Wyatt hadn't gone to him, he'd probably have gone out somewhere else."

"And the Old Man shoved him in extra?"

"Next two Saturdays."

"Are Ripton strong this year?" asked Bob, for lack of anything better to say.

"Very, from all accounts. They whacked the M.C.C. Jolly hot team of M.C.C. too. Stronger than the one we drew with."

"Oh, well, you never know what's going to happen at cricket. I may hold a catch for a change."

Burgess grunted.

Bob went on his way to the nets. Mike was just putting on his pads.

"I say, Mike," said Bob; "I wanted to see you. It's about Wyatt. I've thought of something."

"What's that?"

"A way of getting him out of that bank. If it comes off, that's to say."

"By Jove, he'd jump at anything. What's the idea?"

"Why shouldn't he get a job of sorts out in the Argentine? There ought to be heaps of sound jobs going there for a chap like Wyatt. He's a jolly good shot, to start with. I shouldn't wonder if it wasn't rather a score to be able to shoot out there. And he can ride, I know."

"By Jove, I'll write to father to-night. He must be able to work it, I should think. He never chucked the show altogether, did he?"

Mike, as most other boys of his age would have been, was profoundly ignorant as to the details by which his father's money had been, or was being, made. He only knew vaguely that the source of revenue had something to do with the Argentine. His brother Joe had been born in Buenos Ayres; and once, three years ago, his father had gone over there for a visit, presumably on business. All these things seemed to show that Mr. Jackson senior was a useful man to have about if you wanted a job in that Eldorado, the Argentine Republic.

As a matter of fact, Mike's father owned vast tracts of land up country, where countless sheep lived and had their being. He had long retired from active superintendence of his estate. Like Mr. Spenlow, he had a partner, a stout fellow with the work-taint highly developed, who asked nothing better than to be left in charge. So Mr. Jackson had returned to the home of his fathers, glad to be there again. But he still had a decided voice in the ordering of affairs on the ranches, and Mike was going to the fountain-head of things when he wrote to his father that night, putting forward Wyatt's claims to attention and ability to perform any sort of job with which he might be presented.

The reflection that he had done all that could be done tended to console him for the non-appearance of Wyatt either that night or next morning—a non-appearance which was due to the simple fact that he passed that night in a bed in Mr. Wain's dressing-room, the door of which that cautious pedagogue, who believed in taking no chances, locked from the outside on retiring to rest.

CHAPTER XXVII

THE RIPTON MATCH

Mike got an answer from his father on the morning of the Ripton match.; A letter from Wyatt also lay on his plate when he came down to breakfast.

Mr. Jackson's letter was short, but to the point.; He said he would go and see Wyatt early in the next week.; He added that being expelled from a public school was not the only qualification for success as a sheep-farmer, but that, if Mike's friend added to this a general intelligence and amiability, and a skill for picking off cats with an air-pistol and bull's-eyes with a Lee-Enfield, there was no reason why something should not be done for him.; In any case he would buy him a lunch, so that Wyatt would extract at least some profit from his visit.; He said that he hoped something could be managed.; It was a pity that a boy accustomed to shoot cats should be condemned for the rest of his life to shoot nothing more exciting than his cuffs.

Wyatt's letter was longer.; It might have been published under the title "My First Day in a Bank, by a Beginner."; His advent had apparently caused little sensation.; He had first had a brief conversation with the manager, which had run as follows:;

"Mr. Wyatt?"

"Yes, sir."

"H'm ...; Sportsman?"

"Yes, sir."

"Cricketer?"

"Yes, sir."

"Play football?"

"Yes, sir."

"H'm ...; Racquets?"

"Yes, sir."

"Everything?"

"Yes, sir."

"H'm ...; Well, you won't get any more of it now."

After which a Mr. Blenkinsop had led him up to a vast ledger, in which he was to inscribe the addresses of all out-going letters.; These letters he would then stamp, and subsequently take in bundles to the post office.; Once a week he would be required to buy stamps.; "If I were one of those Napoleons of Finance," wrote Wyatt, "I should cook the accounts, I suppose, and embezzle stamps to an incredible amount.; But it doesn't seem in my line.; I'm afraid I wasn't cut out for a business career.; Still, I have stamped this letter at the expense of the office, and entered it up under the heading 'Sundries,' which is a sort of start.; Look out for an article in the *Wrykynian*, 'Hints for Young Criminals, by J. Wyatt, champion catch-as-catch-can stamp-stealer of the British Isles.'; So long.; I suppose you are playing against Ripton, now that the world of commerce has found that it can't get on without me.; Mind you make a century, and then perhaps Burgess'll give you your first after all.; There were twelve colours given three years ago, because one chap left at half-term and the man who played instead of him came off against Ripton."

* * * * *

This had occurred to Mike independently.; The Ripton match was a special event, and the man who performed any outstanding feat against that school was treated as a sort of Horatius.; Honours were heaped upon him.; If he could only make a century! or even fifty.; Even twenty, if it got the school out of a tight place.; He was as nervous on the Saturday morning as he had been on the morning of the M.C.C. match.; It was Victory or Westminster Abbey now.; To

107

do only averagely well, to be among the ruck, would be as useless as not playing at all, as far as his chance of his first was concerned.

It was evident to those who woke early on the Saturday morning that this Ripton match was not likely to end in a draw.; During the Friday rain had fallen almost incessantly in a steady drizzle.; It had stopped late at night; and at six in the morning there was every prospect of another hot day.; There was that feeling in the air which shows that the sun is trying to get through the clouds.; The sky was a dull grey at breakfast time, except where a flush of deeper colour gave a hint of the sun.; It was a day on which to win the toss, and go in first.; At eleven-thirty, when the match was timed to begin, the wicket would be too wet to be difficult.; Runs would come easily till the sun came out and began to dry the ground.; When that happened there would be trouble for the side that was batting.

Burgess, inspecting the wicket with Mr. Spence during the quarter to eleven interval, was not slow to recognise this fact.

"I should win the toss to-day, if I were you, Burgess," said Mr. Spence.

"Just what I was thinking, sir."

"That wicket's going to get nasty after lunch, if the sun comes out.; A regular Rhodes wicket it's going to be."

"I wish we *had* Rhodes," said Burgess.; "Or even Wyatt.; It would just suit him, this."

Mr. Spence, as a member of the staff, was not going to be drawn into discussing Wyatt and his premature departure, so he diverted the conversation on to the subject of the general aspect of the school's attack.

"Who will go on first with you, Burgess?"

"Who do you think, sir?; Ellerby?; It might be his wicket."

Ellerby bowled medium inclining to slow.; On a pitch that suited him he was apt to turn from leg and get people out caught at the wicket or short slip.

"Certainly, Ellerby.; This end, I think.; The other's yours, though I'm afraid you'll have a poor time bowling fast to-day.; Even with plenty of sawdust I doubt if it will be possible to get a decent foothold till after lunch."

"I must win the toss," said Burgess.; "It's a nuisance too, about our batting.; Marsh will probably be dead out of form after being in the Infirmary so long.; If he'd had a chance of getting a bit of practice yesterday, it might have been all right."

"That rain will have a lot to answer for if we lose.; On a dry, hard wicket I'm certain we should beat them four times out of six.; I was talking to a man who played against them for the Nomads.; He said that on a true wicket there was not a great deal of sting in their bowling, but that they've got a slow leg-break man who might be dangerous on a day like this.; A boy called de Freece.; I don't know of him.; He wasn't in the team last year."

"I know the chap.; He played wing three for them at footer against us this year on their ground.; He was crocked when they came here.; He's a pretty useful chap all round, I believe.; Plays racquets for them too."

"Well, my friend said he had one very dangerous ball, of the Bosanquet type.; Looks as if it were going away, and comes in instead."

"I don't think a lot of that," said Burgess ruefully.; "One consolation is, though, that that sort of ball is easier to watch on a slow wicket.; I must tell the fellows to look out for it."

"I should.; And, above all, win the toss."

* * * * *

Burgess and Maclaine, the Ripton captain, were old acquaintances.; They had been at the same private school, and they had played against one another at football and cricket for two years now.

"We'll go in first, Mac," said Burgess, as they met on the pavilion steps after they had changed.

"It's awfully good of you to suggest it," said Maclaine. "but I think we'll toss.; It's a hobby of mine.; You call."

"Heads."

"Tails it is.; I ought to have warned you that you hadn't a chance.; I've lost the toss five times running, so I was bound to win to-day."

"You'll put us in, I suppose?"

"Yes —after us."

"Oh, well, we sha'n't have long to wait for our knock, that's a comfort.; Buck up and send some one in, and let's get at you."

And Burgess went off to tell the ground-man to have plenty of sawdust ready, as he would want the field paved with it.

* * * * *

The policy of the Ripton team was obvious from the first over.; They meant to force the game.; Already the sun was beginning to peep through the haze.; For about an hour run-getting ought to be a tolerably simple process; but after that hour singles would be as valuable as threes and boundaries an almost unheard-of luxury.

So Ripton went in to hit.

The policy proved successful for a time, as it generally does.; Burgess, who relied on a run that was a series of tiger-like leaps culminating in a spring that suggested that he meant to lower the long jump record, found himself badly handicapped by the state of the ground.; In spite of frequent libations of sawdust, he was compelled to tread cautiously, and this robbed his bowling of much of its pace.; The score mounted rapidly.; Twenty came in ten minutes.; At thirty-five the first wicket fell, run out.

At sixty Ellerby, who had found the pitch too soft for him and had been expensive, gave place to Grant.; Grant bowled what were supposed to be slow leg-breaks, but which did not always break.; The change worked.

Maclaine, after hitting the first two balls to the boundary, skied the third to Bob Jackson in the deep, and Bob, for whom constant practice had robbed this sort of catch of its terrors, held it.

A yorker from Burgess disposed of the next man before he could settle down; but the score, seventy-four for three wickets, was large enough in view of the fact that the pitch was already becoming more difficult, and was certain to get worse, to make Ripton feel that the advantage was with them.; Another hour of play remained before lunch.; The deterioration of the wicket would be slow during that period.; The sun, which was now shining brightly, would put in its deadliest work from two o'clock onwards.; Maclaine's instructions to his men were to go on hitting.

A too liberal interpretation of the meaning of the verb "to hit" led to the departure of two more Riptonians in the course of the next two overs.; There is a certain type of school batsman who considers that to force the game means to swipe blindly at every ball on the chance of taking it half-volley.; This policy sometimes leads to a boundary or two, as it did on this occasion, but it means that wickets will fall, as also happened now.; Seventy-four for three became eighty-six for five.; Burgess began to look happier.

His contentment increased when he got the next man leg-before-wicket with the total unaltered.; At this rate Ripton would be out before lunch for under a hundred.

But the rot stopped with the fall of that wicket.; Dashing tactics were laid aside.; The pitch had begun to play tricks, and the pair now in settled down to watch the ball.; They plodded on, scoring slowly and jerkily till the hands of the clock stood at half-past one.; Then Ellerby, who had gone on again instead of Grant, beat the less steady of the pair with a ball that pitched on the middle stump and shot into the base of the off.; A hundred and twenty had gone up on the board at the beginning of the over.

That period which is always so dangerous, when the wicket is bad, the ten minutes before lunch, proved fatal to two more of the enemy.; The last man had just gone to the wickets, with the score at a hundred and thirty-one, when a quarter to two arrived, and with it the luncheon interval.

So far it was anybody's game.

CHAPTER XXVIII

MIKE WINS HOME

The Ripton last-wicket man was de Freece, the slow bowler.; He was apparently a young gentleman wholly free from the curse of nervousness.; He wore a cheerful smile as he took guard before receiving the first ball after lunch, and Wrykyn had plenty of opportunity of seeing that that was his normal expression when at the wickets.; There is often a certain looseness about the attack after lunch, and the bowler of googlies took advantage of it now.; He seemed to be a batsman with only one hit; but he had also a very accurate eye, and his one hit, a semicircular stroke, which suggested the golf links rather than the cricket field, came off with distressing frequency.; He mowed Burgess's first ball to the square-leg boundary, missed his second, and snicked the third for three over long-slip's head.; The other batsman played out the over, and de Freece proceeded to treat Ellerby's bowling with equal familiarity.; The scoring-board showed an increase of twenty as the result of three overs.; Every run was invaluable now, and the Ripton contingent made the pavilion re-echo as a fluky shot over mid-on's head sent up the hundred and fifty.

There are few things more exasperating to the fielding side than a last-wicket stand.; It resembles in its effect the dragging-out of a book or play after the *dénouement* has been reached.; At the fall of the ninth wicket the fieldsmen nearly always look on their outing as finished.; Just a ball or two to the last man, and it will be their turn to bat.; If the last man insists on keeping them out in the field, they resent it.

What made it especially irritating now was the knowledge that a straight yorker would solve the whole thing.; But when Burgess bowled a yorker, it was not straight.; And when he bowled a straight ball, it was not a yorker.; A four and a three to de Freece, and a four bye sent up a hundred and sixty.

It was beginning to look as if this might go on for ever, when Ellerby, who had been missing the stumps by fractions of an inch, for the last ten minutes, did what Burgess had failed to do.; He bowled a straight, medium-paced yorker, and de Freece, swiping at it with a bright smile, found his leg-stump knocked back.; He had made twenty-eight.; His record score, he explained to Mike, as they walked to the pavilion, for this or any ground.

The Ripton total was a hundred and sixty-six.

* * * * *

With the ground in its usual true, hard condition, Wrykyn would have gone in against a score of a hundred and sixty-six with the cheery intention of knocking off the runs for the loss of two or three wickets.; It would have been a gentle canter for them.

But ordinary standards would not apply here.; On a good wicket Wrykyn that season were a two hundred and fifty to three hundred side.; On a bad wicket—well, they had met the Incogniti on a bad wicket, and their total—with Wyatt playing and making top score—had worked out at a hundred and seven.

A grim determination to do their best, rather than confidence that their best, when done, would be anything record-breaking, was the spirit which animated the team when they opened their innings.

And in five minutes this had changed to a dull gloom.

The tragedy started with the very first ball.; It hardly seemed that the innings had begun, when Morris was seen to leave the crease, and make for the pavilion.

"It's that googly man," said Burgess blankly.

"What's happened?" shouted a voice from the interior of the first eleven room.

"Morris is out."

"Good gracious!; How?" asked Ellerby, emerging from the room with one pad on his leg and the other in his hand.

"L.-b.-w.; First ball."

"My aunt!; Who's in next?; Not me?"

"No.; Berridge.; For goodness sake, Berry, stick a bat in the way, and not your legs.; Watch that de Freece man like a hawk.; He breaks like sin all over the shop.; Hullo, Morris!; Bad luck!; Were you out, do you think?" A batsman who has been given l.-b.-w. is always asked this question on his return to the pavilion, and he answers it in nine cases out of ten in the negative.; Morris was the tenth case.; He thought it was all right, he said.

"Thought the thing was going to break, but it didn't."

"Hear that, Berry?; He doesn't always break.; You must look out for that," said Burgess helpfully.; Morris sat down and began to take off his pads.

"That chap'll have Berry, if he doesn't look out," he said.

But Berridge survived the ordeal.; He turned his first ball to leg for a single.

This brought Marsh to the batting end; and the second tragedy occurred.

It was evident from the way he shaped that Marsh was short of practice.; His visit to the Infirmary had taken the edge off his batting.; He scratched awkwardly at three balls without hitting them.; The last of the over had him in two minds.; He started to play forward, changed his stroke suddenly and tried to step back, and the next moment the bails had shot up like the *débris* of a small explosion, and the wicket-keeper was clapping his gloved hands gently and slowly in the introspective, dreamy way wicket-keepers have on these occasions.

A silence that could be felt brooded over the pavilion.

The voice of the scorer, addressing from his little wooden hut the melancholy youth who was working the telegraph-board, broke it.

"One for two.; Last man duck."

Ellerby echoed the remark.; He got up, and took off his blazer.

"This is all right," he said, "isn't it!; I wonder if the man at the other end is a sort of young Rhodes too!"

Fortunately he was not.; The star of the Ripton attack was evidently de Freece.; The bowler at the other end looked fairly plain.; He sent them down medium-pace, and on a good wicket would probably have been simple.; But to-day there was danger in the most guileless-looking deliveries.

Berridge relieved the tension a little by playing safely through the over, and scoring a couple of twos off it.; And when Ellerby not only survived the destructive de Freece's second over, but actually lifted a loose ball on to the roof of the scoring-hut, the cloud began perceptibly to lift.; A no-ball in the same over sent up the first ten.; Ten for two was not good; but it was considerably better than one for two.

With the score at thirty, Ellerby was missed in the slips off de Freece.; He had been playing with slowly increasing confidence till then, but this seemed to throw him out of his stride.; He played inside the next ball, and was all but bowled:; and then, jumping out to drive, he was smartly stumped.; The cloud began to settle again.

Bob was the next man in.

Ellerby took off his pads, and dropped into the chair next to Mike's.; Mike was silent and thoughtful.; He was in after Bob, and to be on the eve of batting does not make one conversational.

"You in next?" asked Ellerby.

Mike nodded.

"It's getting trickier every minute," said Ellerby.; "The only thing is, if we can only stay in, we might have a chance.; The wicket'll get better, and I don't believe they've any bowling at all bar de Freece.; By George, Bob's out!...; No, he isn't."

Bob had jumped out at one of de Freece's slows, as Ellerby had done, and had nearly met the same fate.; The wicket-keeper, however, had fumbled the ball.

"That's the way I was had," said Ellerby.; "That man's keeping such a jolly good length that you don't know whether to stay in your ground or go out at them.; If only somebody would knock him off his length, I believe we might win yet."

The same idea apparently occurred to Burgess.; He came to where Mike was sitting.

"I'm going to shove you down one, Jackson," he said.; "I shall go in next myself and swipe, and try and knock that man de Freece off."

"All right," said Mike.; He was not quite sure whether he was glad or sorry at the respite.

"It's a pity old Wyatt isn't here," said Ellerby.; "This is just the sort of time when he might have come off."

"Bob's broken his egg," said Mike.

"Good man.; Every little helps….; Oh, you silly ass, get *back*!"

Berridge had called Bob for a short run that was obviously no run.; Third man was returning the ball as the batsmen crossed.; The next moment the wicket-keeper had the bails off.; Berridge was out by a yard.

"Forty-one for four," said Ellerby.; "Help!"

Burgess began his campaign against de Freece by skying his first ball over cover's head to the boundary.; A howl of delight went up from the school, which was repeated, *fortissimo*, when, more by accident than by accurate timing, the captain put on two more fours past extra-cover.; The bowler's cheerful smile never varied.

Whether Burgess would have knocked de Freece off his length or not was a question that was destined to remain unsolved, for in the middle of the other bowler's over Bob hit a single; the batsmen crossed; and Burgess had his leg-stump uprooted while trying a gigantic pull-stroke.

The melancholy youth put up the figures, 54, 5, 12, on the board.

Mike, as he walked out of the pavilion to join Bob, was not conscious of any particular nervousness.; It had been an ordeal having to wait and look on while wickets fell, but now that the time of inaction was at an end he felt curiously composed.; When he had gone out to bat against the M.C.C. on the occasion of his first appearance for the school, he experienced a quaint sensation of unreality.; He seemed to be watching his body walking to the wickets, as if it were some one else's.; There was no sense of individuality.

But now his feelings were different.; He was cool.; He noticed small things —mid-off chewing bits of grass, the bowler re-tying the scarf round his waist, little patches of brown where the turf had been worn away.; He took guard with a clear picture of the positions of the fieldsmen photographed on his brain.

Fitness, which in a batsman exhibits itself mainly in an increased power of seeing the ball, is one of the most inexplicable things connected with cricket.; It has nothing, or very little, to do with actual health.; A man may come out of a sick-room with just that extra quickness in sighting the ball that makes all the difference; or he may be in perfect training and play inside straight half-volleys.; Mike would not have said that he felt more than ordinarily well that day.; Indeed, he was rather painfully conscious of having bolted his food at lunch.; But something seemed to whisper to him, as he settled himself to face the bowler, that he was at the top of his batting form.; A difficult wicket always brought out his latent powers as a bat.; It was a standing mystery with the sporting Press how Joe Jackson managed to collect fifties and sixties on wickets that completely upset men who were, apparently, finer players.; On days when the Olympians of the cricket world were bringing their averages down with ducks and singles, Joe would be in his element, watching the ball and pushing it through the slips as if there were no such thing as a tricky wicket.; And Mike took after Joe.

A single off the fifth ball of the over opened his score and brought him to the opposite end.; Bob played ball number six back to the bowler, and Mike took guard preparatory to facing de Freece.

The Ripton slow bowler took a long run, considering his pace.; In the early part of an innings he often trapped the batsmen in this way, by leading them to expect a faster ball than he actually sent down.; A queer little jump in the middle of the run increased the difficulty of watching him.

The smiting he had received from Burgess in the previous over had not had the effect of knocking de Freece off his length.; The ball was too short to reach with comfort, and not short enough to take liberties with.; It pitched slightly to leg, and whipped in quickly.; Mike had faced half-left, and stepped back.; The increased speed of the ball after it had touched the ground beat him.; The ball hit his right pad.

"'S that?" shouted mid-on.; Mid-on has a habit of appealing for l.-b.-w. in school matches.

De Freece said nothing.; The Ripton bowler was as conscientious in the matter of appeals as a good bowler should be.; He had seen that the ball had pitched off the leg-stump.

The umpire shook his head.; Mid-on tried to look as if he had not spoken.

Mike prepared himself for the next ball with a glow of confidence.; He felt that he knew where he was now.; Till then he had not thought the wicket was so fast.; The two balls he had played at the other end had told him nothing.; They had been well pitched up, and he had smothered them.; He knew what to do now.; He had played on wickets of this pace at home against Saunders's bowling, and Saunders had shown him the right way to cope with them.

The next ball was of the same length, but this time off the off-stump.; Mike jumped out, and hit it before it had time to break.; It flew along the ground through the gap between cover and extra-cover, a comfortable three.

Bob played out the over with elaborate care.

Off the second ball of the other man's over Mike scored his first boundary.; It was a long-hop on the off.; He banged it behind point to the terrace-bank.; The last ball of the over, a half-volley to leg, he lifted over the other boundary.

"Sixty up," said Ellerby, in the pavilion, as the umpire signalled another no-ball.; "By George!; I believe these chaps are going to knock off the runs.; Young Jackson looks as if he was in for a century."

"You ass," said Berridge.; "Don't say that, or he's certain to get out."

Berridge was one of those who are skilled in cricket superstitions.

But Mike did not get out.; He took seven off de Freece's next over by means of two cuts and a drive.; And, with Bob still exhibiting a stolid and rock-like defence, the score mounted to eighty, thence to ninety, and so, mainly by singles, to a hundred.

At a hundred and four, when the wicket had put on exactly fifty, Bob fell to a combination of de Freece and extra-cover.; He had stuck like a limpet for an hour and a quarter, and made twenty-one.

Mike watched him go with much the same feelings as those of a man who turns away from the platform after seeing a friend off on a long railway journey.; His departure upset the scheme of things.; For himself he had no fear now.; He might possibly get out off his next ball, but he felt set enough to stay at the wickets till nightfall.; He had had narrow escapes from de Freece, but he was full of that conviction, which comes to all batsmen on occasion, that this was his day.; He had made twenty-six, and the wicket was getting easier.; He could feel the sting going out of the bowling every over.

Henfrey, the next man in, was a promising rather than an effective bat.; He had an excellent style, but he was uncertain. (Two years later, when he captained the Wrykyn teams, he made a lot of runs.) But this season his batting had been spasmodic.

To-day he never looked like settling down.; He survived an over from de Freece, and hit a fast change bowler who had been put on at the other end for a couple of fluky fours.; Then Mike got the bowling for three consecutive overs, and raised the score to a hundred and twenty-six.; A bye brought Henfrey to the batting end again, and de Freece's pet googly, which had not been much in evidence hitherto, led to his snicking an easy catch into short-slip's hands.

A hundred and twenty-seven for seven against a total of a hundred and sixty-six gives the impression that the batting side has the advantage.; In the present case, however, it was Ripton who were really in the better position.; Apparently, Wrykyn had three more wickets to fall.; Practically they had only one, for neither Ashe, nor Grant, nor Devenish had any pretensions to be considered batsmen.; Ashe was the school wicket-keeper.; Grant and Devenish were bowlers.; Between them the three could not be relied on for a dozen in a decent match.

Mike watched Ashe shape with a sinking heart.; The wicket-keeper looked like a man who feels that his hour has come.; Mike could see him licking his lips.; There was nervousness written all over him.

He was not kept long in suspense.; De Freece's first ball made a hideous wreck of his wicket. "Over," said the umpire.

Mike felt that the school's one chance now lay in his keeping the bowling.; But how was he to do this?; It suddenly occurred to him that it was a delicate position that he was in.; It was not often that he was troubled by an inconvenient modesty, but this happened now.; Grant was a fellow he hardly knew, and a school prefect to boot.; Could he go up to him and explain that he, Jackson, did not consider him competent to bat in this crisis?; Would not this get about and be accounted to him for side?; He had made forty, but even so....

Fortunately Grant solved the problem on his own account.; He came up to Mike and spoke with an earnestness born of nerves.; "For goodness sake," he whispered, "collar the bowling all you know, or we're done.; I shall get outed first ball."

"All right," said Mike, and set his teeth.; Forty to win!; A large order.; But it was going to be done.; His whole existence seemed to concentrate itself on those forty runs.

The fast bowler, who was the last of several changes that had been tried at the other end, was well-meaning but erratic.; The wicket was almost true again now, and it was possible to take liberties.

Mike took them.

A distant clapping from the pavilion, taken up a moment later all round the ground, and echoed by the Ripton fieldsmen, announced that he had reached his fifty.

The last ball of the over he mishit.; It rolled in the direction of third man.

"Come on," shouted Grant.

Mike and the ball arrived at the opposite wicket almost simultaneously.; Another fraction of a second, and he would have been run out.

MIKE AND THE BALL ARRIVED ALMOST SIMULTANEOUSLY

The last balls of the next two overs provided repetitions of this performance.; But each time luck was with him, and his bat was across the crease before the bails were off.; The telegraph-board showed a hundred and fifty.

The next over was doubly sensational.; The original medium-paced bowler had gone on again in place of the fast man, and for the first five balls he could not find his length.; During those five balls Mike raised the score to a hundred and sixty.

But the sixth was of a different kind.; Faster than the rest and of a perfect length, it all but got through Mike's defence.; As it was, he stopped it.; But he did not score.; The umpire called "Over!" and there was Grant at the batting end, with de Freece smiling pleasantly as he walked back to begin his run with the comfortable reflection that at last he had got somebody except Mike to bowl at.

That over was an experience Mike never forgot.

Grant pursued the Fabian policy of keeping his bat almost immovable and trusting to luck.; Point and the slips crowded round.; Mid-off and mid-on moved half-way down the pitch.; Grant looked embarrassed, but determined.; For four balls he baffled the attack, though once nearly caught by point a yard from the wicket.; The fifth curled round his bat, and touched the off-stump.; A bail fell silently to the ground.

Devenish came in to take the last ball of the over.

It was an awe-inspiring moment.; A great stillness was over all the ground.; Mike's knees trembled.; Devenish's face was a delicate grey.

The only person unmoved seemed to be de Freece.; His smile was even more amiable than usual as he began his run.

The next moment the crisis was past.; The ball hit the very centre of Devenish's bat, and rolled back down the pitch.

The school broke into one great howl of joy.; There were still seven runs between them and victory, but nobody appeared to recognise this fact as important.; Mike had got the bowling, and the bowling was not de Freece's.

It seemed almost an anti-climax when a four to leg and two two's through the slips settled the thing.

* * * * *

Devenish was caught and bowled in de Freece's next over; but the Wrykyn total was one hundred and seventy-two.

* * * * *

"Good game," said Maclaine, meeting Burgess in the pavilion.; "Who was the man who made all the runs?; How many, by the way?"

"Eighty-three.; It was young Jackson.; Brother of the other one."

"That family!; How many more of them are you going to have here?"

"He's the last.; I say, rough luck on de Freece.; He bowled rippingly."

Politeness to a beaten foe caused Burgess to change his usual "not bad."

"The funny part of it is," continued he, "that young Jackson was only playing as a sub."

"You've got a rum idea of what's funny," said Maclaine.

CHAPTER XXIX

WYATT AGAIN

It was a morning in the middle of September.; The Jacksons were breakfasting.; Mr. Jackson was reading letters.; The rest, including Gladys Maud, whose finely chiselled features were gradually disappearing behind a mask of bread-and-milk, had settled down to serious work.; The usual catch-as-catch-can contest between Marjory and Phyllis for the jam (referee and time-keeper, Mrs. Jackson) had resulted, after both combatants had been cautioned by the referee, in a victory for Marjory, who had duly secured the stakes.; The hour being nine-fifteen, and the official time for breakfast nine o'clock, Mike's place was still empty.

"I've had a letter from MacPherson," said Mr. Jackson.

MacPherson was the vigorous and persevering gentleman, referred to in a previous chapter, who kept a fatherly eye on the Buenos Ayres sheep.

"He seems very satisfied with Mike's friend Wyatt.; At the moment of writing Wyatt is apparently incapacitated owing to a bullet in the shoulder, but expects to be fit again shortly.; That young man seems to make things fairly lively wherever he is.; I don't wonder he found a public school too restricted a sphere for his energies."

"Has he been fighting a duel?" asked Marjory, interested.

"Bushrangers," said Phyllis.

"There aren't any bushrangers in Buenos Ayres," said Ella.

"How do you know?" said Phyllis clinchingly.

"Bush-ray, bush-ray, bush-ray," began Gladys Maud, conversationally, through the bread-and-milk; but was headed off.

"He gives no details.; Perhaps that letter on Mike's plate supplies them.; I see it comes from Buenos Ayres."

"I wish Mike would come and open it," said Marjory.; "Shall I go and hurry him up?"

The missing member of the family entered as she spoke.

"Buck up, Mike," she shouted.; "There's a letter from Wyatt.; He's been wounded in a duel."

"With a bushranger," added Phyllis.

"Bush-ray," explained Gladys Maud.

"Is there?" said Mike.; "Sorry I'm late."

He opened the letter and began to read.

"What does he say?" inquired Marjory.; "Who was the duel with?"

"How many bushrangers were there?" asked Phyllis.

Mike read on.

"Good old Wyatt!; He's shot a man."

"Killed him?" asked Marjory excitedly.

"No.; Only potted him in the leg.; This is what he says.; First page is mostly about the Ripton match and so on.; Here you are.; 'I'm dictating this to a sportsman of the name of Danvers, a good chap who can't help being ugly, so excuse bad writing.; The fact is we've been having a bust-up here, and I've come out of it with a bullet in the shoulder, which has crocked me for the time being.; It happened like this.; An ass of a Gaucho had gone into the town and got jolly tight, and coming back, he wanted to ride through our place.; The old woman who keeps the lodge wouldn't have it at any price.; Gave him the absolute miss-in-baulk.; So this rotter, instead of shifting off, proceeded to cut the fence, and go through that way.; All the farms out here have their boundaries marked by wire fences, and it is supposed to be a deadly sin to cut these.; Well, the lodge-keeper's son dashed off in search of help.; A chap called Chester, an Old Wykehamist, and I were dipping sheep close by, so he came to us and told us what had happened.; We nipped on to a couple of horses, pulled out our revolvers, and tooled after him.; After a bit we overtook him, and that's when the trouble began.; The johnny had dismounted when we arrived.; I thought he was simply tightening his horse's girths.; What he was really doing was getting a steady aim at us with his revolver.; He fired as we came up, and dropped poor old Chester.; I thought he was killed at first, but it turned out it was only his leg.; I got going then.; I emptied all the six chambers of my revolver, and missed him clean every time.; In the meantime he got me in the right shoulder.; Hurt like sin afterwards, though it was only a sort of dull shock at the moment.; The next item of the programme was a forward move in force on the part of the enemy.; The man had got his knife out now—why he didn't shoot again I don't know—and toddled over in our direction to finish us off.; Chester was unconscious, and it was any money on the Gaucho, when I happened to catch sight of Chester's pistol, which had fallen just by where I came down.; I picked it up, and loosed off.; Missed the first shot, but got him with the second in the ankle at about two yards; and his day's work was done.; That's the painful story.; Danvers says he's getting writer's cramp, so I shall have to stop....'"

"By Jove!" said Mike.

"What a dreadful thing!" said Mrs. Jackson.

"Anyhow, it was practically a bushranger," said Phyllis.

"I told you it was a duel, and so it was," said Marjory.

"What a terrible experience for the poor boy!" said Mrs. Jackson.

"Much better than being in a beastly bank," said Mike, summing up.; "I'm glad he's having such a ripping time.; It must be almost as decent as Wrykyn out there....; I say, what's under that dish?"

CHAPTER XXX

MR. JACKSON MAKES UP HIS MIND

Two years have elapsed and Mike is home again for the Easter holidays.

If Mike had been in time for breakfast that morning he might have gathered from the expression on his father's face, as Mr. Jackson opened the envelope containing his school report and read the contents, that the document in question was not exactly a paean of praise from beginning to end.; But he was late, as usual.; Mike always was late for breakfast in the holidays.

When he came down on this particular morning, the meal was nearly over.; Mr. Jackson had disappeared, taking his correspondence with him; Mrs. Jackson had gone into the kitchen, and when Mike appeared the thing had resolved itself into a mere vulgar brawl between Phyllis and Ella for the jam, while Marjory, who had put her hair up a fortnight before, looked on in a detached sort of way, as if these juvenile gambols distressed her.

"Hullo, Mike," she said, jumping up as he entered; "here you are —I've been keeping everything hot for you."

"Have you?; Thanks awfully.; I say —" his eye wandered in mild surprise round the table.; "I'm a bit late."

Marjory was bustling about, fetching and carrying for Mike, as she always did.; She had adopted him at an early age, and did the thing thoroughly.; She was fond of her other brothers, especially when they made centuries in first-class cricket, but Mike was her favourite.; She would field out in the deep as a natural thing when Mike was batting at the net in the paddock, though for the others, even for Joe, who had played in all five Test Matches in the previous summer, she would do it only as a favour.

Phyllis and Ella finished their dispute and went out.; Marjory sat on the table and watched Mike eat.

"Your report came this morning, Mike," she said.

The kidneys failed to retain Mike's undivided attention.; He looked up interested.; "What did it say?"

"I didn't see —I only caught sight of the Wrykyn crest on the envelope.; Father didn't say anything."

Mike seemed concerned.; "I say, that looks rather rotten!; I wonder if it was awfully bad.; It's the first I've had from Appleby."

"It can't be any worse than the horrid ones Mr. Blake used to write when you were in his form."

"No, that's a comfort," said Mike philosophically.; "Think there's any more tea in that pot?"

"I call it a shame," said Marjory; "they ought to be jolly glad to have you at Wrykyn just for cricket, instead of writing beastly reports that make father angry and don't do any good to anybody."

"Last summer he said he'd take me away if I got another one."

"He didn't mean it really, I *know* he didn't!; He couldn't!; You're the best bat Wrykyn's ever had."

"What ho!" interpolated Mike.

"You *are*.; Everybody says you are.; Why, you got your first the very first term you were there —even Joe didn't do anything nearly so good as that.; Saunders says you're simply bound to play for England in another year or two."

"Saunders is a jolly good chap.; He bowled me a half-volley on the off the first ball I had in a school match.; By the way, I wonder if he's out at the net now.; Let's go and see."

Saunders was setting up the net when they arrived.; Mike put on his pads and went to the wickets, while Marjory and the dogs retired as usual to the far hedge to retrieve.

119

She was kept busy.; Saunders was a good sound bowler of the M.C.C. minor match type, and there had been a time when he had worried Mike considerably, but Mike had been in the Wrykyn team for three seasons now, and each season he had advanced tremendously in his batting.; He had filled out in three years.; He had always had the style, and now he had the strength as well.; Saunders's bowling on a true wicket seemed simple to him.; It was early in the Easter holidays, but already he was beginning to find his form.; Saunders, who looked on Mike as his own special invention, was delighted.

"If you don't be worried by being too anxious now that you're captain, Master Mike," he said, "you'll make a century every match next term."

"I wish I wasn't; it's a beastly responsibility."

Henfrey, the Wrykyn cricket captain of the previous season, was not returning next term, and Mike was to reign in his stead.; He liked the prospect, but it certainly carried with it a rather awe-inspiring responsibility.; At night sometimes he would lie awake, appalled by the fear of losing his form, or making a hash of things by choosing the wrong men to play for the school and leaving the right men out.; It is no light thing to captain a public school at cricket.

As he was walking towards the house, Phyllis met him.; "Oh, I've been hunting for you, Mike; father wants you."

"What for?"

"I don't know."

"Where?"

"He's in the study.; He seems —" added Phyllis, throwing in the information by way of a make-weight, "in a beastly wax."

Mike's jaw fell slightly.; "I hope the dickens it's nothing to do with that bally report," was his muttered exclamation.

Mike's dealings with his father were as a rule of a most pleasant nature.; Mr. Jackson was an understanding sort of man, who treated his sons as companions.; From time to time, however, breezes were apt to ruffle the placid sea of good-fellowship.; Mike's end-of-term report was an unfailing wind-raiser; indeed, on the arrival of Mr. Blake's sarcastic *résumé* of Mike's shortcomings at the end of the previous term, there had been something not unlike a typhoon.; It was on this occasion that Mr. Jackson had solemnly declared his intention of removing Mike from Wrykyn unless the critics became more flattering; and Mr. Jackson was a man of his word.

It was with a certain amount of apprehension, therefore, that Jackson entered the study.

"Come in, Mike," said his father, kicking the waste-paper basket; "I want to speak to you."

Mike, skilled in omens, scented a row in the offing.; Only in moments of emotion was Mr. Jackson in the habit of booting the basket.

There followed an awkward silence, which Mike broke by remarking that he had carted a half-volley from Saunders over the on-side hedge that morning.

"It was just a bit short and off the leg stump, so I stepped out —may I bag the paper-knife for a jiffy?; I'll just show ——"

"Never mind about cricket now," said Mr. Jackson; "I want you to listen to this report."

"Oh, is that my report, father?" said Mike, with a sort of sickly interest, much as a dog about to be washed might evince in his tub.

"It is," replied Mr. Jackson in measured tones, "your report; what is more, it is without exception the worst report you have ever had."

"Oh, I say!" groaned the record-breaker.

"'His conduct,'" quoted Mr. Jackson, "'has been unsatisfactory in the extreme, both in and out of school.'"

"It wasn't anything really.; I only happened ——"

Remembering suddenly that what he had happened to do was to drop a cannon-ball (the school weight) on the form-room floor, not once, but on several occasions, he paused.

"'French bad; conduct disgraceful ——'"

"Everybody rags in French."

"'Mathematics bad.; Inattentive and idle.'"

"Nobody does much work in Math."

"'Latin poor.; Greek, very poor.'"

"We were doing Thucydides, Book Two, last term —all speeches and doubtful readings, and cruxes and things —beastly hard!; Everybody says so."

"Here are Mr. Appleby's remarks:; 'The boy has genuine ability, which he declines to use in the smallest degree.'"

Mike moaned a moan of righteous indignation.

"'An abnormal proficiency at games has apparently destroyed all desire in him to realise the more serious issues of life.'; There is more to the same effect."

Mr. Appleby was a master with very definite ideas as to what constituted a public-school master's duties.; As a man he was distinctly pro-Mike.; He understood cricket, and some of Mike's shots on the off gave him thrills of pure aesthetic joy; but as a master he always made it his habit to regard the manners and customs of the boys in his form with an unbiased eye, and to an unbiased eye Mike in a form-room was about as near the extreme edge as a boy could be, and Mr. Appleby said as much in a clear firm hand.

"You remember what I said to you about your report at Christmas, Mike?" said Mr. Jackson, folding the lethal document and replacing it in its envelope.

Mike said nothing; there was a sinking feeling in his interior.

"I shall abide by what I said."

Mike's heart thumped.

"You will not go back to Wrykyn next term."

Somewhere in the world the sun was shining, birds were twittering; somewhere in the world lambkins frisked and peasants sang blithely at their toil (flat, perhaps, but still blithely), but to Mike at that moment the sky was black, and an icy wind blew over the face of the earth.

The tragedy had happened, and there was an end of it.; He made no attempt to appeal against the sentence.; He knew it would be useless, his father, when he made up his mind, having all the unbending tenacity of the normally easy-going man.

Mr. Jackson was sorry for Mike.; He understood him, and for that reason he said very little now.

"I am sending you to Sedleigh," was his next remark.

Sedleigh!; Mike sat up with a jerk.; He knew Sedleigh by name —one of those schools with about a hundred fellows which you never hear of except when they send up their gymnasium pair to Aldershot, or their Eight to Bisley.; Mike's outlook on life was that of a cricketer, pure and simple.; What had Sedleigh ever done?; What were they ever likely to do?; Whom did they play?; What Old Sedleighan had ever done anything at cricket?; Perhaps they didn't even *play* cricket!

"But it's an awful hole," he said blankly.

Mr. Jackson could read Mike's mind like a book.; Mike's point of view was plain to him.; He did not approve of it, but he knew that in Mike's place and at Mike's age he would have felt the same.; He spoke drily to hide his sympathy.

"It is not a large school," he said, "and I don't suppose it could play Wrykyn at cricket, but it has one merit —boys work there.; Young Barlitt won a Balliol scholarship from Sedleigh last year."; Barlitt was the vicar's son, a silent, spectacled youth who did not enter very largely into Mike's world.; They had met occasionally at tennis-parties, but not much conversation had ensued.; Barlitt's mind was massive, but his topics of conversation were not Mike's.

"Mr. Barlitt speaks very highly of Sedleigh," added Mr. Jackson.

Mike said nothing, which was a good deal better than saying what he would have liked to have said.

CHAPTER XXXI

SEDLEIGH

The train, which had been stopping everywhere for the last half-hour, pulled up again, and Mike, seeing the name of the station, got up, opened the door, and hurled a Gladstone bag out on to the platform in an emphatic and vindictive manner.; Then he got out himself and looked about him.

"For the school, sir?" inquired the solitary porter, bustling up, as if he hoped by sheer energy to deceive the traveller into thinking that Sedleigh station was staffed by a great army of porters.

Mike nodded.; A sombre nod.; The nod Napoleon might have given if somebody had met him in 1812, and said, "So you're back from Moscow, eh?" Mike was feeling thoroughly jaundiced.; The future seemed wholly gloomy.; And, so far from attempting to make the best of things, he had set himself deliberately to look on the dark side.; He thought, for instance, that he had never seen a more repulsive porter, or one more obviously incompetent than the man who had attached himself with a firm grasp to the handle of the bag as he strode off in the direction of the luggage-van.; He disliked his voice, his appearance, and the colour of his hair.; Also the boots he wore.; He hated the station, and the man who took his ticket.

"Young gents at the school, sir," said the porter, perceiving from Mike's *distrait* air that the boy was a stranger to the place, "goes up in the 'bus mostly.; It's waiting here, sir.; Hi, George!"

"I'll walk, thanks," said Mike frigidly.

"It's a goodish step, sir."

"Here you are."

"Thank you, sir.; I'll send up your luggage by the 'bus, sir.; Which 'ouse was it you was going to?"

"Outwood's."

"Right, sir.; It's straight on up this road to the school.; You can't miss it, sir."

"Worse luck," said Mike.

He walked off up the road, sorrier for himself than ever.; It was such absolutely rotten luck.; About now, instead of being on his way to a place where they probably ran a diabolo team instead of a cricket eleven, and played hunt-the-slipper in winter, he would be on the point of arriving at Wrykyn.; And as captain of cricket, at that.; Which was the bitter part of it.; He had never been in command.; For the last two seasons he had been the star man, going in first, and heading the averages easily at the end of the season; and the three captains under whom he had played during his career as a Wrykynian, Burgess, Enderby, and Henfrey had always been sportsmen to him.; But it was not the same thing.; He had meant to do such a lot for Wrykyn cricket this term.; He had had an entirely new system of coaching in his mind.; Now it might never be used.; He had handed it on in a letter to Strachan, who would be captain in his place; but probably Strachan would have some scheme of his own.; There is nobody who could not edit a paper in the ideal way; and there is nobody who has not a theory of his own about cricket-coaching at school.

Wrykyn, too, would be weak this year, now that he was no longer there.; Strachan was a good, free bat on his day, and, if he survived a few overs, might make a century in an hour, but he was not to be depended upon.; There was no doubt that Mike's sudden withdrawal meant that Wrykyn would have a bad time that season.; And it had been such a wretched athletic year for the school.; The football fifteen had been hopeless, and had lost both the Ripton matches, the return by over sixty points.; Sheen's victory in the light-weights at Aldershot had been their one success.; And now, on top of all this, the captain of cricket was removed during the Easter holidays.; Mike's heart bled for Wrykyn, and he found himself loathing Sedleigh and all its works with a great loathing.

The only thing he could find in its favour was the fact that it was set in a very pretty country.; Of a different type from the Wrykyn country, but almost as good.; For three miles Mike made his way through woods and past fields.; Once he crossed a river.; It was soon after this that he caught sight, from the top of a hill, of a group of buildings that wore an unmistakably school-like look.

This must be Sedleigh.

Ten minutes' walk brought him to the school gates, and a baker's boy directed him to Mr. Outwood's.

There were three houses in a row, separated from the school buildings by a cricket-field.; Outwood's was the middle one of these.

Mike went to the front door, and knocked.; At Wrykyn he had always charged in at the beginning of term at the boys' entrance, but this formal reporting of himself at Sedleigh suited his mood.

He inquired for Mr. Outwood, and was shown into a room lined with books.; Presently the door opened, and the house-master appeared.

There was something pleasant and homely about Mr. Outwood.; In appearance he reminded Mike of Smee in "Peter Pan."; He had the same eyebrows and pince-nez and the same motherly look.

"Jackson?" he said mildly.

"Yes, sir."

"I am very glad to see you, very glad indeed.; Perhaps you would like a cup of tea after your journey.; I think you might like a cup of tea.; You come from Crofton, in Shropshire, I understand, Jackson, near Brindleford?; It is a part of the country which I have always wished to visit.; I daresay you have frequently seen the Cluniac Priory of St. Ambrose at Brindleford?"

Mike, who would not have recognised a Cluniac Priory if you had handed him one on a tray, said he had not.

"Dear me!; You have missed an opportunity which I should have been glad to have.; I am preparing a book on Ruined Abbeys and Priories of England, and it has always been my wish to see the Cluniac Priory of St. Ambrose.; A deeply interesting relic of the sixteenth century.; Bishop Geoffrey, 1133-40 — —"

"Shall I go across to the boys' part, sir?"

"What?; Yes.; Oh, yes.; Quite so.; And perhaps you would like a cup of tea after your journey?; No?; Quite so.; Quite so.; You should make a point of visiting the remains of the Cluniac Priory in the summer holidays, Jackson.; You will find the matron in her room.; In many respects it is unique.; The northern altar is in a state of really wonderful preservation.; It consists of a solid block of masonry five feet long and two and a half wide, with chamfered plinth, standing quite free from the apse wall.; It will well repay a visit.; Good-bye for the present, Jackson, good-bye."

Mike wandered across to the other side of the house, his gloom visibly deepened.; All alone in a strange school, where they probably played hopscotch, with a house-master who offered one cups of tea after one's journey and talked about chamfered plinths and apses.; It was a little hard.

He strayed about, finding his bearings, and finally came to a room which he took to be the equivalent of the senior day-room at a Wrykyn house.; Everywhere else he had found nothing but emptiness.; Evidently he had come by an earlier train than was usual.; But this room was occupied.

A very long, thin youth, with a solemn face and immaculate clothes, was leaning against the mantelpiece.; As Mike entered, he fumbled in his top left waistcoat pocket, produced an eyeglass attached to a cord, and fixed it in his right eye.; With the help of this aid to vision he inspected Mike in silence for a while, then, having flicked an invisible speck of dust from the left sleeve of his coat, he spoke.

"Hullo," he said.

He spoke in a tired voice.

"Hullo," said Mike.

"Take a seat," said the immaculate one.; "If you don't mind dirtying your bags, that's to say.; Personally, I don't see any prospect of ever sitting down in this place.; It looks to me as if they meant to use these chairs as mustard-and-cress beds.; A Nursery Garden in the Home.; That sort of idea.; My name," he added pensively, "is Smith.; What's yours?"

CHAPTER XXXII

PSMITH

"Jackson," said Mike.

"Are you the Bully, the Pride of the School, or the Boy who is Led Astray and takes to Drink in Chapter Sixteen?"

"The last, for choice," said Mike, "but I've only just arrived, so I don't know."

"The boy —what will he become?; Are you new here, too, then?"

"Yes!; Why, are you new?"

"Do I look as if I belonged here?; I'm the latest import.; Sit down on yonder settee, and I will tell you the painful story of my life.; By the way, before I start, there's just one thing.; If you ever have occasion to write to me, would you mind sticking a P at the beginning of my name?; P-s-m-i-t-h.; See?; There are too many Smiths, and I don't care for Smythe.; My father's content to worry along in the old-fashioned way, but I've decided to strike out a fresh line.; I shall found a new dynasty.; The resolve came to me unexpectedly this morning, as I was buying a simple penn'orth of butterscotch out of the automatic machine at Paddington.; I jotted it down on the back of an envelope.; In conversation you may address me as Rupert (though I hope you won't), or simply Smith, the P not being sounded.; Cp. the name Zbysco, in which the Z is given a similar miss-in-baulk.; See?"

Mike said he saw.; Psmith thanked him with a certain stately old-world courtesy.

"Let us start at the beginning," he resumed.; "My infancy.; When I was but a babe, my eldest sister was bribed with a shilling an hour by my nurse to keep an eye on me, and see that I did not raise Cain.; At the end of the first day she struck for one-and six, and got it.; We now pass to my boyhood.; At an early age, I was sent to Eton, everybody predicting a bright career for me.; But," said Psmith solemnly, fixing an owl-like gaze on Mike through the eye-glass, "it was not to be."

"No?" said Mike.

"No.; I was superannuated last term."

"Bad luck."

"For Eton, yes.; But what Eton loses, Sedleigh gains."

"But why Sedleigh, of all places?"

"This is the most painful part of my narrative.; It seems that a certain scug in the next village to ours happened last year to collar a Balliol——"

"Not Barlitt!" exclaimed Mike.

"That was the man.; The son of the vicar.; The vicar told the curate, who told our curate, who told our vicar, who told my father, who sent me off here to get a Balliol too.; Do *you* know Barlitt?"

"His pater's vicar of our village.; It was because his son got a Balliol that I was sent here."

"Do you come from Crofton?"

"Yes."

"I've lived at Lower Benford all my life.; We are practically long-lost brothers.; Cheer a little, will you?"

Mike felt as Robinson Crusoe felt when he met Friday.; Here was a fellow human being in this desert place.; He could almost have embraced Psmith.; The very sound of the name Lower Benford was heartening.; His dislike for his new school was not diminished, but now he felt that life there might at least be tolerable.

"Where were you before you came here?" asked Psmith.; "You have heard my painful story.; Now tell me yours."

"Wrykyn.; My pater took me away because I got such a lot of bad reports."

"My reports from Eton were simply scurrilous.; There's a libel action in every sentence.; How do you like this place from what you've seen of it?"

"Rotten."

"I am with you, Comrade Jackson.; You won't mind my calling you Comrade, will you?; I've just become a Socialist.; It's a great scheme.; You ought to be one.; You work for the equal distribution of property, and start by collaring all you can and sitting on it.; We must stick together.; We are companions in misfortune.; Lost lambs.; Sheep that have gone astray.; Divided, we fall, together we may worry through.; Have you seen Professor Radium yet?; I should say Mr. Outwood.; What do you think of him?"

"He doesn't seem a bad sort of chap.; Bit off his nut.; Jawed about apses and things."

"And thereby," said Psmith, "hangs a tale.; I've been making inquiries of a stout sportsman in a sort of Salvation Army uniform, whom I met in the grounds —he's the school sergeant or something, quite a solid man—and I hear that Comrade Outwood's an archaeological cove.; Goes about the country beating up old ruins and fossils and things.; There's an Archaeological Society in the school, run by him.; It goes out on half-holidays, prowling about, and is allowed to break bounds and generally steep itself to the eyebrows in reckless devilry.; And, mark you, laddie, if you belong to the Archaeological Society you get off cricket.; To get off cricket," said Psmith, dusting his right trouser-leg, "was the dream of my youth and the aspiration of my riper years.; A noble game, but a bit too thick for me.; At Eton I used to have to field out at the nets till the soles of my boots wore through.; I suppose you are a blood at the game?; Play for the school against Loamshire, and so on."

"I'm not going to play here, at any rate," said Mike.

He had made up his mind on this point in the train.; There is a certain fascination about making the very worst of a bad job.; Achilles knew his business when he sat in his tent.; The determination not to play cricket for Sedleigh as he could not play for Wrykyn gave Mike a sort of pleasure.; To stand by with folded arms and a sombre frown, as it were, was one way of treating the situation, and one not without its meed of comfort.

Psmith approved the resolve.

"Stout fellow," he said. "'Tis well.; You and I, hand in hand, will search the countryside for ruined abbeys.; We will snare the elusive fossil together.; Above all, we will go out of bounds.; We shall thus improve our minds, and have a jolly good time as well.; I shouldn't wonder if one mightn't borrow a gun from some friendly native, and do a bit of rabbit-shooting here and there.; From what I saw of Comrade Outwood during our brief interview, I shouldn't think he was one of the lynx-eyed contingent.; With tact we ought to be able to slip away from the merry throng of fossil-chasers, and do a bit on our own account."

"Good idea," said Mike.; "We will.; A chap at Wrykyn, called Wyatt, used to break out at night and shoot at cats with an air-pistol."

"It would take a lot to make me do that.; I am all against anything that interferes with my sleep.; But rabbits in the daytime is a scheme.; We'll nose about for a gun at the earliest opp.; Meanwhile we'd better go up to Comrade Outwood, and get our names shoved down for the Society."

"I vote we get some tea first somewhere."

"Then let's beat up a study.; I suppose they have studies here.; Let's go and look."

They went upstairs.; On the first floor there was a passage with doors on either side.; Psmith opened the first of these.

"This'll do us well," he said.

It was a biggish room, looking out over the school grounds.; There were a couple of deal tables, two empty bookcases, and a looking-glass, hung on a nail.

"Might have been made for us," said Psmith approvingly.

"I suppose it belongs to some rotter."

"Not now."

"You aren't going to collar it!"

"That," said Psmith, looking at himself earnestly in the mirror, and straightening his tie, "is the exact programme.; We must stake out our claims.; This is practical Socialism."

"But the real owner's bound to turn up some time or other."

"His misfortune, not ours.; You can't expect two master-minds like us to pig it in that room downstairs.; There are moments when one wants to be alone.; It is imperative that we have a place to retire to after a fatiguing day.; And now, if you want to be really useful, come and help me fetch up my box from downstairs.; It's got an Etna and various things in it."

CHAPTER XXXIII

STAKING OUT A CLAIM

Psmith, in the matter of decorating a study and preparing tea in it, was rather a critic than an executant.; He was full of ideas, but he preferred to allow Mike to carry them out.; It was he who suggested that the wooden bar which ran across the window was unnecessary, but it was Mike who wrenched it from its place.; Similarly, it was Mike who abstracted the key from the door of the next study, though the idea was Psmith's.

"Privacy," said Psmith, as he watched Mike light the Etna, "is what we chiefly need in this age of publicity.; If you leave a study door unlocked in these strenuous times, the first thing you know is, somebody comes right in, sits down, and begins to talk about himself.; I think with a little care we ought to be able to make this room quite decently comfortable.; That putrid calendar must come down, though.; Do you think you could make a long arm, and haul it off the parent tin-tack?; Thanks.; We make progress.; We make progress."

"We shall jolly well make it out of the window," said Mike, spooning up tea from a paper bag with a postcard, "if a sort of young Hackenschmidt turns up and claims the study.; What are you going to do about it?"

"Don't let us worry about it.; I have a presentiment that he will be an insignificant-looking little weed.; How are you getting on with the evening meal?"

"Just ready.; What would you give to be at Eton now?; I'd give something to be at Wrykyn."

"These school reports," said Psmith sympathetically, "are the very dickens.; Many a bright young lad has been soured by them.; Hullo.; What's this, I wonder."

A heavy body had plunged against the door, evidently without a suspicion that there would be any resistance.; A rattling at the handle followed, and a voice outside said, "Dash the door!"

"Hackenschmidt!" said Mike.

"The weed," said Psmith.; "You couldn't make a long arm, could you, and turn the key?; We had better give this merchant audience.; Remind me later to go on with my remarks on school reports.; I had several bright things to say on the subject."

Mike unlocked the door, and flung it open.; Framed in the entrance was a smallish, freckled boy, wearing a bowler hat and carrying a bag.; On his face was an expression of mingled wrath and astonishment.

Psmith rose courteously from his chair, and moved forward with slow stateliness to do the honours.

"What the dickens," inquired the newcomer, "are you doing here?"

"WHAT THE DICKENS ARE YOU DOING HERE?"

"We were having a little tea," said Psmith, "to restore our tissues after our journey.; Come in and join us.; We keep open house, we Psmiths.; Let me introduce you to Comrade Jackson.; A stout fellow.; Homely in appearance, perhaps, but one of us.; I am Psmith.; Your own name will doubtless come up in the course of general chit-chat over the tea-cups."

"My name's Spiller, and this is my study."

Psmith leaned against the mantelpiece, put up his eyeglass, and harangued Spiller in a philosophical vein.

"Of all sad words of tongue or pen," said he, "the saddest are these:; 'It might have been.'; Too late!; That is the bitter cry.; If you had torn yourself from the bosom of the Spiller family by an earlier train, all might have been well.; But no.; Your father held your hand and said huskily, 'Edwin, don't leave us!' Your mother clung to you weeping, and said, 'Edwin, stay!' Your sisters ——"

"I want to know what ——"

"Your sisters froze on to your knees like little octopuses (or octopi), and screamed, 'Don't go, Edwin!' And so," said Psmith, deeply affected by his recital, "you stayed on till the later train; and, on arrival, you find strange faces in the familiar room, a people that know not Spiller.";
Psmith went to the table, and cheered himself with a sip of tea.; Spiller's sad case had moved him greatly.

The victim of Fate seemed in no way consoled.

"It's beastly cheek, that's what I call it.; Are you new chaps?"

"The very latest thing," said Psmith.

"Well, it's beastly cheek."

Mike's outlook on life was of the solid, practical order.; He went straight to the root of the matter.

"What are you going to do about it?" he asked.

Spiller evaded the question.

"It's beastly cheek," he repeated.; "You can't go about the place bagging studies."

"But we do," said Psmith.; "In this life, Comrade Spiller, we must be prepared for every emergency.; We must distinguish between the unusual and the impossible.; It is unusual for people to go about the place bagging studies, so you have rashly ordered your life on the assumption that it is impossible.; Error!; Ah, Spiller, Spiller, let this be a lesson to you."

"Look here, I tell you what it ——"

"I was in a motor with a man once.; I said to him:; 'What would happen if you trod on that pedal thing instead of that other pedal thing?' He said, 'I couldn't.; One's the foot-brake, and the other's the accelerator.'; 'But suppose you did?' I said.; 'I wouldn't,' he said.; 'Now we'll let her rip.'; So he stamped on the accelerator.; Only it turned out to be the foot-brake after all, and we stopped dead, and skidded into a ditch.; The advice I give to every young man starting life is:; 'Never confuse the unusual and the impossible.'; Take the present case.; If you had only realised the possibility of somebody some day collaring your study, you might have thought out dozens of sound schemes for dealing with the matter.; As it is, you are unprepared.; The thing comes on you as a surprise.; The cry goes round:; 'Spiller has been taken unawares.; He cannot cope with the situation.'"

"Can't I!; I'll ——"

"What *are* you going to do about it?" said Mike.

"All I know is, I'm going to have it.; It was Simpson's last term, and Simpson's left, and I'm next on the house list, so, of course, it's my study."

"But what steps," said Psmith, "are you going to take?; Spiller, the man of Logic, we know.; But what of Spiller, the Man of Action?; How do you intend to set about it?; Force is useless.; I was saying to Comrade Jackson before you came in, that I didn't mind betting you were an insignificant-looking little weed.; And you *are* an insignificant-looking little weed."

"We'll see what Outwood says about it."

"Not an unsound scheme.; By no means a scaly project.; Comrade Jackson and myself were about to interview him upon another point.; We may as well all go together."

The trio made their way to the Presence, Spiller pink and determined, Mike sullen, Psmith particularly debonair.; He hummed lightly as he walked, and now and then pointed out to Spiller objects of interest by the wayside.

Mr. Outwood received them with the motherly warmth which was evidently the leading characteristic of his normal manner.

"Ah, Spiller," he said.; "And Smith, and Jackson.; I am glad to see that you have already made friends."

"Spiller's, sir," said Psmith, laying a hand patronisingly on the study-claimer's shoulder — a proceeding violently resented by Spiller —"is a character one cannot help but respect.; His nature expands before one like some beautiful flower."

Mr. Outwood received this eulogy with rather a startled expression, and gazed at the object of the tribute in a surprised way.

"Er—quite so, Smith, quite so," he said at last.; "I like to see boys in my house friendly towards one another."

"There is no vice in Spiller," pursued Psmith earnestly.; "His heart is the heart of a little child."

"Please, sir," burst out this paragon of all the virtues, "I ——"

"But it was not entirely with regard to Spiller that I wished to speak to you, sir, if you were not too busy."

"Not at all, Smith, not at all.; Is there anything ——"

"Please, sir —" began Spiller.

"I understand, sir," said Psmith, "that there is an Archaeological Society in the school."

Mr. Outwood's eyes sparkled behind their pince-nez.; It was a disappointment to him that so few boys seemed to wish to belong to his chosen band.; Cricket and football, games that left him cold, appeared to be the main interest in their lives.; It was but rarely that he could induce new boys to join.; His colleague, Mr. Downing, who presided over the School Fire Brigade, never had any difficulty in finding support.; Boys came readily at his call.; Mr. Outwood pondered wistfully on this at times, not knowing that the Fire Brigade owed its support to the fact that it provided its light-hearted members with perfectly unparalleled opportunities for ragging, while his own band, though small, were in the main earnest.

"Yes, Smith." he said.; "Yes.; We have a small Archaeological Society.; I —er —in a measure look after it.; Perhaps you would care to become a member?"

"Please, sir —" said Spiller.

"One moment, Spiller.; Do you want to join, Smith?"

"Intensely, sir.; Archaeology fascinates me.; A grand pursuit, sir."

"Undoubtedly, Smith.; I am very pleased, very pleased indeed.; I will put down your name at once."

"And Jackson's, sir."

"Jackson, too!" Mr. Outwood beamed.; "I am delighted.; Most delighted.; This is capital.; This enthusiasm is most capital."

"Spiller, sir," said Psmith sadly, "I have been unable to induce to join."

"Oh, he is one of our oldest members."

"Ah," said Psmith, tolerantly, "that accounts for it."

"Please, sir —" said Spiller.

"One moment, Spiller.; We shall have the first outing of the term on Saturday.; We intend to inspect the Roman Camp at Embury Hill, two miles from the school."

"We shall be there, sir."

"Capital!"

"Please, sir —" said Spiller.

"One moment, Spiller," said Psmith.; "There is just one other matter, if you could spare the time, sir."

"Certainly, Smith.; What is that?"

"Would there be any objection to Jackson and myself taking Simpson's old study?"

"By all means, Smith.; A very good idea."

"Yes, sir.; It would give us a place where we could work quietly in the evenings."

"Quite so.; Quite so."

"Thank you very much, sir.; We will move our things in."

"Thank you very much, sir," said Mike.

"Please, sir," shouted Spiller, "aren't I to have it?; I'm next on the list, sir.; I come next after Simpson.; Can't I have it?"

"I'm afraid I have already promised it to Smith, Spiller.; You should have spoken before."

"But, sir——"

Psmith eyed the speaker pityingly.

"This tendency to delay, Spiller," he said, "is your besetting fault.; Correct it, Edwin.; Fight against it."

He turned to Mr. Outwood.

"We should, of course, sir, always be glad to see Spiller in our study.; He would always find a cheery welcome waiting there for him.; There is no formality between ourselves and Spiller."

"Quite so.; An excellent arrangement, Smith.; I like this spirit of comradeship in my house.; Then you will be with us on Saturday?"

"On Saturday, sir."

"All this sort of thing, Spiller," said Psmith, as they closed the door, "is very, very trying for a man of culture.; Look us up in our study one of these afternoons."

CHAPTER XXXIV

GUERRILLA WARFARE

"There are few pleasures," said Psmith, as he resumed his favourite position against the mantelpiece and surveyed the commandeered study with the pride of a householder, "keener to the reflective mind than sitting under one's own roof-tree.; This place would have been wasted on Spiller; he would not have appreciated it properly."

Mike was finishing his tea.; "You're a jolly useful chap to have by you in a crisis, Smith," he said with approval.; "We ought to have known each other before."

"The loss was mine," said Psmith courteously.; "We will now, with your permission, face the future for awhile.; I suppose you realise that we are now to a certain extent up against it.; Spiller's hot Spanish blood is not going to sit tight and do nothing under a blow like this."

"What can he do?; Outwood's given us the study."

"What would you have done if somebody had bagged your study?"

"Made it jolly hot for them!"

"So will Comrade Spiller.; I take it that he will collect a gang and make an offensive movement against us directly he can.; To all appearances we are in a fairly tight place.; It all depends on how big Comrade Spiller's gang will be.; I don't like rows, but I'm prepared to take on a reasonable number of bravoes in defence of the home."

Mike intimated that he was with him on the point.; "The difficulty is, though," he said, "about when we leave this room.; I mean, we're all right while we stick here, but we can't stay all night."

"That's just what I was about to point out when you put it with such admirable clearness.; Here we are in a stronghold, they can only get at us through the door, and we can lock that."

"And jam a chair against it."

"*And*, as you rightly remark, jam a chair against it.; But what of the nightfall?; What of the time when we retire to our dormitory?"

"Or dormitories.; I say, if we're in separate rooms we shall be in the cart."

Psmith eyed Mike with approval.; "He thinks of everything!; You're the man, Comrade Jackson, to conduct an affair of this kind —such foresight! such resource!; We must see to this at once; if they put us in different rooms we're done —we shall be destroyed singly in the watches of the night."

"We'd better nip down to the matron right off."

"Not the matron —Comrade Outwood is the man.; We are as sons to him; there is nothing he can deny us.; I'm afraid we are quite spoiling his afternoon by these interruptions, but we must rout him out once more."

As they got up, the door handle rattled again, and this time there followed a knocking.

"This must be an emissary of Comrade Spiller's," said Psmith.; "Let us parley with the man."

Mike unlocked the door.; A light-haired youth with a cheerful, rather vacant face and a receding chin strolled into the room, and stood giggling with his hands in his pockets.

"I just came up to have a look at you," he explained.

"If you move a little to the left," said Psmith, "you will catch the light and shade effects on Jackson's face better."

The new-comer giggled with renewed vigour.; "Are you the chap with the eyeglass who jaws all the time?"

"I *do* wear an eyeglass," said Psmith; "as to the rest of the description ——"

"My name's Jellicoe."

"Mine is Psmith —P-s-m-i-t-h —one of the Shropshire Psmiths.; The object on the skyline is Comrade Jackson."

"Old Spiller," giggled Jellicoe, "is cursing you like anything downstairs.; You *are* chaps!; Do you mean to say you simply bagged his study?; He's making no end of a row about it."

"Spiller's fiery nature is a byword," said Psmith.

"What's he going to do?" asked Mike, in his practical way.

"He's going to get the chaps to turn you out."

"As I suspected," sighed Psmith, as one mourning over the frailty of human nature.; "About how many horny-handed assistants should you say that he would be likely to bring?; Will you, for instance, join the glad throng?"

"Me?; No fear!; I think Spiller's an ass."

"There's nothing like a common thought for binding people together. *I* think Spiller's an ass."

"How many *will* there be, then?" asked Mike.

"He might get about half a dozen, not more, because most of the chaps don't see why they should sweat themselves just because Spiller's study has been bagged."

"Sturdy common sense," said Psmith approvingly, "seems to be the chief virtue of the Sedleigh character."

"We shall be able to tackle a crowd like that," said Mike.; "The only thing is we must get into the same dormitory."

"This is where Comrade Jellicoe's knowledge of the local geography will come in useful.; Do you happen to know of any snug little room, with, say, about four beds in it?; How many dormitories are there?"

"Five —there's one with three beds in it, only it belongs to three chaps."

"I believe in the equal distribution of property.; We will go to Comrade Outwood and stake out another claim."

Mr. Outwood received them even more beamingly than before.; "Yes, Smith?" he said.

"We must apologise for disturbing you, sir——"

"Not at all, Smith, not at all!; I like the boys in my house to come to me when they wish for my advice or help."

"We were wondering, sir, if you would have any objection to Jackson, Jellicoe and myself sharing the dormitory with the three beds in it.; A very warm friendship —" explained Psmith, patting the gurgling Jellicoe kindly on the shoulder, "has sprung up between Jackson, Jellicoe and myself."

"You make friends easily, Smith.; I like to see it —I like to see it."

"And we can have the room, sir?"

"Certainly —certainly!; Tell the matron as you go down."

"And now," said Psmith, as they returned to the study, "we may say that we are in a fairly winning position.; A vote of thanks to Comrade Jellicoe for his valuable assistance."

"You *are* a chap!" said Jellicoe.

The handle began to revolve again.

"That door," said Psmith, "is getting a perfect incubus!; It cuts into one's leisure cruelly."

This time it was a small boy.; "They told me to come up and tell you to come down," he said. Psmith looked at him searchingly through his eyeglass.

"Who?"

"The senior day-room chaps."

"Spiller?"

"Spiller and Robinson and Stone, and some other chaps."

"They want us to speak to them?"

"They told me to come up and tell you to come down."

"Go and give Comrade Spiller our compliments and say that we can't come down, but shall be delighted to see him up here.; Things," he said, as the messenger departed, "are beginning to move.; Better leave the door open, I think; it will save trouble.; Ah, come in, Comrade Spiller, what can we do for you?"

Spiller advanced into the study; the others waited outside, crowding in the doorway.

"Look here," said Spiller, "are you going to clear out of here or not?"

"After Mr. Outwood's kindly thought in giving us the room?; You suggest a black and ungrateful action, Comrade Spiller."

"You'll get it hot, if you don't."

"We'll risk it," said Mike.

Jellicoe giggled in the background; the drama in the atmosphere appealed to him.; His was a simple and appreciative mind.

"Come on, you chaps," cried Spiller suddenly.

There was an inward rush on the enemy's part, but Mike had been watching.; He grabbed Spiller by the shoulders and ran him back against the advancing crowd.; For a moment the doorway was blocked, then the weight and impetus of Mike and Spiller prevailed, the enemy gave back, and Mike, stepping into the room again, slammed the door and locked it.

"A neat piece of work," said Psmith approvingly, adjusting his tie at the looking-glass.; "The preliminaries may now be considered over, the first shot has been fired.; The dogs of war are now loose."

A heavy body crashed against the door.

"They'll have it down," said Jellicoe.

"We must act, Comrade Jackson!; Might I trouble you just to turn that key quietly, and the handle, and then to stand by for the next attack."

There was a scrambling of feet in the passage outside, and then a repetition of the onslaught on the door.; This time, however, the door, instead of resisting, swung open, and the human battering-ram staggered through into the study.; Mike, turning after re-locking the door, was just in time to see Psmith, with a display of energy of which one would not have believed him capable, grip the invader scientifically by an arm and a leg.

Mike jumped to help, but it was needless; the captive was already on the window-sill.; As Mike arrived, Psmith dropped him on to the flower-bed below.

Psmith closed the window gently and turned to Jellicoe.; "Who was our guest?" he asked, dusting the knees of his trousers where they had pressed against the wall.

"Robinson.; I say, you *are* a chap!"

"Robinson, was it?; Well, we are always glad to see Comrade Robinson, always.; I wonder if anybody else is thinking of calling?"

Apparently frontal attack had been abandoned.; Whisperings could be heard in the corridor.

Somebody hammered on the door.

"Yes?" called Psmith patiently.

"You'd better come out, you know; you'll only get it hotter if you don't."

"Leave us, Spiller; we would be alone."

A bell rang in the distance.

"Tea," said Jellicoe; "we shall have to go now."

"They won't do anything till after tea, I shouldn't think," said Mike.; "There's no harm in going out."

The passage was empty when they opened the door; the call to food was evidently a thing not to be treated lightly by the enemy.

In the dining-room the beleaguered garrison were the object of general attention.; Everybody turned to look at them as they came in.; It was plain that the study episode had been a topic of conversation.; Spiller's face was crimson, and Robinson's coat-sleeve still bore traces of garden mould.

Mike felt rather conscious of the eyes, but Psmith was in his element.; His demeanour throughout the meal was that of some whimsical monarch condescending for a freak to revel with his humble subjects.

Towards the end of the meal Psmith scribbled a note and passed it to Mike.; It read:; "Directly this is over, nip upstairs as quickly as you can."

Mike followed the advice; they were first out of the room.; When they had been in the study a few moments, Jellicoe knocked at the door.; "Lucky you two cut away so quick," he said.; "They were going to try and get you into the senior day-room and scrag you there."

"This," said Psmith, leaning against the mantelpiece, "is exciting, but it can't go on.; We have got for our sins to be in this place for a whole term, and if we are going to do the Hunted Fawn business all the time, life in the true sense of the word will become an impossibility.; My nerves are so delicately attuned that the strain would simply reduce them to hash.; We are not prepared to carry on a long campaign—the thing must be settled at once."

"Shall we go down to the senior day-room, and have it out?" said Mike.

"No, we will play the fixture on our own ground.; I think we may take it as tolerably certain that Comrade Spiller and his hired ruffians will try to corner us in the dormitory to-night.; Well, of course, we could fake up some sort of barricade for the door, but then we should have all the trouble over again to-morrow and the day after that.; Personally I don't propose to be chivvied about indefinitely like this, so I propose that we let them come into the dormitory, and see what happens.; Is this meeting with me?"

"I think that's sound," said Mike.; "We needn't drag Jellicoe into it."

"As a matter of fact—if you don't mind—" began that man of peace.

"Quite right," said Psmith; "this is not Comrade Jellicoe's scene at all; he has got to spend the term in the senior day-room, whereas we have our little wooden *châlet* to retire to in times of stress.; Comrade Jellicoe must stand out of the game altogether.; We shall be glad of his moral support, but otherwise, *ne pas*.; And now, as there won't be anything doing till bedtime, I think I'll collar this table and write home and tell my people that all is well with their Rupert."

CHAPTER XXXV

UNPLEASANTNESS IN THE SMALL HOURS

Jellicoe, that human encyclopaedia, consulted on the probable movements of the enemy, deposed that Spiller, retiring at ten, would make for Dormitory One in the same passage, where Robinson also had a bed.; The rest of the opposing forces were distributed among other and more distant rooms.; It was probable, therefore, that Dormitory One would be the rendezvous.; As to the time when an attack might be expected, it was unlikely that it would occur before half-past eleven.; Mr. Outwood went the round of the dormitories at eleven.

"And touching," said Psmith, "the matter of noise, must this business be conducted in a subdued and *sotto voce* manner, or may we let ourselves go a bit here and there?"

"I shouldn't think old Outwood's likely to hear you —he sleeps miles away on the other side of the house.; He never hears anything.; We often rag half the night and nothing happens."

"This appears to be a thoroughly nice, well-conducted establishment.; What would my mother say if she could see her Rupert in the midst of these reckless youths!"

"All the better," said Mike; "we don't want anybody butting in and stopping the show before it's half started."

"Comrade Jackson's Berserk blood is up —I can hear it sizzling.; I quite agree these things are all very disturbing and painful, but it's as well to do them thoroughly when one's once in for them.; Is there nobody else who might interfere with our gambols?"

"Barnes might," said Jellicoe, "only he won't."

"Who is Barnes?"

"Head of the house —a rotter.; He's in a funk of Stone and Robinson; they rag him; he'll simply sit tight."

"Then I think," said Psmith placidly, "we may look forward to a very pleasant evening.; Shall we be moving?"

Mr. Outwood paid his visit at eleven, as predicted by Jellicoe, beaming vaguely into the darkness over a candle, and disappeared again, closing the door.

"How about that door?" said Mike.; "Shall we leave it open for them?"

"Not so, but far otherwise.; If it's shut we shall hear them at it when they come.; Subject to your approval, Comrade Jackson, I have evolved the following plan of action.; I always ask myself on these occasions, 'What would Napoleon have done?' I think Napoleon would have sat in a chair by his washhand-stand, which is close to the door; he would have posted you by your washhand-stand, and he would have instructed Comrade Jellicoe, directly he heard the door-handle turned, to give his celebrated imitation of a dormitory breathing heavily in its sleep.; He would then——"

"I tell you what," said Mike, "how about tying a string at the top of the steps?"

"Yes, Napoleon would have done that, too.; Hats off to Comrade Jackson, the man with the big brain!"

The floor of the dormitory was below the level of the door.; There were three steps leading down to it.; Psmith lit a candle and they examined the ground.; The leg of a wardrobe and the leg of Jellicoe's bed made it possible for the string to be fastened in a satisfactory manner across the lower step.; Psmith surveyed the result with approval.

"Dashed neat!" he said.; "Practically the sunken road which dished the Cuirassiers at Waterloo.; I seem to see Comrade Spiller coming one of the finest purlers in the world's history."

"If they've got a candle——"

"They won't have.; If they have, stand by with your water-jug and douse it at once; then they'll charge forward and all will be well.; If they have no candle, fling the water at a venture —fire into the brown!; Lest we forget, I'll collar Comrade Jellicoe's jug now and keep it handy.; A couple of sheets would also not be amiss —we will enmesh the enemy!"

"Right ho!" said Mike.

"These humane preparations being concluded," said Psmith, "we will retire to our posts and wait.; Comrade Jellicoe, don't forget to breathe like an asthmatic sheep when you hear the door opened; they may wait at the top of the steps, listening."

"You *are* a chap!" said Jellicoe.

Waiting in the dark for something to happen is always a trying experience, especially if, as on this occasion, silence is essential.; Mike found his thoughts wandering back to the vigil he had kept with Mr. Wain at Wrykyn on the night when Wyatt had come in through the window and found authority sitting on his bed, waiting for him.; Mike was tired after his journey, and he had begun to doze when he was jerked back to wakefulness by the stealthy turning of the door-handle; the faintest rustle from Psmith's direction followed, and a slight giggle, succeeded by a series of deep breaths, showed that Jellicoe, too, had heard the noise.

There was a creaking sound.

It was pitch-dark in the dormitory, but Mike could follow the invaders' movements as clearly as if it had been broad daylight.; They had opened the door and were listening.; Jellicoe's breathing grew more asthmatic; he was flinging himself into his part with the whole-heartedness of the true artist.

The creak was followed by a sound of whispering, then another creak.; The enemy had advanced to the top step....; Another creak....; The vanguard had reached the second step....; In another moment — —

CRASH!

And at that point the proceedings may be said to have formally opened.

A struggling mass bumped against Mike's shins as he rose from his chair; he emptied his jug on to this mass, and a yell of anguish showed that the contents had got to the right address.

Then a hand grabbed his ankle and he went down, a million sparks dancing before his eyes as a fist, flying out at a venture, caught him on the nose.

Mike had not been well-disposed towards the invaders before, but now he ran amok, hitting out right and left at random.; His right missed, but his left went home hard on some portion of somebody's anatomy.; A kick freed his ankle and he staggered to his feet.; At the same moment a sudden increase in the general volume of noise spoke eloquently of good work that was being put in by Psmith.

Even at that crisis, Mike could not help feeling that if a row of this calibre did not draw Mr. Outwood from his bed, he must be an unusual kind of house-master.

He plunged forward again with outstretched arms, and stumbled and fell over one of the on-the-floor section of the opposing force.; They seized each other earnestly and rolled across the room till Mike, contriving to secure his adversary's head, bumped it on the floor with such abandon that, with a muffled yell, the other let go, and for the second time he rose.; As he did so he was conscious of a curious thudding sound that made itself heard through the other assorted noises of the battle.

All this time the fight had gone on in the blackest darkness, but now a light shone on the proceedings.; Interested occupants of other dormitories, roused from their slumbers, had come to observe the sport.; They were crowding in the doorway with a candle.

By the light of this Mike got a swift view of the theatre of war.; The enemy appeared to number five.; The warrior whose head Mike had bumped on the floor was Robinson, who was sitting up feeling his skull in a gingerly fashion.; To Mike's right, almost touching him, was Stone.; In the direction of the door, Psmith, wielding in his right hand the cord of a dressing-gown, was engaging the remaining three with a patient smile.; They were clad in pyjamas, and appeared to be feeling the dressing-gown cord acutely.

The sudden light dazed both sides momentarily.; The defence was the first to recover, Mike, with a swing, upsetting Stone, and Psmith, having seized and emptied Jellicoe's jug over Spiller, getting to work again with the cord in a manner that roused the utmost enthusiasm of the spectators.

PSMITH SEIZED AND EMPTIED JELLICOE'S JUG OVER SPILLER

Agility seemed to be the leading feature of Psmith's tactics.; He was everywhere —on Mike's bed, on his own, on Jellicoe's (drawing a passionate complaint from that non-combatant, on whose face he inadvertently trod), on the floor —he ranged the room, sowing destruction.

The enemy were disheartened; they had started with the idea that this was to be a surprise attack, and it was disconcerting to find the garrison armed at all points.; Gradually they edged to the door, and a final rush sent them through.

"Hold the door for a second," cried Psmith, and vanished.; Mike was alone in the doorway.

139

It was a situation which exactly suited his frame of mind; he stood alone in direct opposition to the community into which Fate had pitchforked him so abruptly.; He liked the feeling; for the first time since his father had given him his views upon school reports that morning in the Easter holidays, he felt satisfied with life.; He hoped, outnumbered as he was, that the enemy would come on again and not give the thing up in disgust; he wanted more.

On an occasion like this there is rarely anything approaching concerted action on the part of the aggressors.; When the attack came, it was not a combined attack; Stone, who was nearest to the door, made a sudden dash forward, and Mike hit him under the chin.

Stone drew back, and there was another interval for rest and reflection.

It was interrupted by the reappearance of Psmith, who strolled back along the passage swinging his dressing-gown cord as if it were some clouded cane.

"Sorry to keep you waiting, Comrade Jackson," he said politely.; "Duty called me elsewhere.; With the kindly aid of a guide who knows the lie of the land, I have been making a short tour of the dormitories.; I have poured divers jugfuls of water over Comrade Spiller's bed, Comrade Robinson's bed, Comrade Stone's —Spiller, Spiller, these are harsh words; where you pick them up I can't think —not from me.; Well, well, I suppose there must be an end to the pleasantest of functions.; Good-night, good-night."

The door closed behind Mike and himself.; For ten minutes shufflings and whisperings went on in the corridor, but nobody touched the handle.

Then there was a sound of retreating footsteps, and silence reigned.

On the following morning there was a notice on the house-board.; It ran:;

INDOOR GAMES

Dormitory-raiders are informed that in future neither Mr. Psmith nor Mr. Jackson will be at home to visitors. This nuisance must now cease.

                        R. PSMITH.
                        M. JACKSON.

CHAPTER XXXVI

ADAIR

On the same morning Mike met Adair for the first time.

He was going across to school with Psmith and Jellicoe, when a group of three came out of the gate of the house next door.

"That's Adair," said Jellicoe, "in the middle."

His voice had assumed a tone almost of awe.

"Who's Adair?" asked Mike.

"Captain of cricket, and lots of other things."

Mike could only see the celebrity's back.; He had broad shoulders and wiry, light hair, almost white.; He walked well, as if he were used to running.; Altogether a fit-looking sort of man.; Even Mike's jaundiced eye saw that.

As a matter of fact, Adair deserved more than a casual glance.; He was that rare type, the natural leader.; Many boys and men, if accident, or the passage of time, places them in a position where they are expected to lead, can handle the job without disaster; but that is a very different thing from being a born leader.; Adair was of the sort that comes to the top by sheer force of character and determination.; He was not naturally clever at work, but he had gone at it with a dogged resolution which had carried him up the school, and landed him high in the Sixth.; As a cricketer he was almost entirely self-taught.; Nature had given him a good eye, and left the thing at that.; Adair's doggedness had triumphed over her failure to do her work thoroughly.; At the cost of more trouble than most people give to their life-work he had made himself into a bowler.; He read the authorities, and watched first-class players, and thought the thing out on his own account, and he divided the art of bowling into three sections.; First, and most important —pitch.; Second on the list —break.; Third —pace.; He set himself to acquire pitch.; He acquired it.; Bowling at his own pace and without any attempt at break, he could now drop the ball on an envelope seven times out of ten.

Break was a more uncertain quantity.; Sometimes he could get it at the expense of pitch, sometimes at the expense of pace.; Some days he could get all three, and then he was an uncommonly bad man to face on anything but a plumb wicket.

Running he had acquired in a similar manner.; He had nothing approaching style, but he had twice won the mile and half-mile at the Sports off elegant runners, who knew all about stride and the correct timing of the sprints and all the rest of it.

Briefly, he was a worker.; He had heart.

A boy of Adair's type is always a force in a school.; In a big public school of six or seven hundred, his influence is felt less; but in a small school like Sedleigh he is like a tidal wave, sweeping all before him.; There were two hundred boys at Sedleigh, and there was not one of them in all probability who had not, directly or indirectly, been influenced by Adair.; As a small boy his sphere was not large, but the effects of his work began to be apparent even then.; It is human nature to want to get something which somebody else obviously values very much; and when it was observed by members of his form that Adair was going to great trouble and inconvenience to secure a place in the form eleven or fifteen, they naturally began to think, too, that it was worth being in those teams.; The consequence was that his form always played hard.; This made other forms play hard.; And the net result was that, when Adair succeeded to the captaincy of football and cricket in the same year, Sedleigh, as Mr. Downing, Adair's housemaster and the nearest approach to a cricket-master that Sedleigh possessed, had a fondness for saying, was a keen school.; As a whole, it both worked and played with energy.

All it wanted now was opportunity.

This Adair was determined to give it.; He had that passionate fondness for his school which every boy is popularly supposed to have, but which really is implanted in about one in every thousand.; The average public-school boy *likes* his school.; He hopes it will lick Bedford at footer and Malvern at cricket, but he rather bets it won't.; He is sorry to leave, and he likes going back at the end of the holidays, but as for any passionate, deep-seated love of the place, he would think it rather bad form than otherwise.; If anybody came up to him, slapped him on the back, and cried, "Come along, Jenkins, my boy!; Play up for the old school, Jenkins!; The dear old school!; The old place you love so!" he would feel seriously ill.

Adair was the exception.

To Adair, Sedleigh was almost a religion.; Both his parents were dead; his guardian, with whom he spent the holidays, was a man with neuralgia at one end of him and gout at the other; and the only really pleasant times Adair had had, as far back as he could remember, he owed to Sedleigh.; The place had grown on him, absorbed him.; Where Mike, violently transplanted from Wrykyn, saw only a wretched little hole not to be mentioned in the same breath with Wrykyn, Adair, dreaming of the future, saw a colossal establishment, a public school among public schools, a lump of human radium, shooting out Blues and Balliol Scholars year after year without ceasing.

It would not be so till long after he was gone and forgotten, but he did not mind that.; His devotion to Sedleigh was purely unselfish.; He did not want fame.; All he worked for was that the school should grow and grow, keener and better at games and more prosperous year by year, till it should take its rank among *the* schools, and to be an Old Sedleighan should be a badge passing its owner everywhere.

"He's captain of cricket and footer," said Jellicoe impressively.; "He's in the shooting eight.; He's won the mile and half two years running.; He would have boxed at Aldershot last term, only he sprained his wrist.; And he plays fives jolly well!"

"Sort of little tin god," said Mike, taking a violent dislike to Adair from that moment.

Mike's actual acquaintance with this all-round man dated from the dinner-hour that day.; Mike was walking to the house with Psmith.; Psmith was a little ruffled on account of a slight passage-of-arms he had had with his form-master during morning school.

"'There's a P before the Smith,' I said to him.; 'Ah, P. Smith, I see,' replied the goat.; 'Not Peasmith,' I replied, exercising wonderful self-restraint, 'just Psmith.'; It took me ten minutes to drive the thing into the man's head; and when I *had* driven it in, he sent me out of the room for looking at him through my eye-glass.; Comrade Jackson, I fear me we have fallen among bad men.; I suspect that we are going to be much persecuted by scoundrels."

"Both you chaps play cricket, I suppose?"

They turned.; It was Adair.; Seeing him face to face, Mike was aware of a pair of very bright blue eyes and a square jaw.; In any other place and mood he would have liked Adair at sight.; His prejudice, however, against all things Sedleighan was too much for him.; "I don't," he said shortly.

"Haven't you *ever* played?"

"My little sister and I sometimes play with a soft ball at home."

Adair looked sharply at him.; A temper was evidently one of his numerous qualities.

"Oh," he said.; "Well, perhaps you wouldn't mind turning out this afternoon and seeing what you can do with a hard ball —if you can manage without your little sister."

"I should think the form at this place would be about on a level with hers.; But I don't happen to be playing cricket, as I think I told you."

Adair's jaw grew squarer than ever.; Mike was wearing a gloomy scowl.

Psmith joined suavely in the dialogue.

"My dear old comrades," he said, "don't let us brawl over this matter.; This is a time for the honeyed word, the kindly eye, and the pleasant smile.; Let me explain to Comrade Adair.; Speaking for Comrade Jackson and myself, we should both be delighted to join in the mimic warfare of our National Game, as you suggest, only the fact is, we happen to be the Young Archaeologists.; We gave in our names last night.; When you are being carried back to the pavilion after your century against Loamshire —do you play Loamshire? —we shall be grubbing in the hard ground for ruined abbeys.; The old choice between Pleasure and Duty, Comrade Adair.; A Boy's Cross-Roads."

"Then you won't play?"

"No," said Mike.

"Archaeology," said Psmith, with a deprecatory wave of the hand, "will brook no divided allegiance from her devotees."

Adair turned, and walked on.

Scarcely had he gone, when another voice hailed them with precisely the same question.

"Both you fellows are going to play cricket, eh?"

It was a master.; A short, wiry little man with a sharp nose and a general resemblance, both in manner and appearance, to an excitable bullfinch.

"I saw Adair speaking to you.; I suppose you will both play.; I like every new boy to begin at once.; The more new blood we have, the better.; We want keenness here.; We are, above all, a keen school.; I want every boy to be keen."

"We are, sir," said Psmith, with fervour.

"Excellent."

"On archaeology."

Mr. Downing—for it was no less a celebrity—started, as one who perceives a loathly caterpillar in his salad.

"Archaeology!"

"We gave in our names to Mr. Outwood last night, sir.; Archaeology is a passion with us, sir.; When we heard that there was a society here, we went singing about the house."

"I call it an unnatural pursuit for boys," said Mr. Downing vehemently.; "I don't like it.; I tell you I don't like it.; It is not for me to interfere with one of my colleagues on the staff, but I tell you frankly that in my opinion it is an abominable waste of time for a boy.; It gets him into idle, loafing habits."

"I never loaf, sir," said Psmith.

"I was not alluding to you in particular.; I was referring to the principle of the thing.; A boy ought to be playing cricket with other boys, not wandering at large about the country, probably smoking and going into low public-houses."

"A very wild lot, sir, I fear, the Archaeological Society here," sighed Psmith, shaking his head.

"If you choose to waste your time, I suppose I can't hinder you.; But in my opinion it is foolery, nothing else."

He stumped off.

"Now *he's* cross," said Psmith, looking after him.; "I'm afraid we're getting ourselves disliked here."

"Good job, too."

"At any rate, Comrade Outwood loves us.; Let's go on and see what sort of a lunch that large-hearted fossil-fancier is going to give us."

CHAPTER XXXVII

MIKE FINDS OCCUPATION

There was more than one moment during the first fortnight of term when Mike found himself regretting the attitude he had imposed upon himself with regard to Sedleighan cricket.; He began to realise the eternal truth of the proverb about half a loaf and no bread.; In the first flush of his resentment against his new surroundings he had refused to play cricket.; And now he positively ached for a game.; Any sort of a game.; An innings for a Kindergarten *v.* the Second Eleven of a Home of Rest for Centenarians would have soothed him.; There were times, when the sun shone, and he caught sight of white flannels on a green ground, and heard the "plonk" of bat striking ball, when he felt like rushing to Adair and shouting, "I *will* be good.; I was in the Wrykyn team three years, and had an average of over fifty the last two seasons.; Lead me to the nearest net, and let me feel a bat in my hands again."

But every time he shrank from such a climb down.; It couldn't be done.

What made it worse was that he saw, after watching behind the nets once or twice, that Sedleigh cricket was not the childish burlesque of the game which he had been rash enough to assume that it must be.; Numbers do not make good cricket.; They only make the presence of good cricketers more likely, by the law of averages.

Mike soon saw that cricket was by no means an unknown art at Sedleigh.; Adair, to begin with, was a very good bowler indeed.; He was not a Burgess, but Burgess was the only Wrykyn bowler whom, in his three years' experience of the school, Mike would have placed above him.; He was a long way better than Neville-Smith, and Wyatt, and Milton, and the others who had taken wickets for Wrykyn.

The batting was not so good, but there were some quite capable men.; Barnes, the head of Outwood's, he who preferred not to interfere with Stone and Robinson, was a mild, rather timid-looking youth —not unlike what Mr. Outwood must have been as a boy —but he knew how to keep balls out of his wicket.; He was a good bat of the old plodding type.

Stone and Robinson themselves, that swash-buckling pair, who now treated Mike and Psmith with cold but consistent politeness, were both fair batsmen, and Stone was a good slow bowler.

There were other exponents of the game, mostly in Downing's house.

Altogether, quite worthy colleagues even for a man who had been a star at Wrykyn.

* * * * *

One solitary overture Mike made during that first fortnight.; He did not repeat the experiment.; It was on a Thursday afternoon, after school.; The day was warm, but freshened by an almost imperceptible breeze.; The air was full of the scent of the cut grass which lay in little heaps behind the nets.; This is the real cricket scent, which calls to one like the very voice of the game.

Mike, as he sat there watching, could stand it no longer.

He went up to Adair.

"May I have an innings at this net?" he asked.; He was embarrassed and nervous, and was trying not to show it.; The natural result was that his manner was offensively abrupt.

Adair was taking off his pads after his innings.; He looked up.; "This net," it may be observed, was the first eleven net.

"What?" he said.

Mike repeated his request.; More abruptly this time, from increased embarrassment.

"This is the first eleven net," said Adair coldly.; "Go in after Lodge over there."

"Over there" was the end net, where frenzied novices were bowling on a corrugated pitch to a red-haired youth with enormous feet, who looked as if he were taking his first lesson at the game.

Mike walked away without a word.

* * * * *

The Archaeological Society expeditions, even though they carried with them the privilege of listening to Psmith's views on life, proved but a poor substitute for cricket.; Psmith, who had no counter-attraction shouting to him that he ought to be elsewhere, seemed to enjoy them hugely, but Mike almost cried sometimes from boredom.; It was not always possible to slip away from the throng, for Mr. Outwood evidently looked upon them as among the very faithful, and kept them by his aide.

Mike on these occasions was silent and jumpy, his brow "sicklied o'er with the pale cast of care."; But Psmith followed his leader with the pleased and indulgent air of a father whose infant son is showing him round the garden.; Psmith's attitude towards archaeological research struck a new note in the history of that neglected science.; He was amiable, but patronising.; He patronised fossils, and he patronised ruins.; If he had been confronted with the Great Pyramid, he would have patronised that.

He seemed to be consumed by a thirst for knowledge.

That this was not altogether a genuine thirst was proved on the third expedition.; Mr. Outwood and his band were pecking away at the site of an old Roman camp.; Psmith approached Mike.

"Having inspired confidence," he said, "by the docility of our demeanour, let us slip away, and brood apart for awhile.; Roman camps, to be absolutely accurate, give me the pip.; And I never want to see another putrid fossil in my life.; Let us find some shady nook where a man may lie on his back for a bit."

Mike, over whom the proceedings connected with the Roman camp had long since begun to shed a blue depression, offered no opposition, and they strolled away down the hill.

Looking back, they saw that the archaeologists were still hard at it.; Their departure had passed unnoticed.

"A fatiguing pursuit, this grubbing for mementoes of the past," said Psmith.; "And, above all, dashed bad for the knees of the trousers.; Mine are like some furrowed field.; It's a great grief to a man of refinement, I can tell you, Comrade Jackson.; Ah, this looks a likely spot."

They had passed through a gate into the field beyond.; At the further end there was a brook, shaded by trees and running with a pleasant sound over pebbles.

"Thus far," said Psmith, hitching up the knees of his trousers, and sitting down, "and no farther.; We will rest here awhile, and listen to the music of the brook.; In fact, unless you have anything important to say, I rather think I'll go to sleep.; In this busy life of ours these naps by the wayside are invaluable.; Call me in about an hour."; And Psmith, heaving the comfortable sigh of the worker who by toil has earned rest, lay down, with his head against a mossy tree-stump, and closed his eyes.

Mike sat on for a few minutes, listening to the water and making centuries in his mind, and then, finding this a little dull, he got up, jumped the brook, and began to explore the wood on the other side.

He had not gone many yards when a dog emerged suddenly from the undergrowth, and began to bark vigorously at him.

Mike liked dogs, and, on acquaintance, they always liked him.; But when you meet a dog in some one else's wood, it is as well not to stop in order that you may get to understand each other.; Mike began to thread his way back through the trees.

He was too late.

"Stop!; What the dickens are you doing here?" shouted a voice behind him.

In the same situation a few years before, Mike would have carried on, and trusted to speed to save him.; But now there seemed a lack of dignity in the action.; He came back to where the man was standing.

145

"I'm sorry if I'm trespassing," he said.; "I was just having a look round."

"The dickens you —Why, you're Jackson!"

Mike looked at him.; He was a short, broad young man with a fair moustache.; Mike knew that he had seen him before somewhere, but he could not place him.

"I played against you, for the Free Foresters last summer.; In passing, you seem to be a bit of a free forester yourself, dancing in among my nesting pheasants."

"I'm frightfully sorry."

"That's all right.; Where do you spring from?"

"Of course —I remember you now.; You're Prendergast.; You made fifty-eight not out."

"Thanks.; I was afraid the only thing you would remember about me was that you took a century mostly off my bowling."

"You ought to have had me second ball, only cover dropped it."

"Don't rake up forgotten tragedies.; How is it you're not at Wrykyn?; What are you doing down here?"

"I've left Wrykyn."

Prendergast suddenly changed the conversation.; When a fellow tells you that he has left school unexpectedly, it is not always tactful to inquire the reason.; He began to talk about himself.

"I hang out down here.; I do a little farming and a good deal of pottering about."

"Get any cricket?" asked Mike, turning to the subject next his heart.

"Only village.; Very keen, but no great shakes.; By the way, how are you off for cricket now?; Have you ever got a spare afternoon?"

Mike's heart leaped.

"Any Wednesday or Saturday.; Look here, I'll tell you how it is."

And he told how matters stood with him.

"So, you see," he concluded, "I'm supposed to be hunting for ruins and things" —Mike's ideas on the subject of archaeology were vague —"but I could always slip away.; We all start out together, but I could nip back, get on to my bike —I've got it down here —and meet you anywhere you liked.; By Jove, I'm simply dying for a game.; I can hardly keep my hands off a bat."

"I'll give you all you want.; What you'd better do is to ride straight to Lower Borlock —that's the name of the place —and I'll meet you on the ground.; Any one will tell you where Lower Borlock is.; It's just off the London road.; There's a sign-post where you turn off.; Can you come next Saturday?"

"Rather.; I suppose you can fix me up with a bat and pads?; I don't want to bring mine."

"I'll lend you everything.; I say, you know, we can't give you a Wrykyn wicket.; The Lower Borlock pitch isn't a shirt-front."

"I'll play on a rockery, if you want me to," said Mike.

* * * * *

"You're going to what?" asked Psmith, sleepily, on being awakened and told the news.

"I'm going to play cricket, for a village near here.; I say, don't tell a soul, will you?; I don't want it to get about, or I may get lugged in to play for the school."

"My lips are sealed.; I think I'll come and watch you.; Cricket I dislike, but watching cricket is one of the finest of Britain's manly sports.; I'll borrow Jellicoe's bicycle."

* * * * *

That Saturday, Lower Borlock smote the men of Chidford hip and thigh.; Their victory was due to a hurricane innings of seventy-five by a new-comer to the team, M. Jackson.

CHAPTER XXXVIII

THE FIRE BRIGADE MEETING

Cricket is the great safety-valve.; If you like the game, and are in a position to play it at least twice a week, life can never be entirely grey.; As time went on, and his average for Lower Borlock reached the fifties and stayed there, Mike began, though he would not have admitted it, to enjoy himself.; It was not Wrykyn, but it was a very decent substitute.

The only really considerable element making for discomfort now was Mr. Downing.; By bad luck it was in his form that Mike had been placed on arrival; and Mr. Downing, never an easy form-master to get on with, proved more than usually difficult in his dealings with Mike.

They had taken a dislike to each other at their first meeting; and it grew with further acquaintance.; To Mike, Mr. Downing was all that a master ought not to be, fussy, pompous, and openly influenced in his official dealings with his form by his own private likes and dislikes.; To Mr. Downing, Mike was simply an unamiable loafer, who did nothing for the school and apparently had none of the instincts which should be implanted in the healthy boy.; Mr. Downing was rather strong on the healthy boy.

The two lived in a state of simmering hostility, punctuated at intervals by crises, which usually resulted in Lower Borlock having to play some unskilled labourer in place of their star batsman, employed doing "over-time."

One of the most acute of these crises, and the most important, in that it was the direct cause of Mike's appearance in Sedleigh cricket, had to do with the third weekly meeting of the School Fire Brigade.

It may be remembered that this well-supported institution was under Mr. Downing's special care.; It was, indeed, his pet hobby and the apple of his eye.

Just as you had to join the Archaeological Society to secure the esteem of Mr. Outwood, so to become a member of the Fire Brigade was a safe passport to the regard of Mr. Downing.; To show a keenness for cricket was good, but to join the Fire Brigade was best of all.; The Brigade was carefully organised.; At its head was Mr. Downing, a sort of high priest; under him was a captain, and under the captain a vice-captain.; These two officials were those sportive allies, Stone and Robinson, of Outwood's house, who, having perceived at a very early date the gorgeous opportunities for ragging which the Brigade offered to its members, had joined young and worked their way up.

Under them were the rank and file, about thirty in all, of whom perhaps seven were earnest workers, who looked on the Brigade in the right, or Downing, spirit.; The rest were entirely frivolous.

The weekly meetings were always full of life and excitement.

At this point it is as well to introduce Sammy to the reader.

Sammy, short for Sampson, was a young bull-terrier belonging to Mr. Downing.; If it is possible for a man to have two apples of his eye, Sammy was the other.; He was a large, light-hearted dog with a white coat, an engaging expression, the tongue of an ant-eater, and a manner which was a happy blend of hurricane and circular saw.; He had long legs, a tenor voice, and was apparently made of india-rubber.

Sammy was a great favourite in the school, and a particular friend of Mike's, the Wrykynian being always a firm ally of every dog he met after two minutes' acquaintance.

In passing, Jellicoe owned a clock-work rat, much in request during French lessons.

We will now proceed to the painful details.

* * * * *

The meetings of the Fire Brigade were held after school in Mr. Downing's form-room.; The proceedings always began in the same way, by the reading of the minutes of the last meeting.; After that the entertainment varied according to whether the members happened to be fertile or not in ideas for the disturbing of the peace.

To-day they were in very fair form.

As soon as Mr. Downing had closed the minute-book, Wilson, of the School House, held up his hand.

"Well, Wilson?"

"Please, sir, couldn't we have a uniform for the Brigade?"

"A uniform?" Mr. Downing pondered

"Red, with green stripes, sir,"

Red, with a thin green stripe, was the Sedleigh colour.

"Shall I put it to the vote, sir?" asked Stone.

"One moment, Stone."

"Those in favour of the motion move to the left, those against it to the right."

A scuffling of feet, a slamming of desk-lids and an upset blackboard, and the meeting had divided.

Mr. Downing rapped irritably on his desk.

"Sit down!" he said, "sit down!; I won't have this noise and disturbance.; Stone, sit down — Wilson, get back to your place."

"Please, sir, the motion is carried by twenty-five votes to six."

"Please, sir, may I go and get measured this evening?"

"Please, sir — —"

"Si-*lence*!; The idea of a uniform is, of course, out of the question."

"Oo-oo-oo-oo, sir-r-r!"

"Be *quiet!* Entirely out of the question.; We cannot plunge into needless expense.; Stone, listen to me.; I cannot have this noise and disturbance!; Another time when a point arises it must be settled by a show of hands.; Well, Wilson?"

"Please, sir, may we have helmets?"

"Very useful as a protection against falling timbers, sir," said Robinson.

"I don't think my people would be pleased, sir, if they knew I was going out to fires without a helmet," said Stone.

The whole strength of the company:; "Please, sir, may we have helmets?"

"Those in favour —" began Stone.

Mr. Downing banged on his desk.; "Silence!; Silence!!; Silence!!!; Helmets are, of course, perfectly preposterous."

"Oo-oo-oo-oo, sir-r-r!"

"But, sir, the danger!"

"Please, sir, the falling timbers!"

The Fire Brigade had been in action once and once only in the memory of man, and that time it was a haystack which had burnt itself out just as the rescuers had succeeded in fastening the hose to the hydrant.

"Silence!"

"Then, please, sir, couldn't we have an honour cap?; It wouldn't be expensive, and it would be just as good as a helmet for all the timbers that are likely to fall on our heads."

Mr. Downing smiled a wry smile.

"Our Wilson is facetious," he remarked frostily.

"Sir, no, sir!; I wasn't facetious!; Or couldn't we have footer-tops, like the first fifteen have?; They — —"

"Wilson, leave the room!"

"Sir, *please*, sir!"

"This moment, Wilson.; And," as he reached the door, "do me one hundred lines."

A pained "OO-oo-oo, sir-r-r," was cut off by the closing door.

Mr. Downing proceeded to improve the occasion.; "I deplore this growing spirit of flippancy," he said.; "I tell you I deplore it!; It is not right!; If this Fire Brigade is to be of solid use, there must be less of this flippancy.; We must have keenness.; I want you boys above all to be keen.; I—What is that noise?"

From the other side of the door proceeded a sound like water gurgling from a bottle, mingled with cries half-suppressed, as if somebody were being prevented from uttering them by a hand laid over his mouth.; The sufferer appeared to have a high voice.

There was a tap at the door and Mike walked in.; He was not alone.; Those near enough to see, saw that he was accompanied by Jellicoe's clock-work rat, which moved rapidly over the floor in the direction of the opposite wall.

"May I fetch a book from my desk, sir?" asked Mike.

"Very well—be quick, Jackson; we are busy."

Being interrupted in one of his addresses to the Brigade irritated Mr. Downing.

The muffled cries grew more distinct.

"What—is—that—noise?" shrilled Mr. Downing.

"Noise, sir?" asked Mike, puzzled.

"I think it's something outside the window, sir," said Stone helpfully.

"A bird, I think, sir," said Robinson.

"Don't be absurd!" snapped Mr. Downing.; "It's outside the door.; Wilson!"

"Yes, sir?" said a voice "off."

"Are you making that whining noise?"

"Whining noise, sir?; No, sir, I'm not making a whining noise."

"What *sort* of noise, sir?" inquired Mike, as many Wrykynians had asked before him.; It was a question invented by Wrykyn for use in just such a case as this.

"I do not propose," said Mr. Downing acidly, "to imitate the noise; you can all hear it perfectly plainly.; It is a curious whining noise."

"They are mowing the cricket field, sir," said the invisible Wilson.; "Perhaps that's it."

"It may be one of the desks squeaking, sir," put in Stone.; "They do sometimes."

"Or somebody's boots, sir," added Robinson.

"Silence!; Wilson?"

"Yes, sir?" bellowed the unseen one.

"Don't shout at me from the corridor like that.; Come in."

"Yes, sir!"

As he spoke the muffled whining changed suddenly to a series of tenor shrieks, and the india-rubber form of Sammy bounded into the room like an excited kangaroo.

Willing hands had by this time deflected the clockwork rat from the wall to which it had been steering, and pointed it up the alley-way between the two rows of desks.; Mr. Downing, rising from his place, was just in time to see Sammy with a last leap spring on his prey and begin worrying it.

Chaos reigned.

"A rat!" shouted Robinson.

The twenty-three members of the Brigade who were not earnest instantly dealt with the situation, each in the manner that seemed proper to him.; Some leaped on to forms, others flung books, all shouted.; It was a stirring, bustling scene.

Sammy had by this time disposed of the clock-work rat, and was now standing, like Marius, among the ruins barking triumphantly.

The banging on Mr. Downing's desk resembled thunder.; It rose above all the other noises till in time they gave up the competition and died away.

Mr. Downing shot out orders, threats, and penalties with the rapidity of a Maxim gun.

"Stone, sit down!; Donovan, if you do not sit down, you will be severely punished.; Henderson, one hundred lines for gross disorder!; Windham, the same!; Go to your seat, Vincent.;

What are you doing, Broughton-Knight?; I will not have this disgraceful noise and disorder!; The meeting is at an end; go quietly from the room, all of you.; Jackson and Wilson, remain. *Quietly*, I said, Durand!; Don't shuffle your feet in that abominable way."

Crash!

"Wolferstan, I distinctly saw you upset that black-board with a movement of your hand —one hundred lines.; Go quietly from the room, everybody."

The meeting dispersed.

"Jackson and Wilson, come here.; What's the meaning of this disgraceful conduct?; Put that dog out of the room, Jackson."

Mike removed the yelling Sammy and shut the door on him.

"Well, Wilson?"

"Please, sir, I was playing with a clock-work rat ——"

"What business have you to be playing with clock-work rats?"

"Then I remembered," said Mike, "that I had left my Horace in my desk, so I came in ——"

"And by a fluke, sir," said Wilson, as one who tells of strange things, "the rat happened to be pointing in the same direction, so he came in, too."

"I met Sammy on the gravel outside and he followed me."

"I tried to collar him, but when you told me to come in, sir, I had to let him go, and he came in after the rat."

It was plain to Mr. Downing that the burden of sin was shared equally by both culprits.; Wilson had supplied the rat, Mike the dog; but Mr. Downing liked Wilson and disliked Mike.; Wilson was in the Fire Brigade, frivolous at times, it was true, but nevertheless a member.; Also he kept wicket for the school.; Mike was a member of the Archaeological Society, and had refused to play cricket.

Mr. Downing allowed these facts to influence him in passing sentence.

"One hundred lines, Wilson," he said.; "You may go."

Wilson departed with the air of a man who has had a great deal of fun, and paid very little for it.

Mr. Downing turned to Mike.; "You will stay in on Saturday afternoon, Jackson; it will interfere with your Archaeological studies, I fear, but it may teach you that we have no room at Sedleigh for boys who spend their time loafing about and making themselves a nuisance.; We are a keen school; this is no place for boys who do nothing but waste their time.; That will do, Jackson."

And Mr. Downing walked out of the room.; In affairs of this kind a master has a habit of getting the last word.

CHAPTER XXXIX

ACHILLES LEAVES HIS TENT

They say misfortunes never come singly.; As Mike sat brooding over his wrongs in his study, after the Sammy incident, Jellicoe came into the room, and, without preamble, asked for the loan of a sovereign.

When one has been in the habit of confining one's lendings and borrowings to sixpences and shillings, a request for a sovereign comes as something of a blow.

"What on earth for?" asked Mike.

"I say, do you mind if I don't tell you?; I don't want to tell anybody.; The fact is, I'm in a beastly hole."

"Oh, sorry," said Mike.; "As a matter of fact, I do happen to have a quid.; You can freeze on to it, if you like.; But it's about all I have got, so don't be shy about paying it back."

Jellicoe was profuse in his thanks, and disappeared in a cloud of gratitude.

Mike felt that Fate was treating him badly.; Being kept in on Saturday meant that he would be unable to turn out for Little Borlock against Claythorpe, the return match.; In the previous game he had scored ninety-eight, and there was a lob bowler in the Claythorpe ranks whom he was particularly anxious to meet again.; Having to yield a sovereign to Jellicoe —why on earth did the man want all that? —meant that, unless a carefully worded letter to his brother Bob at Oxford had the desired effect, he would be practically penniless for weeks.

In a gloomy frame of mind he sat down to write to Bob, who was playing regularly for the 'Varsity this season, and only the previous week had made a century against Sussex, so might be expected to be in a sufficiently softened mood to advance the needful. (Which, it may be stated at once, he did, by return of post.)

Mike was struggling with the opening sentences of this letter —he was never a very ready writer —when Stone and Robinson burst into the room.

Mike put down his pen, and got up.; He was in warlike mood, and welcomed the intrusion.; If Stone and Robinson wanted battle, they should have it.

But the motives of the expedition were obviously friendly.; Stone beamed.; Robinson was laughing.

"You're a sportsman," said Robinson.

"What did he give you?" asked Stone.

They sat down, Robinson on the table, Stone in Psmith's deck-chair.; Mike's heart warmed to them.; The little disturbance in the dormitory was a thing of the past, done with, forgotten, contemporary with Julius Caesar.; He felt that he, Stone and Robinson must learn to know and appreciate one another.

There was, as a matter of fact, nothing much wrong with Stone and Robinson.; They were just ordinary raggers of the type found at every public school, small and large.; They were absolutely free from brain.; They had a certain amount of muscle, and a vast store of animal spirits.; They looked on school life purely as a vehicle for ragging.; The Stones and Robinsons are the swashbucklers of the school world.; They go about, loud and boisterous, with a whole-hearted and cheerful indifference to other people's feelings, treading on the toes of their neighbour and shoving him off the pavement, and always with an eye wide open for any adventure.; As to the kind of adventure, they are not particular so long as it promises excitement.; Sometimes they go through their whole school career without accident.; More often they run up against a snag in the shape of some serious-minded and muscular person who objects to having his toes trodden on and being shoved off the pavement, and then they usually sober down, to the mutual advantage of themselves and the rest of the community.

One's opinion of this type of youth varies according to one's point of view.; Small boys whom they had occasion to kick, either from pure high spirits or as a punishment for some slip from the narrow path which the ideal small boy should tread, regarded Stone and Robinson as bullies of the genuine "Eric" and "St. Winifred's" brand.; Masters were rather afraid of them.; Adair had a smouldering dislike for them.; They were useful at cricket, but apt not to take Sedleigh as seriously as he could have wished.

As for Mike, he now found them pleasant company, and began to get out the tea-things.

"Those Fire Brigade meetings," said Stone, "are a rag.; You can do what you like, and you never get more than a hundred lines."

"Don't you!" said Mike.; "I got Saturday afternoon."

"What!"

"Is Wilson in too?"

"No.; He got a hundred lines."

Stone and Robinson were quite concerned.

"What a beastly swindle!"

"That's because you don't play cricket.; Old Downing lets you do what you like if you join the Fire Brigade and play cricket."

"'We are, above all, a keen school,'" quoted Stone.; "Don't you ever play?"

"I have played a bit," said Mike.

"Well, why don't you have a shot?; We aren't such flyers here.; If you know one end of a bat from the other, you could get into some sort of a team.; Were you at school anywhere before you came here?"

"I was at Wrykyn."

"Why on earth did you leave?" asked Stone.; "Were you sacked?"

"No.; My pater took me away."

"Wrykyn?" said Robinson.; "Are you any relation of the Jacksons there—J.; W. and the others?"

"Brother."

"What!"

"Well, didn't you play at all there?"

"Yes," said Mike, "I did.; I was in the team three years, and I should have been captain this year, if I'd stopped on."

There was a profound and gratifying sensation.; Stone gaped, and Robinson nearly dropped his tea-cup.

Stone broke the silence.

"But I mean to say—look here!; What I mean is, why aren't you playing?; Why don't you play now?"

"I do.; I play for a village near here.; Place called Little Borlock.; A man who played against Wrykyn for the Free Foresters captains them.; He asked me if I'd like some games for them."

"But why not for the school?"

"Why should I?; It's much better fun for the village.; You don't get ordered about by Adair, for a start."

"Adair sticks on side," said Stone.

"Enough for six," agreed Robinson.

"By Jove," said Stone, "I've got an idea.; My word, what a rag!"

"What's wrong now?" inquired Mike politely.

"Why, look here.; To-morrow's Mid-term Service day.; It's nowhere near the middle of the term, but they always have it in the fourth week.; There's chapel at half-past nine till half-past ten.; Then the rest of the day's a whole holiday.; There are always house matches.; We're playing Downing's.; Why don't you play and let's smash them?"

"By Jove, yes," said Robinson.; "Why don't you?; They're always sticking on side because they've won the house cup three years running.; I say, do you bat or bowl?"

"Bat.; Why?"

Robinson rocked on the table.

"Why, old Downing fancies himself as a bowler.; You *must* play, and knock the cover off him."

"Masters don't play in house matches, surely?"

"This isn't a real house match.; Only a friendly.; Downing always turns out on Mid-term Service day.; I say, do play."

"Think of the rag."

"But the team's full," said Mike.

"The list isn't up yet.; We'll nip across to Barnes' study, and make him alter it."

They dashed out of the room.; From down the passage Mike heard yells of "*Barnes!*" the closing of a door, and a murmur of excited conversation.; Then footsteps returning down the passage.

Barnes appeared, on his face the look of one who has seen visions.

"I say," he said, "is it true?; Or is Stone rotting?; About Wrykyn, I mean."

"Yes, I was in the team."

Barnes was an enthusiastic cricketer.; He studied his *Wisden*, and he had an immense respect for Wrykyn cricket.

"Are you the M. Jackson, then, who had an average of fifty-one point nought three last year?"

"ARE YOU THE M. JACKSON, THEN, WHO HAD AN AVERAGE OF FIFTY-ONE POINT NOUGHT THREE LAST YEAR?"

p. 225

"Yes."

Barnes's manner became like that of a curate talking to a bishop.

"I say," he said, "then —er —will you play against Downing's to-morrow?"

"Rather," said Mike.; "Thanks awfully.; Have some tea?"

CHAPTER XL

THE MATCH WITH DOWNING'S

It is the curious instinct which prompts most people to rub a thing in that makes the lot of the average convert an unhappy one.; Only the very self-controlled can refrain from improving the occasion and scoring off the convert.; Most leap at the opportunity.

It was so in Mike's case.; Mike was not a genuine convert, but to Mr. Downing he had the outward aspect of one.; When you have been impressing upon a non-cricketing boy for nearly a month that (*a*) the school is above all a keen school, (*b*) that all members of it should play cricket, and (*c*) that by not playing cricket he is ruining his chances in this world and imperilling them in the next; and when, quite unexpectedly, you come upon this boy dressed in cricket flannels, wearing cricket boots and carrying a cricket bag, it seems only natural to assume that you have converted him, that the seeds of your eloquence have fallen on fruitful soil and sprouted.

Mr. Downing assumed it.

He was walking to the field with Adair and another member of his team when he came upon Mike.

"What!" he cried.; "Our Jackson clad in suit of mail and armed for the fray!"

This was Mr. Downing's No. 2 manner—the playful.

"This is indeed Saul among the prophets.; Why this sudden enthusiasm for a game which I understood that you despised?; Are our opponents so reduced?"

Psmith, who was with Mike, took charge of the affair with a languid grace which had maddened hundreds in its time, and which never failed to ruffle Mr. Downing.

"We are, above all, sir," he said, "a keen house.; Drones are not welcomed by us.; We are essentially versatile.; Jackson, the archaeologist of yesterday, becomes the cricketer of to-day.; It is the right spirit, sir," said Psmith earnestly.; "I like to see it."

"Indeed, Smith?; You are not playing yourself, I notice.; Your enthusiasm has bounds."

"In our house, sir, competition is fierce, and the Selection Committee unfortunately passed me over."

* * * * *

There were a number of pitches dotted about over the field, for there was always a touch of the London Park about it on Mid-term Service day.; Adair, as captain of cricket, had naturally selected the best for his own match.; It was a good wicket, Mike saw.; As a matter of fact the wickets at Sedleigh were nearly always good.; Adair had infected the ground-man with some of his own keenness, with the result that that once-leisurely official now found himself sometimes, with a kind of mild surprise, working really hard.; At the beginning of the previous season Sedleigh had played a scratch team from a neighbouring town on a wicket which, except for the creases, was absolutely undistinguishable from the surrounding turf, and behind the pavilion after the match Adair had spoken certain home truths to the ground-man.; The latter's reformation had dated from that moment.

* * * * *

Barnes, timidly jubilant, came up to Mike with the news that he had won the toss, and the request that Mike would go in first with him.

In stories of the "Not Really a Duffer" type, where the nervous new boy, who has been found crying in the boot-room over the photograph of his sister, contrives to get an innings in a game, nobody suspects that he is really a prodigy till he hits the Bully's first ball out of the ground for six.

With Mike it was different. There was no pitying smile on Adair's face as he started his run preparatory to sending down the first ball. Mike, on the cricket field, could not have looked anything but a cricketer if he had turned out in a tweed suit and hobnail boots. Cricketer was written all over him—in his walk, in the way he took guard, in his stand at the wickets. Adair started to bowl with the feeling that this was somebody who had more than a little knowledge of how to deal with good bowling and punish bad.

Mike started cautiously. He was more than usually anxious to make runs to-day, and he meant to take no risks till he could afford to do so. He had seen Adair bowl at the nets, and he knew that he was good.

The first over was a maiden, six dangerous balls beautifully played. The fieldsmen changed over.

The general interest had now settled on the match between Outwood's and Downing's. The fact in Mike's case had gone round the field, and, as several of the other games had not yet begun, quite a large crowd had collected near the pavilion to watch. Mike's masterly treatment of the opening over had impressed the spectators, and there was a popular desire to see how he would deal with Mr. Downing's slows. It was generally anticipated that he would do something special with them.

Off the first ball of the master's over a leg-bye was run.

Mike took guard.

Mr. Downing was a bowler with a style of his own. He took two short steps, two long steps, gave a jump, took three more short steps, and ended with a combination of step and jump, during which the ball emerged from behind his back and started on its slow career to the wicket. The whole business had some of the dignity of the old-fashioned minuet, subtly blended with the careless vigour of a cake-walk. The ball, when delivered, was billed to break from leg, but the programme was subject to alterations.

If the spectators had expected Mike to begin any firework effects with the first ball, they were disappointed. He played the over through with a grace worthy of his brother Joe. The last ball he turned to leg for a single.

His treatment of Adair's next over was freer. He had got a sight of the ball now. Half-way through the over a beautiful square cut forced a passage through the crowd by the pavilion, and dashed up against the rails. He drove the sixth ball past cover for three.

The crowd was now reluctantly dispersing to its own games, but it stopped as Mr. Downing started his minuet-cake-walk, in the hope that it might see something more sensational.

This time the hope was fulfilled.

The ball was well up, slow, and off the wicket on the on-side. Perhaps if it had been allowed to pitch, it might have broken in and become quite dangerous. Mike went out at it, and hit it a couple of feet from the ground. The ball dropped with a thud and a spurting of dust in the road that ran along one side of the cricket field.

It was returned on the instalment system by helpers from other games, and the bowler began his manoeuvres again. A half-volley this time. Mike slammed it back, and mid-on, whose heart was obviously not in the thing, failed to stop it.

"Get to them, Jenkins," said Mr. Downing irritably, as the ball came back from the boundary. "Get to them."

"Sir, please, sir——"

"Don't talk in the field, Jenkins."

Having had a full-pitch hit for six and a half-volley for four, there was a strong probability that Mr. Downing would pitch his next ball short.

The expected happened. The third ball was a slow long-hop, and hit the road at about the same spot where the first had landed. A howl of untuneful applause rose from the watchers in the pavilion, and Mike, with the feeling that this sort of bowling was too good to be true, waited in position for number four.

There are moments when a sort of panic seizes a bowler.; This happened now with Mr. Downing.; He suddenly abandoned science and ran amok.; His run lost its stateliness and increased its vigour.; He charged up to the wicket as a wounded buffalo sometimes charges a gun.; His whole idea now was to bowl fast.

When a slow bowler starts to bowl fast, it is usually as well to be batting, if you can manage it.

By the time the over was finished, Mike's score had been increased by sixteen, and the total of his side, in addition, by three wides.

And a shrill small voice, from the neighbourhood of the pavilion, uttered with painful distinctness the words, "Take him off!"

That was how the most sensational day's cricket began that Sedleigh had known.

A description of the details of the morning's play would be monotonous.; It is enough to say that they ran on much the same lines as the third and fourth overs of the match.; Mr. Downing bowled one more over, off which Mike helped himself to sixteen runs, and then retired moodily to cover-point, where, in Adair's fifth over, he missed Barnes —the first occasion since the game began on which that mild batsman had attempted to score more than a single.; Scared by this escape, Outwood's captain shrank back into his shell, sat on the splice like a limpet, and, offering no more chances, was not out at lunch time with a score of eleven.

Mike had then made a hundred and three.

* * * * *

As Mike was taking off his pads in the pavilion, Adair came up.

"Why did you say you didn't play cricket?" he asked abruptly.

"WHY DID YOU SAY YOU DIDN'T PLAY CRICKET?" HE ASKED

When one has been bowling the whole morning, and bowling well, without the slightest success, one is inclined to be abrupt.

Mike finished unfastening an obstinate strap. Then he looked up.

"I didn't say anything of the kind. I said I wasn't going to play here. There's a difference. As a matter of fact, I was in the Wrykyn team before I came here. Three years."

Adair was silent for a moment.

"Will you play for us against the Old Sedleighans to-morrow?" he said at length.

Mike tossed his pads into his bag and got up.

"No, thanks."

There was a silence.

"Above it, I suppose?"

"Not a bit. Not up to it. I shall want a lot of coaching at that end net of yours before I'm fit to play for Sedleigh."

There was another pause.

"Then you won't play?" asked Adair.

"I'm not keeping you, am I?" said Mike, politely.

It was remarkable what a number of members of Outwood's house appeared to cherish a personal grudge against Mr. Downing. It had been that master's somewhat injudicious practice for many years to treat his own house as a sort of Chosen People. Of all masters, the most unpopular is he who by the silent tribunal of a school is convicted of favouritism. And the dislike deepens if it is a house which he favours and not merely individuals. On occasions when boys in his own house and boys from other houses were accomplices and partners in wrong-doing, Mr. Downing distributed his thunderbolts unequally, and the school noticed it. The result was that not only he himself, but also —which was rather unfair—his house, too, had acquired a good deal of unpopularity.

The general consensus of opinion in Outwood's during the luncheon interval was that, having got Downing's up a tree, they would be fools not to make the most of the situation.

Barnes's remark that he supposed, unless anything happened and wickets began to fall a bit faster, they had better think of declaring somewhere about half-past three or four, was met with a storm of opposition.

"Declare!" said Robinson. "Great Scott, what on earth are you talking about?"

"Declare!" Stone's voice was almost a wail of indignation. "I never saw such a chump."

"They'll be rather sick if we don't, won't they?" suggested Barnes.

"Sick!; I should think they would," said Stone. "That's just the gay idea. Can't you see that by a miracle we've got a chance of getting a jolly good bit of our own back against those Downing's ticks? What we've got to do is to jolly well keep them in the field all day if we can, and be jolly glad it's so beastly hot. If they lose about a dozen pounds each through sweating about in the sun after Jackson's drives, perhaps they'll stick on less side about things in general in future. Besides, I want an innings against that bilge of old Downing's, if I can get it."

"So do I," said Robinson.

"If you declare, I swear I won't field. Nor will Robinson."

"Rather not."

"Well, I won't then," said Barnes unhappily. "Only you know they're rather sick already."

"Don't you worry about that," said Stone with a wide grin. "They'll be a lot sicker before we've finished."

And so it came about that that particular Mid-term Service-day match made history. Big scores had often been put up on Mid-term Service day. Games had frequently been one-sided. But it had never happened before in the annals of the school that one side, going in first early in the morning, had neither completed its innings nor declared it closed when stumps were drawn at 6.30. In no previous Sedleigh match, after a full day's play, had the pathetic words "Did not bat" been written against the whole of one of the contending teams.

These are the things which mark epochs.

Play was resumed at 2.15. For a quarter of an hour Mike was comparatively quiet. Adair, fortified by food and rest, was bowling really well, and his first half-dozen overs had to be watched carefully.; But the wicket was too good to give him a chance, and Mike, playing himself in again, proceeded to get to business once more.; Bowlers came and went.; Adair pounded away at one end with brief intervals between the attacks.; Mr. Downing took a couple more overs, in one of which a horse, passing in the road, nearly had its useful life cut suddenly short.; Change-bowlers of various actions and paces, each weirder and more futile than the last, tried their luck.; But still the first-wicket stand continued.

The bowling of a house team is all head and no body.; The first pair probably have some idea of length and break.; The first-change pair are poor.; And the rest, the small change, are simply the sort of things one sees in dreams after a heavy supper, or when one is out without one's gun.

Time, mercifully, generally breaks up a big stand at cricket before the field has suffered too much, and that is what happened now.; At four o'clock, when the score stood at two hundred and twenty for no wicket, Barnes, greatly daring, smote lustily at a rather wide half-volley and was caught at short-slip for thirty-three.; He retired blushfully to the pavilion, amidst applause, and Stone came out.

As Mike had then made a hundred and eighty-seven, it was assumed by the field, that directly he had topped his second century, the closure would be applied and their ordeal finished.; There was almost a sigh of relief when frantic cheering from the crowd told that the feat had been accomplished.; The fieldsmen clapped in quite an indulgent sort of way, as who should say, "Capital, capital.; And now let's start *our* innings."; Some even began to edge towards the pavilion.; But the next ball was bowled, and the next over, and the next after that, and still Barnes made no sign. (The conscience-stricken captain of Outwood's was, as a matter of fact, being practically held down by Robinson and other ruffians by force.)

A grey dismay settled on the field.

The bowling had now become almost unbelievably bad.; Lobs were being tried, and Stone, nearly weeping with pure joy, was playing an innings of the How-to-brighten-cricket type.; He had an unorthodox style, but an excellent eye, and the road at this period of the game became absolutely unsafe for pedestrians and traffic.

Mike's pace had become slower, as was only natural, but his score, too, was mounting steadily.

"This is foolery," snapped Mr. Downing, as the three hundred and fifty went up on the board.; "Barnes!" he called.

There was no reply.; A committee of three was at that moment engaged in sitting on Barnes's head in the first eleven changing-room, in order to correct a more than usually feverish attack of conscience.

"Barnes!"

"Please, sir," said Stone, some species of telepathy telling him what was detaining his captain.; "I think Barnes must have left the field.; He has probably gone over to the house to fetch something."

"This is absurd.; You must declare your innings closed.; The game has become a farce."

"Declare!; Sir, we can't unless Barnes does.; He might be awfully annoyed if we did anything like that without consulting him."

"Absurd."

"He's very touchy, sir."

"It is perfect foolery."

"I think Jenkins is just going to bowl, sir."

Mr. Downing walked moodily to his place.

* * * * *

In a neat wooden frame in the senior day-room at Outwood's, just above the mantelpiece, there was on view, a week later, a slip of paper.; The writing on it was as follows:;

OUTWOOD'S *v*.; DOWNING'S

Outwood's.; First innings.

J. P. Barnes, *c.*; Hammond, *b.*; Hassall...	33
M. Jackson, not out..........................	277
W. J. Stone, not out........................	124
Extras................................	37
;	—
Total (for one wicket)......	471

Downing's did not bat.

CHAPTER XLI

THE SINGULAR BEHAVIOUR OF JELLICOE

Outwood's rollicked considerably that night.; Mike, if he had cared to take the part, could have been the Petted Hero.; But a cordial invitation from the senior day-room to be the guest of the evening at about the biggest rag of the century had been refused on the plea of fatigue.; One does not make two hundred and seventy-seven runs on a hot day without feeling the effects, even if one has scored mainly by the medium of boundaries; and Mike, as he lay back in Psmith's deck-chair, felt that all he wanted was to go to bed and stay there for a week.; His hands and arms burned as if they were red-hot, and his eyes were so tired that he could not keep them open.

Psmith, leaning against the mantelpiece, discoursed in a desultory way on the day's happenings — the score off Mr. Downing, the undeniable annoyance of that battered bowler, and the probability of his venting his annoyance on Mike next day.

"In theory," said he, "the manly what-d'you-call-it of cricket and all that sort of thing ought to make him fall on your neck to-morrow and weep over you as a foeman worthy of his steel.; But I am prepared to bet a reasonable sum that he will give no Jiu-jitsu exhibition of this kind.; In fact, from what I have seen of our bright little friend, I should say that, in a small way, he will do his best to make it distinctly hot for you, here and there."

"I don't care," murmured Mike, shifting his aching limbs in the chair.

"In an ordinary way, I suppose, a man can put up with having his bowling hit a little.; But your performance was cruelty to animals.; Twenty-eight off one over, not to mention three wides, would have made Job foam at the mouth.; You will probably get sacked.; On the other hand, it's worth it.; You have lit a candle this day which can never be blown out.; You have shown the lads of the village how Comrade Downing's bowling ought to be treated.; I don't suppose he'll ever take another wicket."

"He doesn't deserve to."

Psmith smoothed his hair at the glass and turned round again.

"The only blot on this day of mirth and good-will is," he said, "the singular conduct of our friend Jellicoe.; When all the place was ringing with song and merriment, Comrade Jellicoe crept to my side, and, slipping his little hand in mine, touched me for three quid."

This interested Mike, fagged as he was.

"What!; Three quid!"

"Three jingling, clinking sovereigns.; He wanted four."

"But the man must be living at the rate of I don't know what.; It was only yesterday that he borrowed a quid from *me*!"

"He must be saving money fast.; There appear to be the makings of a financier about Comrade Jellicoe.; Well, I hope, when he's collected enough for his needs, he'll pay me back a bit.; I'm pretty well cleaned out."

"I got some from my brother at Oxford."

"Perhaps he's saving up to get married.; We may be helping towards furnishing the home.; There was a Siamese prince fellow at my dame's at Eton who had four wives when he arrived, and gathered in a fifth during his first summer holidays.; It was done on the correspondence system.; His Prime Minister fixed it up at the other end, and sent him the glad news on a picture post-card.; I think an eye ought to be kept on Comrade Jellicoe."

* * * * *

Mike tumbled into bed that night like a log, but he could not sleep.; He ached all over.; Psmith chatted for a time on human affairs in general, and then dropped gently off.; Jellicoe, who appeared to be wrapped in gloom, contributed nothing to the conversation.

After Psmith had gone to sleep, Mike lay for some time running over in his mind, as the best substitute for sleep, the various points of his innings that day.; He felt very hot and uncomfortable.

Just as he was wondering whether it would not be a good idea to get up and have a cold bath, a voice spoke from the darkness at his side.

"Are you asleep, Jackson?"

"Who's that?"

"Me —Jellicoe.; I can't get to sleep."

"Nor can I. I'm stiff all over."

"I'll come over and sit on your bed."

There was a creaking, and then a weight descended in the neighbourhood of Mike's toes.

Jellicoe was apparently not in conversational mood.; He uttered no word for quite three minutes.; At the end of which time he gave a sound midway between a snort and a sigh.

"I say, Jackson!" he said.

"Yes?"

"Have you —oh, nothing."

Silence again.

"Jackson."

"Hullo?"

"I say, what would your people say if you got sacked?"

"All sorts of things.; Especially my pater.; Why?"

"Oh, I don't know.; So would mine."

"Everybody's would, I expect."

"Yes."

The bed creaked, as Jellicoe digested these great thoughts.; Then he spoke again.

"It would be a jolly beastly thing to get sacked."

Mike was too tired to give his mind to the subject.; He was not really listening.; Jellicoe droned on in a depressed sort of way.

"You'd get home in the middle of the afternoon, I suppose, and you'd drive up to the house, and the servant would open the door, and you'd go in.; They might all be out, and then you'd have to hang about, and wait; and presently you'd hear them come in, and you'd go out into the passage, and they'd say 'Hullo!'"

Jellicoe, in order to give verisimilitude, as it were, to an otherwise bald and unconvincing narrative, flung so much agitated surprise into the last word that it woke Mike from a troubled doze into which he had fallen.

"Hullo?" he said.; "What's up?"

"Then you'd say.; 'Hullo!' And then they'd say, 'What are you doing here?; 'And you'd say——"

"What on earth are you talking about?"

"About what would happen."

"Happen when?"

"When you got home.; After being sacked, you know."

"Who's been sacked?" Mike's mind was still under a cloud.

"Nobody.; But if you were, I meant.; And then I suppose there'd be an awful row and general sickness, and all that.; And then you'd be sent into a bank, or to Australia, or something."

Mike dozed off again.

"My pater would be frightfully sick.; My mater would be sick.; My sister would be jolly sick, too.; Have you got any sisters, Jackson?; I say, Jackson!"

"Hullo!; What's the matter?; Who's that?"

"Me —Jellicoe."

"What's up?"

"I asked you if you'd got any sisters."

"Any *what*?"

"Sisters."

"Whose sisters?"

"Yours.; I asked if you'd got any."

"Any what?"

"Sisters."

"What about them?"

The conversation was becoming too intricate for Jellicoe.; He changed the subject.

"I say, Jackson!"

"Well?"

"I say, you don't know any one who could lend me a pound, do you?"

"What!" cried Mike, sitting up in bed and staring through the darkness in the direction whence the numismatist's voice was proceeding.; "Do *what*?"

"I say, look out.; You'll wake Smith."

"Did you say you wanted some one to lend you a quid?"

"Yes," said Jellicoe eagerly.; "Do you know any one?"

Mike's head throbbed.; This thing was too much.; The human brain could not be expected to cope with it.; Here was a youth who had borrowed a pound from one friend the day before, and three pounds from another friend that very afternoon, already looking about him for further loans.; Was it a hobby, or was he saving up to buy an aeroplane?

"What on earth do you want a pound for?"

"I don't want to tell anybody.; But it's jolly serious.; I shall get sacked if I don't get it."

Mike pondered.

Those who have followed Mike's career as set forth by the present historian will have realised by this time that he was a good long way from being perfect.; As the Blue-Eyed Hero he would have been a rank failure.; Except on the cricket field, where he was a natural genius, he was just ordinary.; He resembled ninety per cent. of other members of English public schools.; He had some virtues and a good many defects.; He was as obstinate as a mule, though people whom he liked could do as they pleased with him.; He was good-natured as a general thing, but on occasion his temper could be of the worst, and had, in his childhood, been the subject of much adverse comment among his aunts.; He was rigidly truthful, where the issue concerned only himself.; Where it was a case of saving a friend, he was prepared to act in a manner reminiscent of an American expert witness.

He had, in addition, one good quality without any defect to balance it.; He was always ready to help people.; And when he set himself to do this, he was never put off by discomfort or risk.; He went at the thing with a singleness of purpose that asked no questions.

Bob's postal order, which had arrived that evening, was reposing in the breast-pocket of his coat.

It was a wrench, but, if the situation was so serious with Jellicoe, it had to be done.

* * * * *

Two minutes later the night was being made hideous by Jellicoe's almost tearful protestations of gratitude, and the postal order had moved from one side of the dormitory to the other.

CHAPTER XLII

JELLICOE GOES ON THE SICK-LIST

Mike woke next morning with a confused memory of having listened to a great deal of incoherent conversation from Jellicoe, and a painfully vivid recollection of handing over the bulk of his worldly wealth to him.; The thought depressed him, though it seemed to please Jellicoe, for the latter carolled in a gay undertone as he dressed, till Psmith, who had a sensitive ear, asked as a favour that these farm-yard imitations might cease until he was out of the room.

There were other things to make Mike low-spirited that morning.; To begin with, he was in detention, which in itself is enough to spoil a day.; It was a particularly fine day, which made the matter worse.; In addition to this, he had never felt stiffer in his life.; It seemed to him that the creaking of his joints as he walked must be audible to every one within a radius of several yards.; Finally, there was the interview with Mr. Downing to come.; That would probably be unpleasant.; As Psmith had said, Mr. Downing was the sort of master who would be likely to make trouble.; The great match had not been an ordinary match.; Mr. Downing was a curious man in many ways, but he did not make a fuss on ordinary occasions when his bowling proved expensive.; Yesterday's performance, however, stood in a class by itself.; It stood forth without disguise as a deliberate rag.; One side does not keep another in the field the whole day in a one-day match except as a grisly kind of practical joke.; And Mr. Downing and his house realised this.; The house's way of signifying its comprehension of the fact was to be cold and distant as far as the seniors were concerned, and abusive and pugnacious as regards the juniors.; Young blood had been shed overnight, and more flowed during the eleven o'clock interval that morning to avenge the insult.

Mr. Downing's methods of retaliation would have to be, of necessity, more elusive; but Mike did not doubt that in some way or other his form-master would endeavour to get a bit of his own back.

As events turned out, he was perfectly right.; When a master has got his knife into a boy, especially a master who allows himself to be influenced by his likes and dislikes, he is inclined to single him out in times of stress, and savage him as if he were the official representative of the evildoers.; Just as, at sea, the skipper, when he has trouble with the crew, works it off on the boy.

Mr. Downing was in a sarcastic mood when he met Mike.; That is to say, he began in a sarcastic strain.; But this sort of thing is difficult to keep up.; By the time he had reached his peroration, the rapier had given place to the bludgeon.; For sarcasm to be effective, the user of it must be met half-way.; His hearer must appear to be conscious of the sarcasm and moved by it.; Mike, when masters waxed sarcastic towards him, always assumed an air of stolid stupidity, which was as a suit of mail against satire.

So Mr. Downing came down from the heights with a run, and began to express himself with a simple strength which it did his form good to listen to.; Veterans who had been in the form for terms said afterwards that there had been nothing to touch it, in their experience of the orator, since the glorious day when Dunster, that prince of raggers, who had left at Christmas to go to a crammer's, had introduced three lively grass-snakes into the room during a Latin lesson.

"You are surrounded," concluded Mr. Downing, snapping his pencil in two in his emotion, "by an impenetrable mass of conceit and vanity and selfishness.; It does not occur to you to admit your capabilities as a cricketer in an open, straightforward way and place them at the disposal of the school.; No, that would not be dramatic enough for you.; It would be too commonplace altogether.; Far too commonplace!" Mr. Downing laughed bitterly.; "No, you must conceal your capabilities.; You must act a lie.; You must —who is that shuffling his feet?; I will not have it, I *will* have silence —you must hang back in order to make a more effective entrance, like some wretched actor who —I will *not* have this shuffling.; I have spoken of this before.; Macpherson, are you shuffling your feet?"

"Sir, no, sir."

"Please, sir."

"Well, Parsons?"

"I think it's the noise of the draught under the door, sir."

Instant departure of Parsons for the outer regions.; And, in the excitement of this side-issue, the speaker lost his inspiration, and abruptly concluded his remarks by putting Mike on to translate in Cicero.; Which Mike, who happened to have prepared the first half-page, did with much success.

* * * * *

The Old Boys' match was timed to begin shortly after eleven o'clock.; During the interval most of the school walked across the field to look at the pitch.; One or two of the Old Boys had already changed and were practising in front of the pavilion.

It was through one of these batsmen that an accident occurred which had a good deal of influence on Mike's affairs.

Mike had strolled out by himself.; Half-way across the field Jellicoe joined him.; Jellicoe was cheerful, and rather embarrassingly grateful.; He was just in the middle of his harangue when the accident happened.

To their left, as they crossed the field, a long youth, with the faint beginnings of a moustache and a blazer that lit up the surrounding landscape like a glowing beacon, was lashing out recklessly at a friend's bowling.; Already he had gone within an ace of slaying a small boy.; As Mike and Jellicoe proceeded on their way, there was a shout of "Heads!"

The almost universal habit of batsmen of shouting "Heads!" at whatever height from the ground the ball may be, is not a little confusing.; The average person, on hearing the shout, puts his hands over his skull, crouches down and trusts to luck.; This is an excellent plan if the ball is falling, but is not much protection against a skimming drive along the ground.

When "Heads!" was called on the present occasion, Mike and Jellicoe instantly assumed the crouching attitude.

Jellicoe was the first to abandon it.; He uttered a yell and sprang into the air.; After which he sat down and began to nurse his ankle.

The bright-blazered youth walked up.

"Awfully sorry, you know, man.; Hurt?"

Jellicoe was pressing the injured spot tenderly with his finger-tips, uttering sharp howls whenever, zeal outrunning discretion, he prodded himself too energetically.

"Silly ass, Dunster," he groaned, "slamming about like that."

"Awfully sorry.; But I did yell."

"It's swelling up rather," said Mike; "You'd better get over to the house and have it looked at.; Can you walk?"

Jellicoe tried, but sat down again with a loud "Ow!" At that moment the bell rang.

"I shall have to be going in," said Mike, "or I'd have helped you over."

"I'll give you a hand," said Dunster.

He helped the sufferer to his feet and they staggered off together, Jellicoe hopping, Dunster advancing with a sort of polka step.; Mike watched them start and then turned to go in.

CHAPTER XLIII

MIKE RECEIVES A COMMISSION

There is only one thing to be said in favour of detention on a fine summer's afternoon, and that is that it is very pleasant to come out of.; The sun never seems so bright or the turf so green as during the first five minutes after one has come out of the detention-room.; One feels as if one were entering a new and very delightful world.; There is also a touch of the Rip van Winkle feeling.; Everything seems to have gone on and left one behind.; Mike, as he walked to the cricket field, felt very much behind the times.

Arriving on the field he found the Old Boys batting.; He stopped and watched an over of Adair's.; The fifth ball bowled a man.; Mike made his way towards the pavilion.

Before he got there he heard his name called, and turning, found Psmith seated under a tree with the bright-blazered Dunster.

"Return of the exile," said Psmith.; "A joyful occasion tinged with melancholy.; Have a cherry? —take one or two.; These little acts of unremembered kindness are what one needs after a couple of hours in extra pupil-room.; Restore your tissues, Comrade Jackson, and when you have finished those, apply again."

"Is your name Jackson?" inquired Dunster, "because Jellicoe wants to see you."

"Alas, poor Jellicoe!" said Psmith.; "He is now prone on his bed in the dormitory —there a sheer hulk lies poor Tom Jellicoe, the darling of the crew, faithful below he did his duty, but Comrade Dunster has broached him to.; I have just been hearing the melancholy details."

"Old Smith and I," said Dunster, "were at a private school together.; I'd no idea I should find him here."

"It was a wonderfully stirring sight when we met," said Psmith; "not unlike the meeting of Ulysses and the hound Argos, of whom you have doubtless read in the course of your dabblings in the classics.; I was Ulysses; Dunster gave a life-like representation of the faithful dawg."

"You still jaw as much as ever, I notice," said the animal delineator, fondling the beginnings of his moustache.

"More," sighed Psmith, "more.; Is anything irritating you?" he added, eyeing the other's manoeuvres with interest.

"You needn't be a funny ass, man," said Dunster, pained; "heaps of people tell me I ought to have it waxed."

"What it really wants is top-dressing with guano.; Hullo! another man out.; Adair's bowling better to-day than he did yesterday."

"I heard about yesterday," said Dunster.; "It must have been a rag!; Couldn't we work off some other rag on somebody before I go?; I shall be stopping here till Monday in the village.; Well hit, sir —Adair's bowling is perfectly simple if you go out to it."

"Comrade Dunster went out to it first ball," said Psmith to Mike.

"Oh! chuck it, man; the sun was in my eyes.; I hear Adair's got a match on with the M.C.C. at last."

"Has he?" said Psmith; "I hadn't heard.; Archaeology claims so much of my time that I have little leisure for listening to cricket chit-chat."

"What was it Jellicoe wanted?" asked Mike; "was it anything important?"

"He seemed to think so —he kept telling me to tell you to go and see him."

"I fear Comrade Jellicoe is a bit of a weak-minded blitherer— —"

"Did you ever hear of a rag we worked off on Jellicoe once?" asked Dunster.; "The man has absolutely no sense of humour —can't see when he's being rotted.; Well it was like this— Hullo!; We're all out —I shall have to be going out to field again, I suppose, dash it!; I'll tell you when I see you again."

"I shall count the minutes," said Psmith.

Mike stretched himself; the sun was very soothing after his two hours in the detention-room; he felt disinclined for exertion.

"I don't suppose it's anything special about Jellicoe, do you?" he said.; "I mean, it'll keep till tea-time; it's no catch having to sweat across to the house now."

"Don't dream of moving," said Psmith.; "I have several rather profound observations on life to make and I can't make them without an audience.; Soliloquy is a knack.; Hamlet had got it, but probably only after years of patient practice.; Personally, I need some one to listen when I talk.; I like to feel that I am doing good.; You stay where you are —don't interrupt too much."

Mike tilted his hat over his eyes and abandoned Jellicoe.

It was not until the lock-up bell rang that he remembered him.; He went over to the house and made his way to the dormitory, where he found the injured one in a parlous state, not so much physical as mental.; The doctor had seen his ankle and reported that it would be on the active list in a couple of days.; It was Jellicoe's mind that needed attention now.

Mike found him in a condition bordering on collapse.

"I say, you might have come before!" said Jellicoe.

"What's up?; I didn't know there was such a hurry about it —what did you want?"

"It's no good now," said Jellicoe gloomily; "it's too late, I shall get sacked."

"What on earth are you talking about?; What's the row?"

"It's about that money."

"What about it?"

"I had to pay it to a man to-day, or he said he'd write to the Head —then of course I should get sacked.; I was going to take the money to him this afternoon, only I got crocked, so I couldn't move.; I wanted to get hold of you to ask you to take it for me —it's too late now!"

Mike's face fell.; "Oh, hang it!" he said, "I'm awfully sorry.; I'd no idea it was anything like that —what a fool I was!; Dunster did say he thought it was something important, only like an ass I thought it would do if I came over at lock-up."

"It doesn't matter," said Jellicoe miserably; "it can't be helped."

"Yes, it can," said Mike.; "I know what I'll do —it's all right.; I'll get out of the house after lights-out."

Jellicoe sat up.; "You can't!; You'd get sacked if you were caught."

"Who would catch me?; There was a chap at Wrykyn I knew who used to break out every night nearly and go and pot at cats with an air-pistol; it's as easy as anything."

The toad-under-the-harrow expression began to fade from Jellicoe's face.; "I say, do you think you could, really?"

"Of course I can!; It'll be rather a rag."

"I say, it's frightfully decent of you."

"What absolute rot!"

"But, look here, are you certain — —"

"I shall be all right.; Where do you want me to go?"

"It's a place about a mile or two from here, called Lower Borlock."

"Lower Borlock?"

"Yes, do you know it?"

"Rather!; I've been playing cricket for them all the term."

"I say, have you?; Do you know a man called Barley?"

"Barley?; Rather —he runs the 'White Boar'."

"He's the chap I owe the money to."

"Old Barley!"

Mike knew the landlord of the "White Boar" well; he was the wag of the village team.; Every village team, for some mysterious reason, has its comic man.; In the Lower Borlock eleven Mr. Barley filled the post.; He was a large, stout man, with a red and cheerful face, who looked exactly like the jovial inn-keeper of melodrama.; He was the last man Mike would have expected to do the "money by Monday-week or I write to the headmaster" business.

But he reflected that he had only seen him in his leisure moments, when he might naturally be expected to unbend and be full of the milk of human kindness.; Probably in business hours he was quite different.; After all, pleasure is one thing and business another.

Besides, five pounds is a large sum of money, and if Jellicoe owed it, there was nothing strange in Mr. Barley's doing everything he could to recover it.

He wondered a little what Jellicoe could have been doing to run up a bill as big as that, but it did not occur to him to ask, which was unfortunate, as it might have saved him a good deal of inconvenience.; It seemed to him that it was none of his business to inquire into Jellicoe's private affairs.; He took the envelope containing the money without question.

"I shall bike there, I think," he said, "if I can get into the shed."

The school's bicycles were stored in a shed by the pavilion.

"You can manage that," said Jellicoe; "it's locked up at night, but I had a key made to fit it last summer, because I used to go out in the early morning sometimes before it was opened."

"Got it on you?"

"Smith's got it."

"I'll get it from him."

"I say!"

"Well?"

"Don't tell Smith why you want it, will you?; I don't want anybody to know —if a thing once starts getting about it's all over the place in no time."

"All right, I won't tell him."

"I say, thanks most awfully!; I don't know what I should have done, I — —"

"Oh, chuck it!" said Mike.

CHAPTER XLIV

AND FULFILS IT

Mike started on his ride to Lower Borlock with mixed feelings.; It is pleasant to be out on a fine night in summer, but the pleasure is to a certain extent modified when one feels that to be detected will mean expulsion.

Mike did not want to be expelled, for many reasons.; Now that he had grown used to the place he was enjoying himself at Sedleigh to a certain extent.; He still harboured a feeling of resentment against the school in general and Adair in particular, but it was pleasant in Outwood's now that he had got to know some of the members of the house, and he liked playing cricket for Lower Borlock; also, he was fairly certain that his father would not let him go to Cambridge if he were expelled from Sedleigh.; Mr. Jackson was easy-going with his family, but occasionally his foot came down like a steam-hammer, as witness the Wrykyn school report affair.

So Mike pedalled along rapidly, being wishful to get the job done without delay.

Psmith had yielded up the key, but his inquiries as to why it was needed had been embarrassing.; Mike's statement that he wanted to get up early and have a ride had been received by Psmith, with whom early rising was not a hobby, with honest amazement and a flood of advice and warning on the subject.

"One of the Georges," said Psmith, "I forget which, once said that a certain number of hours' sleep a day—I cannot recall for the moment how many—made a man something, which for the time being has slipped my memory.; However, there you are.; I've given you the main idea of the thing; and a German doctor says that early rising causes insanity.; Still, if you're bent on it——" After which he had handed over the key.

Mike wished he could have taken Psmith into his confidence.; Probably he would have volunteered to come, too; Mike would have been glad of a companion.

It did not take him long to reach Lower Borlock.; The "White Boar" stood at the far end of the village, by the cricket field.; He rode past the church—standing out black and mysterious against the light sky—and the rows of silent cottages, until he came to the inn.

The place was shut, of course, and all the lights were out—it was some time past eleven.

The advantage an inn has over a private house, from the point of view of the person who wants to get into it when it has been locked up, is that a nocturnal visit is not so unexpected in the case of the former.; Preparations have been made to meet such an emergency.; Where with a private house you would probably have to wander round heaving rocks and end by climbing up a water-spout, when you want to get into an inn you simply ring the night-bell, which, communicating with the boots' room, has that hard-worked menial up and doing in no time.

After Mike had waited for a few minutes there was a rattling of chains and a shooting of bolts and the door opened.

"Yes, sir?" said the boots, appearing in his shirt-sleeves.; "Why, 'ullo!; Mr. Jackson, sir!"

Mike was well known to all dwellers in Lower Borlock, his scores being the chief topic of conversation when the day's labours were over.

"I want to see Mr. Barley, Jack."

"He's bin in bed this half-hour back, Mr. Jackson."

"I must see him.; Can you get him down?"

The boots looked doubtful.; "Roust the guv'nor outer bed?" he said.

Mike quite admitted the gravity of the task.; The landlord of the "White Boar" was one of those men who need a beauty sleep.

"I wish you would—it's a thing that can't wait.; I've got some money to give to him."

"Oh, if it's *that* —" said the boots.

Five minutes later mine host appeared in person, looking more than usually portly in a check dressing-gown and red bedroom slippers of the *Dreadnought* type.

"You can pop off, Jack."

Exit boots to his slumbers once more.

"Well, Mr. Jackson, what's it all about?"

"Jellicoe asked me to come and bring you the money."

"The money?; What money?"

"What he owes you; the five pounds, of course."

"The five —" Mr. Barley stared open-mouthed at Mike for a moment; then he broke into a roar of laughter which shook the sporting prints on the wall and drew barks from dogs in some distant part of the house.; He staggered about laughing and coughing till Mike began to expect a fit of some kind.; Then he collapsed into a chair, which creaked under him, and wiped his eyes.

"Oh dear!" he said, "oh dear! the five pounds!"

Mike was not always abreast of the rustic idea of humour, and now he felt particularly fogged.; For the life of him he could not see what there was to amuse any one so much in the fact that a person who owed five pounds was ready to pay it back.; It was an occasion for rejoicing, perhaps, but rather for a solemn, thankful, eyes-raised-to-heaven kind of rejoicing.

"What's up?" he asked.

"Five pounds!"

"You might tell us the joke."

Mr. Barley opened the letter, read it, and had another attack; when this was finished he handed the letter to Mike, who was waiting patiently by, hoping for light, and requested him to read it.

"Dear, dear!" chuckled Mr. Barley, "five pounds!; They may teach you young gentlemen to talk Latin and Greek and what not at your school, but it 'ud do a lot more good if they'd teach you how many beans make five; it 'ud do a lot more good if they'd teach you to come in when it rained, it 'ud do — —"

Mike was reading the letter.

> "DEAR MR. BARLEY," it ran. —"I send the £5, which I could not get before.; I hope it is in time, because I don't want you to write to the headmaster.; I am sorry Jane and John ate your wife's hat and the chicken and broke the vase."

There was some more to the same effect; it was signed "T.; G. Jellicoe."

"What on earth's it all about?" said Mike, finishing this curious document.

Mr. Barley slapped his leg.; "Why, Mr. Jellicoe keeps two dogs here; I keep 'em for him till the young gentlemen go home for their holidays.; Aberdeen terriers, they are, and as sharp as mustard.; Mischief!; I believe you, but, love us! they don't do no harm!; Bite up an old shoe sometimes and such sort of things.; The other day, last Wednesday it were, about 'ar parse five, Jane —she's the worst of the two, always up to it, she is —she got hold of my old hat and had it in bits before you could say knife.; John upset a china vase in one of the bedrooms chasing a mouse, and they got on the coffee-room table and ate half a cold chicken what had been left there.; So I says to myself, 'I'll have a game with Mr. Jellicoe over this,' and I sits down and writes off saying the little dogs have eaten a valuable hat and a chicken and what not, and the damage'll be five pounds, and will he kindly remit same by Saturday night at the latest or I write to his headmaster.; Love us!" Mr. Barley slapped his thigh, "he took it all in, every word —and here's the five pounds in cash in this envelope here!; I haven't had such a laugh since we got old Tom Raxley out of bed at twelve of a winter's night by telling him his house was a-fire."

It is not always easy to appreciate a joke of the practical order if one has been made even merely part victim of it.; Mike, as he reflected that he had been dragged out of his house in the middle of the night, in contravention of all school rules and discipline, simply in order to satisfy Mr. Barley's sense of humour, was more inclined to be abusive than mirthful.; Running risks is all very well when they are necessary, or if one chooses to run them for one's own amusement, but to be placed in a dangerous position, a position imperilling one's chance of going to the 'Varsity, is another matter altogether.

But it is impossible to abuse the Barley type of man.; Barley's enjoyment of the whole thing was so honest and child-like.; Probably it had given him the happiest quarter of an hour he had known for years, since, in fact, the affair of old Tom Raxley.; It would have been cruel to damp the man.

So Mike laughed perfunctorily, took back the envelope with the five pounds, accepted a stone ginger beer and a plateful of biscuits, and rode off on his return journey.

* * * * *

Mention has been made above of the difference which exists between getting into an inn after lock-up and into a private house.; Mike was to find this out for himself.

His first act on arriving at Sedleigh was to replace his bicycle in the shed.; This he accomplished with success.; It was pitch-dark in the shed, and as he wheeled his machine in, his foot touched something on the floor.; Without waiting to discover what this might be, he leaned his bicycle against the wall, went out, and locked the door, after which he ran across to Outwood's.

Fortune had favoured his undertaking by decreeing that a stout drain-pipe should pass up the wall within a few inches of his and Psmith's study.; On the first day of term, it may be remembered he had wrenched away the wooden bar which bisected the window-frame, thus rendering exit and entrance almost as simple as they had been for Wyatt during Mike's first term at Wrykyn.

He proceeded to scale this water-pipe.

He had got about half-way up when a voice from somewhere below cried, "Who's that?"

CHAPTER XLV

PURSUIT

These things are Life's Little Difficulties.; One can never tell precisely how one will act in a sudden emergency.; The right thing for Mike to have done at this crisis was to have ignored the voice, carried on up the water-pipe, and through the study window, and gone to bed.; It was extremely unlikely that anybody could have recognised him at night against the dark background of the house.; The position then would have been that somebody in Mr. Outwood's house had been seen breaking in after lights-out; but it would have been very difficult for the authorities to have narrowed the search down any further than that.; There were thirty-four boys in Outwood's, of whom about fourteen were much the same size and build as Mike.

The suddenness, however, of the call caused Mike to lose his head.; He made the strategic error of sliding rapidly down the pipe, and running.

There were two gates to Mr. Outwood's front garden.; The carriage drive ran in a semicircle, of which the house was the centre.; It was from the right-hand gate, nearest to Mr. Downing's house, that the voice had come, and, as Mike came to the ground, he saw a stout figure galloping towards him from that direction.; He bolted like a rabbit for the other gate.; As he did so, his pursuer again gave tongue.

"Oo-oo-oo yer!" was the exact remark.

Whereby Mike recognised him as the school sergeant.

"Oo-oo-oo yer!" was that militant gentleman's habitual way of beginning a conversation.

With this knowledge, Mike felt easier in his mind.; Sergeant Collard was a man of many fine qualities, (notably a talent for what he was wont to call "spott'n," a mysterious gift which he exercised on the rifle range), but he could not run.; There had been a time in his hot youth when he had sprinted like an untamed mustang in pursuit of volatile Pathans in Indian hill wars, but Time, increasing his girth, had taken from him the taste for such exercise.; When he moved now it was at a stately walk.; The fact that he ran to-night showed how the excitement of the chase had entered into his blood.

"Oo-oo-oo yer!" he shouted again, as Mike, passing through the gate, turned into the road that led to the school.; Mike's attentive ear noted that the bright speech was a shade more puffily delivered this time.; He began to feel that this was not such bad fun after all.; He would have liked to be in bed, but, if that was out of the question, this was certainly the next best thing.

He ran on, taking things easily, with the sergeant panting in his wake, till he reached the entrance to the school grounds.; He dashed in and took cover behind a tree.

Presently the sergeant turned the corner, going badly and evidently cured of a good deal of the fever of the chase.; Mike heard him toil on for a few yards and then stop.; A sound of panting was borne to him.

Then the sound of footsteps returning, this time at a walk.; They passed the gate and went on down the road.

The pursuer had given the thing up.

Mike waited for several minutes behind his tree.; His programme now was simple.; He would give Sergeant Collard about half an hour, in case the latter took it into his head to "guard home" by waiting at the gate.; Then he would trot softly back, shoot up the water-pipe once more, and so to bed.; It had just struck a quarter to something—twelve, he supposed—on the school clock.; He would wait till a quarter past.

Meanwhile, there was nothing to be gained from lurking behind a tree.; He left his cover, and started to stroll in the direction of the pavilion.; Having arrived there, he sat on the steps, looking out on to the cricket field.

His thoughts were miles away, at Wrykyn, when he was recalled to Sedleigh by the sound of somebody running.; Focussing his gaze, he saw a dim figure moving rapidly across the cricket field straight for him.

His first impression, that he had been seen and followed, disappeared as the runner, instead of making for the pavilion, turned aside, and stopped at the door of the bicycle shed.; Like Mike, he was evidently possessed of a key, for Mike heard it grate in the lock.; At this point he left the pavilion and hailed his fellow rambler by night in a cautious undertone.

The other appeared startled.

"Who the dickens is that?" he asked.; "Is that you, Jackson?"

Mike recognised Adair's voice.; The last person he would have expected to meet at midnight obviously on the point of going for a bicycle ride.

"What are you doing out here, Jackson?"

"What are you, if it comes to that?"

Adair was lighting his lamp.

"I'm going for the doctor.; One of the chaps in our house is bad."

"Oh!"

"What are you doing out here?"

"Just been for a stroll."

"Hadn't you better be getting back?"

"Plenty of time."

"I suppose you think you're doing something tremendously brave and dashing?"

"Hadn't you better be going to the doctor?"

"If you want to know what I think — —"

"I don't.; So long."

Mike turned away, whistling between his teeth.; After a moment's pause, Adair rode off.; Mike saw his light pass across the field and through the gate.; The school clock struck the quarter.

It seemed to Mike that Sergeant Collard, even if he had started to wait for him at the house, would not keep up the vigil for more than half an hour.; He would be safe now in trying for home again.

He walked in that direction.

Now it happened that Mr. Downing, aroused from his first sleep by the news, conveyed to him by Adair, that MacPhee, one of the junior members of Adair's dormitory, was groaning and exhibiting other symptoms of acute illness, was disturbed in his mind.; Most housemasters feel uneasy in the event of illness in their houses, and Mr. Downing was apt to get jumpy beyond the ordinary on such occasions.; All that was wrong with MacPhee, as a matter of fact, was a very fair stomach-ache, the direct and legitimate result of eating six buns, half a cocoa-nut, three doughnuts, two ices, an apple, and a pound of cherries, and washing the lot down with tea.; But Mr. Downing saw in his attack the beginnings of some deadly scourge which would sweep through and decimate the house.; He had despatched Adair for the doctor, and, after spending a few minutes prowling restlessly about his room, was now standing at his front gate, waiting for Adair's return.

It came about, therefore, that Mike, sprinting lightly in the direction of home and safety, had his already shaken nerves further maltreated by being hailed, at a range of about two yards, with a cry of "Is that you, Adair?" The next moment Mr. Downing emerged from his gate.

Mike stood not upon the order of his going.; He was off like an arrow —a flying figure of Guilt.; Mr. Downing, after the first surprise, seemed to grasp the situation.; Ejaculating at intervals the words, "Who is that?; Stop!; Who is that?; Stop!" he dashed after the much-enduring Wrykynian at an extremely creditable rate of speed.; Mr. Downing was by way of being a sprinter.; He had won handicap events at College sports at Oxford, and, if Mike had not got such a good start, the race might have been over in the first fifty yards.; As it was, that victim of Fate, going well, kept ahead.; At the entrance to the school grounds he led by a dozen yards.; The procession passed into the field, Mike heading as before for the pavilion.

As they raced across the soft turf, an idea occurred to Mike which he was accustomed in after years to attribute to genius, the one flash of it which had ever illumined his life.

It was this.

One of Mr. Downing's first acts, on starting the Fire Brigade at Sedleigh, had been to institute an alarm bell.; It had been rubbed into the school officially—in speeches from the daïs—by the headmaster, and unofficially—in earnest private conversations—by Mr. Downing, that at the sound of this bell, at whatever hour of day or night, every member of the school must leave his house in the quickest possible way, and make for the open.; The bell might mean that the school was on fire, or it might mean that one of the houses was on fire.; In any case, the school had its orders—to get out into the open at once.

Nor must it be supposed that the school was without practice at this feat.; Every now and then a notice would be found posted up on the board to the effect that there would be fire drill during the dinner hour that day.; Sometimes the performance was bright and interesting, as on the occasion when Mr. Downing, marshalling the brigade at his front gate, had said, "My house is supposed to be on fire.; Now let's do a record!" which the Brigade, headed by Stone and Robinson, obligingly did.; They fastened the hose to the hydrant, smashed a window on the ground floor (Mr. Downing having retired for a moment to talk with the headmaster), and poured a stream of water into the room.; When Mr. Downing was at liberty to turn his attention to the matter, he found that the room selected was his private study, most of the light furniture of which was floating on a miniature lake.; That episode had rather discouraged his passion for realism, and fire drill since then had taken the form, for the most part, of "practising escaping."; This was done by means of canvas shoots, kept in the dormitories.; At the sound of the bell the prefect of the dormitory would heave one end of the shoot out of window, the other end being fastened to the sill.; He would then go down it himself, using his elbows as a brake.; Then the second man would follow his example, and these two, standing below, would hold the end of the shoot so that the rest of the dormitory could fly rapidly down it without injury, except to their digestions.

After the first novelty of the thing had worn off, the school had taken a rooted dislike to fire drill.; It was a matter for self-congratulation among them that Mr. Downing had never been able to induce the headmaster to allow the alarm bell to be sounded for fire drill at night.; The headmaster, a man who had his views on the amount of sleep necessary for the growing boy, had drawn the line at night operations.; "Sufficient unto the day" had been the gist of his reply.; If the alarm bell were to ring at night when there was no fire, the school might mistake a genuine alarm of fire for a bogus one, and refuse to hurry themselves.

So Mr. Downing had had to be content with day drill.

The alarm bell hung in the archway leading into the school grounds.; The end of the rope, when not in use, was fastened to a hook half-way up the wall.

Mike, as he raced over the cricket field, made up his mind in a flash that his only chance of getting out of this tangle was to shake his pursuer off for a space of time long enough to enable him to get to the rope and tug it.; Then the school would come out.; He would mix with them, and in the subsequent confusion get back to bed unnoticed.

The task was easier than it would have seemed at the beginning of the chase.; Mr. Downing, owing to the two facts that he was not in the strictest training, and that it is only an Alfred Shrubb who can run for any length of time at top speed shouting "Who is that?; Stop!; Who is that?; Stop!" was beginning to feel distressed.; There were bellows to mend in the Downing camp.; Mike perceived this, and forced the pace.; He rounded the pavilion ten yards to the good.; Then, heading for the gate, he put all he knew into one last sprint.; Mr. Downing was not equal to the effort.; He worked gamely for a few strides, then fell behind.; When Mike reached the gate, a good forty yards separated them.

As far as Mike could judge —he was not in a condition to make nice calculations —he had about four seconds in which to get busy with that bell rope.

Probably nobody has ever crammed more energetic work into four seconds than he did then.

The night was as still as only an English summer night can be, and the first clang of the clapper sounded like a million iron girders falling from a height on to a sheet of tin.; He tugged away furiously, with an eye on the now rapidly advancing and loudly shouting figure of the housemaster.

And from the darkened house beyond there came a gradually swelling hum, as if a vast hive of bees had been disturbed.

The school was awake.

CHAPTER XLVI

THE DECORATION OF SAMMY

Psmith leaned against the mantelpiece in the senior day-room at Outwood's —since Mike's innings against Downing's the Lost Lambs had been received as brothers by that centre of disorder, so that even Spiller was compelled to look on the hatchet as buried —and gave his views on the events of the preceding night, or, rather, of that morning, for it was nearer one than twelve when peace had once more fallen on the school.

"Nothing that happens in this luny-bin," said Psmith, "has power to surprise me now.; There was a time when I might have thought it a little unusual to have to leave the house through a canvas shoot at one o'clock in the morning, but I suppose it's quite the regular thing here.; Old school tradition, &c.; Men leave the school, and find that they've got so accustomed to jumping out of window that they look on it as a sort of affectation to go out by the door.; I suppose none of you merchants can give me any idea when the next knockabout entertainment of this kind is likely to take place?"

"I wonder who rang that bell!" said Stone.; "Jolly sporting idea."

"I believe it was Downing himself.; If it was, I hope he's satisfied."

Jellicoe, who was appearing in society supported by a stick, looked meaningly at Mike, and giggled, receiving in answer a stony stare.; Mike had informed Jellicoe of the details of his interview with Mr. Barley at the "White Boar," and Jellicoe, after a momentary splutter of wrath against the practical joker, was now in a particularly light-hearted mood.; He hobbled about, giggling at nothing and at peace with all the world.

"It was a stirring scene," said Psmith.; "The agility with which Comrade Jellicoe boosted himself down the shoot was a triumph of mind over matter.; He seemed to forget his ankle.; It was the nearest thing to a Boneless Acrobatic Wonder that I have ever seen."

"I was in a beastly funk, I can tell you."

Stone gurgled.

"So was I," he said, "for a bit.; Then, when I saw that it was all a rag, I began to look about for ways of doing the thing really well.; I emptied about six jugs of water on a gang of kids under my window."

"I rushed into Downing's, and ragged some of the beds," said Robinson.

"It was an invigorating time," said Psmith.; "A sort of pageant.; I was particularly struck with the way some of the bright lads caught hold of the idea.; There was no skimping.; Some of the kids, to my certain knowledge, went down the shoot a dozen times.; There's nothing like doing a thing thoroughly.; I saw them come down, rush upstairs, and be saved again, time after time.; The thing became chronic with them.; I should say Comrade Downing ought to be satisfied with the high state of efficiency to which he has brought us.; At any rate I hope ——"

There was a sound of hurried footsteps outside the door, and Sharpe, a member of the senior day-room, burst excitedly in.; He seemed amused.

"I say, have you chaps seen Sammy?"

"Seen who?" said Stone.; "Sammy?; Why?"

"You'll know in a second.; He's just outside.; Here, Sammy, Sammy, Sammy!; Sam!; Sam!"

A bark and a patter of feet outside.

"Come on, Sammy.; Good dog."

There was a moment's silence.; Then a great yell of laughter burst forth.; Even Psmith's massive calm was shattered.; As for Jellicoe, he sobbed in a corner.

Sammy's beautiful white coat was almost entirely concealed by a thick covering of bright red paint.; His head, with the exception of the ears, was untouched, and his serious, friendly eyes seemed to emphasise the weirdness of his appearance.; He stood in the doorway, barking and wagging his tail, plainly puzzled at his reception.; He was a popular dog, and was always well received when he visited any of the houses, but he had never before met with enthusiasm like this.

"Good old Sammy!"

"What on earth's been happening to him?"

"Who did it?"

Sharpe, the introducer, had no views on the matter.

"I found him outside Downing's, with a crowd round him.; Everybody seems to have seen him.; I wonder who on earth has gone and mucked him up like that!"

Mike was the first to show any sympathy for the maltreated animal.

"Poor old Sammy," he said, kneeling on the floor beside the victim, and scratching him under the ear.; "What a beastly shame!; It'll take hours to wash all that off him, and he'll hate it."

"It seems to me," said Psmith, regarding Sammy dispassionately through his eyeglass, "that it's not a case for mere washing.; They'll either have to skin him bodily, or leave the thing to time.; Time, the Great Healer.; In a year or two he'll fade to a delicate pink.; I don't see why you shouldn't have a pink bull-terrier.; It would lend a touch of distinction to the place.; Crowds would come in excursion trains to see him.; By charging a small fee you might make him self-supporting.; I think I'll suggest it to Comrade Downing."

"There'll be a row about this," said Stone.

"Rows are rather sport when you're not mixed up in them," said Robinson, philosophically.; "There'll be another if we don't start off for chapel soon.; It's a quarter to."

There was a general move.; Mike was the last to leave the room.; As he was going, Jellicoe stopped him.; Jellicoe was staying in that Sunday, owing to his ankle.

"I say," said Jellicoe, "I just wanted to thank you again about that——"

"Oh, that's all right."

"No, but it really was awfully decent of you.; You might have got into a frightful row.; Were you nearly caught?"

"Jolly nearly."

"It *was* you who rang the bell, wasn't it?"

"Yes, it was.; But for goodness sake don't go gassing about it, or somebody will get to hear who oughtn't to, and I shall be sacked."

"All right.; But, I say, you *are* a chap!"

"What's the matter now?"

"I mean about Sammy, you know.; It's a jolly good score off old Downing.; He'll be frightfully sick."

"Sammy!" cried Mike.; "My good man, you don't think I did that, do you?; What absolute rot!; I never touched the poor brute."

"Oh, all right," said Jellicoe.; "But I wasn't going to tell any one, of course."

"What do you mean?"

"You *are* a chap!" giggled Jellicoe.

Mike walked to chapel rather thoughtfully.

CHAPTER XLVII

MR. DOWNING ON THE SCENT

There was just one moment, the moment in which, on going down to the junior day-room of his house to quell an unseemly disturbance, he was boisterously greeted by a vermilion bull terrier, when Mr. Downing was seized with a hideous fear lest he had lost his senses.; Glaring down at the crimson animal that was pawing at his knees, he clutched at his reason for one second as a drowning man clutches at a lifebelt.

Then the happy laughter of the young onlookers reassured him.

"Who—" he shouted, "WHO has done this?"

"WHO——" HE SHOUTED. "WHO HAS DONE THIS?"

"Please, sir, we don't know," shrilled the chorus.
"Please, sir, he came in like that."

178

"Please, sir, we were sitting here when he suddenly ran in, all red."

A voice from the crowd:; "Look at old Sammy!"

The situation was impossible.; There was nothing to be done.; He could not find out by verbal inquiry who had painted the dog.; The possibility of Sammy being painted red during the night had never occurred to Mr. Downing, and now that the thing had happened he had no scheme of action.; As Psmith would have said, he had confused the unusual with the impossible, and the result was that he was taken by surprise.

While he was pondering on this the situation was rendered still more difficult by Sammy, who, taking advantage of the door being open, escaped and rushed into the road, thus publishing his condition to all and sundry.; You can hush up a painted dog while it confines itself to your own premises, but once it has mixed with the great public this becomes out of the question.; Sammy's state advanced from a private trouble into a row.; Mr. Downing's next move was in the same direction that Sammy had taken, only, instead of running about the road, he went straight to the headmaster.

The Head, who had had to leave his house in the small hours in his pyjamas and a dressing-gown, was not in the best of tempers.; He had a cold in the head, and also a rooted conviction that Mr. Downing, in spite of his strict orders, had rung the bell himself on the previous night in order to test the efficiency of the school in saving themselves in the event of fire.; He received the housemaster frostily, but thawed as the latter related the events which had led up to the ringing of the bell.

"Dear me!" he said, deeply interested.; "One of the boys at the school, you think?"

"I am certain of it," said Mr. Downing.

"Was he wearing a school cap?"

"He was bare-headed.; A boy who breaks out of his house at night would hardly run the risk of wearing a distinguishing cap."

"No, no, I suppose not.; A big boy, you say?"

"Very big."

"You did not see his face?"

"It was dark and he never looked back — he was in front of me all the time."

"Dear me!"

"There is another matter ——"

"Yes?"

"This boy, whoever he was, had done something before he rang the bell — he had painted my dog Sampson red."

The headmaster's eyes protruded from their sockets.; "He — he — *what*, Mr. Downing?"

"He painted my dog red — bright red."; Mr. Downing was too angry to see anything humorous in the incident.; Since the previous night he had been wounded in his tenderest feelings.; His Fire Brigade system had been most shamefully abused by being turned into a mere instrument in the hands of a malefactor for escaping justice, and his dog had been held up to ridicule to all the world.; He did not want to smile, he wanted revenge.

The headmaster, on the other hand, did want to smile.; It was not his dog, he could look on the affair with an unbiased eye, and to him there was something ludicrous in a white dog suddenly appearing as a red dog.

"It is a scandalous thing!" said Mr. Downing.

"Quite so!; Quite so!" said the headmaster hastily.; "I shall punish the boy who did it most severely.; I will speak to the school in the Hall after chapel."

Which he did, but without result.; A cordial invitation to the criminal to come forward and be executed was received in wooden silence by the school, with the exception of Johnson III., of Outwood's, who, suddenly reminded of Sammy's appearance by the headmaster's words, broke into a wild screech of laughter, and was instantly awarded two hundred lines.

The school filed out of the Hall to their various lunches, and Mr. Downing was left with the conviction that, if he wanted the criminal discovered, he would have to discover him for himself.

The great thing in affairs of this kind is to get a good start, and Fate, feeling perhaps that it had been a little hard upon Mr. Downing, gave him a most magnificent start.; Instead of having to hunt for a needle in a haystack, he found himself in a moment in the position of being set to find it in a mere truss of straw.

It was Mr. Outwood who helped him.; Sergeant Collard had waylaid the archaeological expert on his way to chapel, and informed him that at close on twelve the night before he had observed a youth, unidentified, attempting to get into his house *via* the water-pipe.; Mr. Outwood, whose thoughts were occupied with apses and plinths, not to mention cromlechs, at the time, thanked the sergeant with absent-minded politeness and passed on.; Later he remembered the fact *à propos* of some reflections on the subject of burglars in mediaeval England, and passed it on to Mr. Downing as they walked back to lunch.

"Then the boy was in your house!" exclaimed Mr. Downing.

"Not actually in, as far as I understand.; I gather from the sergeant that he interrupted him before——"

"I mean he must have been one of the boys in your house."

"But what was he doing out at that hour?"

"He had broken out."

"Impossible, I think.; Oh yes, quite impossible!; I went round the dormitories as usual at eleven o'clock last night, and all the boys were asleep—all of them."

Mr. Downing was not listening.; He was in a state of suppressed excitement and exultation which made it hard for him to attend to his colleague's slow utterances.; He had a clue!; Now that the search had narrowed itself down to Outwood's house, the rest was comparatively easy.; Perhaps Sergeant Collard had actually recognised the boy.; Or reflection he dismissed this as unlikely, for the sergeant would scarcely have kept a thing like that to himself; but he might very well have seen more of him than he, Downing, had seen.; It was only with an effort that he could keep himself from rushing to the sergeant then and there, and leaving the house lunch to look after itself.; He resolved to go the moment that meal was at an end.

Sunday lunch at a public-school house is probably one of the longest functions in existence.; It drags its slow length along like a languid snake, but it finishes in time.; In due course Mr. Downing, after sitting still and eyeing with acute dislike everybody who asked for a second helping, found himself at liberty.

Regardless of the claims of digestion, he rushed forth on the trail.

* * * * *

Sergeant Collard lived with his wife and a family of unknown dimensions in the lodge at the school front gate.; Dinner was just over when Mr. Downing arrived, as a blind man could have told.

The sergeant received his visitor with dignity, ejecting the family, who were torpid after roast beef and resented having to move, in order to ensure privacy.

Having requested his host to smoke, which the latter was about to do unasked, Mr. Downing stated his case.

"Mr. Outwood," he said, "tells me that last night, sergeant, you saw a boy endeavouring to enter his house."

The sergeant blew a cloud of smoke.; "Oo-oo-oo, yer," he said; "I did, sir—spotted 'im, I did.; Feeflee good at spottin', I am, sir.; Dook of Connaught, he used to say, 'Ere comes Sergeant Collard,' he used to say, 'e's feeflee good at spottin'.'"

"What did you do?"

"Do?; Oo-oo-oo!; I shouts 'Oo-oo-oo yer, yer young monkey, what yer doin' there?'"

"Yes?"

"But 'e was off in a flash, and I doubles after 'im prompt."

"But you didn't catch him?"

"No, sir," admitted the sergeant reluctantly.

"Did you catch sight of his face, sergeant?"

"No, sir, 'e was doublin' away in the opposite direction."

"Did you notice anything at all about his appearance?"

"'E was a long young chap, sir, with a pair of legs on him—feeflee fast 'e run, sir.; Oo-oo-oo, feeflee!"

"You noticed nothing else?"

"'E wasn't wearing no cap of any sort, sir."

"Ah!"

"Bare-'eaded, sir," added the sergeant, rubbing the point in.

"It was undoubtedly the same boy, undoubtedly!; I wish you could have caught a glimpse of his face, sergeant."

"So do I, sir."

"You would not be able to recognise him again if you saw him, you think?"

"Oo-oo-oo!; Wouldn't go so far as to say that, sir, 'cos yer see, I'm feeflee good at spottin', but it was a dark night."

Mr. Downing rose to go.

"Well," he said, "the search is now considerably narrowed down, considerably!; It is certain that the boy was one of the boys in Mr. Outwood's house."

"Young monkeys!" interjected the sergeant helpfully.

"Good-afternoon, sergeant."

"Good-afternoon to you, sir."

"Pray do not move, sergeant."

The sergeant had not shown the slightest inclination of doing anything of the kind.

"I will find my way out.; Very hot to-day, is it not?"

"Feeflee warm, sir; weather's goin' to break—workin' up for thunder."

"I hope not.; The school plays the M.C.C. on Wednesday, and it would be a pity if rain were to spoil our first fixture with them.; Good afternoon."

And Mr. Downing went out into the baking sunlight, while Sergeant Collard, having requested Mrs. Collard to take the children out for a walk at once, and furthermore to give young Ernie a clip side of the 'ead, if he persisted in making so much noise, put a handkerchief over his face, rested his feet on the table, and slept the sleep of the just.

CHAPTER XLVIII

THE SLEUTH-HOUND

For the Doctor Watsons of this world, as opposed to the Sherlock Holmeses, success in the province of detective work must always be, to a very large extent, the result of luck.; Sherlock Holmes can extract a clue from a wisp of straw or a flake of cigar-ash.; But Doctor Watson has got to have it taken out for him, and dusted, and exhibited clearly, with a label attached.

The average man is a Doctor Watson.; We are wont to scoff in a patronising manner at that humble follower of the great investigator, but, as a matter of fact, we should have been just as dull ourselves.; We should not even have risen to the modest level of a Scotland Yard Bungler.; We should simply have hung around, saying:;

"My dear Holmes, how—?" and all the rest of it, just as the downtrodden medico did.

It is not often that the ordinary person has any need to see what he can do in the way of detection.; He gets along very comfortably in the humdrum round of life without having to measure footprints and smile quiet, tight-lipped smiles.; But if ever the emergency does arise, he thinks naturally of Sherlock Holmes, and his methods.

Mr. Downing had read all the Holmes stories with great attention, and had thought many times what an incompetent ass Doctor Watson was; but, now that he had started to handle his own first case, he was compelled to admit that there was a good deal to be said in extenuation of Watson's inability to unravel tangles.; It certainly was uncommonly hard, he thought, as he paced the cricket field after leaving Sergeant Collard, to detect anybody, unless you knew who had really done the crime.; As he brooded over the case in hand, his sympathy for Dr. Watson increased with every minute, and he began to feel a certain resentment against Sir Arthur Conan Doyle.; It was all very well for Sir Arthur to be so shrewd and infallible about tracing a mystery to its source, but he knew perfectly well who had done the thing before he started!

Now that he began really to look into this matter of the alarm bell and the painting of Sammy, the conviction was creeping over him that the problem was more difficult than a casual observer might imagine.; He had got as far as finding that his quarry of the previous night was a boy in Mr. Outwood's house, but how was he to get any farther?; That was the thing.; There were, of course, only a limited number of boys in Mr. Outwood's house as tall as the one he had pursued; but even if there had been only one other, it would have complicated matters.; If you go to a boy and say, "Either you or Jones were out of your house last night at twelve o'clock," the boy does not reply, "Sir, I cannot tell a lie—I was out of my house last night at twelve o'clock."; He simply assumes the animated expression of a stuffed fish, and leaves the next move to you.; It is practically Stalemate.

All these things passed through Mr. Downing's mind as he walked up and down the cricket field that afternoon.

What he wanted was a clue.; But it is so hard for the novice to tell what is a clue and what isn't.; Probably, if he only knew, there were clues lying all over the place, shouting to him to pick them up.

What with the oppressive heat of the day and the fatigue of hard thinking, Mr. Downing was working up for a brain-storm, when Fate once more intervened, this time in the shape of Riglett, a junior member of his house.

Riglett slunk up in the shamefaced way peculiar to some boys, even when they have done nothing wrong, and, having capped Mr. Downing with the air of one who has been caught in the act of doing something particularly shady, requested that he might be allowed to fetch his bicycle from the shed.

"Your bicycle?" snapped Mr. Downing.; Much thinking had made him irritable.; "What do you want with your bicycle?"

Riglett shuffled, stood first on his left foot, then on his right, blushed, and finally remarked, as if it were not so much a sound reason as a sort of feeble excuse for the low and blackguardly fact that he wanted his bicycle, that he had got leave for tea that afternoon.

Then Mr. Downing remembered.; Riglett had an aunt resident about three miles from the school, whom he was accustomed to visit occasionally on Sunday afternoons during the term.

He felt for his bunch of keys, and made his way to the shed, Riglett shambling behind at an interval of two yards.

Mr. Downing unlocked the door, and there on the floor was the Clue!

A clue that even Dr. Watson could not have overlooked.

Mr. Downing saw it, but did not immediately recognise it for what it was.; What he saw at first was not a Clue, but just a mess.; He had a tidy soul and abhorred messes.; And this was a particularly messy mess.; The greater part of the flooring in the neighbourhood of the door was a sea of red paint.; The tin from which it had flowed was lying on its side in the middle of the shed.; The air was full of the pungent scent.

"Pah!" said Mr. Downing.

Then suddenly, beneath the disguise of the mess, he saw the clue.; A foot-mark!; No less.; A crimson foot-mark on the grey concrete!

Riglett, who had been waiting patiently two yards away, now coughed plaintively.; The sound recalled Mr. Downing to mundane matters.

"Get your bicycle, Riglett," he said, "and be careful where you tread.; Somebody has upset a pot of paint on the floor."

Riglett, walking delicately through dry places, extracted his bicycle from the rack, and presently departed to gladden the heart of his aunt, leaving Mr. Downing, his brain fizzing with the enthusiasm of the detective, to lock the door and resume his perambulation of the cricket field.

Give Dr. Watson a fair start, and he is a demon at the game.; Mr. Downing's brain was now working with a rapidity and clearness which a professional sleuth might have envied.

Paint.; Red paint.; Obviously the same paint with which Sammy had been decorated.; A foot-mark.; Whose foot-mark?; Plainly that of the criminal who had done the deed of decoration.

Yoicks!

There were two things, however, to be considered.; Your careful detective must consider everything.; In the first place, the paint might have been upset by the ground-man.; It was the ground-man's paint.; He had been giving a fresh coating to the wood-work in front of the pavilion scoring-box at the conclusion of yesterday's match. (A labour of love which was the direct outcome of the enthusiasm for work which Adair had instilled into him.) In that case the foot-mark might be his.

Note one:; Interview the ground-man on this point.

In the second place Adair might have upset the tin and trodden in its contents when he went to get his bicycle in order to fetch the doctor for the suffering MacPhee.; This was the more probable of the two contingencies, for it would have been dark in the shed when Adair went into it.

Note two Interview Adair as to whether he found, on returning to the house, that there was paint on his boots.

Things were moving.

* * * * *

He resolved to take Adair first.; He could get the ground-man's address from him.

Passing by the trees under whose shade Mike and Psmith and Dunster had watched the match on the previous day, he came upon the Head of his house in a deck-chair reading a book.; A summer Sunday afternoon is the time for reading in deck-chairs.

"Oh, Adair," he said.; "No, don't get up.; I merely wished to ask you if you found any paint on your boots when you returned to the house last night?"

"Paint, sir?" Adair was plainly puzzled.; His book had been interesting, and had driven the Sammy incident out of his head.

"I see somebody has spilt some paint on the floor of the bicycle shed.; You did not do that, I suppose, when you went to fetch your bicycle?"

"No, sir."

"It is spilt all over the floor.; I wondered whether you had happened to tread in it.; But you say you found no paint on your boots this morning?"

"No, sir, my bicycle is always quite near the door of the shed.; I didn't go into the shed at all."

"I see.; Quite so.; Thank you, Adair.; Oh, by the way, Adair, where does Markby live?"

"I forget the name of his cottage, sir, but I could show you in a second.; It's one of those cottages just past the school gates, on the right as you turn out into the road.; There are three in a row.; His is the first you come to.; There's a barn just before you get to them."

"Thank you.; I shall be able to find them.; I should like to speak to Markby for a moment on a small matter."

A sharp walk took him to the cottages Adair had mentioned.; He rapped at the door of the first, and the ground-man came out in his shirt-sleeves, blinking as if he had just woke up, as was indeed the case.

"Oh, Markby!"

"Sir?"

"You remember that you were painting the scoring-box in the pavilion last night after the match?"

"Yes, sir.; It wanted a lick of paint bad.; The young gentlemen will scramble about and get through the window.; Makes it look shabby, sir.; So I thought I'd better give it a coating so as to look ship-shape when the Marylebone come down."

"Just so.; An excellent idea.; Tell me, Markby, what did you do with the pot of paint when you had finished?"

"Put it in the bicycle shed, sir."

"On the floor?"

"On the floor, sir?; No.; On the shelf at the far end, with the can of whitening what I use for marking out the wickets, sir."

"Of course, yes.; Quite so.; Just as I thought."

"Do you want it, sir?"

"No, thank you, Markby, no, thank you.; The fact is, somebody who had no business to do so has moved the pot of paint from the shelf to the floor, with the result that it has been kicked over, and spilt.; You had better get some more to-morrow.; Thank you, Markby.; That is all I wished to know."

Mr. Downing walked back to the school thoroughly excited.; He was hot on the scent now.; The only other possible theories had been tested and successfully exploded.; The thing had become simple to a degree.; All he had to do was to go to Mr. Outwood's house —the idea of searching a fellow-master's house did not appear to him at all a delicate task; somehow one grew unconsciously to feel that Mr. Outwood did not really exist as a man capable of resenting liberties —find the paint-splashed boot, ascertain its owner, and denounce him to the headmaster.; Picture, Blue Fire and "God Save the King" by the full strength of the company.; There could be no doubt that a paint-splashed boot must be in Mr. Outwood's house somewhere.; A boy cannot tread in a pool of paint without showing some signs of having done so.; It was Sunday, too, so that the boot would not yet have been cleaned.; Yoicks!; Also Tally-ho!; This really was beginning to be something like business.

Regardless of the heat, the sleuth-hound hurried across to Outwood's as fast as he could walk.

CHAPTER XLIX

A CHECK

The only two members of the house not out in the grounds when he arrived were Mike and Psmith. They were standing on the gravel drive in front of the boys' entrance. Mike had a deck-chair in one hand and a book in the other. Psmith—for even the greatest minds will sometimes unbend—was playing diabolo. That is to say, he was trying without success to raise the spool from the ground.

"There's a kid in France," said Mike disparagingly, as the bobbin rolled off the string for the fourth time, "who can do it three thousand seven hundred and something times."

Psmith smoothed a crease out of his waistcoat and tried again. He had just succeeded in getting the thing to spin when Mr. Downing arrived. The sound of his footsteps disturbed Psmith and brought the effort to nothing.

"Enough of this spoolery," said he, flinging the sticks through the open window of the senior day-room. "I was an ass ever to try it. The philosophical mind needs complete repose in its hours of leisure. Hullo!"

He stared after the sleuth-hound, who had just entered the house.

"What the dickens," said Mike, "does he mean by barging in as if he'd bought the place?"

"Comrade Downing looks pleased with himself. What brings him round in this direction, I wonder! Still, no matter. The few articles which he may sneak from our study are of inconsiderable value. He is welcome to them. Do you feel inclined to wait awhile till I have fetched a chair and book?"

"I'll be going on. I shall be under the trees at the far end of the ground."

"'Tis well. I will be with you in about two ticks."

Mike walked on towards the field, and Psmith, strolling upstairs to fetch his novel, found Mr. Downing standing in the passage with the air of one who has lost his bearings.

"A warm afternoon, sir," murmured Psmith courteously, as he passed.

"Er—Smith!"

"Sir?"

"I—er—wish to go round the dormitories."

It was Psmith's guiding rule in life never to be surprised at anything, so he merely inclined his head gracefully, and said nothing.

"I should be glad if you would fetch the keys and show me where the rooms are."

"With acute pleasure, sir," said Psmith. "Or shall I fetch Mr. Outwood, sir?"

"Do as I tell you, Smith," snapped Mr. Downing.

Psmith said no more, but went down to the matron's room. The matron being out, he abstracted the bunch of keys from her table and rejoined the master.

"Shall I lead the way, sir?" he asked.

Mr. Downing nodded.

"Here, sir," said Psmith, opening a door, "we have Barnes' dormitory. An airy room, constructed on the soundest hygienic principles. Each boy, I understand, has quite a considerable number of cubic feet of air all to himself. It is Mr. Outwood's boast that no boy has ever asked for a cubic foot of air in vain. He argues justly——"

He broke off abruptly and began to watch the other's manoeuvres in silence. Mr. Downing was peering rapidly beneath each bed in turn.

"Are you looking for Barnes, sir?" inquired Psmith politely. "I think he's out in the field."

Mr. Downing rose, having examined the last bed, crimson in the face with the exercise.

"Show me the next dormitory, Smith," he said, panting slightly.

"This," said Psmith, opening the next door and sinking his voice to an awed whisper, "is where *I* sleep!"

185

Mr. Downing glanced swiftly beneath the three beds.; "Excuse me, sir," said Psmith, "but are we chasing anything?"

"Be good enough, Smith," said Mr. Downing with asperity, "to keep your remarks to yourself."

"I was only wondering, sir.; Shall I show you the next in order?"

"Certainly."

They moved on up the passage.

Drawing blank at the last dormitory, Mr. Downing paused, baffled.; Psmith waited patiently by.; An idea struck the master.

"The studies, Smith," he cried.

"Aha!" said Psmith.; "I beg your pardon, sir.; The observation escaped me unawares.; The frenzy of the chase is beginning to enter into my blood.; Here we have — —"

Mr. Downing stopped short.

"Is this impertinence studied, Smith?"

"Ferguson's study, sir?; No, sir.; That's further down the passage.; This is Barnes'."

Mr. Downing looked at him closely.; Psmith's face was wooden in its gravity.; The master snorted suspiciously, then moved on.

"Whose is this?" he asked, rapping a door.

"This, sir, is mine and Jackson's."

"What!; Have you a study?; You are low down in the school for it."

"I think, sir, that Mr. Outwood gave it us rather as a testimonial to our general worth than to our proficiency in school-work."

Mr. Downing raked the room with a keen eye.; The absence of bars from the window attracted his attention.

"Have you no bars to your windows here, such as there are in my house?"

"There appears to be no bar, sir," said Psmith, putting up his eyeglass.

Mr Downing was leaning out of the window.

"A lovely view, is it not, sir?" said Psmith.; "The trees, the field, the distant hills — —"

Mr. Downing suddenly started.; His eye had been caught by the water-pipe at the side of the window.; The boy whom Sergeant Collard had seen climbing the pipe must have been making for this study.

He spun round and met Psmith's blandly inquiring gaze.; He looked at Psmith carefully for a moment.; No.; The boy he had chased last night had not been Psmith.; That exquisite's figure and general appearance were unmistakable, even in the dusk.

"Whom did you say you shared this study with, Smith?"

"Jackson, sir.; The cricketer."

"Never mind about his cricket, Smith," said Mr. Downing with irritation.

"No, sir."

"He is the only other occupant of the room?"

"Yes, sir."

"Nobody else comes into it?"

"If they do, they go out extremely quickly, sir."

"Ah!; Thank you, Smith."

"Not at all, sir."

Mr. Downing pondered.; Jackson!; The boy bore him a grudge.; The boy was precisely the sort of boy to revenge himself by painting the dog Sammy.; And, gadzooks!; The boy whom he had pursued last night had been just about Jackson's size and build!

Mr. Downing was as firmly convinced at that moment that Mike's had been the hand to wield the paint-brush as he had ever been of anything in his life.

"Smith!" he said excitedly.

"On the spot, sir," said Psmith affably.

"Where are Jackson's boots?"

186

There are moments when the giddy excitement of being right on the trail causes the amateur (or Watsonian) detective to be incautious.; Such a moment came to Mr. Downing then.; If he had been wise, he would have achieved his object, the getting a glimpse of Mike's boots, by a devious and snaky route.; As it was, he rushed straight on.

"His boots, sir?; He has them on.; I noticed them as he went out just now."

"Where is the pair he wore yesterday?"

"Where are the boots of yester-year?" murmured Psmith to himself.; "I should say at a venture, sir, that they would be in the basket downstairs.; Edmund, our genial knife-and-boot boy, collects them, I believe, at early dawn."

"Would they have been cleaned yet?"

"If I know Edmund, sir —no."

"Smith," said Mr. Downing, trembling with excitement, "go and bring that basket to me here."

Psmith's brain was working rapidly as he went downstairs.; What exactly was at the back of the sleuth's mind, prompting these manoeuvres, he did not know.; But that there was something, and that that something was directed in a hostile manner against Mike, probably in connection with last night's wild happenings, he was certain.; Psmith had noticed, on leaving his bed at the sound of the alarm bell, that he and Jellicoe were alone in the room.; That might mean that Mike had gone out through the door when the bell sounded, or it might mean that he had been out all the time.; It began to look as if the latter solution were the correct one.

* * * * *

He staggered back with the basket, painfully conscious the while that it was creasing his waistcoat, and dumped it down on the study floor.; Mr. Downing stooped eagerly over it.; Psmith leaned against the wall, and straightened out the damaged garment.

"We have here, sir," he said, "a fair selection of our various bootings."

Mr. Downing looked up.

"You dropped none of the boots on your way up, Smith?"

"Not one, sir.; It was a fine performance."

Mr. Downing uttered a grunt of satisfaction, and bent once more to his task.; Boots flew about the room.; Mr. Downing knelt on the floor beside the basket, and dug like a terrier at a rat-hole.

At last he made a dive, and, with an exclamation of triumph, rose to his feet.; In his hand he held a boot.

"Put those back again, Smith," he said.

The ex-Etonian, wearing an expression such as a martyr might have worn on being told off for the stake, began to pick up the scattered footgear, whistling softly the tune of "I do all the dirty work," as he did so.

"That's the lot, sir," he said, rising.

"Ah.; Now come across with me to the headmaster's house.; Leave the basket here.; You can carry it back when you return."

"Shall I put back that boot, sir?"

"Certainly not.; I shall take this with me, of course."

"Shall I carry it, sir?"

Mr. Downing reflected.

"Yes, Smith," he said.; "I think it would be best."

It occurred to him that the spectacle of a housemaster wandering abroad on the public highway, carrying a dirty boot, might be a trifle undignified.; You never knew whom you might meet on Sunday afternoon.

Psmith took the boot, and doing so, understood what before had puzzled him.

Across the toe of the boot was a broad splash of red paint.

He knew nothing, of course, of the upset tin in the bicycle shed; but when a housemaster's dog has been painted red in the night, and when, on the following day, the housemaster goes about in search of a paint-splashed boot, one puts two and two together.; Psmith looked at the name inside the boot.; It was "Brown, boot-maker, Bridgnorth."; Bridgnorth was only a few miles from his own home and Mike's.; Undoubtedly it was Mike's boot.

"Can you tell me whose boot that is?" asked Mr. Downing.

Psmith looked at it again.

"No, sir.; I can't say the little chap's familiar to me."

"Come with me, then."

Mr. Downing left the room.; After a moment Psmith followed him.

The headmaster was in his garden.; Thither Mr. Downing made his way, the boot-bearing Psmith in close attendance.

The Head listened to the amateur detective's statement with interest.

"Indeed?" he said, when Mr. Downing had finished.

"Indeed?; Dear me!; It certainly seems —It is a curiously well-connected thread of evidence.; You are certain that there was red paint on this boot you discovered in Mr. Outwood's house?"

"I have it with me.; I brought it on purpose to show to you.; Smith!"

"Sir?"

"You have the boot?"

"Ah," said the headmaster, putting on a pair of pince-nez, "now let me look at —This, you say, is the —?; Just so.; Just so.; Just....; But, er, Mr. Downing, it may be that I have not examined this boot with sufficient care, but —Can *you* point out to me exactly where this paint is that you speak of?"

Mr. Downing stood staring at the boot with a wild, fixed stare.; Of any suspicion of paint, red or otherwise, it was absolutely and entirely innocent.

CHAPTER L

THE DESTROYER OF EVIDENCE

The boot became the centre of attraction, the cynosure of all eyes.; Mr. Downing fixed it with the piercing stare of one who feels that his brain is tottering.; The headmaster looked at it with a mildly puzzled expression.; Psmith, putting up his eyeglass, gazed at it with a sort of affectionate interest, as if he were waiting for it to do a trick of some kind.

Mr. Downing was the first to break the silence.

"There was paint on this boot," he said vehemently.; "I tell you there was a splash of red paint across the toe.; Smith will bear me out in this.; Smith, you saw the paint on this boot?"

"Paint, sir!"

"What!; Do you mean to tell me that you did *not* see it?"

"No, sir.; There was no paint on this boot."

"This is foolery.; I saw it with my own eyes.; It was a broad splash right across the toe."

The headmaster interposed.

"You must have made a mistake, Mr. Downing.; There is certainly no trace of paint on this boot.; These momentary optical delusions are, I fancy, not uncommon.; Any doctor will tell you ——"

"I had an aunt, sir," said Psmith chattily, "who was remarkably subject ——"

"It is absurd.; I cannot have been mistaken," said Mr. Downing.; "I am positively certain the toe of this boot was red when I found it."

"It is undoubtedly black now, Mr. Downing."

"A sort of chameleon boot," murmured Psmith.

The goaded housemaster turned on him.

"What did you say, Smith?"

"Did I speak, sir?" said Psmith, with the start of one coming suddenly out of a trance.

Mr. Downing looked searchingly at him.

"You had better be careful, Smith."

"Yes, sir."

"I strongly suspect you of having something to do with this."

"Really, Mr. Downing," said the headmaster, "that is surely improbable.; Smith could scarcely have cleaned the boot on his way to my house.; On one occasion I inadvertently spilt some paint on a shoe of my own.; I can assure you that it does not brush off.; It needs a very systematic cleaning before all traces are removed."

"Exactly, sir," said Psmith.; "My theory, if I may ——?"

"Certainly, Smith."

Psmith bowed courteously and proceeded.

"My theory, sir, is that Mr. Downing was deceived by the light and shade effects on the toe of the boot.; The afternoon sun, streaming in through the window, must have shone on the boot in such a manner as to give it a momentary and fictitious aspect of redness.; If Mr. Downing recollects, he did not look long at the boot.; The picture on the retina of the eye, consequently, had not time to fade.; I remember thinking myself, at the moment, that the boot appeared to have a certain reddish tint.; The mistake ——"

"Bah!" said Mr. Downing shortly.

"Well, really," said the headmaster, "it seems to me that that is the only explanation that will square with the facts.; A boot that is really smeared with red paint does not become black of itself in the course of a few minutes."

"You are very right, sir," said Psmith with benevolent approval.; "May I go now, sir?; I am in the middle of a singularly impressive passage of Cicero's speech De Senectute."

"I am sorry that you should leave your preparation till Sunday, Smith.; It is a habit of which I altogether disapprove."

"I am reading it, sir," said Psmith, with simple dignity, "for pleasure.; Shall I take the boot with me, sir?"

"If Mr. Downing does not want it?"

The housemaster passed the fraudulent piece of evidence to Psmith without a word, and the latter, having included both masters in a kindly smile, left the garden.

Pedestrians who had the good fortune to be passing along the road between the housemaster's house and Mr. Outwood's at that moment saw what, if they had but known it, was a most unusual sight, the spectacle of Psmith running.; Psmith's usual mode of progression was a dignified walk.; He believed in the contemplative style rather than the hustling.

On this occasion, however, reckless of possible injuries to the crease of his trousers, he raced down the road, and turning in at Outwood's gate, bounded upstairs like a highly trained professional athlete.

On arriving at the study, his first act was to remove a boot from the top of the pile in the basket, place it in the small cupboard under the bookshelf, and lock the cupboard.; Then he flung himself into a chair and panted.

"Brain," he said to himself approvingly, "is what one chiefly needs in matters of this kind.; Without brain, where are we?; In the soup, every time.; The next development will be when Comrade Downing thinks it over, and is struck with the brilliant idea that it's just possible that the boot he gave me to carry and the boot I did carry were not one boot but two boots.; Meanwhile ——"

He dragged up another chair for his feet and picked up his novel.

He had not been reading long when there was a footstep in the passage, and Mr. Downing appeared.

The possibility, in fact the probability, of Psmith having substituted another boot for the one with the incriminating splash of paint on it had occurred to him almost immediately on leaving the headmaster's garden.; Psmith and Mike, he reflected, were friends.; Psmith's impulse would be to do all that lay in his power to shield Mike.; Feeling aggrieved with himself that he had not thought of this before, he, too, hurried over to Outwood's.

Mr. Downing was brisk and peremptory.

"I wish to look at these boots again," he said.; Psmith, with a sigh, laid down his novel, and rose to assist him.

"Sit down, Smith," said the housemaster.; "I can manage without your help."

Psmith sat down again, carefully tucking up the knees of his trousers, and watched him with silent interest through his eyeglass.

The scrutiny irritated Mr. Downing.

"Put that thing away, Smith," he said.

"That thing, sir?"

"Yes, that ridiculous glass.; Put it away."

"Why, sir?"

"Why!; Because I tell you to do so."

"I guessed that that was the reason, sir," sighed Psmith replacing the eyeglass in his waistcoat pocket.; He rested his elbows on his knees, and his chin on his hands, and resumed his contemplative inspection of the boot-expert, who, after fidgeting for a few moments, lodged another complaint.

"Don't sit there staring at me, Smith."

"I was interested in what you were doing, sir."

"Never mind.; Don't stare at me in that idiotic way."

"May I read, sir?" asked Psmith, patiently.

"Yes, read if you like."

"Thank you, sir."

Psmith took up his book again, and Mr. Downing, now thoroughly irritated, pursued his investigations in the boot-basket.

He went through it twice, but each time without success.; After the second search, he stood up, and looked wildly round the room.; He was as certain as he could be of anything that the missing piece of evidence was somewhere in the study.; It was no use asking Psmith point-blank where it was, for Psmith's ability to parry dangerous questions with evasive answers was quite out of the common.

His eye roamed about the room.; There was very little cover there, even for so small a fugitive as a number nine boot.; The floor could be acquitted, on sight, of harbouring the quarry.

Then he caught sight of the cupboard, and something seemed to tell him that there was the place to look.

"Smith!" he said.

Psmith had been reading placidly all the while.

"Yes, sir?"

"What is in this cupboard?"

"That cupboard, sir?"

"Yes.; This cupboard."; Mr. Downing rapped the door irritably.

"Just a few odd trifles, sir.; We do not often use it.; A ball of string, perhaps.; Possibly an old note-book.; Nothing of value or interest."

"Open it."

"I think you will find that it is locked, sir."

"Unlock it."

"But where is the key, sir?"

"Have you not got the key?"

"If the key is not in the lock, sir, you may depend upon it that it will take a long search to find it."

"Where did you see it last?"

"It was in the lock yesterday morning.; Jackson might have taken it."

"Where is Jackson?"

"Out in the field somewhere, sir."

Mr. Downing thought for a moment.

"I don't believe a word of it," he said shortly.; "I have my reasons for thinking that you are deliberately keeping the contents of that cupboard from me.; I shall break open the door."

Psmith got up.

"I'm afraid you mustn't do that, sir."

Mr. Downing stared, amazed.

"Are you aware whom you are talking to, Smith?" he inquired acidly.

"Yes, sir.; And I know it's not Mr. Outwood, to whom that cupboard happens to belong.; If you wish to break it open, you must get his permission.; He is the sole lessee and proprietor of that cupboard.; I am only the acting manager."

Mr. Downing paused.; He also reflected.; Mr. Outwood in the general rule did not count much in the scheme of things, but possibly there were limits to the treating of him as if he did not exist.; To enter his house without his permission and search it to a certain extent was all very well.; But when it came to breaking up his furniture, perhaps — —!

On the other hand, there was the maddening thought that if he left the study in search of Mr. Outwood, in order to obtain his sanction for the house-breaking work which he proposed to carry through, Smith would be alone in the room.; And he knew that, if Smith were left alone in the room, he would instantly remove the boot to some other hiding-place.; He thoroughly disbelieved the story of the lost key.; He was perfectly convinced that the missing boot was in the cupboard.

He stood chewing these thoughts for awhile, Psmith in the meantime standing in a graceful attitude in front of the cupboard, staring into vacancy.

Then he was seized with a happy idea.; Why should he leave the room at all?; If he sent Smith, then he himself could wait and make certain that the cupboard was not tampered with.

"Smith," he said, "go and find Mr. Outwood, and ask him to be good enough to come here for a moment."

CHAPTER LI

MAINLY ABOUT BOOTS

"Be quick, Smith," he said, as the latter stood looking at him without making any movement in the direction of the door.

"*Quick*, sir?" said Psmith meditatively, as if he had been asked a conundrum.

"Go and find Mr. Outwood at once."

Psmith still made no move.

"Do you intend to disobey me, Smith?" Mr. Downing's voice was steely.

"Yes, sir."

"What!"

"Yes, sir."

There was one of those you-could-have-heard-a-pin-drop silences.; Psmith was staring reflectively at the ceiling.; Mr. Downing was looking as if at any moment he might say, "Thwarted to me face, ha, ha!; And by a very stripling!"

It was Psmith, however, who resumed the conversation.; His manner was almost too respectful; which made it all the more a pity that what he said did not keep up the standard of docility.

"I take my stand," he said, "on a technical point.; I say to myself, 'Mr. Downing is a man I admire as a human being and respect as a master.; In ——'"

"This impertinence is doing you no good, Smith."

Psmith waved a hand deprecatingly.

"If you will let me explain, sir.; I was about to say that in any other place but Mr. Outwood's house, your word would be law.; I would fly to do your bidding.; If you pressed a button, I would do the rest.; But in Mr. Outwood's house I cannot do anything except what pleases me or what is ordered by Mr. Outwood.; I ought to have remembered that before.; One cannot," he continued, as who should say, "Let us be reasonable," "one cannot, to take a parallel case, imagine the colonel commanding the garrison at a naval station going on board a battleship and ordering the crew to splice the jibboom spanker.; It might be an admirable thing for the Empire that the jibboom spanker *should* be spliced at that particular juncture, but the crew would naturally decline to move in the matter until the order came from the commander of the ship.; So in my case.; If you will go to Mr. Outwood, and explain to him how matters stand, and come back and say to me, 'Psmith, Mr. Outwood wishes you to ask him to be good enough to come to this study,' then I shall be only too glad to go and find him.; You see my difficulty, sir?"

"Go and fetch Mr. Outwood, Smith.; I shall not tell you again."

Psmith flicked a speck of dust from his coat-sleeve.

"Very well, Smith."

"I can assure you, sir, at any rate, that if there is a boot in that cupboard now, there will be a boot there when you return."

Mr. Downing stalked out of the room.

"But," added Psmith pensively to himself, as the footsteps died away, "I did not promise that it would be the same boot."

He took the key from his pocket, unlocked the cupboard, and took out the boot.; Then he selected from the basket a particularly battered specimen.; Placing this in the cupboard, he re-locked the door.

His next act was to take from the shelf a piece of string.; Attaching one end of this to the boot that he had taken from the cupboard, he went to the window.; His first act was to fling the cupboard-key out into the bushes.; Then he turned to the boot.; On a level with the sill the water-pipe, up which Mike had started to climb the night before, was fastened to the wall by an iron band.; He tied the other end of the string to this, and let the boot swing free.; He noticed with approval, when it had stopped swinging, that it was hidden from above by the window-sill.

193

He returned to his place at the mantelpiece.

As an after-thought he took another boot from the basket, and thrust it up the chimney. A shower of soot fell into the grate, blackening his hand.

The bathroom was a few yards down the corridor. He went there, and washed off the soot.

When he returned, Mr. Downing was in the study, and with him Mr. Outwood, the latter looking dazed, as if he were not quite equal to the intellectual pressure of the situation.

"Where have you been, Smith?" asked Mr. Downing sharply.

"I have been washing my hands, sir."

"H'm!" said Mr. Downing suspiciously.

"Yes, I saw Smith go into the bathroom," said Mr. Outwood. "Smith, I cannot quite understand what it is Mr. Downing wishes me to do."

"My dear Outwood," snapped the sleuth, "I thought I had made it perfectly clear. Where is the difficulty?"

"I cannot understand why you should suspect Smith of keeping his boots in a cupboard, and," added Mr. Outwood with spirit, catching sight of a Good-Gracious-has-the-man-*no*-sense look on the other's face, "why he should not do so if he wishes it."

"Exactly, sir," said Psmith, approvingly. "You have touched the spot."

"If I must explain again, my dear Outwood, will you kindly give me your attention for a moment. Last night a boy broke out of your house, and painted my dog Sampson red."

"He painted —!" said Mr. Outwood, round-eyed. "Why?"

"I don't know why. At any rate, he did. During the escapade one of his boots was splashed with the paint. It is that boot which I believe Smith to be concealing in this cupboard. Now, do you understand?"

Mr. Outwood looked amazedly at Smith, and Psmith shook his head sorrowfully at Mr. Outwood. Psmith'a expression said, as plainly as if he had spoken the words, "We must humour him."

"So with your permission, as Smith declares that he has lost the key, I propose to break open the door of this cupboard. Have you any objection?"

Mr. Outwood started.

"Objection? None at all, my dear fellow, none at all. Let me see, *what* is it you wish to do?"

"This," said Mr. Downing shortly.

There was a pair of dumb-bells on the floor, belonging to Mike. He never used them, but they always managed to get themselves packed with the rest of his belongings on the last day of the holidays. Mr. Downing seized one of these, and delivered two rapid blows at the cupboard-door. The wood splintered. A third blow smashed the flimsy lock. The cupboard, with any skeletons it might contain, was open for all to view.

Mr. Downing uttered a cry of triumph, and tore the boot from its resting-place.

"I told you," he said. "I told you."

"I wondered where that boot had got to," said Psmith. "I've been looking for it for days."

Mr. Downing was examining his find. He looked up with an exclamation of surprise and wrath.

"This boot has no paint on it," he said, glaring at Psmith. "This is not the boot."

"It certainly appears, sir," said Psmith sympathetically, "to be free from paint. There's a sort of reddish glow just there, if you look at it sideways," he added helpfully.

"Did you place that boot there, Smith?"

"I must have done. Then, when I lost the key ——"

"Are you satisfied now, Downing?" interrupted Mr. Outwood with asperity, "or is there any more furniture you wish to break?"

The excitement of seeing his household goods smashed with a dumb-bell had made the archaeological student quite a swashbuckler for the moment. A little more, and one could imagine him giving Mr. Downing a good, hard knock.

The sleuth-hound stood still for a moment, baffled.; But his brain was working with the rapidity of a buzz-saw.; A chance remark of Mr. Outwood's set him fizzing off on the trail once more.; Mr. Outwood had caught sight of the little pile of soot in the grate.; He bent down to inspect it.

"Dear me," he said, "I must remember to have the chimneys swept.; It should have been done before."

Mr. Downing's eye, rolling in a fine frenzy from heaven to earth, from earth to heaven, also focussed itself on the pile of soot; and a thrill went through him.; Soot in the fireplace!; Smith washing his hands! ("You know my methods, my dear Watson.; Apply them.")

Mr. Downing's mind at that moment contained one single thought; and that thought was "What ho for the chimney!"

He dived forward with a rush, nearly knocking Mr. Outwood off his feet, and thrust an arm up into the unknown.; An avalanche of soot fell upon his hand and wrist, but he ignored it, for at the same instant his fingers had closed upon what he was seeking.

"Ah," he said.; "I thought as much.; You were not quite clever enough, after all, Smith."

"No, sir," said Psmith patiently.; "We all make mistakes."

"You would have done better, Smith, not to have given me all this trouble.; You have done yourself no good by it."

"It's been great fun, though, sir," argued Psmith.

"Fun!" Mr. Downing laughed grimly.; "You may have reason to change your opinion of what constitutes — —"

His voice failed as his eye fell on the all-black toe of the boot.; He looked up, and caught Psmith's benevolent gaze.; He straightened himself and brushed a bead of perspiration from his face with the back of his hand.; Unfortunately, he used the sooty hand, and the result was like some gruesome burlesque of a nigger minstrel.

"Did —you —put —that —boot —there, Smith?" he asked slowly.

"DID—YOU—PUT—THAT—BOOT—THERE, SMITH?"

"Yes, sir."
"Then what did you *MEAN* by putting it there?" roared Mr. Downing.
"Animal spirits, sir," said Psmith.
"WHAT!"
"Animal spirits, sir."

What Mr. Downing would have replied to this one cannot tell, though one can guess roughly.; For, just as he was opening his mouth, Mr. Outwood, catching sight of his Chirgwin-like countenance, intervened.

"My dear Downing," he said, "your face.; It is positively covered with soot, positively.; You must come and wash it.; You are quite black.; Really, you present a most curious appearance, most.; Let me show you the way to my room."

In all times of storm and tribulation there comes a breaking-point, a point where the spirit definitely refuses to battle any longer against the slings and arrows of outrageous fortune.; Mr. Downing could not bear up against this crowning blow.; He went down beneath it.; In the language of the Ring, he took the count.; It was the knock-out.

"Soot!" he murmured weakly.; "Soot!"

"Your face is covered, my dear fellow, quite covered."

"It certainly has a faintly sooty aspect, sir," said Psmith.

His voice roused the sufferer to one last flicker of spirit.

"You will hear more of this, Smith," he said.; "I say you will hear more of it."

Then he allowed Mr. Outwood to lead him out to a place where there were towels, soap, and sponges.

* * * * *

When they had gone, Psmith went to the window, and hauled in the string.; He felt the calm after-glow which comes to the general after a successfully conducted battle.; It had been trying, of course, for a man of refinement, and it had cut into his afternoon, but on the whole it had been worth it.

The problem now was what to do with the painted boot.; It would take a lot of cleaning, he saw, even if he could get hold of the necessary implements for cleaning it.; And he rather doubted if he would be able to do so.; Edmund, the boot-boy, worked in some mysterious cell, far from the madding crowd, at the back of the house.; In the boot-cupboard downstairs there would probably be nothing likely to be of any use.

His fears were realised.; The boot-cupboard was empty.; It seemed to him that, for the time being, the best thing he could do would be to place the boot in safe hiding, until he should have thought out a scheme.

Having restored the basket to its proper place, accordingly, he went up to the study again, and placed the red-toed boot in the chimney, at about the same height where Mr. Downing had found the other.; Nobody would think of looking there a second time, and it was improbable that Mr. Outwood really would have the chimneys swept, as he had said.; The odds were that he had forgotten about it already.

Psmith went to the bathroom to wash his hands again, with the feeling that he had done a good day's work.

CHAPTER LII

ON THE TRAIL AGAIN

The most massive minds are apt to forget things at times.; The most adroit plotters make their little mistakes.; Psmith was no exception to the rule.; He made the mistake of not telling Mike of the afternoon's happenings.

It was not altogether forgetfulness.; Psmith was one of those people who like to carry through their operations entirely by themselves.; Where there is only one in a secret the secret is more liable to remain unrevealed.; There was nothing, he thought, to be gained from telling Mike.; He forgot what the consequences might be if he did not.

So Psmith kept his own counsel, with the result that Mike went over to school on the Monday morning in pumps.

Edmund, summoned from the hinterland of the house to give his opinion why only one of Mike's boots was to be found, had no views on the subject.; He seemed to look on it as one of those things which no fellow can understand.

"'Ere's one of 'em, Mr. Jackson," he said, as if he hoped that Mike might be satisfied with a compromise.

"One?; What's the good of that, Edmund, you chump?; I can't go over to school in one boot."

Edmund turned this over in his mind, and then said, "No, sir," as much as to say, "I may have lost a boot, but, thank goodness, I can still understand sound reasoning."

"Well, what am I to do?; Where is the other boot?"

"Don't know, Mr. Jackson," replied Edmund to both questions.

"Well, I mean —Oh, dash it, there's the bell."

And Mike sprinted off in the pumps he stood in.

It is only a deviation from those ordinary rules of school life, which one observes naturally and without thinking, that enables one to realise how strong public-school prejudices really are.; At a school, for instance, where the regulations say that coats only of black or dark blue are to be worn, a boy who appears one day in even the most respectable and unostentatious brown finds himself looked on with a mixture of awe and repulsion, which would be excessive if he had sand-bagged the headmaster.; So in the case of boots.; School rules decree that a boy shall go to his form-room in boots, There is no real reason why, if the day is fine, he should not wear shoes, should he prefer them.; But, if he does, the thing creates a perfect sensation.; Boys say, "Great Scott, what *have* you got on?" Masters say, "Jones, *what* are you wearing on your feet?" In the few minutes which elapse between the assembling of the form for call-over and the arrival of the form-master, some wag is sure either to stamp on the shoes, accompanying the act with some satirical remark, or else to pull one of them off, and inaugurate an impromptu game of football with it.; There was once a boy who went to school one morning in elastic-sided boots....

Mike had always been coldly distant in his relations to the rest of his form, looking on them, with a few exceptions, as worms; and the form, since his innings against Downing's on the Friday, had regarded Mike with respect.; So that he escaped the ragging he would have had to undergo at Wrykyn in similar circumstances.; It was only Mr. Downing who gave trouble.

There is a sort of instinct which enables some masters to tell when a boy in their form is wearing shoes instead of boots, just as people who dislike cats always know when one is in a room with them.; They cannot see it, but they feel it in their bones.

Mr. Downing was perhaps the most bigoted anti-shoeist in the whole list of English schoolmasters.; He waged war remorselessly against shoes.; Satire, abuse, lines, detention —every weapon was employed by him in dealing with their wearers.; It had been the late Dunster's practice always to go over to school in shoes when, as he usually did, he felt shaky in the morning's lesson.; Mr. Downing always detected him in the first five minutes, and that meant a lecture of anything from ten minutes to a quarter of an hour on Untidy Habits and Boys Who Looked like Loafers—which broke the back of the morning's work nicely.; On one occasion, when a particularly tricky bit of Livy was on the bill of fare, Dunster had entered the form-room in heel-less Turkish bath-slippers, of a vivid crimson; and the subsequent proceedings, including his journey over to the house to change the heel-less atrocities, had seen him through very nearly to the quarter to eleven interval.

Mike, accordingly, had not been in his place for three minutes when Mr. Downing, stiffening like a pointer, called his name.

"Yes, sir?" said Mike.

"*What* are you wearing on your feet, Jackson?"

"Pumps, sir."

"You are wearing pumps?; Are you not aware that PUMPS are not the proper things to come to school in?; Why are you wearing *PUMPS*?"

The form, leaning back against the next row of desks, settled itself comfortably for the address from the throne.

"I have lost one of my boots, sir."

A kind of gulp escaped from Mr. Downing's lips.; He stared at Mike for a moment in silence.; Then, turning to Stone, he told him to start translating.

Stone, who had been expecting at least ten minutes' respite, was taken unawares.; When he found the place in his book and began to construe, he floundered hopelessly.; But, to his growing surprise and satisfaction, the form-master appeared to notice nothing wrong.; He said "Yes, yes," mechanically, and finally "That will do," whereupon Stone resumed his seat with the feeling that the age of miracles had returned.

Mr. Downing's mind was in a whirl.; His case was complete.; Mike's appearance in shoes, with the explanation that he had lost a boot, completed the chain.; As Columbus must have felt when his ship ran into harbour, and the first American interviewer, jumping on board, said, "Wal, sir, and what are your impressions of our glorious country?" so did Mr. Downing feel at that moment.

When the bell rang at a quarter to eleven, he gathered up his gown, and sped to the headmaster.

CHAPTER LIII

THE KETTLE METHOD

It was during the interval that day that Stone and Robinson, discussing the subject of cricket over a bun and ginger-beer at the school shop, came to a momentous decision, to wit, that they were fed up with Adair administration and meant to strike.; The immediate cause of revolt was early-morning fielding-practice, that searching test of cricket keenness.; Mike himself, to whom cricket was the great and serious interest of life, had shirked early-morning fielding-practice in his first term at Wrykyn.; And Stone and Robinson had but a luke-warm attachment to the game, compared with Mike's.

As a rule, Adair had contented himself with practice in the afternoon after school, which nobody objects to; and no strain, consequently, had been put upon Stone's and Robinson's allegiance.; In view of the M.C.C. match on the Wednesday, however, he had now added to this an extra dose to be taken before breakfast.; Stone and Robinson had left their comfortable beds that day at six o'clock, yawning and heavy-eyed, and had caught catches and fielded drives which, in the cool morning air, had stung like adders and bitten like serpents.; Until the sun has really got to work, it is no joke taking a high catch.; Stone's dislike of the experiment was only equalled by Robinson's.; They were neither of them of the type which likes to undergo hardships for the common good.; They played well enough when on the field, but neither cared greatly whether the school had a good season or not.; They played the game entirely for their own sakes.

The result was that they went back to the house for breakfast with a never-again feeling, and at the earliest possible moment met to debate as to what was to be done about it.; At all costs another experience like to-day's must be avoided.

"It's all rot," said Stone.; "What on earth's the good of sweating about before breakfast?; It only makes you tired."

"I shouldn't wonder," said Robinson, "if it wasn't bad for the heart.; Rushing about on an empty stomach, I mean, and all that sort of thing."

"Personally," said Stone, gnawing his bun, "I don't intend to stick it."

"Nor do I."

"I mean, it's such absolute rot.; If we aren't good enough to play for the team without having to get up overnight to catch catches, he'd better find somebody else."

"Yes."

At this moment Adair came into the shop.

"Fielding-practice again to-morrow," he said briskly, "at six."

"Before breakfast?" said Robinson.

"Rather.; You two must buck up, you know.; You were rotten to-day."; And he passed on, leaving the two malcontents speechless.

Stone was the first to recover.

"I'm hanged if I turn out to-morrow," he said, as they left the shop.;"He can do what he likes about it.; Besides, what can he do, after all?; Only kick us out of the team.; And I don't mind that."

"Nor do I."

"I don't think he will kick us out, either.; He can't play the M.C.C. with a scratch team.; If he does, we'll go and play for that village Jackson plays for.; We'll get Jackson to shove us into the team."

"All right," said Robinson.; "Let's."

Their position was a strong one.; A cricket captain may seem to be an autocrat of tremendous power, but in reality he has only one weapon, the keenness of those under him.; With the majority, of course, the fear of being excluded or ejected from a team is a spur that drives.;

200

The majority, consequently, are easily handled.; But when a cricket captain runs up against a boy who does not much care whether he plays for the team or not, then he finds himself in a difficult position, and, unless he is a man of action, practically helpless.

Stone and Robinson felt secure.; Taking it all round, they felt that they would just as soon play for Lower Borlock as for the school.; The bowling of the opposition would be weaker in the former case, and the chance of making runs greater.; To a certain type of cricketer runs are runs, wherever and however made.

The result of all this was that Adair, turning out with the team next morning for fielding-practice, found himself two short.; Barnes was among those present, but of the other two representatives of Outwood's house there were no signs.

Barnes, questioned on the subject, had no information to give, beyond the fact that he had not seen them about anywhere.; Which was not a great help.; Adair proceeded with the fielding-practice without further delay.

At breakfast that morning he was silent and apparently wrapped in thought.; Mr. Downing, who sat at the top of the table with Adair on his right, was accustomed at the morning meal to blend nourishment of the body with that of the mind.; As a rule he had ten minutes with the daily paper before the bell rang, and it was his practice to hand on the results of his reading to Adair and the other house-prefects, who, not having seen the paper, usually formed an interested and appreciative audience.; To-day, however, though the house-prefects expressed varying degrees of excitement at the news that Tyldesley had made a century against Gloucestershire, and that a butter famine was expected in the United States, these world-shaking news-items seemed to leave Adair cold.; He champed his bread and marmalade with an abstracted air.

He was wondering what to do in this matter of Stone and Robinson.

Many captains might have passed the thing over.; To take it for granted that the missing pair had overslept themselves would have been a safe and convenient way out of the difficulty.; But Adair was not the sort of person who seeks for safe and convenient ways out of difficulties.; He never shirked anything, physical or moral.

He resolved to interview the absentees.

It was not until after school that an opportunity offered itself.; He went across to Outwood's and found the two non-starters in the senior day-room, engaged in the intellectual pursuit of kicking the wall and marking the height of each kick with chalk.; Adair's entrance coincided with a record effort by Stone, which caused the kicker to overbalance and stagger backwards against the captain.

"Sorry," said Stone.; "Hullo, Adair!"

"Don't mention it.; Why weren't you two at fielding-practice this morning?"

Robinson, who left the lead to Stone in all matters, said nothing.; Stone spoke.

"We didn't turn up," he said.

"I know you didn't.; Why not?"

Stone had rehearsed this scene in his mind, and he spoke with the coolness which comes from rehearsal.

"We decided not to."

"Oh?"

"Yes.; We came to the conclusion that we hadn't any use for early-morning fielding."

Adair's manner became ominously calm.

"You were rather fed-up, I suppose?"

"That's just the word."

"Sorry it bored you."

"It didn't.; We didn't give it the chance to."

Robinson laughed appreciatively.

"What's the joke, Robinson?" asked Adair.

"There's no joke," said Robinson, with some haste.; "I was only thinking of something."

"I'll give you something else to think about soon."

Stone intervened.

"It's no good making a row about it, Adair.; You must see that you can't do anything.; Of course, you can kick us out of the team, if you like, but we don't care if you do.; Jackson will get us a game any Wednesday or Saturday for the village he plays for.; So we're all right.; And the school team aren't such a lot of flyers that you can afford to go chucking people out of it whenever you want to.; See what I mean?"

"You and Jackson seem to have fixed it all up between you."

"What are you going to do?; Kick us out?"

"No."

"Good.; I thought you'd see it was no good making a beastly row.; We'll play for the school all right.; There's no earthly need for us to turn out for fielding-practice before breakfast."

"You don't think there is?; You may be right.; All the same, you're going to to-morrow morning."

"What!"

"Six sharp.; Don't be late."

"Don't be an ass, Adair.; We've told you we aren't going to."

"That's only your opinion.; I think you are.; I'll give you till five past six, as you seem to like lying in bed."

"You can turn out if you feel like it.; You won't find me there."

"That'll be a disappointment.; Nor Robinson?"

"No," said the junior partner in the firm; but he said it without any deep conviction.; The atmosphere was growing a great deal too tense for his comfort.

"You've quite made up your minds?"

"Yes," said Stone.

"Right," said Adair quietly, and knocked him down.

He was up again in a moment.; Adair had pushed the table back, and was standing in the middle of the open space.

"You cad," said Stone.; "I wasn't ready."

"Well, you are now.; Shall we go on?"

Stone dashed in without a word, and for a few moments the two might have seemed evenly matched to a not too intelligent spectator.; But science tells, even in a confined space.; Adair was smaller and lighter than Stone, but he was cooler and quicker, and he knew more about the game.; His blow was always home a fraction of a second sooner than his opponent's.; At the end of a minute Stone was on the floor again.

He got up slowly and stood leaning with one hand on the table.

"Suppose we say ten past six?" said Adair.; "I'm not particular to a minute or two."

Stone made no reply.

"Will ten past six suit you for fielding-practice to-morrow?" said Adair.

"All right," said Stone.

"Thanks.; How about you, Robinson?"

Robinson had been a petrified spectator of the Captain-Kettle-like manoeuvres of the cricket captain, and it did not take him long to make up his mind.; He was not altogether a coward.; In different circumstances he might have put up a respectable show.; But it takes a more than ordinarily courageous person to embark on a fight which he knows must end in his destruction.; Robinson knew that he was nothing like a match even for Stone, and Adair had disposed of Stone in a little over one minute.; It seemed to Robinson that neither pleasure nor profit was likely to come from an encounter with Adair.

"All right," he said hastily, "I'll turn up."

"Good," said Adair.; "I wonder if either of you chaps could tell me which is Jackson's study."

Stone was dabbing at his mouth with a handkerchief, a task which precluded anything in the shape of conversation; so Robinson replied that Mike's study was the first you came to on the right of the corridor at the top of the stairs.

"Thanks," said Adair.; "You don't happen to know if he's in, I suppose?"

"He went up with Smith a quarter of an hour ago.; I don't know if he's still there."

"I'll go and see," said Adair.; "I should like a word with him if he isn't busy."

CHAPTER LIV

ADAIR HAS A WORD WITH MIKE

Mike, all unconscious of the stirring proceedings which had been going on below stairs, was peacefully reading a letter he had received that morning from Strachan at Wrykyn, in which the successor to the cricket captaincy which should have been Mike's had a good deal to say in a lugubrious strain.; In Mike's absence things had been going badly with Wrykyn.; A broken arm, contracted in the course of some rash experiments with a day-boy's motor-bicycle, had deprived the team of the services of Dunstable, the only man who had shown any signs of being able to bowl a side out.; Since this calamity, wrote Strachan, everything had gone wrong.; The M.C.C., led by Mike's brother Reggie, the least of the three first-class-cricketing Jacksons, had smashed them by a hundred and fifty runs.; Geddington had wiped them off the face of the earth.; The Incogs, with a team recruited exclusively from the rabbit-hutch —not a well-known man on the side except Stacey, a veteran who had been playing for the club since Fuller Pilch's time —had got home by two wickets.; In fact, it was Strachan's opinion that the Wrykyn team that summer was about the most hopeless gang of dead-beats that had ever made an exhibition of itself on the school grounds.; The Ripton match, fortunately, was off, owing to an outbreak of mumps at that shrine of learning and athletics —the second outbreak of the malady in two terms.; Which, said Strachan, was hard lines on Ripton, but a bit of jolly good luck for Wrykyn, as it had saved them from what would probably have been a record hammering, Ripton having eight of their last year's team left, including Dixon, the fast bowler, against whom Mike alone of the Wrykyn team had been able to make runs in the previous season.; Altogether, Wrykyn had struck a bad patch.

Mike mourned over his suffering school.; If only he could have been there to help.; It might have made all the difference.; In school cricket one good batsman, to go in first and knock the bowlers off their length, may take a weak team triumphantly through a season.; In school cricket the importance of a good start for the first wicket is incalculable.

As he put Strachan's letter away in his pocket, all his old bitterness against Sedleigh, which had been ebbing during the past few days, returned with a rush.; He was conscious once more of that feeling of personal injury which had made him hate his new school on the first day of term.

And it was at this point, when his resentment was at its height, that Adair, the concrete representative of everything Sedleighan, entered the room.

There are moments in life's placid course when there has got to be the biggest kind of row.; This was one of them.

* * * * *

Psmith, who was leaning against the mantelpiece, reading the serial story in a daily paper which he had abstracted from the senior day-room, made the intruder free of the study with a dignified wave of the hand, and went on reading.; Mike remained in the deck-chair in which he was sitting, and contented himself with glaring at the newcomer.

Psmith was the first to speak.

"If you ask my candid opinion," he said, looking up from his paper, "I should say that young Lord Antony Trefusis was in the soup already.; I seem to see the *consommé* splashing about his ankles.; He's had a note telling him to be under the oak-tree in the Park at midnight.; He's just off there at the end of this instalment.; I bet Long Jack, the poacher, is waiting there with a sandbag.; Care to see the paper, Comrade Adair?; Or don't you take any interest in contemporary literature?"

"Thanks," said Adair.; "I just wanted to speak to Jackson for a minute."

"Fate," said Psmith, "has led your footsteps to the right place.; That is Comrade Jackson, the Pride of the School, sitting before you."

"What do you want?" said Mike.

He suspected that Adair had come to ask him once again to play for the school.; The fact that the M.C.C. match was on the following day made this a probable solution of the reason for his visit.; He could think of no other errand that was likely to have set the head of Downing's paying afternoon calls.

"I'll tell you in a minute.; It won't take long."

"That," said Psmith approvingly, "is right.; Speed is the key-note of the present age.; Promptitude.; Despatch.; This is no time for loitering.; We must be strenuous.; We must hustle.; We must Do It Now.; We ——"

"Buck up," said Mike.

"Certainly," said Adair.; "I've just been talking to Stone and Robinson."

"An excellent way of passing an idle half-hour," said Psmith.

"We weren't exactly idle," said Adair grimly.; "It didn't last long, but it was pretty lively while it did.; Stone chucked it after the first round."

Mike got up out of his chair.; He could not quite follow what all this was about, but there was no mistaking the truculence of Adair's manner.; For some reason, which might possibly be made clear later, Adair was looking for trouble, and Mike in his present mood felt that it would be a privilege to see that he got it.

Psmith was regarding Adair through his eyeglass with pain and surprise.

"Surely," he said, "you do not mean us to understand that you have been *brawling* with Comrade Stone!; This is bad hearing.; I thought that you and he were like brothers.; Such a bad example for Comrade Robinson, too.; Leave us, Adair.; We would brood.; Oh, go thee, knave, I'll none of thee.; Shakespeare."

Psmith turned away, and resting his elbows on the mantelpiece, gazed at himself mournfully in the looking-glass.

"I'm not the man I was," he sighed, after a prolonged inspection.; "There are lines on my face, dark circles beneath my eyes.; The fierce rush of life at Sedleigh is wasting me away."

"Stone and I had a discussion about early-morning fielding-practice," said Adair, turning to Mike.

Mike said nothing.

"I thought his fielding wanted working up a bit, so I told him to turn out at six to-morrow morning.; He said he wouldn't, so we argued it out.; He's going to all right.; So is Robinson."

Mike remained silent.

"So are you," added Adair.

"I get thinner and thinner," said Psmith from the mantelpiece.

Mike looked at Adair, and Adair looked at Mike, after the manner of two dogs before they fly at one another.; There was an electric silence in the study.; Psmith peered with increased earnestness into the glass.

"Oh?" said Mike at last.; "What makes you think that?"

"I don't think.; I know."

"Any special reason for my turning out?"

"Yes."

"What's that?"

"You're going to play for the school against the M.C.C. to-morrow, and I want you to get some practice."

"I wonder how you got that idea!"

"Curious I should have done, isn't it?"

"Very.; You aren't building on it much, are you?" said Mike politely.

"I am, rather," replied Adair with equal courtesy.

"I'm afraid you'll be disappointed."

"I don't think so."

"My eyes," said Psmith regretfully, "are a bit close together.; However," he added philosophically, "it's too late to alter that now."

Mike drew a step closer to Adair.

"What makes you think I shall play against the M.C.C.?" he asked curiously.

"I'm going to make you."

Mike took another step forward.; Adair moved to meet him.

"Would you care to try now?" said Mike.

For just one second the two drew themselves together preparatory to beginning the serious business of the interview, and in that second Psmith, turning from the glass, stepped between them.

"Get out of the light, Smith," said Mike.

Psmith waved him back with a deprecating gesture.

"My dear young friends," he said placidly, "if you *will* let your angry passions rise, against the direct advice of Doctor Watts, I suppose you must, But when you propose to claw each other in my study, in the midst of a hundred fragile and priceless ornaments, I lodge a protest.; If you really feel that you want to scrap, for goodness sake do it where there's some room.; I don't want all the study furniture smashed.; I know a bank whereon the wild thyme grows, only a few yards down the road, where you can scrap all night if you want to.; How would it be to move on there?; Any objections?; None?; Then shift ho! and let's get it over."

CHAPTER LV

CLEARING THE AIR

Psmith was one of those people who lend a dignity to everything they touch.; Under his auspices the most unpromising ventures became somehow enveloped in an atmosphere of measured stateliness.; On the present occasion, what would have been, without his guiding hand, a mere unscientific scramble, took on something of the impressive formality of the National Sporting Club.

"The rounds," he said, producing a watch, as they passed through a gate into a field a couple of hundred yards from the house gate, "will be of three minutes' duration, with a minute rest in between.; A man who is down will have ten seconds in which to rise.; Are you ready, Comrades Adair and Jackson?; Very well, then.; Time."

After which, it was a pity that the actual fight did not quite live up to its referee's introduction.; Dramatically, there should have been cautious sparring for openings and a number of tensely contested rounds, as if it had been the final of a boxing competition.; But school fights, when they do occur—which is only once in a decade nowadays, unless you count junior school scuffles—are the outcome of weeks of suppressed bad blood, and are consequently brief and furious.; In a boxing competition, however much one may want to win, one does not dislike one's opponent.; Up to the moment when "time" was called, one was probably warmly attached to him, and at the end of the last round one expects to resume that attitude of mind.; In a fight each party, as a rule, hates the other.

So it happened that there was nothing formal or cautious about the present battle.; All Adair wanted was to get at Mike, and all Mike wanted was to get at Adair.; Directly Psmith called "time," they rushed together as if they meant to end the thing in half a minute.

It was this that saved Mike.; In an ordinary contest with the gloves, with his opponent cool and boxing in his true form, he could not have lasted three rounds against Adair.; The latter was a clever boxer, while Mike had never had a lesson in his life.; If Adair had kept away and used his head, nothing could have prevented him winning.

As it was, however, he threw away his advantages, much as Tom Brown did at the beginning of his fight with Slogger Williams, and the result was the same as on that historic occasion.; Mike had the greater strength, and, thirty seconds from the start, knocked his man clean off his feet with an unscientific but powerful right-hander.

This finished Adair's chances.; He rose full of fight, but with all the science knocked out of him.; He went in at Mike with both hands.; The Irish blood in him, which for the ordinary events of life made him merely energetic and dashing, now rendered him reckless.; He abandoned all attempt at guarding.; It was the Frontal Attack in its most futile form, and as unsuccessful as a frontal attack is apt to be.; There was a swift exchange of blows, in the course of which Mike's left elbow, coming into contact with his opponent's right fist, got a shock which kept it tingling for the rest of the day; and then Adair went down in a heap.

He got up slowly and with difficulty.; For a moment he stood blinking vaguely.; Then he lurched forward at Mike.

In the excitement of a fight—which is, after all, about the most exciting thing that ever happens to one in the course of one's life—it is difficult for the fighters to see what the spectators see.; Where the spectators see an assault on an already beaten man, the fighter himself only sees a legitimate piece of self-defence against an opponent whose chances are equal to his own.; Psmith saw, as anybody looking on would have seen, that Adair was done.; Mike's blow had taken him within a fraction of an inch of the point of the jaw, and he was all but knocked out.; Mike could not see this.; All he understood was that his man was on his feet again and coming at him, so he hit out with all his strength; and this time Adair went down and stayed down.

"Brief," said Psmith, coming forward, "but exciting.; We may take that, I think, to be the conclusion of the entertainment.; I will now have a dash at picking up the slain.; I shouldn't stop, if I were you.; He'll be sitting up and taking notice soon, and if he sees you he may want to go on with the combat, which would do him no earthly good.; If it's going to be continued in our next, there had better be a bit of an interval for alterations and repairs first."

"Is he hurt much, do you think?" asked Mike.; He had seen knock-outs before in the ring, but this was the first time he had ever effected one on his own account, and Adair looked unpleasantly corpse-like.

"*He's* all right," said Psmith.; "In a minute or two he'll be skipping about like a little lambkin.; I'll look after him.; You go away and pick flowers."

Mike put on his coat and walked back to the house.; He was conscious of a perplexing whirl of new and strange emotions, chief among which was a curious feeling that he rather liked Adair.; He found himself thinking that Adair was a good chap, that there was something to be said for his point of view, and that it was a pity he had knocked him about so much.; At the same time, he felt an undeniable thrill of pride at having beaten him.; The feat presented that interesting person, Mike Jackson, to him in a fresh and pleasing light, as one who had had a tough job to face and had carried it through.; Jackson, the cricketer, he knew, but Jackson, the deliverer of knock-out blows, was strange to him, and he found this new acquaintance a man to be respected.

The fight, in fact, had the result which most fights have, if they are fought fairly and until one side has had enough.; It revolutionised Mike's view of things.; It shook him up, and drained the bad blood out of him.; Where, before, he had seemed to himself to be acting with massive dignity, he now saw that he had simply been sulking like some wretched kid.; There had appeared to him something rather fine in his policy of refusing to identify himself in any way with Sedleigh, a touch of the stone-walls-do-not-a-prison-make sort of thing.; He now saw that his attitude was to be summed up in the words, "Sha'n't play."

It came upon Mike with painful clearness that he had been making an ass of himself.

He had come to this conclusion, after much earnest thought, when Psmith entered the study.

"How's Adair?" asked Mike.

"Sitting up and taking nourishment once more.; We have been chatting.; He's not a bad cove."

"He's all right," said Mike.

There was a pause.; Psmith straightened his tie.

"Look here," he said, "I seldom interfere in terrestrial strife, but it seems to me that there's an opening here for a capable peace-maker, not afraid of work, and willing to give his services in exchange for a comfortable home.; Comrade Adair's rather a stoutish fellow in his way.; I'm not much on the 'Play up for the old school, Jones,' game, but every one to his taste.; I shouldn't have thought anybody would get overwhelmingly attached to this abode of wrath, but Comrade Adair seems to have done it.; He's all for giving Sedleigh a much-needed boost-up.; It's not a bad idea in its way.; I don't see why one shouldn't humour him.; Apparently he's been sweating since early childhood to buck the school up.; And as he's leaving at the end of the term, it mightn't be a scaly scheme to give him a bit of a send-off, if possible, by making the cricket season a bit of a banger.; As a start, why not drop him a line to say that you'll play against the M.C.C. to-morrow?"

Mike did not reply at once.; He was feeling better disposed towards Adair and Sedleigh than he had felt, but he was not sure that he was quite prepared to go as far as a complete climb-down.

"It wouldn't be a bad idea," continued Psmith; "There's nothing like giving a man a bit in every now and then.; It broadens the soul and improves the action of the skin.; What seems to have fed up Comrade Adair, to a certain extent, is that Stone apparently led him to understand that you had offered to give him and Robinson places in your village team.; You didn't, of course?"

"Of course not," said Mike indignantly.

"I told him he didn't know the old *noblesse oblige* spirit of the Jacksons.; I said that you would scorn to tarnish the Jackson escutcheon by not playing the game.; My eloquence convinced him.; However, to return to the point under discussion, why not?"

"I don't—What I mean to say—" began Mike.

"If your trouble is," said Psmith, "that you fear that you may be in unworthy company———"

"Don't be an ass."

"———Dismiss it. *I* am playing."

Mike stared.

"You're what?; You?"

"I," said Psmith, breathing on a coat-button, and polishing it with his handkerchief.

"Can you play cricket?"

"You have discovered," said Psmith, "my secret sorrow."

"You're rotting."

"You wrong me, Comrade Jackson."

"Then why haven't you played?"

"Why haven't you?"

"Why didn't you come and play for Lower Borlock, I mean?"

"The last time I played in a village cricket match I was caught at point by a man in braces.; It would have been madness to risk another such shock to my system.; My nerves are so exquisitely balanced that a thing of that sort takes years off my life."

"No, but look here, Smith, bar rotting.; Are you really any good at cricket?"

"Competent judges at Eton gave me to understand so.; I was told that this year I should be a certainty for Lord's.; But when the cricket season came, where was I?; Gone.; Gone like some beautiful flower that withers in the night."

"But you told me you didn't like cricket.; You said you only liked watching it."

"Quite right.; I do.; But at schools where cricket is compulsory you have to overcome your private prejudices.; And in time the thing becomes a habit.; Imagine my feelings when I found that I was degenerating, little by little, into a slow left-hand bowler with a swerve.; I fought against it, but it was useless, and after a while I gave up the struggle, and drifted with the stream.; Last year, in a house match"—Psmith's voice took on a deeper tone of melancholy—"I took seven for thirteen in the second innings on a hard wicket.; I did think, when I came here, that I had found a haven of rest, but it was not to be.; I turn out to-morrow.; What Comrade Outwood will say, when he finds that his keenest archaeological disciple has deserted, I hate to think.; However———"

Mike felt as if a young and powerful earthquake had passed.; The whole face of his world had undergone a quick change.; Here was he, the recalcitrant, wavering on the point of playing for the school, and here was Psmith, the last person whom he would have expected to be a player, stating calmly that he had been in the running for a place in the Eton eleven.

Then in a flash Mike understood.; He was not by nature intuitive, but he read Psmith's mind now.; Since the term began, he and Psmith had been acting on precisely similar motives.; Just as he had been disappointed of the captaincy of cricket at Wrykyn, so had Psmith been disappointed of his place in the Eton team at Lord's.; And they had both worked it off, each in his own way—Mike sullenly, Psmith whimsically, according to their respective natures—on Sedleigh.

If Psmith, therefore, did not consider it too much of a climb-down to renounce his resolution not to play for Sedleigh, there was nothing to stop Mike doing so, as—at the bottom of his heart—he wanted to do.

"By Jove," he said, "if you're playing, I'll play.; I'll write a note to Adair now.; But, I say—" he stopped—"I'm hanged if I'm going to turn out and field before breakfast to-morrow."

"That's all right.; You won't have to.; Adair won't be there himself.; He's not playing against the M.C.C.; He's sprained his wrist."

CHAPTER LVI

IN WHICH PEACE IS DECLARED

"Sprained his wrist?" said Mike.; "How did he do that?"

"During the brawl.; Apparently one of his efforts got home on your elbow instead of your expressive countenance, and whether it was that your elbow was particularly tough or his wrist particularly fragile, I don't know.; Anyhow, it went.; It's nothing bad, but it'll keep him out of the game to-morrow."

"I say, what beastly rough luck!; I'd no idea.; I'll go round."

"Not a bad scheme.; Close the door gently after you, and if you see anybody downstairs who looks as if he were likely to be going over to the shop, ask him to get me a small pot of some rare old jam and tell the man to chalk it up to me.; The jam Comrade Outwood supplies to us at tea is all right as a practical joke or as a food for those anxious to commit suicide, but useless to anybody who values life."

On arriving at Mr. Downing's and going to Adair's study, Mike found that his late antagonist was out.; He left a note informing him of his willingness to play in the morrow's match.; The lock-up bell rang as he went out of the house.

A spot of rain fell on his hand.; A moment later there was a continuous patter, as the storm, which had been gathering all day, broke in earnest.; Mike turned up his coat-collar, and ran back to Outwood's.; "At this rate," he said to himself, "there won't be a match at all to-morrow."

* * * * *

When the weather decides, after behaving well for some weeks, to show what it can do in another direction, it does the thing thoroughly.; When Mike woke the next morning the world was grey and dripping.; Leaden-coloured clouds drifted over the sky, till there was not a trace of blue to be seen, and then the rain began again, in the gentle, determined way rain has when it means to make a day of it.

It was one of those bad days when one sits in the pavilion, damp and depressed, while figures in mackintoshes, with discoloured buckskin boots, crawl miserably about the field in couples.

Mike, shuffling across to school in a Burberry, met Adair at Downing's gate.

These moments are always difficult.; Mike stopped —he could hardly walk on as if nothing had happened —and looked down at his feet.

"Coming across?" he said awkwardly.

"Right ho!" said Adair.

They walked on in silence.

"It's only about ten to, isn't it?" said Mike.

Adair fished out his watch, and examined it with an elaborate care born of nervousness.

"About nine to."

"Good.; We've got plenty of time."

"Yes."

"I hate having to hurry over to school."

"So do I."

"I often do cut it rather fine, though."

"Yes.; So do I."

"Beastly nuisance when one does."

"Beastly."

"It's only about a couple of minutes from the houses to the school, I should think, shouldn't you?"

"Not much more.; Might be three."

"Yes.; Three if one didn't hurry."

"Oh, yes, if one didn't hurry."

Another silence.

"Beastly day," said Adair.

"Rotten."

Silence again.

"I say," said Mike, scowling at his toes, "awfully sorry about your wrist."

"Oh, that's all right.; It was my fault."

"Does it hurt?"

"Oh, no, rather not, thanks."

"I'd no idea you'd crocked yourself."

"Oh, no, that's all right.; It was only right at the end.; You'd have smashed me anyhow."

"Oh, rot."

"I bet you anything you like you would."

"I bet you I shouldn't....; Jolly hard luck, just before the match."

"Oh, no....; I say, thanks awfully for saying you'd play."

"Oh, rot....; Do you think we shall get a game?"

Adair inspected the sky carefully.

"I don't know.; It looks pretty bad, doesn't it?"

"Rotten.; I say, how long will your wrist keep you out of cricket?"

"Be all right in a week.; Less, probably."

"Good."

"Now that you and Smith are going to play, we ought to have a jolly good season."

"Rummy, Smith turning out to be a cricketer."

"Yes.; I should think he'd be a hot bowler, with his height."

"He must be jolly good if he was only just out of the Eton team last year."

"Yes."

"What's the time?" asked Mike.

Adair produced his watch once more.

"Five to."

"We've heaps of time."

"Yes, heaps."

"Let's stroll on a bit down the road, shall we?"

"Right ho!"

Mike cleared his throat.

"I say."

"Hullo?"

"I've been talking to Smith.; He was telling me that you thought I'd promised to give Stone and Robinson places in the ——"

"Oh, no, that's all right.; It was only for a bit.; Smith told me you couldn't have done, and I saw that I was an ass to think you could have.; It was Stone seeming so dead certain that he could play for Lower Borlock if I chucked him from the school team that gave me the idea."

"He never even asked me to get him a place."

"No, I know."

"Of course, I wouldn't have done it, even if he had."

"Of course not."

"I didn't want to play myself, but I wasn't going to do a rotten trick like getting other fellows away from the team."

"No, I know."

"It was rotten enough, really, not playing myself."

"Oh, no.; Beastly rough luck having to leave Wrykyn just when you were going to be captain, and come to a small school like this."

The excitement of the past few days must have had a stimulating effect on Mike's mind — shaken it up, as it were:; for now, for the second time in two days, he displayed quite a creditable amount of intuition.; He might have been misled by Adair's apparently deprecatory attitude towards Sedleigh, and blundered into a denunciation of the place.; Adair had said "a small school like this" in the sort of voice which might have led his hearer to think that he was expected to say, "Yes, rotten little hole, isn't it?" or words to that effect.; Mike, fortunately, perceived that the words were used purely from politeness, on the Chinese principle.; When a Chinaman wishes to pay a compliment, he does so by belittling himself and his belongings.

He eluded the pitfall.

"What rot!" he said.; "Sedleigh's one of the most sporting schools I've ever come across.; Everybody's as keen as blazes.; So they ought to be, after the way you've sweated."

Adair shuffled awkwardly.

"I've always been fairly keen on the place," he said.; "But I don't suppose I've done anything much."

"You've loosened one of my front teeth," said Mike, with a grin, "if that's any comfort to you."

"I couldn't eat anything except porridge this morning.; My jaw still aches."

For the first time during the conversation their eyes met, and the humorous side of the thing struck them simultaneously.; They began to laugh.

"What fools we must have looked!" said Adair.

"*You* were all right.; I must have looked rotten.; I've never had the gloves on in my life.; I'm jolly glad no one saw us except Smith, who doesn't count.; Hullo, there's the bell.; We'd better be moving on.; What about this match?; Not much chance of it from the look of the sky at present."

"It might clear before eleven.; You'd better get changed, anyhow, at the interval, and hang about in case."

"All right.; It's better than doing Thucydides with Downing.; We've got math, till the interval, so I don't see anything of him all day; which won't hurt me."

"He isn't a bad sort of chap, when you get to know him," said Adair.

"I can't have done, then.; I don't know which I'd least soon be, Downing or a black-beetle, except that if one was Downing one could tread on the black-beetle.; Dash this rain.; I got about half a pint down my neck just then.; We sha'n't get a game to-day, of anything like it.; As you're crocked, I'm not sure that I care much.; You've been sweating for years to get the match on, and it would be rather rot playing it without you."

"I don't know that so much.; I wish we could play, because I'm certain, with you and Smith, we'd walk into them.; They probably aren't sending down much of a team, and really, now that you and Smith are turning out, we've got a jolly hot lot.; There's quite decent batting all the way through, and the bowling isn't so bad.; If only we could have given this M.C.C. lot a really good hammering, it might have been easier to get some good fixtures for next season.; You see, it's all right for a school like Wrykyn, but with a small place like this you simply can't get the best teams to give you a match till you've done something to show that you aren't absolute rotters at the game.; As for the schools, they're worse.; They'd simply laugh at you.; You were cricket secretary at Wrykyn last year.; What would you have done if you'd had a challenge from Sedleigh?; You'd either have laughed till you were sick, or else had a fit at the mere idea of the thing."

Mike stopped.

"By Jove, you've struck about the brightest scheme on record.; I never thought of it before.; Let's get a match on with Wrykyn."

"What!; They wouldn't play us."

"Yes, they would.; At least, I'm pretty sure they would.; I had a letter from Strachan, the captain, yesterday, saying that the Ripton match had had to be scratched owing to illness.; So they've got a vacant date.; Shall I try them?; I'll write to Strachan to-night, if you like.; And they aren't strong this year.; We'll smash them.; What do you say?"

Adair was as one who has seen a vision.
"By Jove," he said at last, "if we only could!"

CHAPTER LVII

MR. DOWNING MOVES

The rain continued without a break all the morning.; The two teams, after hanging about dismally, and whiling the time away with stump-cricket in the changing-rooms, lunched in the pavilion at one o'clock.; After which the M.C.C. captain, approaching Adair, moved that this merry meeting be considered off and himself and his men permitted to catch the next train back to town.; To which Adair, seeing that it was out of the question that there should be any cricket that afternoon, regretfully agreed, and the first Sedleigh *v.*; M.C.C. match was accordingly scratched.

Mike and Psmith, wandering back to the house, were met by a damp junior from Downing's, with a message that Mr. Downing wished to see Mike as soon as he was changed.

"What's he want me for?" inquired Mike.

The messenger did not know.; Mr. Downing, it seemed, had not confided in him.; All he knew was that the housemaster was in the house, and would be glad if Mike would step across.

"A nuisance," said Psmith, "this incessant demand for you.; That's the worst of being popular.; If he wants you to stop to tea, edge away.; A meal on rather a sumptuous scale will be prepared in the study against your return."

Mike changed quickly, and went off, leaving Psmith, who was fond of simple pleasures in his spare time, earnestly occupied with a puzzle which had been scattered through the land by a weekly paper.; The prize for a solution was one thousand pounds, and Psmith had already informed Mike with some minuteness of his plans for the disposition of this sum.; Meanwhile, he worked at it both in and out of school, generally with abusive comments on its inventor.

He was still fiddling away at it when Mike returned.

Mike, though Psmith was at first too absorbed to notice it, was agitated.

"I don't wish to be in any way harsh," said Psmith, without looking up, "but the man who invented this thing was a blighter of the worst type.; You come and have a shot.; For the moment I am baffled.; The whisper flies round the clubs, 'Psmith is baffled.'"

"The man's an absolute drivelling ass," said Mike warmly.

"Me, do you mean?"

"What on earth would be the point of my doing it?"

"You'd gather in a thousand of the best.; Give you a nice start in life."

"I'm not talking about your rotten puzzle."

"What are you talking about?"

"That ass Downing.; I believe he's off his nut."

"Then your chat with Comrade Downing was not of the old-College-chums-meeting-unexpectedly-after-years'-separation type?; What has he been doing to you?"

"He's off his nut."

"I know.; But what did he do?; How did the brainstorm burst?; Did he jump at you from behind a door and bite a piece out of your leg, or did he say he was a tea-pot?"

Mike sat down.

"You remember that painting Sammy business?"

"As if it were yesterday," said Psmith.; "Which it was, pretty nearly."

"He thinks I did it."

"Why?; Have you ever shown any talent in the painting line?"

"The silly ass wanted me to confess that I'd done it.; He as good as asked me to.; Jawed a lot of rot about my finding it to my advantage later on if I behaved sensibly."

"Then what are you worrying about?; Don't you know that when a master wants you to do the confessing-act, it simply means that he hasn't enough evidence to start in on you with?; You're all right.; The thing's a stand-off."

"Evidence!" said Mike, "My dear man, he's got enough evidence to sink a ship.; He's absolutely sweating evidence at every pore.; As far as I can see, he's been crawling about, doing the Sherlock Holmes business for all he's worth ever since the thing happened, and now he's dead certain that I painted Sammy."

"*Did* you, by the way?" asked Psmith.

"No," said Mike shortly, "I didn't.; But after listening to Downing I almost began to wonder if I hadn't.; The man's got stacks of evidence to prove that I did."

"Such as what?"

"It's mostly about my boots.; But, dash it, you know all about that.; Why, you were with him when he came and looked for them."

"It is true," said Psmith, "that Comrade Downing and I spent a very pleasant half-hour together inspecting boots, but how does he drag you into it?"

"He swears one of the boots was splashed with paint."

"Yes.; He babbled to some extent on that point when I was entertaining him.; But what makes him think that the boot, if any, was yours?"

"He's certain that somebody in this house got one of his boots splashed, and is hiding it somewhere.; And I'm the only chap in the house who hasn't got a pair of boots to show, so he thinks it's me.; I don't know where the dickens my other boot has gone.; Edmund swears he hasn't seen it, and it's nowhere about.; Of course I've got two pairs, but one's being soled.; So I had to go over to school yesterday in pumps.; That's how he spotted me."

Psmith sighed.

"Comrade Jackson," he said mournfully, "all this very sad affair shows the folly of acting from the best motives.; In my simple zeal, meaning to save you unpleasantness, I have landed you, with a dull, sickening thud, right in the cart.; Are you particular about dirtying your hands?; If you aren't, just reach up that chimney a bit?"

Mike stared, "What the dickens are you talking about?"

"Go on.; Get it over.; Be a man, and reach up the chimney."

"I don't know what the game is," said Mike, kneeling beside the fender and groping, "but — *Hullo!*"

"Ah ha!" said Psmith moodily.

Mike dropped the soot-covered object in the fender, and glared at it.

MIKE DROPPED THE SOOT-COVERED OBJECT IN THE FENDER

"It's my boot!" he said at last.

"It *is*," said Psmith, "your boot.; And what is that red stain across the toe?; Is it blood?; No, 'tis not blood.; It is red paint."

Mike seemed unable to remove his eyes from the boot.

"How on earth did —By Jove!; I remember now.; I kicked up against something in the dark when I was putting my bicycle back that night.; It must have been the paint-pot."

"Then you were out that night?"

"Rather.; That's what makes it so jolly awkward.; It's too long to tell you now — —"

"Your stories are never too long for me," said Psmith.; "Say on!"

"Well, it was like this."; And Mike related the events which had led up to his midnight excursion.; Psmith listened attentively.

"This," he said, when Mike had finished, "confirms my frequently stated opinion that Comrade Jellicoe is one of Nature's blitherers.; So that's why he touched us for our hard-earned, was it?"

"Yes.; Of course there was no need for him to have the money at all."

"And the result is that you are in something of a tight place.; You're *absolutely* certain you didn't paint that dog?; Didn't do it, by any chance, in a moment of absent-mindedness, and forgot all about it?; No?; No, I suppose not.; I wonder who did!"

"It's beastly awkward.; You see, Downing chased me that night.; That was why I rang the alarm bell.; So, you see, he's certain to think that the chap he chased, which was me, and the chap who painted Sammy, are the same.; I shall get landed both ways."

Psmith pondered.

"It *is* a tightish place," he admitted.

"I wonder if we could get this boot clean," said Mike, inspecting it with disfavour.

"Not for a pretty considerable time."

"I suppose not.; I say, I *am* in the cart.; If I can't produce this boot, they're bound to guess why."

"What exactly," asked Psmith, "was the position of affairs between you and Comrade Downing when you left him?; Had you definitely parted brass-rags?; Or did you simply sort of drift apart with mutual courtesies?"

"Oh, he said I was ill-advised to continue that attitude, or some rot, and I said I didn't care, I hadn't painted his bally dog, and he said very well, then, he must take steps, and —well, that was about all."

"Sufficient, too," said Psmith, "quite sufficient.; I take it, then, that he is now on the war-path, collecting a gang, so to speak."

"I suppose he's gone to the Old Man about it."

"Probably.; A very worrying time our headmaster is having, taking it all round, in connection with this painful affair.; What do you think his move will be?"

"I suppose he'll send for me, and try to get something out of me."

"*He'll* want you to confess, too.; Masters are all whales on confession.; The worst of it is, you can't prove an alibi, because at about the time the foul act was perpetrated, you were playing Round-and-round-the-mulberry-bush with Comrade Downing.; This needs thought.; You had better put the case in my hands, and go out and watch the dandelions growing.; I will think over the matter."

"Well, I hope you'll be able to think of something.; I can't."

"Possibly.; You never know."

There was a tap at the door.

"See how we have trained them," said Psmith.; "They now knock before entering.; There was a time when they would have tried to smash in a panel.; Come in."

A small boy, carrying a straw hat adorned with the school-house ribbon, answered the invitation.

"Oh, I say, Jackson," he said, "the headmaster sent me over to tell you he wants to see you."

"I told you so," said Mike to Psmith.

"Don't go," suggested Psmith.; "Tell him to write."

Mike got up.

"All this is very trying," said Psmith.; "I'm seeing nothing of you to-day."; He turned to the small boy.; "Tell Willie," he added, "that Mr. Jackson will be with him in a moment."

The emissary departed.

"*You're* all right," said Psmith encouragingly.; "Just you keep on saying you're all right.; Stout denial is the thing.; Don't go in for any airy explanations.; Simply stick to stout denial.; You can't beat it."

With which expert advice, he allowed Mike to go on his way.

He had not been gone two minutes, when Psmith, who had leaned back in his chair, wrapped in thought, heaved himself up again.; He stood for a moment straightening his tie at the looking-glass; then he picked up his hat and moved slowly out of the door and down the passage.; Thence, at the same dignified rate of progress, out of the house and in at Downing's front gate.

The postman was at the door when he got there, apparently absorbed in conversation with the parlour-maid.; Psmith stood by politely till the postman, who had just been told it was like his impudence, caught sight of him, and, having handed over the letters in an ultra-formal and professional manner, passed away.

"Is Mr. Downing at home?" inquired Psmith.

He was, it seemed.; Psmith was shown into the dining-room on the left of the hall, and requested to wait.; He was examining a portrait of Mr. Downing which hung on the wall, when the housemaster came in.

"An excellent likeness, sir," said Psmith, with a gesture of the hand towards the painting.

"Well, Smith," said Mr. Downing shortly, "what do you wish to see me about?"

"It was in connection with the regrettable painting of your dog, sir."

"Ha!" said Mr. Downing.

"I did it, sir," said Psmith, stopping and flicking a piece of fluff off his knee.

CHAPTER LVIII

THE ARTIST CLAIMS HIS WORK

The line of action which Psmith had called Stout Denial is an excellent line to adopt, especially if you really are innocent, but it does not lead to anything in the shape of a bright and snappy dialogue between accuser and accused.; Both Mike and the headmaster were oppressed by a feeling that the situation was difficult.; The atmosphere was heavy, and conversation showed a tendency to flag.; The headmaster had opened brightly enough, with a summary of the evidence which Mr. Downing had laid before him, but after that a massive silence had been the order of the day.; There is nothing in this world quite so stolid and uncommunicative as a boy who has made up his mind to be stolid and uncommunicative; and the headmaster, as he sat and looked at Mike, who sat and looked past him at the bookshelves, felt awkward.; It was a scene which needed either a dramatic interruption or a neat exit speech.; As it happened, what it got was the dramatic interruption.

The headmaster was just saying, "I do not think you fully realise, Jackson, the extent to which appearances ——" ——which was practically going back to the beginning and starting again ——when there was a knock at the door.; A voice without said, "Mr. Downing to see you, sir," and the chief witness for the prosecution burst in.

"I would not have interrupted you," said Mr. Downing, "but ——"

"Not at all, Mr. Downing.; Is there anything I can ——?"

"I have discovered —I have been informed —In short, it was not Jackson, who committed the —who painted my dog."

Mike and the headmaster both looked at the speaker.; Mike with a feeling of relief—for Stout Denial, unsupported by any weighty evidence, is a wearing game to play —the headmaster with astonishment.

"Not Jackson?" said the headmaster.

"No.; It was a boy in the same house.; Smith."

Psmith!; Mike was more than surprised.; He could not believe it.; There is nothing which affords so clear an index to a boy's character as the type of rag which he considers humorous.; Between what is a rag and what is merely a rotten trick there is a very definite line drawn.; Masters, as a rule, do not realise this, but boys nearly always do.; Mike could not imagine Psmith doing a rotten thing like covering a housemaster's dog with red paint, any more than he could imagine doing it himself.; They had both been amused at the sight of Sammy after the operation, but anybody, except possibly the owner of the dog, would have thought it funny at first.; After the first surprise, their feeling had been that it was a scuggish thing to have done and beastly rough luck on the poor brute.; It was a kid's trick.; As for Psmith having done it, Mike simply did not believe it.

"Smith!" said the headmaster.; "What makes you think that?"

"Simply this," said Mr. Downing, with calm triumph, "that the boy himself came to me a few moments ago and confessed."

Mike was conscious of a feeling of acute depression.; It did not make him in the least degree jubilant, or even thankful, to know that he himself was cleared of the charge.; All he could think of was that Psmith was done for.; This was bound to mean the sack.; If Psmith had painted Sammy, it meant that Psmith had broken out of his house at night:; and it was not likely that the rules about nocturnal wandering were less strict at Sedleigh than at any other school in the kingdom.; Mike felt, if possible, worse than he had felt when Wyatt had been caught on a similar occasion.; It seemed as if Fate had a special grudge against his best friends.; He did not make friends very quickly or easily, though he had always had scores of acquaintances —and with Wyatt and Psmith he had found himself at home from the first moment he had met them.

He sat there, with a curious feeling of having swallowed a heavy weight, hardly listening to what Mr. Downing was saying.; Mr. Downing was talking rapidly to the headmaster, who was nodding from time to time.

Mike took advantage of a pause to get up.; "May I go, sir?" he said.

"Certainly, Jackson, certainly," said the Head; "Oh, and er —, if you are going back to your house, tell Smith that I should like to see him."

"Yes, sir."

He had reached the door, when again there was a knock.

"Come in," said the headmaster.

It was Adair.

"Yes, Adair?"

Adair was breathing rather heavily, as if he had been running.

"It was about Sammy —Sampson, sir," he said, looking at Mr. Downing.

"Ah, we know —.; Well, Adair, what did you wish to say?"

"It wasn't Jackson who did it, sir."

"No, no, Adair.; So Mr. Downing — —"

"It was Dunster, sir."

Terrific sensation!; The headmaster gave a sort of strangled yelp of astonishment.; Mr. Downing leaped in his chair.; Mike's eyes opened to their fullest extent.

"Adair!"

There was almost a wail in the headmaster's voice.; The situation had suddenly become too much for him.; His brain was swimming.; That Mike, despite the evidence against him, should be innocent, was curious, perhaps, but not particularly startling.; But that Adair should inform him, two minutes after Mr. Downing's announcement of Psmith's confession, that Psmith, too, was guiltless, and that the real criminal was Dunster —it was this that made him feel that somebody, in the words of an American author, had played a mean trick on him, and substituted for his brain a side-order of cauliflower.; Why Dunster, of all people?; Dunster, who, he remembered dizzily, had left the school at Christmas.; And why, if Dunster had really painted the dog, had Psmith asserted that he himself was the culprit?; Why —why anything?; He concentrated his mind on Adair as the only person who could save him from impending brain-fever.

"Adair!"

"Yes, sir?"

"What —*what* do you mean?"

"It *was* Dunster, sir.; I got a letter from him only five minutes ago, in which he said that he had painted Sammy —Sampson, the dog, sir, for a rag —for a joke, and that, as he didn't want any one here to get into a row —be punished for it, I'd better tell Mr. Downing at once.; I tried to find Mr. Downing, but he wasn't in the house.; Then I met Smith outside the house, and he told me that Mr. Downing had gone over to see you, sir."

"Smith told you?" said Mr. Downing.

"Yes, sir."

"Did you say anything to him about your having received this letter from Dunster?"

"I gave him the letter to read, sir."

"And what was his attitude when he had read it?"

"He laughed, sir."

"*Laughed!*" Mr. Downing's voice was thunderous.

"Yes, sir.; He rolled about."

Mr. Downing snorted.

"But Adair," said the headmaster, "I do not understand how this thing could have been done by Dunster.; He has left the school."

"He was down here for the Old Sedleighans' match, sir.; He stopped the night in the village."

"And that was the night the —it happened?"

"Yes, sir."

"I see.; Well, I am glad to find that the blame cannot be attached to any boy in the school.; I am sorry that it is even an Old Boy.; It was a foolish, discreditable thing to have done, but it is not as bad as if any boy still at the school had broken out of his house at night to do it."

"The sergeant," said Mr. Downing, "told me that the boy he saw was attempting to enter Mr. Outwood's house."

"Another freak of Dunster's, I suppose," said the headmaster.; "I shall write to him."

"If it was really Dunster who painted my dog," said Mr. Downing, "I cannot understand the part played by Smith in this affair.; If he did not do it, what possible motive could he have had for coming to me of his own accord and deliberately confessing?"

"To be sure," said the headmaster, pressing a bell.; "It is certainly a thing that calls for explanation.; Barlow," he said, as the butler appeared, "kindly go across to Mr. Outwood's house and inform Smith that I should like to see him."

"If you please, sir, Mr. Smith is waiting in the hall."

"In the hall!"

"Yes, sir.; He arrived soon after Mr. Adair, sir, saying that he would wait, as you would probably wish to see him shortly."

"H'm.; Ask him to step up, Barlow."

"Yes, sir."

There followed one of the tensest "stage waits" of Mike's experience.; It was not long, but, while it lasted, the silence was quite solid.; Nobody seemed to have anything to say, and there was not even a clock in the room to break the stillness with its ticking.; A very faint drip-drip of rain could be heard outside the window.

Presently there was a sound of footsteps on the stairs.; The door was opened.

"Mr. Smith, sir."

The old Etonian entered as would the guest of the evening who is a few moments late for dinner.; He was cheerful, but slightly deprecating.; He gave the impression of one who, though sure of his welcome, feels that some slight apology is expected from him.; He advanced into the room with a gentle half-smile which suggested good-will to all men.

"It is still raining," he observed.; "You wished to see me, sir?"

"Sit down, Smith."

"Thank you, sir."

He dropped into a deep arm-chair (which both Adair and Mike had avoided in favour of less luxurious seats) with the confidential cosiness of a fashionable physician calling on a patient, between whom and himself time has broken down the barriers of restraint and formality.

Mr. Downing burst out, like a reservoir that has broken its banks.

"Smith."

Psmith turned his gaze politely in the housemaster's direction.

"Smith, you came to me a quarter of an hour ago and told me that it was you who had painted my dog Sampson."

"Yes, sir."

"It was absolutely untrue?"

"I am afraid so, sir."

"But, Smith —" began the headmaster.

Psmith bent forward encouragingly.

"——This is a most extraordinary affair.; Have you no explanation to offer?; What induced you to do such a thing?"

Psmith sighed softly.

"The craze for notoriety, sir," he replied sadly.; "The curse of the present age."

"What!" cried the headmaster.

"It is remarkable," proceeded Psmith placidly, with the impersonal touch of one lecturing on generalities, "how frequently, when a murder has been committed, one finds men confessing that they have done it when it is out of the question that they should have committed it.; It is one of the most interesting problems with which anthropologists are confronted.; Human nature — —"

The headmaster interrupted.

"Smith," he said, "I should like to see you alone for a moment.; Mr. Downing might I trouble —?; Adair, Jackson."

He made a motion towards the door.

When he and Psmith were alone, there was silence.; Psmith leaned back comfortably in his chair.; The headmaster tapped nervously with his foot on the floor.

"Er — Smith."

"Sir?"

The headmaster seemed to have some difficulty in proceeding.; He paused again.; Then he went on.

"Er — Smith, I do not for a moment wish to pain you, but have you — er, do you remember ever having had, as a child, let us say, any — er — severe illness?; Any — er — *mental* illness?"

"No, sir."

"There is no — forgive me if I am touching on a sad subject — there is no — none of your near relatives have ever suffered in the way I — er — have described?"

"There isn't a lunatic on the list, sir," said Psmith cheerfully.

"Of course, Smith, of course," said the headmaster hurriedly, "I did not mean to suggest — quite so, quite so....; You think, then, that you confessed to an act which you had not committed purely from some sudden impulse which you cannot explain?"

"Strictly between ourselves, sir — —"

Privately, the headmaster found Psmith's man-to-man attitude somewhat disconcerting, but he said nothing.

"Well, Smith?"

"I should not like it to go any further, sir."

"I will certainly respect any confidence — —"

"I don't want anybody to know, sir.; This is strictly between ourselves."

"I think you are sometimes apt to forget, Smith, the proper relations existing between boy and — Well, never mind that for the present.; We can return to it later.; For the moment, let me hear what you wish to say.; I shall, of course, tell nobody, if you do not wish it."

"Well, it was like this, sir," said Psmith.; "Jackson happened to tell me that you and Mr. Downing seemed to think he had painted Mr. Downing's dog, and there seemed some danger of his being expelled, so I thought it wouldn't be an unsound scheme if I were to go and say I had done it.; That was the whole thing.; Of course, Dunster writing created a certain amount of confusion."

There was a pause.

"It was a very wrong thing to do, Smith," said the headmaster, at last, "but....; You are a curious boy, Smith.; Good-night."

He held out his hand.

"Good-night, sir," said Psmith.

"Not a bad old sort," said Psmith meditatively to himself, as he walked downstairs.; "By no means a bad old sort.; I must drop in from time to time and cultivate him."

* * * * *

Mike and Adair were waiting for him outside the front door.

"Well?" said Mike.

"You *are* the limit," said Adair.; "What's he done?"

"Nothing.; We had a very pleasant chat, and then I tore myself away."

"Do you mean to say he's not going to do a thing?"

"Not a thing."

"Well, you're a marvel," said Adair.

Psmith thanked him courteously.; They walked on towards the houses.

"By the way, Adair," said Mike, as the latter started to turn in at Downing's, "I'll write to Strachan to-night about that match."

"What's that?" asked Psmith.

"Jackson's going to try and get Wrykyn to give us a game," said Adair.; "They've got a vacant date.; I hope the dickens they'll do it."

"Oh, I should think they're certain to," said Mike.; "Good-night."

"And give Comrade Downing, when you see him," said Psmith, "my very best love.; It is men like him who make this Merrie England of ours what it is."

* * * * *

"I say, Psmith," said Mike suddenly, "what really made you tell Downing you'd done it?"

"The craving for — —"

"Oh, chuck it.; You aren't talking to the Old Man now.; I believe it was simply to get me out of a jolly tight corner."

Psmith's expression was one of pain.

"My dear Comrade Jackson," said he, "you wrong me.; You make me writhe.; I'm surprised at you.; I never thought to hear those words from Michael Jackson."

"Well, I believe you did, all the same," said Mike obstinately.; "And it was jolly good of you, too."

Psmith moaned.

CHAPTER LIX

SEDLEIGH v. WRYKYN

The Wrykyn match was three-parts over, and things were going badly for Sedleigh. In a way one might have said that the game was over, and that Sedleigh had lost; for it was a one day match, and Wrykyn, who had led on the first innings, had only to play out time to make the game theirs.

Sedleigh were paying the penalty for allowing themselves to be influenced by nerves in the early part of the day. Nerves lose more school matches than good play ever won. There is a certain type of school batsman who is a gift to any bowler when he once lets his imagination run away with him. Sedleigh, with the exception of Adair, Psmith, and Mike, had entered upon this match in a state of the most azure funk. Ever since Mike had received Strachan's answer and Adair had announced on the notice-board that on Saturday, July the twentieth, Sedleigh would play Wrykyn, the team had been all on the jump. It was useless for Adair to tell them, as he did repeatedly, on Mike's authority, that Wrykyn were weak this season, and that on their present form Sedleigh ought to win easily. The team listened, but were not comforted. Wrykyn might be below their usual strength, but then Wrykyn cricket, as a rule, reached such a high standard that this probably meant little. However weak Wrykyn might be—for them—there was a very firm impression among the members of the Sedleigh first eleven that the other school was quite strong enough to knock the cover off *them*. Experience counts enormously in school matches. Sedleigh had never been proved. The teams they played were the sort of sides which the Wrykyn second eleven would play. Whereas Wrykyn, from time immemorial, had been beating Ripton teams and Free Foresters teams and M.C.C. teams packed with county men and sending men to Oxford and Cambridge who got their blues as freshmen.

Sedleigh had gone on to the field that morning a depressed side.

It was unfortunate that Adair had won the toss. He had had no choice but to take first innings. The weather had been bad for the last week, and the wicket was slow and treacherous. It was likely to get worse during the day, so Adair had chosen to bat first.

Taking into consideration the state of nerves the team was in, this in itself was a calamity. A school eleven are always at their worst and nerviest before lunch. Even on their own ground they find the surroundings lonely and unfamiliar. The subtlety of the bowlers becomes magnified. Unless the first pair make a really good start, a collapse almost invariably ensues.

To-day the start had been gruesome beyond words. Mike, the bulwark of the side, the man who had been brought up on Wrykyn bowling, and from whom, whatever might happen to the others, at least a fifty was expected—Mike, going in first with Barnes and taking first over, had played inside one from Bruce, the Wrykyn slow bowler, and had been caught at short slip off his second ball.

That put the finishing-touch on the panic. Stone, Robinson, and the others, all quite decent punishing batsmen when their nerves allowed them to play their own game, crawled to the wickets, declined to hit out at anything, and were clean bowled, several of them, playing back to half-volleys. Adair did not suffer from panic, but his batting was not equal to his bowling, and he had fallen after hitting one four. Seven wickets were down for thirty when Psmith went in.

Psmith had always disclaimed any pretensions to batting skill, but he was undoubtedly the right man for a crisis like this. He had an enormous reach, and he used it. Three consecutive balls from Bruce he turned into full-tosses and swept to the leg-boundary, and, assisted by Barnes, who had been sitting on the splice in his usual manner, he raised the total to seventy-one before being yorked, with his score at thirty-five. Ten minutes later the innings was over, with Barnes not out sixteen, for seventy-nine.

Wrykyn had then gone in, lost Strachan for twenty before lunch, and finally completed their innings at a quarter to four for a hundred and thirty-one.

This was better than Sedleigh had expected. At least eight of the team had looked forward dismally to an afternoon's leather-hunting. But Adair and Psmith, helped by the wicket, had never been easy, especially Psmith, who had taken six wickets, his slows playing havoc with the tail.

It would be too much to say that Sedleigh had any hope of pulling the game out of the fire; but it was a comfort, they felt, at any rate, having another knock. As is usual at this stage of a match, their nervousness had vanished, and they felt capable of better things than in the first innings.

It was on Mike's suggestion that Psmith and himself went in first. Mike knew the limitations of the Wrykyn bowling, and he was convinced that, if they could knock Bruce off, it might be possible to rattle up a score sufficient to give them the game, always provided that Wrykyn collapsed in the second innings. And it seemed to Mike that the wicket would be so bad then that they easily might.

So he and Psmith had gone in at four o'clock to hit. And they had hit. The deficit had been wiped off, all but a dozen runs, when Psmith was bowled, and by that time Mike was set and in his best vein. He treated all the bowlers alike. And when Stone came in, restored to his proper frame of mind, and lashed out stoutly, and after him Robinson and the rest, it looked as if Sedleigh had a chance again. The score was a hundred and twenty when Mike, who had just reached his fifty, skied one to Strachan at cover. The time was twenty-five past five.

As Mike reached the pavilion, Adair declared the innings closed.

Wrykyn started batting at twenty-five minutes to six, with sixty-nine to make if they wished to make them, and an hour and ten minutes during which to keep up their wickets if they preferred to take things easy and go for a win on the first innings.

At first it looked as if they meant to knock off the runs, for Strachan forced the game from the first ball, which was Psmith's, and which he hit into the pavilion. But, at fifteen, Adair bowled him. And when, two runs later, Psmith got the next man stumped, and finished up his over with a c-and-b, Wrykyn decided that it was not good enough. Seventeen for three, with an hour all but five minutes to go, was getting too dangerous. So Drummond and Rigby, the next pair, proceeded to play with caution, and the collapse ceased.

This was the state of the game at the point at which this chapter opened. Seventeen for three had become twenty-four for three, and the hands of the clock stood at ten minutes past six. Changes of bowling had been tried, but there seemed no chance of getting past the batsmen's defence. They were playing all the good balls, and refused to hit at the bad.

A quarter past six struck, and then Psmith made a suggestion which altered the game completely.

"Why don't you have a shot this end?" he said to Adair, as they were crossing over. "There's a spot on the off which might help you a lot. You can break like blazes if only you land on it. It doesn't help my leg-breaks a bit, because they won't hit at them."

Barnes was on the point of beginning to bowl, when Adair took the ball from him. The captain of Outwood's retired to short leg with an air that suggested that he was glad to be relieved of his prominent post.

The next moment Drummond's off-stump was lying at an angle of forty-five. Adair was absolutely accurate as a bowler, and he had dropped his first ball right on the worn patch.

Two minutes later Drummond's successor was retiring to the pavilion, while the wicket-keeper straightened the stumps again.

There is nothing like a couple of unexpected wickets for altering the atmosphere of a game. Five minutes before, Sedleigh had been lethargic and without hope. Now there was a stir and buzz all round the ground. There were twenty-five minutes to go, and five wickets were down. Sedleigh was on top again.

The next man seemed to take an age coming out. As a matter of fact, he walked more rapidly than a batsman usually walks to the crease.

Adair's third ball dropped just short of the spot. The batsman, hitting out, was a shade too soon. The ball hummed through the air a couple of feet from the ground in the direction of mid-off, and Mike, diving to the right, got to it as he was falling, and chucked it up.

After that the thing was a walk-over. Psmith clean bowled a man in his next over; and the tail, demoralised by the sudden change in the game, collapsed uncompromisingly. Sedleigh won by thirty-five runs with eight minutes in hand.

* * * * *

Psmith and Mike sat in their study after lock-up, discussing things in general and the game in particular.

"I feel like a beastly renegade, playing against Wrykyn," said Mike. "Still, I'm glad we won. Adair's a jolly good sort, and it'll make him happy for weeks."

"When I last saw Comrade Adair," said Psmith, "he was going about in a sort of trance, beaming vaguely and wanting to stand people things at the shop."

"He bowled awfully well."

"Yes," said Psmith. "I say, I don't wish to cast a gloom over this joyful occasion in any way, but you say Wrykyn are going to give Sedleigh a fixture again next year?"

"Well?"

"Well, have you thought of the massacre which will ensue? You will have left, Adair will have left. Incidentally, I shall have left. Wrykyn will swamp them."

"I suppose they will. Still, the great thing, you see, is to get the thing started. That's what Adair was so keen on. Now Sedleigh has beaten Wrykyn, he's satisfied. They can get on fixtures with decent clubs, and work up to playing the big schools. You've got to start somehow. So it's all right, you see."

"And, besides," said Psmith, reflectively, "in an emergency they can always get Comrade Downing to bowl for them, what? Let us now sally out and see if we can't promote a rag of some sort in this abode of wrath. Comrade Outwood has gone over to dinner at the School House, and it would be a pity to waste a somewhat golden opportunity. Shall we stagger?"

They staggered.

Mike and Psmith

1

MR. JACKSON MAKES UP HIS MIND

If Mike had been in time for breakfast that fatal Easter morning he might have gathered from the expression on his father's face, as Mr. Jackson opened the envelope containing his school report and read the contents, that the document in question was not exactly a paean of praise from beginning to end. But he was late, as usual. Mike always was late for breakfast in the holidays.

When he came down on this particular morning, the meal was nearly over. Mr. Jackson had disappeared, taking his correspondence with him; Mrs. Jackson had gone into the kitchen, and when Mike appeared the thing had resolved itself into a mere vulgar brawl between Phyllis and Ella for the jam, while Marjory, recently affecting a grown-up air, looked on in a detached sort of way, as if these juvenile gambols distressed her.

"Hello, Mike," she said, jumping up as he entered, "here you are —I've been keeping everything hot for you."

"Have you? Thanks awfully. I say…" His eye wandered in mild surprise round the table. "I'm a bit late."

Marjory was bustling about, fetching and carrying for Mike, as she always did. She had adopted him at an early age, and did the thing thoroughly. She was fond of her other brothers, especially when they made centuries in first-class cricket, but Mike was her favorite. She would field out in the deep as a natural thing when Mike was batting at the net in the paddock, though for the others, even for Joe, who had played in all five Test Matches in the previous summer, she would do it only as a favor.

Phyllis and Ella finished their dispute and went out. Marjory sat on the table and watched Mike eat.

"Your report came this morning, Mike," she said.

The kidneys failed to retain Mike's undivided attention. He looked up interested. "What did it say?"

"I didn't see —I only caught sight of the Wrykyn crest on the envelope. Father didn't say anything."

Mike seemed concerned. "I say, that looks rather rotten! I wonder if it was awfully bad. It's the first I've had from Appleby."

"It can't be any worse than the horrid ones Mr. Blake used to write when you were in his form."

"No, that's a comfort," said Mike philosophically. "Think there's any more tea in that pot?"

"I call it a shame," said Marjory; "they ought to be jolly glad to have you at Wrykyn just for cricket, instead of writing beastly reports that make father angry and don't do any good to anybody."

"Last Christmas he said he'd take me away if I got another one."

"He didn't mean it really, I *know* he didn't! He couldn't! You're the best bat Wrykyn's ever had."

"What ho!" interpolated Mike.

"You *are*. Everybody says you are. Why, you got your first the very first term you were there-even Joe didn't do anything nearly so good as that. Saunders says you're simply bound to play for England in another year or two."

"Saunders is a jolly good chap. He bowled me a half volley on the off the first ball I had in a school match. By the way, I wonder if he's out at the net now. Let's go and see."

Saunders the professional was setting up the net when they arrived. Mike put on his pads and went to the wicket, while Marjory and the dogs retired as usual to the far hedge to retrieve.

She was kept busy. Saunders was a good sound bowler of the M.C.C. minor match type, and there had been a time when he had worried Mike considerably, but Mike had been in the Wrykyn team for three seasons now, and each season he had advanced tremendously in his batting. He had filled out in three years. He had always had the style, and now he had the strength as well, Saunder's bowling on a true wicket seemed simple to him. It was early in the Easter holidays, but already he was beginning to find his form. Saunders, who looked on Mike as his own special invention, was delighted.

"If you don't be worried by being too anxious now that you're captain, Master Mike," he said, "you'll make a century every match next term."

"I wish I wasn't; it's a beastly responsibility."

Henfrey, the Wrykyn cricket captain of the previous season, was not returning next term, and Mike was to reign in his stead. He liked the prospect, but it certainly carried with it a rather awe-inspiring responsibility. At night sometimes he would lie awake, appalled by the fear of losing his form, or making a hash of things by choosing the wrong men to play for the school and leaving the right men out. It is no light thing to captain a public school at cricket.

As he was walking toward the house, Phyllis met him. "Oh, I've been hunting for you, Mike; Father wants you."

"What for?"

"I don't know."

"Where?"

"He's in the study. He seems..." added Phyllis, throwing in the information by a way of a makeweight, "in a beastly temper."

Mike's jaw fell slightly. "I hope the dickens it's nothing to do with that bally report," was his muttered exclamation.

Mike's dealings with his father were as a rule of a most pleasant nature. Mr. Jackson was an understanding sort of man, who treated his sons as companions. From time to time, however, breezes were apt to ruffle the placid sea of good fellowship. Mike's end-of-term report was an unfailing wind raiser; indeed, on the arrival of Mr. Blake's sarcastic resume of Mike's shortcomings at the end of the previous term, there had been something not unlike a typhoon. It was on this occasion that Mr. Jackson had solemnly declared his intention of removing Mike from Wrykyn unless the critics became more flattering; and Mr. Jackson was a man of his word.

It was with a certain amount of apprehension, therefore, that Jackson entered the study.

"Come in, Mike," said his father, kicking the waste-paper basket; "I want to speak to you."

Mike, skilled in omens, scented a row in the offing. Only in moments of emotion was Mr. Jackson in the habit of booting the basket.

There followed an awkward silence, which Mike broke by remarking that he had carted a half volley from Saunders over the on-side hedge that morning.

"It was just a bit short and off the leg stump, so I stepped out-may I bag the paper knife for a jiffy? I'll just show —"

"Never mind about cricket now," said Mr. Jackson; "I want you to listen to this report."

"Oh, is that my report, Father?" said Mike, with a sort of sickly interest, much as a dog about to be washed might evince in his tub.

"It is," replied Mr. Jackson in measured tones, "your report; what is more, it is without exception the worst report you have ever had."

"Oh, I say!" groaned the record-breaker.

"'His conduct,'" quoted Mr. Jackson, "'has been unsatisfactory in the extreme, both in and out of school.'"

"It wasn't anything really. I only happened —"

Remembering suddenly that what he had happened to do was to drop a cannonball (the school weight) on the form-room floor, not once, but on several occasions, he paused.

"'French bad; conduct disgraceful —'"

"Everybody rags in French."

"'Mathematics bad. Inattentive and idle.'"

"Nobody does much work in Math."

"'Latin poor. Greek, very poor.'"

"We were doing Thucydides, Book Two, last term-all speeches and doubtful readings, and cruxes and things-beastly hard! Everybody says so."

"Here are Mr. Appleby's remarks: 'The boy has genuine ability, which he declines to use in the smallest degree.'"

Mike moaned a moan of righteous indignation.

"'An abnormal proficiency at games has apparently destroyed all desire in him to realize the more serious issues of life.' There is more to the same effect."

Mr. Appleby was a master with very definite ideas as to what constituted a public-school master's duties. As a man he was distinctly pro-Mike. He understood cricket, and some of Mike's strokes on the off gave him thrills of pure aesthetic joy; but as a master he always made it his habit to regard the manners and customs of the boys in his form with an unbiased eye, and to an unbiased eye Mike in a form room was about as near the extreme edge as a boy could be, and Mr. Appleby said as much in a clear firm hand.

"You remember what I said to you about your report at Christmas, Mike?" said Mr. Jackson, folding the lethal document and replacing it in its envelope.

Mike said nothing; there was a sinking feeling in his interior.

"I shall abide by what I said."

Mike's heart thumped.

"You will not go back to Wrykyn next term."

Somewhere in the world the sun was shining, birds were twittering; somewhere in the world lambkins frisked and peasants sang blithely at their toil (flat, perhaps, but still blithely), but to Mike at that moment the sky was black, and an icy wind blew over the face of the earth.

The tragedy had happened, and there was an end of it. He made no attempt to appeal against the sentence. He knew it would be useless, his father, when he made up his mind, having all the unbending tenacity of the normally easygoing man.

Mr. Jackson was sorry for Mike. He understood him, and for that reason he said very little now.

"I am sending you to Sedleigh," was his next remark.

Sedleigh! Mike sat up with a jerk. He knew Sedleigh by name-one of those schools with about a hundred boys which you never hear of except when they send up their gym team to Aldershot, or their Eight to Bisley. Mike's outlook on life was that of a cricketer, pure and simple. What had Sedleigh ever done? What were they ever likely to do? Whom did they play? What Old Sedleighan had ever done anything at cricket? Perhaps they didn't even *play* cricket!

"But it's an awful hole," he said blankly.

Mr. Jackson could read Mike's mind like a book. Mike's point of view was plain to him. He did not approve of it, but he knew that in Mike's place and at Mike's age he would have felt the same. He spoke dryly to hide his sympathy.

"It is not a large school," he said, "and I don't suppose it could play Wrykyn at cricket, but it has one merit-boys work there. Young Barlitt won a Balliol scholarship from Sedleigh last year." Barlitt was the vicar's son, a silent, spectacled youth who did not enter very largely into Mike's world. They had met occasionally at tennis parties, but not much conversation had ensued. Barlitt's mind was massive, but his topics of conversation were not Mike's.

"Mr. Barlitt speaks very highly of Sedleigh," added Mr. Jackson.

Mike said nothing, which was a good deal better than saying what he would have liked to have said.

2

SEDLEIGH

The train, which had been stopping everywhere for the last half hour, pulled up again, and Mike, seeing the name of the station, got up, opened the door, and hurled a bag out on to the platform in an emphatic and vindictive manner. Then he got out himself and looked about him.

"For the school, sir?" inquired the solitary porter, bustling up, as if he hoped by sheer energy to deceive the traveler into thinking that Sedleigh station was staffed by a great army of porters.

Mike nodded. A somber nod. The nod Napoleon might have given if somebody had met him in 1812, and said, "So you're back from Moscow, eh?" Mike was feeling thoroughly jaundiced. The future seemed wholly gloomy. And, so far from attempting to make the best of things, he had set himself deliberately to look on the dark side. He thought, for instance, that he had never seen a more repulsive porter, or one more obviously incompetent than the man who had attached himself with a firm grasp to the handle of the bag as he strode off in the direction of the luggage van. He disliked his voice, his appearance, and the color of his hair. Also the boots he wore. He hated the station, and the man who took his ticket.

"Young gents at the school, sir," said the porter, perceiving from Mike's *distrait* air that the boy was a stranger to the place, "goes up in the bus mostly. It's waiting here, sir. Hi, George!"

"I'll walk, thanks," said Mike frigidly.

"It's a goodish step, sir."

"Here you are."

"Thank you, sir. I'll send up your luggage by the bus, sir. Which 'ouse was it you was going to?"

"Outwood's."

"Right, sir. It's straight on up this road to the school. You can't miss it, sir."

"Worse luck," said Mike.

He walked off up the road, sorrier for himself than ever. It was such absolutely rotten luck. About now, instead of being on his way to a place where they probably ran a Halma team instead of a cricket eleven, and played hunt-the-slipper in winter, he would be on the point of arriving at Wrykyn. And as captain of cricket, at that. Which was the bitter part of it. He had never been in command. For the last two seasons he had been the star man, going in first, and heading the averages easily at the end of the season; and the three captains under whom he had played during his career as a Wrykynian, Burgess, Enderby, and Henfrey, had always been sportsmen to him. But it was not the same thing. He had meant to do such a lot for Wrykyn cricket this term. He had had an entirely new system of coaching in his mind. Now it might never be used. He had handed it on in a letter to Strachan, who would be captain in his place; but probably Strachan would have some scheme of his own. There is nobody who could not edit a paper in the ideal way; and there is nobody who has not a theory of his own about cricket coaching at school.

Wrykyn, too, would be weak this year, now that he was no longer there. Strachan was a good, free bat on his day, and, if he survived a few overs, might make a century in an hour, but he was not to be depended upon. There was no doubt that Mike's sudden withdrawal meant that Wrykyn would have a bad time that season. And it had been such a wretched athletic year for the school. The football fifteen had been hopeless, and had lost both the Ripton matches, the return by over sixty points. Sheen's victory in the light weights at Aldershot had been their one success. And now, on top of all this, the captain of cricket was removed during the Easter holidays. Mike's heart bled for Wrykyn, and he found himself loathing Sedleigh and all its works with a great loathing.

The only thing he could find in its favor was the fact that it was set in a very pretty country. Of a different type from the Wrykyn country, but almost as good. For three miles Mike made his way through woods and past fields. Once he crossed a river. It was soon after this that he caught sight, from the top of a hill, of a group of buildings that wore an unmistakably schoollike look.

This must be Sedleigh.

Ten minutes' walk brought him to the school gates, and a baker's boy directed him to Mr. Outwood's.

There were three houses in a row, separated from the school buildings by a cricket field. Outwood's was the middle one of these.

Mike went to the front door and knocked. At Wrykyn he had always charged in at the beginning of term at the boys' entrance, but this formal reporting of himself at Sedleigh suited his mood.

He inquired for Mr. Outwood, and was shown into a room lined with books.

Presently the door opened, and the housemaster appeared.

There was something pleasant and homely about Mr. Outwood. In appearance he reminded Mike of Smee in *Peter Pan*. He had the same eyebrows and pince-nez and the same motherly look.

"Jackson?" he said mildly.

"Yes, sir."

"I am very glad to see you, very glad indeed. Perhaps you would like a cup of tea after your journey. I think you might like a cup of tea. You come from Crofton, in Shropshire, I understand, Jackson, near Brindleford? It is a part of the country which I have always wished to visit. I dare say you have frequently seen the Cluniac Priory of St. Ambrose at Brindleford?"

Mike, who would not have recognized a Cluniac Priory if you had handed him one on a tray, said he had not.

"Dear me! You have missed an opportunity which I should have been glad to have. I am preparing a book on Ruined Abbeys and Priories of England, and it has always been my wish to see the Cluniac Priory of St. Ambrose. A deeply interesting relic of the sixteenth century. Bishop Geoffrey, 1133-40 —"

"Shall I go across to the boys' part, sir?"

"What? Yes. Oh, yes. Quite so. And perhaps you would like a cup of tea after your journey? No? Quite so. Quite so. You should make a point of visiting the remains of the Cluniac Priory in the summer holidays, Jackson. You will find the matron in her room. In many respects it is unique. The northern altar is in a state of really wonderful preservation. It consists of a solid block of masonry five feet long and two and a half wide, with chamfered plinth, standing quite free from the apse wall. It will well repay a visit. Good-bye for the present, Jackson, good-bye."

Mike wandered across to the other side of the house, his gloom visibly deepened. All alone in a strange school, where they probably played hopscotch, with a housemaster who offered one cups of tea after one's journey and talked about chamfered plinths and apses. It was a little hard.

He strayed about, finding his bearings, and finally came to a room which he took to be the equivalent of the senior day room at a Wrykyn house. Everywhere else he had found nothing but emptiness. Evidently he had come by an earlier train than was usual. But this room was occupied.

A very long, thin youth, with a solemn face and immaculate clothes, was leaning against the mantelpiece. As Mike entered, he fumbled in his top left waistcoat pocket, produced an eyeglass attached to a cord, and fixed it in his right eye. With the help of this aid to vision he inspected Mike in silence for a while, then, having flicked an invisible speck of dust from the left sleeve of his coat, he spoke.

"Hello," he said.

He spoke in a tired voice.

"Hello," said Mike.

"Take a seat," said the immaculate one. "If you don't mind dirtying your bags, that's to say. Personally, I don't see any prospect of ever sitting down in this place. It looks to me as if they meant to use these chairs as mustard-and-cress beds. A Nursery Garden in the Home. That sort of idea. My name," he added pensively, "is Smith. What's yours?"

3

PSMITH

"Jackson," said Mike.

"Are you the Bully, the Pride of the School, or the Boy who is Led Astray and takes to Drink in Chapter Sixteen?"

"The last, for choice," said Mike, "but I've only just arrived, so I don't know."

"The boy-what will he become? Are you new here, too, then?"

"Yes! Why, are you new?"

"Do I look as if I belonged here? I'm the latest import. Sit down on yonder settee, and I will tell you the painful story of my life. By the way, before I start, there's just one thing. If you ever have occasion to write to me, would you mind sticking a P at the beginning of my name? P-s-m-i-t-h. See? There are too many Smiths, and I don't care for Smythe. My father's content to worry along in the old-fashioned way, but I've decided to strike out a fresh line. I shall found a new dynasty. The resolve came to me unexpectedly this morning. I jotted it down on the back of an envelope. In conversation you may address me as Rupert (though I hope you won't), or simply Smith, the *P* not being sounded. Compare the name Zbysco, in which the Z is given a similar miss-in-balk. See?"

Mike said he saw. Psmith thanked him with a certain stately old world courtesy.

"Let us start at the beginning," he resumed. "My infancy. When I was but a babe, my eldest sister was bribed with a shilling an hour by my nurse to keep an eye on me, and see that I did not raise Cain. At the end of the first day she struck for one-and-six, and got it. We now pass to my boyhood. At an early age, I was sent to Eton, everybody predicting a bright career for me. But," said Psmith solemnly, fixing an owl-like gaze on Mike through the eyeglass, "it was not to be."

"No?" said Mike.

"No. I was superannuated last term."

"Bad luck."

"For Eton, yes. But what Eton loses, Sedleigh gains."

"But why Sedleigh, of all places?"

"This is the most painful part of my narrative. It seems that a certain scug in the next village to ours happened last year to collar a Balliol —"

"Not Barlitt!" exclaimed Mike.

"That was the man. The son of the vicar. The vicar told the curate, who told our curate, who told our vicar, who told my father, who sent me off here to get a Balliol too. Do *you* know Barlitt?"

"His father's vicar of our village. It was because his son got a Balliol that I was sent here."

"Do you come from Crofton?"

"Yes."

"I've lived at Lower Benford all my life. We are practically long-lost brothers. Cheer a little, will you?"

Mike felt as Robinson Crusoe felt when he met Friday. Here was a fellow human being in this desert place. He could almost have embraced Psmith. The very sound of the name Lower Benford was heartening. His dislike for his new school was not diminished, but now he felt that life there might at least be tolerable.

"Where were you before you came here?" asked Psmith. "You have heard my painful story. Now tell me yours."

"Wrykyn. My father took me away because I got such a lot of bad reports."

"My reports from Eton were simply scurrilous. There's a libel action in every sentence. How do you like this place, from what you've seen of it?"

"Rotten."

"I am with you, Comrade Jackson. You won't mind my calling you Comrade, will you? I've just become a socialist. It's a great scheme. You ought to be one. You work for the equal distribution of property, and start by collaring all you can and sitting on it. We must stick together. We are companions in misfortune. Lost lambs. Sheep that have gone astray. Divided, we fall, together we may worry through. Have you seen Professor Radium yet? I should say Mr. Outwood. What do you think of him?"

"He doesn't seem a bad sort of chap. Bit off his nut. Jawed about apses and things."

"And thereby," said Psmith, "hangs a tale. I've been making inquiries of a stout sportsman in a sort of Salvation Army uniform, whom I met in the grounds-he's the school sergeant or something, quite a solid man-and I hear that Comrade Outwood's an archaeological cove. Goes about the country beating up old ruins and fossils and things. There's an Archaeological Society in the school, run by him. It goes out on half-holidays, prowling about, and is allowed to break bounds and generally steep itself to the eyebrows in reckless devilry. And, mark you, laddie, if you belong to the Archaeological Society you get off cricket. To get off cricket," said Psmith, dusting his right trouser leg, "was the dream of my youth and the aspiration of my riper years. A noble game, but a bit too thick for me. At Eton I used to have to field out at the nets till the soles of my boots wore through. I suppose you are a blood at the game? Play for the school against Loamshire, and so on."

"I'm not going to play here, at any rate," said Mike.

He had made up his mind on this point in the train. There is a certain fascination about making the very worst of a bad job. Achilles knew his business when he sat in his tent. The determination not to play cricket for Sedleigh as he could not play for Wrykyn gave Mike a sort of pleasure. To stand by with folded arms and a somber frown, as it were, was one way of treating the situation, and one not without its meed of comfort.

Psmith approved the resolve.

"Stout fellow," he said. "'Tis well. You and I, hand in hand, will search the countryside for ruined abbeys. We will snare the elusive fossil together. Above all, we will go out of bounds. We shall thus improve our minds, and have a jolly good time as well. I shouldn't wonder if one mightn't borrow a gun from some friendly native, and do a bit of rabbit shooting here and there. From what I saw of Comrade Outwood during our brief interview, I shouldn't think he was one of the lynx-eyed contingent. With tact we ought to be able to slip away from the merry throng of fossil chasers, and do a bit on our own account."

"Good idea," said Mike. "We will. A chap at Wrykyn, called Wyatt, used to break out at night and shoot at cats with an air pistol."

"It would take a lot to make me do that. I am all against anything that interferes with my sleep. But rabbits in the daytime is a scheme. We'll nose about for a gun at the earliest opp. Meanwhile we'd better go up to Comrade Outwood, and get our names shoved down for the Society."

"I vote we get some tea first somewhere."

"Then let's beat up a study. I suppose they have studies here. Let's go and look."

They went upstairs. On the first floor there was a passage with doors on either side. Psmith opened the first of these.

"This'll do us well," he said.

It was a biggish room, looking out over the school grounds. There were a couple of deal tables, two empty bookcases, and a looking glass, hung on a nail.

"Might have been made for us," said Psmith approvingly.

"I suppose it belongs to some rotter."

"Not now."

"You aren't going to collar it!"

"That," said Psmith, looking at himself earnestly in the mirror, and straightening his tie, "is the exact program. We must stake out our claims. This is practical socialism."

235

"But the real owner's bound to turn up some time or other."

"His misfortune, not ours. You can't expect two masterminds like us to pig it in that room downstairs. There are moments when one wants to be alone. It is imperative that we have a place to retire to after a fatiguing day. And now, if you want to be really useful, come and help me fetch up my box from downstairs. It's got a gas ring and various things in it."

4

STAKING OUT A CLAIM

Psmith, in the matter of decorating a study and preparing tea in it, was rather a critic than an executant. He was full of ideas, but he preferred to allow Mike to carry them out. It was he who suggested that the wooden bar which ran across the window was unnecessary, but it was Mike who wrenched it from its place. Similarly, it was Mike who abstracted the key from the door of the next study, though the idea was Psmith's.

"Privacy," said Psmith, as he watched Mike light the gas ring, "is what we chiefly need in this age of publicity. If you leave a study door unlocked in these strenuous times, the first thing you know is, somebody comes right in, sits down, and begins to talk about himself. I think with a little care we ought to be able to make this room quite decently comfortable. That putrid calendar must come down, though. Do you think you could make a long arm, and haul it off the parent tintack? Thanks. We make progress. We make progress."

"We shall jolly well make it out of the window," said Mike, spooning up tea from a paperbag with a postcard, "if a sort of young Hackenschmidt turns up and claims the study. What are you going to do about it?"

"Don't let us worry about it. I have a presentiment that he will be an insignificant-looking little weed. How are you getting on with the evening meal?"

"Just ready. What would you give to be at Eton now? I'd give something to be at Wrykyn."

"These school reports," said Psmith sympathetically, "are the very dickens. Many a bright young lad has been soured by them. Hello, what's this, I wonder."

A heavy body had plunged against the door, evidently without a suspicion that there would be any resistance. A rattling of the handle followed, and a voice outside said, "Dash the door!"

"Hackenschmidt!" said Mike.

"The weed," said Psmith. "You couldn't make a long arm, could you, and turn the key? We had better give this merchant audience. Remind me later to go on with my remarks on school reports. I had several bright things to say on the subject."

Mike unlocked the door, and flung it open. Framed in the entrance was a smallish, freckled boy, wearing a pork-pie hat and carrying a bag. On his face was an expression of mingled wrath and astonishment.

Psmith rose courteously from his chair, and moved forward with slow stateliness to do the honors.

"What the dickens," inquired the newcomer, "are you doing here?"

"We were having a little tea," said Psmith, "to restore our tissues after our journey. Come in and join us. We keep open house, we Psmiths. Let me introduce you to Comrade Jackson. A stout fellow. Homely in appearance, perhaps, but one of us. I am Psmith. Your own name will doubtless come up in the course of general chitchat over the teacups."

"My name's Spiller, and this is my study."

Psmith leaned against the mantelpiece, put up his eyeglass, and harangued Spiller in a philosophical vein.

"Of all sad words of tongue or pen," said he, "the saddest are these: 'It might have been.' Too late! That is the bitter cry. If you had torn yourself from the bosom of the Spiller family by an earlier train, all might have been well. But no. Your father held your hand and said huskily, 'Edwin, don't leave us!' Your mother clung to you weeping, and said, 'Edwin, stay!' Your sisters —"

"I want to know what —"

"Your sisters froze on to your knees like little octopuses (or octopi), and screamed, 'Don't go, Edwin!' And so," said Psmith, deeply affected by his recital, "you stayed on till the later train; and, on arrival, you find strange faces in the familiar room, a people that know not Spiller."

Psmith went to the table, and cheered himself with a sip of tea. Spiller's sad case had moved him greatly.

The victim of Fate seemed in no way consoled.

"It's beastly cheek, that's what I call it. Are you new chaps?"

"The very latest thing," said Psmith.

"Well, it's beastly cheek."

Mike's outlook on life was of the solid, practical order. He went straight to the root of the matter.

"What are you going to do about it?" he asked.

Spiller evaded the question.

"It's beastly cheek," he repeated. "You can't go about the place bagging studies."

"But we do," said Psmith. "In this life, Comrade Spiller, we must be prepared for every emergency. We must distinguish between the unusual and the impossible. It is unusual for people to go about the place bagging studies, so you have rashly ordered your life on the assumption that it is impossible. Error! Ah, Spiller, Spiller, let this be a lesson to you."

"Look here, I tell you what it —"

"I was in a car with a man once. I said to him: 'What would happen if you trod on that pedal thing instead of that other pedal thing?' He said, 'I couldn't. One's the foot brake, and the other's the accelerator.' 'But suppose you did?' I said. 'I wouldn't,' he said. 'Now we'll let her rip.' So he stamped on the accelerator. Only it turned out to be the foot brake after all, and we stopped dead, and skidded into a ditch. The advice I give to every young man starting life is: 'Never confuse the unusual and the impossible.' Take the present case. If you had only realized the possibility of somebody someday collaring your study, you might have thought out dozens of sound schemes for dealing with the matter. As it is, you are unprepared. The thing comes on you as a surprise. The cry goes round: 'Spiller has been taken unawares. He cannot cope with the situation.'"

"Can't I! I'll —"

"What *are* you going to do about it?" said Mike.

"All I know is, I'm going to have it. It was Simpson's last term, and Simpson's left, and I'm next on the house list, so, of course, it's my study."

"But what steps," said Psmith, "are you going to take? Spiller, the man of Logic, we know. But what of Spiller, the Man of Action? How do you intend to set about it? Force is useless. I was saying to Comrade Jackson before you came in, that I didn't mind betting you were an insignificant-looking little weed. And you *are* an insignificant-looking little weed."

"We'll see what Outwood says about it."

"Not an unsound scheme. By no means a scaly project. Comrade Jackson and myself were about to interview him upon another point. We may as well all go together."

The trio made their way to the Presence, Spiller pink and determined, Mike sullen, Psmith particularly debonair. He hummed lightly as he walked, and now and then pointed out to Spiller objects of interest by the wayside.

Mr. Outwood received them with the motherly warmth which was evidently the leading characteristic of his normal manner.

"Ah, Spiller," he said. "And Smith, and Jackson. I am glad to see you have already made friends."

"Spiller's, sir," said Psmith, laying a hand patronizingly on the study-claimer's shoulder — a proceeding violently resented by Spiller — "is a character one cannot help but respect. His nature expands before one like some beautiful flower."

Mr. Outwood received this eulogy with rather a startled expression, and gazed at the object of the tribute in a surprised way.

"Er-quite so, Smith, quite so," he said at last. "I like to see boys in my house friendly toward one another."

"There is no vice in Spiller," pursued Psmith earnestly. "His heart is the heart of a little child."

"Please, sir," burst out this paragon of all the virtues, "I —"

"But it was not entirely with regard to Spiller that I wished to speak to you, sir, if you were not too busy."

"Not at all, Smith, not at all. Is there anything..."

"Please, sir —" began Spiller

"I understand, sir," said Psmith, "that there is an Archaeological Society in the school."

Mr. Outwood's eyes sparkled behind their pince-nez. It was a disappointment to him that so few boys seemed to wish to belong to his chosen band. Cricket and football, games that left him cold, appeared to be the main interest in their lives. It was but rarely that he could induce new boys to join. His colleague, Mr. Downing, who presided over the School Fire Brigade, never had any difficulty in finding support. Boys came readily at his call. Mr. Outwood pondered wistfully on this at times, not knowing that the Fire Brigade owed its support to the fact that it provided its lighthearted members with perfectly unparalleled opportunities for ragging, while his own band, though small, was, in the main, earnest.

"Yes, Smith," he said, "Yes. We have a small Archaeological Society. I —er-in a measure look after it. Perhaps you would care to become a member?"

"Please, sir —" said Spiller.

"One moment, Spiller. Do you want to join, Smith?"

"Intensely, sir. Archaeology fascinates me. A grand pursuit, sir."

"Undoubtedly, Smith. I am very pleased, very pleased indeed. I will put down your name at once."

"And Jackson's, sir."

"Jackson, too!" Mr. Outwood beamed. "I am delighted. Most delighted. This is capital. This enthusiasm is most capital."

"Spiller, sir," said Psmith sadly, "I have been unable to induce to join."

"Oh, he is one of our oldest members."

"Ah," said Psmith, tolerantly, "that accounts for it."

"Please, sir —" said Spiller.

"One moment, Spiller. We shall have the first outing of the term on Saturday. We intend to inspect the Roman Camp at Embury Hill, two miles from the school."

"We shall be there, sir."

"Capital!"

"Please, sir —" said Spiller.

"One moment, Spiller," said Psmith. "There is just one other matter, if you could spare the time, sir."

"Certainly, Smith. What is that?"

"Would there be any objection to Jackson and myself taking Simpson's old study?"

"By all means, Smith. A very good idea."

"Yes, sir. It would give us a place where we could work quietly in the evenings."

"Quite so. Quite so."

"Thank you very much, sir. We will move our things in."

"Thank you very much, sir," said Mike.

"Please, sir," shouted Spiller, "aren't I to have it? I'm next on the list, sir. I come next after Simpson. Can't I have it?"

"I'm afraid I have already promised it to Smith, Spiller. You should have spoken before."

"But sir —"

Psmith eyed the speaker pityingly.

"This tendency to delay, Spiller," he said, "is your besetting fault. Correct it, Edwin. Fight against it."

He turned to Mr. Outwood.

"We should, of course, sir, always be glad to see Spiller in our study. He would always find a cheery welcome waiting there for him. There is no formality between ourselves and Spiller."

"Quite so. An excellent arrangement, Smith. I like this spirit of comradeship in my house. Then you will be with us on Saturday?"

"On Saturday, sir."

"All this sort of thing, Spiller," said Psmith, as they closed the door, "is very, very trying for a man of culture. Look us up in our study one of these afternoons."

5

GUERRILLA WARFARE

"There are few pleasures," said Psmith, as he resumed his favorite position against the mantelpiece and surveyed the commandeered study with the pride of a householder, "keener to the reflective mind than sitting under one's own rooftree. This place would have been wasted on Spiller; he would not have appreciated it properly."

Mike was finishing his tea. "You're a jolly useful chap to have by you in a crisis, Smith," he said with approval. "We ought to have known each other before."

"The loss was mine," said Psmith courteously. "We will now, with your permission, face the future for a while. I suppose you realize that we are now to a certain extent up against it. Spiller's hot Spanish blood is not going to sit tight and do nothing under a blow like this."

"What can he do? Outwood's given us the study."

"What would you have done if somebody had bagged your study?"

"Made it jolly hot for them!"

"So will Comrade Spiller. I take it that he will collect a gang and make an offensive movement against us directly he can. To all appearances we are in a fairly tight place. It all depends on how big Comrade Spiller's gang will be. I don't like rows, but I'm prepared to take on a reasonable number of assailants in defense of the home."

Mike intimated that he was with him on the point. "The difficulty is, though," he said, "about when we leave this room. I mean, we're all right while we stick here, but we can't stay all night."

"That's just what I was about to point out when you put it with such admirable clearness. Here we are in a stronghold; they can only get at us through the door, and we can lock that."

"And jam a chair against it."

"*And*, as you rightly remark, jam a chair against it. But what of the nightfall? What of the time when we retire to our dormitory?"

"Or dormitories. I say, if we're in separate rooms we shall be in the cart."

Psmith eyed Mike with approval. "He thinks of everything! You're the man, Comrade Jackson, to conduct an affair of this kind-such foresight! such resource! We must see to this at once; if they put us in different rooms we're done-we shall be destroyed singly in the watches of the night."

"We'd better nip down to the matron right off."

"Not the matron-Comrade Outwood is the man. We are as sons to him; there is nothing he can deny us. I'm afraid we are quite spoiling his afternoon by these interruptions, but we must rout him out once more."

As they got up, the door handle rattled again, and this time there followed a knocking.

"This must be an emissary of Comrade Spiller's," said Psmith. "Let us parley with the man."

Mike unlocked the door. A light-haired youth with a cheerful, rather vacant face and a receding chin strolled into the room, and stood giggling with his hands in his pockets.

"I just came up to have a look at you," he explained.

"If you move a little to the left," said Psmith, "you will catch the light-and-shade effects on Jackson's face better."

The newcomer giggled with renewed vigor. "Are you the chap with the eyeglass who jaws all the time?"

"I *do* wear an eyeglass," said Psmith; "as to the rest of the description —"

"My name's Jellicoe."

"Mine is Psmith —P-s-m-i-t-h —one of the Shropshire Psmiths. The object on the skyline is Comrade Jackson."

"Old Spiller," giggled Jellicoe, "is cursing you like anything downstairs. You *are* chaps! Do you mean to say you simply bagged his study? He's making no end of a row about it."

"Spiller's fiery nature is a byword," said Psmith.

"What's he going to do?" asked Mike, in his practical way.

"He's going to get the chaps to turn you out."

"As I suspected," sighed Psmith, as one mourning over the frailty of human nature. "About how many horny-handed assistants should you say that he would be likely to bring? Will you, for instance, join the glad throng?"

"Me? No fear! I think Spiller's an ass."

"There's nothing like a common thought for binding people together. *I* think Spiller's an ass."

"How many *will* there be, then?" asked Mike.

"He might get about half a dozen, not more, because most of the chaps don't see why they should sweat themselves just because Spiller's study has been bagged."

"Sturdy common sense," said Psmith approvingly, "seems to be the chief virtue of the Sedleigh character."

"We shall be able to tackle a crowd like that," said Mike. "The only thing is we must get into the same dormitory."

"This is where Comrade Jellicoe's knowledge of the local geography will come in useful. Do you happen to know of any snug little room, with, say, about four beds in it? How many dormitories are there?"

"Five-there's one with three beds in it, only it belongs to three chaps."

"I believe in the equal distribution of property. We will go to Comrade Outwood and stake out another claim."

Mr. Outwood received them even more beamingly than before. "Yes, Smith?" he said.

"We must apologize for disturbing you, sir —"

"Not at all, Smith, not at all! I like the boys in my house to come to me when they wish for my advice or help."

"We were wondering, sir, if you would have any objection to Jackson, Jellicoe and myself sharing the dormitory with the three beds in it. A very warm friendship..." explained Psmith, patting the gurgling Jellicoe kindly on the shoulder, "has sprung up between Jackson, Jellicoe and myself."

"You make friends easily, Smith. I like to see it —I like to see it."

"And we can have the room, sir?"

"Certainly-certainly! Tell the matron as you go down."

"And now," said Psmith, as they returned to the study, "we may say that we are in a fairly winning position. A vote of thanks to Comrade Jellicoe for his valuable assistance."

"You *are* a chap!" said Jellicoe.

The handle began to revolve again.

"That door," said Psmith, "is getting a perfect incubus! It cuts into one's leisure cruelly."

This time it was a small boy. "They told me to come up and tell you to come down," he said. Psmith looked at him searchingly through his eyeglass.

"Who?"

"The senior day room chaps."

"Spiller?"

"Spiller and Robinson and Stone, and some other chaps."

"They want us to speak to them?"

"They told me to come up and tell you to come down."

"Go and give Comrade Spiller our compliments and say that we can't come down, but shall be delighted to see him up here. Things," he said, as the messenger departed, "are beginning to move. Better leave the door open, I think; it will save trouble. Ah, come in, Comrade Spiller, what can we do for you?"

Spiller advanced into the study; the others waited outside, crowding in the doorway.

"Look here," said Spiller, "are you going to clear out of here or not?"

"After Mr. Outwood's kindly thought in giving us the room? You suggest a black and ungrateful action, Comrade Spiller."

"You'll get it hot, if you don't."

"We'll risk it," said Mike.

Jellicoe giggled in the background; the drama in the atmosphere appealed to him. His was a simple and appreciative mind.

"Come on, you chaps," cried Spiller suddenly.

There was an inward rush on the enemy's part, but Mike had been watching. He grabbed Spiller by the shoulders and ran him back against the advancing crowd. For a moment the doorway was blocked, then the weight and impetus of Mike and Spiller prevailed, the enemy gave back, and Mike, stepping into the room again, slammed the door and locked it.

"A neat piece of work," said Psmith approvingly, adjusting his tie at the looking glass. "The preliminaries may now be considered over, the first shot has been fired. The dogs of war are now loose."

A heavy body crashed against the door.

"They'll have it down," said Jellicoe.

"We must act, Comrade Jackson! Might I trouble you just to turn that key quietly, and the handle, and then to stand by for the next attack."

There was a scrambling of feet in the passage outside, and then a repetition of the onslaught on the door. This time, however, the door, instead of resisting, swung open, and the human battering ram staggered through into the study. Mike, turning after relocking the door, was just in time to see Psmith, with a display of energy of which one would not have believed him capable, grip the invader scientifically by an arm and a leg.

Mike jumped to help, but it was needless; the captive was already on the windowsill. As Mike arrived, Psmith dropped him onto the flowerbed below.

Psmith closed the window gently and turned to Jellicoe. "Who was our guest?" he asked, dusting the knees of his trousers where they had pressed against the wall.

"Robinson. I say, you *are* a chap!"

"Robinson, was it? Well, we are always glad to see Comrade Robinson, always. I wonder if anybody else is thinking of calling?"

Apparently frontal attack had been abandoned. Whisperings could be heard in the corridor. Somebody hammered on the door.

"Yes?" called Psmith patiently.

"You'd better come out, you know; you'll only get it hotter if you don't."

"Leave us, Spiller; we would be alone."

A bell rang in the distance.

"Tea," said Jellicoe; "we shall have to go now."

"They won't do anything till after tea, I shouldn't think," said Mike.

"There's no harm in going out."

The passage was empty when they opened the door; the call to food was evidently a thing not to be treated lightly by the enemy.

In the dining room the beleaguered garrison were the object of general attention. Everybody turned to look at them as they came in. It was plain that the study episode had been a topic of conversation. Spiller's face was crimson, and Robinson's coat sleeve still bore traces of garden mold.

Mike felt rather conscious of the eyes, but Psmith was in his element. His demeanor throughout the meal was that of some whimsical monarch condescending for a freak to revel with his humble subjects.

Toward the end of the meal Psmith scribbled a note and passed it to Mike. It read: "Directly this is over, nip upstairs as quickly as you can."

Mike followed the advice; they were first out of the room. When they had been in the study a few moments, Jellicoe knocked at the door. "Lucky you two cut away so quick," he said. "They were going to try and get you into the senior day room and scrag you there."

"This," said Psmith, leaning against the mantelpiece, "is exciting, but it can't go on. We have got for our sins to be in this place for a whole term, and if we are going to do the Hunted Fawn business all the time, life in the true sense of the word will become an impossibility. My nerves are so delicately attuned that the strain would simply reduce them to hash. We are not prepared to carry on a long campaign-the thing must be settled at once."

"Shall we go down to the senior day room, and have it out?" said Mike.

"No, we will play the fixture on our own ground. I think we may take it as tolerably certain that Comrade Spiller and his hired ruffians will try to corner us in the dormitory tonight. Well, of course, we could fake up some sort of barricade for the door, but then we should have all the trouble over again tomorrow and the day after that. Personally I don't propose to be chivied about indefinitely like this, so I propose that we let them come into the dormitory, and see what happens. Is this meeting with me?"

"I think that's sound," said Mike. "We needn't drag Jellicoe into it."

"As a matter of fact-if you don't mind..." began that man of peace.

"Quite right," said Psmith; "this is not Comrade Jellicoe's scene at all; he has got to spend the term in the senior day room, whereas we have our little wooden *châlet* to retire to in times of stress. Comrade Jellicoe must stand out of the game altogether. We shall be glad of his moral support, but otherwise, *ne pas*. And now, as there won't be anything doing till bedtime, I think I'll collar this table and write home and tell my people that all is well with their Rupert."

6

UNPLEASANTNESS IN THE SMALL HOURS

Jellicoe, that human encyclopedia, consulted on the probable movements of the enemy, deposed that Spiller, retiring at ten, would make for Dormitory One in the same passage, where Robinson also had a bed. The rest of the opposing forces were distributed among other and more distant rooms. It was probable, therefore, that Dormitory One would be the rendezvous. As to the time when an attack might be expected, it was unlikely that it would occur before half past eleven. Mr. Outwood went the round of the dormitories at eleven.

"And touching," said Psmith, "the matter of noise, must this business be conducted in a subdued and *sotto voce* manner, or may we let ourselves go a bit here and there?"

"I shouldn't think old Outwood's likely to hear you-he sleeps miles away on the other side of the house. He never hears anything. We often rag half the night and nothing happens."

"This appears to be a thoroughly nice, well-conducted establishment. What would my mother say if she could see her Rupert in the midst of these reckless youths!"

"All the better," said Mike; "we don't want anybody butting in and stopping the show before it's half started."

"Comrade Jackson's berserk blood is up—I can hear it sizzling. I quite agree these things are all very disturbing and painful, but it's as well to do them thoroughly when one's once in for them. Is there nobody else who might interfere with our gambols?"

"Barnes might," said Jellicoe, "only he won't."

"Who is Barnes?"

"Head of the house—a rotter. He's in a funk of Stone and Robinson; they rag him; he'll simply sit tight."

"Then I think," said Psmith placidly, "we may look forward to a very pleasant evening. Shall we be moving?"

Mr. Outwood paid his visit at eleven, as predicted by Jellicoe, beaming vaguely into the darkness over a torch, and disappeared again, closing the door.

"How about that door?" said Mike. "Shall we leave it open for them?"

"Not so, but far otherwise. If it's shut we shall hear them at it when they come. Subject to your approval, Comrade Jackson, I have evolved the following plan of action. I always ask myself on these occasions, 'What would Napoleon have done?' I think Napoleon would have sat in a chair by his washhand stand, which is close to the door; he would have posted you by your washhand stand, and he would have instructed Comrade Jellicoe, directly he heard the door handle turned, to give his celebrated imitation of a dormitory breathing heavily in its sleep. He would then—"

"I tell you what," said Mike, "How about tying a string at the top of the steps?"

"Yes, Napoleon would have done that, too. Hats off to Comrade Jackson, the man with the big brain!"

The floor of the dormitory was below the level of the door. There were three steps leading down to it. Psmith switched on his torch and they examined the ground. The leg of a wardrobe and the leg of Jellicoe's bed made it possible for the string to be fastened in a satisfactory manner across the lower step. Psmith surveyed the result with approval.

"Dashed neat!" he said. "Practically the sunken road which dished the Cuirassiers at Waterloo. I seem to see Comrade Spiller coming one of the finest purlers in the world's history."

"If they've got a torch—"

"They won't have. If they have, stand by and grab it at once; then they'll charge forward and all will be well. If they have no light, fire into the brown with a jug of water. Lest we forget, I'll collar Comrade Jellicoe's jug now and keep it handy. A couple of sheets would also not be amiss-we will enmesh the enemy!"

"Right ho!" said Mike.

"These humane preparations being concluded," said Psmith, "we will retire to our posts and wait. Comrade Jellicoe, don't forget to breathe like an asthmatic sheep when you hear the door opened; they may wait at the top of the steps, listening."

"You *are* a lad!" said Jellicoe.

Waiting in the dark for something to happen is always a trying experience, especially if, as on this occasion, silence is essential. Mike was tired after his journey, and he had begun to doze when he was jerked back to wakefulness by the stealthy turning of the door handle; the faintest rustle from Psmith's direction followed, and a slight giggle, succeeded by a series of deep breaths, showed that Jellicoe, too, had heard the noise.

There was a creaking sound.

It was pitch-dark in the dormitory, but Mike could follow the invaders' movements as clearly as if it had been broad daylight. They had opened the door and were listening. Jellicoe's breathing grew more asthmatic; he was flinging himself into his part with the wholeheartedness of the true artist.

The creak was followed by a sound of whispering, then another creak. The enemy had advanced to the top step.... Another creak.... The vanguard had reached the second step.... In another moment —

CRASH!

And at that point the proceedings may be said to have formally opened.

A struggling mass bumped against Mike's shins as he rose from his chair; he emptied his jug onto this mass, and a yell of anguish showed that the contents had got to the right address.

Then a hand grabbed his ankle and he went down, a million sparks dancing before his eyes as a fist, flying out at a venture, caught him on the nose.

Mike had not been well disposed toward the invaders before, but now he ran amok, hitting out right and left at random. His right missed, but his left went home hard on some portion of somebody's anatomy. A kick freed his ankle and he staggered to his feet. At the same moment a sudden increase in the general volume of noise spoke eloquently of good work that was being put in by Psmith.

Even at that crisis, Mike could not help feeling that if a row of this caliber did not draw Mr. Outwood from his bed, he must be an unusual kind of housemaster.

He plunged forward again with outstretched arms, and stumbled and fell over one of the on-the-floor section of the opposing force. They seized each other earnestly and rolled across the room till Mike, contriving to secure his adversary's head, bumped it on the floor with such abandon that, with a muffled yell, the other let go, and for the second time he rose. As he did so he was conscious of a curious thudding sound that made itself heard through the other assorted noises of the battle.

All this time the fight had gone on in the blackest darkness, but now a light shone on the proceedings. Interested occupants of other dormitories, roused from their slumbers, had come to observe the sport. They had switched on the light and were crowding in the doorway.

By the light of this Mike got a swift view of the theater of war. The enemy appeared to number five. The warrior whose head Mike had bumped on the floor was Robinson, who was sitting up feeling his skull in a gingerly fashion. To Mike's right, almost touching him, was Stone. In the direction of the door, Psmith, wielding in his right hand the cord of a dressing gown, was engaging the remaining three with a patient smile.

They were clad in pajamas, and appeared to be feeling the dressing-gown cord acutely.

The sudden light dazed both sides momentarily. The defense was the first to recover, Mike, with a swing, upsetting Stone, and Psmith, having seized and emptied Jellicoe's jug over Spiller, getting to work again with the cord in a manner that roused the utmost enthusiasm of the spectators.

246

Agility seemed to be the leading feature of Psmith's tactics. He was everywhere-on Mike's bed, on his own, on Jellicoe's (drawing a passionate complaint from that noncombatant, on whose face he inadvertently trod), on the floor-he ranged the room, sowing destruction.

The enemy were disheartened; they had started with the idea that this was to be a surprise attack, and it was disconcerting to find the garrison armed at all points. Gradually they edged to the door, and a final rush sent them through.

"Hold the door for a second," cried Psmith, and vanished. Mike was alone in the doorway.

It was a situation which exactly suited his frame of mind; he stood alone in direct opposition to the community into which Fate had pitchforked him so abruptly. He liked the feeling; for the first time since his father had given him his views upon school reports that morning in the Easter holidays, he felt satisfied with life. He hoped, outnumbered as he was, that the enemy would come on again and not give the thing up in disgust; he wanted more.

On an occasion like this there is rarely anything approaching concerted action on the part of the aggressors. When the attack came, it was not a combined attack; Stone, who was nearest to the door, made a sudden dash forward, and Mike hit him under the chin.

Stone drew back, and there was another interval for rest and reflection.

It was interrupted by the reappearance of Psmith, who strolled back along the passage swinging his dressing-gown cord as if it were some clouded cane.

"Sorry to keep you waiting, Comrade Jackson," he said politely. "Duty called me elsewhere. With the kindly aid of a guide who knows the lie of the land, I have been making a short tour of the dormitories. I have poured divers jugfuls of water over Comrade Spiller's bed, Comrade Robinson's bed, Comrade Stone's —Spiller, Spiller, these are harsh words; where you pick them up I can't think-not from me. Well, well, I suppose there must be an end to the pleasantest of functions. Good night, good night."

The door closed behind Mike and himself. For ten minutes shufflings and whisperings went on in the corridor, but nobody touched the handle.

Then there was a sound of retreating footsteps, and silence reigned.

On the following morning there was a notice on the house board. It ran: IND

7

ADAIR

On the same morning Mike met Adair for the first time.

He was going across to school with Psmith and Jellicoe, when a group of three came out of the gate of the house next door.

"That's Adair," said Jellicoe, "in the middle."

His voice had assumed a tone almost of awe.

"Who's Adair?" asked Mike.

"Captain of cricket, and lots of other things."

Mike could only see the celebrity's back. He had broad shoulders and wiry, light hair, almost white. He walked well, as if he were used to running. Altogether a fit-looking sort of man. Even Mike's jaundiced eye saw that.

As a matter of fact, Adair deserved more than a casual glance. He was that rare type, the natural leader. Many boys and men, if accident, or the passage of time, places them in a position where they are expected to lead, can handle the job without disaster; but that is a very different thing from being a born leader. Adair was of the sort that comes to the top by sheer force of character and determination. He was not naturally clever at work, but he had gone at it with a dogged resolution which had carried him up the school, and landed him high in the Sixth. As a cricketer he was almost entirely self-taught. Nature had given him a good eye, and left the thing at that. Adair's doggedness had triumphed over her failure to do her work thoroughly. At the cost of more trouble than most people give to their life work he had made himself into a bowler. He read the authorities, and watched first-class players, and thought the thing out on his own account, and he divided the art of bowling into three sections. First, and most important-pitch. Second on the list-break. Third-pace. He set himself to acquire pitch. He acquired it. Bowling at his own pace and without any attempt at break, he could now drop the ball on an envelope seven times out of ten.

Break was a more uncertain quantity. Sometimes he could get it at the expense of pitch, sometimes at the expense of pace. Some days he could get all three, and then he was an uncommonly bad man to face on anything but a plumb wicket.

Running he had acquired in a similar manner. He had nothing approaching style, but he had twice won the mile and half mile at the Sports off elegant runners, who knew all about stride and the correct timing of the sprints and all the rest of it.

Briefly, he was a worker. He had heart.

A boy of Adair's type is always a force in a school. In a big public school or six or seven hundred, his influence is felt less; but in a small school like Sedleigh he is like a tidal wave, sweeping all before him. There were two hundred boys at Sedleigh, and there was not one of them in all probability who had not, directly or indirectly, been influenced by Adair. As a small boy his sphere was not large, but the effects of his work began to be apparent even then. It is human nature to want to get something which somebody else obviously values very much; and when it was observed by members of his form that Adair was going to great trouble and inconvenience to secure a place in the form eleven or fifteen, they naturally began to think, too, that it was worth being in those teams. The consequence was that his form always played hard. This made other forms play hard. And the net result was that, when Adair succeeded to the captaincy of Rugger and cricket in the same year, Sedleigh, as Mr. Downing, Adair's housemaster and the nearest approach to a cricket master that Sedleigh possessed, had a fondness for saying, was a keen school. As a whole, it both worked and played with energy.

All it wanted now was opportunity.

This Adair was determined to give it. He had that passionate fondness for his school which every boy is popularly supposed to have, but which really is implanted in about one in every thousand. The average public-school boy *likes* his school. He hopes it will lick Bedford at Rugger and Malvern at cricket, but he rather bets it won't. He is sorry to leave, and he likes going back at the end of the holidays, but as for any passionate, deep-seated love of the place, he would think it rather bad form than otherwise. If anybody came up to him, slapped him on the back, and cried, "Come along, Jenkins, my boy! Play up for the old school, Jenkins! The dear old school! The old place you love so!" he would feel seriously ill.

Adair was the exception.

To Adair, Sedleigh was almost a religion. Both his parents were dead; his guardian, with whom he spent the holidays, was a man with neuralgia at one end of him and gout at the other; and the only really pleasant times Adair had had, as far back as he could remember, he owed to Sedleigh. The place had grown on him, absorbed him. Where Mike, violently transplanted from Wrykyn, saw only a wretched little hole not to be mentioned in the same breath with Wrykyn, Adair, dreaming of the future, saw a colossal establishment, a public school among public schools, a lump of human radium, shooting out Blues and Balliol Scholars year after year without ceasing.

It would not be so till long after he was gone and forgotten, but he did not mind that. His devotion to Sedleigh was purely unselfish. He did not want fame. All he worked for was that the school should grow and grow, keener and better at games and more prosperous year by year, till it should take its rank among *the* schools, and to be an Old Sedleighan should be a badge passing its owner everywhere.

"He's captain of cricket and Rugger," said Jellicoe impressively. "He's in the shooting eight. He's won the mile and half mile two years running. He would have boxed at Aldershot last term, only he sprained his wrist. And he plays fives jolly well!"

"Sort of little tin god," said Mike, taking a violent dislike to Adair from that moment.

Mike's actual acquaintance with this all-round man dated from the dinner hour that day. Mike was walking to the house with Psmith. Psmith was a little ruffled on account of a slight passage-of-arms he had had with his form master during morning school.

"'There's a P before the Smith,' I said to him. 'Ah, P. Smith, I see,' replied the goat. 'Not Peasmith,' I replied, exercising wonderful self-restraint, 'just Psmith.' It took me ten minutes to drive the thing into the man's head; and when I *had* driven it in, he sent me out of the room for looking at him through my eyeglass. Comrade Jackson, I fear me we have fallen among bad men. I suspect that we are going to be much persecuted by scoundrels."

"Both you chaps play cricket, I suppose?"

They turned. It was Adair. Seeing him face to face, Mike was aware of a pair of very bright blue eyes and a square jaw. In any other place and mood he would have liked Adair at sight. His prejudice, however, against all things Sedleighan was too much for him. "I don't," he said shortly.

"Haven't you *ever* played?"

"My little sister and I sometimes play with a soft ball at home."

Adair looked sharply at him. A temper was evidently one of his numerous qualities.

"Oh," he said. "Well, perhaps you wouldn't mind turning out this afternoon and seeing what you can do with a hard ball-if you can manage without your little sister."

"I should think the form at this place would be about on a level with hers. But I don't happen to be playing cricket, as I think I told you."

Adair's jaw grew squarer than ever. Mike was wearing a gloomy scowl.

Psmith joined suavely in the dialogue.

"My dear old comrades," he said, "Don't let us brawl over this matter. This is a time for the honeyed word, the kindly eye, and the pleasant smile. Let me explain to Comrade Adair. Speaking for Comrade Jackson and myself, we should both be delighted to join in the mimic warfare of our National Game, as you suggest, only the fact is, we happen to be the Young Archaeologists. We gave in our names last night. When you are being carried back to the pavilion after your century against Loamshire-do you play Loamshire? —we shall be grubbing in the hard ground for ruined abbeys. The old choice between Pleasure and Duty, Comrade Adair. A Boy's Crossroads."

"Then you won't play?"

"No," said Mike.

"Archaeology," said Psmith, with a deprecatory wave of the hand, "will brook no divided allegiance from her devotees."

Adair turned, and walked on.

Scarcely had he gone, when another voice hailed them with precisely the same question.

"Both you fellows are going to play cricket, eh?"

It was a master. A short, wiry little man with a sharp nose and a general resemblance, both in manner and appearance, to an excitable bullfinch.

"I saw Adair speaking to you. I suppose you will both play. I like every new boy to begin at once. The more new blood we have, the better. We want keenness here. We are, above all, a keen school. I want every boy to be keen."

"We are, sir," said Psmith, with fervor.

"Excellent."

"On archaeology."

Mr. Downing-for it was no less a celebrity-started, as one who perceives a loathly caterpillar in his salad.

"Archaeology!"

"We gave in our names to Mr. Outwood last night, sir. Archaeology is a passion with us, sir. When we heard that there was a society here, we went singing about the house."

"I call it an unnatural pursuit for boys," said Mr. Downing vehemently. "I don't like it. I tell you I don't like it. It is not for me to interfere with one of my colleagues on the staff, but I tell you frankly that in my opinion it is an abominable waste of time for a boy. It gets him into idle, loafing habits."

"I never loaf, sir," said Psmith.

"I was not alluding to you in particular. I was referring to the principle of the thing. A boy ought to be playing cricket with other boys, not wandering at large about the country, probably smoking and going into low public houses."

"A very wild lot, sir, I fear, the Archaeological Society here," sighed
Psmith, shaking his head.

"If you choose to waste your time, I suppose I can't hinder you. But in my opinion it is foolery, nothing else."

He stumped off.

"Now *he's* cross," said Psmith, looking after him. "I'm afraid we're getting ourselves disliked here."

"Good job, too."

"At any rate, Comrade Outwood loves us. Let's go on and see what sort of a lunch that large-hearted fossil fancier is going to give us."

8

MIKE FINDS OCCUPATION

There was more than one moment during the first fortnight of term when Mike found himself regretting the attitude he had imposed upon himself with regard to Sedleighan cricket. He began to realize the eternal truth of the proverb about half a loaf and no bread. In the first flush of his resentment against his new surroundings he had refused to play cricket. And now he positively ached for a game. Any sort of a game. An innings for a Kindergarten v. the Second Eleven of a Home of Rest for Centenarians would have soothed him. There were times, when the sun shone, and he caught sight of white flannels on a green ground, and heard the "plonk" of bat striking ball, when he felt like rushing to Adair and shouting, "I *will* be good. I was in the Wrykyn team three years, and had an average of over fifty the last two seasons. Lead me to the nearest net, and let me feel a bat in my hands again."

But every time he shrank from such a climb down. It couldn't be done.

What made it worse was that he saw, after watching behind the nets once or twice, that Sedleigh cricket was not the childish burlesque of the game which he had been rash enough to assume that it must be. Numbers do not make good cricket. They only make the presence of good cricketers more likely, by the law of averages.

Mike soon saw that cricket was by no means an unknown art at Sedleigh. Adair, to begin with, was a very good bowler indeed. He was not a Burgess, but Burgess was the only Wrykyn bowler whom, in his three years' experience of the school, Mike would have placed above him. He was a long way better than Neville-Smith, and Wyatt, and Milton, and the others who had taken wickets for Wrykyn.

The batting was not so good, but there were some quite capable men. Barnes, the head of Outwood's, he who preferred not to interfere with Stone and Robinson, was a mild, rather timid-looking youth-not unlike what Mr. Outwood must have been as a boy-but he knew how to keep balls out of his wicket. He was a good bat of the old plodding type.

Stone and Robinson themselves, that swashbuckling pair, who now treated Mike and Psmith with cold but consistent politeness, were both fair batsmen, and Stone was a good slow bowler.

There were other exponents of the game, mostly in Downing's house.

Altogether, quite worthy colleagues even for a man who had been a star at Wrykyn.

* * * * *

One solitary overture Mike made during that first fortnight. He did not repeat the experiment.

It was on a Thursday afternoon, after school. The day was warm, but freshened by an almost imperceptible breeze. The air was full of the scent of the cut grass which lay in little heaps behind the nets. This is the real cricket scent, which calls to one like the very voice of the game.

Mike, as he sat there watching, could stand it no longer.

He went up to Adair.

"May I have an innings at this net?" he asked. He was embarrassed and nervous, and was trying not to show it. The natural result was that his manner was offensively abrupt.

Adair was taking off his pads after his innings. He looked up. "This net," it may be observed, was the first eleven net.

"What?" he said.

Mike repeated his request. More abruptly this time, from increased embarrassment.

"This is the first eleven net," said Adair coldly. "Go in after Lodge over there."

"Over there" was the end net, where frenzied novices were bowling on a corrugated pitch to a red-haired youth with enormous feet, who looked as if he were taking his first lesson at the game.

Mike walked away without a word.

* * * * *

The Archaeological Society expeditions, even though they carried with them the privilege of listening to Psmith's views of life, proved but a poor substitute for cricket. Psmith, who had no counterattraction shouting to him that he ought to be elsewhere, seemed to enjoy them hugely, but Mike almost cried sometimes from boredom. It was not always possible to slip away from the throng, for Mr. Outwood evidently looked upon them as among the very faithful, and kept them by his side.

Mike on these occasions was silent and jumpy, his brow "sicklied o'er with the pale cast of care." But Psmith followed his leader with the pleased and indulgent air of a father whose infant son is showing him round the garden. Psmith's attitude toward archaeological research struck a new note in the history of that neglected science. He was amiable, but patronizing. He patronized fossils, and he patronized ruins. If he had been confronted with the Great Pyramid, he would have patronized that.

He seemed to be consumed by a thirst for knowledge.

That this was not altogether a genuine thirst was proved in the third expedition. Mr. Outwood and his band were pecking away at the site of an old Roman camp. Psmith approached Mike.

"Having inspired confidence," he said, "by the docility of our demeanor, let us slip away, and brood apart for awhile. Roman camps, to be absolutely accurate, give me the pip. And I never want to see another putrid fossil in my life. Let us find some shady nook where a man may lie on his back for a bit."

Mike, over whom the proceedings connected with the Roman camp had long since begun to shed a blue depression, offered no opposition, and they strolled away down the hill.

Looking back, they saw that the archaeologists were still hard at it. Their departure had passed unnoticed.

"A fatiguing pursuit, this grubbing for mementos of the past," said Psmith. "And, above all, dashed bad for the knees of the trousers. Mine are like some furrowed field. It's a great grief to a man of refinement, I can tell you, Comrade Jackson. Ah, this looks a likely spot."

They had passed through a gate into the field beyond. At the farther end there was a brook, shaded by trees and running with a pleasant sound over pebbles.

"Thus far," said Psmith, hitching up the knees of his trousers, and sitting down, "and no farther. We will rest here awhile, and listen to the music of the brook. In fact, unless you have anything important to say, I rather think I'll go to sleep. In this busy life of ours these naps by the wayside are invaluable. Call me in about an hour." And Psmith, heaving the comfortable sigh of the worker who by toil has earned rest, lay down, with his head against a mossy tree stump, and closed his eyes.

Mike sat on for a few minutes, listening to the water and making centuries in his mind, and then, finding this a little dull, he got up, jumped the brook, and began to explore the wood on the other side.

He had not gone many yards when a dog emerged suddenly from the undergrowth, and began to bark vigorously at him.

Mike liked dogs, and, on acquaintance, they always liked him. But when you meet a dog in someone else's wood, it is as well not to stop in order that you may get to understand each other. Mike began to thread his way back through the trees.

He was too late.

"Stop! What the dickens are you doing here?" shouted a voice behind him.

In the same situation a few years before, Mike would have carried on, and trusted to speed to save him. But now there seemed a lack of dignity in the action. He came back to where the man was standing.

"I'm sorry if I'm trespassing," he said. "I was just having a look round."

"The dickens you-Why, you're Jackson!"

Mike looked at him. He was a short, broad young man with a fair moustache. Mike knew that he had seen him before somewhere, but he could not place him.

"I played against you, for the Free Foresters last summer. In passing you seem to be a bit of a free forester yourself, dancing in among my nesting pheasants."

"I'm frightfully sorry."

"That's all right. Where do you spring from?"

"Of course —I remember you now. You're Prendergast. You made fifty-eight not out."

"Thanks. I was afraid the only thing you would remember about me was that you took a century mostly off my bowling."

"You ought to have had me second ball, only cover dropped it."

"Don't rake up forgotten tragedies. How is it you're not at Wrykyn? What are you doing down here?"

"I've left Wrykyn."

Prendergast suddenly changed the conversation. When a fellow tells you that he has left school unexpectedly, it is not always tactful to inquire the reason. He began to talk about himself.

"I hang out down here. I do a little farming and a good deal of puttering about."

"Get any cricket?" asked Mike, turning to the subject next his heart.

"Only village. Very keen, but no great shakes. By the way, how are you off for cricket now? Have you ever got a spare afternoon?"

Mike's heart leaped.

"Any Wednesday or Saturday. Look here, I'll tell you how it is."

And he told how matters stood with him.

"So, you see," he concluded, "I'm supposed to be hunting for ruins and things" —Mike's ideas on the subject of archaeology were vague —"but I could always slip away. We all start out together, but I could nip back, get onto my bike —I've got it down here-and meet you anywhere you liked. By Jove, I'm simply dying for a game. I can hardly keep my hands off a bat."

"I'll give you all you want. What you'd better do is to ride straight to Lower Borlock-that's the name of the place-and I'll meet you on the ground. Anyone will tell you where Lower Borlock is. It's just off the London road. There's a signpost where you turn off. Can you come next Saturday?"

"Rather. I suppose you can fix me up with a bat and pads? I don't want to bring mine."

"I'll lend you everything. I say, you know, we can't give you a Wrykyn wicket. The Lower Borlock pitch isn't a shirt front."

"I'll play on a rockery, if you want me to," said Mike.

* * * * *

"You're going to what?" asked Psmith, sleepily, on being awakened and told the news.

"I'm going to play cricket, for a village near here. I say, don't tell a soul, will you? I don't want it to get about, or I may get lugged in to play for the school."

"My lips are sealed. I think I'll come and watch you. Cricket I dislike, but watching cricket is one of the finest of Britain's manly sports. I'll borrow Jellicoe's bicycle."

* * * * *

That Saturday, Lower Borlock smote the men of Chidford hip and thigh. Their victory was due to a hurricane innings of seventy-five by a newcomer to the team, M. Jackson.

9

THE FIRE BRIGADE MEETING

Cricket is the great safety valve. If you like the game, and are in a position to play it at least twice a week, life can never be entirely gray. As time went on, and his average for Lower Borlock reached the fifties and stayed there, Mike began, though he would not have admitted it, to enjoy himself. It was not Wrykyn, but it was a very decent substitute.

The only really considerable element making for discomfort now was Mr. Downing. By bad luck it was in his form that Mike had been placed on arrival; and Mr. Downing, never an easy form master to get on with, proved more than usually difficult in his dealings with Mike.

They had taken a dislike to each other at their first meeting; and it grew with further acquaintance. To Mike, Mr. Downing was all that a master ought not to be, fussy, pompous, and openly influenced in his official dealings with his form by his own private likes and dislikes. To Mr. Downing, Mike was simply an unamiable loafer, who did nothing for the school and apparently had none of the healthy instincts which should be implanted in the healthy boy. Mr. Downing was rather strong on the healthy boy.

The two lived in a state of simmering hostility, punctuated at intervals by crises, which usually resulted in Lower Borlock having to play some unskilled laborer in place of their star batsman, employed doing "overtime."

One of the most acute of these crises, and the most important, in that it was the direct cause of Mike's appearance in Sedleigh cricket, had to do with the third weekly meeting of the School Fire Brigade.

It may be remembered that this well-supported institution was under Mr. Downing's special care. It was, indeed, his pet hobby and the apple of his eye.

Just as you had to join the Archaeological Society to secure the esteem of Mr. Outwood, so to become a member of the Fire Brigade was a safe passport to the regard of Mr. Downing. To show a keenness for cricket was good, but to join the Fire Brigade was best of all.

The Brigade was carefully organized. At its head was Mr. Downing, a sort of high priest; under him was a captain, and under the captain a vice-captain. These two officials were those sportive allies, Stone and Robinson, of Outwood's house, who, having perceived at a very early date the gorgeous opportunities for ragging which the Brigade offered to its members, had joined young and worked their way up.

Under them were the rank and file, about thirty in all, of whom perhaps seven were earnest workers, who looked on the Brigade in the right, or Downing, spirit. The rest were entirely frivolous.

The weekly meetings were always full of life and excitement.

At this point it is as well to introduce Sammy to the reader.

Sammy, short for Sampson, was a young bull terrier belonging to Mr. Downing. If it is possible for a man to have two apples of his eye, Sammy was the other. He was a large, lighthearted dog with a white coat, an engaging expression, the tongue of an anteater, and a manner which was a happy blend of hurricane and circular saw. He had long legs, a tenor voice, and was apparently made of India rubber.

Sammy was a great favorite in the school, and a particular friend of Mike's, the Wrykynian being always a firm ally of every dog he met after two minutes' acquaintance.

In passing, Jellicoe owned a clockwork rat, much in request during
French lessons.

We will now proceed to the painful details.

* * * * *

The meetings of the Fire Brigade were held after school in Mr. Downing's form room. The proceedings always began in the same way, by the reading of the minutes of the last meeting. After that the entertainment varied according to whether the members happened to be fertile or not in ideas for the disturbing of the peace.

Today they were in very fair form.

As soon as Mr. Downing had closed the minute book, Wilson, of the School House, held up his hand.

"Well, Wilson?"

"Please, sir, couldn't we have a uniform for the Brigade?"

"A uniform?" Mr. Downing pondered.

"Red, with green stripes, sir."

Red, with a thin green stripe, was the Sedleigh color.

"Shall I put it to the vote, sir?" asked Stone.

"One moment, Stone."

"Those in favor of the motion move to the left, those against it to the right."

A scuffling of feet, a slamming of desk lids and an upset blackboard, and the meeting had divided.

Mr. Downing rapped irritably on his desk.

"Sit down!" he said. "Sit down! I won't have this noise and disturbance. Stone, sit down-Wilson, get back to your place."

"Please, sir, the motion is carried by twenty-five votes to six."

"Please, sir, may I go and get measured this evening?"

"Please, sir —"

"Si-*lence!* The idea of a uniform is, of course, out of the question."

"Oo-oo-oo-oo, sir-r-r!"

"Be *quiet!* Entirely out of the question. We cannot plunge into needless expense. Stone, listen to me. I cannot have this noise and disturbance! Another time when a point arises it must be settled by a show of hands. Well, Wilson?"

"Please, sir, may we have helmets?"

"Very useful as a protection against falling timbers, sir," said Robinson.

"I don't think my people would be pleased, sir, if they knew I was going out to fires without a helmet," said Stone.

The whole strength of the company: "Please, sir, may we have helmets?"

"Those in favor..." began Stone.

Mr. Downing banged on his desk. "Silence! Silence!! Silence!!! Helmets are, of course, perfectly preposterous."

"Oo-oo-oo-oo, sir-r-r!"

"But, sir, the danger!"

"Please, sir, the falling timbers!"

The Fire Brigade had been in action once and once only in the memory of man, and that time it was a haystack which had burned itself out just as the rescuers had succeeded in fastening the hose to the hydrant.

"Silence!"

"Then, please, sir, couldn't we have an honor cap? It wouldn't be expensive, and it would be just as good as a helmet for all the timbers that are likely to fall on our heads."

Mr. Downing smiled a wry smile.

"Our Wilson is facetious," he remarked frostily.

"Sir, no, sir! I wasn't facetious! Or couldn't we have tasseled caps like the first fifteen have? They —"

"Wilson, leave the room!"

"Sir, *please*, sir!"

"This moment, Wilson. And," as he reached the door, "do me one hundred lines."

A pained "OO-oo-oo, sir-r-r," was cut off by the closing door.

Mr. Downing proceeded to improve the occasion. "I deplore this growing spirit of flippancy," he said. "I tell you I deplore it! It is not right! If this Fire Brigade is to be of solid use, there must be less of this flippancy. We must have keenness. I want you boys above all to be keen. I...? What is that noise?"

From the other side of the door proceeded a sound like water gurgling from a bottle, mingled with cries half suppressed, as if somebody were being prevented from uttering them by a hand laid over his mouth. The sufferer appeared to have a high voice.

There was a tap at the door and Mike walked in. He was not alone. Those near enough to see, saw that he was accompanied by Jellicoe's clockwork rat, which moved rapidly over the floor in the direction of the opposite wall.

"May I fetch a book from my desk, sir?" asked Mike.

"Very well-be quick, Jackson; we are busy."

Being interrupted in one of his addresses to the Brigade irritated Mr. Downing.

The muffled cries grew more distinct.

"What...is...that...noise?" shrilled Mr. Downing.

"Noise, sir?" asked Mike, puzzled.

"I think it's something outside the window, sir," said Stone helpfully.

"A bird, I think, sir," said Robinson.

"Don't be absurd!" snapped Mr. Downing. "It's outside the door. Wilson!"

"Yes, sir?" said a voice "off."

"Are you making that whining noise?"

"Whining noise, sir? No, sir, I'm not making a whining noise."

"What *sort* of noise, sir?" inquired Mike, as many Wrykynians had asked before him. It was a question invented by Wrykyn for use in just such a case as this.

"I do not propose," said Mr. Downing acidly, "to imitate the noise; you can all hear it perfectly plainly. It is a curious whining noise."

"They are mowing the cricket field, sir," said the invisible Wilson.

"Perhaps that's it."

"It may be one of the desks squeaking, sir," put in Stone. "They do sometimes."

"Or somebody's shoes, sir," added Robinson.

"Silence! Wilson?"

"Yes, sir?" bellowed the unseen one.

"Don't shout at me from the corridor like that. Come in."

"Yes, sir!"

As he spoke the muffled whining changed suddenly to a series of tenor shrieks, and the India-rubber form of Sammy bounded into the room like an excited kangaroo.

Willing hands had by this time deflected the clockwork rat from the wall to which it had been steering, and pointed it up the alleyway between the two rows of desks. Mr. Downing, rising from his place, was just in time to see Sammy with a last leap spring on his prey and begin worrying it.

Chaos reigned.

"A rat!" shouted Robinson.

The twenty-three members of the Brigade who were not earnest instantly dealt with the situation, each in the manner that seemed proper to him. Some leaped onto forms, others flung books, all shouted. It was a stirring, bustling scene.

Sammy had by this time disposed of the clockwork rat, and was now standing, like Marius, among the ruins barking triumphantly.

The banging on Mr. Downing's desk resembled thunder. It rose above all the other noises till in time they gave up the competition and died away.

Mr. Downing shot out orders, threats, and penalties with the rapidity of a Bren gun.

"Stone, sit down! Donovan, if you do not sit down you will be severely punished. Henderson, one hundred lines for gross disorder! Windham, the same! Go to your seat, Vincent. What are you doing, Broughton-Knight? I will not have this disgraceful noise and disorder! The meeting is at an end; go quietly from the room, all of you. Jackson and Wilson, remain. *Quietly*, I said, Durand! Don't shuffle your feet in that abominable way."

Crash!

"Wolferstan, I distinctly saw you upset that blackboard with a movement of your hand-one hundred lines. Go quietly from the room, everybody."

The meeting dispersed.

"Jackson and Wilson, come here. What's the meaning of this disgraceful conduct? Put that dog out of the room, Jackson."

Mike removed the yelling Sammy and shut the door on him.

"Well, Wilson?"

"Please, sir, I was playing with a clockwork rat —"

"What business have you to be playing with clockwork rats?"

"Then I remembered," said Mike, "that I had left my Horace in my desk, so I came in —"

"And by a fluke, sir," said Wilson, as one who tells of strange things, "the rat happened to be pointing in the same direction, so he came in, too."

"I met Sammy on the gravel outside and he followed me."

"I tried to collar him, but when you told me to come in, sir, I had to let him go, and he came in after the rat."

It was plain to Mr. Downing that the burden of sin was shared equally by both culprits. Wilson had supplied the rat, Mike the dog; but Mr. Downing liked Wilson and disliked Mike. Wilson was in the Fire Brigade, frivolous at times, it was true, but nevertheless a member. Also he kept wicket for the school. Mike was a member of the Archaeological Society, and had refused to play cricket.

Mr. Downing allowed these facts to influence him in passing sentence.

"One hundred lines, Wilson," he said. "You may go."

Wilson departed with the air of a man who has had a great deal of fun, and paid very little for it.

Mr. Downing turned to Mike. "You will stay in on Saturday afternoon, Jackson; it will interfere with your Archaeological studies, I fear, but it may teach you that we have no room at Sedleigh for boys who spend their time loafing about and making themselves a nuisance. We are a keen school; this is no place for boys who do nothing but waste their time. That will do, Jackson."

And Mr. Downing walked out of the room. In affairs of this kind a master has a habit of getting the last word.

10

ACHILLES LEAVES HIS TENT

They say misfortunes never come singly. As Mike sat brooding over his wrongs in his study, after the Sammy incident, Jellicoe came into the room, and, without preamble, asked for the loan of a pound.

When one has been in the habit of confining one's lendings and borrowings to sixpences and shillings, a request for a pound comes as something of a blow.

"What on earth for?" asked Mike.

"I say, do you mind if I don't tell you? I don't want to tell anybody. The fact is, I'm in a beastly hole."

"Oh, sorry," said Mike. "As a matter of fact, I do happen to have a quid. You can freeze on to it, if you like. But it's about all I have got, so don't be shy about paying it back."

Jellicoe was profuse in his thanks, and disappeared in a cloud of gratitude.

Mike felt that Fate was treating him badly. Being kept in on Saturday meant that he would be unable to turn out for Little Borlock against Claythorpe, the return match. In the previous game he had scored ninety-eight, and there was a lob bowler in the Claythorpe ranks whom he was particularly anxious to meet again. Having to yield a sovereign to Jellicoe-why on earth did the man want all that? —meant that, unless a carefully worded letter to his brother Bob at Oxford had the desired effect, he would be practically penniless for weeks.

In a gloomy frame of mind he sat down to write to Bob, who was playing regularly for the Varsity this season, and only the previous week had made a century against Sussex, so might be expected to be in a sufficiently softened mood to advance the needful. (Which, it may be stated at once, he did, by return of post.)

Mike was struggling with the opening sentences of this letter-he was never a very ready writer-when Stone and Robinson burst into the room.

Mike put down his pen, and got up. He was in warlike mood, and welcomed the intrusion. If Stone and Robinson wanted battle, they should have it.

But the motives of the expedition were obviously friendly. Stone beamed. Robinson was laughing.

"You're a sportsman," said Robinson.

"What did he give you?" asked Stone.

They sat down, Robinson on the table, Stone in Psmith's deck chair. Mike's heart warmed to them. The little disturbance in the dormitory was a thing of the past, done with, forgotten, contemporary with Julius Caesar. He felt that he, Stone and Robinson must learn to know and appreciate one another.

There was, as a matter of fact, nothing much wrong with Stone and Robinson. They were just ordinary raggers of the type found at every public school, small and large. They were absolutely free from brain. They had a certain amount of muscle, and a vast store of animal spirits. They looked on school life purely as a vehicle for ragging. The Stones and Robinsons are the swashbucklers of the school world. They go about, loud and boisterous, with a wholehearted and cheerful indifference to other people's feelings, treading on the toes of their neighbor and shoving him off the pavement, and always with an eye wide open for any adventure. As to the kind of adventure, they are not particular so long as it promises excitement. Sometimes they go through their whole school career without accident. More often they run up against a snag in the shape of some serious-minded and muscular person, who objects to having his toes trodden on and being shoved off the pavement, and then they usually sober down, to the mutual advantage of themselves and the rest of the community.

One's opinion of this type of youth varies according to one's point of view. Small boys whom they had occasion to kick, either from pure high spirits or as a punishment for some slip from the narrow path which the ideal small boy should tread, regarded Stone and Robinson as bullies of the genuine "Eric" and "St. Winifred's" brand. Masters were rather afraid of them. Adair had a smouldering dislike for them. They were useful at cricket, but apt not to take Sedleigh as seriously as he could have wished.

As for Mike, he now found them pleasant company, and began to get out the tea things.

"Those Fire Brigade meetings," said Stone, "are a rag. You can do what you like, and you never get more than a hundred lines."

"Don't you!" said Mike. "I got Saturday afternoon."

"What!"

"Is Wilson in too?"

"No. He got a hundred lines."

Stone and Robinson were quite concerned.

"What a beastly swindle!"

"That's because you don't play cricket. Old Downing lets you do what you like if you join the Fire Brigade and play cricket."

"'We are, above all, a keen school,'" quoted Stone. "Don't you ever play?"

"I have played a bit," said Mike.

"Well, why don't you have a shot? We aren't such flyers here. If you know one end of a bat from the other, you could get into some sort of a team. Were you at school anywhere before you came here?"

"I was at Wrykyn."

"Why on earth did you leave?" asked Stone. "Were you sacked?"

"No. My father took me away."

"Wrykyn?" said Robinson. "Are you any relation of the Jacksons there —J.W. and the others?"

"Brother."

"What!"

"Well, didn't you play at all there?"

"Yes," said Mike, "I did. I was in the team three years, and I should have been captain this year, if I'd stopped on."

There was a profound and gratifying sensation. Stone gaped, and Robinson nearly dropped his teacup.

Stone broke the silence.

"But I mean to say-look here? What I mean is, why aren't you playing? Why don't you play now?"

"I do. I play for a village near here. Place called Lower Borlock. A man who played against Wrykyn for the Free Foresters captains them. He asked me if I'd like some games for them."

"But why not for the school?"

"Why should I? It's much better fun for the village. You don't get ordered about by Adair, for a start."

"Adair sticks on side," said Stone.

"Enough for six," agreed Robinson.

"By Jove," said Stone, "I've got an idea. My word, what a rag!"

"What's wrong now?" inquired Mike politely.

"Why, look here. Tomorrow's Mid-Term Service Day. It's nowhere near the middle of the term, but they always have it in the fourth week. There's chapel at half past nine till half past ten. Then the rest of the day's a whole holiday. There are always house matches. We're playing Downing's. Why don't you play and let's smash them?"

"By Jove, yes," said Robinson. "Why don't you? They're always sticking on side because they've won the house cup three years running. I say, do you bat or bowl?"

"Bat. Why?"

Robinson rocked on the table.

"Why, old Downing fancies himself as a bowler. You *must* play, and knock the cover off him."

"Masters don't play in house matches, surely?"

"This isn't a real house match. Only a friendly. Downing always turns out on Mid-Term Service Day. I say, do play."

"Think of the rag."

"But the team's full," said Mike.

"The list isn't up yet. We'll nip across to Barnes's study, and make him alter it."

They dashed out of the room. From down the passage Mike heard yells of "*Barnes!*" the closing of a door, and a murmur of excited conversation. Then footsteps returning down the passage.

Barnes appeared, on his face the look of one who has seen visions.

"I say," he said, "is it true? Or is Stone rotting? About Wrykyn, I mean."

"Yes, I was in the team."

Barnes was an enthusiastic cricketer. He studied his *Wisden*, and he had an immense respect for Wrykyn cricket.

"Are you the M. Jackson, then, who had an average of fifty-one point naught three last year?"

"Yes."

Barnes's manner became like that of a curate talking to a bishop.

"I say," he said, "then-er-will you play against Downing's tomorrow?"

"Rather," said Mike. "Thanks awfully. Have some tea?"

11

THE MATCH WITH DOWNING'S

It is the curious instinct which prompts most people to rub a thing in that makes the lot of the average convert an unhappy one. Only the very self-controlled can refrain from improving the occasion and scoring off the convert. Most leap at the opportunity.

It was so in Mike's case. Mike was not a genuine convert, but to Mr. Downing he had the outward aspect of one. When you have been impressing upon a noncricketing boy for nearly a month that (*a*) the school is above all a keen school, (*b*) that all members of it should play cricket, and (*c*) that by not playing cricket he is ruining his chances in this world and imperiling them in the next; and when, quite unexpectedly, you come upon this boy dressed in cricket flannels, wearing cricket boots and carrying a cricket bag, it seems only natural to assume that you have converted him, that the seeds of your eloquence have fallen on fruitful soil and sprouted.

Mr. Downing assumed it.

He was walking to the field with Adair and another member of his team when he came upon Mike.

"What!" he cried. "Our Jackson clad in suit of mail and armed for the fray!"

This was Mr. Downing's No. 2 manner-the playful.

"This is indeed Saul among the prophets. Why this sudden enthusiasm for a game which I understood that you despised? Are our opponents so reduced?"

Psmith, who was with Mike, took charge of the affair with a languid grace which had maddened hundreds in its time, and which never failed to ruffle Mr. Downing.

"We are, above all, sir," he said, "a keen house. Drones are not welcomed by us. We are essentially versatile. Jackson, the archaeologist of yesterday, becomes the cricketer of today. It is the right spirit, sir," said Psmith earnestly. "I like to see it."

"Indeed, Smith? You are not playing yourself, I notice. Your enthusiasm has bounds."

"In our house, sir, competition is fierce, and the Selection Committee unfortunately passed me over."

* * * * *

There were a number of pitches dotted about over the field, for there was always a touch of the London Park about it on Mid-Term Service Day. Adair, as captain of cricket, had naturally selected the best for his own match. It was a good wicket, Mike saw. As a matter of fact the wickets at Sedleigh were nearly always good. Adair had infected the groundsman with some of his own keenness, with the result that that once-leisurely official now found himself sometimes, with a kind of mild surprise, working really hard. At the beginning of the previous season Sedleigh had played a scratch team from a neighboring town on a wicket which, except for the creases, was absolutely undistinguishable from the surrounding turf, and behind the pavilion after the match Adair had spoken certain home truths to the groundsman. The latter's reformation had dated from that moment.

* * * * *

Barnes, timidly jubilant, came up to Mike with the news that he had won the toss, and the request that Mike would go in first with him.

In stories of the "Not Really a Duffer" type, where the nervous new boy, who has been found crying in the changing room over the photograph of his sister, contrives to get an innings in a game, nobody suspects that he is really a prodigy till he hits the Bully's first ball out of the ground for six.

With Mike it was different. There was no pitying smile on Adair's face as he started his run preparatory to sending down the first ball. Mike, on the cricket field, could not have looked anything but a cricketer if he had turned out in a tweed suit and hobnail boots. Cricketer was written all over him-in his walk, in the way he took guard, in his stand at the wicket. Adair started to bowl with the feeling that this was somebody who had more than a little knowledge of how to deal with good bowling and punish bad.

Mike started cautiously. He was more than usually anxious to make runs today, and he meant to take no risks till he could afford to do so. He had seen Adair bowl at the nets, and he knew that he was good.

The first over was a maiden, six dangerous balls beautifully played. The fieldsmen changed over.

The general interest had now settled on the match between Outwood's and Downing's. The facts in Mike's case had gone around the field, and, as several of the other games had not yet begun, quite a large crowd had collected near the pavilion to watch. Mike's masterly treatment of the opening over had impressed the spectators, and there was a popular desire to see how he would deal with Mr. Downing's slows. It was generally anticipated that he would do something special with them.

Off the first ball of the master's over a leg-bye was run.

Mike took guard.

Mr. Downing was a bowler with a style of his own. He took two short steps, two long steps, gave a jump, took three more short steps, and ended with a combination of step and jump, during which the ball emerged from behind his back and started on its slow career to the wicket. The whole business had some of the dignity of the old-fashioned minuet, subtly blended with the careless vigor of a cakewalk. The ball, when delivered, was billed to break from leg, but the program was subject to alterations.

If the spectators had expected Mike to begin any firework effects with the first ball, they were disappointed. He played the over through with a grace worthy of his brother Joe. The last ball he turned to leg for a single.

His treatment of Adair's next over was freer. He had got a sight of the ball now. Halfway through the over a beautiful square cut forced a passage through the crowd by the pavilion, and dashed up against the rails. He drove the sixth ball past cover for three.

The crowd was now reluctantly dispersing to its own games, but it stopped as Mr. Downing started his minuet-cakewalk, in the hope that it might see something more sensational.

This time the hope was fulfilled.

The ball was well up, slow, and off the wicket on the on-side. Perhaps if it had been allowed to pitch, it might have broken in and become quite dangerous. Mike went out at it, and hit it a couple of feet from the ground. The ball dropped with a thud and a spurting of dust in the road that ran along one side of the cricket field.

It was returned on the installment system by helpers from other games, and the bowler began his maneuvers again. A half volley this time. Mike slammed it back, and mid on, whose heart was obviously not in the thing, failed to stop it.

"Get to them, Jenkins," said Mr. Downing irritably, as the ball came back from the boundary. "Get to them."

"Sir, please, sir —"

"Don't talk in the field, Jenkins."

Having had a full pitch hit for six and a half volley for four, there was a strong probability that Mr. Downing would pitch his next ball short.

The expected happened. The third ball was a slow long hop, and hit the road at about the same spot where the first had landed. A howl of untuneful applause rose from the watchers in the pavilion, and Mike, with the feeling that this sort of bowling was too good to be true, waited in position for number four.

There are moments when a sort of panic seizes a bowler. This happened now with Mr. Downing. He suddenly abandoned science and ran amok. His run lost its stateliness and increased its vigor. He charged up to the wicket as a wounded buffalo sometimes charges a gun. His whole idea now was to bowl fast.

When a slow bowler starts to bowl fast, it is usually as well to be batting, if you can manage it.

By the time the over was finished, Mike's score had been increased by sixteen, and the total of his side, in addition, by three wides.

And a shrill small voice, from the neighborhood of the pavilion, uttered with painful distinctness the words, "Take him off!"

That was how the most sensational day's cricket began that Sedleigh had known.

A description of the details of the morning's play would be monotonous. It is enough to say that they ran on much the same lines as the third and fourth overs of the match. Mr. Downing bowled one more over, off which Mike helped himself to sixteen runs, and then retired moodily to cover point, where, in Adair's fifth over, he missed Barnes-the first occasion since the game began on which that mild batsman had attempted to score more than a single. Scared by this escape, Outwood's captain shrank back into his shell, sat on the splice like a limpet, and, offering no more chances, was not out at lunchtime with a score of eleven. Mike had then made a hundred and three.

* * * * *

As Mike was taking off his pads in the pavilion, Adair came up.

"Why did you say you didn't play cricket?" he asked abruptly.

When one has been bowling the whole morning, and bowling well, without the slightest success, one is inclined to be abrupt.

Mike finished unfastening an obstinate strap. Then he looked up.

"I didn't say anything of the kind. I said I wasn't going to play here. There's a difference. As a matter of fact, I was in the Wrykyn team before I came here. Three years."

Adair was silent for a moment.

"Will you play for us against the Old Sedleighans tomorrow?" he said at length.

Mike tossed his pads into his bag and got up.

"No, thanks."

There was a silence.

"Above it, I suppose?"

"Not a bit. Not up to it. I shall want a lot of coaching at that end net of yours before I'm fit to play for Sedleigh."

There was another pause.

"Then you won't play?" asked Adair.

"I'm not keeping you, am I?" said Mike, politely.

It was remarkable what a number of members of Outwood's house appeared to cherish a personal grudge against Mr. Downing. It had been that master's somewhat injudicious practice for many years to treat his own house as a sort of Chosen People. Of all masters, the most unpopular is he who by the silent tribunal of a school is convicted of favoritism. And the dislike deepens if it is a house which he favors and not merely individuals. On occasions when boys in his own house and boys from other houses were accomplices and partners in wrongdoing, Mr. Downing distributed his thunderbolts unequally, and the school noticed it. The result was that not only he himself, but also-which was rather unfair-his house, too, had acquired a good deal of unpopularity.

The general consensus of opinion in Outwood's during the luncheon interval was that having got Downing's up a tree, they would be fools not to make the most of the situation.

Barnes's remark that he supposed, unless anything happened and wickets began to fall a bit faster, they had better think of declaring somewhere about half past three or four, was met with a storm of opposition.

"Declare!" said Robinson. "Great Scot, what on earth are you talking about?"

"Declare!" Stone's voice was almost a wail of indignation. "I never saw such a chump."

"They'll be rather sick if we don't, won't they?" suggested Barnes.

"Sick! I should think they would," said Stone. "That's just the gay idea. Can't you see that by a miracle we've got a chance of getting a jolly good bit of our own back against those Downing's ticks? What we've got to do is to jolly well keep them in the field all day if we can, and be jolly glad it's so beastly hot. If they lose about a dozen pounds each through sweating about in the sun after Jackson's drives, perhaps they'll stick on less side about things in general in future. Besides, I want an innings against that bilge of old Downing's, if I can get it."

"So do I," said Robinson.

"If you declare, I swear I won't field. Nor will Robinson."

"Rather not."

"Well, I won't then," said Barnes unhappily. "Only you know they're rather sick already."

"Don't you worry about that," said Stone with a wide grin. "They'll be a lot sicker before we've finished."

And so it came about that that particular Mid-Term Service-Day match made history. Big scores had often been put up on Mid-Term Service Day. Games had frequently been one-sided. But it had never happened before in the annals of the school that one side, going in first early in the morning, had neither completed its innings nor declared it closed when stumps were drawn at 6.30. In no previous Sedleigh match, after a full day's play, had the pathetic words "Did not bat" been written against the whole of one of the contending teams.

These are the things which mark epochs.

Play was resumed at 2.15. For a quarter of an hour Mike was comparatively quiet. Adair, fortified by food and rest, was bowling really well, and his first half dozen overs had to be watched carefully. But the wicket was too good to give him a chance, and Mike, playing himself in again, proceeded to get to business once more. Bowlers came and went. Adair pounded away at one end with brief intervals between the attacks. Mr. Downing took a couple more overs, in one of which a horse, passing in the road, nearly had its useful life cut suddenly short. Change bowlers of various actions and paces, each weirder and more futile than the last, tried their luck. But still the first-wicket stand continued.

The bowling of a house team is all head and no body. The first pair probably have some idea of length and break. The first-change pair are poor. And the rest, the small change, are simply the sort of things one sees in dreams after a heavy supper, or when one is out without one's gun.

Time, mercifully, generally breaks up a big stand at cricket before the field has suffered too much, and that is what happened now. At four o'clock, when the score stood at two hundred and twenty for no wicket, Barnes, greatly daring, smote lustily at a rather wide half volley and was caught at short slip for thirty-three. He retired blushfully to the pavilion, amidst applause, and Stone came out.

As Mike had then made a hundred and eighty-seven, it was assumed by the field, that directly he had topped his second century, the closure would be applied and their ordeal finished. There was almost a sigh of relief when frantic cheering from the crowd told that the feat had been accomplished. The fieldsmen clapped in quite an indulgent sort of way, as who should say, "Capital, capital. And now let's start *our* innings." Some even began to edge toward the pavilion.

But the next ball was bowled, and the next over, and the next after that, and still Barnes made no sign. (The conscience stricken captain of Outwood's was, as a matter of fact, being practically held down by Robinson and other ruffians by force.)

A gray dismay settled on the field.

The bowling had now become almost unbelievably bad. Lobs were being tried, and Stone, nearly weeping with pure joy, was playing an innings of the "How-to-brighten-cricket" type. He had an unorthodox style, but an excellent eye, and the road at this period of the game became absolutely unsafe for pedestrians and traffic.

Mike's pace had become slower, as was only natural, but his score, too, was mounting steadily.

"This is foolery," snapped Mr. Downing, as the three hundred and fifty went up on the board. "Barnes!" he called.

There was no reply. A committee of three was at that moment engaged in sitting on Barnes's head in the first eleven changing room, in order to correct a more than usually feverish attack of conscience.

"Barnes!"

"Please, sir," said Stone, some species of telepathy telling him what was detaining his captain. "I think Barnes must have left the field. He has probably gone over to the house to fetch something."

"This is absurd. You must declare your innings closed. The game has become a farce."

"Declare! Sir, we can't unless Barnes does. He might be awfully annoyed if we did anything like that without consulting him."

"Absurd."

"He's very touchy, sir."

"It is perfect foolery."

"I think Jenkins is just going to bowl, sir."

Mr. Downing walked moodily to his place.

In a neat wooden frame in the senior day room at Outwood's, just above the mantlepiece, there was on view, a week later, a slip of paper.

The writing on it was as follows:

OUTWOOD'S *v.* DOWNING'S

Outwood's. First innings.

    J.P. Barnes, *c.* Hammond, *b.* Hassall 33
    M. Jackson, not out 277
    W.J. Stone, not out 124
    Extras 37

    Total (for one wicket) 471

Downing's did not bat.

12

THE SINGULAR BEHAVIOR OF JELLICOE

Outwood's rollicked considerably that night. Mike, if he had cared to take the part, could have been the Petted Hero. But a cordial invitation from the senior day room to be the guest of the evening at about the biggest rag of the century had been refused on the plea of fatigue. One does not make two hundred and seventy-seven runs on a hot day without feeling the effects, even if one has scored mainly by the medium of boundaries; and Mike, as he lay back in Psmith's deck chair, felt that all he wanted was to go to bed and stay there for a week. His hands and arms burned as if they were red-hot, and his eyes were so tired that he could not keep them open.

Psmith, leaning against the mantlepiece, discoursed in a desultory way on the day's happenings-the score off Mr. Downing, the undeniable annoyance of that battered bowler, and the probability of his venting his annoyance on Mike next day.

"In theory," said he, "the manly what-d'you-call-it of cricket and all that sort of thing ought to make him fall on your neck tomorrow and weep over you as a foeman worthy of his steel. But I am prepared to bet a reasonable sum that he will give no jujitsu exhibition of this kind. In fact, from what I have seen of our bright little friend, I should say that, in a small way, he will do his best to make it distinctly hot for you, here and there."

"I don't care," murmured Mike, shifting his aching limbs in the chair.

"In an ordinary way, I suppose, a man can put up with having his bowling hit a little. But your performance was cruelty to animals. Twenty-eight off one over, not to mention three wides, would have made Job foam at the mouth. You will probably get sacked. On the other hand, it's worth it. You have lit a candle this day which can never be blown out. You have shown the lads of the village how Comrade Downing's bowling ought to be treated. I don't suppose he'll ever take another wicket."

"He doesn't deserve to."

Psmith smoothed his hair at the glass and turned round again.

"The only blot on this day of mirth and goodwill is," he said, "the singular conduct of our friend Jellicoe. When all the place was ringing with song and merriment, Comrade Jellicoe crept to my side, and, slipping his little hand in mine, touched me for three quid."

This interested Mike, tired as he was.

"What! Three quid!"

"Three crisp, crackling quid. He wanted four."

"But the man must be living at the rate of I don't know what. It was only yesterday that he borrowed a quid from *me*!"

"He must be saving money fast. There appear to be the makings of a financier about Comrade Jellicoe. Well, I hope, when he's collected enough for his needs, he'll pay me back a bit. I'm pretty well cleaned out."

"I got some from my brother at Oxford."

"Perhaps he's saving up to get married. We may be helping toward furnishing the home. There was a Siamese prince fellow at my dame's at Eton who had four wives when he arrived, and gathered in a fifth during his first summer holidays. It was done on the correspondence system. His Prime Minister fixed it up at the other end, and sent him the glad news on a picture post card. I think an eye ought to be kept on Comrade Jellicoe."

* * * * *

Mike tumbled into bed that night like a log, but he could not sleep. He ached all over. Psmith chatted for a time on human affairs in general, and then dropped gently off. Jellicoe, who appeared to be wrapped in gloom, contributed nothing to the conversation.

After Psmith had gone to sleep, Mike lay for some time running over in his mind, as the best substitute for sleep, the various points of his innings that day. He felt very hot and uncomfortable.

Just as he was wondering whether it would not be a good idea to get up and have a cold bath, a voice spoke from the darkness at his side.

"Are you asleep, Jackson?"

"Who's that?"

"Me-Jellicoe. I can't get to sleep."

"Nor can I. I'm stiff all over."

"I'll come over and sit on your bed."

There was a creaking, and then a weight descended in the neighborhood of Mike's toes.

Jellicoe was apparently not in conversational mood. He uttered no word for quite three minutes. At the end of which time he gave a sound midway between a snort and a sigh.

"I say, Jackson!" he said.

"Yes?"

"Have you-oh, nothing."

Silence again.

"Jackson."

"Hello?"

"I say, what would your people say if you got sacked?"

"All sorts of things. Especially my father. Why?"

"Oh, I don't know. So would mine."

"Everybody's would, I expect."

"Yes."

The bed creaked, as Jellicoe digested these great thoughts. Then he spoke again.

"It would be a jolly beastly thing to get sacked."

Mike was too tired to give his mind to the subject. He was not really listening. Jellicoe droned on in a depressed sort of way.

"You'd get home in the middle of the afternoon, I suppose, and you'd drive up to the house, and the servant would open the door, and you'd go in. They might all be out, and then you'd have to hang about, and wait; and presently you'd hear them come in, and you'd go out into the passage, and they'd say 'Hello!'"

Jellicoe, in order to give verisimilitude, as it were, to an otherwise bald and unconvincing narrative, flung so much agitated surprise into the last word that it woke Mike from a troubled doze into which he had fallen.

"Hello?" he said. "What's up?"

"Then you'd say, 'Hello!' And then they'd say, 'What are you doing here?' And you'd say —"

"What on earth are you talking about?"

"About what would happen."

"Happen when?"

"When you got home. After being sacked, you know."

"Who's been sacked?" Mike's mind was still under a cloud.

"Nobody. But if you were, I meant. And then I suppose there'd be an awful row and general sickness, and all that. And then you'd be sent into a bank, or to Australia, or something."

Mike dozed off again.

"My father would be frightfully sick. My mater would be sick. My sister would be jolly sick, too. Have you got any sisters, Jackson? I say, Jackson!"

"Hello! What's the matter? Who's that?"

"Me-Jellicoe."

"What's up?"

"I asked you if you'd got any sisters."

"Any *what?*"

"Sisters."

"Whose sisters?"

"Yours. I asked if you'd got any."

"Any what?"

"Sisters."

"What about them?"

The conversation was becoming too intricate for Jellicoe. He changed the subject.

"I say, Jackson!"

"Well?"

"I say, you don't know anyone who could lend me a pound, do you?"

"What!" cried Mike, sitting up in bed and staring through the darkness in the direction whence the numismatist's voice was proceeding. "Do *what?*"

"I say, look out. You'll wake Psmith."

"Did you say you wanted someone to lend you a quid?"

"Yes," said Jellicoe eagerly. "Do you know anyone?"

Mike's head throbbed. This thing was too much. The human brain could not be expected to cope with it. Here was a youth who had borrowed a pound from one friend the day before, and three pounds from another friend that very afternoon, already looking about him for further loans. Was it a hobby, or was he saving up to buy an airplane?

"What on earth do you want a pound for?"

"I don't want to tell anybody. But it's jolly serious. I shall get sacked if I don't get it."

Mike pondered.

Those who have followed Mike's career as set forth by the present historian will have realized by this time that he was a good long way from being perfect. As the Blue-Eyed Hero he would have been a rank failure. Except on the cricket field, where he was a natural genius, he was just ordinary. He resembled ninety percent of other members of English public schools. He had some virtues and a good many defects. He was as obstinate as a mule, though people whom he liked could do as they pleased with him. He was good-natured as a general thing, but on occasion his temper could be of the worst, and had, in his childhood, been the subject of much adverse comment among his aunts. He was rigidly truthful, where the issue concerned only himself. Where it was a case of saving a friend, he was prepared to act in a manner reminiscent of an American expert witness.

He had, in addition, one good quality without any defect to balance it. He was always ready to help people. And when he set himself to do this, he was never put off by discomfort or risk. He went at the thing with a singleness of purpose that asked no questions.

Bob's postal order which had arrived that evening, was reposing in the breast pocket of his coat.

It was a wrench, but, if the situation was so serious with Jellicoe, it had to be done.

Two minutes later the night was being made hideous by Jellicoe's almost tearful protestations of gratitude, and the postal order had moved from one side of the dormitory to the other.

13

JELLICOE GOES ON THE SICK LIST

Mike woke next morning with a confused memory of having listened to a great deal of incoherent conversation from Jellicoe, and a painfully vivid recollection of handing over the bulk of his worldly wealth to him. The thought depressed him, though it seemed to please Jellicoe, for the latter caroled in a gay undertone as he dressed, till Psmith, who had a sensitive ear, asked as a favor that these farmyard imitations might cease until he was out of the room.

There were other things to make Mike low-spirited that morning. To begin with, he was in detention, which in itself is enough to spoil a day. It was a particularly fine day, which made the matter worse. In addition to this, he had never felt stiffer in his life. It seemed to him that the creaking of his joints as he walked must be audible to everyone within a radius of several yards. Finally, there was the interview with Mr. Downing to come. That would probably be unpleasant. As Psmith had said, Mr. Downing was the sort of master who would be likely to make trouble. The great match had not been an ordinary match. Mr. Downing was a curious man in many ways, but he did not make a fuss on ordinary occasions when his bowling proved expensive. Yesterday's performance, however, stood in a class by itself. It stood forth without disguise as a deliberate rag. One side does not keep another in the field the whole day in a one-day match except as a grisly kind of practical joke. And Mr. Downing and his house realized this. The house's way of signifying its comprehension of the fact was to be cold and distant as far as the seniors were concerned, and abusive and pugnacious as regards the juniors. Young blood had been shed overnight, and more flowed during the eleven-o'-clock interval that morning to avenge the insult.

Mr. Downing's methods of retaliation would have to be, of necessity, more elusive; but Mike did not doubt that in some way or other his form master would endeavor to get a bit of his own back.

As events turned out, he was perfectly right. When a master has got his knife into a boy, especially a master who allows himself to be influenced by his likes and dislikes, he is inclined to single him out in times of stress, and savage him as if he were the official representative of the evildoers. Just as, at sea, the skipper when he has trouble with the crew, works it off on the boy.

Mr. Downing was in a sarcastic mood when he met Mike. That is to say, he began in a sarcastic strain. But this sort of thing is difficult to keep up. By the time he had reached his peroration, the rapier had given place to the bludgeon. For sarcasm to be effective, the user of it must be met halfway. His hearer must appear to be conscious of the sarcasm and moved by it. Mike, when masters waxed sarcastic toward him, always assumed an air of stolid stupidity, which was as a suit of mail against satire.

So Mr. Downing came down from the heights with a run, and began to express himself with a simple strength which it did his form good to listen to. Veterans who had been in the form for terms said afterward that there had been nothing to touch it, in their experience of the orator, since the glorious day when Dunster, that prince of raggers, who had left at Christmas to go to a crammer's, had introduced three lively grass snakes into the room during a Latin lesson.

"You are surrounded," concluded Mr. Downing, snapping his pencil in two in his emotion, "by an impenetrable mass of conceit and vanity and selfishness. It does not occur to you to admit your capabilities as a cricketer in an open, straightforward way and place them at the disposal of the school. No, that would not be dramatic enough for you. It would be too commonplace altogether. Far too commonplace!" Mr. Downing laughed bitterly. "No, you must conceal your capabilities. You must act a lie. You must—who is that shuffling his feet? I will not have it, I *will* have silence-you must hang back in order to make a more effective entrance, like some wretched actor who —I will *not* have this shuffling. I have spoken of this before. Macpherson, are you shuffling your feet?"

"Sir, no, sir."

"Please, sir."

"Well, Parsons?"

"I think it's the noise of the draft under the door, sir."

Instant departure of Parsons for the outer regions. And, in the excitement of this side issue, the speaker lost his inspiration, and abruptly concluded his remarks by putting Mike on to translate in Cicero. Which Mike, who happened to have prepared the first half-page, did with much success.

The Old Boys' match was timed to begin shortly after eleven o'clock. During the interval most of the school walked across the field to look at the pitch. One or two of the Old Boys had already changed and were practicing in front of the pavilion.

It was through one of these batsmen that an accident occurred which had a good deal of influence on Mike's affairs.

Mike had strolled out by himself. Halfway across the field Jellicoe joined him. Jellicoe was cheerful, and rather embarrassingly grateful. He was just in the middle of his harangue when the accident happened.

To their left, as they crossed the field, a long youth, with the faint beginnings of a moustache and a blazer that lit up the surrounding landscape like a glowing beacon, was lashing out recklessly at a friend's bowling. Already he had gone within an ace of slaying a small boy. As Mike and Jellicoe proceeded on their way, there was a shout of "Heads!"

The almost universal habit of batsmen of shouting "Heads!" at whatever height from the ground the ball may be, is not a little confusing. The average person, on hearing the shout, puts his hands over his skull, crouches down and trusts to luck. This is an excellent plan if the ball is falling, but is not much protection against a skimming drive along the ground.

When "Heads!" was called on the present occasion, Mike and Jellicoe instantly assumed the crouching attitude.

Jellicoe was the first to abandon it. He uttered a yell and sprang into the air. After which he sat down and began to nurse his ankle.

The bright-blazered youth walked up.

"Awfully sorry, you know. Hurt?"

Jellicoe was pressing the injured spot tenderly with his fingertips, uttering sharp howls whenever, zeal outrunning discretion, he prodded himself too energetically.

"Silly ass, Dunster," he groaned, "slamming about like that."

"Awfully sorry. But I did yell."

"It's swelling up rather," said Mike. "You'd better get over to the house and have it looked at. Can you walk?"

Jellicoe tried, but sat down again with a loud "Ow!" At that moment the bell rang.

"I shall have to be going in," said Mike, "or I'd have helped you over."

"I'll give you a hand," said Dunster.

He helped the sufferer to his feet and they staggered off together, Jellicoe hopping, Dunster advancing with a sort of polka step. Mike watched them start and then turned to go in.

MIKE RECEIVES A COMMISSION

There is only one thing to be said in favor of detention on a fine summer's afternoon, and that is that it is very pleasant to come out of. The sun never seems so bright or the turf so green as during the first five minutes after one has come out of the detention room. One feels as if one were entering a new and very delightful world. There is also a touch of the Rip van Winkle feeling. Everything seems to have gone on and left one behind. Mike, as he walked to the cricket field, felt very much behind the times.

Arriving on the field he found the Old Boys batting. He stopped and watched an over of Adair's. The fifth ball bowled a man. Mike made his way toward the pavilion.

Before he got there he heard his name called, and turning, found Psmith seated under a tree with the bright-blazered Dunster.

"Return of the exile," said Psmith. "A joyful occasion tinged with melancholy. Have a cherry?—take one or two. These little acts of unremembered kindness are what one needs after a couple of hours in extra pupil room. Restore your tissues, Comrade Jackson, and when you have finished those, apply again."

"Is your name Jackson?" inquired Dunster, "because Jellicoe wants to see you."

"Alas, poor Jellicoe!" said Psmith. "He is now prone on his bed in the dormitory-there a sheer hulk lies poor Tom Jellicoe, the darling of the crew, faithful below he did his duty, but Comrade Dunster has broached him to. I have just been hearing the melancholy details."

"Old Smith and I," said Dunster, "were at prep school together. I'd no idea I should find him here."

"It was a wonderfully stirring sight when we met," said Psmith; "not unlike the meeting of Ulysses and the hound Argos, of whom you have doubtless read in the course of your dabblings in the classics. I was Ulysses; Dunster gave a lifelike representation of the faithful dawg."

"You still jaw as much as ever, I notice," said the animal delineator, fondling the beginnings of his moustache.

"More," sighed Psmith, "more. Is anything irritating you?" he added, eyeing the other's maneuvers with interest.

"You needn't be a funny ass, man," said Dunster, pained; "heaps of people tell me I ought to have it waxed."

"What it really wants is top-dressing with guano. Hello! another man out. Adair's bowling better today than he did yesterday."

"I heard about yesterday," said Dunster. "It must have been a rag! Couldn't we work off some other rag on somebody before I go? I shall be stopping here till Monday in the village. Well hit, sir-Adair's bowling is perfectly simple if you go out to it."

"Comrade Dunster went out to it first ball," said Psmith to Mike.

"Oh! chuck it, man; the sun was in my eyes. I hear Adair's got a match on with the M.C.C. at last."

"Has he?" said Psmith; "I hadn't heard. Archaeology claims so much of my time that I have little leisure for listening to cricket chitchat."

"What was it Jellicoe wanted?" asked Mike; "was it anything important?"

"He seemed to think so-he kept telling me to tell you to go and see him."

"I fear Comrade Jellicoe is a bit of a weak-minded blitherer—"

"Did you ever hear of a rag we worked off on Jellicoe once?" asked Dunster. "The man has absolutely no sense of humor-can't see when he's being rotted. Well, it was like this-hello! We're all out—I shall have to be going out to field again, I suppose, dash it! I'll tell you when I see you again."

"I shall count the minutes," said Psmith.

Mike stretched himself; the sun was very soothing after his two hours in the detention room; he felt disinclined for exertion.

"I don't suppose it's anything special about Jellicoe, do you?" he said. "I mean, it'll keep till teatime; it's no catch having to sweat across to the house now."

"Don't dream of moving," said Psmith. "I have several rather profound observations on life to make and I can't make them without an audience. Soliloquy is a knack. Hamlet had got it, but probably only after years of patient practice. Personally, I need someone to listen when I talk. I like to feel that I am doing good. You stay where you are-don't interrupt too much."

Mike tilted his hat over his eyes and abandoned Jellicoe.

It was not until the lock-up bell rang that he remembered him. He went over to the house and made his way to the dormitory, where he found the injured one in a parlous state, not so much physical as mental. The doctor had seen his ankle and reported that it would be on the active list in a couple of days. It was Jellicoe's mind that needed attention now.

Mike found him in a condition bordering on collapse. "I say, you might have come before!" said Jellicoe.

"What's up? I didn't know there was such a hurry about it-what did you want?"

"It's no good now," said Jellicoe gloomily; "it's too late, I shall get sacked."

"What on earth are you talking about? What's the row?"

"It's about that money."

"What about it?"

"I had to pay it to a man today, or he said he'd write to the Head-then of course I should get sacked. I was going to take the money to him this afternoon, only I got crocked, so I couldn't move. I wanted to get hold of you to ask you to take it for me-it's too late now!"

Mike's face fell. "Oh, hang it!" he said, "I'm awfully sorry. I'd no idea it was anything like that-what a fool I was! Dunster did say he thought it was something important, only like an ass I thought it would do if I came over at lockup."

"It doesn't matter," said Jellicoe miserably; "it can't be helped."

"Yes, it can," said Mike. "I know what I'll do-it's all right. I'll get out of the house after lights-out."

Jellicoe sat up. "You can't! You'd get sacked if you were caught."

"Who would catch me? There was a chap at Wrykyn I knew who used to break out every night nearly and go and pot at cats with an air pistol; it's as easy as anything."

The toad-under-the-harrow expression began to fade from Jellicoe's face.
"I say, do you think you could, really?"

"Of course I can! It'll be rather a rag."

"I say, it's frightfully decent of you."

"What absolute rot!"

"But look here, are you certain —"

"I shall be all right. Where do you want me to go?"

"It's a place about a mile or two from here, called Lower Borlock."

"Lower Borlock?"

"Yes, do you know it?"

"Rather! I've been playing cricket for them all the term."

"I say, have you? Do you know a man called Barley?"

"Barley? Rather-he runs the White Boar."

"He's the chap I owe the money to."

"Old Barley!"

Mike knew the landlord of the White Boar well; he was the wag of the village team. Every village team, for some mysterious reason, has its comic man. In the Lower Borlock eleven Mr. Barley filled the post. He was a large, stout man, with a red and cheerful face, who looked exactly like the jovial innkeeper of melodrama. He was the last man Mike would have expected to do the "money by Monday-week or I write to the headmaster" business.

But he reflected that he had only seen him in his leisure moments, when he might naturally be expected to unbend and be full of the milk of human kindness. Probably in business hours he was quite different. After all, pleasure is one thing and business another.

Besides, five pounds is a large sum of money, and if Jellicoe owed it, there was nothing strange in Mr. Barley's doing everything he could to recover it.

He wondered a little what Jellicoe could have been doing to run up a bill as big as that, but it did not occur to him to ask, which was unfortunate, as it might have saved him a good deal of inconvenience. It seemed to him that it was none of his business to inquire into Jellicoe's private affairs. He took the envelope containing the money without question.

"I shall bike there, I think," he said, "if I can get into the shed."

The school's bicycles were stored in a shed by the pavilion.

"You can manage that," said Jellicoe; "it's locked up at night, but I had a key made to fit it last summer, because I used to get out in the early morning sometimes before it was opened."

"Got it on you?"

"Smith's got it."

"I'll get it from him."

"I say!"

"Well?"

"Don't tell Smith why you want it, will you? I don't want anybody to know-if a thing once starts getting about it's all over the place in no time."

"All right, I won't tell him."

"I say, thanks most awfully! I don't know what I should have done, I —"

"Oh, chuck it!" said Mike.

15

...AND FULFILLS IT

Mike started on his ride to Lower Borlock with mixed feelings. It is pleasant to be out on a fine night in summer, but the pleasure is to a certain extent modified when one feels that to be detected will mean expulsion.

Mike did not want to be expelled, for many reasons. Now that he had grown used to the place he was enjoying himself at Sedleigh to a certain extent. He still harbored a feeling of resentment against the school in general and Adair in particular, but it was pleasant in Outwood's now that he had got to know some of the members of the house, and he liked playing cricket for Lower Borlock; also, he was fairly certain that his father would not let him go to Cambridge if he were expelled from Sedleigh. Mr. Jackson was easygoing with his family, but occasionally his foot came down like a steam hammer, as witness the Wrykyn school-report affair.

So Mike pedaled along rapidly, being wishful to get the job done without delay.

Psmith had yielded up the key, but his inquiries as to why it was needed had been embarrassing. Mike's statement that he wanted to get up early and have a ride had been received by Psmith, with whom early rising was not a hobby, with honest amazement and a flood of advice and warning on the subject.

"One of the Georges," said Psmith, "I forget which, once said that a certain number of hours' sleep a day—I cannot recall for the moment how many-made a man something, which for the time being has slipped my memory. However, there you are. I've given you the main idea of the thing; and a German doctor says that early rising causes insanity. Still, if you're bent on it...." After which he had handed over the key.

Mike wished he could have taken Psmith into his confidence. Probably he would have volunteered to come, too; Mike would have been glad of a companion.

It did not take him long to reach Lower Borlock. The White Boar stood at the far end of the village, by the cricket field. He rode past the church-standing out black and mysterious against the light sky-and the rows of silent cottages, until he came to the inn.

The place was shut, of course, and all the lights were out-it was sometime past eleven.

The advantage an inn has over a private house, from the point of view of the person who wants to get into it when it has been locked up, is that a nocturnal visit is not so unexpected in the case of the former. Preparations have been made to meet such an emergency. Where with a private house you would probably have to wander around heaving rocks and end by climbing up a waterspout, when you want to get into an inn you simply ring the night bell, which, communicating with the boots' room, has that hard-worked menial up and doing in no time.

After Mike had waited for a few minutes there was a rattling of chains and a shooting of bolts and the door opened.

"Yes, sir?" said the boots, appearing in his shirt sleeves. "Why, 'ello! Mr. Jackson, sir!"

Mike was well known to all dwellers in Lower Borlock, his scores being the chief topic of conversation when the day's labors were over.

"I want to see Mr. Barley, Jack."

"He's bin' in bed this half hour back, Mr. Jackson."

"I must see him. Can you get him down?"

The boots looked doubtful. "Roust the guv'nor outer bed?" he said.

Mike quite admitted the gravity of the task. The landlord of the White Boar was one of those men who need a beauty sleep.

"I wish you would-it's a thing that can't wait. I've got some money to give to him."

"Oh, if it's *that* ..." said the boots.

Five minutes later mine host appeared in person, looking more than usually portly in a check dressing gown and red bedroom slippers.

"You can pop off, Jack."

Exit boots to his slumbers once more.

"Well, Mr. Jackson, what's it all about?"

"Jellicoe asked me to come and bring you the money."

"The money? What money?"

"What he owes you; the five pounds, of course."

"The five —" Mr. Barley stared openmouthed at Mike for a moment; then he broke into a roar of laughter which shook the sporting prints on the wall and drew barks from dogs in some distant part of the house. He staggered about laughing and coughing till Mike began to expect a fit of some kind. Then he collapsed into a chair, which creaked under him, and wiped his eyes.

"Oh dear!" he said, "Oh dear! The five pounds!"

Mike was not always abreast of the rustic idea of humor, and now he felt particularly fogged. For the life of him he could not see what there was to amuse anyone so much in the fact that a person who owed five pounds was ready to pay it back. It was an occasion for rejoicing, perhaps, but rather for a solemn, thankful, eyes-raised-to-heaven kind of rejoicing.

"What's up?" he asked.

"Five pounds!"

"You might tell us the joke."

Mr. Barley opened the letter, read it, and had another attack; when this was finished he handed the letter to Mike, who was waiting patiently by, hoping for light, and requested him to read it.

"Dear, dear!" chuckled Mr. Barley, "five pounds! They may teach you young gentlemen to talk Latin and Greek and what-not at your school, but it 'ud do a lot more good if they'd teach you how many beans make five; it 'ud do a lot more good if they'd teach you to come in when it rained; it 'ud do..."

Mike was reading the letter.

"Dear Mr. Barley," it ran.

"I send the £5, which I could not get before. I hope it is in time, because I don't want you to write to the headmaster. I am sorry Jane and John ate your wife's hat and the chicken and broke the vase."

There was some more to the same effect; it was signed "T.G. Jellicoe."

"What on earth's it all about?" said Mike, finishing this curious document.

Mr. Barley slapped his leg. "Why, Mr. Jellicoe keeps two dogs here; I keep 'em for him till the young gentlemen go home for their holidays. Aberdeen terriers, they are, and as sharp as mustard. Mischief! I believe you, but, love us! they don't do no harm! Bite up an old shoe sometimes and such sort of things. The other day, last Wednesday it were, about 'ar parse five, Jane-she's the worst of the two, always up to it, she is-she got hold of my old hat and had it in bits before you could say knife. John upset a china vase in one of the bedrooms chasing a mouse, and they got on the coffee-room table and ate half a cold chicken what had been left there. So I says to myself, 'I'll have a game with Mr. Jellicoe over this,' and I sits down and writes off saying the little dogs have eaten a valuable hat and a chicken and what not, and the damage'll be five pounds, and will he kindly remit same by Saturday night at the latest or I write to his headmaster. Love us!" Mr. Barley slapped his thigh, "he took it all in, every word-and here's the five pounds in cash in this envelope here! I haven't had such a laugh since we got old Tom Raxley out of bed at twelve of a winter's night by telling him his house was afire."

It is not always easy to appreciate a joke of the practical order if one has been made even merely part victim of it. Mike, as he reflected that he had been dragged out of his house in the middle of the night, in contravention of all school rules and discipline, simply in order to satisfy Mr. Barley's sense of humor, was more inclined to be abusive than mirthful. Running risks is

276

all very well when they are necessary, or if one chooses to run them for one's own amusement, but to be placed in a dangerous position, a position imperiling one's chance of going to the 'Varsity, is another matter altogether.

But it is impossible to abuse the Barley type of man. Barley's enjoyment of the whole thing was so honest and childlike. Probably it had given him the happiest quarter of an hour he had known for years, since, in fact, the affair of old Tom Raxley. It would have been cruel to damp the man.

So Mike laughed perfunctorily, took back the envelope with the five pounds, accepted a ginger beer and a plateful of biscuits, and rode off on his return journey.

* * * * *

Mention has been made above of the difference which exists between getting into an inn after lockup and into a private house. Mike was to find this out for himself.

His first act on arriving at Sedleigh was to replace his bicycle in the shed. This he accomplished with success. It was pitch-dark in the shed, and as he wheeled his machine in, his foot touched something on the floor. Without waiting to discover what this might be, he leaned his bicycle against the wall, went out, and locked the door, after which he ran across to Outwood's.

Fortune had favored his undertaking by decreeing that a stout drainpipe should pass up the wall within a few inches of his and Psmith's study. On the first day of term, it may be remembered he had wrenched away the wooden bar which bisected the window frame, thus rendering exit and entrance almost as simple as they had been for Wyatt during Mike's first term at Wrykyn.

He proceeded to scale this water pipe.

He had got about halfway up when a voice from somewhere below cried, "Who's that?"

16

PURSUIT

These things are Life's Little Difficulties. One can never tell precisely how one will act in a sudden emergency. The right thing for Mike to have done at this crisis was to have ignored the voice, carried on up the water pipe, and through the study window, and gone to bed. It was extremely unlikely that anybody could have recognized him at night against the dark background of the house. The position then would have been that somebody in Mr. Outwood's house had been seen breaking in after lights-out; but it would have been very difficult for the authorities to have narrowed the search down any further than that. There were thirty-four boys in Outwood's, of whom about fourteen were much the same size and build as Mike.

The suddenness, however, of the call caused Mike to lose his head. He made the strategic error of sliding rapidly down the pipe, and running.

There were two gates to Mr. Outwood's front garden. The drive ran in a semicircle, of which the house was the center. It was from the right-hand gate, nearest to Mr. Downing's house, that the voice had come, and, as Mike came to the ground, he saw a stout figure galloping toward him from that direction. He bolted like a rabbit for the other gate. As he did so, his pursuer again gave tongue.

"Oo-oo-oo yer!" was the exact remark.

Whereby Mike recognized him as the school sergeant. "Oo-oo-oo yer!" was that militant gentleman's habitual way of beginning a conversation.

With this knowledge, Mike felt easier in his mind. Sergeant Collard was a man of many fine qualities (notably a talent for what he was wont to call "spott'n," a mysterious gift which he exercised on the rifle range), but he could not run. There had been a time in his hot youth when he had sprinted like an untamed mustang in pursuit of volatile Pathans in Indian hill wars, but Time, increasing his girth, had taken from him the taste for such exercise. When he moved now it was at a stately walk. The fact that he ran tonight showed how the excitement of the chase had entered into his blood.

"Oo-oo-oo yer!" he shouted again, as Mike, passing through the gate, turned into the road that led to the school. Mike's attentive ear noted that the bright speech was a shade more puffily delivered this time. He began to feel that this was not such bad fun after all. He would have liked to be in bed, but, if that was out of the question, this was certainly the next-best thing.

He ran on, taking things easily, with the sergeant panting in his wake, till he reached the entrance to the school grounds. He dashed in and took cover behind a tree.

Presently the sergeant turned the corner, going badly and evidently cured of a good deal of the fever of the chase. Mike heard him toil on for a few yards and then stop. A sound of panting was borne to him.

Then the sound of footsteps returning, this time at a walk. They passed the gate and went on down the road.

The pursuer had given the thing up.

Mike waited for several minutes behind his tree. His program now was simple. He would give Sergeant Collard about half an hour, in case the latter took it into his head to "guard home" by waiting at the gate. Then he would trot softly back, shoot up the water pipe once more, and so to bed. It had just struck a quarter to something-twelve, he supposed-on the school clock. He would wait till a quarter past.

Meanwhile, there was nothing to be gained from lurking behind a tree. He left his cover, and started to stroll in the direction of the pavilion. Having arrived there, he sat on the steps, looking out onto the cricket field.

His thoughts were miles away, at Wrykyn, when he was recalled to Sedleigh by the sound of somebody running. Focusing his gaze, he saw a dim figure moving rapidly across the cricket field straight for him.

His first impression, that he had been seen and followed, disappeared as the runner, instead of making for the pavilion, turned aside, and stopped at the door of the bicycle shed. Like Mike, he was evidently possessed of a key, for Mike heard it grate in the lock. At this point he left the pavilion and hailed his fellow rambler by night in a cautious undertone.

The other appeared startled.

"Who the dickens is that?" he asked. "Is that you, Jackson?"

Mike recognized Adair's voice. The last person he would have expected to meet at midnight obviously on the point of going for a bicycle ride.

"What are you doing out here. Jackson?"

"What are you, if it comes to that?"

Adair was adjusting his front light.

"I'm going for the doctor. One of the chaps in our house is bad."

"Oh!"

"What are you doing out here?"

"Just been for a stroll."

"Hadn't you better be getting back?"

"Plenty of time."

"I suppose you think you're doing something tremendously brave and dashing?"

"Hadn't you better be going to the doctor?"

"If you want to know what I think —"

"I don't. So long."

Mike turned away, whistling between his teeth. After a moment's pause, Adair rode off. Mike saw his light pass across the field and through the gate. The school clock struck the quarter.

It seemed to Mike that Sergeant Collard, even if he had started to wait for him at the house, would not keep up the vigil for more than half an hour. He would be safe now in trying for home again.

He walked in that direction.

Now it happened that Mr. Downing, aroused from his first sleep by the news, conveyed to him by Adair, that MacPhee, one of the junior members of Adair's dormitory, was groaning and exhibiting other symptoms of acute illness, was disturbed in his mind. Most housemasters feel uneasy in the event of illness in their houses, and Mr. Downing was apt to get jumpy beyond the ordinary on such occasions. All that was wrong with MacPhee, as a matter of fact, was a very fair stomachache, the direct and legitimate result of eating six buns, half a coconut, three doughnuts, two ices, an apple, and a pound of cherries, and washing the lot down with tea. But Mr. Downing saw in his attack the beginnings of some deadly scourge which would sweep through and decimate the house. He had dispatched Adair for the doctor, and, after spending a few minutes prowling restlessly about his room, was now standing at his front gate, waiting for Adair's return.

It came about, therefore, that Mike, sprinting lightly in the direction of home and safety, had his already shaken nerves further maltreated by being hailed, at a range of about two yards, with a cry of "Is that you, Adair?" The next moment Mr. Downing emerged from his gate.

Mike stood not upon the order of his going. He was off like an arrow — a flying figure of Guilt. Mr. Downing, after the first surprise, seemed to grasp the situation. Ejaculating at intervals the words, "Who is that? Stop! Who is that? Stop!" he dashed after the much-enduring Wrykynian at an extremely creditable rate of speed. Mr. Downing was by way of being a sprinter. He had won handicap events at College sports at Oxford, and, if Mike had not got such a good start, the race might have been over in the first fifty yards. As it was, that victim of Fate, going well, kept ahead. At the entrance to the school grounds he led by a dozen yards. The procession passed into the field, Mike heading as before for the pavilion.

As they raced across the soft turf, an idea occurred to Mike, which he was accustomed in after years to attribute to genius, the one flash of it which had ever illumined his life.

It was this.

One of Mr. Downing's first acts, on starting the Fire Brigade at Sedleigh, had been to institute an alarm bell. It had been rubbed into the school officially-in speeches from the dais-by the headmaster, and unofficially-in earnest private conversations-by Mr. Downing, that at the sound of this bell, at whatever hour of day or night, every member of the school must leave his house in the quickest possible way, and make for the open. The bell might mean that the school was on fire, or it might mean that one of the houses was on fire. In any case, the school had its orders-to get out into the open at once.

Nor must it be supposed that the school was without practice at this feat. Every now and then a notice would be found posted up on the board to the effect that there would be fire drill during the dinner hour that day. Sometimes the performance was bright and interesting, as on the occasion when Mr. Downing, marshaling the brigade at his front gate, had said, "My house is supposed to be on fire. Now let's do a record!" which the Brigade, headed by Stone and Robinson, obligingly did. They fastened the hose to the hydrant, smashed a window on the ground floor (Mr. Downing having retired for a moment to talk with the headmaster), and poured a stream of water into the room. When Mr. Downing was at liberty to turn his attention to the matter, he found that the room selected was his private study, most of the light furniture of which was floating in a miniature lake. That episode had rather discouraged his passion for realism, and fire drill since then had taken the form, for the most part, of "practicing escaping." This was done by means of canvas chutes, kept in the dormitories. At the sound of the bell the prefect of the dormitory would heave one end of the chute out of the window, the other end being fastened to the sill. He would then go down it himself, using his elbows as a brake. Then the second man would follow his example, and these two, standing below, would hold the end of the chute so that the rest of the dormitory could fly rapidly down it without injury, except to their digestions.

After the first novelty of the thing had worn off, the school had taken a rooted dislike to fire drill. It was a matter for self-congratulation among them that Mr. Downing had never been able to induce the headmaster to allow the alarm bell to be sounded for fire drill at night. The headmaster, a man who had his views on the amount of sleep necessary for the growing boy, had drawn the line at night operations. "Sufficient unto the day" had been the gist of his reply. If the alarm bell were to ring at night when there was no fire, the school might mistake a genuine alarm of fire for a bogus one, and refuse to hurry themselves.

So Mr. Downing had had to be content with day drill.

The alarm bell hung in the archway, leading into the school grounds. The end of the rope, when not in use, was fastened to a hook halfway up the wall.

Mike, as he raced over the cricket field, made up his mind in a flash that his only chance of getting out of this tangle was to shake his pursuer off for a space of time long enough to enable him to get to the rope and tug it. Then the school would come out. He would mix with them, and in the subsequent confusion get back to bed unnoticed.

The task was easier than it would have seemed at the beginning of the chase. Mr. Downing, owing to the two facts that he was not in the strictest training, and that it is only a Bannister who can run for any length of time at top speed shouting "Who is that? Stop! Who is that? Stop!" was beginning to feel distressed. There were bellows to mend in the Downing camp. Mike perceived this, and forced the pace. He rounded the pavilion ten yards to the good. Then, heading for the gate, he put all he knew into one last sprint. Mr. Downing was not equal to the effort. He worked gamely for a few strides, then fell behind. When Mike reached the gate, a good forty yards separated them.

As far as Mike could judge-he was not in a condition to make nice calculations-he had about four seconds in which to get busy with that bell rope.

Probably nobody has ever crammed more energetic work into four seconds than he did then.

The night was as still as only an English summer night can be, and the first clang of the clapper sounded like a million iron girders falling from a height onto a sheet of tin. He tugged away furiously, with an eye on the now rapidly advancing and loudly shouting figure of the housemaster.

And from the darkened house beyond there came a gradually swelling hum, as if a vast hive of bees had been disturbed.

The school was awake.

17

THE DECORATION OF SAMMY

Psmith leaned against the mantelpiece in the senior day room at Outwood's—since Mike's innings against Downing's the Lost Lambs had been received as brothers by the center of disorder, so that even Spiller was compelled to look on the hatchet as buried-and gave his views on the events of the preceding night, or, rather, of that morning, for it was nearer one than twelve when peace had once more fallen on the school.

"Nothing that happens in this loony bin," said Psmith, "has power to surprise me now. There was a time when I might have thought it a little unusual to have to leave the house through a canvas chute at one o'clock in the morning, but I suppose it's quite the regular thing here. Old school tradition, etc. Men leave the school, and find that they've got so accustomed to jumping out of windows that they look on it as a sort of affectation to go out by the door. I suppose none of you merchants can give me any idea when the next knockabout entertainment of this kind is likely to take place?"

"I wonder who rang that bell!" said Stone. "Jolly sporting idea."

"I believe it was Downing himself. If it was, I hope he's satisfied."

Jellicoe, who was appearing in society supported by a stick, looked meaningly at Mike, and giggled, receiving in answer a stony stare. Mike had informed Jellicoe of the details of his interview with Mr. Barley at the White Boar, and Jellicoe, after a momentary splutter of wrath against the practical joker, was now in a particular lighthearted mood. He hobbled about, giggling at nothing and at peace with all the world.

"It was a stirring scene," said Psmith. "The agility with which Comrade Jellicoe boosted himself down the chute was a triumph of mind over matter. He seemed to forget his ankle. It was the nearest thing to a Boneless Acrobatic Wonder that I have ever seen."

"I was in a beastly funk, I can tell you."

Stone gurgled.

"So was I," he said, "for a bit. Then, when I saw that it was all a rag, I began to look about for ways of doing the thing really well. I emptied about six jugs of water on a gang of kids under my window."

"I rushed into Downing's, and ragged some of the beds," said Robinson.

"It was an invigorating time," said Psmith. "A sort of pageant. I was particularly struck with the way some of the bright lads caught hold of the idea. There was no skimping. Some of the kids, to my certain knowledge, went down the chute a dozen times. There's nothing like doing a thing thoroughly. I saw them come down, rush upstairs, and be saved again, time after time. The thing became chronic with them. I should say Comrade Downing ought to be satisfied with the high state of efficiency to which he has brought us. At any rate I hope—"

There was a sound of hurried footsteps outside the door, and Sharpe, a member of the senior day room, burst excitedly in. He seemed amused.

"I say, have you chaps seen Sammy?"

"Seen who?" said Stone. "Sammy? Why?"

"You'll know in a second. He's just outside. Here, Sammy, Sammy, Sammy! Sam! Sam!"

A bark and a patter of feet outside.

"Come on, Sammy. Good dog."

There was a moment's silence. Then a great yell of laughter burst forth. Even Psmith's massive calm was shattered. As for Jellicoe, he sobbed in a corner.

Sammy's beautiful white coat was almost entirely concealed by a thick covering of bright-red paint. His head, with the exception of the ears, was untouched, and his serious, friendly eyes seemed to emphasise the weirdness of his appearance. He stood in the doorway, barking and wagging his tail, plainly puzzled at his reception. He was a popular dog, and was always well received when he visited any of the houses, but he had never before met with enthusiasm like this.

"Good old Sammy!"

"What on earth's been happening to him?"

"Who did it?"

Sharpe, the introducer, had no views on the matter.

"I found him outside Downing's, with a crowd round him. Everybody seems to have seen him. I wonder who on earth has gone and mucked him up like that!"

Mike was the first to show any sympathy for the maltreated animal.

"Poor old Sammy," he said, kneeling on the floor beside the victim, and scratching him under the ear. "What a beastly shame! It'll take hours to wash all that off him, and he'll hate it."

"It seems to me," said Psmith, regarding Sammy dispassionately through his eyeglass, "that it's not a case for mere washing. They'll either have to skin him bodily, or leave the thing to time. Time, the Great Healer. In a year or two he'll fade to a delicate pink. I don't see why you shouldn't have a pink bull terrier. It would lend a touch of distinction to the place. Crowds would come in excursion trains to see him. By charging a small fee you might make him self-supporting. I think I'll suggest it to Comrade Downing."

"There'll be a row about this," said Stone.

"Rows are rather sport when you're not mixed up in them," said Robinson, philosophically. "There'll be another if we don't start off for chapel soon. It's a quarter to."

There was a general move. Mike was the last to leave the room. As he was going, Jellicoe stopped him. Jellicoe was staying in that Sunday, owing to his ankle.

"I say," said Jellicoe, "I just wanted to thank you again about that —"

"Oh, that's all right."

"No, but it really was awfully decent of you. You might have got into a frightful row. Were you nearly caught?"

"Jolly nearly."

"It *was* you who rang the bell, wasn't it?"

"Yes, it was. But for goodness' sake don't go gassing about it, or somebody will get to hear who oughtn't to, and I shall be sacked."

"All right. But, I say, you *are* a chap!"

"What's the matter now?"

"I mean about Sammy, you know. It's a jolly good score off old Downing. He'll be frightfully sick."

"Sammy!" cried Mike. "My good man, you don't think I did that, do you? What absolute rot! I never touched the poor brute."

"Oh, all right," said Jellicoe. "But I wasn't going to tell anyone, of course."

"What do you mean?"

"You *are* a chap!" giggled Jellicoe.

Mike walked to chapel rather thoughtfully.

18

MR. DOWNING ON THE SCENT

There was just one moment, the moment in which, on going down to the junior day room of his house to quell an unseemly disturbance, he was boisterously greeted by a vermilion bull terrier, when Mr. Downing was seized with a hideous fear lest he had lost his senses. Glaring down at the crimson animal that was pawing at his knees, he clutched at his reason for one second as a drowning man clutches at a life belt.

Then the happy laughter of the young onlookers reassured him.

"Who—" he shouted, "WHO has done this?"

"Please, sir, we don't know," shrilled the chorus.

"Please, sir, he came in like that."

"Please, sir, we were sitting here when he suddenly ran in, all red."

A voice from the crowd: "Look at old Sammy!"

The situation was impossible. There was nothing to be done. He could not find out by verbal inquiry who had painted the dog. The possibility of Sammy being painted red during the night had never occurred to Mr. Downing, and now that the thing had happened he had no scheme of action. As Psmith would have said, he had confused the unusual with the impossible, and the result was that he was taken by surprise.

While he was pondering on this, the situation was rendered still more difficult by Sammy, who, taking advantage of the door being open, escaped and rushed into the road, thus publishing his condition to all and sundry. You can hush up a painted dog while it confines itself to your own premises, but once it has mixed with the great public, this becomes out of the question. Sammy's state advanced from a private trouble into a row. Mr. Downing's next move was in the same direction that Sammy had taken, only, instead of running about the road, he went straight to the headmaster.

The Head, who had had to leave his house in the small hours in his pajamas and a dressing gown, was not in the best of tempers. He had a cold in the head, and also a rooted conviction that Mr. Downing, in spite of his strict orders, had rung the bell himself on the previous night in order to test the efficiency of the school in saving themselves in the event of fire. He received the housemaster frostily, but thawed as the latter related the events which had led up to the ringing of the bell.

"Dear me!" he said, deeply interested. "One of the boys at the school, you think?"

"I am certain of it," said Mr. Downing.

"Was he wearing a school cap?"

"He was bareheaded. A boy who breaks out of his house at night would hardly run the risk of wearing a distinguishing cap."

"No, no, I suppose not. A big boy, you say?"

"Very big."

"You did not see his face?"

"It was dark and he never looked back-he was in front of me all the time."

"Dear me!"

"There is another matter…"

"Yes?"

"This boy, whoever he was, had done something before he rang the bell-he had painted my dog Sampson red."

The headmaster's eyes protruded from their sockets. "He-he —*what*, Mr. Downing?"

"He painted my dog red-bright red." Mr. Downing was too angry to see anything humorous in the incident. Since the previous night he had been wounded in his tenderest feelings, his Fire Brigade system had been most shamefully abused by being turned into a mere instrument in the hands of a malefactor for escaping justice, and his dog had been held up to ridicule to all the world. He did not want to smile; he wanted revenge.

The headmaster, on the other hand, did want to smile. It was not his dog, he could look on the affair with an unbiased eye, and to him there was something ludicrous in a white dog suddenly appearing as a red dog.

"It is a scandalous thing!" said Mr. Downing.

"Quite so! Quite so!" said the headmaster hastily. "I shall punish the boy who did it most severely. I will speak to the school in the Hall after chapel."

Which he did, but without result. A cordial invitation to the criminal to come forward and be executed was received in wooden silence by the school, with the exception of Johnson III, of Outwood's, who, suddenly reminded of Sammy's appearance by the headmaster's words, broke into a wild screech of laughter, and was instantly awarded two hundred lines.

The school filed out of the Hall to their various lunches, and Mr. Downing was left with the conviction that, if he wanted the criminal discovered, he would have to discover him for himself.

The great thing in affairs of this kind is to get a good start, and Fate, feeling perhaps that it had been a little hard upon Mr. Downing, gave him a most magnificent start. Instead of having to hunt for a needle in a haystack, he found himself in a moment in the position of being set to find it in a mere truss of straw.

It was Mr. Outwood who helped him. Sergeant Collard had waylaid the archaeological expert on his way to chapel, and informed him that at close on twelve the night before he had observed a youth, unidentified, attempting to get into his house *via* the water pipe. Mr. Outwood, whose thoughts were occupied with apses and plinths, not to mention cromlechs, at the time, thanked the sergeant with absent minded politeness and passed on. Later he remembered the fact apropos of some reflections on the subject of burglars in medieval England, and passed it on to Mr. Downing as they walked back to lunch.

"Then the boy was in your house!" exclaimed Mr. Downing.

"Not actually in, as far as I understand. I gather from the sergeant that he interrupted him before —"

"I mean he must have been one of the boys in your house."

"But what was he doing out at that hour?"

"He had broken out."

"Impossible, I think. Oh yes, quite impossible! I went around the dormitories as usual at eleven o'clock last night, and all the boys were asleep-all of them."

Mr. Downing was not listening. He was in a state of suppressed excitement and exultation, which made it hard for him to attend to his colleague's slow utterances. He had a clue! Now that the search had narrowed itself down to Outwood's house, the rest was comparatively easy. Perhaps Sergeant Collard had actually recognized the boy. On reflection he dismissed this as unlikely, for the sergeant would scarcely have kept a thing like that to himself; but he might very well have seen more of him than he, Downing, had seen. It was only with an effort that he could keep himself from rushing to the sergeant then and there, and leaving the house lunch to look after itself. He resolved to go the moment that meal was at an end.

Sunday lunch at a public-school house is probably one of the longest functions in existence. It drags its slow length along like a languid snake, but it finishes in time. In due course Mr. Downing, after sitting still and eyeing with acute dislike everybody who asked for a second helping, found himself at liberty.

Regardless of the claims of digestion, he rushed forth on the trail.

Sergeant Collard lived with his wife and a family of unknown dimensions in the lodge at the school front gate. Dinner was just over when Mr. Downing arrived, as a blind man could have told.

The sergeant received his visitor with dignity, ejecting the family, who were torpid after roast beef and resented having to move, in order to ensure privacy.

Having requested his host to smoke, which the latter was about to do unasked, Mr. Downing stated his case.

"Mr. Outwood," he said, "tells me that last night, Sergeant, you saw a boy endeavoring to enter his house."

The sergeant blew a cloud of smoke. "Oo-oo-oo, yer," he said; "I did, sir-spotted 'im, I did. Feeflee good at spottin', I am, sir. Dook of Connaught, he used to say, 'Ere comes Sergeant Collard,' 'e used to say, ''e's feeflee good at spottin'.'"

"What did you do?"

"Do? Oo-oo-oo! I shouts 'Oo-oo-oo yer, yer young monkey, what yer doin' there?'"

"Yes?"

"But 'e was off in a flash, and I doubles after 'im prompt."

"But you didn't catch him?"

"No, sir," admitted the sergeant reluctantly.

"Did you catch sight of his face, Sergeant?"

"No, sir, 'e was doublin' away in the opposite direction."

"Did you notice anything at all about his appearance?"

"'E was a long young chap, sir, with a pair of legs on him-feeflee fast 'e run, sir. Oo-oo-oo, feeflee!"

"You noticed nothing else?"

"'E wasn't wearing no cap of any sort, sir."

"Ah!"

"Bare'eaded, sir," added the sergeant, rubbing the point in.

"It was undoubtedly the same boy, undoubtedly! I wish you could have caught a glimpse of his face, Sergeant."

"So do I, sir."

"You would not be able to recognize him again if you saw him, you think?"

"Oo-oo-oo! Wouldn't go as far as to say that, sir, 'cos yer see, I'm feeflee good at spottin', but it was a dark night."

Mr. Downing rose to go.

"Well," he said, "the search is now considerably narrowed down, considerably! It is certain that the boy was one of the boys in Mr. Outwood's house."

"Young monkeys!" interjected the sergeant helpfully

"Good afternoon, Sergeant."

"Good afternoon to you, sir."

"Pray do not move, Sergeant."

The sergeant had not shown the slightest inclination of doing anything of the kind.

"I will find my way out. Very hot today, is it not?"

"Feeflee warm, sir; weather's goin' to break' workin' up for thunder."

"I hope not. The school plays the M.C.C. on Wednesday, and it would be a pity if rain were to spoil our first fixture with them. Good afternoon."

And Mr. Downing went out into the baking sunlight, while Sergeant Collard, having requested Mrs. Collard to take the children out for a walk at once, and furthermore to give young Ernie a clip side of the 'ead, if he persisted in making so much noise, put a handkerchief over his face, rested his feet on the table, and slept the sleep of the just.

19

THE SLEUTH-HOUND

For the Doctor Watsons of this world, as opposed to the Sherlock Holmeses, success in the province of detective work must be, to a very large extent, the result of luck. Sherlock Holmes can extract a clue from a wisp of straw or a flake of cigar ash. But Doctor Watson has got to have it taken out for him, and dusted, and exhibited clearly, with a label attached.

The average man is a Doctor Watson. We are wont to scoff in a patronizing manner at that humbler follower of the great investigator, but, as a matter of fact, we should have been just as dull ourselves. We should not even have risen to the modest level of a Scotland Yard bungler. We should simply have hung around, saying: "My dear Holmes, how...?" and all the rest of it, just as the downtrodden medico did.

It is not often that the ordinary person has any need to see what he can do in the way of detection. He gets along very comfortably in the humdrum round of life without having to measure footprints and smile quiet, tight-lipped smiles. But if ever the emergency does arise, he thinks naturally of Sherlock Holmes, and his methods.

Mr. Downing had read all the Holmes stories with great attention, and had thought many times what an incompetent ass Doctor Watson was; but, now that he had started to handle his own first case, he was compelled to admit that there was a good deal to be said in extenuation of Watson's inability to unravel tangles. It certainly was uncommonly hard, he thought, as he paced the cricket field after leaving Sergeant Collard, to detect anybody, unless you knew who had really done the crime. As he brooded over the case in hand, his sympathy for Doctor Watson increased with every minute, and he began to feel a certain resentment against Sir Arthur Conan Doyle. It was all very well for Sir Arthur to be so shrewd and infallible about tracing a mystery to its source, but he knew perfectly well who had done the thing before he started!

Now that he began really to look into this matter of the alarm bell and the painting of Sammy, the conviction was creeping over him that the problem was more difficult than a casual observer might imagine. He had got as far as finding that his quarry of the previous night was a boy in Mr. Outwood's house, but how was he to get any further? That was the thing. There was, of course, only a limited number of boys in Mr. Outwood's house as tall as the one he had pursued; but even if there had been only one other, it would have complicated matters. If you go to a boy and say, "Either you or Jones were out of your house last night at twelve o'clock," the boy does not reply, "Sir, I cannot tell a lie —I was out of my house last night at twelve o'clock." He simply assumes the animated expression of a stuffed fish, and leaves the next move to you. It is practically stalemate.

All these things passed through Mr. Downing's mind as he walked up and down the cricket field that afternoon.

What he wanted was a clue. But it is so hard for the novice to tell what is a clue and what isn't. Probably, if he only knew, there were clues lying all over the place, shouting to him to pick them up.

What with the oppressive heat of the day and the fatigue of hard thinking, Mr. Downing was working up for a brainstorm when Fate once more intervened, this time in the shape of Riglett, a junior member of his house.

Riglett slunk up in the shamefaced way peculiar to some boys, even when they have done nothing wrong, and, having "capped" Mr. Downing with the air of one who had been caught in the act of doing something particularly shady, requested that he might be allowed to fetch his bicycle from the shed.

"Your bicycle?" snapped Mr. Downing. Much thinking had made him irritable. "What do you want with your bicycle?"

Riglett shuffled, stood first on his left foot, then on his right, blushed, and finally remarked, as if it were not so much a sound reason as a sort of feeble excuse for the low and blackguardly fact that he wanted his bicycle, that he had got leave for tea that afternoon.

Then Mr. Downing remembered. Riglett had an aunt resident about three miles from the school, whom he was accustomed to visit occasionally on Sunday afternoons during the term.

He felt for his bunch of keys, and made his way to the shed, Riglett shambling behind at an interval of two yards.

Mr. Downing unlocked the door, and there on the floor was the Clue!

A clue that even Doctor Watson could not have overlooked.

Mr. Downing saw it, but did not immediately recognize it for what it was. What he saw at first was not a clue, but just a mess. He had a tidy soul and abhorred messes. And this was a particularly messy mess. The greater part of the flooring in the neighborhood of the door was a sea of red paint. The tin from which it had flowed was lying on its side in the middle of the shed. The air was full of the pungent scent.

"Pah!" said Mr. Downing.

Then suddenly, beneath the disguise of the mess, he saw the clue. A footmark! No less. A crimson footmark on the gray concrete!

Riglett, who had been waiting patiently two yards away, now coughed plaintively. The sound recalled Mr. Downing to mundane matters.

"Get your bicycle, Riglett," he said, "and be careful where you tread. Somebody has upset a pot of paint on the floor."

Riglett, walking delicately through dry places, extracted his bicycle from the rack, and presently departed to gladden the heart of his aunt, leaving Mr. Downing, his brain fizzing with the enthusiasm of the detective, to lock the door and resume his perambulation of the cricket field.

Give Doctor Watson a fair start, and he is a demon at the game. Mr. Downing's brain was now working with a rapidity and clearness which a professional sleuth might have envied.

Paint. Red paint. Obviously the same paint with which Sammy had been decorated. A footmark. Whose footmark? Plainly that of the criminal who had done the deed of decoration. Yoicks!

There were two things, however, to be considered. Your careful detective must consider everything. In the first place, the paint might have been upset by the groundsman. It was the groundsman's paint. He had been giving a fresh coating to the woodwork in front of the pavilion scoring box at the conclusion of yesterday's match. (A labor of love which was the direct outcome of the enthusiasm for work which Adair had instilled into him.) In that case the footmark might be his.

Note one: Interview the groundsman on this point.

In the second place Adair might have upset the tin and trodden in its contents when he went to get his bicycle in order to fetch the doctor for the suffering MacPhee. This was the more probable of the two contingencies, for it would have been dark in the shed when Adair went into it.

Note two: Interview Adair as to whether he found, on returning to the house, that there was paint on his shoes.

Things were moving.

* * * * *

He resolved to take Adair first. He could get the groundsman's address from him.

Passing by the trees under whose shade Mike and Psmith and Dunster had watched the match on the previous day, he came upon the Head of his house in a deck chair reading a book. A summer Sunday afternoon is the time for reading in deck chairs.

"Oh, Adair," he said. "No, don't get up. I merely wished to ask you if you found any paint on your shoes when you returned to the house last night."

"Paint, sir?" Adair was plainly puzzled. His book had been interesting, and had driven the Sammy incident out of his head.

"I see somebody has spilled some paint on the floor of the bicycle shed. You did not do that, I suppose, when you went to fetch your bicycle?"

"No, sir."

"It is spilled all over the floor. I wondered whether you had happened to tread in it. But you say you found no paint on your shoes this morning?"

"No, sir, my bicycle is always quite near the door of the shed. I didn't go into the shed at all."

"I see. Quite so. Thank you, Adair. Oh, by the way, Adair, where does Markby live?"

"I forget the name of his cottage, sir, but I could show you in a second. It's one of those cottages just past the school gates, on the right as you turn out into the road. There are three in a row. His is the first you come to. There's a barn just before you get to them."

"Thank you. I shall be able to find them. I should like to speak to Markby for a moment on a small matter."

A sharp walk took him to the cottages Adair had mentioned. He rapped at the door of the first, and the groundsman came out in his shirt sleeves, blinking as if he had just waked up, as was indeed the case.

"Oh, Markby!"

"Sir?"

"You remember that you were painting the scoring box in the pavilion last night after the match?"

"Yes, sir. It wanted a lick of paint bad. The young gentlemen will scramble about and get through the window. Makes it look shabby, sir. So I thought I'd better give it a coating so as to look shipshape when the Marylebone come down."

"Just so. An excellent idea. Tell me, Markby, what did you do with the pot of paint when you had finished?"

"Put it in the bicycle shed, sir."

"On the floor?"

"On the floor, sir? No. On the shelf at the far end, with the can of whitening what I use for marking out the wickets, sir."

"Of course, yes. Quite so. Just as I thought."

"Do you want it, sir?"

"No, thank you, Markby, no, thank you. The fact is, somebody who had no business to do so has moved the pot of paint from the shelf to the floor, with the result that it has been kicked over and spilled. You had better get some more tomorrow. Thank you, Markby. That is all I wished to know."

Mr. Downing walked back to the school thoroughly excited. He was hot on the scent now. The only other possible theories had been tested and successfully exploded. The thing had become simple to a degree. All he had to do was to go to Mr. Outwood's house-the idea of searching a fellow master's house did not appear to him at all a delicate task; somehow one grew unconsciously to feel that Mr. Outwood did not really exist as a man capable of resenting liberties-find the paint-splashed shoe, ascertain its owner, and denounce him to the headmaster. There could be no doubt that a paint-splashed shoe must be in Mr. Outwood's house somewhere. A boy cannot tread in a pool of paint without showing some signs of having done so.

It was Sunday, too, so that the shoe would not yet have been cleaned. Yoicks! Also tally-ho! This really was beginning to be something like business.

Regardless of the heat, the sleuth-hound hurried across to Outwood's as fast as he could walk.

20

A CHECK

The only two members of the house not out in the grounds when he arrived were Mike and Psmith. They were standing on the gravel drive in front of the boys' entrance. Mike had a deck chair in one hand and a book in the other. Psmith-for even the greatest minds will sometimes unbend-was wrestling with a Yo-Yo. That is to say, he was trying without success to keep the spool spinning. He smoothed a crease out of his waistcoat and tried again. He had just succeeded in getting the thing to spin when Mr. Downing arrived. The sound of his footsteps disturbed Psmith and brought the effort to nothing.

"Enough of this spoolery," said he, flinging the spool through the open window of the senior day room. "I was an ass ever to try it. The philosophical mind needs complete repose in its hours of leisure. Hello!"

He stared after the sleuth-hound, who had just entered the house.

"What the dickens," said Mike, "does he mean by barging in as if he'd bought the place?"

"Comrade Downing looks pleased with himself. What brings him around in this direction, I wonder! Still, no matter. The few articles which he may sneak from our study are of inconsiderable value. He is welcome to them. Do you feel inclined to wait awhile till I have fetched a chair and book?"

"I'll be going on. I shall be under the trees at the far end of the ground."

"'Tis well. I will be with you in about two ticks."

Mike walked on toward the field, and Psmith, strolling upstairs to fetch his novel, found Mr. Downing standing in the passage with the air of one who has lost his bearings.

"A warm afternoon, sir," murmured Psmith courteously, as he passed.

"Er-Smith!"

"Sir?"

"I —er-wish to go round the dormitories."

It was Psmith's guiding rule in life never to be surprised at anything, so he merely inclined his head gracefully, and said nothing.

"I should be glad if you would fetch the keys and show me where the rooms are."

"With acute pleasure, sir," said Psmith. "Or shall I fetch Mr. Outwood, sir?"

"Do as I tell you Smith," snapped Mr. Downing.

Psmith said no more, but went down to the matron's room. The matron being out, he abstracted the bunch of keys from her table and rejoined the master.

"Shall I lead the way, sir?" he asked.

Mr. Downing nodded.

"Here, sir," said Psmith, opening the door, "we have Barnes's dormitory. An airy room, constructed on the soundest hygienic principles. Each boy, I understand, has quite a considerable number of cubic feet of air all to himself. It is Mr. Outwood's boast that no boy has ever asked for a cubic foot of air in vain. He argues justly —"

He broke off abruptly and began to watch the other's maneuvers in silence. Mr. Downing was peering rapidly beneath each bed in turn.

"Are you looking for Barnes, sir?" inquired Psmith politely. "I think he's out in the field."

Mr. Downing rose, having examined the last bed, crimson in the face with the exercise.

"Show me the next dormitory, Smith," he said, panting slightly.

"This," said Psmith, opening the next door and sinking his voice to an awed whisper, "is where *I* sleep!"

Mr. Downing glanced swiftly beneath the three beds.

"Excuse me, sir," said Psmith, "but are we chasing anything?"

291

"Be good enough, Smith," said Mr. Downing with asperity, "to keep your remarks to yourself."

"I was only wondering sir. Shall I show you the next in order?"

"Certainly."

They moved on up the passage.

Drawing blank at the last dormitory, Mr. Downing paused, baffled. Psmith waited patiently by. An idea struck the master.

"The studies, Smith," he cried.

"Aha!" said Psmith. "I beg your pardon, sir. The observation escaped me unawares. The frenzy of the chase is beginning to enter into my blood. Here we have —"

Mr. Downing stopped short.

"Is this impertinence studied, Smith?"

"Ferguson's study, sir? No, sir. That's farther down the passage. This is Barnes's."

Mr. Downing looked at him closely. Psmith's face was wooden in its gravity. The master snorted suspiciously, then moved on.

"Whose is this?" he asked, rapping a door.

"This, sir, is mine and Jackson's."

"What! Have you a study? You are low down in the school for it."

"I think, sir, that Mr. Outwood gave it us rather as a testimonial to our general worth than to our proficiency in schoolwork."

Mr. Downing raked the room with a keen eye. The absence of bars from the window attracted his attention.

"Have you no bars to your windows here, such as there are in my house?"

"There appears to be no bar, sir," said Psmith, putting up his eyeglass.

Mr. Downing was leaning out of the window.

"A lovely view, is it not, sir?" said Psmith. "The trees, the field, the distant hills..."

Mr. Downing suddenly started. His eye had been caught by the water pipe at the side of the window. The boy whom Sergeant Collard had seen climbing the pipe must have been making for this study.

He spun around and met Psmith's blandly inquiring gaze. He looked at Psmith carefully for a moment. No. The boy he had chased last night had not been Psmith. That exquisite's figure and general appearance were unmistakable, even in the dusk.

"Whom did you say you shared this study with, Smith?"

"Jackson, sir. The cricketer."

"Never mind about his cricket, Smith," said Mr. Downing with irritation.

"No, sir."

"He is the only other occupant of the room?"

"Yes, sir."

"Nobody else comes into it?"

"If they do, they go out extremely quickly, sir."

"Ah! Thank you, Smith."

"Not at all, sir."

Mr. Downing pondered. Jackson! The boy bore him a grudge. The boy was precisely the sort of boy to revenge himself by painting the dog Sammy. And, gadzooks! The boy whom he had pursued last night had been just about Jackson's size and build!

Mr. Downing was as firmly convinced at that moment that Mike's had been the hand to wield the paintbrush as he had ever been of anything in his life.

"Smith!" he said excitedly.

"On the spot, sir," said Psmith affably.

"Where are Jackson's shoes?"

There are moments when the giddy excitement of being right on the trail causes the amateur (or Watsonian) detective to be incautious. Such a moment came to Mr. Downing then. If he had been wise, he would have achieved his object, the getting a glimpse of Mike's shoes, by a devious and snaky route. As it was, he rushed straight on.

"His shoes, sir? He has them on. I noticed them as he went out just now."

"Where is the pair he wore yesterday?"

"Where are the shoes of yesteryear?" murmured Psmith to himself. "I should say at a venture, sir, that they would be in the basket, downstairs. Edmund, our genial knife-and-boot boy, collects them, I believe, at early dawn."

"Would they have been cleaned yet?"

"If I know Edmund, sir-no."

"Smith," said Mr. Downing, trembling with excitement, "go and bring that basket to me here."

Psmith's brain was working rapidly as he went downstairs. What exactly was at the back of the sleuth's mind, prompting these maneuvers, he did not know. But that there was something, and that that something was directed in a hostile manner against Mike, probably in connection with last night's wild happenings, he was certain. Psmith had noticed, on leaving his bed at the sound of the alarm bell, that he and Jellicoe were alone in the room. That might mean that Mike had gone out through the door when the bell sounded, or it might mean that he had been out all the time. It began to look as if the latter solution were the correct one.

He staggered back with the basket, painfully conscious all the while that it was creasing his waistcoat, and dumped it down on the study floor. Mr. Downing stooped eagerly over it. Psmith leaned against the wall, and straightened out the damaged garment.

"We have here, sir," he said, "a fair selection of our various bootings."

Mr. Downing looked up.

"You dropped none of the shoes on your way up, Smith?"

"Not one, sir. It was a fine performance."

Mr. Downing uttered a grunt of satisfaction, and bent once more to his task. Shoes flew about the room. Mr. Downing knelt on the floor beside the basket, and dug like a terrier at a rathole.

At last he made a dive, and, with an exclamation of triumph, rose to his feet. In his hand he held a shoe.

"Put those back again, Smith," he said.

The ex-Etonian, wearing an expression such as a martyr might have worn on being told off for the stake, began to pick up the scattered footgear, whistling softly the tune of "I do all the dirty work," as he did so.

"That's the lot, sir," he said, rising.

"Ah. Now come across with me to the headmaster's house. Leave the basket here. You can carry it back when you return."

"Shall I put back that shoe, sir?"

"Certainly not. I shall take this with me, of course."

"Shall I carry it, sir?"

Mr. Downing reflected.

"Yes, Smith," he said. "I think it would be best."

It occurred to him that the spectacle of a house master wandering abroad on the public highway, carrying a dirty shoe, might be a trifle undignified. You never knew whom you might meet on Sunday afternoon.

Psmith took the shoe, and doing so, understood what before had puzzled him.

Across the toe of the shoe was a broad splash of red paint.

He knew nothing, of course, of the upset tin in the bicycle shed; but when a housemaster's dog has been painted red in the night, and when, on the following day, the housemaster goes about in search of a paint splashed shoe, one puts two and two together. Psmith looked at the name inside the shoe. It was "Brown bootmaker, Bridgnorth." Bridgnorth was only a few miles from his own home and Mike's. Undoubtedly it was Mike's shoe.

"Can you tell me whose shoe that is?" asked Mr. Downing.

Psmith looked at it again.

"No, sir. I can't say the little chap's familiar to me."

"Come with me, then."

Mr. Downing left the room. After a moment Psmith followed him.

The headmaster was in his garden. Thither Mr. Downing made his way, the shoe-bearing Psmith in close attendance.

The Head listened to the amateur detective's statement with interest.

"Indeed?" he said, when Mr. Downing had finished, "Indeed? Dear me! It certainly seems... It is a curiously well-connected thread of evidence. You are certain that there was red paint on this shoe you discovered in Mr. Outwood's house?"

"I have it with me. I brought it on purpose to show to you. Smith!"

"Sir?"

"You have the shoe?"

"Ah," said the headmaster, putting on a pair of pince-nez, "now let me look at-This, you say, is the —? Just so. Just so. Just... But, er, Mr. Downing, it may be that I have not examined this shoe with sufficient care, but-Can *you* point out to me exactly where this paint is that you speak of?"

Mr. Downing stood staring at the shoe with a wild, fixed stare. Of any suspicion of paint, red or otherwise, it was absolutely and entirely innocent.

21

THE DESTROYER OF EVIDENCE

The shoe became the center of attention, the cynosure of all eyes. Mr. Downing fixed it with the piercing stare of one who feels that his brain is tottering. The headmaster looked at it with a mildly puzzled expression. Psmith, putting up his eyeglass, gazed at it with a sort of affectionate interest, as if he were waiting for it to do a trick of some kind.

Mr. Downing was the first to break the silence.

"There was paint on this shoe," he said vehemently. "I tell you there was a splash of red paint across the toe. Smith will bear me out in this. Smith, you saw the paint on this shoe?"

"Paint, sir?"

"What! Do you mean to tell me that you did *not* see it?"

"No, sir. There was no paint on this shoe."

"This is foolery. I saw it with my own eyes. It was a broad splash right across the toe."

The headmaster interposed.

"You must have made a mistake, Mr. Downing. There is certainly no trace of paint on this shoe. These momentary optical delusions are, I fancy, not uncommon. Any doctor will tell you —"

"I had an aunt, sir," said Psmith chattily, "who was remarkably subject —"

"It is absurd. I cannot have been mistaken," said Mr. Downing. "I am positively certain the toe of this shoe was red when I found it."

"It is undoubtedly black now, Mr. Downing."

"A sort of chameleon shoe," murmured Psmith.

The goaded housemaster turned on him.

"What did you say, Smith?"

"Did I speak, sir?" said Psmith, with the start of one coming suddenly out of a trance.

Mr. Downing looked searchingly at him.

"You had better be careful, Smith."

"Yes, sir."

"I strongly suspect you of having something to do with this."

"Really, Mr. Downing," said the headmaster, "this is surely improbable. Smith could scarcely have cleaned the shoe on his way to my house. On one occasion I inadvertently spilled some paint on a shoe of my own. I can assure you that it does not brush off. It needs a very systematic cleaning before all traces are removed."

"Exactly, sir," said Psmith. "My theory, if I may...?"

"Certainly Smith."

Psmith bowed courteously and proceeded.

"My theory, sir, is that Mr. Downing was deceived by the light-and-shade effects on the toe of the shoe. The afternoon sun, streaming in through the window, must have shone on the shoe in such a manner as to give it a momentary and fictitious aspect of redness. If Mr. Downing recollects, he did not look long at the shoe. The picture on the retina of the eye, consequently, had not time to fade. I remember thinking myself, at the moment, that the shoe appeared to have a certain reddish tint. The mistake...."

"Bag!" said Mr. Downing shortly.

"Well, really," said the headmaster, "it seems to me that that is the only explanation that will square with the facts. A shoe that is really smeared with red paint does not become black of itself in the course of a few minutes."

"You are very right, sir," said Psmith with benevolent approval. "May I go now, sir? I am in the middle of a singularly impressive passage of Cicero's speech *De senectute*."

"I am sorry that you should leave your preparation till Sunday, Smith. It is a habit of which I altogether disapprove."

"I am reading it, sir," said Psmith, with simple dignity, "for pleasure. Shall I take the shoe with me, sir?"

"If Mr. Downing does not want it?"

The housemaster passed the fraudulent piece of evidence to Psmith without a word, and the latter, having included both masters in a kindly smile, left the garden.

Pedestrians who had the good fortune to be passing along the road between the headmaster's house and Mr. Outwood's at that moment saw what, if they had but known it, was a most unusual sight, the spectacle of Psmith running. Psmith's usual mode of progression was a dignified walk. He believed in the contemplative style rather than the hustling.

On this occasion, however, reckless of possible injuries to the crease of his trousers, he raced down the road, and turning in at Outwood's gate, bounded upstairs like a highly trained professional athlete.

On arriving at the study, his first act was to remove a shoe from the top of the pile in the basket, place it in the small cupboard under the bookshelf, and lock the cupboard. Then he flung himself into a chair and panted.

"Brain," he said to himself approvingly, "is what one chiefly needs in matters of this kind. Without brain, where are we? In the soup, every time. The next development will be when Comrade Downing thinks it over, and is struck with the brilliant idea that it's just possible that the shoe he gave me to carry and the shoe I did carry were not one shoe but two shoes. Meanwhile..."

He dragged up another chair for his feet and picked up his novel.

He had not been reading long when there was a footstep in the passage, and Mr. Downing appeared.

The possibility, in fact the probability, of Psmith's having substituted another shoe for the one with the incriminating splash of paint on it had occurred to him almost immediately on leaving the headmaster's garden. Psmith and Mike, he reflected, were friends. Psmith's impulse would be to do all that lay in his power to shield Mike. Feeling aggrieved with himself that he had not thought of this before, he, too, hurried over to Outwood's.

Mr. Downing was brisk and peremptory.

"I wish to look at these shoes again," he said. Psmith, with a sigh, laid down his novel, and rose to assist him.

"Sit down, Smith," said the housemaster. "I can manage without your help."

Psmith sat down again, carefully tucking up the knees of his trousers, and watched him with silent interest through his eyeglass.

The scrutiny irritated Mr. Downing.

"Put that thing away, Smith," he said.

"That thing, sir?"

"Yes, that ridiculous glass. Put it away."

"Why, sir?"

"Why! Because I tell you to do so."

"I guessed that that was the reason, sir," sighed Psmith, replacing the eyeglass in his waistcoat pocket. He rested his elbows on his knees, and his chin on his hands, and resumed his contemplative inspection of the shoe expert, who, after fidgeting for a few moments, lodged another complaint.

"Don't sit there staring at me, Smith."

"I was interested in what you were doing, sir."

"Never mind. Don't stare at me in that idiotic way."

"May I read, sir?" asked Psmith, patiently.

"Yes, read if you like."

"Thank you, sir."

Psmith took up his book again, and Mr. Downing, now thoroughly irritated, pursued his investigations in the boot basket.

He went through it twice, but each time without success. After the second search, he stood up, and looked wildly round the room. He was as certain as he could be of anything that the missing piece of evidence was somewhere in the study. It was no use asking Psmith point-blank where it was, for Psmith's ability to parry dangerous questions with evasive answers was quite out of the common.

His eye roamed about the room. There was very little cover there, even for so small a fugitive as a number nine shoe. The floor could be acquitted, on sight, of harboring the quarry.

Then he caught sight of the cupboard, and something seemed to tell him that there was the place to look.

"Smith!" he said.

Psmith had been reading placidly all the while.

"Yes, sir?"

"What is in this cupboard?"

"That cupboard, sir?"

"Yes. This cupboard." Mr. Downing rapped the door irritably.

"Just a few odd trifles, sir. We do not often use it. A ball of string, perhaps. Possibly an old notebook. Nothing of value or interest.

"Open it."

"I think you will find that it is locked, sir."

"Unlock it."

"But where is the key, sir?"

"Have you not got the key?"

"If the key is not in the lock, sir, you may depend upon it that it will take a long search to find it."

"Where did you see it last?"

"It was in the lock yesterday morning. Jackson might have taken it."

"Where is Jackson?"

"Out in the field somewhere, sir."

Mr. Downing thought for a moment.

"I don't believe a word of it," he said shortly. "I have my reasons for thinking that you are deliberately keeping the contents of that cupboard from me. I shall break open the door."

Psmith got up.

"I'm afraid you mustn't do that, sir."

Mr. Downing stared, amazed.

"Are you aware whom you are talking to, Smith?" he inquired icily.

"Yes, sir. And I know it's not Mr. Outwood, to whom that cupboard happens to belong. If you wish to break it open, you must get his permission. He is the sole lessee and proprietor of that cupboard. I am only the acting manager."

Mr. Downing paused. He also reflected. Mr. Outwood in the general rule did not count much in the scheme of things, but possibly there were limits to the treating of him as if he did not exist. To enter his house without his permission and search it to a certain extent was all very well. But when it came to breaking up his furniture, perhaps...!

On the other hand, there was the maddening thought that if he left the study in search of Mr. Outwood, in order to obtain his sanction for the house-breaking work which he proposed to carry through, Smith would be alone in the room. And he knew that if Smith were left alone in the room, he would instantly remove the shoe to some other hiding place. He thoroughly disbelieved the story of the lost key. He was perfectly convinced that the missing shoe was in the cupboard.

He stood chewing these thoughts for a while, Psmith in the meantime standing in a graceful attitude in front of the cupboard, staring into vacancy.

Then he was seized with a happy idea. Why should he leave the room at all? If he sent Smith, then he himself could wait and make certain that the cupboard was not tampered with.

"Smith," he said, "go and find Mr. Outwood, and ask him to be good enough to come here for a moment."

22

MAINLY ABOUT SHOES

"Be quick, Smith," he said, as the latter stood looking at him without making any movement in the direction of the door.

"*Quick*, sir?" said Psmith meditatively, as if he had been asked a conundrum.

"Go and find Mr. Outwood at once."

Psmith still made no move.

"Do you intend to disobey me, Smith?" Mr. Downing's voice was steely.

"Yes, sir."

"What!"

"Yes, sir."

There was one of those you-could-have-heard-a-pin-drop silences. Psmith was staring reflectively at the ceiling. Mr. Downing was looking as if at any moment he might say, "Thwarted to me face, ha, ha! And by a very stripling!"

It was Psmith, however, who resumed the conversation. His manner was almost too respectful; which made it all the more a pity that what he said did not keep up the standard of docility.

"I take my stand," he said, "on a technical point. I say to myself, 'Mr. Downing is a man I admire as a human being and respect as a master. In —' "

"This impertinence is doing you no good, Smith."

Psmith waved a hand deprecatingly.

"If you will let me explain, sir. I was about to say that in any other place but Mr. Outwood's house, your word would be law. I would fly to do your bidding. If you pressed a button, I would do the rest. But in Mr. Outwood's house I cannot do anything except what pleases me or what is ordered by Mr. Outwood. I ought to have remembered that before. One cannot," he continued, as who should say, "Let us be reasonable," "one cannot, to take a parallel case, imagine the colonel commanding the garrison at a naval station going on board a battleship and ordering the crew to splice the jibboom spanker. It might be an admirable thing for the Empire that the jibboom spanker *should* be spliced at that particular juncture, but the crew would naturally decline to move in the matter until the order came from the commander of the ship. So in my case. If you will go to Mr. Outwood, explain to him how matters stand, and come back and say to me, 'Psmith, Mr. Outwood wishes you to ask him to be good enough to come to this study,' then I shall be only too glad to go and find him. You see my difficulty, sir?"

"Go and fetch Mr. Outwood, Smith. I shall not tell you again."

Psmith flicked a speck of dust from his coat sleeve.

"Very well, Smith."

"I can assure you, sir, at any rate, that if there is a shoe in that cupboard now, there will be a shoe there when you return."

Mr. Downing stalked out of the room.

"But," added Psmith pensively to himself, as the footsteps died away, "I did not promise that it would be the same shoe."

He took the key from his pocket, unlocked the cupboard, and took out the shoe. Then he selected from the basket a particularly battered specimen. Placing this in the cupboard, he relocked the door.

His next act was to take from the shelf a piece of string. Attaching one end of this to the shoe that he had taken from the cupboard, he went to the window. His first act was to fling the cupboard key out into the bushes. Then he turned to the shoe. On a level with the sill the water pipe, up which Mike had started to climb the night before, was fastened to the wall by an iron band. He tied the other end of the string to this, and let the shoe swing free. He noticed with approval, when it had stopped swinging, that it was hidden from above by the windowsill.

299

He returned to his place at the mantelpiece.

As an afterthought he took another shoe from the basket, and thrust it up the chimney. A shower of soot fell into the grate, blackening his hand.

The bathroom was a few yards down the corridor. He went there, and washed off the soot.

When he returned, Mr. Downing was in the study, and with him Mr. Outwood, the latter looking dazed, as if he were not quite equal to the intellectual pressure of the situation.

"Where have you been, Smith?" asked Mr. Downing sharply.

"I have been washing my hands, sir."

"H'm!" said Mr. Downing suspiciously.

"Yes, I saw Smith go into the bathroom," said Mr. Outwood. "Smith, I cannot quite understand what it is Mr. Downing wishes me to do."

"My dear Outwood," snapped the sleuth, "I thought I had made it perfectly clear. Where is the difficulty?"

"I cannot understand why you should suspect Smith of keeping his shoes in a cupboard, and," added Mr. Outwood with spirit, catching sight of a good-gracious-has-the-man-*no*-sense look on the other's face, "Why he should not do so if he wishes it."

"Exactly, sir," said Psmith, approvingly. "You have touched the spot."

"If I must explain again, my dear Outwood, will you kindly give me your attention for a moment. Last night a boy broke out of your house, and painted my dog Sampson red."

"He painted...!" said Mr. Outwood, round-eyed. "Why?"

"I don't know why. At any rate, he did. During the escapade one of his shoes was splashed with the paint. It is that shoe which I believe Smith to be concealing in this cupboard. Now, do you understand?"

Mr. Outwood looked amazedly at Psmith, and Psmith shook his head sorrowfully at Mr. Outwood. Psmith's expression said, as plainly as if he had spoken the words, "We must humor him."

"So with your permission, as Smith declares that he has lost the key, I propose to break open the door of this cupboard. Have you any objection?"

Mr. Outwood started.

"Objection? None at all, my dear fellow, none at all. Let me see, *what* is it you wish to do?"

"This," said Mr. Downing shortly.

There was a pair of dumbbells on the floor, belonging to Mike. He never used them, but they always managed to get themselves packed with the rest of his belongings on the last day of the holidays. Mr. Downing seized one of these, and delivered two rapid blows at the cupboard door. The wood splintered. A third blow smashed the flimsy lock. The cupboard, with any skeletons it might contain, was open for all to view.

Mr. Downing uttered a cry of triumph, and tore the shoe from its resting place.

"I told you," he said. "I told you."

"I wondered where that shoe had got to," said Psmith. "I've been looking for it for days."

Mr. Downing was examining his find. He looked up with an exclamation of surprise and wrath.

"This shoe has no paint on it," he said, glaring at Psmith. "This is not the shoe."

"It certainly appears, sir," said Psmith sympathetically, "to be free from paint. There's a sort of reddish glow just there, if you look at it sideways," he added helpfully.

"Did you place that shoe there, Smith?"

"I must have done. Then, when I lost the key —"

"Are you satisfied now, Downing?" interrupted Mr. Outwood with asperity, "or is there any more furniture you wish to break?"

The excitement of seeing his household goods smashed with a dumbbell had made the archaeological student quite a swashbuckler for the moment. A little more, and one could imagine him giving Mr. Downing a good, hard knock.

The sleuth-hound stood still for a moment, baffled. But his brain was working with the rapidity of a buzz saw. A chance remark of Mr. Outwood's set him fizzing off on the trail once more. Mr. Outwood had caught sight of the little pile of soot in the grate. He bent down to inspect it.

"Dear me," he said, "I must remember to have the chimneys swept. It should have been done before."

Mr. Downing's eye, rolling in a fine frenzy from heaven to earth, from earth to heaven, also focused itself on the pile of soot; and a thrill went through him. Soot in the fireplace! Smith washing his hands! ("You know my methods, my dear Watson. Apply them.")

Mr. Downing's mind at that moment contained one single thought; and that thought was, "What ho for the chimney!"

He dived forward with a rush, nearly knocking Mr. Outwood off his feet, and thrust an arm up into the unknown. An avalanche of soot fell upon his hand and wrist, but he ignored it, for at the same instant his fingers had closed upon what he was seeking.

"Ah," he said. "I thought as much. You were not quite clever enough, after all, Smith."

"No, sir," said Psmith patiently. "We all make mistakes."

"You would have done better, Smith, not to have given me all this trouble. You have done yourself no good by it."

"It's been great fun, though, sir," argued Psmith.

"Fun!" Mr. Downing laughed grimly. "You may have reason to change your opinion of what constitutes —"

His voice failed as his eye fell on the all-black toe of the shoe. He looked up, and caught Psmith's benevolent gaze. He straightened himself and brushed a bead of perspiration from his face with the back of his hand. Unfortunately, he used the sooty hand, and the result was that he looked like a chimney sweep at work.

"Did-you-put-that-shoe-there, Smith?" he asked slowly.

"Yes, sir."

"Then what did you *MEAN* by putting it there?" roared Mr. Downing.

"Animal spirits, sir," said Psmith.

"WHAT?"

"Animal spirits, sir."

What Mr. Downing would have replied to this one cannot tell, though one can guess roughly. For, just as he was opening his mouth, Mr. Outwood, catching sight of his soot-covered countenance, intervened.

"My dear Downing," he said, "your face. It is positively covered with soot, positively. You must come and wash it. You are quite black. Really you present a most curious appearance, most. Let me show you the way to my room."

In all times of storm and tribulation there comes a breaking point, a point where the spirit definitely refuses to battle any longer against the slings and arrows of outrageous fortune. Mr. Downing could not bear up against this crowning blow. He went down beneath it. In the language of the ring, he took the count. It was the knockout.

"Soot!" he murmured weakly. "Soot!"

"Your face is covered, my dear fellow, quite covered."

"It certainly has a faintly sooty aspect, sir," said Psmith.

His voice roused the sufferer to one last flicker of spirit.

"You will hear more of this, Smith," he said. "I say you will hear more of it."

Then he allowed Mr. Outwood to lead him out to a place where there were towels, soap, and sponges.

* * * * *

When they had gone, Psmith went to the window, and hauled in the string. He felt the calm afterglow which comes to the general after a successfully conducted battle. It had been trying, of course, for a man of refinement, and it had cut into his afternoon, but on the whole it had been worth it.

The problem now was what to do with the painted shoe. It would take a lot of cleaning, he saw, even if he could get hold of the necessary implements for cleaning it. And he rather doubted if he would be able to do so. Edmund, the boot-boy, worked in some mysterious cell far from the madding crowd, at the back of the house. In the boot cupboard downstairs there would probably be nothing likely to be of any use.

His fears were realized. The boot cupboard was empty. It seemed to him that, for the time being, the best thing he could do would be to place the shoe in safe hiding, until he would have thought out a scheme.

Having restored the basket to its proper place, accordingly, he went up to the study again, and placed the red-toed shoe in the chimney, at about the same height where Mr. Downing had found the other. Nobody would think of looking there a second time, and it was improbable that Mr. Outwood really would have the chimneys swept, as he had said. The odds were that he had forgotten about it already.

Psmith went to the bathroom to wash his hands again, with the feeling that he had done a good day's work.

23

ON THE TRAIL AGAIN

The most massive minds are apt to forget things at times. The most adroit plotters make their little mistakes. Psmith was no exception to the rule. He made the mistake of not telling Mike of the afternoon's happenings.

It was not altogether forgetfulness. Psmith was one of those people who like to carry through their operations entirely by themselves. Where there is only one in a secret, the secret is more liable to remain unrevealed. There was nothing, he thought, to be gained from telling Mike. He forgot what the consequences might be if he did not.

So Psmith kept his own counsel, with the result that Mike went over to school on the Monday morning in gym shoes.

Edmund, summoned from the hinterland of the house to give his opinion why only one of Mike's shoes was to be found, had no views on the subject. He seemed to look on it as one of these things which no fellow can understand.

"'Ere's one of 'em, Mr. Jackson," he said, as if he hoped that Mike might be satisfied with a compromise.

"One? What's the good of that, Edmund, you chump? I can't go over to school in one shoe."

Edmund turned this over in his mind, and then said, "No, sir," as much as to say, "I may have lost a shoe, but, thank goodness, I can still understand sound reasoning."

"Well, what am I to do? Where *is* the other shoe?"

"Don't know, Mr. Jackson," replied Edmund to both questions.

"Well, I mean... Oh, dash it, there's the bell." And Mike sprinted off in the gym shoes he stood in.

It is only a deviation from those ordinary rules of school life, which one observes naturally and without thinking, that enables one to realize how strong public-school prejudices really are. At a school, for instance, where the regulations say that coats only of black or dark blue are to be worn, a boy who appears one day in even the most respectable and unostentatious brown finds himself looked on with a mixture of awe and repulsion, which would be excessive if he had sandbagged the headmaster. So in the case of shoes. School rules decree that a boy shall go to his form room in shoes. There is no real reason why, if the day is fine, he should not wear gym shoes, should he prefer them. But, if he does, the thing creates a perfect sensation. Boys say, "Great Scott, what *have* you got on?" Masters say, "Jones, *what* are you wearing on your feet?" In the few minutes which elapse between the assembling of the form for call-over and the arrival of the form master, some wag is sure either to stamp on the gym shoes, accompanying the act with some satirical remark, or else to pull one of them off, and inaugurate an impromptu game of football with it. There was once a boy who went to school one morning in elastic-sided boots.

Mike had always been coldly distant in his relations to the rest of his form, looking on them, with a few exceptions, as worms; and the form, since his innings against Downing's on the Friday, had regarded Mike with respect. So that he escaped the ragging he would have had to undergo at Wrykyn in similar circumstance. It was only Mr. Downing who gave trouble.

There is a sort of instinct which enables some masters to tell when a boy in their form is wearing gym shoes instead of the more formal kind, just as people who dislike cats always know when one is in a room with them. They cannot see it but they feel it in their bones.

Mr. Downing was perhaps the most bigoted anti-gym-shoeist in the whole list of English schoolmasters. He waged war remorselessly against gym shoes. Satire, abuse, lines, detention—every weapon was employed by him in dealing with their wearers. It had been the late Dunster's practice always to go over to school in gym shoes when, as he usually did, he felt shaky in the morning's lesson. Mr. Downing always detected him in the first five minutes, and that meant a lecture of anything from ten minutes to a quarter of an hour on Untidy Habits and Boys Who

Looked Like Loafers-which broke the back of the morning's work nicely. On one occasion, when a particularly tricky bit of Livy was on the bill of fare, Dunster had entered the form room in heelless Turkish bath slippers, of a vivid crimson; and the subsequent proceedings, including his journey over to the house to change the heelless atrocities, had seen him through very nearly to the quarter-to-eleven interval.

Mike, accordingly, had not been in his place for three minutes when Mr. Downing, stiffening like a pointer, called his name.

"Yes, sir?" said Mike.

"*What* are you wearing on your feet, Jackson?"

"Gym shoes, sir."

"You are wearing gym shoes? Are you not aware that gym shoes are not the proper things to come to school in? Why are you wearing gym shoes?"

The form, leaning back against the next row of desks, settled itself comfortably for the address from the throne.

"I have lost one of my shoes, sir."

A kind of gulp escaped from Mr. Downing's lips. He stared at Mike for a moment in silence. Then, turning to Stone, he told him to start translating.

Stone, who had been expecting at least ten minutes' respite, was taken unawares. When he found the place in his book and began to construe, he floundered hopelessly. But, to his growing surprise and satisfaction, the form master appeared to notice nothing wrong. He said "Yes, yes," mechanically, and finally, "That will do," whereupon Stone resumed his seat with the feeling that the age of miracles had returned.

Mr. Downing's mind was in a whirl. His case was complete. Mike's appearance in gym shoes, with the explanation that he had lost a shoe, completed the chain. As Columbus must have felt when his ship ran into harbor, and the first American interviewer, jumping on board, said, "Wal, sir, and what are your impressions of our glorious country?" so did Mr. Downing feel at that moment.

When the bell rang at a quarter to eleven, he gathered up his gown and sped to the headmaster.

24

THE ADAIR METHOD

It was during the interval that day that Stone and Robinson, discussing the subject of cricket over a bun and ginger beer at the school shop, came to a momentous decision, to wit, that they were fed up with the Adair administration and meant to strike. The immediate cause of revolt was early-morning fielding practice, that searching test of cricket keenness. Mike himself, to whom cricket was the great and serious interest in life, had shirked early-morning fielding practice in his first term at Wrykyn. And Stone and Robinson had but a lukewarm attachment to the game, compared with Mike's.

As a rule, Adair had contented himself with practice in the afternoon after school, which nobody objects to; and no strain, consequently, had been put upon Stone's and Robinson's allegiance. In view of the M.C.C. match on the Wednesday, however, he had now added to this an extra dose to be taken before breakfast. Stone and Robinson had left their comfortable beds that day at six o'clock, yawning and heavy-eyed, and had caught catches and fielded drives which, in the cool morning air, had stung like adders and bitten like serpents. Until the sun has really got to work, it is no joke taking a high catch. Stone's dislike of the experiment was only equaled by Robinson's. They were neither of them of the type which likes to undergo hardships for the common good. They played well enough when on the field, but neither cared greatly whether the school had a good season or not. They played the games entirely for their own sakes.

The result was that they went back to the house for breakfast with a never-again feeling, and at the earliest possible moment met to debate as to what was to be done about it. At all costs another experience like today's must be avoided.

"It's all rot," said Stone. "What on earth's the good of sweating about before breakfast? It only makes you tired."

"I shouldn't wonder," said Robinson, "if it wasn't bad for the heart.
Rushing about on an empty stomach, I mean, and all that sort of thing."

"Personally," said Stone, gnawing his bun, "I don't intend to stick it."

"Nor do I."

"I mean, it's such absolute rot. If we aren't good enough to play for the team without having to get up overnight to catch catches, he'd better find somebody else."

"Yes."

At this moment Adair came into the shop.

"Fielding practice again tomorrow," he said briskly, "at six."

"Before breakfast?" said Robinson.

"Rather. You two must buck up, you know. You were rotten today." And he passed on, leaving the two malcontents speechless.

Stone was the first to recover.

"I'm hanged if I turn out tomorrow," he said, as they left the shop. "He can do what he likes about it. Besides, what can he do, after all? Only kick us out of the team. And I don't mind that."

"Nor do I."

"I don't think he will kick us out, either. He can't play the M.C.C. with a scratch team. If he does, we'll go and play for that village Jackson plays for. We'll get Jackson to shove us into the team."

"All right," said Robinson. "Let's."

Their position was a strong one. A cricket captain may seem to be an autocrat of tremendous power, but in reality he has only one weapon, the keenness of those under him. With the majority, of course, the fear of being excluded or ejected from a team is a spur that drives. The majority, consequently, are easily handled. But when a cricket captain runs up against a boy who does not much care whether he plays for the team or not, then he finds himself in a difficult position, and, unless he is a man of action, practically helpless.

Stone and Robinson felt secure. Taking it all around, they felt that they would just as soon play for Lower Borlock as for the school. The bowling of the opposition would be weaker in the former case, and the chance of making runs greater. To a certain type of cricketer runs are runs, wherever and however made.

The result of all this was that Adair, turning out with the team next morning for fielding practice, found himself two short. Barnes was among those present, but of the other two representatives of Outwood's house there were no signs.

Barnes, questioned on the subject, had no information to give, beyond the fact that he had not seen them about anywhere. Which was not a great help. Adair proceeded with the fielding practice without further delay.

At breakfast that morning he was silent and apparently rapt in thought. Mr. Downing, who sat at the top of the table with Adair on his right, was accustomed at the morning meal to blend nourishment of the body with that of the mind. As a rule he had ten minutes with the daily paper before the bell rang, and it was his practice to hand on the results of his reading to Adair and the other house prefects, who, not having seen the paper, usually formed an interested and appreciative audience. Today, however, though the house prefects expressed varying degrees of excitement at the news that Sheppard had made a century against Gloucestershire, and that a butter famine was expected in the United States, these world-shaking news items seemed to leave Adair cold. He champed his bread and marmalade with an abstracted air.

He was wondering what to do in the matter of Stone and Robinson.

Many captains might have passed the thing over. To take it for granted that the missing pair had overslept themselves would have been a safe and convenient way out of the difficulty. But Adair was not the sort of person who seeks for safe and convenient ways out of difficulties. He never shirked anything, physical or moral.

He resolved to interview the absentees.

It was not until after school that an opportunity offered itself. He went across to Outwood's and found the two nonstarters in the senior day room, engaged in the intellectual pursuit of kicking the wall and marking the height of each kick with chalk. Adair's entrance coincided with a record effort by Stone, which caused the kicker to overbalance and stagger backward against the captain.

"Sorry," said Stone. "Hello, Adair!"

"Don't mention it. Why weren't you two at fielding practice this morning?"

Robinson, who left the lead to Stone in all matters, said nothing. Stone spoke.

"We didn't turn up," he said.

"I know you didn't. Why not?"

Stone had rehearsed this scene in his mind, and he spoke with the coolness which comes from rehearsal.

"We decided not to."

"Oh?"

"Yes. We came to the conclusion that we hadn't any use for early-morning fielding."

Adair's manner became ominously calm.

"You were rather fed up, I suppose?"

"That's just the word."

"Sorry it bored you."

"It didn't. We didn't give it the chance to."

Robinson laughed appreciatively.

"What's the joke, Robinson?" asked Adair.

"There's no joke," said Robinson, with some haste. "I was only thinking of something."

"I'll give you something else to think about soon."

Stone intervened.

"It's no good making a row about it, Adair. You must see that you can't do anything. Of course, you can kick us out of the team, if you like, but we don't care if you do. Jackson will get us a game any Wednesday or Saturday for the village he plays for. So we're all right. And the school team aren't such a lot of flyers that you can afford to go chucking people out of it whenever you want to. See what I mean?"

"You and Jackson seem to have fixed it all up between you."

"What are you going to do? Kick us out?"

"No."

"Good. I thought you'd see it was no good making a beastly row. We'll play for the school all right. There's no earthly need for us to turn out for fielding practice before breakfast."

"You don't think there is? You may be right. All the same, you're going to tomorrow morning."

"What!"

"Six sharp. Don't be late."

"Don't be an ass, Adair. We've told you we aren't going to."

"That's only your opinion. I think you are. I'll give you till five past six, as you seem to like lying in bed."

"You can turn out if you feel like it. You won't find me there."

"That'll be a disappointment. Nor Robinson?"

"No," said the junior partner in the firm; but he said it without any deep conviction. The atmosphere was growing a great deal too tense for his comfort.

"You've quite made up your minds?"

"Yes," said Stone.

"Right," said Adair quietly, and knocked him down.

He was up again in a moment. Adair had pushed the table back, and was standing in the middle of the open space.

"You cad," said Stone. "I wasn't ready."

"Well, you are now. Shall we go on?"

Stone dashed in without a word, and for a few moments the two might have seemed evenly matched to a not too intelligent spectator. But science tells, even in a confined space. Adair was smaller and lighter than Stone, but he was cooler and quicker, and he knew more about the game. His blow was always home a fraction of a second sooner than his opponent's. At the end of a minute Stone was on the floor again.

He got up slowly and stood leaning with one hand on the table.

"Suppose we say ten past six!" said Adair. "I'm not particular to a minute or two."

Stone made no reply.

"Will ten past six suit you for fielding practice tomorrow?" said Adair.

"All right," said Stone.

"Thanks. How about you, Robinson?"

Robinson had been a petrified spectator of the Captain-Kettle-like maneuvers of the cricket captain, and it did not take him long to make up his mind. He was not altogether a coward. In different circumstances he might have put up a respectable show. But it takes a more than ordinarily courageous person to embark on a fight which he knows must end in his destruction. Robinson knew that he was nothing like a match even for Stone, and Adair had disposed of Stone in a little over one minute. It seemed to Robinson that neither pleasure nor profit was likely to come from an encounter with Adair.

"All right," he said hastily, "I'll turn up."

"Good," said Adair. "I wonder if either of you chaps could tell me which is Jackson's study."

Stone was dabbing at his mouth with a handkerchief, a task which precluded anything in the shape of conversation; so Robinson replied that Mike's study was the first you came to on the right of the corridor at the top of the stairs.

"Thanks," said Adair. "You don't happen to know if he's in, I suppose?"

"He went up with Smith a quarter of an hour ago. I don't know if he's still there."

"I'll go and see," said Adair. "I should like a word with him if he isn't busy."

25

ADAIR HAS A WORD WITH MIKE

Mike, all unconscious of the stirring proceedings which had been going on below stairs, was peacefully reading a letter he had received that morning from Strachan at Wrykyn, in which the successor to the cricket captaincy which should have been Mike's had a good deal to say in a lugubrious strain. In Mike's absence things had been going badly with Wrykyn. A broken arm, contracted in the course of some rash experiments with a day boy's motor bicycle, had deprived the team of the services of Dunstable, the only man who had shown any signs of being able to bowl a side out. Since this calamity, wrote Strachan, everything had gone wrong. The M.C.C., led by Mike's brother Reggie, the least of the three first-class cricketing Jacksons, had smashed them by a hundred and fifty runs. Geddington had wiped them off the face of the earth. The Incogs, with a team recruited exclusively from the rabbit hutch-not a well-known man on the side except Stacey, a veteran who had been playing for the club for nearly half a century-had got home by two wickets. In fact, it was Strachan's opinion that the Wrykyn team that summer was about the most hopeless gang of deadbeats that had ever made exhibition of itself on the school grounds. The Ripton match, fortunately, was off, owing to an outbreak of mumps at that shrine of learning and athletics-the second outbreak of the malady in two terms. Which, said Strachan, was hard lines on Ripton, but a bit of jolly good luck for Wrykyn, as it had saved them from what would probably have been a record hammering, Ripton having eight of their last year's team left, including Dixon, the fast bowler, against whom Mike alone of the Wrykyn team had been able to make runs in the previous season. Altogether, Wrykyn had struck a bad patch.

Mike mourned over his suffering school. If only he could have been there to help. It might have made all the difference. In school cricket one good batsman, to go in first and knock the bowlers off their length, may take a weak team triumphantly through a season. In school cricket the importance of a good start for the first wicket is incalculable.

As he put Strachan's letter away in his pocket, all his old bitterness against Sedleigh, which had been ebbing during the past few days, returned with a rush. He was conscious once more of that feeling of personal injury which had made him hate his new school on the first day of term.

And it was at this point, when his resentment was at its height, that Adair, the concrete representative of everything Sedleighan, entered the room.

There are moments in life's placid course when there has got to be the biggest kind of row. This was one of them.

Psmith, who was leaning against the mantelpiece, reading the serial story in a daily paper which he had abstracted from the senior day room, made the intruder free of the study with a dignified wave of the hand, and went on reading. Mike remained in the deck chair in which he was sitting, and contented himself with glaring at the newcomer.

Psmith was the first to speak.

"If you ask my candid opinion," he said, looking up from his paper, "I should say that young Lord Antony Trefusis was in the soup already. I seem to see the consommé splashing about his ankles. He's had a note telling him to be under the oak tree in the Park at midnight. He's just off there at the end of this installment. I bet Long Jack, the poacher, is waiting there with a sandbag. Care to see the paper, Comrade Adair? Or don't you take any interest in contemporary literature?"

"Thanks," said Adair. "I just wanted to speak to Jackson for a minute."

"Fate," said Psmith, "has led your footsteps to the right place. This is Comrade Jackson, the Pride of the School, sitting before you."

"What do you want?" said Mike.

309

He suspected that Adair had come to ask him once again to play for the school. The fact that the M.C.C. match was on the following day made this a probable solution of the reason for his visit. He could think of no other errand that was likely to have set the head of Downing's paying afternoon calls.

"I'll tell you in a minute. It won't take long."

"That," said Psmith approvingly, "is right. Speed is the keynote of the present age. Promptitude. Dispatch. This is no time for loitering. We must be strenuous. We must hustle. We must Do It Now. We —"

"Buck up," said Mike.

"Certainly," said Adair. "I've just been talking to Stone and Robinson."

"An excellent way of passing an idle half hour," said Psmith.

"We weren't exactly idle," said Adair grimly. "It didn't last long, but it was pretty lively while it did. Stone chucked it after the first round."

Mike got up out of his chair. He could not quite follow what all this was about, but there was no mistaking the truculence of Adair's manner. For some reason, which might possibly be made clear later, Adair was looking for trouble, and Mike in his present mood felt that it would be a privilege to see that he got it.

Psmith was regarding Adair through his eyeglass with pain and surprise.

"Surely," he said, "you do not mean us to understand that you have been *brawling* with Comrade Stone! This is bad hearing. I thought that you and he were like brothers. Such a bad example for Comrade Robinson, too. Leave us, Adair. We would brood. 'Oh, go thee, knave, I'll none of thee.' Shakespeare."

Psmith turned away, and resting his elbows on the mantelpiece, gazed at himself mournfully in the looking glass.

"I'm not the man I was," he sighed, after a prolonged inspection. "There are lines on my face, dark circles beneath my eyes. The fierce rush of life at Sedleigh is wasting me away."

"Stone and I had a discussion about early-morning fielding practice," said Adair, turning to Mike.

Mike said nothing.

"I thought his fielding wanted working up a bit, so I told him to turn out at six tomorrow morning. He said he wouldn't, so we argued it out. He's going to all right. So is Robinson."

Mike remained silent.

"So are you," said Adair.

"I get thinner and thinner," said Psmith from the mantelpiece.

Mike looked at Adair, and Adair looked at Mike, after the manner of two dogs before they fly at one another. There was an electric silence in the study. Psmith peered with increased earnestness into the glass.

"Oh?" said Mike at last. "What makes you think that?"

"I don't think. I know."

"Any special reason for my turning out?"

"Yes."

"What's that?"

"You're going to play for the school against the M.C.C. tomorrow, and I want you to get some practice."

"I wonder how you got that idea!"

"Curious I should have done, isn't it?"

"Very. You aren't building on it much, are you?" said Mike politely.

"I am, rather," replied Adair, with equal courtesy.

"I'm afraid you'll be disappointed."

"I don't think so."

"My eyes," said Psmith regretfully, "are a bit close together. However," he added philosophically, "it's too late to alter that now."

310

Mike drew a step closer to Adair.

"What makes you think I shall play against the M.C.C.?" he asked curiously.

"I'm going to make you."

Mike took another step forward. Adair moved to meet him.

"Would you care to try now?" said Mike.

For just one second the two drew themselves together preparatory to beginning the serious business of the interview, and in that second Psmith, turning from the glass, stepped between them.

"Get out of the light, Smith," said Mike.

Psmith waved him back with a deprecating gesture.

"My dear young friends," he said placidly, "if you *will* let your angry passions rise, against the direct advice of Doctor Watts, I suppose you must. But when you propose to claw each other in my study, in the midst of a hundred fragile and priceless ornaments, I lodge a protest. If you really feel that you want to scrap, for goodness' sake do it where there's some room. I don't want all the study furniture smashed. I know a bank whereon the wild thyme grows, only a few yards down the road, where you can scrap all night if you want to. How would it be to move on there? Any objections? None. Then shift ho! And let's get it over."

26

CLEARING THE AIR

Psmith was one of those people who lend a dignity to everything they touch. Under his auspices the most unpromising ventures became somehow enveloped in an atmosphere of measured stateliness. On the present occasion, what would have been, without his guiding hand, a mere unscientific scramble, took on something of the impressive formality of the National Sporting Club.

"The rounds," he said, producing a watch, as they passed through a gate into a field a couple of hundred yards from the house gate, "will be of three minutes' duration, with a minute rest in between. A man who is down will have ten seconds in which to rise. Are you ready, Comrades Adair and Jackson? Very well, then. Time."

After which, it was a pity that the actual fight did not quite live up to its referee's introduction. Dramatically, there should have been cautious sparring for openings and a number of tensely contested rounds, as if it had been the final of a boxing competition. But school fights, when they do occur-which is only once in a decade nowadays, unless you count junior school scuffles-are the outcome of weeks of suppressed bad blood, and are consequently brief and furious. In a boxing competition, however much one may want to win, one does not dislike one's opponent. Up to the moment when "time" was called, one was probably warmly attached to him, and at the end of the last round one expects to resume that attitude of mind. In a fight each party, as a rule, hates the other.

So it happened that there was nothing formal or cautious about the present battle. All Adair wanted was to get at Mike, and all Mike wanted was to get at Adair. Directly Psmith called "time," they rushed together as if they meant to end the thing in half a minute.

It was this that saved Mike. In an ordinary contest with the gloves, with his opponent cool and boxing in his true form, he could not have lasted three rounds against Adair. The latter was a clever boxer, while Mike had never had a lesson in his life. If Adair had kept away and used his head, nothing could have prevented his winning.

As it was, however, he threw away his advantages, much as Tom Brown did at the beginning of his fight with Slogger Williams, and the result was the same as on that historic occasion. Mike had the greater strength, and, thirty seconds from the start, knocked his man clean off his feet with an unscientific but powerful righthander.

This finished Adair's chances. He rose full of fight, but with all the science knocked out of him. He went in at Mike with both hands. The Irish blood in him, which for the ordinary events of life made him merely energetic and dashing, now rendered him reckless. He abandoned all attempt at guarding. It was the Frontal Attack in its most futile form, and as unsuccessful as a frontal attack is apt to be. There was a swift exchange of blows, in the course of which Mike's left elbow, coming into contact with his opponent's right fist, got a shock which kept it tingling for the rest of the day; and then Adair went down in a heap.

He got up slowly and with difficulty. For a moment he stood blinking vaguely. Then he lurched forward at Mike.

In the excitement of a fight-which is, after all, about the most exciting thing that ever happens to one in the course of one's life-it is difficult for the fighters to see what the spectators see. Where the spectators see an assault on an already beaten man, the fighter himself only sees a legitimate piece of self-defense against an opponent whose chances are equal to his own. Psmith saw, as anybody looking on would have seen, that Adair was done. Mike's blow had taken him within a fraction of an inch of the point of the jaw, and he was all but knocked out. Mike could not see this. All he understood was that his man was on his feet again and coming at him, so he hit out with all his strength; and this time Adair went down and stayed down.

"Brief," said Psmith, coming forward, "but exciting. We may take that, I think, to be the conclusion of the entertainment. I will now have a dash at picking up the slain. I shouldn't stop, if I were you. He'll be sitting up and taking notice soon, and if he sees you he may want to go on with the combat, which would do him no earthly good. If it's going to be continued in our next, there had better be a bit of an interval for alterations and repairs first."

"Is he hurt much, do you think?" asked Mike. He had seen knockouts before in the ring, but this was the first time he had ever effected one on his own account, and Adair looked unpleasantly corpselike.

"*He's* all right," said Psmith. "In a minute or two he'll be skipping about like a little lambkin. I'll look after him. You go away and pick flowers."

Mike put on his coat and walked back to the house. He was conscious of a perplexing whirl of new and strange emotions, chief among which was a curious feeling that he rather liked Adair. He found himself thinking that Adair was a good chap, that there was something to be said for his point of view, and that it was a pity he had knocked him about so much. At the same time, he felt an undeniable thrill of pride at having beaten him. The feat presented that interesting person, Mike Jackson, to him in a fresh and pleasing light, as one who had had a tough job to face and had carried it through. Jackson the cricketer he knew, but Jackson the deliverer of knockout blows was strange to him, and he found this new acquaintance a man to be respected.

The fight, in fact, had the result which most fights have, if they are fought fairly and until one side has had enough. It revolutionized Mike's view of things. It shook him up, and drained the bad blood out of him. Where before he had seemed to himself to be acting with massive dignity, he now saw that he had simply been sulking like some wretched kid. There had appeared to him something rather fine in his policy of refusing to identify himself in any way with Sedleigh, a touch of the stone-walls-do-not-a-prison-make sort of thing. He now saw that his attitude was to be summed up in the words, "Sha'n't play."

It came upon Mike with painful clearness that he had been making an ass of himself.

He had come to this conclusion, after much earnest thought, when Psmith entered the study.

"How's Adair?" asked Mike.

"Sitting up and taking nourishment once more. We have been chatting. He's not a bad cove."

"He's all right," said Mike.

There was a pause. Psmith straightened his tie.

"Look here," he said, "I seldom interfere in terrestrial strife, but it seems to me that there's an opening here for a capable peacemaker, not afraid of work, and willing to give his services in exchange for a comfortable home. Comrade Adair's rather a stoutish fellow in his way. I'm not much on the 'Play up for the old school, Jones,' game, but everyone to his taste. I shouldn't have thought anybody would get overwhelmingly attached to this abode of wrath, but Comrade Adair seems to have done it. He's all for giving Sedleigh a much-needed boost-up. It's not a bad idea in its way. I don't see why one shouldn't humor him. Apparently he's been sweating since early childhood to buck the school up. And as he's leaving at the end of the term, it mightn't be a scaly scheme to give him a bit of a send-off, if possible, by making the cricket season a bit of a banger. As a start, why not drop him a line to say that you'll play against the M.C.C. tomorrow?"

Mike did not reply at once. He was feeling better disposed toward Adair and Sedleigh then he had felt, but he was not sure that he was quite prepared to go as far as a complete climb-down.

"It wouldn't be a bad idea," continued Psmith. "There's nothing like giving in to a man a bit every now and then. It broadens the soul and improves the action of the skin. What seems to have fed up Comrade Adair, to a certain extent, is that Stone apparently led him to understand that you had offered to give him and Robinson places in your village team. You didn't, of course?"

"Of course not," said Mike indignantly.

"I told him he didn't know the old *noblesse oblige* spirit of the Jacksons. I said that you would scorn to tarnish the Jackson escutcheon by not playing the game. My eloquence convinced him. However, to return to the point under discussion, why not?"

"I don't...What I mean to say..." began Mike.

"If your trouble is," said Psmith, "that you fear that you may be in unworthy company —"

"Don't be an ass."

"—Dismiss it. *I* am playing."

Mike stared.

"You're *what? You?*"

"I," said Psmith, breathing on a coat button, and polishing it with his handkerchief.

"Can you play cricket?"

"You have discovered," said Psmith, "my secret sorrow."

"You're rotting."

"You wrong me, Comrade Jackson."

"Then why haven't you played?"

"Why haven't you?"

"Why didn't you come and play for Lower Borlock, I mean?"

"The last time I played in a village cricket match I was caught at point by a man in braces. It would have been madness to risk another such shock to my system. My nerves are so exquisitely balanced that a thing of that sort takes years off my life."

"No, but look here, Smith, bar rotting. Are you really any good at cricket?"

"Competent judges at Eton gave me to understand so. I was told that this year I should be a certainty for Lord's. But when the cricket season came, where was I? Gone. Gone like some beautiful flower that withers in the night."

"But you told me you didn't like cricket. You said you only liked watching it."

"Quite right. I do. But at schools where cricket is compulsory you have to overcome your private prejudices. And in time the thing becomes a habit. Imagine my feelings when I found that I was degenerating, little by little, into a slow left-hand bowler with a swerve. I fought against it, but it was useless, and after a while I gave up the struggle, and drifted with the stream. Last year in a house match" —Psmith's voice took on a deeper tone of melancholy —"I took seven for thirteen in the second innings on a hard wicket. I did think, when I came here, that I had found a haven of rest, but it was not to be. I turn out tomorrow. What Comrade Outwood will say, when he finds that his keenest archaeological disciple has deserted, I hate to think. However..."

Mike felt as if a young and powerful earthquake had passed. The whole face of his world had undergone a quick change. Here was he, the recalcitrant, wavering on the point of playing for the school, and here was Psmith, the last person whom he would have expected to be a player, stating calmly that he had been in the running for a place in the Eton eleven.

Then in a flash Mike understood. He was not by nature intuitive, but he read Psmith's mind now. Since the term began, he and Psmith had been acting on precisely similar motives. Just as he had been disappointed of the captaincy of cricket at Wrykyn, so had Psmith been disappointed of his place in the Eton team at Lord's. And they had both worked it off, each in his own way-Mike sullenly, Psmith whimsically, according to their respective natures-on Sedleigh.

If Psmith, therefore, did not consider it too much of a climb-down to renounce his resolution not to play for Sedleigh, there was nothing to stop Mike doing so, as-at the bottom of his heart-he wanted to do.

"By Jove," he said, "if you're playing, I'll play. I'll write a note to Adair now. But, I say" —he stopped —"I'm hanged if I'm going to turn out and field before breakfast tomorrow."

"That's all right. You won't have to. Adair won't be there himself. He's not playing against the M.C.C. He's sprained his wrist."

27

IN WHICH PEACE IS DECLARED

"Sprained his wrist?" said Mike. "How did he do that?"

"During the brawl. Apparently one of his efforts got home on your elbow instead of your expressive countenance, and whether it was that your elbow was particularly tough or his wrist particularly fragile, I don't know. Anyhow, it went. It's nothing bad, but it'll keep him out of the game tomorrow."

"I say, what beastly rough luck! I'd no idea. I'll go around."

"Not a bad scheme. Close the door gently after you, and if you see anybody downstairs who looks as if he were likely to be going over to the shop, ask him to get me a small pot of some rare old jam and tell the man to chalk it up to me. The jam Comrade Outwood supplies to us at tea is all right as a practical joke or as a food for those anxious to commit suicide, but useless to anybody who values life."

On arriving at Mr. Downing's and going to Adair's study, Mike found that his late antagonist was out. He left a note informing him of his willingness to play in the morrow's match. The lock-up bell rang as he went out of the house.

A spot of rain fell on his hand. A moment later there was a continuous patter, as the storm, which had been gathering all day, broke in earnest. Mike turned up his coat collar, and ran back to Outwood's. "At this rate," he said to himself, "there won't be a match at all tomorrow."

* * * * *

When the weather decides, after behaving well for some weeks, to show what it can do in another direction, it does the thing thoroughly. When Mike woke the next morning the world was gray and dripping. Leaden-colored clouds drifted over the sky, till there was not a trace of blue to be seen, and then the rain began again, in the gentle, determined way rain has when it means to make a day of it.

It was one of those bad days when one sits in the pavilion, damp and depressed, while figures in mackintoshes, with discolored buckskin boots, crawl miserably about the field in couples.

Mike, shuffling across to school in a Burberry, met Adair at Downing's gate.

These moments are always difficult. Mike stopped—he could hardly walk on as if nothing had happened—and looked down at his feet.

"Coming across?" he said awkwardly.

"Right ho!" said Adair.

They walked on in silence.

"It's only about ten to, isn't it?" said Mike.

Adair fished out his watch, and examined it with an elaborate care born of nervousness.

"About nine to."

"Good. We've got plenty of time."

"Yes."

"I hate having to hurry over to school."

"So do I."

"I often do cut it rather fine, though."

"Yes. So do I."

"Beastly nuisance when one does."

"Beastly."

"It's only about a couple of minutes from the houses to the school, I should think, shouldn't you?"

"Not much more. Might be three."

"Yes. Three if one didn't hurry."
Another silence.
"Beastly day," said Adair.
"Rotten."
Silence again.
"I say," said Mike, scowling at his toes, "awfully sorry about your wrist."
"Oh, that's all right. It was my fault."
"Does it hurt?"
"Oh, no, rather not, thanks."
"I'd no idea you'd crocked yourself."
"Oh, no, that's all right. It was only right at the end. You'd have smashed me anyhow."
"Oh, rot."
"I bet you anything you like you would."
"I bet you I shouldn't.... Jolly hard luck, just before the match."
"Oh, no.... I say, thanks awfully for saying you'd play."
"Oh, rot.... Do you think we shall get a game?"
Adair inspected the sky carefully.
"I don't know. It looks pretty bad, doesn't it?"
"Rotten. I say, how long will your wrist keep you out of cricket?"
"Be all right in a week. Less, probably."
"Good."
"Now that you and Smith are going to play, we ought to have a jolly good season."
"Rummy, Smith turning out to be a cricketer."
"Yes. I should think he'd be a hot bowler, with his height."
"He must be jolly good if he was only just out of the Eton team last year."
"Yes."
"What's the time?" asked Mike.
Adair produced his watch once more.
"Five to."
"We've heaps of time."
"Yes, heaps."
"Let's stroll on a bit down the road, shall we?"
"Right ho!"
Mike cleared his throat.
"I say."
"Hello?"
"I've been talking to Smith. He was telling me that you thought I'd promised to give Stone and Robinson places in the —"
"Oh, no, that's all right. It was only for a bit. Smith told me you couldn't have done, and I saw that I was an ass to think you could have. It was Stone seeming so dead certain that he could play for Lower Borlock if I chucked him from the school team that gave me the idea."

"He never even asked me to get him a place."
"No, I know."
"Of course, I wouldn't have done it, even if he had."
"Of course not."
"I didn't want to play myself, but I wasn't going to do a rotten trick like getting other fellows away from the team."
"No, I know."
"It was rotten enough, really, not playing myself."

"Oh, no. Beastly rough luck having to leave Wrykyn just when you were going to be captain, and come to a small school like this."

The excitement of the past few days must have had a stimulating effect on Mike's mind-shaken it up, as it were, for now, for the second time in two days, he displayed quite a creditable amount of intuition. He might have been misled by Adair's apparently deprecatory attitude toward Sedleigh, and blundered into a denunciation of the place. Adair had said, "a small school like this" in the sort of voice which might have led his hearer to think that he was expected to say, "Yes, rotten little hole, isn't it?" or words to that effect. Mike, fortunately, perceived that the words were used purely from politeness, on the Chinese principle. When a Chinese man wishes to pay a compliment, he does so by belittling himself and his belongings.

He eluded the pitfall.

"What rot!" he said. "Sedleigh's one of the most sporting schools I've ever come across. Everybody's as keen as blazes. So they ought to be, after the way you've sweated."

Adair shuffled awkwardly.

"I've always been fairly keen on the place," he said. "But I don't suppose I've done anything much."

"You've loosened one of my front teeth," said Mike, with a grin, "if that's any comfort to you."

"I couldn't eat anything except porridge this morning. My jaw still aches."

For the first time during the conversation their eyes met, and the humorous side of the thing struck them simultaneously. They began to laugh.

"What fools we must have looked," said Adair.

"*You* were all right. I must have looked rotten. I've never had the gloves on in my life. I'm jolly glad no one saw us except Smith, who doesn't count. Hello, there's the bell. We'd better be moving on. What about this match? Not much chance of it from the look of the sky at present."

"It might clear before eleven. You'd better get changed, anyhow, at the interval, and hang about in case."

"All right. It's better than doing Thucydides with Downing. We've got math till the interval, so I don't see anything of him all day; which won't hurt me."

"He isn't a bad sort of chap, when you get to know him," said Adair.

"I can't have done, then. I don't know which I'd least soon be, Downing or a black beetle, except that if one was Downing one could tread on the black beetle. Dash this rain. I got about half a pint down my neck just then. We shan't get a game today, or anything like it. As you're crocked, I'm not sure that I care much. You've been sweating for years to get the match on, and it would be rather rot playing it without you."

"I don't know that so much. I wish we could play because I'm certain, with you and Smith, we'd walk into them. They probably aren't sending down much of a team, and really, now that you and Smith are turning out, we've got a jolly hot lot. There's quite decent batting all the way through, and the bowling isn't so bad. If only we could have given this M.C.C. lot a really good hammering, it might have been easier to get some good fixtures for next season. You see, it's all right for a school like Wrykyn, but with a small place like this you simply can't get the best teams to give you a match till you've done something to show that you aren't absolute rotters at the game. As for the schools, they're worse. They'd simply laugh at you. You were cricket secretary at Wrykyn last year. What would you have done if you'd had a challenge from Sedleigh? You'd either have laughed till you were sick, or else had a fit at the mere idea of the thing."

Mike stopped.

"By Jove, you've struck about the brightest scheme on record. I never thought of it before. Let's get a match on with Wrykyn."

"What! They wouldn't play us."

"Yes, they would. At least, I'm pretty sure they would. I had a letter from Strachan, the captain, yesterday, saying that the Ripton match had had to be scratched owing to illness. So they've got a vacant date. Shall I try them? I'll write to Strachan tonight, if you like. And they aren't strong this year. We'll smash them. What do you say?"

Adair was as one who has seen a vision.

"By Jove," he said at last, "if we only could!"

28

MR. DOWNING MOVES

The rain continued without a break all the morning. The two teams, after hanging about dismally, and whiling the time away with stump-cricket in the changing rooms, lunched in the pavilion at one o'clock. After which the M.C.C. captain, approaching Adair, moved that this merry meeting be considered off and he and his men permitted to catch the next train back to town. To which Adair, seeing that it was out of the question that there should be any cricket that afternoon, regretfully agreed, and the first Sedleigh v. M.C.C. match was accordingly scratched.

Mike and Psmith, wandering back to the house, were met by a damp junior from Downing's, with a message that Mr. Downing wished to see Mike as soon as he was changed.

"What's he want me for?" inquired Mike.

The messenger did not know. Mr. Downing, it seemed, had not confided in him. All he knew was that the housemaster was in the house, and would be glad if Mike would step across.

"A nuisance," said Psmith, "this incessant demand for you. That's the worst of being popular. If he wants you to stop to tea, edge away. A meal on rather a sumptuous scale will be prepared in the study against your return."

Mike changed quickly, and went off, leaving Psmith, who was fond of simple pleasures in his spare time, earnestly occupied with a puzzle which had been scattered through the land by a weekly paper. The prize for a solution was one thousand pounds, and Psmith had already informed Mike with some minuteness of his plans for the disposition of this sum. Meanwhile, he worked at it both in and out of school, generally with abusive comments on its inventor.

He was still fiddling away at it when Mike returned.

Mike, though Psmith was at first too absorbed to notice it, was agitated.

"I don't wish to be in any way harsh," said Psmith, without looking up, "but the man who invented this thing was a blighter of the worst type. You come and have a shot. For the moment I am baffled. The whisper flies round the clubs, 'Psmith is baffled.'"

"The man's an absolute driveling ass," said Mike warmly.

"Me, do you mean?"

"What on earth would be the point of my doing it?"

"You'd gather in a thousand of the best. Give you a nice start in life."

"I'm not talking about your rotten puzzle."

"What *are* you talking about?"

"That ass Downing. I believe he's off his nut."

"Then your chat with Comrade Downing was not of the old-College-chums-meeting-unexpectedly-after-years'-separation type? What has he been doing to you?"

"He's off his nut."

"I know. But what did he do? How did the brainstorm burst? Did he jump at you from behind a door and bite a piece out of your leg, or did he say he was a teapot?"

Mike sat down.

"You remember that painting-Sammy business?"

"As if it were yesterday," said Psmith. "Which it was, pretty nearly."

"He thinks I did it."

"Why? Have you ever shown any talent in the painting line?"

"The silly ass wanted me to confess that I'd done it. He as good as asked me to. Jawed a lot of rot about my finding it to my advantage later on if I behaved sensibly."

"Then what are you worrying about? Don't you know that when a master wants you to do the confessing act, it simply means that he hasn't enough evidence to start in on you with? You're all right. The thing's a stand-off."

"Evidence!" said Mike. "My dear man, he's got enough evidence to sink a ship. He's absolutely sweating evidence at every pore. As far as I can see, he's been crawling about, doing the Sherlock Holmes business for all he's worth ever since the thing happened, and now he's dead certain that I painted Sammy."

"*Did* you, by the way?" said Psmith.

"No," said Mike shortly, "I didn't. But after listening to Downing I almost began to wonder if I hadn't. The man's got stacks of evidence to prove that I did."

"Such as what?"

"It's mostly about my shoes. But, dash it, you know all about that. Why, you were with him when he came and looked for them."

"It is true," said Psmith, "that Comrade Downing and I spent a very pleasant half hour together inspecting shoes, but how does he drag you into it?"

"He swears one of the shoes was splashed with paint."

"Yes. He babbled to some extent on that point when I was entertaining him. But what makes him think that the shoe, if any, was yours?"

"He's certain that somebody in this house got one of his shoes splashed, and is hiding it somewhere. And I'm the only chap in the house who hasn't got a pair of shoes to show, so he thinks it's me. I don't know where the dickens my other shoe has gone. Of course I've got two pairs, but one's being soled. So I had to go over to school yesterday in gym shoes. That's how he spotted me."

Psmith sighed.

"Comrade Jackson," he said mournfully, "all this very sad affair shows the folly of acting from the best motives. In my simple zeal, meaning to save you unpleasantness, I have landed you, with a dull, sickening thud, right in the cart. Are you particular about dirtying your hands? If you aren't, just reach up that chimney a bit!"

Mike stared.

"What the dickens are you talking about?"

"Go on. Get it over. Be a man, and reach up the chimney."

"I don't know what the game is," said Mike, kneeling beside the fender and groping, "but — *Hello!*"

"Ah ha!" said Psmith moodily.

Mike dropped the soot-covered object in the fender, and glared at it.

"It's my shoe!" he said at last.

"It *is*," said Psmith, "your shoe. And what is that red stain across the toe? Is it blood? No, 'tis not blood. It is red paint."

Mike seemed unable to remove his eyes from the shoe.

"How on earth did-By Jove! I remember now. I kicked up against something in the dark when I was putting my bicycle back that night. It must have been the paint pot."

"Then you were out that night?"

"Rather. That's what makes it so jolly awkward. It's too long to tell you now —"

"Your stories are never too long for me," said Psmith. "Say on!"

"Well, it was like this." And Mike related the events which had led up to his midnight excursion. Psmith listened attentively.

"This," he said, when Mike had finished, "confirms my frequently stated opinion that Comrade Jellicoe is one of Nature's blitherers. So that's why he touched us for our hard-earned, was it?"

"Yes. Of course there was no need for him to have the money at all."

"And the result is that you are in something of a tight place. You're *absolutely* certain you didn't paint that dog? Didn't do it, by any chance, in a moment of absent-mindedness, and forgot all about it? No? No, I suppose not. I wonder who did!"

"It's beastly awkward. You see, Downing chased me that night. That was why I rang the alarm bell. So, you see, he's certain to think that the chap he chased, which was me, and the chap who painted Sammy, are the same. I shall get landed both ways."

Psmith pondered.

"It *is* a tightish place," he admitted.

"I wonder if we could get this shoe clean," said Mike, inspecting it with disfavor.

"Not for a pretty considerable time."

"I suppose not. I say, I *am* in the cart. If I can't produce this shoe, they're bound to guess why."

"What exactly," asked Psmith, "was the position of affairs between you and Comrade Downing when you left him? Had you definitely parted brass rags? Or did you simply sort of drift apart with mutual courtesies?"

"Oh, he said I was ill advised to continue that attitude, or some rot, and I said I didn't care, I hadn't painted his bally dog, and he said very well, then, he must take steps, and-well, that was about all."

"Sufficient, too," said Psmith, "quite sufficient, I take it, then, that he is now on the warpath, collecting a gang, so to speak."

"I suppose he's gone to the Old Man about it."

"Probably. A very worrying time our headmaster is having, taking it all round, in connection with this painful affair. What do you think his move will be?"

"I suppose he'll send for me, and try to get something out of me."

"*He'll* want you to confess, too. Masters are all whales on confession. The worst of it is, you can't prove an alibi, because at about the time the foul act was perpetrated, you were playing Round-and-round-the- mulberry-bush with Comrade Downing. This needs thought. You had better put the case in my hands, and go out and watch the dandelions growing. I will think over the matter."

"Well, I hope you'll be able to think of something. I can't."

"Possibly. You never know."

There was a tap at the door.

"See how we have trained them," said Psmith. "They now knock before entering. There was a time when they would have tried to smash in a panel. Come in."

A small boy, carrying a straw hat adorned with the School House ribbon, answered the invitation.

"Oh, I say, Jackson," he said, "the headmaster sent me over to tell you he wants to see you."

"I told you so," said Mike to Psmith.

"Don't go," suggested Psmith. "Tell him to write."

Mike got up.

"All this is very trying," said Psmith. "I'm seeing nothing of you today." He turned to the small boy. "Tell Willie," he added, "that Mr. Jackson will be with him in a moment."

The emissary departed.

"*You're* all right," said Psmith encouragingly. "Just you keep on saying you're all right. Stout denial is the thing. Don't go in for any airy explanations. Simply stick to stout denial. You can't beat it."

With which expert advice, he allowed Mike to go on his way.

He had not been gone two minutes, when Psmith, who had leaned back in his chair, rapt in thought, heaved himself up again. He stood for a moment straightening his tie at the looking glass; then he picked up his hat and moved slowly out of the door and down the passage. Thence, at the same dignified rate of progress, out of the house and in at Downing's front gate.

The postman was at the door when he got there, apparently absorbed in conversation with the parlor maid. Psmith stood by politely till the postman, who had just been told it was like his impudence, caught sight of him, and, having handed over the letters in an ultraformal and professional manner, passed away.

"Is Mr. Downing at home?" inquired Psmith.

He was, it seemed. Psmith was shown into the dining room on the left of the hall, and requested to wait. He was examining a portrait of Mr. Downing which hung on the wall when the housemaster came in.

"An excellent likeness, sir," said Psmith, with a gesture of the hand toward the painting.

"Well, Smith," said Mr. Downing shortly, "what do you wish to see me about?"

"It was in connection with the regrettable painting of your dog, sir."

"Ha!" said Mr. Downing.

"I did it, sir," said Psmith, stopping and flicking a piece of fluff off his knee.

29

THE ARTIST CLAIMS HIS WORK

The line of action which Psmith had called Stout Denial is an excellent line to adopt, especially if you really are innocent, but it does not lead to anything in the shape of a bright and snappy dialogue between accuser and accused. Both Mike and the headmaster were oppressed by a feeling that the situation was difficult. The atmosphere was heavy, and conversation showed a tendency to flag. The headmaster had opened brightly enough, with a summary of the evidence which Mr. Downing had laid before him, but after that a massive silence had been the order of the day. There is nothing in this world quite so stolid and uncommunicative as a boy who has made up his mind to be stolid and uncommunicative; and the headmaster, as he sat and looked at Mike, who sat and looked past him at the bookshelves, felt awkward. It was a scene which needed either a dramatic interruption or a neat exit speech. As it happened, what it got was the dramatic interruption.

The headmaster was just saying, "I do not think you fully realize, Jackson, the extent to which appearances..."—which was practically going back to the beginning and starting again-when there was a knock at the door. A voice without said, "Mr. Downing to see you, sir," and the chief witness for the prosecution burst in.

"I would not have interrupted you," said Mr. Downing, "but—"

"Not at all, Mr. Downing. Is there anything I can..."

"I have discovered...I have been informed...In short, it was not Jackson, who committed the-who painted my dog."

Mike and the headmaster both looked at the speaker. Mike with a feeling of relief-for Stout Denial, unsupported by any weighty evidence, is a wearing game to play-the headmaster with astonishment.

"Not Jackson?" said the headmaster.

"No. It was a boy in the same house. Smith."

Psmith! Mike was more than surprised. He could not believe it. There is nothing which affords so clear an index to a boy's character as the type of rag which he considers humorous. Between what is a rag and what is merely a rotten trick there is a very definite line drawn. Masters, as a rule, do not realize this, but boys nearly always do. Mike could not imagine Psmith doing a rotten thing like covering a housemaster's dog with red paint, any more than he could imagine doing it himself. They had both been amused at the sight of Sammy after the operation, but anybody, except possibly the owner of the dog, would have thought it funny at first. After the first surprise, their feeling had been that it was a rotten thing to have done and beastly rough luck on the poor brute. It was a kid's trick. As for Psmith having done it, Mike simply did not believe it.

"Smith!" said the headmaster. "What makes you think that?"

"Simply this," said Mr. Downing, with calm triumph, "that the boy himself came to me a few moments ago and confessed."

Mike was conscious of a feeling of acute depression. It did not make him in the least degree jubilant, or even thankful, to know that he himself was cleared of the charge. All he could think of was that Psmith was done for. This was bound to mean the sack. If Psmith had painted Sammy it meant that Psmith had broken out of his house at night; and it was not likely that the rules about nocturnal wandering were less strict at Sedleigh than at any other school in the kingdom. Mike felt, if possible, worse than he had felt when Wyatt had been caught on a similar occasion. It seemed as if Fate had a special grudge against his best friends. He did not make friends very quickly or easily, though he had always had scores of acquaintances-and with Wyatt and Psmith he had found himself at home from the first moment he had met them.

323

He sat there, with a curious feeling of having swallowed a heavy weight, hardly listening to what Mr. Downing was saying. Mr. Downing was talking rapidly to the headmaster, who was nodding from time to time.

Mike took advantage of a pause to get up. "May I go, sir?" he said.

"Certainly, Jackson, certainly," said the Head. "Oh, and er-if you are going back to your house, tell Smith that I should like to see him."

"Yes, sir."

He had reached the door, when again there was a knock.

"Come in," said the headmaster.

It was Adair.

"Yes, Adair?"

Adair was breathing rather heavily, as if he had been running.

"It was about Sammy-Sampson, sir," he said, looking at Mr. Downing.

"Ah, we know... Well, Adair, what did you wish to say?"

"It wasn't Jackson who did it, sir."

"No, no, Adair. So Mr. Downing—"

"It was Dunster, sir."

Terrific sensation! The headmaster gave a sort of strangled yelp of astonishment. Mr. Downing leaped in his chair. Mike's eyes opened to their fullest extent.

"Adair!"

There was almost a wail in the headmaster's voice. The situation had suddenly become too much for him. His brain was swimming. That Mike, despite the evidence against him, should be innocent, was curious, perhaps, but not particularly startling. But that Adair should inform him, two minutes after Mr. Downing's announcement of Psmith's confession, that Psmith, too, was guiltless, and that the real criminal was Dunster-it was this that made him feel that somebody, in the words of an American author, had played a mean trick on him, and substituted for his brain a side order of cauliflower. Why Dunster, of all people? Dunster, who, he remembered dizzily, had left the school at Christmas. And why, if Dunster had really painted the dog, had Psmith asserted that he himself was the culprit? Why-why anything? He concentrated his mind on Adair as the only person who could save him from impending brain fever.

"Adair!"

"Yes, sir?"

"What—*what* do you mean?"

"It *was* Dunster, sir. I got a letter from him only five minutes ago, in which he said that he had painted Sammy-Sampson, the dog, sir, for a rag-for a joke, and that, as he didn't want anyone here to get into a row-be punished for it, I'd better tell Mr. Downing at once. I tried to find Mr. Downing, but he wasn't in the house. Then I met Smith outside the house, and he told me that Mr. Downing had gone over to see you, sir."

"Smith told you?" said Mr. Downing.

"Yes, sir."

"Did you say anything to him about your having received this letter from Dunster?"

"I gave him the letter to read, sir."

"And what was his attitude when he had read it?"

"He laughed, sir."

"*Laughed*!" Mr. Downing's voice was thunderous.

"Yes, sir. He rolled about."

Mr. Downing snorted.

"But Adair," said the headmaster, "I do not understand how this thing could have been done by Dunster. He has left the school."

"He was down here for the Old Sedleighans' match, sir. He stopped the night in the village."

"And that was the night the-it happened?"

"Yes, sir."

"I see. Well, I am glad to find that the blame can not be attached to any boy in the school. I am sorry that it is even an Old Boy. It was a foolish, discreditable thing to have done, but it is not as bad as if any boy still at the school had broken out of his house at night to do it."

"The sergeant," said Mr. Downing, "told me that the boy he saw was attempting to enter Mr. Outwood's house."

"Another freak of Dunster's, I suppose," said the headmaster. "I shall write to him."

"If it was really Dunster who painted my dog," said Mr. Downing, "I cannot understand the part played by Smith in this affair. If he did not do it, what possible motive could he have had for coming to me of his own accord and deliberately confessing?"

"To be sure," said the headmaster, pressing a bell. "It is certainly a thing that calls for explanation. Barlow," he said, as the butler appeared, "kindly go across to Mr. Outwood's house and inform Smith that I should like to see him."

"If you please, sir, Mr. Smith is waiting in the hall."

"In the hall!"

"Yes, sir. He arrived soon after Mr. Adair, sir, saying that he would wait, as you would probably wish to see him shortly."

"H'm. Ask him to step up, Barlow."

"Yes, sir."

There followed one of the tensest "stage waits" of Mike's experience. It was not long, but, while it lasted, the silence was quite solid. Nobody seemed to have anything to say, and there was not even a clock in the room to break the stillness with its ticking. A very faint drip-drip of rain could be heard outside the window.

Presently there was a sound of footsteps on the stairs. The door was opened.

"Mr. Smith, sir."

The Old Etonian entered as would the guest of the evening who is a few moments late for dinner. He was cheerful, but slightly deprecating. He gave the impression of one who, though sure of his welcome, feels that some slight apology is expected from him. He advanced into the room with a gentle half-smile which suggested good will to all men.

"It is still raining," he observed. "You wished to see me, sir?"

"Sit down, Smith."

"Thank you, sir."

He dropped into a deep armchair (which both Adair and Mike had avoided in favor of less luxurious seats) with the confidential cosiness of a fashionable physician calling on a patient, between whom and himself time has broken down the barriers of restraint and formality.

Mr. Downing burst out, like a reservoir that has broken its banks.

"Smith."

Psmith turned his gaze politely in the housemaster's direction.

"Smith, you came to me a quarter of an hour ago and told me that it was you who had painted my dog Sampson."

"Yes, sir."

"It was absolutely untrue?"

"I am afraid so, sir."

"But, Smith..." began the headmaster.

Psmith bent forward encouragingly.

"...This is a most extraordinary affair. Have you no explanation to offer? What induced you to do such a thing?"

Psmith sighed softly.

"The craze of notoriety, sir," he replied sadly. "The curse of the present age."

"What!" replied the headmaster.

"It is remarkable," proceeded Psmith placidly, with the impersonal touch of one lecturing on generalities, "how frequently, when a murder has been committed, one finds men confessing that they have done it when it is out of the question that they should have committed it. It is one of the most interesting problems with which anthropologists are confronted. Human nature —"

The headmaster interrupted.

"Smith," he said, "I should like to see you alone for a moment. Mr. Downing, might I trouble...? Adair, Jackson."

He made a motion toward the door.

When he and Psmith were alone, there was silence. Psmith leaned back comfortably in his chair. The headmaster tapped nervously with his foot on the floor.

"Er...Smith."

"Sir?"

The headmaster seemed to have some difficulty in proceeding. He paused again. Then he went on.

"Er...Smith, I do not for a moment wish to pain you, but have you...er, do you remember ever having had, as a child, let us say, any...er...severe illness? Any...er...*mental* illness?"

"No, sir."

"There is no-forgive me if I am touching on a sad subject-there is no...none of your near relatives have ever suffered in the way I...er...have described?"

"There isn't a lunatic on the list, sir," said Psmith cheerfully.

"Of course, Smith, of course," said the headmaster hurriedly, "I did not mean to suggest-quite so, quite so.... You think, then, that you confessed to an act which you had not committed purely from some sudden impulse which you cannot explain?"

"Strictly between ourselves, sir..."

Privately, the headmaster found Psmith's man-to-man attitude somewhat disconcerting, but he said nothing.

"Well, Smith?"

"I should not like it to go any further, sir."

"I will certainly respect any confidence..."

"I don't want anybody to know, sir. This is strictly between ourselves."

"I think you are sometimes apt to forget, Smith, the proper relations existing between boy and-Well, never mind that for the present. We can return to it later. For the moment, let me hear what you wish to say. I shall, of course, tell nobody, if you do not wish it."

"Well, it was like this, sir," said Psmith, "Jackson happened to tell me that you and Mr. Downing seemed to think he had painted Mr. Downing's dog, and there seemed some danger of his being expelled, so I thought it wouldn't be an unsound scheme if I were to go and say I had done it. That was the whole thing. Of course, Dunster writing created a certain amount of confusion."

There was a pause.

"It was a very wrong thing to do, Smith," said the headmaster, at last, "but.... You are a curious boy, Smith. Good night."

He held out his hand.

"Good night, sir," said Psmith.

"Not a bad old sort," said Psmith meditatively to himself, as he walked downstairs. "By no means a bad old sort. I must drop in from time to time and cultivate him."

Mike and Adair were waiting for him outside the front door.

"Well?" said Mike.

"You *are* the limit," said Adair. "What's he done?"

"Nothing. We had a very pleasant chat, and then I tore myself away."

"Do you mean to say he's not going to do a thing?"

"Not a thing."

"Well, you're a marvel," said Adair.

Psmith thanked him courteously. They walked on toward the houses.

"By the way, Adair," said Mike, as the latter started to turn in at Downing's, "I'll write to Strachan tonight about that match."

"What's that?" asked Psmith.

"Jackson's going to try and get Wrykyn to give us a game," said Adair. "They've got a vacant date. I hope the dickens they'll do it."

"Oh, I should think they're certain to," said Mike. "Good night."

"And give Comrade Downing, when you see him," said Psmith, "my very best love. It is men like him who make this Merrie England of ours what it is."

* * * * *

"I say, Psmith," said Mike suddenly, "what really made you tell Downing you'd done it?"

"The craving for —"

"Oh, chuck it. You aren't talking to the Old Man now. I believe it was simply to get me out of a jolly tight corner."

Psmith's expression was one of pain.

"My dear Comrade Jackson," said he, "you wrong me. You make me writhe. I'm surprised at you. I never thought to hear those words from Michael Jackson."

"Well, I believe you did, all the same," said Mike obstinately. "And it was jolly good of you, too."

Psmith moaned.

SEDLEIGH V. WRYKYN

The Wrykyn match was three parts over, and things were going badly for Sedleigh. In a way one might have said that the game was over, and that Sedleigh had lost; for it was a one-day match, and Wrykyn, who had led on the first innings, had only to play out time to make the game theirs.

Sedleigh were paying the penalty for allowing themselves to be influenced by nerves in the early part of the day. Nerves lose more school matches than good play ever won. There is a certain type of school batsman who is a gift to any bowler when he once lets his imagination run away with him. Sedleigh, with the exception of Adair, Psmith, and Mike, had entered upon this match in a state of the most azure funk. Ever since Mike had received Strachan's answer and Adair had announced on the notice board that on Saturday, July the twentieth, Sedleigh would play Wrykyn, the team had been all on the jump. It was useless for Adair to tell them, as he did repeatedly, on Mike's authority, that Wrykyn were weak this season, and that on their present form Sedleigh ought to win easily. The team listened, but were not comforted. Wrykyn might be below their usual strength, but then Wrykyn cricket, as a rule, reached such a high standard that this probably meant little. However weak Wrykyn might be-for them-there was a very firm impression among the members of the Sedleigh first eleven that the other school was quite strong enough to knock the cover off *them*. Experience counts enormously in school matches. Sedleigh had never been proved. The teams they played were the sort of sides which the Wrykyn second eleven would play. Whereas Wrykyn, from time immemorial, had been beating Ripton teams and Free Foresters teams and M.C.C. teams packed with county men and sending men to Oxford and Cambridge who got their blues as freshmen.

Sedleigh had gone onto the field that morning a depressed side.

It was unfortunate that Adair had won the toss. He had had no choice but to take first innings. The weather had been bad for the last week, and the wicket was slow and treacherous. It was likely to get worse during the day, so Adair had chosen to bat first.

Taking into consideration the state of nerves the team was in, this in itself was a calamity. A school eleven are always at their worst and nerviest before lunch. Even on their own ground they find the surroundings lonely and unfamiliar. The subtlety of the bowlers becomes magnified. Unless the first pair make a really good start, a collapse almost invariably ensues.

Today the start had been gruesome beyond words. Mike, the bulwark of the side, the man who had been brought up on Wrykyn bowling, and from whom, whatever might happen to the others, at least a fifty was expected-Mike, going in first with Barnes and taking first over, had played inside one from Bruce, the Wrykyn slow bowler, and had been caught at short slip off his second ball.

That put the finishing touch on the panic. Stone, Robinson, and the others, all quite decent punishing batsmen when their nerves allowed them to play their own game, crawled to the wickets, declined to hit out at anything, and were clean bowled, several of them, playing back to half volleys. Adair did not suffer from panic, but his batting was not equal to his bowling, and he had fallen after hitting one four. Seven wickets were down for thirty when Psmith went in.

Psmith had always disclaimed any pretensions to batting skill, but he was undoubtedly the right man for a crisis like this. He had an enormous reach, and he used it. Three consecutive balls from Bruce he turned into full tosses and swept to the leg boundary, and, assisted by Barnes, who had been sitting on the splice in his usual manner, he raised the total to seventy-one before being yorked, with his score at thirty-five. Ten minutes later the innings was over, with Barnes not out sixteen, for seventy-nine.

Wrykyn had then gone in, lost Strachan for twenty before lunch, and finally completed their innings at a quarter to four for a hundred and thirty-one.

This was better than Sedleigh had expected. At least eight of the team had looked forward dismally to an afternoon's leather hunting. But Adair and Psmith, helped by the wicket, had never been easy, especially Psmith, who had taken six wickets, his slows playing havoc with the tail.

It would be too much to say that Sedleigh had any hope of pulling the game out of the fire; but it was a comfort, they felt, at any rate, having another knock. As is usual at this stage of a match, their nervousness had vanished, and they felt capable of better things than in the first innings.

It was on Mike's suggestion that Psmith and he went in first. Mike knew the limitations of the Wrykyn bowling, and he was convinced that, if they could knock Bruce off, it might be possible to rattle up a score sufficient to give them the game, always provided Wrykyn collapsed in the second innings. And it seemed to Mike that the wicket would be so bad then that they easily might.

So he and Psmith had gone in at four o'clock to hit. And they had hit. The deficit had been wiped off, all but a dozen runs, when Psmith was bowled, and by that time Mike was set and in his best vein. He treated all the bowlers alike. And when Stone came in, restored to his proper frame of mind, and lashed out stoutly, and after him Robinson and the rest, it looked as if Sedleigh had a chance again. The score was a hundred and twenty when Mike, who had just reached his fifty, skied one to Strachan at cover. The time was twenty-five past five.

As Mike reached the pavilion, Adair declared the innings closed.

Wrykyn started batting at twenty-five minutes to six, with sixty-nine to make if they wished to make them, and an hour and ten minutes during which to keep up their wickets if they preferred to take things easy and go for a win on the first innings.

At first it looked as if they meant to knock off the runs, for Strachan forced the game from the first ball, which was Psmith's, and which he hit into the pavilion. But, at fifteen, Adair bowled him. And when, two runs later, Psmith got the next man stumped, and finished up his over with a c-and-b, Wrykyn decided that it was not good enough. Seventeen for three, with an hour all but five minutes to go, was getting too dangerous. So Drummond and Rigby, the next pair, proceeded to play with caution, and the collapse ceased.

This was the state of the game at the point at which this chapter opened. Seventeen for three had become twenty-four for three, and the hands of the clock stood at ten minutes past six. Changes of bowling had been tried, but there seemed no chance of getting past the batsmen's defence. They were playing all the good balls, and refused to hit at the bad.

A quarter past six struck, and then Psmith made a suggestion which altered the game completely.

"Why don't you have a shot this end?" he said to Adair, as they were crossing over. "There's a spot on the off which might help you a lot. You can break like blazes if only you land on it. It doesn't help my leg breaks a bit, because they won't hit at them."

Barnes was on the point of beginning to bowl when Adair took the ball from him. The captain of Outwood's retired to short leg with an air that suggested that he was glad to be relieved of his prominent post. The next moment Drummond's off stump was lying at an angle of forty-five. Adair was absolutely accurate as a bowler, and he had dropped his first ball right on the worn patch.

Two minutes later Drummond's successor was retiring to the pavilion, while the wicket keeper straightened the stumps again.

There is nothing like a couple of unexpected wickets for altering the atmosphere of a game. Five minutes before, Sedleigh had been lethargic and without hope. Now there was a stir and buzz all around the ground. There were twenty-five minutes to go, and five wickets were down. Sedleigh was on top again.

The next man seemed to take an age coming out. As a matter of fact, he walked more rapidly than a batsman usually walks to the crease.

Adair's third ball dropped just short of the spot. The batsman, hitting out, was a shade too soon. The ball hummed through the air a couple of feet from the ground in the direction of mid off, and Mike, diving to the right, got to it as he was falling, and chucked it up.

After that the thing was a walk over. Psmith clean bowled a man in his next over: and the tail, demoralized by the sudden change in the game, collapsed uncompromisingly. Sedleigh won by thirty-five runs with eight minutes in hand.

* * * * *

Psmith and Mike sat in their study after lockup, discussing things in general and the game in particular. "I feel like a beastly renegade, playing against Wrykyn," said Mike. "Still, I'm glad we won. Adair's a jolly good sort and it'll make him happy for weeks."

"When I last saw Comrade Adair," said Psmith, "he was going about in a sort of trance, beaming vaguely and wanting to stand people things at the shop."

"He bowled awfully well."

"Yes," said Psmith. "I say, I don't wish to cast a gloom over this joyful occasion in any way, but you say Wrykyn are going to give Sedleigh a fixture again next year?"

"Well?"

"Well, have you thought of the massacre which will ensue? You will have left, Adair will have left. Incidentally, I shall have left. Wrykyn will swamp them."

"I suppose they will. Still, the great thing, you see, is to get the thing started. That's what Adair was so keen on. Now Sedleigh has beaten Wrykyn, he's satisfied. They can get fixtures with decent clubs, and work up to playing the big schools. You've got to start somehow. So it's all right, you see."

"And, besides," said Psmith, reflectively, "in an emergency they can always get Comrade Downing to bowl for them, what? Let us now sally out and see if we can't promote a rag of some sort in this abode of wrath. Comrade Outwood has gone over to dinner at the School House, and it would be a pity to waste a somewhat golden opportunity. Shall we stagger?"

They staggered.

Psmith in the City

1. Mr Bickersdyke Walks behind the Bowler's Arm

Considering what a prominent figure Mr John Bickersdyke was to be in Mike Jackson's life, it was only appropriate that he should make a dramatic entry into it. This he did by walking behind the bowler's arm when Mike had scored ninety-eight, causing him thereby to be clean bowled by a long-hop.

It was the last day of the Ilsworth cricket week, and the house team were struggling hard on a damaged wicket. During the first two matches of the week all had been well. Warm sunshine, true wickets, tea in the shade of the trees. But on the Thursday night, as the team champed their dinner contentedly after defeating the Incogniti by two wickets, a pattering of rain made itself heard upon the windows. By bedtime it had settled to a steady downpour. On Friday morning, when the team of the local regiment arrived in their brake, the sun was shining once more in a watery, melancholy way, but play was not possible before lunch. After lunch the bowlers were in their element. The regiment, winning the toss, put together a hundred and thirty, due principally to a last wicket stand between two enormous corporals, who swiped at everything and had luck enough for two whole teams. The house team followed with seventy-eight, of which Psmith, by his usual golf methods, claimed thirty. Mike, who had gone in first as the star bat of the side, had been run out with great promptitude off the first ball of the innings, which his partner had hit in the immediate neighbourhood of point. At close of play the regiment had made five without loss. This, on the Saturday morning, helped by another shower of rain which made the wicket easier for the moment, they had increased to a hundred and forty-eight, leaving the house just two hundred to make on a pitch which looked as if it were made of linseed.

It was during this week that Mike had first made the acquaintance of Psmith's family. Mr Smith had moved from Shropshire, and taken Ilsworth Hall in a neighbouring county. This he had done, as far as could be ascertained, simply because he had a poor opinion of Shropshire cricket. And just at the moment cricket happened to be the pivot of his life.

'My father,' Psmith had confided to Mike, meeting him at the station in the family motor on the Monday, 'is a man of vast but volatile brain. He has not that calm, dispassionate outlook on life which marks your true philosopher, such as myself. I —'

'I say,' interrupted Mike, eyeing Psmith's movements with apprehension, 'you aren't going to drive, are you?'

'Who else? As I was saying, I am like some contented spectator of a Pageant. My pater wants to jump in and stage-manage. He is a man of hobbies. He never has more than one at a time, and he never has that long. But while he has it, it's all there. When I left the house this morning he was all for cricket. But by the time we get to the ground he may have chucked cricket and taken up the Territorial Army. Don't be surprised if you find the wicket being dug up into trenches, when we arrive, and the pro. moving in echelon towards the pavilion. No,' he added, as the car turned into the drive, and they caught a glimpse of white flannels and blazers in the distance, and heard the sound of bat meeting ball, 'cricket seems still to be topping the bill. Come along, and I'll show you your room. It's next to mine, so that, if brooding on Life in the still hours of the night, I hit on any great truth, I shall pop in and discuss it with you.'

While Mike was changing, Psmith sat on his bed, and continued to discourse.

'I suppose you're going to the 'Varsity?' he said.

'Rather,' said Mike, lacing his boots. 'You are, of course? Cambridge, I hope. I'm going to King's.'

'Between ourselves,' confided Psmith, 'I'm dashed if I know what's going to happen to me. I am the thingummy of what's-its-name.'

'You look it,' said Mike, brushing his hair.

'Don't stand there cracking the glass,' said Psmith. 'I tell you I am practically a human three-shies-a-penny ball. My father is poising me lightly in his hand, preparatory to flinging me at one of the milky cocos of Life. Which one he'll aim at I don't know. The least thing fills him with a whirl of new views as to my future. Last week we were out shooting together, and he said that the life of the gentleman-farmer was the most manly and independent on earth, and that he had a good mind to start me on that. I pointed out that lack of early training had rendered me unable to distinguish between a threshing-machine and a mangel-wurzel, so he chucked that. He has now worked round to Commerce. It seems that a blighter of the name of Bickersdyke is coming here for the week-end next Saturday. As far as I can say without searching the Newgate Calendar, the man Bickersdyke's career seems to have been as follows. He was at school with my pater, went into the City, raked in a certain amount of doubloons-probably dishonestly-and is now a sort of Captain of Industry, manager of some bank or other, and about to stand for Parliament. The result of these excesses is that my pater's imagination has been fired, and at time of going to press he wants me to imitate Comrade Bickersdyke. However, there's plenty of time. That's one comfort. He's certain to change his mind again. Ready? Then suppose we filter forth into the arena?'

Out on the field Mike was introduced to the man of hobbies. Mr Smith, senior, was a long, earnest-looking man who might have been Psmith in a grey wig but for his obvious energy. He was as wholly on the move as Psmith was wholly statuesque. Where Psmith stood like some dignified piece of sculpture, musing on deep questions with a glassy eye, his father would be trying to be in four places at once. When Psmith presented Mike to him, he shook hands warmly with him and started a sentence, but broke off in the middle of both performances to dash wildly in the direction of the pavilion in an endeavour to catch an impossible catch some thirty yards away. The impetus so gained carried him on towards Bagley, the Ilsworth Hall ground-man, with whom a moment later he was carrying on an animated discussion as to whether he had or had not seen a dandelion on the field that morning. Two minutes afterwards he had skimmed away again. Mike, as he watched him, began to appreciate Psmith's reasons for feeling some doubt as to what would be his future walk in life.

At lunch that day Mike sat next to Mr Smith, and improved his acquaintance with him; and by the end of the week they were on excellent terms. Psmith's father had Psmith's gift of getting on well with people.

On this Saturday, as Mike buckled on his pads, Mr Smith bounded up, full of advice and encouragement.

'My boy,' he said, 'we rely on you. These others' —he indicated with a disparaging wave of the hand the rest of the team, who were visible through the window of the changing-room —'are all very well. Decent club bats. Good for a few on a billiard-table. But you're our hope on a wicket like this. I have studied cricket all my life' —till that summer it is improbable that Mr Smith had ever handled a bat —'and I know a first-class batsman when I see one. I've seen your brothers play. Pooh, you're better than any of them. That century of yours against the Green Jackets was a wonderful innings, wonderful. Now look here, my boy. I want you to be careful. We've a lot of runs to make, so we mustn't take any risks. Hit plenty of boundaries, of course, but be careful. Careful. Dash it, there's a youngster trying to climb up the elm. He'll break his neck. It's young Giles, my keeper's boy. Hi! Hi, there!'

He scudded out to avert the tragedy, leaving Mike to digest his expert advice on the art of batting on bad wickets.

Possibly it was the excellence of this advice which induced Mike to play what was, to date, the best innings of his life. There are moments when the batsman feels an almost super-human fitness. This came to Mike now. The sun had begun to shine strongly. It made the wicket more difficult, but it added a cheerful touch to the scene. Mike felt calm and masterful. The bowling had no terrors for him. He scored nine off his first over and seven off his second, half-way through which he lost his partner. He was to undergo a similar bereavement several times that afternoon, and at frequent intervals. However simple the bowling might seem to him, it had enough sting in it to worry the rest of the team considerably. Batsmen came and went at the other end with such rapidity that it seemed hardly worth while their troubling to come in at all. Every now and then one would give promise of better things by lifting the slow bowler into the pavilion or over the boundary, but it always happened that a similar stroke, a few balls later, ended in an easy catch. At five o'clock the Ilsworth score was eighty-one for seven wickets, last man nought, Mike not out fifty-nine. As most of the house team, including Mike, were dispersing to their homes or were due for visits at other houses that night, stumps were to be drawn at six. It was obvious that they could not hope to win. Number nine on the list, who was Bagley, the ground-man, went in with instructions to play for a draw, and minute advice from Mr Smith as to how he was to do it. Mike had now begun to score rapidly, and it was not to be expected that he could change his game; but Bagley, a dried-up little man of the type which bowls for five hours on a hot August day without exhibiting any symptoms of fatigue, put a much-bound bat stolidly in front of every ball he received; and the Hall's prospects of saving the game grew brighter.

At a quarter to six the professional left, caught at very silly point for eight. The score was a hundred and fifteen, of which Mike had made eighty-five.

A lengthy young man with yellow hair, who had done some good fast bowling for the Hall during the week, was the next man in. In previous matches he had hit furiously at everything, and against the Green Jackets had knocked up forty in twenty minutes while Mike was putting the finishing touches to his century. Now, however, with his host's warning ringing in his ears, he adopted the unspectacular, or Bagley, style of play. His manner of dealing with the ball was that of one playing croquet. He patted it gingerly back to the bowler when it was straight, and left it icily alone when it was off the wicket. Mike, still in the brilliant vein, clumped a half-volley past point to the boundary, and with highly scientific late cuts and glides brought his score to ninety-eight. With Mike's score at this, the total at a hundred and thirty, and the hands of the clock at five minutes to six, the yellow-haired croquet exponent fell, as Bagley had fallen, a victim to silly point, the ball being the last of the over.

Mr Smith, who always went in last for his side, and who so far had not received a single ball during the week, was down the pavilion steps and half-way to the wicket before the retiring batsman had taken half a dozen steps.

'Last over,' said the wicket-keeper to Mike. 'Any idea how many you've got? You must be near your century, I should think.'

'Ninety-eight,' said Mike. He always counted his runs.

'By Jove, as near as that? This is something like a finish.'

Mike left the first ball alone, and the second. They were too wide of the off-stump to be hit at safely. Then he felt a thrill as the third ball left the bowler's hand. It was a long-hop. He faced square to pull it.

And at that moment Mr John Bickersdyke walked into his life across the bowling-screen.

He crossed the bowler's arm just before the ball pitched. Mike lost sight of it for a fraction of a second, and hit wildly. The next moment his leg stump was askew; and the Hall had lost the match.

'I'm sorry,' he said to Mr Smith. 'Some silly idiot walked across the screen just as the ball was bowled.'

'What!' shouted Mr Smith. 'Who was the fool who walked behind the bowler's arm?' he yelled appealingly to Space.

'Here he comes, whoever he is,' said Mike.

A short, stout man in a straw hat and a flannel suit was walking towards them. As he came nearer Mike saw that he had a hard, thin-lipped mouth, half-hidden by a rather ragged moustache, and that behind a pair of gold spectacles were two pale and slightly protruding eyes, which, like his mouth, looked hard.

'How are you, Smith,' he said.

'Hullo, Bickersdyke.' There was a slight internal struggle, and then Mr Smith ceased to be the cricketer and became the host. He chatted amiably to the new-comer.

'You lost the game, I suppose,' said Mr Bickersdyke.

The cricketer in Mr Smith came to the top again, blended now, however, with the host. He was annoyed, but restrained in his annoyance.

'I say, Bickersdyke, you know, my dear fellow,' he said complainingly, 'you shouldn't have walked across the screen. You put Jackson off, and made him get bowled.'

'The screen?'

'That curious white object,' said Mike. 'It is not put up merely as an ornament. There's a sort of rough idea of giving the batsman a chance of seeing the ball, as well. It's a great help to him when people come charging across it just as the bowler bowls.'

Mr Bickersdyke turned a slightly deeper shade of purple, and was about to reply, when what sporting reporters call 'the veritable ovation' began.

Quite a large crowd had been watching the game, and they expressed their approval of Mike's performance.

There is only one thing for a batsman to do on these occasions. Mike ran into the pavilion, leaving Mr Bickersdyke standing.

2. Mike Hears Bad News

It seemed to Mike, when he got home, that there was a touch of gloom in the air. His sisters were as glad to see him as ever. There was a good deal of rejoicing going on among the female Jacksons because Joe had scored his first double century in first-class cricket. Double centuries are too common, nowadays, for the papers to take much notice of them; but, still, it is not everybody who can make them, and the occasion was one to be marked. Mike had read the news in the evening paper in the train, and had sent his brother a wire from the station, congratulating him. He had wondered whether he himself would ever achieve the feat in first-class cricket. He did not see why he should not. He looked forward through a long vista of years of county cricket. He had a birth qualification for the county in which Mr Smith had settled, and he had played for it once already at the beginning of the holidays. His *debut* had not been sensational, but it had been promising. The fact that two members of the team had made centuries, and a third seventy odd, had rather eclipsed his own twenty-nine not out; but it had been a faultless innings, and nearly all the papers had said that here was yet another Jackson, evidently well up to the family standard, who was bound to do big things in the future.

The touch of gloom was contributed by his brother Bob to a certain extent, and by his father more noticeably. Bob looked slightly thoughtful. Mr Jackson seemed thoroughly worried.

Mike approached Bob on the subject in the billiard-room after dinner.

Bob was practising cannons in rather a listless way.

'What's up, Bob?' asked Mike.

Bob laid down his cue.

'I'm hanged if I know,' said Bob. 'Something seems to be. Father's worried about something.'

'He looked as if he'd got the hump rather at dinner.'

'I only got here this afternoon, about three hours before you did. I had a bit of a talk with him before dinner. I can't make out what's up. He seemed awfully keen on my finding something to do now I've come down from Oxford. Wanted to know whether I couldn't get a tutoring job or a mastership at some school next term. I said I'd have a shot. I don't see what all the hurry's about, though. I was hoping he'd give me a bit of travelling on the Continent somewhere before I started in.'

'Rough luck,' said Mike. 'I wonder why it is. Jolly good about Joe, wasn't it? Let's have fifty up, shall we?'

Bob's remarks had given Mike no hint of impending disaster. It seemed strange, of course, that his father, who had always been so easy-going, should have developed a hustling Get On or Get Out spirit, and be urging Bob to Do It Now; but it never occurred to him that there could be any serious reason for it. After all, fellows had to start working some time or other. Probably his father had merely pointed this out to Bob, and Bob had made too much of it.

Half-way through the game Mr Jackson entered the room, and stood watching in silence.

'Want a game, father?' asked Mike.

'No, thanks, Mike. What is it? A hundred up?'

'Fifty.'

'Oh, then you'll be finished in a moment. When you are, I wish you'd just look into the study for a moment, Mike. I want to have a talk with you.'

'Rum,' said Mike, as the door closed. 'I wonder what's up?'

For a wonder his conscience was free. It was not as if a bad school-report might have arrived in his absence. His Sedleigh report had come at the beginning of the holidays, and had been, on the whole, fairly decent—nothing startling either way. Mr Downing, perhaps through remorse at having harried Mike to such an extent during the Sammy episode, had exercised a studied moderation in his remarks. He had let Mike down far more easily than he really deserved. So it could not be a report that was worrying Mr Jackson. And there was nothing else on his conscience.

Bob made a break of sixteen, and ran out. Mike replaced his cue, and walked to the study.

His father was sitting at the table. Except for the very important fact that this time he felt that he could plead Not Guilty on every possible charge, Mike was struck by the resemblance in the general arrangement of the scene to that painful ten minutes at the end of the previous holidays, when his father had announced his intention of taking him away from Wrykyn and sending him to Sedleigh. The resemblance was increased by the fact that, as Mike entered, Mr Jackson was kicking at the waste-paper basket—a thing which with him was an infallible sign of mental unrest.

'Sit down, Mike,' said Mr Jackson. 'How did you get on during the week?'

'Topping. Only once out under double figures. And then I was run out. Got a century against the Green Jackets, seventy-one against the Incogs, and today I made ninety-eight on a beast of a wicket, and only got out because some silly goat of a chap—'

He broke off. Mr Jackson did not seem to be attending. There was a silence. Then Mr Jackson spoke with an obvious effort.

'Look here, Mike, we've always understood one another, haven't we?'

'Of course we have.'

'You know I wouldn't do anything to prevent you having a good time, if I could help it. I took you away from Wrykyn, I know, but that was a special case. It was necessary. But I understand perfectly how keen you are to go to Cambridge, and I wouldn't stand in the way for a minute, if I could help it.'

Mike looked at him blankly. This could only mean one thing. He was not to go to the 'Varsity. But why? What had happened? When he had left for the Smith's cricket week, his name had been down for King's, and the whole thing settled. What could have happened since then?

'But I can't help it,' continued Mr Jackson.

'Aren't I going up to Cambridge, father?' stammered Mike.

'I'm afraid not, Mike. I'd manage it if I possibly could. I'm just as anxious to see you get your Blue as you are to get it. But it's kinder to be quite frank. I can't afford to send you to Cambridge. I won't go into details which you would not understand; but I've lost a very large sum of money since I saw you last. So large that we shall have to economize in every way. I shall let this house and take a much smaller one. And you and Bob, I'm afraid, will have to start earning your living. I know it's a terrible disappointment to you, old chap.'

'Oh, that's all right,' said Mike thickly. There seemed to be something sticking in his throat, preventing him from speaking.

'If there was any possible way—'

'No, it's all right, father, really. I don't mind a bit. It's awfully rough luck on you losing all that.'

There was another silence. The clock ticked away energetically on the mantelpiece, as if glad to make itself heard at last. Outside, a plaintive snuffle made itself heard. John, the bull-dog, Mike's inseparable companion, who had followed him to the study, was getting tired of waiting on the mat. Mike got up and opened the door. John lumbered in.

The movement broke the tension.

'Thanks, Mike,' said Mr Jackson, as Mike started to leave the room, 'you're a sportsman.'

3. The New Era Begins

Details of what were in store for him were given to Mike next morning. During his absence at Ilsworth a vacancy had been got for him in that flourishing institution, the New Asiatic Bank; and he was to enter upon his duties, whatever they might be, on the Tuesday of the following week. It was short notice, but banks have a habit of swallowing their victims rather abruptly. Mike remembered the case of Wyatt, who had had just about the same amount of time in which to get used to the prospect of Commerce.

On the Monday morning a letter arrived from Psmith. Psmith was still perturbed. 'Commerce,' he wrote, 'continues to boom. My pater referred to Comrade Bickersdyke last night as a Merchant Prince. Comrade B. and I do not get on well together. Purely for his own good, I drew him aside yesterday and explained to him at great length the frightfulness of walking across the bowling-screen. He seemed restive, but I was firm. We parted rather with the Distant Stare than the Friendly Smile. But I shall persevere. In many ways the casual observer would say that he was hopeless. He is a poor performer at Bridge, as I was compelled to hint to him on Saturday night. His eyes have no animated sparkle of intelligence. And the cut of his clothes jars my sensitive soul to its foundations. I don't wish to speak ill of a man behind his back, but I must confide in you, as my Boyhood's Friend, that he wore a made-up tie at dinner. But no more of a painful subject. I am working away at him with a brave smile. Sometimes I think that I am succeeding. Then he seems to slip back again. However,' concluded the letter, ending on an optimistic note, 'I think that I shall make a man of him yet-some day.'

Mike re-read this letter in the train that took him to London. By this time Psmith would know that his was not the only case in which Commerce was booming. Mike had written to him by return, telling him of the disaster which had befallen the house of Jackson. Mike wished he could have told him in person, for Psmith had a way of treating unpleasant situations as if he were merely playing at them for his own amusement. Psmith's attitude towards the slings and arrows of outrageous Fortune was to regard them with a bland smile, as if they were part of an entertainment got up for his express benefit.

Arriving at Paddington, Mike stood on the platform, waiting for his box to emerge from the luggage-van, with mixed feelings of gloom and excitement. The gloom was in the larger quantities, perhaps, but the excitement was there, too. It was the first time in his life that he had been entirely dependent on himself. He had crossed the Rubicon. The occasion was too serious for him to feel the same helplessly furious feeling with which he had embarked on life at Sedleigh. It was possible to look on Sedleigh with quite a personal enmity. London was too big to be angry with. It took no notice of him. It did not care whether he was glad to be there or sorry, and there was no means of making it care. That is the peculiarity of London. There is a sort of cold unfriendliness about it. A city like New York makes the new arrival feel at home in half an hour; but London is a specialist in what Psmith in his letter had called the Distant Stare. You have to buy London's good-will.

Mike drove across the Park to Victoria, feeling very empty and small. He had settled on Dulwich as the spot to get lodgings, partly because, knowing nothing about London, he was under the impression that rooms anywhere inside the four-mile radius were very expensive, but principally because there was a school at Dulwich, and it would be a comfort being near a school. He might get a game of fives there sometimes, he thought, on a Saturday afternoon, and, in the summer, occasional cricket.

Wandering at a venture up the asphalt passage which leads from Dulwich station in the direction of the College, he came out into Acacia Road. There is something about Acacia Road which inevitably suggests furnished apartments. A child could tell at a glance that it was bristling with bed-sitting rooms.

Mike knocked at the first door over which a card hung.

There is probably no more depressing experience in the world than the process of engaging furnished apartments. Those who let furnished apartments seem to take no joy in the act. Like Pooh-Bah, they do it, but it revolts them.

In answer to Mike's knock, a female person opened the door. In appearance she resembled a pantomime 'dame', inclining towards the restrained melancholy of Mr Wilkie Bard rather than the joyous abandon of Mr George Robey. Her voice she had modelled on the gramophone. Her most recent occupation seemed to have been something with a good deal of yellow soap in it. As a matter of fact-there are no secrets between our readers and ourselves-she had been washing a shirt. A useful occupation, and an honourable, but one that tends to produce a certain homeliness in the appearance.

She wiped a pair of steaming hands on her apron, and regarded Mike with an eye which would have been markedly expressionless in a boiled fish.

'Was there anything?' she asked.

Mike felt that he was in for it now. He had not sufficient ease of manner to back gracefully away and disappear, so he said that there was something. In point of fact, he wanted a bed-sitting room.

'Orkup stays,' said the pantomime dame. Which Mike interpreted to mean, would he walk upstairs?

The procession moved up a dark flight of stairs until it came to a door. The pantomime dame opened this, and shuffled through. Mike stood in the doorway, and looked in.

It was a repulsive room. One of those characterless rooms which are only found in furnished apartments. To Mike, used to the comforts of his bedroom at home and the cheerful simplicity of a school dormitory, it seemed about the most dismal spot he had ever struck. A sort of Sargasso Sea among bedrooms.

He looked round in silence. Then he said: 'Yes.' There did not seem much else to say.

'It's a nice room,' said the pantomime dame. Which was a black lie. It was not a nice room. It never had been a nice room. And it did not seem at all probable that it ever would be a nice room. But it looked cheap. That was the great thing. Nobody could have the assurance to charge much for a room like that. A landlady with a conscience might even have gone to the length of paying people some small sum by way of compensation to them for sleeping in it.

'About what?' queried Mike. Cheapness was the great consideration. He understood that his salary at the bank would be about four pounds ten a month, to begin with, and his father was allowing him five pounds a month. One does not do things *en prince* on a hundred and fourteen pounds a year.

The pantomime dame became slightly more animated. Prefacing her remarks by a repetition of her statement that it was a nice room, she went on to say that she could 'do' it at seven and sixpence per week 'for him'—giving him to understand, presumably, that, if the Shah of Persia or Mr Carnegie ever applied for a night's rest, they would sigh in vain for such easy terms. And that included lights. Coals were to be looked on as an extra. 'Sixpence a scuttle.' Attendance was thrown in.

Having stated these terms, she dribbled a piece of fluff under the bed, after the manner of a professional Association footballer, and relapsed into her former moody silence.

Mike said he thought that would be all right. The pantomime dame exhibited no pleasure.

''Bout meals?' she said. 'You'll be wanting breakfast. Bacon, aigs, an' that, I suppose?'

Mike said he supposed so.

'That'll be extra,' she said. 'And dinner? A chop, or a nice steak?'

Mike bowed before this original flight of fancy. A chop or a nice steak seemed to be about what he might want.

'That'll be extra,' said the pantomime dame in her best Wilkie Bard manner.

Mike said yes, he supposed so. After which, having put down seven and sixpence, one week's rent in advance, he was presented with a grubby receipt and an enormous latchkey, and the *seance* was at an end. Mike wandered out of the house. A few steps took him to the railings that bounded the College grounds. It was late August, and the evenings had begun to close in. The cricket-field looked very cool and spacious in the dim light, with the school buildings looming vague and shadowy through the slight mist. The little gate by the railway bridge was not locked. He went in, and walked slowly across the turf towards the big clump of trees which marked the division between the cricket and football fields. It was all very pleasant and soothing after the pantomime dame and her stuffy bed-sitting room. He sat down on a bench beside the second eleven telegraph-board, and looked across the ground at the pavilion. For the first time that day he began to feel really home-sick. Up till now the excitement of a strange venture had borne him up; but the cricket-field and the pavilion reminded him so sharply of Wrykyn. They brought home to him with a cutting distinctness, the absolute finality of his break with the old order of things. Summers would come and go, matches would be played on this ground with all the glory of big scores and keen finishes; but he was done. 'He was a jolly good bat at school. Top of the Wrykyn averages two years. But didn't do anything after he left. Went into the city or something.' That was what they would say of him, if they didn't quite forget him.

The clock on the tower over the senior block chimed quarter after quarter, but Mike sat on, thinking. It was quite late when he got up, and began to walk back to Acacia Road. He felt cold and stiff and very miserable.

4. First Steps in a Business Career

The City received Mike with the same aloofness with which the more western portion of London had welcomed him on the previous day. Nobody seemed to look at him. He was permitted to alight at St Paul's and make his way up Queen Victoria Street without any demonstration. He followed the human stream till he reached the Mansion House, and eventually found himself at the massive building of the New Asiatic Bank, Limited.

The difficulty now was to know how to make an effective entrance. There was the bank, and here was he. How had he better set about breaking it to the authorities that he had positively arrived and was ready to start earning his four pound ten *per mensem*? Inside, the bank seemed to be in a state of some confusion. Men were moving about in an apparently irresolute manner. Nobody seemed actually to be working. As a matter of fact, the business of a bank does not start very early in the morning. Mike had arrived before things had really begun to move. As he stood near the doorway, one or two panting figures rushed up the steps, and flung themselves at a large book which stood on the counter near the door. Mike was to come to know this book well. In it, if you were an *employe* of the New Asiatic Bank, you had to inscribe your name every morning. It was removed at ten sharp to the accountant's room, and if you reached the bank a certain number of times in the year too late to sign, bang went your bonus.

After a while things began to settle down. The stir and confusion gradually ceased. All down the length of the bank, figures could be seen, seated on stools and writing hieroglyphics in large letters. A benevolent-looking man, with spectacles and a straggling grey beard, crossed the gangway close to where Mike was standing. Mike put the thing to him, as man to man.

'Could you tell me,' he said, 'what I'm supposed to do? I've just joined the bank.' The benevolent man stopped, and looked at him with a pair of mild blue eyes. 'I think, perhaps, that your best plan would be to see the manager,' he said. 'Yes, I should certainly do that. He will tell you what work you have to do. If you will permit me, I will show you the way.'

'It's awfully good of you,' said Mike. He felt very grateful. After his experience of London, it was a pleasant change to find someone who really seemed to care what happened to him. His heart warmed to the benevolent man.

'It feels strange to you, perhaps, at first, Mr—'

'Jackson.'

'Mr Jackson. My name is Waller. I have been in the City some time, but I can still recall my first day. But one shakes down. One shakes down quite quickly. Here is the manager's room. If you go in, he will tell you what to do.'

'Thanks awfully,' said Mike.

'Not at all.' He ambled off on the quest which Mike had interrupted, turning, as he went, to bestow a mild smile of encouragement on the new arrival. There was something about Mr Waller which reminded Mike pleasantly of the White Knight in 'Alice through the Looking-glass.'

Mike knocked at the managerial door, and went in.

Two men were sitting at the table. The one facing the door was writing when Mike went in. He continued to write all the time he was in the room. Conversation between other people in his presence had apparently no interest for him, nor was it able to disturb him in any way.

The other man was talking into a telephone. Mike waited till he had finished. Then he coughed. The man turned round. Mike had thought, as he looked at his back and heard his voice, that something about his appearance or his way of speaking was familiar. He was right. The man in the chair was Mr Bickersdyke, the cross-screen pedestrian.

These reunions are very awkward. Mike was frankly unequal to the situation. Psmith, in his place, would have opened the conversation, and relaxed the tension with some remark on the weather or the state of the crops. Mike merely stood wrapped in silence, as in a garment.

That the recognition was mutual was evident from Mr Bickersdyke's look. But apart from this, he gave no sign of having already had the pleasure of making Mike's acquaintance. He merely stared at him as if he were a blot on the arrangement of the furniture, and said, 'Well?'

The most difficult parts to play in real life as well as on the stage are those in which no 'business' is arranged for the performer. It was all very well for Mr Bickersdyke. He had been 'discovered sitting'. But Mike had had to enter, and he wished now that there was something he could do instead of merely standing and speaking.

'I've come,' was the best speech he could think of. It was not a good speech. It was too sinister. He felt that even as he said it. It was the sort of thing Mephistopheles would have said to Faust by way of opening conversation. And he was not sure, either, whether he ought not to have added, 'Sir.'

Apparently such subtleties of address were not necessary, for Mr Bickersdyke did not start up and shout, 'This language to me!' or anything of that kind. He merely said, 'Oh! And who are you?'

'Jackson,' said Mike. It was irritating, this assumption on Mr Bickersdyke's part that they had never met before.

'Jackson? Ah, yes. You have joined the staff?'

Mike rather liked this way of putting it. It lent a certain dignity to the proceedings, making him feel like some important person for whose services there had been strenuous competition. He seemed to see the bank's directors being reassured by the chairman. ('I am happy to say, gentlemen, that our profits for the past year are 3,000,006-2-2 1/2 pounds —(cheers) —and' —impressively —'that we have finally succeeded in inducing Mr Mike Jackson —(sensation) —to-er-in fact, to join the staff!' (Frantic cheers, in which the chairman joined.)

'Yes,' he said.

Mr Bickersdyke pressed a bell on the table beside him, and picking up a pen, began to write. Of Mike he took no further notice, leaving that toy of Fate standing stranded in the middle of the room.

After a few moments one of the men in fancy dress, whom Mike had seen hanging about the gangway, and whom he afterwards found to be messengers, appeared. Mr Bickersdyke looked up.

'Ask Mr Bannister to step this way,' he said.

The messenger disappeared, and presently the door opened again to admit a shock-headed youth with paper cuff-protectors round his wrists.

'This is Mr Jackson, a new member of the staff. He will take your place in the postage department. You will go into the cash department, under Mr Waller. Kindly show him what he has to do.'

Mike followed Mr Bannister out. On the other side of the door the shock-headed one became communicative.

'Whew!' he said, mopping his brow. 'That's the sort of thing which gives me the pip. When William came and said old Bick wanted to see me, I said to him, "William, my boy, my number is up. This is the sack." I made certain that Rossiter had run me in for something. He's been waiting for a chance to do it for weeks, only I've been as good as gold and haven't given it him. I pity you going into the postage. There's one thing, though. If you can stick it for about a month, you'll get through all right. Men are always leaving for the East, and then you get shunted on into another department, and the next new man goes into the postage. That's the best of this place. It's not like one of those banks where you stay in London all your life. You only have three years here, and then you get your orders, and go to one of the branches in the East, where you're the dickens of a big pot straight away, with a big screw and a dozen native Johnnies under you. Bit of all right, that. I shan't get my orders for another two and a half years and more, worse luck. Still, it's something to look forward to.'

'Who's Rossiter?' asked Mike.

'The head of the postage department. Fussy little brute. Won't leave you alone. Always trying to catch you on the hop. There's one thing, though. The work in the postage is pretty simple. You can't make many mistakes, if you're careful. It's mostly entering letters and stamping them.'

They turned in at the door in the counter, and arrived at a desk which ran parallel to the gangway. There was a high rack running along it, on which were several ledgers. Tall, green-shaded electric lamps gave it rather a cosy look.

As they reached the desk, a little man with short, black whiskers buzzed out from behind a glass screen, where there was another desk.

'Where have you been, Bannister, where have you been? You must not leave your work in this way. There are several letters waiting to be entered. Where have you been?'

'Mr Bickersdyke sent for me,' said Bannister, with the calm triumph of one who trumps an ace.

'Oh! Ah! Oh! Yes, very well. I see. But get to work, get to work. Who is this?'

'This is a new man. He's taking my place. I've been moved on to the cash.'

'Oh! Ah! Is your name Smith?' asked Mr Rossiter, turning to Mike.

Mike corrected the rash guess, and gave his name. It struck him as a curious coincidence that he should be asked if his name were Smith, of all others. Not that it is an uncommon name.

'Mr Bickersdyke told me to expect a Mr Smith. Well, well, perhaps there are two new men. Mr Bickersdyke knows we are short-handed in this department. But, come along, Bannister, come along. Show Jackson what he has to do. We must get on. There is no time to waste.'

He buzzed back to his lair. Bannister grinned at Mike. He was a cheerful youth. His normal expression was a grin.

'That's a sample of Rossiter,' he said. 'You'd think from the fuss he's made that the business of the place was at a standstill till we got to work. Perfect rot! There's never anything to do here till after lunch, except checking the stamps and petty cash, and I've done that ages ago. There are three letters. You may as well enter them. It all looks like work. But you'll find the best way is to wait till you get a couple of dozen or so, and then work them off in a batch. But if you see Rossiter about, then start stamping something or writing something, or he'll run you in for neglecting your job. He's a nut. I'm jolly glad I'm under old Waller now. He's the pick of the bunch. The other heads of departments are all nuts, and Bickersdyke's the nuttiest of the lot. Now, look here. This is all you've got to do. I'll just show you, and then you can manage for yourself. I shall have to be shunting off to my own work in a minute.'

5. The Other Man

As Bannister had said, the work in the postage department was not intricate. There was nothing much to do except enter and stamp letters, and, at intervals, take them down to the post office at the end of the street. The nature of the work gave Mike plenty of time for reflection.

His thoughts became gloomy again. All this was very far removed from the life to which he had looked forward. There are some people who take naturally to a life of commerce. Mike was not of these. To him the restraint of the business was irksome. He had been used to an open-air life, and a life, in its way, of excitement. He gathered that he would not be free till five o'clock, and that on the following day he would come at ten and go at five, and the same every day, except Saturdays and Sundays, all the year round, with a ten days' holiday. The monotony of the prospect appalled him. He was not old enough to know what a narcotic is Habit, and that one can become attached to and interested in the most unpromising jobs. He worked away dismally at his letters till he had finished them. Then there was nothing to do except sit and wait for more.

He looked through the letters he had stamped, and re-read the addresses. Some of them were directed to people living in the country, one to a house which he knew quite well, near to his own home in Shropshire. It made him home-sick, conjuring up visions of shady gardens and country sounds and smells, and the silver Severn gleaming in the distance through the trees. About now, if he were not in this dismal place, he would be lying in the shade in the garden with a book, or wandering down to the river to boat or bathe. That envelope addressed to the man in Shropshire gave him the worst moment he had experienced that day.

The time crept slowly on to one o'clock. At two minutes past Mike awoke from a day-dream to find Mr Waller standing by his side. The cashier had his hat on.

'I wonder,' said Mr Waller, 'if you would care to come out to lunch. I generally go about this time, and Mr Rossiter, I know, does not go out till two. I thought perhaps that, being unused to the City, you might have some difficulty in finding your way about.'

'It's awfully good of you,' said Mike. 'I should like to.'

The other led the way through the streets and down obscure alleys till they came to a chop-house. Here one could have the doubtful pleasure of seeing one's chop in its various stages of evolution. Mr Waller ordered lunch with the care of one to whom lunch is no slight matter. Few workers in the City do regard lunch as a trivial affair. It is the keynote of their day. It is an oasis in a desert of ink and ledgers. Conversation in city office deals, in the morning, with what one is going to have for lunch, and in the afternoon with what one has had for lunch.

At intervals during the meal Mr Waller talked. Mike was content to listen. There was something soothing about the grey-bearded one.

'What sort of a man is Bickersdyke?' asked Mike.

'A very able man. A very able man indeed. I'm afraid he's not popular in the office. A little inclined, perhaps, to be hard on mistakes. I can remember the time when he was quite different. He and I were fellow clerks in Morton and Blatherwick's. He got on better than I did. A great fellow for getting on. They say he is to be the Unionist candidate for Kenningford when the time comes. A great worker, but perhaps not quite the sort of man to be generally popular in an office.'

'He's a blighter,' was Mike's verdict. Mr Waller made no comment. Mike was to learn later that the manager and the cashier, despite the fact that they had been together in less prosperous days-or possibly because of it-were not on very good terms. Mr Bickersdyke was a man of strong prejudices, and he disliked the cashier, whom he looked down upon as one who had climbed to a lower rung of the ladder than he himself had reached.

As the hands of the chop-house clock reached a quarter to two, Mr Waller rose, and led the way back to the office, where they parted for their respective desks. Gratitude for any good turn done to him was a leading characteristic of Mike's nature, and he felt genuinely grateful to the cashier for troubling to seek him out and be friendly to him.

His three-quarters-of-an-hour absence had led to the accumulation of a small pile of letters on his desk. He sat down and began to work them off. The addresses continued to exercise a fascination for him. He was miles away from the office, speculating on what sort of a man J. B. Garside, Esq, was, and whether he had a good time at his house in Worcestershire, when somebody tapped him on the shoulder.

He looked up.

Standing by his side, immaculately dressed as ever, with his eye-glass fixed and a gentle smile on his face, was Psmith.

Mike stared.

'Commerce,' said Psmith, as he drew off his lavender gloves, 'has claimed me for her own. Comrade of old, I, too, have joined this blighted institution.'

As he spoke, there was a whirring noise in the immediate neighbourhood, and Mr Rossiter buzzed out from his den with the *esprit* and animation of a clock-work toy.

'Who's here?' said Psmith with interest, removing his eye-glass, polishing it, and replacing it in his eye.

'Mr Jackson,' exclaimed Mr Rossiter. 'I really must ask you to be good enough to come in from your lunch at the proper time. It was fully seven minutes to two when you returned, and —'

'That little more,' sighed Psmith, 'and how much is it!'

'Who are you?' snapped Mr Rossiter, turning on him.

'I shall be delighted, Comrade —'

'Rossiter,' said Mike, aside.

'Comrade Rossiter. I shall be delighted to furnish you with particulars of my family history. As follows. Soon after the Norman Conquest, a certain Sieur de Psmith grew tired of work — a family failing, alas! — and settled down in this country to live peacefully for the remainder of his life on what he could extract from the local peasantry. He may be described as the founder of the family which ultimately culminated in Me. Passing on —'

Mr Rossiter refused to pass on.

'What are you doing here? What have you come for?'

'Work,' said Psmith, with simple dignity. 'I am now a member of the staff of this bank. Its interests are my interests. Psmith, the individual, ceases to exist, and there springs into being Psmith, the cog in the wheel of the New Asiatic Bank; Psmith, the link in the bank's chain; Psmith, the Worker. I shall not spare myself,' he proceeded earnestly. 'I shall toil with all the accumulated energy of one who, up till now, has only known what work is like from hearsay. Whose is that form sitting on the steps of the bank in the morning, waiting eagerly for the place to open? It is the form of Psmith, the Worker. Whose is that haggard, drawn face which bends over a ledger long after the other toilers have sped blithely westwards to dine at Lyons' Popular Cafe? It is the face of Psmith, the Worker.'

'I —' began Mr Rossiter.

'I tell you,' continued Psmith, waving aside the interruption and tapping the head of the department rhythmically in the region of the second waistcoat-button with a long finger, 'I tell *you*, Comrade Rossiter, that you have got hold of a good man. You and I together, not forgetting Comrade Jackson, the pet of the Smart Set, will toil early and late till we boost up this Postage Department into a shining model of what a Postage Department should be. What that is, at present, I do not exactly know. However. Excursion trains will be run from distant shires to see this Postage Department. American visitors to London will do it before going on to the Tower. And now,' he broke off, with a crisp, businesslike intonation, 'I must ask you to excuse me. Much as I have enjoyed this little chat, I fear it must now cease. The time has come to work. Our trade rivals are getting ahead of us. The whisper goes round, "Rossiter and Psmith are talking, not working," and other firms prepare to pinch our business. Let me Work.'

Two minutes later, Mr Rossiter was sitting at his desk with a dazed expression, while Psmith, perched gracefully on a stool, entered figures in a ledger.

6. Psmith Explains

For the space of about twenty-five minutes Psmith sat in silence, concentrated on his ledger, the picture of the model bank-clerk. Then he flung down his pen, slid from his stool with a satisfied sigh, and dusted his waistcoat. 'A commercial crisis,' he said, 'has passed. The job of work which Comrade Rossiter indicated for me has been completed with masterly skill. The period of anxiety is over. The bank ceases to totter. Are you busy, Comrade Jackson, or shall we chat awhile?'

Mike was not busy. He had worked off the last batch of letters, and there was nothing to do but to wait for the next, or-happy thought-to take the present batch down to the post, and so get out into the sunshine and fresh air for a short time. 'I rather think I'll nip down to the post-office,' said he, 'You couldn't come too, I suppose?'

'On the contrary,' said Psmith, 'I could, and will. A stroll will just restore those tissues which the gruelling work of the last half-hour has wasted away. It is a fearful strain, this commercial toil. Let us trickle towards the post office. I will leave my hat and gloves as a guarantee of good faith. The cry will go round, "Psmith has gone! Some rival institution has kidnapped him!" Then they will see my hat,' —he built up a foundation of ledgers, planted a long ruler in the middle, and hung his hat on it —'my gloves,' —he stuck two pens into the desk and hung a lavender glove on each —'and they will sink back swooning with relief. The awful suspense will be over. They will say, "No, he has not gone permanently. Psmith will return. When the fields are white with daisies he'll return." And now, Comrade Jackson, lead me to this picturesque little post-office of yours of which I have heard so much.'

Mike picked up the long basket into which he had thrown the letters after entering the addresses in his ledger, and they moved off down the aisle. No movement came from Mr Rossiter's lair. Its energetic occupant was hard at work. They could just see part of his hunched-up back.

'I wish Comrade Downing could see us now,' said Psmith. 'He always set us down as mere idlers. Triflers. Butterflies. It would be a wholesome corrective for him to watch us perspiring like this in the cause of Commerce.'

'You haven't told me yet what on earth you're doing here,' said Mike. 'I thought you were going to the 'Varsity. Why the dickens are you in a bank? Your pater hasn't lost his money, has he?'

'No. There is still a tolerable supply of doubloons in the old oak chest. Mine is a painful story.'

'It always is,' said Mike.

'You are very right, Comrade Jackson. I am the victim of Fate. Ah, so you put the little chaps in there, do you?' he said, as Mike, reaching the post-office, began to bundle the letters into the box. 'You seem to have grasped your duties with admirable promptitude. It is the same with me. I fancy we are both born men of Commerce. In a few years we shall be pinching Comrade Bickersdyke's job. And talking of Comrade B. brings me back to my painful story. But I shall never have time to tell it to you during our walk back. Let us drift aside into this tea-shop. We can order a buckwheat cake or a butter-nut, or something equally succulent, and carefully refraining from consuming these dainties, I will tell you all.'

'Right O!' said Mike.

'When last I saw you,' resumed Psmith, hanging Mike's basket on the hat-stand and ordering two portions of porridge, 'you may remember that a serious crisis in my affairs had arrived. My father inflamed with the idea of Commerce had invited Comrade Bickersdyke —'

'When did you know he was a manager here?' asked Mike.

'At an early date. I have my spies everywhere. However, my pater invited Comrade Bickersdyke to our house for the weekend. Things turned out rather unfortunately. Comrade B. resented my purely altruistic efforts to improve him mentally and morally. Indeed, on one occasion he went so far as to call me an impudent young cub, and to add that he wished he had me under him in his bank, where, he asserted, he would knock some of the nonsense out of me. All very painful. I tell you, Comrade Jackson, for the moment it reduced my delicately vibrating ganglions to a mere frazzle. Recovering myself, I made a few blithe remarks, and we then parted. I cannot say that we parted friends, but at any rate I bore him no ill-will. I was still determined to make him a credit to me. My feelings towards him were those of some kindly father to his prodigal son. But he, if I may say so, was fairly on the hop. And when my pater, after dinner the same night, played into his hands by mentioning that he thought I ought to plunge into a career of commerce, Comrade B. was, I gather, all over him. Offered to make a vacancy for me in the bank, and to take me on at once. My pater, feeling that this was the real hustle which he admired so much, had me in, stated his case, and said, in effect, "How do we go?" I intimated that Comrade Bickersdyke was my greatest chum on earth. So the thing was fixed up and here I am. But you are not getting on with your porridge, Comrade Jackson. Perhaps you don't care for porridge? Would you like a finnan haddock, instead? Or a piece of shortbread? You have only to say the word.'

'It seems to me,' said Mike gloomily, 'that we are in for a pretty rotten time of it in this bally bank. If Bickersdyke's got his knife into us, he can make it jolly warm for us. He's got his knife into me all right about that walking-across-the-screen business.'

'True,' said Psmith, 'to a certain extent. It is an undoubted fact that Comrade Bickersdyke will have a jolly good try at making life a nuisance to us; but, on the other hand, I propose, so far as in me lies, to make things moderately unrestful for him, here and there.'

'But you can't,' objected Mike. 'What I mean to say is, it isn't like a school. If you wanted to score off a master at school, you could always rag and so on. But here you can't. How can you rag a man who's sitting all day in a room of his own while you're sweating away at a desk at the other end of the building?'

'You put the case with admirable clearness, Comrade Jackson,' said Psmith approvingly. 'At the hard-headed, common-sense business you sneak the biscuit every time with ridiculous ease. But you do not know all. I do not propose to do a thing in the bank except work. I shall be a model as far as work goes. I shall be flawless. I shall bound to do Comrade Rossiter's bidding like a highly trained performing dog. It is outside the bank, when I have staggered away dazed with toil, that I shall resume my attention to the education of Comrade Bickersdyke.'

'But, dash it all, how can you? You won't see him. He'll go off home, or to his club, or —'

Psmith tapped him earnestly on the chest.

'There, Comrade Jackson,' he said, 'you have hit the bull's-eye, rung the bell, and gathered in the cigar or cocoanut according to choice. He *will* go off to his club. And I shall do precisely the same.'

'How do you mean?'

'It is this way. My father, as you may have noticed during your stay at our stately home of England, is a man of a warm, impulsive character. He does not always do things as other people would do them. He has his own methods. Thus, he has sent me into the City to do the hard-working, bank-clerk act, but at the same time he is allowing me just as large an allowance as he would have given me if I had gone to the 'Varsity. Moreover, while I was still at Eton he put my name up for his clubs, the Senior Conservative among others. My pater belongs to four clubs altogether, and in course of time, when my name comes up for election, I shall do the same. Meanwhile, I belong to one, the Senior Conservative. It is a bigger club than the others, and your name comes up for election sooner. About the middle of last month a great yell of joy made the West End of London shake like a jelly. The three thousand members of the Senior Conservative had just learned that I had been elected.'

Psmith paused, and ate some porridge.

'I wonder why they call this porridge,' he observed with mild interest. 'It would be far more manly and straightforward of them to give it its real name. To resume. I have gleaned, from casual chit-chat with my father, that Comrade Bickersdyke also infests the Senior Conservative. You might think that that would make me, seeing how particular I am about whom I mix with, avoid the club. Error. I shall go there every day. If Comrade Bickersdyke wishes to emend any little traits in my character of which he may disapprove, he shall never say that I did not give him the opportunity. I shall mix freely with Comrade Bickersdyke at the Senior Conservative Club. I shall be his constant companion. I shall, in short, haunt the man. By these strenuous means I shall, as it were, get a bit of my own back. And now,' said Psmith, rising, 'it might be as well, perhaps, to return to the bank and resume our commercial duties. I don't know how long you are supposed to be allowed for your little trips to and from the post-office, but, seeing that the distance is about thirty yards, I should say at a venture not more than half an hour. Which is exactly the space of time which has flitted by since we started out on this important expedition. Your devotion to porridge, Comrade Jackson, has led to our spending about twenty-five minutes in this hostelry.'

'Great Scott,' said Mike, 'there'll be a row.'

'Some slight temporary breeze, perhaps,' said Psmith. 'Annoying to men of culture and refinement, but not lasting. My only fear is lest we may have worried Comrade Rossiter at all. I regard Comrade Rossiter as an elder brother, and would not cause him a moment's heart-burning for worlds. However, we shall soon know,' he added, as they passed into the bank and walked up the aisle, 'for there is Comrade Rossiter waiting to receive us in person.'

The little head of the Postage Department was moving restlessly about in the neighbourhood of Psmith's and Mike's desk.

'Am I mistaken,' said Psmith to Mike, 'or is there the merest suspicion of a worried look on our chief's face? It seems to me that there is the slightest soupcon of shadow about that broad, calm brow.'

7. Going into Winter Quarters

There was.

Mr Rossiter had discovered Psmith's and Mike's absence about five minutes after they had left the building. Ever since then, he had been popping out of his lair at intervals of three minutes, to see whether they had returned. Constant disappointment in this respect had rendered him decidedly jumpy. When Psmith and Mike reached the desk, he was a kind of human soda-water bottle. He fizzed over with questions, reproofs, and warnings.

'What does it mean? What does it mean?' he cried. 'Where have you been? Where have you been?'

'Poetry,' said Psmith approvingly.

'You have been absent from your places for over half an hour. Why? Why? Why? Where have you been? Where have you been? I cannot have this. It is preposterous. Where have you been? Suppose Mr Bickersdyke had happened to come round here. I should not have known what to say to him.'

'Never an easy man to chat with, Comrade Bickersdyke,' agreed Psmith.

'You must thoroughly understand that you are expected to remain in your places during business hours.'

'Of course,' said Psmith, 'that makes it a little hard for Comrade Jackson to post letters, does it not?'

'Have you been posting letters?'

'We have,' said Psmith. 'You have wronged us. Seeing our absent places you jumped rashly to the conclusion that we were merely gadding about in pursuit of pleasure. Error. All the while we were furthering the bank's best interests by posting letters.'

'You had no business to leave your place. Jackson is on the posting desk.'

'You are very right,' said Psmith, 'and it shall not occur again. It was only because it was the first day, Comrade Jackson is not used to the stir and bustle of the City. His nerve failed him. He shrank from going to the post-office alone. So I volunteered to accompany him. And,' concluded Psmith, impressively, 'we won safely through. Every letter has been posted.'

'That need not have taken you half an hour.'

'True. And the actual work did not. It was carried through swiftly and surely. But the nerve-strain had left us shaken. Before resuming our more ordinary duties we had to refresh. A brief breathing-space, a little coffee and porridge, and here we are, fit for work once more.'

'If it occurs again, I shall report the matter to Mr Bickersdyke.'

'And rightly so,' said Psmith, earnestly. 'Quite rightly so. Discipline, discipline. That is the cry. There must be no shirking of painful duties. Sentiment must play no part in business. Rossiter, the man, may sympathise, but Rossiter, the Departmental head, must be adamant.'

Mr Rossiter pondered over this for a moment, then went off on a side-issue.

'What is the meaning of this foolery?' he asked, pointing to Psmith's gloves and hat. 'Suppose Mr Bickersdyke had come round and seen them, what should I have said?'

'You would have given him a message of cheer. You would have said, "All is well. Psmith has not left us. He will come back. And Comrade Bickersdyke, relieved, would have —"'

'You do not seem very busy, Mr Smith.'

Both Psmith and Mr Rossiter were startled.

Mr Rossiter jumped as if somebody had run a gimlet into him, and even Psmith started slightly. They had not heard Mr Bickersdyke approaching. Mike, who had been stolidly entering addresses in his ledger during the latter part of the conversation, was also taken by surprise.

Psmith was the first to recover. Mr Rossiter was still too confused for speech, but Psmith took the situation in hand.

'Apparently no,' he said, swiftly removing his hat from the ruler. 'In reality, yes. Mr Rossiter and I were just scheming out a line of work for me as you came up. If you had arrived a moment later, you would have found me toiling.'

'H'm. I hope I should. We do not encourage idling in this bank.'

'Assuredly not,' said Psmith warmly. 'Most assuredly not. I would not have it otherwise. I am a worker. A bee, not a drone. A *Lusitania,* not a limpet. Perhaps I have not yet that grip on my duties which I shall soon acquire; but it is coming. It is coming. I see daylight.'

'H'm. I have only your word for it.' He turned to Mr Rossiter, who had now recovered himself, and was as nearly calm as it was in his nature to be. 'Do you find Mr Smith's work satisfactory, Mr Rossiter?'

Psmith waited resignedly for an outburst of complaint respecting the small matter that had been under discussion between the head of the department and himself; but to his surprise it did not come.

'Oh-ah-quite, quite, Mr Bickersdyke. I think he will very soon pick things up.'

Mr Bickersdyke turned away. He was a conscientious bank manager, and one can only suppose that Mr Rossiter's tribute to the earnestness of one of his *employes* was gratifying to him. But for that, one would have said that he was disappointed.

'Oh, Mr Bickersdyke,' said Psmith.

The manager stopped.

'Father sent his kind regards to you,' said Psmith benevolently.

Mr Bickersdyke walked off without comment.

'An uncommonly cheery, companionable feller,' murmured Psmith, as he turned to his work.

The first day anywhere, if one spends it in a sedentary fashion, always seemed unending; and Mike felt as if he had been sitting at his desk for weeks when the hour for departure came. A bank's day ends gradually, reluctantly, as it were. At about five there is a sort of stir, not unlike the stir in a theatre when the curtain is on the point of falling. Ledgers are closed with a bang. Men stand about and talk for a moment or two before going to the basement for their hats and coats. Then, at irregular intervals, forms pass down the central aisle and out through the swing doors. There is an air of relaxation over the place, though some departments are still working as hard as ever under a blaze of electric light. Somebody begins to sing, and an instant chorus of protests and maledictions rises from all sides. Gradually, however, the electric lights go out. The procession down the centre aisle becomes more regular; and eventually the place is left to darkness and the night watchman.

The postage department was one of the last to be freed from duty. This was due to the inconsiderateness of the other departments, which omitted to disgorge their letters till the last moment. Mike as he grew familiar with the work, and began to understand it, used to prowl round the other departments during the afternoon and wrest letters from them, usually receiving with them much abuse for being a nuisance and not leaving honest workers alone. Today, however, he had to sit on till nearly six, waiting for the final batch of correspondence.

Psmith, who had waited patiently with him, though his own work was finished, accompanied him down to the post office and back again to the bank to return the letter basket; and they left the office together.

'By the way,' said Psmith, 'what with the strenuous labours of the bank and the disturbing interviews with the powers that be, I have omitted to ask you where you are digging. Wherever it is, of course you must clear out. It is imperative, in this crisis, that we should be together. I have acquired a quite snug little flat in Clement's Inn. There is a spare bedroom. It shall be yours.'

'My dear chap,' said Mike, 'it's all rot. I can't sponge on you.'

'You pain me, Comrade Jackson. I was not suggesting such a thing. We are business men, hard-headed young bankers. I make you a business proposition. I offer you the post of confidential secretary and adviser to me in exchange for a comfortable home. The duties will be light. You will be required to refuse invitations to dinner from crowned heads, and to listen attentively to my views on Life. Apart from this, there is little to do. So that's settled.'

'It isn't,' said Mike. 'I —'

'You will enter upon your duties tonight. Where are you suspended at present?'

'Dulwich. But, look here —'

'A little more, and you'll get the sack. I tell you the thing is settled. Now, let us hail yon taximeter cab, and desire the stern-faced aristocrat on the box to drive us to Dulwich. We will then collect a few of your things in a bag, have the rest off by train, come back in the taxi, and go and bite a chop at the Carlton. This is a momentous day in our careers, Comrade Jackson. We must buoy ourselves up.'

Mike made no further objections. The thought of that bed-sitting room in Acacia Road and the pantomime dame rose up and killed them. After all, Psmith was not like any ordinary person. There would be no question of charity. Psmith had invited him to the flat in exactly the same spirit as he had invited him to his house for the cricket week.

'You know,' said Psmith, after a silence, as they flitted through the streets in the taximeter, 'one lives and learns. Were you so wrapped up in your work this afternoon that you did not hear my very entertaining little chat with Comrade Bickersdyke, or did it happen to come under your notice? It did? Then I wonder if you were struck by the singular conduct of Comrade Rossiter?'

'I thought it rather decent of him not to give you away to that blighter Bickersdyke.'

'Admirably put. It was precisely that that struck me. He had his opening, all ready made for him, but he refrained from depositing me in the soup. I tell you, Comrade Jackson, my rugged old heart was touched. I said to myself, "There must be good in Comrade Rossiter, after all. I must cultivate him." I shall make it my business to be kind to our Departmental head. He deserves the utmost consideration. His action shone like a good deed in a wicked world. Which it was, of course. From today onwards I take Comrade Rossiter under my wing. We seem to be getting into a tolerably benighted quarter. Are we anywhere near? "Through Darkest Dulwich in a Taximeter."'

The cab arrived at Dulwich station, and Mike stood up to direct the driver. They whirred down Acacia Road. Mike stopped the cab and got out. A brief and somewhat embarrassing interview with the pantomime dame, during which Mike was separated from a week's rent in lieu of notice, and he was in the cab again, bound for Clement's Inn.

His feelings that night differed considerably from the frame of mind in which he had gone to bed the night before. It was partly a very excellent dinner and partly the fact that Psmith's flat, though at present in some disorder, was obviously going to be extremely comfortable, that worked the change. But principally it was due to his having found an ally. The gnawing loneliness had gone. He did not look forward to a career of Commerce with any greater pleasure than before; but there was no doubt that with Psmith, it would be easier to get through the time after office hours. If all went well in the bank he might find that he had not drawn such a bad ticket after all.

8. The Friendly Native

'The first principle of warfare,' said Psmith at breakfast next morning, doling out bacon and eggs with the air of a medieval monarch distributing largesse, 'is to collect a gang, to rope in allies, to secure the cooperation of some friendly native. You may remember that at Sedleigh it was partly the sympathetic cooperation of that record blitherer, Comrade Jellicoe, which enabled us to nip the pro-Spiller movement in the bud. It is the same in the present crisis. What Comrade Jellicoe was to us at Sedleigh, Comrade Rossiter must be in the City. We must make an ally of that man. Once I know that he and I are as brothers, and that he will look with a lenient and benevolent eye on any little shortcomings in my work, I shall be able to devote my attention whole-heartedly to the moral reformation of Comrade Bickersdyke, that man of blood. I look on Comrade Bickersdyke as a bargee of the most pronounced type; and anything I can do towards making him a decent member of Society shall be done freely and ungrudgingly. A trifle more tea, Comrade Jackson?'

'No, thanks,' said Mike. 'I've done. By Jove, Smith, this flat of yours is all right.'

'Not bad,' assented Psmith, 'not bad. Free from squalor to a great extent. I have a number of little objects of *vertu* coming down shortly from the old homestead. Pictures, and so on. It will be by no means un-snug when they are up. Meanwhile, I can rough it. We are old campaigners, we Psmiths. Give us a roof, a few comfortable chairs, a sofa or two, half a dozen cushions, and decent meals, and we do not repine. Reverting once more to Comrade Rossiter —'

'Yes, what about him?' said Mike. 'You'll have a pretty tough job turning him into a friendly native, I should think. How do you mean to start?'

Psmith regarded him with a benevolent eye.

'There is but one way,' he said. 'Do you remember the case of Comrade Outwood, at Sedleigh? How did we corral him, and become to him practically as long-lost sons?'

'We got round him by joining the Archaeological Society.'

'Precisely,' said Psmith. 'Every man has his hobby. The thing is to find it out. In the case of comrade Rossiter, I should say that it would be either postage stamps, dried seaweed, or Hall Caine. I shall endeavour to find out today. A few casual questions, and the thing is done. Shall we be putting in an appearance at the busy hive now? If we are to continue in the running for the bonus stakes, it would be well to start soon.'

Mike's first duty at the bank that morning was to check the stamps and petty cash. While he was engaged on this task, he heard Psmith conversing affably with Mr Rossiter.

'Good morning,' said Psmith.

'Morning,' replied his chief, doing sleight-of-hand tricks with a bundle of letters which lay on his desk. 'Get on with your work, Psmith. We have a lot before us.'

'Undoubtedly. I am all impatience. I should say that in an institution like this, dealing as it does with distant portions of the globe, a philatelist would have excellent opportunities of increasing his collection. With me, stamp-collecting has always been a positive craze. I —'

'I have no time for nonsense of that sort myself,' said Mr Rossiter. 'I should advise you, if you mean to get on, to devote more time to your work and less to stamps.'

'I will start at once. Dried seaweed, again —'

'Get on with your work, Smith.'

Psmith retired to his desk.

'This,' he said to Mike, 'is undoubtedly something in the nature of a set-back. I have drawn blank. The papers bring out posters, "Psmith Baffled." I must try again. Meanwhile, to work. Work, the hobby of the philosopher and the poor man's friend.'

The morning dragged slowly on without incident. At twelve o'clock Mike had to go out and buy stamps, which he subsequently punched in the punching-machine in the basement, a not very exhilarating job in which he was assisted by one of the bank messengers, who discoursed learnedly on roses during the *seance*. Roses were his hobby. Mike began to see that Psmith had reason in his assumption that the way to every man's heart was through his hobby. Mike made

352

a firm friend of William, the messenger, by displaying an interest and a certain knowledge of roses. At the same time the conversation had the bad effect of leading to an acute relapse in the matter of homesickness. The rose-garden at home had been one of Mike's favourite haunts on a summer afternoon. The contrast between it and the basement of the new Asiatic Bank, the atmosphere of which was far from being roselike, was too much for his feelings. He emerged from the depths, with his punched stamps, filled with bitterness against Fate.

He found Psmith still baffled.

'Hall Caine,' said Psmith regretfully, 'has also proved a frost. I wandered round to Comrade Rossiter's desk just now with a rather brainy excursus on "The Eternal City", and was received with the Impatient Frown rather than the Glad Eye. He was in the middle of adding up a rather tricky column of figures, and my remarks caused him to drop a stitch. So far from winning the man over, I have gone back. There now exists between Comrade Rossiter and myself a certain coldness. Further investigations will be postponed till after lunch.'

The postage department received visitors during the morning. Members of other departments came with letters, among them Bannister. Mr Rossiter was away in the manager's room at the time.

'How are you getting on?' said Bannister to Mike.

'Oh, all right,' said Mike.

'Had any trouble with Rossiter yet?'

'No, not much.'

'He hasn't run you in to Bickersdyke?'

'No.'

'Pardon my interrupting a conversation between old college chums,' said Psmith courteously, 'but I happened to overhear, as I toiled at my desk, the name of Comrade Rossiter.'

Bannister looked somewhat startled. Mike introduced them.

'This is Smith,' he said. 'Chap I was at school with. This is Bannister, Smith, who used to be on here till I came.'

'In this department?' asked Psmith.

'Yes.'

'Then, Comrade Bannister, you are the very man I have been looking for. Your knowledge will be invaluable to us. I have no doubt that, during your stay in this excellently managed department, you had many opportunities of observing Comrade Rossiter?'

'I should jolly well think I had,' said Bannister with a laugh. 'He saw to that. He was always popping out and cursing me about something.'

'Comrade Rossiter's manners are a little restive,' agreed Psmith. 'What used you to talk to him about?'

'What used I to talk to him about?'

'Exactly. In those interviews to which you have alluded, how did you amuse, entertain Comrade Rossiter?'

'I didn't. He used to do all the talking there was.'

Psmith straightened his tie, and clicked his tongue, disappointed.

'This is unfortunate,' he said, smoothing his hair. 'You see, Comrade Bannister, it is this way. In the course of my professional duties, I find myself continually coming into contact with Comrade Rossiter.'

'I bet you do,' said Bannister.

'On these occasions I am frequently at a loss for entertaining conversation. He has no difficulty, as apparently happened in your case, in keeping up his end of the dialogue. The subject of my shortcomings provides him with ample material for speech. I, on the other hand, am dumb. I have nothing to say.'

'I should think that was a bit of a change for you, wasn't it?'

'Perhaps, so,' said Psmith, 'perhaps so. On the other hand, however restful it may be to myself, it does not enable me to secure Comrade Rossiter's interest and win his esteem.'

'What Smith wants to know,' said Mike, 'is whether Rossiter has any hobby of any kind. He thinks, if he has, he might work it to keep in with him.'

Psmith, who had been listening with an air of pleased interest, much as a father would listen to his child prattling for the benefit of a visitor, confirmed this statement.

'Comrade Jackson,' he said, 'has put the matter with his usual admirable clearness. That is the thing in a nutshell. Has Comrade Rossiter any hobby that you know of? Spillikins, brass-rubbing, the Near Eastern Question, or anything like that? I have tried him with postage-stamps (which you'd think, as head of a postage department, he ought to be interested in), and dried seaweed, Hall Caine, but I have the honour to report total failure. The man seems to have no pleasures. What does he do with himself when the day's toil is ended? That giant brain must occupy itself somehow.'

'I don't know,' said Bannister, 'unless it's football. I saw him once watching Chelsea. I was rather surprised.'

'Football,' said Psmith thoughtfully, 'football. By no means a scaly idea. I rather fancy, Comrade Bannister, that you have whanged the nail on the head. Is he strong on any particular team? I mean, have you ever heard him, in the intervals of business worries, stamping on his desk and yelling, "Buck up Cottagers!" or "Lay 'em out, Pensioners!" or anything like that? One moment.' Psmith held up his hand. 'I will get my Sherlock Holmes system to work. What was the other team in the modern gladiatorial contest at which you saw Comrade Rossiter?'

'Manchester United.'

'And Comrade Rossiter, I should say, was a Manchester man.'

'I believe he is.'

'Then I am prepared to bet a small sum that he is nuts on Manchester United. My dear Holmes, how —! Elementary, my dear fellow, quite elementary. But here comes the lad in person.'

Mr Rossiter turned in from the central aisle through the counter-door, and, observing the conversational group at the postage-desk, came bounding up. Bannister moved off.

'Really, Smith,' said Mr Rossiter, 'you always seem to be talking. I have overlooked the matter once, as I did not wish to get you into trouble so soon after joining; but, really, it cannot go on. I must take notice of it.'

Psmith held up his hand.

'The fault was mine,' he said, with manly frankness. 'Entirely mine. Bannister came in a purely professional spirit to deposit a letter with Comrade Jackson. I engaged him in conversation on the subject of the Football League, and I was just trying to correct his view that Newcastle United were the best team playing, when you arrived.'

'It is perfectly absurd,' said Mr Rossiter, 'that you should waste the bank's time in this way. The bank pays you to work, not to talk about professional football.'

'Just so, just so,' murmured Psmith.

'There is too much talking in this department.'

'I fear you are right.'

'It is nonsense.'

'My own view,' said Psmith, 'was that Manchester United were by far the finest team before the public.'

'Get on with your work, Smith.'

Mr Rossiter stumped off to his desk, where he sat as one in thought.

'Smith,' he said at the end of five minutes.

Psmith slid from his stool, and made his way deferentially towards him.

'Bannister's a fool,' snapped Mr Rossiter.

'So I thought,' said Psmith.

'A perfect fool. He always was.'

Psmith shook his head sorrowfully, as who should say, 'Exit Bannister.'

'There is no team playing today to touch Manchester United.'

'Precisely what I said to Comrade Bannister.'

'Of course. You know something about it.'

'The study of League football,' said Psmith, 'has been my relaxation for years.'

'But we have no time to discuss it now.'

'Assuredly not, sir. Work before everything.'

'Some other time, when —'

' —We are less busy. Precisely.'

Psmith moved back to his seat.

'I fear,' he said to Mike, as he resumed work, 'that as far as Comrade Rossiter's friendship and esteem are concerned, I have to a certain extent landed Comrade Bannister in the bouillon; but it was in a good cause. I fancy we have won through. Half an hour's thoughtful perusal of the "Footballers' Who's Who", just to find out some elementary facts about Manchester United, and I rather think the friendly Native is corralled. And now once more to work. Work, the hobby of the hustler and the deadbeat's dread.'

9. The Haunting of Mr Bickersdyke

Anything in the nature of a rash and hasty move was wholly foreign to Psmith's tactics. He had the patience which is the chief quality of the successful general. He was content to secure his base before making any offensive movement. It was a fortnight before he turned his attention to the education of Mr Bickersdyke. During that fortnight he conversed attractively, in the intervals of work, on the subject of League football in general and Manchester United in particular. The subject is not hard to master if one sets oneself earnestly to it; and Psmith spared no pains. The football editions of the evening papers are not reticent about those who play the game: and Psmith drank in every detail with the thoroughness of the conscientious student. By the end of the fortnight he knew what was the favourite breakfast-food of J. Turnbull; what Sandy Turnbull wore next his skin; and who, in the opinion of Meredith, was England's leading politician. These facts, imparted to and discussed with Mr Rossiter, made the progress of the *entente cordiale* rapid. It was on the eighth day that Mr Rossiter consented to lunch with the Old Etonian. On the tenth he played the host. By the end of the fortnight the flapping of the white wings of Peace over the Postage Department was setting up a positive draught. Mike, who had been introduced by Psmith as a distant relative of Moger, the goalkeeper, was included in the great peace.

'So that now,' said Psmith, reflectively polishing his eye-glass, 'I think that we may consider ourselves free to attend to Comrade Bickersdyke. Our bright little Mancunian friend would no more run us in now than if we were the brothers Turnbull. We are as inside forwards to him.'

The club to which Psmith and Mr Bickersdyke belonged was celebrated for the steadfastness of its political views, the excellence of its cuisine, and the curiously Gorgonzolaesque marble of its main staircase. It takes all sorts to make a world. It took about four thousand of all sorts to make the Senior Conservative Club. To be absolutely accurate, there were three thousand seven hundred and eighteen members.

To Mr Bickersdyke for the next week it seemed as if there was only one.

There was nothing crude or overdone about Psmith's methods. The ordinary man, having conceived the idea of haunting a fellow clubman, might have seized the first opportunity of engaging him in conversation. Not so Psmith. The first time he met Mr Bickersdyke in the club was on the stairs after dinner one night. The great man, having received practical proof of the excellence of cuisine referred to above, was coming down the main staircase at peace with all men, when he was aware of a tall young man in the 'faultless evening dress' of which the female novelist is so fond, who was regarding him with a fixed stare through an eye-glass. The tall young man, having caught his eye, smiled faintly, nodded in a friendly but patronizing manner, and passed on up the staircase to the library. Mr Bickersdyke sped on in search of a waiter.

As Psmith sat in the library with a novel, the waiter entered, and approached him.

'Beg pardon, sir,' he said. 'Are you a member of this club?'

Psmith fumbled in his pocket and produced his eye-glass, through which he examined the waiter, button by button.

'I am Psmith,' he said simply.

'A member, sir?'

'*The* member,' said Psmith. 'Surely you participated in the general rejoicings which ensued when it was announced that I had been elected? But perhaps you were too busy working to pay any attention. If so, I respect you. I also am a worker. A toiler, not a flatfish. A sizzler, not a squab. Yes, I am a member. Will you tell Mr Bickersdyke that I am sorry, but I have been elected, and have paid my entrance fee and subscription.'

'Thank you, sir.'

The waiter went downstairs and found Mr Bickersdyke in the lower smoking-room.

'The gentleman says he is, sir.'

'H'm,' said the bank-manager. 'Coffee and Benedictine, and a cigar.'

'Yes, sir.'

On the following day Mr Bickersdyke met Psmith in the club three times, and on the day after that seven. Each time the latter's smile was friendly, but patronizing. Mr Bickersdyke began to grow restless.

On the fourth day Psmith made his first remark. The manager was reading the evening paper in a corner, when Psmith sinking gracefully into a chair beside him, caused him to look up.

'The rain keeps off,' said Psmith.

Mr Bickersdyke looked as if he wished his employee would imitate the rain, but he made no reply.

Psmith called a waiter.

'Would you mind bringing me a small cup of coffee?' he said. 'And for you,' he added to Mr Bickersdyke.

'Nothing,' growled the manager.

'And nothing for Mr Bickersdyke.'

The waiter retired. Mr Bickersdyke became absorbed in his paper.

'I see from my morning paper,' said Psmith, affably, 'that you are to address a meeting at the Kenningford Town Hall next week. I shall come and hear you. Our politics differ in some respects, I fear—I incline to the Socialist view-but nevertheless I shall listen to your remarks with great interest, great interest.'

The paper rustled, but no reply came from behind it.

'I heard from father this morning,' resumed Psmith.

Mr Bickersdyke lowered his paper and glared at him.

'I don't wish to hear about your father,' he snapped.

An expression of surprise and pain came over Psmith's face.

'What!' he cried. 'You don't mean to say that there is any coolness between my father and you? I am more grieved than I can say. Knowing, as I do, what a genuine respect my father has for your great talents, I can only think that there must have been some misunderstanding. Perhaps if you would allow me to act as a mediator —'

Mr Bickersdyke put down his paper and walked out of the room.

Psmith found him a quarter of an hour later in the card-room. He sat down beside his table, and began to observe the play with silent interest. Mr Bickersdyke, never a great performer at the best of times, was so unsettled by the scrutiny that in the deciding game of the rubber he revoked, thereby presenting his opponents with the rubber by a very handsome majority of points. Psmith clicked his tongue sympathetically.

Dignified reticence is not a leading characteristic of the bridge-player's manner at the Senior Conservative Club on occasions like this. Mr Bickersdyke's partner did not bear his calamity with manly resignation. He gave tongue on the instant. 'What on earth's', and 'Why on earth's' flowed from his mouth like molten lava. Mr Bickersdyke sat and fermented in silence. Psmith clicked his tongue sympathetically throughout.

Mr Bickersdyke lost that control over himself which every member of a club should possess. He turned on Psmith with a snort of frenzy.

'How can I keep my attention fixed on the game when you sit staring at me like a —like a —'

'I am sorry,' said Psmith gravely, 'if my stare falls short in any way of your ideal of what a stare should be; but I appeal to these gentlemen. Could I have watched the game more quietly?'

'Of course not,' said the bereaved partner warmly. 'Nobody could have any earthly objection to your behaviour. It was absolute carelessness. I should have thought that one might have expected one's partner at a club like this to exercise elementary —'

But Mr Bickersdyke had gone. He had melted silently away like the driven snow.

Psmith took his place at the table.

'A somewhat nervous excitable man, Mr Bickersdyke, I should say,' he observed.

'A somewhat dashed, blanked idiot,' emended the bank-manager's late partner. 'Thank goodness he lost as much as I did. That's some light consolation.'

Psmith arrived at the flat to find Mike still out. Mike had repaired to the Gaiety earlier in the evening to refresh his mind after the labours of the day. When he returned, Psmith was sitting in an armchair with his feet on the mantelpiece, musing placidly on Life.

'Well?' said Mike.

'Well? And how was the Gaiety? Good show?'

'Jolly good. What about Bickersdyke?'

Psmith looked sad.

'I cannot make Comrade Bickersdyke out,' he said. 'You would think that a man would be glad to see the son of a personal friend. On the contrary, I may be wronging Comrade B., but I should almost be inclined to say that my presence in the Senior Conservative Club tonight irritated him. There was no *bonhomie* in his manner. He seemed to me to be giving a spirited imitation of a man about to foam at the mouth. I did my best to entertain him. I chatted. His only reply was to leave the room. I followed him to the card-room, and watched his very remarkable and brainy tactics at bridge, and he accused me of causing him to revoke. A very curious personality, that of Comrade Bickersdyke. But let us dismiss him from our minds. Rumours have reached me,' said Psmith, 'that a very decent little supper may be obtained at a quaint, old-world eating-house called the Savoy. Will you accompany me thither on a tissue-restoring expedition? It would be rash not to probe these rumours to their foundation, and ascertain their exact truth.'

10. Mr Bickersdyke Addresses His Constituents

It was noted by the observant at the bank next morning that Mr Bickersdyke had something on his mind. William, the messenger, knew it, when he found his respectful salute ignored. Little Briggs, the accountant, knew it when his obsequious but cheerful 'Good morning' was acknowledged only by a 'Morn" which was almost an oath. Mr Bickersdyke passed up the aisle and into his room like an east wind. He sat down at his table and pressed the bell. Harold, William's brother and co-messenger, entered with the air of one ready to duck if any missile should be thrown at him. The reports of the manager's frame of mind had been circulated in the office, and Harold felt somewhat apprehensive. It was on an occasion very similar to this that George Barstead, formerly in the employ of the New Asiatic Bank in the capacity of messenger, had been rash enough to laugh at what he had taken for a joke of Mr Bickersdyke's, and had been instantly presented with the sack for gross impertinence.

'Ask Mr Smith—' began the manager. Then he paused. 'No, never mind,' he added.

Harold remained in the doorway, puzzled.

'Don't stand there gaping at me, man,' cried Mr Bickersdyke, 'Go away.'

Harold retired and informed his brother, William, that in his, Harold's, opinion, Mr Bickersdyke was off his chump.

'Off his onion,' said William, soaring a trifle higher in poetic imagery.

'Barmy,' was the terse verdict of Samuel Jakes, the third messenger. 'Always said so.' And with that the New Asiatic Bank staff of messengers dismissed Mr Bickersdyke and proceeded to concentrate themselves on their duties, which consisted principally of hanging about and discussing the prophecies of that modern seer, Captain Coe.

What had made Mr Bickersdyke change his mind so abruptly was the sudden realization of the fact that he had no case against Psmith. In his capacity of manager of the bank he could not take official notice of Psmith's behaviour outside office hours, especially as Psmith had done nothing but stare at him. It would be impossible to make anybody understand the true inwardness of Psmith's stare. Theoretically, Mr Bickersdyke had the power to dismiss any subordinate of his whom he did not consider satisfactory, but it was a power that had to be exercised with discretion. The manager was accountable for his actions to the Board of Directors. If he dismissed Psmith, Psmith would certainly bring an action against the bank for wrongful dismissal, and on the evidence he would infallibly win it. Mr Bickersdyke did not welcome the prospect of having to explain to the Directors that he had let the shareholders of the bank in for a fine of whatever a discriminating jury cared to decide upon, simply because he had been stared at while playing bridge. His only hope was to catch Psmith doing his work badly.

He touched the bell again, and sent for Mr Rossiter.

The messenger found the head of the Postage Department in conversation with Psmith. Manchester United had been beaten by one goal to nil on the previous afternoon, and Psmith was informing Mr Rossiter that the referee was a robber, who had evidently been financially interested in the result of the game. The way he himself looked at it, said Psmith, was that the thing had been a moral victory for the United. Mr Rossiter said yes, he thought so too. And it was at this moment that Mr Bickersdyke sent for him to ask whether Psmith's work was satisfactory.

The head of the Postage Department gave his opinion without hesitation. Psmith's work was about the hottest proposition he had ever struck. Psmith's work-well, it stood alone. You couldn't compare it with anything. There are no degrees in perfection. Psmith's work was perfect, and there was an end to it.

He put it differently, but that was the gist of what he said.

Mr Bickersdyke observed he was glad to hear it, and smashed a nib by stabbing the desk with it.

It was on the evening following this that the bank-manager was due to address a meeting at the Kenningford Town Hall.

He was looking forward to the event with mixed feelings. He had stood for Parliament once before, several years back, in the North. He had been defeated by a couple of thousand votes, and he hoped that the episode had been forgotten. Not merely because his defeat had been heavy. There was another reason. On that occasion he had stood as a Liberal. He was standing for Kenningford as a Unionist. Of course, a man is at perfect liberty to change his views, if he wishes to do so, but the process is apt to give his opponents a chance of catching him (to use the inspired language of the music-halls) on the bend. Mr Bickersdyke was rather afraid that the light-hearted electors of Kenningford might avail themselves of this chance.

Kenningford, S.E., is undoubtedly by way of being a tough sort of place. Its inhabitants incline to a robust type of humour, which finds a verbal vent in catch phrases and expends itself physically in smashing shop-windows and kicking policemen. He feared that the meeting at the Town Hall might possibly be a trifle rowdy.

All political meetings are very much alike. Somebody gets up and introduces the speaker of the evening, and then the speaker of the evening says at great length what he thinks of the scandalous manner in which the Government is behaving or the iniquitous goings-on of the Opposition. From time to time confederates in the audience rise and ask carefully rehearsed questions, and are answered fully and satisfactorily by the orator. When a genuine heckler interrupts, the orator either ignores him, or says haughtily that he can find him arguments but cannot find him brains. Or, occasionally, when the question is an easy one, he answers it. A quietly conducted political meeting is one of England's most delightful indoor games. When the meeting is rowdy, the audience has more fun, but the speaker a good deal less.

Mr Bickersdyke's introducer was an elderly Scotch peer, an excellent man for the purpose in every respect, except that he possessed a very strong accent.

The audience welcomed that accent uproariously. The electors of Kenningford who really had any definite opinions on politics were fairly equally divided. There were about as many earnest Liberals as there were earnest Unionists. But besides these there was a strong contingent who did not care which side won. These looked on elections as Heaven-sent opportunities for making a great deal of noise. They attended meetings in order to extract amusement from them; and they voted, if they voted at all, quite irresponsibly. A funny story at the expense of one candidate told on the morning of the polling, was quite likely to send these brave fellows off in dozens filling in their papers for the victim's opponent.

There was a solid block of these gay spirits at the back of the hall. They received the Scotch peer with huge delight. He reminded them of Harry Lauder and they said so. They addressed him affectionately as 'Arry', throughout his speech, which was rather long. They implored him to be a pal and sing 'The Saftest of the Family'. Or, failing that, 'I love a lassie'. Finding they could not induce him to do this, they did it themselves. They sang it several times. When the peer, having finished his remarks on the subject of Mr Bickersdyke, at length sat down, they cheered for seven minutes, and demanded an encore.

The meeting was in excellent spirits when Mr Bickersdyke rose to address it.

The effort of doing justice to the last speaker had left the free and independent electors at the back of the hall slightly limp. The bank-manager's opening remarks were received without any demonstration.

Mr Bickersdyke spoke well. He had a penetrating, if harsh, voice, and he said what he had to say forcibly. Little by little the audience came under his spell. When, at the end of a well-turned sentence, he paused and took a sip of water, there was a round of applause, in which many of the admirers of Mr Harry Lauder joined.

He resumed his speech. The audience listened intently. Mr Bickersdyke, having said some nasty things about Free Trade and the Alien Immigrant, turned to the Needs of the Navy and the necessity of increasing the fleet at all costs.

'This is no time for half-measures,' he said. 'We must do our utmost. We must burn our boats —'

'Excuse me,' said a gentle voice.

Mr Bickersdyke broke off. In the centre of the hall a tall figure had risen. Mr Bickersdyke found himself looking at a gleaming eye-glass which the speaker had just polished and inserted in his eye.

The ordinary heckler Mr Bickersdyke would have taken in his stride. He had got his audience, and simply by continuing and ignoring the interruption, he could have won through in safety. But the sudden appearance of Psmith unnerved him. He remained silent.

'How,' asked Psmith, 'do you propose to strengthen the Navy by burning boats?'

The inanity of the question enraged even the pleasure-seekers at the back.

'Order! Order!' cried the earnest contingent.

'Sit down, fice!' roared the pleasure-seekers.

Psmith sat down with a patient smile.

Mr Bickersdyke resumed his speech. But the fire had gone out of it. He had lost his audience. A moment before, he had grasped them and played on their minds (or what passed for minds down Kenningford way) as on a stringed instrument. Now he had lost his hold.

He spoke on rapidly, but he could not get into his stride. The trivial interruption had broken the spell. His words lacked grip. The dead silence in which the first part of his speech had been received, that silence which is a greater tribute to the speaker than any applause, had given place to a restless medley of little noises; here a cough; there a scraping of a boot along the floor, as its wearer moved uneasily in his seat; in another place a whispered conversation. The audience was bored.

Mr Bickersdyke left the Navy, and went on to more general topics. But he was not interesting. He quoted figures, saw a moment later that he had not quoted them accurately, and instead of carrying on boldly, went back and corrected himself.

'Gow up top!' said a voice at the back of the hall, and there was a general laugh.

Mr Bickersdyke galloped unsteadily on. He condemned the Government. He said they had betrayed their trust.

And then he told an anecdote.

'The Government, gentlemen,' he said, 'achieves nothing worth achieving, and every individual member of the Government takes all the credit for what is done to himself. Their methods remind me, gentlemen, of an amusing experience I had while fishing one summer in the Lake District.'

In a volume entitled 'Three Men in a Boat' there is a story of how the author and a friend go into a riverside inn and see a very large trout in a glass case. They make inquiries about it, have men assure them, one by one, that the trout was caught by themselves. In the end the trout turns out to be made of plaster of Paris.

Mr Bickersdyke told that story as an experience of his own while fishing one summer in the Lake District.

It went well. The meeting was amused. Mr Bickersdyke went on to draw a trenchant comparison between the lack of genuine merit in the trout and the lack of genuine merit in the achievements of His Majesty's Government.

There was applause.

When it had ceased, Psmith rose to his feet again.

'Excuse me,' he said.

11. Misunderstood

Mike had refused to accompany Psmith to the meeting that evening, saying that he got too many chances in the ordinary way of business of hearing Mr Bickersdyke speak, without going out of his way to make more. So Psmith had gone off to Kenningford alone, and Mike, feeling too lazy to sally out to any place of entertainment, had remained at the flat with a novel.

He was deep in this, when there was the sound of a key in the latch, and shortly afterwards Psmith entered the room. On Psmith's brow there was a look of pensive care, and also a slight discoloration. When he removed his overcoat, Mike saw that his collar was burst and hanging loose and that he had no tie. On his erstwhile speckless and gleaming shirt front were number of finger-impressions, of a boldness and clearness of outline which would have made a Bertillon expert leap with joy.

'Hullo!' said Mike dropping his book.

Psmith nodded in silence, went to his bedroom, and returned with a looking-glass. Propping this up on a table, he proceeded to examine himself with the utmost care. He shuddered slightly as his eye fell on the finger-marks; and without a word he went into his bathroom again. He emerged after an interval of ten minutes in sky-blue pyjamas, slippers, and an Old Etonian blazer. He lit a cigarette; and, sitting down, stared pensively into the fire.

'What the dickens have you been playing at?' demanded Mike.

Psmith heaved a sigh.

'That,' he replied, 'I could not say precisely. At one moment it seemed to be Rugby football, at another a jiu-jitsu *seance*. Later, it bore a resemblance to a pantomime rally. However, whatever it was, it was all very bright and interesting. A distinct experience.'

'Have you been scrapping?' asked Mike. 'What happened? Was there a row?'

'There was,' said Psmith, 'in a measure what might be described as a row. At least, when you find a perfect stranger attaching himself to your collar and pulling, you begin to suspect that something of that kind is on the bill.'

'Did they do that?'

Psmith nodded.

'A merchant in a moth-eaten bowler started warbling to a certain extent with me. It was all very trying for a man of culture. He was a man who had, I should say, discovered that alcohol was a food long before the doctors found it out. A good chap, possibly, but a little boisterous in his manner. Well, well.'

Psmith shook his head sadly.

'He got you one on the forehead,' said Mike, 'or somebody did. Tell us what happened. I wish the dickens I'd come with you. I'd no notion there would be a rag of any sort. What did happen?'

'Comrade Jackson,' said Psmith sorrowfully, 'how sad it is in this life of ours to be consistently misunderstood. You know, of course, how wrapped up I am in Comrade Bickersdyke's welfare. You know that all my efforts are directed towards making a decent man of him; that, in short, I am his truest friend. Does he show by so much as a word that he appreciates my labours? Not he. I believe that man is beginning to dislike me, Comrade Jackson.'

'What happened, anyhow? Never mind about Bickersdyke.'

'Perhaps it was mistaken zeal on my part.... Well, I will tell you all. Make a long arm for the shovel, Comrade Jackson, and pile on a few more coals. I thank you. Well, all went quite smoothly for a while. Comrade B. in quite good form. Got his second wind, and was going strong for the tape, when a regrettable incident occurred. He informed the meeting, that while up in the Lake country, fishing, he went to an inn and saw a remarkably large stuffed trout in a glass case. He made inquiries, and found that five separate and distinct people had caught —'

'Why, dash it all,' said Mike, 'that's a frightful chestnut.'

Psmith nodded.

'It certainly has appeared in print,' he said. 'In fact I should have said it was rather a well-known story. I was so interested in Comrade Bickersdyke's statement that the thing had happened to himself that, purely out of good-will towards him, I got up and told him that I thought it was my duty, as a friend, to let him know that a man named Jerome had pinched his story, put it in a book, and got money by it. Money, mark you, that should by rights have been Comrade Bickersdyke's. He didn't appear to care much about sifting the matter thoroughly. In fact, he seemed anxious to get on with his speech, and slur the matter over. But, tactlessly perhaps, I continued rather to harp on the thing. I said that the book in which the story had appeared was published in 1889. I asked him how long ago it was that he had been on his fishing tour, because it was important to know in order to bring the charge home against Jerome. Well, after a bit, I was amazed, and pained, too, to hear Comrade Bickersdyke urging certain bravoes in the audience to turn me out. If ever there was a case of biting the hand that fed him.... Well, well.... By this time the meeting had begun to take sides to some extent. What I might call my party, the Earnest Investigators, were whistling between their fingers, stamping on the floor, and shouting, "Chestnuts!" while the opposing party, the bravoes, seemed to be trying, as I say, to do jiu-jitsu tricks with me. It was a painful situation. I know the cultivated man of affairs should have passed the thing off with a short, careless laugh; but, owing to the above-mentioned alcohol-expert having got both hands under my collar, short, careless laughs were off. I was compelled, very reluctantly, to conclude the interview by tapping the bright boy on the jaw. He took the hint, and sat down on the floor. I thought no more of the matter, and was making my way thoughtfully to the exit, when a second man of wrath put the above on my forehead. You can't ignore a thing like that. I collected some of his waistcoat and one of his legs, and hove him with some vim into the middle distance. By this time a good many of the Earnest Investigators were beginning to join in; and it was just there that the affair began to have certain points of resemblance to a pantomime rally. Everybody seemed to be shouting a good deal and hitting everybody else. It was no place for a man of delicate culture, so I edged towards the door, and drifted out. There was a cab in the offing. I boarded it. And, having kicked a vigorous politician in the stomach, as he was endeavouring to climb in too, I drove off home.'

Psmith got up, looked at his forehead once more in the glass, sighed, and sat down again.

'All very disturbing,' he said.

'Great Scott,' said Mike, 'I wish I'd come. Why on earth didn't you tell me you were going to rag? I think you might as well have done. I wouldn't have missed it for worlds.'

Psmith regarded him with raised eyebrows.

'Rag!' he said. 'Comrade Jackson, I do not understand you. You surely do not think that I had any other object in doing what I did than to serve Comrade Bickersdyke? It's terrible how one's motives get distorted in this world of ours.'

'Well,' said Mike, with a grin, 'I know one person who'll jolly well distort your motives, as you call it, and that's Bickersdyke.'

Psmith looked thoughtful.

'True,' he said, 'true. There is that possibility. I tell you, Comrade Jackson, once more that my bright young life is being slowly blighted by the frightful way in which that man misunderstands me. It seems almost impossible to try to do him a good turn without having the action misconstrued.'

'What'll you say to him tomorrow?'

'I shall make no allusion to the painful affair. If I happen to meet him in the ordinary course of business routine, I shall pass some light, pleasant remark-on the weather, let us say, or the Bank rate-and continue my duties.'

'How about if he sends for you, and wants to do the light, pleasant remark business on his own?'

'In that case I shall not thwart him. If he invites me into his private room, I shall be his guest, and shall discuss, to the best of my ability, any topic which he may care to introduce. There shall be no constraint between Comrade Bickersdyke and myself.'

'No, I shouldn't think there would be. I wish I could come and hear you.'

'I wish you could,' said Psmith courteously.

'Still, it doesn't matter much to you. You don't care if you do get sacked.'

Psmith rose.

'In that way possibly, as you say, I am agreeably situated. If the New Asiatic Bank does not require Psmith's services, there are other spheres where a young man of spirit may carve a place for himself. No, what is worrying me, Comrade Jackson, is not the thought of the push. It is the growing fear that Comrade Bickersdyke and I will never thoroughly understand and appreciate one another. A deep gulf lies between us. I do what I can do to bridge it over, but he makes no response. On his side of the gulf building operations appear to be at an entire standstill. That is what is carving these lines of care on my forehead, Comrade Jackson. That is what is painting these purple circles beneath my eyes. Quite inadvertently to be disturbing Comrade Bickersdyke, annoying him, preventing him from enjoying life. How sad this is. Life bulges with these tragedies.'

Mike picked up the evening paper.

'Don't let it keep you awake at night,' he said. 'By the way, did you see that Manchester United were playing this afternoon? They won. You'd better sit down and sweat up some of the details. You'll want them tomorrow.'

'You are very right, Comrade Jackson,' said Psmith, reseating himself. 'So the Mancunians pushed the bulb into the meshes beyond the uprights no fewer than four times, did they? Bless the dear boys, what spirits they do enjoy, to be sure. Comrade Jackson, do not disturb me. I must concentrate myself. These are deep waters.'

12. In a Nutshell

Mr Bickersdyke sat in his private room at the New Asiatic Bank with a pile of newspapers before him. At least, the casual observer would have said that it was Mr Bickersdyke. In reality, however, it was an active volcano in the shape and clothes of the bank-manager. It was freely admitted in the office that morning that the manager had lowered all records with ease. The staff had known him to be in a bad temper before-frequently; but his frame of mind on all previous occasions had been, compared with his present frame of mind, that of a rather exceptionally good-natured lamb. Within ten minutes of his arrival the entire office was on the jump. The messengers were collected in a pallid group in the basement, discussing the affair in whispers and endeavouring to restore their nerve with about sixpenn'orth of the beverage known as 'unsweetened'. The heads of departments, to a man, had bowed before the storm. Within the space of seven minutes and a quarter Mr Bickersdyke had contrived to find some fault with each of them. Inward Bills was out at an A.B.C. shop snatching a hasty cup of coffee, to pull him together again. Outward Bills was sitting at his desk with the glazed stare of one who has been struck in the thorax by a thunderbolt. Mr Rossiter had been torn from Psmith in the middle of a highly technical discussion of the Manchester United match, just as he was showing-with the aid of a ball of paper-how he had once seen Meredith centre to Sandy Turnbull in a Cup match, and was now leaping about like a distracted grasshopper. Mr Waller, head of the Cash Department, had been summoned to the Presence, and after listening meekly to a rush of criticism, had retired to his desk with the air of a beaten spaniel.

Only one man of the many in the building seemed calm and happy-Psmith.

Psmith had resumed the chat about Manchester United, on Mr Rossiter's return from the lion's den, at the spot where it had been broken off; but, finding that the head of the Postage Department was in no mood for discussing football (or any thing else), he had postponed his remarks and placidly resumed his work.

Mr Bickersdyke picked up a paper, opened it, and began searching the columns. He had not far to look. It was a slack season for the newspapers, and his little trouble, which might have received a paragraph in a busy week, was set forth fully in three-quarters of a column.

The column was headed, 'Amusing Heckling'.

Mr Bickersdyke read a few lines, and crumpled the paper up with a snort.

The next he examined was an organ of his own shade of political opinion. It too, gave him nearly a column, headed 'Disgraceful Scene at Kenningford'. There was also a leaderette on the subject.

The leaderette said so exactly what Mr Bickersdyke thought himself that for a moment he was soothed. Then the thought of his grievance returned, and he pressed the bell.

'Send Mr Smith to me,' he said.

William, the messenger, proceeded to inform Psmith of the summons.

Psmith's face lit up.

'I am always glad to sweeten the monotony of toil with a chat with
Little Clarence,' he said. 'I shall be with him in a moment.'

He cleaned his pen very carefully, placed it beside his ledger, flicked a little dust off his coatsleeve, and made his way to the manager's room.

Mr Bickersdyke received him with the ominous restraint of a tiger crouching for its spring. Psmith stood beside the table with languid grace, suggestive of some favoured confidential secretary waiting for instructions.

A ponderous silence brooded over the room for some moments. Psmith broke it by remarking that the Bank Rate was unchanged. He mentioned this fact as if it afforded him a personal gratification.

Mr Bickersdyke spoke.

'Well, Mr Smith?' he said.

'You wished to see me about something, sir?' inquired Psmith, ingratiatingly.

'You know perfectly well what I wished to see you about. I want to hear your explanation of what occurred last night.'

'May I sit, sir?'

He dropped gracefully into a chair, without waiting for permission, and, having hitched up the knees of his trousers, beamed winningly at the manager.

'A deplorable affair,' he said, with a shake of his head. 'Extremely deplorable. We must not judge these rough, uneducated men too harshly, however. In a time of excitement the emotions of the lower classes are easily stirred. Where you or I would —'

Mr Bickersdyke interrupted.

'I do not wish for any more buffoonery, Mr Smith —'

Psmith raised a pained pair of eyebrows.

'Buffoonery, sir!'

'I cannot understand what made you act as you did last night, unless you are perfectly mad, as I am beginning to think.'

'But, surely, sir, there was nothing remarkable in my behaviour? When a merchant has attached himself to your collar, can you do less than smite him on the other cheek? I merely acted in self-defence. You saw for yourself—'

'You know what I am alluding to. Your behaviour during my speech.'

'An excellent speech,' murmured Psmith courteously.

'Well?' said Mr Bickersdyke.

'It was, perhaps, mistaken zeal on my part, sir, but you must remember that I acted purely from the best motives. It seemed to me —'

'That is enough, Mr Smith. I confess that I am absolutely at a loss to understand you —'

'It is too true, sir,' sighed Psmith.

'You seem,' continued Mr Bickersdyke, warming to his subject, and turning gradually a richer shade of purple, 'you seem to be determined to endeavour to annoy me.' ('No no,' from Psmith.) 'I can only assume that you are not in your right senses. You follow me about in my club —'

'Our club, sir,' murmured Psmith.

'Be good enough not to interrupt me, Mr Smith. You dog my footsteps in my club —'

'Purely accidental, sir. We happen to meet-that is all.'

'You attend meetings at which I am speaking, and behave in a perfectly imbecile manner.'

Psmith moaned slightly.

'It may seem humorous to you, but I can assure you it is extremely bad policy on your part. The New Asiatic Bank is no place for humour, and I think —'

'Excuse me, sir,' said Psmith.

The manager started at the familiar phrase. The plum-colour of his complexion deepened.

'I entirely agree with you, sir,' said Psmith, 'that this bank is no place for humour.'

'Very well, then. You —'

'And I am never humorous in it. I arrive punctually in the morning, and I work steadily and earnestly till my labours are completed. I think you will find, on inquiry, that Mr Rossiter is satisfied with my work.'

'That is neither here nor —'

'Surely, sir,' said Psmith, 'you are wrong? Surely your jurisdiction ceases after office hours? Any little misunderstanding we may have at the close of the day's work cannot affect you officially. You could not, for instance, dismiss me from the service of the bank if we were partners at bridge at the club and I happened to revoke.'

'I can dismiss you, let me tell you, Mr Smith, for studied insolence, whether in the office or not.'

'I bow to superior knowledge,' said Psmith politely, 'but I confess I doubt it. And,' he added, 'there is another point. May I continue to some extent?'

'If you have anything to say, say it.'

Psmith flung one leg over the other, and settled his collar.

'It is perhaps a delicate matter,' he said, 'but it is best to be frank. We should have no secrets. To put my point quite clearly, I must go back a little, to the time when you paid us that very welcome week-end visit at our house in August.'

'If you hope to make capital out of the fact that I have been a guest of your father —'

'Not at all,' said Psmith deprecatingly. 'Not at all. You do not take me. My point is this. I do not wish to revive painful memories, but it cannot be denied that there was, here and there, some slight bickering between us on that occasion. The fault,' said Psmith magnanimously, 'was possibly mine. I may have been too exacting, too capricious. Perhaps so. However, the fact remains that you conceived the happy notion of getting me into this bank, under the impression that, once I was in, you would be able to-if I may use the expression-give me beans. You said as much to me, if I remember. I hate to say it, but don't you think that if you give me the sack, although my work is satisfactory to the head of my department, you will be by way of admitting that you bit off rather more than you could chew? I merely make the suggestion.'

Mr Bickersdyke half rose from his chair.

'You —'

'Just so, just so, but-to return to the main point-don't you? The whole painful affair reminds me of the story of Agesilaus and the Petulant Pterodactyl, which as you have never heard, I will now proceed to relate. Agesilaus —'

Mr Bickersdyke made a curious clucking noise in his throat.

'I am boring you,' said Psmith, with ready tact. 'Suffice it to say that Comrade Agesilaus interfered with the pterodactyl, which was doing him no harm; and the intelligent creature, whose motto was "Nemo me impune lacessit", turned and bit him. Bit him good and hard, so that Agesilaus ever afterwards had a distaste for pterodactyls. His reluctance to disturb them became quite a byword. The Society papers of the period frequently commented upon it. Let us draw the parallel.'

Here Mr Bickersdyke, who had been clucking throughout this speech, essayed to speak; but Psmith hurried on.

'You are Agesilaus,' he said. 'I am the Petulant Pterodactyl. You, if I may say so, butted in of your own free will, and took me from a happy home, simply in order that you might get me into this place under you, and give me beans. But, curiously enough, the major portion of that vegetable seems to be coming to you. Of course, you can administer the push if you like; but, as I say, it will be by way of a confession that your scheme has sprung a leak. Personally,' said Psmith, as one friend to another, 'I should advise you to stick it out. You never know what may happen. At any moment I may fall from my present high standard of industry and excellence; and then you have me, so to speak, where the hair is crisp.'

He paused. Mr Bickersdyke's eyes, which even in their normal state protruded slightly, now looked as if they might fall out at any moment. His face had passed from the plum-coloured stage to something beyond. Every now and then he made the clucking noise, but except for that he was silent. Psmith, having waited for some time for something in the shape of comment or criticism on his remarks, now rose.

'It has been a great treat to me, this little chat,' he said affably, 'but I fear that I must no longer allow purely social enjoyments to interfere with my commercial pursuits. With your permission, I will rejoin my department, where my absence is doubtless already causing comment and possibly dismay. But we shall be meeting at the club shortly, I hope. Good-bye, sir, good-bye.'

He left the room, and walked dreamily back to the Postage Department, leaving the manager still staring glassily at nothing.

13. Mike is Moved On

This episode may be said to have concluded the first act of the commercial drama in which Mike and Psmith had been cast for leading parts. And, as usually happens after the end of an act, there was a lull for a while until things began to work up towards another climax. Mike, as day succeeded day, began to grow accustomed to the life of the bank, and to find that it had its pleasant side after all. Whenever a number of people are working at the same thing, even though that thing is not perhaps what they would have chosen as an object in life, if left to themselves, there is bound to exist an atmosphere of good-fellowship; something akin to, though a hundred times weaker than, the public school spirit. Such a community lacks the main motive of the public school spirit, which is pride in the school and its achievements. Nobody can be proud of the achievements of a bank. When the business of arranging a new Japanese loan was given to the New Asiatic Bank, its employees did not stand on stools, and cheer. On the contrary, they thought of the extra work it would involve; and they cursed a good deal, though there was no denying that it was a big thing for the bank-not unlike winning the Ashburton would be to a school. There is a cold impersonality about a bank. A school is a living thing.

Setting aside this important difference, there was a good deal of the public school about the New Asiatic Bank. The heads of departments were not quite so autocratic as masters, and one was treated more on a grown-up scale, as man to man; but, nevertheless, there remained a distinct flavour of a school republic. Most of the men in the bank, with the exception of certain hard-headed Scotch youths drafted in from other establishments in the City, were old public school men. Mike found two Old Wrykinians in the first week. Neither was well known to him. They had left in his second year in the team. But it was pleasant to have them about, and to feel that they had been educated at the right place.

As far as Mike's personal comfort went, the presence of these two Wrykinians was very much for the good. Both of them knew all about his cricket, and they spread the news. The New Asiatic Bank, like most London banks, was keen on sport, and happened to possess a cricket team which could make a good game with most of the second-rank clubs. The disappearance to the East of two of the best bats of the previous season caused Mike's advent to be hailed with a good deal of enthusiasm. Mike was a county man. He had only played once for his county, it was true, but that did not matter. He had passed the barrier which separates the second-class bat from the first-class, and the bank welcomed him with awe. County men did not come their way every day.

Mike did not like being in the bank, considered in the light of a career. But he bore no grudge against the inmates of the bank, such as he had borne against the inmates of Sedleigh. He had looked on the latter as bound up with the school, and, consequently, enemies. His fellow workers in the bank he regarded as companions in misfortune. They were all in the same boat together. There were men from Tonbridge, Dulwich, Bedford, St Paul's, and a dozen other schools. One or two of them he knew by repute from the pages of Wisden. Bannister, his cheerful predecessor in the Postage Department, was the Bannister, he recollected now, who had played for Geddington against Wrykyn in his second year in the Wrykyn team. Munroe, the big man in the Fixed Deposits, he remembered as leader of the Ripton pack. Every day brought fresh discoveries of this sort, and each made Mike more reconciled to his lot. They were a pleasant set of fellows in the New Asiatic Bank, and but for the dreary outlook which the future held-for Mike, unlike most of his follow workers, was not attracted by the idea of a life in the East-he would have been very fairly content.

The hostility of Mr Bickersdyke was a slight drawback. Psmith had developed a habit of taking Mike with him to the club of an evening; and this did not do anything towards wiping out of the manager's mind the recollection of his former passage of arms with the Old Wrykinian. The glass remaining Set Fair as far as Mr Rossiter's approval was concerned, Mike was enabled to keep off the managerial carpet to a great extent; but twice, when he posted letters without going through the preliminary formality of stamping them, Mr Bickersdyke had opportunities of which he availed himself. But for these incidents life was fairly enjoyable. Owing to Psmith's benevolent efforts, the Postage Department became quite a happy family, and ex-occupants of the postage desk, Bannister especially, were amazed at the change that had come over Mr Rossiter. He no longer darted from his lair like a pouncing panther. To report his subordinates to the manager seemed now to be a lost art with him. The sight of Psmith and Mr Rossiter proceeding high and disposedly to a mutual lunch became quite common, and ceased to excite remark.

'By kindness,' said Psmith to Mike, after one of these expeditions. 'By tact and kindness. That is how it is done. I do not despair of training Comrade Rossiter one of these days to jump through paper hoops.'

So that, altogether, Mike's life in the bank had become very fairly pleasant.

Out of office-hours he enjoyed himself hugely. London was strange to him, and with Psmith as a companion, he extracted a vast deal of entertainment from it. Psmith was not unacquainted with the West End, and he proved an excellent guide. At first Mike expostulated with unfailing regularity at the other's habit of paying for everything, but Psmith waved aside all objections with languid firmness.

'I need you, Comrade Jackson,' he said, when Mike lodged a protest on finding himself bound for the stalls for the second night in succession. 'We must stick together. As my confidential secretary and adviser, your place is by my side. Who knows but that between the acts tonight I may not be seized with some luminous thought? Could I utter this to my next-door neighbour or the programme-girl? Stand by me, Comrade Jackson, or we are undone.'

So Mike stood by him.

By this time Mike had grown so used to his work that he could tell to within five minutes when a rush would come; and he was able to spend a good deal of his time reading a surreptitious novel behind a pile of ledgers, or down in the tea-room. The New Asiatic Bank supplied tea to its employees. In quality it was bad, and the bread-and-butter associated with it was worse. But it had the merit of giving one an excuse for being away from one's desk. There were large printed notices all over the tea-room, which was in the basement, informing gentlemen that they were only allowed ten minutes for tea, but one took just as long as one thought the head of one's department would stand, from twenty-five minutes to an hour and a quarter.

This state of things was too good to last. Towards the beginning of the New Year a new man arrived, and Mike was moved on to another department.

14. Mr Waller Appears in a New Light

The department into which Mike was sent was the Cash, or, to be more exact, that section of it which was known as Paying Cashier. The important task of shooting doubloons across the counter did not belong to Mike himself, but to Mr Waller. Mike's work was less ostentatious, and was performed with pen, ink, and ledgers in the background. Occasionally, when Mr Waller was out at lunch, Mike had to act as substitute for him, and cash cheques; but Mr Waller always went out at a slack time, when few customers came in, and Mike seldom had any very startling sum to hand over.

He enjoyed being in the Cash Department. He liked Mr Waller. The work was easy; and when he did happen to make mistakes, they were corrected patiently by the grey-bearded one, and not used as levers for boosting him into the presence of Mr Bickersdyke, as they might have been in some departments. The cashier seemed to have taken a fancy to Mike; and Mike, as was usually the way with him when people went out of their way to be friendly, was at his best. Mike at his ease and unsuspicious of hostile intentions was a different person from Mike with his prickles out.

Psmith, meanwhile, was not enjoying himself. It was an unheard-of thing, he said, depriving a man of his confidential secretary without so much as asking his leave.

'It has caused me the greatest inconvenience,' he told Mike, drifting round in a melancholy way to the Cash Department during a slack spell one afternoon. 'I miss you at every turn. Your keen intelligence and ready sympathy were invaluable to me. Now where am I? In the cart. I evolved a slightly bright thought on life just now. There was nobody to tell it to except the new man. I told it him, and the fool gaped. I tell you, Comrade Jackson, I feel like some lion that has been robbed of its cub. I feel as Marshall would feel if they took Snelgrove away from him, or as Peace might if he awoke one morning to find Plenty gone. Comrade Rossiter does his best. We still talk brokenly about Manchester United-they got routed in the first round of the Cup yesterday and Comrade Rossiter is wearing black-but it is not the same. I try work, but that is no good either. From ledger to ledger they hurry me, to stifle my regret. And when they win a smile from me, they think that I forget. But I don't. I am a broken man. That new exhibit they've got in your place is about as near to the Extreme Edge as anything I've ever seen. One of Nature's blighters. Well, well, I must away. Comrade Rossiter awaits me.'

Mike's successor, a youth of the name of Bristow, was causing Psmith a great deal of pensive melancholy. His worst defect-which he could not help-was that he was not Mike. His others-which he could-were numerous. His clothes were cut in a way that harrowed Psmith's sensitive soul every time he looked at them. The fact that he wore detachable cuffs, which he took off on beginning work and stacked in a glistening pile on the desk in front of him, was no proof of innate viciousness of disposition, but it prejudiced the Old Etonian against him. It was part of Psmith's philosophy that a man who wore detachable cuffs had passed beyond the limit of human toleration. In addition, Bristow wore a small black moustache and a ring and that, as Psmith informed Mike, put the lid on it.

Mike would sometimes stroll round to the Postage Department to listen to the conversations between the two. Bristow was always friendliness itself. He habitually addressed Psmith as Smithy, a fact which entertained Mike greatly but did not seem to amuse Psmith to any overwhelming extent. On the other hand, when, as he generally did, he called Mike 'Mister Cricketer', the humour of the thing appeared to elude Mike, though the mode of address always drew from Psmith a pale, wan smile, as of a broken heart made cheerful against its own inclination.

The net result of the coming of Bristow was that Psmith spent most of his time, when not actually oppressed by a rush of work, in the precincts of the Cash Department, talking to Mike and Mr Waller. The latter did not seem to share the dislike common among the other heads of departments of seeing his subordinates receiving visitors. Unless the work was really heavy, in which case a mild remonstrance escaped him, he offered no objection to Mike being at home to Psmith. It was this tolerance which sometimes got him into trouble with Mr Bickersdyke. The manager did not often perambulate the office, but he did occasionally, and the interview which ensued upon his finding Hutchinson, the underling in the Cash Department at that time, with his stool tilted comfortably against the wall, reading the sporting news from a pink paper to a friend from the Outward Bills Department who lay luxuriously on the floor beside him, did not rank among Mr Waller's pleasantest memories. But Mr Waller was too soft-hearted to interfere with his assistants unless it was absolutely necessary. The truth of the matter was that the New Asiatic Bank was over-staffed. There were too many men for the work. The London branch of the bank was really only a nursery. New men were constantly wanted in the Eastern branches, so they had to be put into the London branch to learn the business, whether there was any work for them to do or not.

It was after one of these visits of Psmith's that Mr Waller displayed a new and unsuspected side to his character. Psmith had come round in a state of some depression to discuss Bristow, as usual. Bristow, it seemed, had come to the bank that morning in a fancy waistcoat of so emphatic a colour-scheme that Psmith stoutly refused to sit in the same department with it.

'What with Comrades Bristow and Bickersdyke combined,' said Psmith plaintively, 'the work is becoming too hard for me. The whisper is beginning to circulate, "Psmith's number is up-As a reformer he is merely among those present. He is losing his dash." But what can I do? I cannot keep an eye on both of them at the same time. The moment I concentrate myself on Comrade Bickersdyke for a brief spell, and seem to be doing him a bit of good, what happens? Why, Comrade Bristow sneaks off and buys a sort of woollen sunset. I saw the thing unexpectedly. I tell you I was shaken. It is the suddenness of that waistcoat which hits you. It's discouraging, this sort of thing. I try always to think well of my fellow man. As an energetic Socialist, I do my best to see the good that is in him, but it's hard. Comrade Bristow's the most striking argument against the equality of man I've ever come across.'

Mr Waller intervened at this point.

'I think you must really let Jackson go on with his work, Smith,' he said. 'There seems to be too much talking.'

'My besetting sin,' said Psmith sadly. 'Well, well, I will go back and do my best to face it, but it's a tough job.'

He tottered wearily away in the direction of the Postage Department.

'Oh, Jackson,' said Mr Waller, 'will you kindly take my place for a few minutes? I must go round and see the Inward Bills about something. I shall be back very soon.'

Mike was becoming accustomed to deputizing for the cashier for short spaces of time. It generally happened that he had to do so once or twice a day. Strictly speaking, perhaps, Mr Waller was wrong to leave such an important task as the actual cashing of cheques to an inexperienced person of Mike's standing; but the New Asiatic Bank differed from most banks in that there was not a great deal of cross-counter work. People came in fairly frequently to cash cheques of two or three pounds, but it was rare that any very large dealings took place.

Having completed his business with the Inward Bills, Mr Waller made his way back by a circuitous route, taking in the Postage desk.

He found Psmith with a pale, set face, inscribing figures in a ledger. The Old Etonian greeted him with the faint smile of a persecuted saint who is determined to be cheerful even at the stake.

'Comrade Bristow,' he said.

'Hullo, Smithy?' said the other, turning.

Psmith sadly directed Mr Waller's attention to the waistcoat, which was certainly definite in its colouring.

'Nothing,' said Psmith. 'I only wanted to look at you.'

'Funny ass,' said Bristow, resuming his work. Psmith glanced at Mr Waller, as who should say, 'See what I have to put up with. And yet I do not give way.'

'Oh-er-Smith,' said Mr Waller, 'when you were talking to Jackson just now—'

'Say no more,' said Psmith. 'It shall not occur again. Why should I dislocate the work of your department in my efforts to win a sympathetic word? I will bear Comrade Bristow like a man here. After all, there are worse things at the Zoo.'

'No, no,' said Mr Waller hastily, 'I did not mean that. By all means pay us a visit now and then, if it does not interfere with your own work. But I noticed just now that you spoke to Bristow as Comrade Bristow.'

'It is too true,' said Psmith. 'I must correct myself of the habit. He will be getting above himself.'

'And when you were speaking to Jackson, you spoke of yourself as a Socialist.'

'Socialism is the passion of my life,' said Psmith.

Mr Waller's face grew animated. He stammered in his eagerness.

'I am delighted,' he said. 'Really, I am delighted. I also —'

'A fellow worker in the Cause?' said Psmith.

'Er-exactly.'

Psmith extended his hand gravely. Mr Waller shook it with enthusiasm.

'I have never liked to speak of it to anybody in the office,' said Mr Waller, 'but I, too, am heart and soul in the movement.'

'Yours for the Revolution?' said Psmith.

'Just so. Just so. Exactly. I was wondering-the fact is, I am in the habit of speaking on Sundays in the open air, and —'

'Hyde Park?'

'No. No. Clapham Common. It is-er-handier for me where I live. Now, as you are interested in the movement, I was thinking that perhaps you might care to come and hear me speak next Sunday. Of course, if you have nothing better to do.'

'I should like to excessively,' said Psmith.

'Excellent. Bring Jackson with you, and both of you come to supper afterwards, if you will.'

'Thanks very much.'

'Perhaps you would speak yourself?'

'No,' said Psmith. 'No. I think not. My Socialism is rather of the practical sort. I seldom speak. But it would be a treat to listen to you. What-er-what type of oratory is yours?'

'Oh, well,' said Mr Waller, pulling nervously at his beard, 'of course I —. Well, I am perhaps a little bitter —'

'Yes, yes.'

'A little mordant and ironical.'

'You would be,' agreed Psmith. 'I shall look forward to Sunday with every fibre quivering. And Comrade Jackson shall be at my side.'

'Excellent,' said Mr Waller. 'I will go and tell him now.'

15. Stirring Times on the Common

'The first thing to do,' said Psmith, 'is to ascertain that such a place as Clapham Common really exists. One has heard of it, of course, but has its existence ever been proved? I think not. Having accomplished that, we must then try to find out how to get to it. I should say at a venture that it would necessitate a sea-voyage. On the other hand, Comrade Waller, who is a native of the spot, seems to find no difficulty in rolling to the office every morning. Therefore-you follow me, Jackson?—it must be in England. In that case, we will take a taximeter cab, and go out into the unknown, hand in hand, trusting to luck.'

'I expect you could get there by tram,' said Mike.

Psmith suppressed a slight shudder.

'I fear, Comrade Jackson,' he said, 'that the old noblesse oblige traditions of the Psmiths would not allow me to do that. No. We will stroll gently, after a light lunch, to Trafalgar Square, and hail a taxi.'

'Beastly expensive.'

'But with what an object! Can any expenditure be called excessive which enables us to hear Comrade Waller being mordant and ironical at the other end?'

'It's a rum business,' said Mike. 'I hope the dickens he won't mix us up in it. We should look frightful fools.'

'I may possibly say a few words,' said Psmith carelessly, 'if the spirit moves me. Who am I that I should deny people a simple pleasure?'

Mike looked alarmed.

'Look here,' he said, 'I say, if you *are* going to play the goat, for goodness' sake don't go lugging me into it. I've got heaps of troubles without that.'

Psmith waved the objection aside.

'You,' he said, 'will be one of the large, and, I hope, interested audience. Nothing more. But it is quite possible that the spirit may not move me. I may not feel inspired to speak. I am not one of those who love speaking for speaking's sake. If I have no message for the many-headed, I shall remain silent.'

'Then I hope the dickens you won't have,' said Mike. Of all things he hated most being conspicuous before a crowd-except at cricket, which was a different thing-and he had an uneasy feeling that Psmith would rather like it than otherwise.

'We shall see,' said Psmith absently. 'Of course, if in the vein, I might do something big in the way of oratory. I am a plain, blunt man, but I feel convinced that, given the opportunity, I should haul up my slacks to some effect. But-well, we shall see. We shall see.'

And with this ghastly state of doubt Mike had to be content.

It was with feelings of apprehension that he accompanied Psmith from the flat to Trafalgar Square in search of a cab which should convey them to Clapham Common.

They were to meet Mr Waller at the edge of the Common nearest the old town of Clapham. On the journey down Psmith was inclined to be *debonnaire*. Mike, on the other hand, was silent and apprehensive. He knew enough of Psmith to know that, if half an opportunity were offered him, he would extract entertainment from this affair after his own fashion; and then the odds were that he himself would be dragged into it. Perhaps-his scalp bristled at the mere idea-he would even be let in for a speech.

This grisly thought had hardly come into his head, when Psmith spoke.

'I'm not half sure,' he said thoughtfully, 'I sha'n't call on you for a speech, Comrade Jackson.'

'Look here, Psmith —' began Mike agitatedly.

'I don't know. I think your solid, incisive style would rather go down with the masses. However, we shall see, we shall see.'

Mike reached the Common in a state of nervous collapse.

Mr Waller was waiting for them by the railings near the pond. The apostle of the Revolution was clad soberly in black, except for a tie of vivid crimson. His eyes shone with the light of enthusiasm, vastly different from the mild glow of amiability which they exhibited for six days in every week. The man was transformed.

'Here you are,' he said. 'Here you are. Excellent. You are in good time. Comrades Wotherspoon and Prebble have already begun to speak. I shall commence now that you have come. This is the way. Over by these trees.'

They made their way towards a small clump of trees, near which a fair-sized crowd had already begun to collect. Evidently listening to the speakers was one of Clapham's fashionable Sunday amusements. Mr Waller talked and gesticulated incessantly as he walked. Psmith's demeanour was perhaps a shade patronizing, but he displayed interest. Mike proceeded to the meeting with the air of an about-to-be-washed dog. He was loathing the whole business with a heartiness worthy of a better cause. Somehow, he felt he was going to be made to look a fool before the afternoon was over. But he registered a vow that nothing should drag him on to the small platform which had been erected for the benefit of the speaker.

As they drew nearer, the voices of Comrades Wotherspoon and Prebble became more audible. They had been audible all the time, very much so, but now they grew in volume. Comrade Wotherspoon was a tall, thin man with side-whiskers and a high voice. He scattered his aitches as a fountain its sprays in a strong wind. He was very earnest. Comrade Prebble was earnest, too. Perhaps even more so than Comrade Wotherspoon. He was handicapped to some extent, however, by not having a palate. This gave to his profoundest thoughts a certain weirdness, as if they had been uttered in an unknown tongue. The crowd was thickest round his platform. The grown-up section plainly regarded him as a comedian, pure and simple, and roared with happy laughter when he urged them to march upon Park Lane and loot the same without mercy or scruple. The children were more doubtful. Several had broken down, and been led away in tears.

When Mr Waller got up to speak on platform number three, his audience consisted at first only of Psmith, Mike, and a fox-terrier. Gradually however, he attracted others. After wavering for a while, the crowd finally decided that he was worth hearing. He had a method of his own. Lacking the natural gifts which marked Comrade Prebble out as an entertainer, he made up for this by his activity. Where his colleagues stood comparatively still, Mr Waller behaved with the vivacity generally supposed to belong only to peas on shovels and cats on hot bricks. He crouched to denounce the House of Lords. He bounded from side to side while dissecting the methods of the plutocrats. During an impassioned onslaught on the monarchical system he stood on one leg and hopped. This was more the sort of thing the crowd had come to see. Comrade Wotherspoon found himself deserted, and even Comrade Prebble's shortcomings in the way of palate were insufficient to keep his flock together. The entire strength of the audience gathered in front of the third platform.

Mike, separated from Psmith by the movement of the crowd, listened with a growing depression. That feeling which attacks a sensitive person sometimes at the theatre when somebody is making himself ridiculous on the stage-the illogical feeling that it is he and not the actor who is floundering-had come over him in a wave. He liked Mr Waller, and it made his gorge rise to see him exposing himself to the jeers of a crowd. The fact that Mr Waller himself did not know that they were jeers, but mistook them for applause, made it no better. Mike felt vaguely furious.

His indignation began to take a more personal shape when the speaker, branching off from the main subject of Socialism, began to touch on temperance. There was no particular reason why Mr Waller should have introduced the subject of temperance, except that he happened to be an enthusiast. He linked it on to his remarks on Socialism by attributing the lethargy of the masses to their fondness for alcohol; and the crowd, which had been inclined rather to pat itself on the back during the assaults on Rank and Property, finding itself assailed in its turn, resented it. They were there to listen to speakers telling them that they were the finest fellows on earth, not pointing out their little failings to them. The feeling of the meeting became hostile. The jeers grew more frequent and less good-tempered.

'Comrade Waller means well,' said a voice in Mike's ear, 'but if he shoots it at them like this much more there'll be a bit of an imbroglio.'

'Look here, Smith,' said Mike quickly, 'can't we stop him? These chaps are getting fed up, and they look bargees enough to do anything. They'll be going for him or something soon.'

'How can we switch off the flow? I don't see. The man is wound up. He means to get it off his chest if it snows. I feel we are by way of being in the soup once more, Comrade Jackson. We can only sit tight and look on.'

The crowd was becoming more threatening every minute. A group of young men of the loafer class who stood near Mike were especially fertile in comment. Psmith's eyes were on the speaker; but Mike was watching this group closely. Suddenly he saw one of them, a thick-set youth wearing a cloth cap and no collar, stoop.

When he rose again there was a stone in his hand.

The sight acted on Mike like a spur. Vague rage against nobody in particular had been simmering in him for half an hour. Now it concentrated itself on the cloth-capped one.

Mr Waller paused momentarily before renewing his harangue. The man in the cloth cap raised his hand. There was a swirl in the crowd, and the first thing that Psmith saw as he turned was Mike seizing the would-be marksman round the neck and hurling him to the ground, after the manner of a forward at football tackling an opponent during a line-out from touch.

There is one thing which will always distract the attention of a crowd from any speaker, and that is a dispute between two of its units. Mr Waller's views on temperance were forgotten in an instant. The audience surged round Mike and his opponent.

The latter had scrambled to his feet now, and was looking round for his assailant.

'That's 'im, Bill!' cried eager voices, indicating Mike.

''E's the bloke wot 'it yer, Bill,' said others, more precise in detail.

Bill advanced on Mike in a sidelong, crab-like manner.

''Oo're you, I should like to know?' said Bill.

Mike, rightly holding that this was merely a rhetorical question and that Bill had no real thirst for information as to his family history, made no reply. Or, rather, the reply he made was not verbal. He waited till his questioner was within range, and then hit him in the eye. A reply far more satisfactory, if not to Bill himself, at any rate to the interested onlookers, than any flow of words.

A contented sigh went up from the crowd. Their Sunday afternoon was going to be spent just as they considered Sunday afternoons should be spent.

'Give us your coat,' said Psmith briskly, 'and try and get it over quick. Don't go in for any fancy sparring. Switch it on, all you know, from the start. I'll keep a thoughtful eye open to see that none of his friends and relations join in.'

Outwardly Psmith was unruffled, but inwardly he was not feeling so composed. An ordinary turn-up before an impartial crowd which could be relied upon to preserve the etiquette of these matters was one thing. As regards the actual little dispute with the cloth-capped Bill, he felt that he could rely on Mike to handle it satisfactorily. But there was no knowing how long the crowd would be content to remain mere spectators. There was no doubt which way its sympathies lay. Bill, now stripped of his coat and sketching out in a hoarse voice a scenario of what he intended to do-knocking Mike down and stamping him into the mud was one of the milder feats he promised to perform for the entertainment of an indulgent audience-was plainly the popular favourite.

Psmith, though he did not show it, was more than a little apprehensive.

Mike, having more to occupy his mind in the immediate present, was not anxious concerning the future. He had the great advantage over Psmith of having lost his temper. Psmith could look on the situation as a whole, and count the risks and possibilities. Mike could only see Bill shuffling towards him with his head down and shoulders bunched.

'Gow it, Bill!' said someone.

'Pliy up, the Arsenal!' urged a voice on the outskirts of the crowd.

A chorus of encouragement from kind friends in front: 'Step up, Bill!'
And Bill stepped.

16. Further Developments

Bill (surname unknown) was not one of your ultra-scientific fighters. He did not favour the American crouch and the artistic feint. He had a style wholly his own. It seemed to have been modelled partly on a tortoise and partly on a windmill. His head he appeared to be trying to conceal between his shoulders, and he whirled his arms alternately in circular sweeps.

Mike, on the other hand, stood upright and hit straight, with the result that he hurt his knuckles very much on his opponent's skull, without seeming to disturb the latter to any great extent. In the process he received one of the windmill swings on the left ear. The crowd, strong pro-Billites, raised a cheer.

This maddened Mike. He assumed the offensive. Bill, satisfied for the moment with his success, had stepped back, and was indulging in some fancy sparring, when Mike sprang upon him like a panther. They clinched, and Mike, who had got the under grip, hurled Bill forcibly against a stout man who looked like a publican. The two fell in a heap, Bill underneath.

At the same time Bill's friends joined in.

The first intimation Mike had of this was a violent blow across the shoulders with a walking-stick. Even if he had been wearing his overcoat, the blow would have hurt. As he was in his jacket it hurt more than anything he had ever experienced in his life. He leapt up with a yell, but Psmith was there before him. Mike saw his assailant lift the stick again, and then collapse as the old Etonian's right took him under the chin.

He darted to Psmith's side.

'This is no place for us,' observed the latter sadly. 'Shift ho, I think. Come on.'

They dashed simultaneously for the spot where the crowd was thinnest. The ring which had formed round Mike and Bill had broken up as the result of the intervention of Bill's allies, and at the spot for which they ran only two men were standing. And these had apparently made up their minds that neutrality was the best policy, for they made no movement to stop them. Psmith and Mike charged through the gap, and raced for the road.

The suddenness of the move gave them just the start they needed. Mike looked over his shoulder. The crowd, to a man, seemed to be following. Bill, excavated from beneath the publican, led the field. Lying a good second came a band of three, and after them the rest in a bunch.

They reached the road in this order.

Some fifty yards down the road was a stationary tram. In the ordinary course of things it would probably have moved on long before Psmith and Mike could have got to it; but the conductor, a man with sporting blood in him, seeing what appeared to be the finish of some Marathon Race, refrained from giving the signal, and moved out into the road to observe events more clearly, at the same time calling to the driver, who joined him. Passengers on the roof stood up to get a good view. There was some cheering.

Psmith and Mike reached the tram ten yards to the good; and, if it had been ready to start then, all would have been well. But Bill and his friends had arrived while the driver and conductor were both out in the road.

The affair now began to resemble the doings of Horatius on the bridge. Psmith and Mike turned to bay on the platform at the foot of the tram steps. Bill, leading by three yards, sprang on to it, grabbed Mike, and fell with him on to the road. Psmith, descending with a dignity somewhat lessened by the fact that his hat was on the side of his head, was in time to engage the runners-up.

Psmith, as pugilist, lacked something of the calm majesty which characterized him in the more peaceful moments of life, but he was undoubtedly effective. Nature had given him an enormous reach and a lightness on his feet remarkable in one of his size; and at some time in his career he appeared to have learned how to use his hands. The first of the three runners, the walking-stick manipulator, had the misfortune to charge straight into the old Etonian's left. It was a well-timed blow, and the force of it, added to the speed at which the victim was running, sent him on to the pavement, where he spun round and sat down. In the subsequent proceedings he took no part.

The other two attacked Psmith simultaneously, one on each side. In doing so, the one on the left tripped over Mike and Bill, who were still in the process of sorting themselves out, and fell, leaving Psmith free to attend to the other. He was a tall, weedy youth. His conspicuous features were a long nose and a light yellow waistcoat. Psmith hit him on the former with his left and on the latter with his right. The long youth emitted a gurgle, and collided with Bill, who had wrenched himself free from Mike and staggered to his feet. Bill, having received a second blow in the eye during the course of his interview on the road with Mike, was not feeling himself. Mistaking the other for an enemy, he proceeded to smite him in the parts about the jaw. He had just upset him, when a stern official voice observed, "Ere, now, what's all this?'

There is no more unfailing corrective to a scene of strife than the 'What's all this?' of the London policeman. Bill abandoned his intention of stamping on the prostrate one, and the latter, sitting up, blinked and was silent.

'What's all this?' asked the policeman again. Psmith, adjusting his hat at the correct angle again, undertook the explanations.

'A distressing scene, officer,' he said. 'A case of that unbridled brawling which is, alas, but too common in our London streets. These two, possibly till now the closest friends, fall out over some point, probably of the most trivial nature, and what happens? They brawl. They—'

'He 'it me,' said the long youth, dabbing at his face with a handkerchief and pointing an accusing finger at Psmith, who regarded him through his eyeglass with a look in which pity and censure were nicely blended.

Bill, meanwhile, circling round restlessly, in the apparent hope of getting past the Law and having another encounter with Mike, expressed himself in a stream of language which drew stern reproof from the shocked constable.

'You 'op it,' concluded the man in blue. 'That's what you do. You 'op it.'

'I should,' said Psmith kindly. 'The officer is speaking in your best interests. A man of taste and discernment, he knows what is best. His advice is good, and should be followed.'

The constable seemed to notice Psmith for the first time. He turned and stared at him. Psmith's praise had not had the effect of softening him. His look was one of suspicion.

'And what might *you* have been up to?' he inquired coldly. 'This man says you hit him.'

Psmith waved the matter aside.

'Purely in self-defence,' he said, 'purely in self-defence. What else could the man of spirit do? A mere tap to discourage an aggressive movement.'

The policeman stood silent, weighing matters in the balance. He produced a notebook and sucked his pencil. Then he called the conductor of the tram as a witness.

'A brainy and admirable step,' said Psmith, approvingly. 'This rugged, honest man, all unused to verbal subtleties, shall give us his plain account of what happened. After which, as I presume this tram-little as I know of the habits of trams-has got to go somewhere today, I would suggest that we all separated and moved on.'

He took two half-crowns from his pocket, and began to clink them meditatively together. A slight softening of the frigidity of the constable's manner became noticeable. There was a milder beam in the eyes which gazed into Psmith's.

Nor did the conductor seem altogether uninfluenced by the sight.

The conductor deposed that he had bin on the point of pushing on, seeing as how he'd hung abart long enough, when he see'd them two gents, the long 'un with the heye-glass (Psmith bowed) and t'other 'un, a-legging of it dahn the road towards him, with the other blokes pelting after 'em. He added that, when they reached the trem, the two gents had got aboard, and was then set upon by the blokes. And after that, he concluded, well, there was a bit of a scrap, and that's how it was.

'Lucidly and excellently put,' said Psmith. 'That is just how it was. Comrade Jackson, I fancy we leave the court without a stain on our characters. We win through. Er-constable, we have given you a great deal of trouble. Possibly —?'

'Thank you, sir.' There was a musical clinking. 'Now then, all of you, you 'op it. You're all bin poking your noses in 'ere long enough. Pop off. Get on with that tram, conductor.' Psmith and Mike settled themselves in a seat on the roof. When the conductor came along, Psmith gave him half a crown, and asked after his wife and the little ones at home. The conductor thanked goodness that he was a bachelor, punched the tickets, and retired.

'Subject for a historical picture,' said Psmith. 'Wounded leaving the field after the Battle of Clapham Common. How are your injuries, Comrade Jackson?'

'My back's hurting like blazes,' said Mike. 'And my ear's all sore where that chap got me. Anything the matter with you?'

'Physically,' said Psmith, 'no. Spiritually much. Do you realize, Comrade Jackson, the thing that has happened? I am riding in a tram. I, Psmith, have paid a penny for a ticket on a tram. If this should get about the clubs! I tell you, Comrade Jackson, no such crisis has ever occurred before in the course of my career.'

'You can always get off, you know,' said Mike.

'He thinks of everything,' said Psmith, admiringly. 'You have touched the spot with an unerring finger. Let us descend. I observe in the distance a cab. That looks to me more the sort of thing we want. Let us go and parley with the driver.'

17. Sunday Supper

The cab took them back to the flat, at considerable expense, and Psmith requested Mike to make tea, a performance in which he himself was interested purely as a spectator. He had views on the subject of tea-making which he liked to expound from an armchair or sofa, but he never got further than this. Mike, his back throbbing dully from the blow he had received, and feeling more than a little sore all over, prepared the Etna, fetched the milk, and finally produced the finished article.

Psmith sipped meditatively.

'How pleasant,' he said, 'after strife is rest. We shouldn't have appreciated this simple cup of tea had our sensibilities remained unstirred this afternoon. We can now sit at our ease, like warriors after the fray, till the time comes for setting out to Comrade Waller's once more.'

Mike looked up.

'What! You don't mean to say you're going to sweat out to Clapham again?'

'Undoubtedly. Comrade Waller is expecting us to supper.'

'What absolute rot! We can't fag back there.'

'Noblesse oblige. The cry has gone round the Waller household, "Jackson and Psmith are coming to supper," and we cannot disappoint them now. Already the fatted blanc-mange has been killed, and the table creaks beneath what's left of the midday beef. We must be there; besides, don't you want to see how the poor man is? Probably we shall find him in the act of emitting his last breath. I expect he was lynched by the enthusiastic mob.'

'Not much,' grinned Mike. 'They were too busy with us. All right, I'll come if you really want me to, but it's awful rot.'

One of the many things Mike could never understand in Psmith was his fondness for getting into atmospheres that were not his own. He would go out of his way to do this. Mike, like most boys of his age, was never really happy and at his ease except in the presence of those of his own years and class. Psmith, on the contrary, seemed to be bored by them, and infinitely preferred talking to somebody who lived in quite another world. Mike was not a snob. He simply had not the ability to be at his ease with people in another class from his own. He did not know what to talk to them about, unless they were cricket professionals. With them he was never at a loss.

But Psmith was different. He could get on with anyone. He seemed to have the gift of entering into their minds and seeing things from their point of view.

As regarded Mr Waller, Mike liked him personally, and was prepared, as we have seen, to undertake considerable risks in his defence; but he loathed with all his heart and soul the idea of supper at his house. He knew that he would have nothing to say. Whereas Psmith gave him the impression of looking forward to the thing as a treat.

* * * * *

The house where Mr Waller lived was one of a row of semi-detached villas on the north side of the Common. The door was opened to them by their host himself. So far from looking battered and emitting last breaths, he appeared particularly spruce. He had just returned from Church, and was still wearing his gloves and tall hat. He squeaked with surprise when he saw who were standing on the mat.

'Why, dear me, dear me,' he said. 'Here you are! I have been wondering what had happened to you. I was afraid that you might have been seriously hurt. I was afraid those ruffians might have injured you. When last I saw you, you were being —'

'Chivvied,' interposed Psmith, with dignified melancholy. 'Do not let us try to wrap the fact up in pleasant words. We were being chivvied. We were legging it with the infuriated mob at our heels. An ignominious position for a Shropshire Psmith, but, after all, Napoleon did the same.'

'But what happened? I could not see. I only know that quite suddenly the people seemed to stop listening to me, and all gathered round you and Jackson. And then I saw that Jackson was engaged in a fight with a young man.'

'Comrade Jackson, I imagine, having heard a great deal about all men being equal, was anxious to test the theory, and see whether Comrade Bill was as good a man as he was. The experiment was broken off prematurely, but I personally should be inclined to say that Comrade Jackson had a shade the better of the exchanges.'

Mr Waller looked with interest at Mike, who shuffled and felt awkward. He was hoping that Psmith would say nothing about the reason of his engaging Bill in combat. He had an uneasy feeling that Mr Waller's gratitude would be effusive and overpowering, and he did not wish to pose as the brave young hero. There are moments when one does not feel equal to the *role*.

Fortunately, before Mr Waller had time to ask any further questions, the supper-bell sounded, and they went into the dining-room.

Sunday supper, unless done on a large and informal scale, is probably the most depressing meal in existence. There is a chill discomfort in the round of beef, an icy severity about the open jam tart. The blancmange shivers miserably.

Spirituous liquor helps to counteract the influence of these things, and so does exhilarating conversation. Unfortunately, at Mr Waller's table there was neither. The cashier's views on temperance were not merely for the platform; they extended to the home. And the company was not of the exhilarating sort. Besides Psmith and Mike and their host, there were four people present—Comrade Prebble, the orator; a young man of the name of Richards; Mr Waller's niece, answering to the name of Ada, who was engaged to Mr Richards; and Edward.

Edward was Mr Waller's son. He was ten years old, wore a very tight Eton suit, and had the peculiarly loathsome expression which a snub nose sometimes gives to the young.

It would have been plain to the most casual observer that Mr Waller was fond and proud of his son. The cashier was a widower, and after five minutes' acquaintance with Edward, Mike felt strongly that Mrs Waller was the lucky one. Edward sat next to Mike, and showed a tendency to concentrate his conversation on him. Psmith, at the opposite end of the table, beamed in a fatherly manner upon the pair through his eyeglass.

Mike got on with small girls reasonably well. He preferred them at a distance, but, if cornered by them, could put up a fairly good show. Small boys, however, filled him with a sort of frozen horror. It was his view that a boy should not be exhibited publicly until he reached an age when he might be in the running for some sort of colours at a public school.

Edward was one of those well-informed small boys. He opened on Mike with the first mouthful.

'Do you know the principal exports of Marseilles?' he inquired.

'What?' said Mike coldly.

'Do you know the principal exports of Marseilles? I do.'

'Oh?' said Mike.

'Yes. Do you know the capital of Madagascar?'

Mike, as crimson as the beef he was attacking, said he did not.

'I do.'

'Oh?' said Mike.

'Who was the first king —'

'You mustn't worry Mr Jackson, Teddy,' said Mr Waller, with a touch of pride in his voice, as who should say 'There are not many boys of his age, I can tell you, who *could* worry you with questions like that.'

'No, no, he likes it,' said Psmith, unnecessarily. 'He likes it. I always hold that much may be learned by casual chit-chat across the dinner-table. I owe much of my own grasp of —'

'I bet *you* don't know what's the capital of Madagascar,' interrupted Mike rudely.

'I do,' said Edward. 'I can tell you the kings of Israel?' he added, turning to Mike. He seemed to have no curiosity as to the extent of Psmith's knowledge. Mike's appeared to fascinate him.

Mike helped himself to beetroot in moody silence.

His mouth was full when Comrade Prebble asked him a question. Comrade Prebble, as has been pointed out in an earlier part of the narrative, was a good chap, but had no roof to his mouth.

'I beg your pardon?' said Mike.

Comrade Prebble repeated his observation. Mike looked helplessly at Psmith, but Psmith's eyes were on his plate.

Mike felt he must venture on some answer.

'No,' he said decidedly.

Comrade Prebble seemed slightly taken aback. There was an awkward pause. Then Mr Waller, for whom his fellow Socialist's methods of conversation held no mysteries, interpreted.

'The mustard, Prebble? Yes, yes. Would you mind passing Prebble the mustard, Mr Jackson?'

'Oh, sorry,' gasped Mike, and, reaching out, upset the water-jug into the open jam-tart.

Through the black mist which rose before his eyes as he leaped to his feet and stammered apologies came the dispassionate voice of Master Edward Waller reminding him that mustard was first introduced into Peru by Cortez.

His host was all courtesy and consideration. He passed the matter off genially. But life can never be quite the same after you have upset a water-jug into an open jam-tart at the table of a comparative stranger. Mike's nerve had gone. He ate on, but he was a broken man.

At the other end of the table it became gradually apparent that things were not going on altogether as they should have done. There was a sort of bleakness in the atmosphere. Young Mr Richards was looking like a stuffed fish, and the face of Mr Waller's niece was cold and set.

'Why, come, come, Ada,' said Mr Waller, breezily, 'what's the matter? You're eating nothing. What's George been saying to you?' he added jocularly.

'Thank you, uncle Robert,' replied Ada precisely, 'there's nothing the matter. Nothing that Mr Richards can say to me can upset me.'

'Mr Richards!' echoed Mr Waller in astonishment. How was he to know that, during the walk back from church, the world had been transformed, George had become Mr Richards, and all was over?

'I assure you, Ada —' began that unfortunate young man. Ada turned a frigid shoulder towards him.

'Come, come,' said Mr Waller disturbed. 'What's all this? What's all this?'

His niece burst into tears and left the room.

If there is anything more embarrassing to a guest than a family row, we have yet to hear of it. Mike, scarlet to the extreme edges of his ears, concentrated himself on his plate. Comrade Prebble made a great many remarks, which were probably illuminating, if they could have been understood. Mr Waller looked, astonished, at Mr Richards. Mr Richards, pink but dogged, loosened his collar, but said nothing. Psmith, leaning forward, asked Master Edward Waller his opinion on the Licensing Bill.

'We happened to have a word or two,' said Mr Richards at length, 'on the way home from church on the subject of Women's Suffrage.'

'That fatal topic!' murmured Psmith.

'In Australia —' began Master Edward Waller.

'I was rayther-well, rayther facetious about it,' continued Mr Richards.

Psmith clicked his tongue sympathetically.

'In Australia —' said Edward.

'I went talking on, laughing and joking, when all of a sudden she flew out at me. How was I to know she was 'eart and soul in the movement? You never told me,' he added accusingly to his host.

'In Australia —' said Edward.

'I'll go and try and get her round. How was I to know?'

Mr Richards thrust back his chair and bounded from the room.

'Now, iawinyaw, iear oiler —' said Comrade Prebble judicially, but was interrupted.

'How very disturbing!' said Mr Waller. 'I am so sorry that this should have happened. Ada is such a touchy, sensitive girl. She —'

'In Australia,' said Edward in even tones, 'they've *got* Women's Suffrage already. Did *you* know that?' he said to Mike.

Mike made no answer. His eyes were fixed on his plate. A bead of perspiration began to roll down his forehead. If his feelings could have been ascertained at that moment, they would have been summed up in the words, 'Death, where is thy sting?'

18. Psmith Makes a Discovery

'Women,' said Psmith, helping himself to trifle, and speaking with the air of one launched upon his special subject, 'are, one must recollect, like-like-er, well, in fact, just so. Passing on lightly from that conclusion, let us turn for a moment to the Rights of Property, in connection with which Comrade Prebble and yourself had so much that was interesting to say this afternoon. Perhaps you'—he bowed in Comrade Prebble's direction—'would resume, for the benefit of Comrade Jackson—a novice in the Cause, but earnest-your very lucid—'

Comrade Prebble beamed, and took the floor. Mike began to realize that, till now, he had never known what boredom meant. There had been moments in his life which had been less interesting than other moments, but nothing to touch this for agony. Comrade Prebble's address streamed on like water rushing over a weir. Every now and then there was a word or two which was recognizable, but this happened so rarely that it amounted to little. Sometimes Mr Waller would interject a remark, but not often. He seemed to be of the opinion that Comrade Prebble's was the master mind and that to add anything to his views would be in the nature of painting the lily and gilding the refined gold. Mike himself said nothing. Psmith and Edward were equally silent. The former sat like one in a trance, thinking his own thoughts, while Edward, who, prospecting on the sideboard, had located a rich biscuit-mine, was too occupied for speech.

After about twenty minutes, during which Mike's discomfort changed to a dull resignation, Mr Waller suggested a move to the drawing-room, where Ada, he said, would play some hymns.

The prospect did not dazzle Mike, but any change, he thought, must be for the better. He had sat staring at the ruin of the blancmange so long that it had begun to hypnotize him. Also, the move had the excellent result of eliminating the snub-nosed Edward, who was sent to bed. His last words were in the form of a question, addressed to Mike, on the subject of the hypotenuse and the square upon the same.

'A remarkably intelligent boy,' said Psmith. 'You must let him come to tea at our flat one day. I may not be in myself—I have many duties which keep me away-but Comrade Jackson is sure to be there, and will be delighted to chat with him.'

On the way upstairs Mike tried to get Psmith to himself for a moment to suggest the advisability of an early departure; but Psmith was in close conversation with his host. Mike was left to Comrade Prebble, who, apparently, had only touched the fringe of his subject in his lecture in the dining-room.

When Mr Waller had predicted hymns in the drawing-room, he had been too sanguine (or too pessimistic). Of Ada, when they arrived, there were no signs. It seemed that she had gone straight to bed. Young Mr Richards was sitting on the sofa, moodily turning the leaves of a photograph album, which contained portraits of Master Edward Waller in geometrically progressing degrees of repulsiveness-here, in frocks, looking like a gargoyle; there, in sailor suit, looking like nothing on earth. The inspection of these was obviously deepening Mr Richards' gloom, but he proceeded doggedly with it.

Comrade Prebble backed the reluctant Mike into a corner, and, like the Ancient Mariner, held him with a glittering eye. Psmith and Mr Waller, in the opposite corner, were looking at something with their heads close together. Mike definitely abandoned all hope of a rescue from Psmith, and tried to buoy himself up with the reflection that this could not last for ever.

Hours seemed to pass, and then at last he heard Psmith's voice saying good-bye to his host.

He sprang to his feet. Comrade Prebble was in the middle of a sentence, but this was no time for polished courtesy. He felt that he must get away, and at once. 'I fear,' Psmith was saying, 'that we must tear ourselves away. We have greatly enjoyed our evening. You must look us up at our flat one day, and bring Comrade Prebble. If I am not in, Comrade Jackson is certain to be, and he will be more than delighted to hear Comrade Prebble speak further on the subject of which he is such a master.' Comrade Prebble was understood to say that he would certainly come. Mr Waller beamed. Mr Richards, still steeped in gloom, shook hands in silence.

Out in the road, with the front door shut behind them, Mike spoke his mind.

'Look here, Smith,' he said definitely, 'if being your confidential secretary and adviser is going to let me in for any more of that sort of thing, you can jolly well accept my resignation.'

'The orgy was not to your taste?' said Psmith sympathetically.

Mike laughed. One of those short, hollow, bitter laughs.

'I am at a loss, Comrade Jackson,' said Psmith, 'to understand your attitude. You fed sumptuously. You had fun with the crockery-that knockabout act of yours with the water-jug was alone worth the money-and you had the advantage of listening to the views of a master of his subject. What more do you want?'

'What on earth did you land me with that man Prebble for?'

'Land you! Why, you courted his society. I had practically to drag you away from him. When I got up to say good-bye, you were listening to him with bulging eyes. I never saw such a picture of rapt attention. Do you mean to tell me, Comrade Jackson, that your appearance belied you, that you were not interested? Well, well. How we misread our fellow creatures.'

'I think you might have come and lent a hand with Prebble. It was a bit thick.'

'I was too absorbed with Comrade Waller. We were talking of things of vital moment. However, the night is yet young. We will take this cab, wend our way to the West, seek a cafe, and cheer ourselves with light refreshments.'

Arrived at a cafe whose window appeared to be a sort of museum of every kind of German sausage, they took possession of a vacant table and ordered coffee. Mike soon found himself soothed by his bright surroundings, and gradually his impressions of blancmange, Edward, and Comrade Prebble faded from his mind. Psmith, meanwhile, was preserving an unusual silence, being deep in a large square book of the sort in which Press cuttings are pasted. As Psmith scanned its contents a curious smile lit up his face. His reflections seemed to be of an agreeable nature.

'Hullo,' said Mike, 'what have you got hold of there? Where did you get that?'

'Comrade Waller very kindly lent it to me. He showed it to me after supper, knowing how enthusiastically I was attached to the Cause. Had you been less tensely wrapped up in Comrade Prebble's conversation, I would have desired you to step across and join us. However, you now have your opportunity.'

'But what is it?' asked Mike.

'It is the record of the meetings of the Tulse Hill Parliament,' said Psmith impressively. 'A faithful record of all they said, all the votes of confidence they passed in the Government, and also all the nasty knocks they gave it from time to time.'

'What on earth's the Tulse Hill Parliament?'

'It is, alas,' said Psmith in a grave, sad voice, 'no more. In life it was beautiful, but now it has done the Tom Bowling act. It has gone aloft. We are dealing, Comrade Jackson, not with the live, vivid present, but with the far-off, rusty past. And yet, in a way, there is a touch of the live, vivid present mixed up in it.'

'I don't know what the dickens you're talking about,' said Mike. 'Let's have a look, anyway.'

Psmith handed him the volume, and, leaning back, sipped his coffee, and watched him. At first Mike's face was bored and blank, but suddenly an interested look came into it.

'Aha!' said Psmith.

'Who's Bickersdyke? Anything to do with our Bickersdyke?'

'No other than our genial friend himself.'

Mike turned the pages, reading a line or two on each.

'Hullo!' he said, chuckling. 'He lets himself go a bit, doesn't he!'

'He does,' acknowledged Psmith. 'A fiery, passionate nature, that of Comrade Bickersdyke.'

'He's simply cursing the Government here. Giving them frightful beans.'

Psmith nodded.

'I noticed the fact myself.'

'But what's it all about?'

'As far as I can glean from Comrade Waller,' said Psmith, 'about twenty years ago, when he and Comrade Bickersdyke worked hand-in-hand as fellow clerks at the New Asiatic, they were both members of the Tulse Hill Parliament, that powerful institution. At that time Comrade Bickersdyke was as fruity a Socialist as Comrade Waller is now. Only, apparently, as he began to get on a bit in the world, he altered his views to some extent as regards the iniquity of freezing on to a decent share of the doubloons. And that, you see, is where the dim and rusty past begins to get mixed up with the live, vivid present. If any tactless person were to publish those very able speeches made by Comrade Bickersdyke when a bulwark of the Tulse Hill Parliament, our revered chief would be more or less caught bending, if I may employ the expression, as regards his chances of getting in as Unionist candidate at Kenningford. You follow me, Watson? I rather fancy the light-hearted electors of Kenningford, from what I have seen of their rather acute sense of humour, would be, as it were, all over it. It would be very, very trying for Comrade Bickersdyke if these speeches of his were to get about.'

'You aren't going to —!'

'I shall do nothing rashly. I shall merely place this handsome volume among my treasured books. I shall add it to my "Books that have helped me" series. Because I fancy that, in an emergency, it may not be at all a bad thing to have about me. And now,' he concluded, 'as the hour is getting late, perhaps we had better be shoving off for home.'

19. The Illness of Edward

Life in a bank is at its pleasantest in the winter. When all the world outside is dark and damp and cold, the light and warmth of the place are comforting. There is a pleasant air of solidity about the interior of a bank. The green shaded lamps look cosy. And, the outside world offering so few attractions, the worker, perched on his stool, feels that he is not so badly off after all. It is when the days are long and the sun beats hot on the pavement, and everything shouts to him how splendid it is out in the country, that he begins to grow restless.

Mike, except for a fortnight at the beginning of his career in the New Asiatic Bank, had not had to stand the test of sunshine. At present, the weather being cold and dismal, he was almost entirely contented. Now that he had got into the swing of his work, the days passed very quickly; and with his life after office-hours he had no fault to find at all.

His life was very regular. He would arrive in the morning just in time to sign his name in the attendance-book before it was removed to the accountant's room. That was at ten o'clock. From ten to eleven he would potter. There was nothing going on at that time in his department, and Mr Waller seemed to take it for granted that he should stroll off to the Postage Department and talk to Psmith, who had generally some fresh grievance against the ring-wearing Bristow to air. From eleven to half past twelve he would put in a little gentle work. Lunch, unless there was a rush of business or Mr Waller happened to suffer from a spasm of conscientiousness, could be spun out from half past twelve to two. More work from two till half past three. From half past three till half past four tea in the tearoom, with a novel. And from half past four till five either a little more work or more pottering, according to whether there was any work to do or not. It was by no means an unpleasant mode of spending a late January day.

Then there was no doubt that it was an interesting little community, that of the New Asiatic Bank. The curiously amateurish nature of the institution lent a certain air of light-heartedness to the place. It was not like one of those banks whose London office is their main office, where stern business is everything and a man becomes a mere machine for getting through a certain amount of routine work. The employees of the New Asiatic Bank, having plenty of time on their hands, were able to retain their individuality. They had leisure to think of other things besides their work. Indeed, they had so much leisure that it is a wonder they thought of their work at all.

The place was full of quaint characters. There was West, who had been requested to leave Haileybury owing to his habit of borrowing horses and attending meets in the neighbourhood, the same being always out of bounds and necessitating a complete disregard of the rules respecting evening chapel and lock-up. He was a small, dried-up youth, with black hair plastered down on his head. He went about his duties in a costume which suggested the sportsman of the comic papers.

There was also Hignett, who added to the meagre salary allowed him by the bank by singing comic songs at the minor music halls. He confided to Mike his intention of leaving the bank as soon as he had made a name, and taking seriously to the business. He told him that he had knocked them at the Bedford the week before, and in support of the statement showed him a cutting from the Era, in which the writer said that 'Other acceptable turns were the Bounding Zouaves, Steingruber's Dogs, and Arthur Hignett.' Mike wished him luck.

And there was Raymond who dabbled in journalism and was the author of 'Straight Talks to Housewives' in *Trifles*, under the pseudonym of 'Lady Gussie'; Wragge, who believed that the earth was flat, and addressed meetings on the subject in Hyde Park on Sundays; and many others, all interesting to talk to of a morning when work was slack and time had to be filled in.

Mike found himself, by degrees, growing quite attached to the New Asiatic Bank.

One morning, early in February, he noticed a curious change in Mr Waller. The head of the Cash Department was, as a rule, mildly cheerful on arrival, and apt (excessively, Mike thought, though he always listened with polite interest) to relate the most recent sayings and doings of his snub-nosed son, Edward. No action of this young prodigy was withheld from Mike. He had heard, on different occasions, how he had won a prize at his school for General Information (which Mike could well believe); how he had trapped young Mr Richards, now happily reconciled to Ada, with an ingenious verbal catch; and how he had made a sequence of diverting puns on the name of the new curate, during the course of that cleric's first Sunday afternoon visit.

On this particular day, however, the cashier was silent and absent-minded. He answered Mike's good-morning mechanically, and sitting down at his desk, stared blankly across the building. There was a curiously grey, tired look on his face.

Mike could not make it out. He did not like to ask if there was anything the matter. Mr Waller's face had the unreasonable effect on him of making him feel shy and awkward. Anything in the nature of sorrow always dried Mike up and robbed him of the power of speech. Being naturally sympathetic, he had raged inwardly in many a crisis at this devil of dumb awkwardness which possessed him and prevented him from putting his sympathy into words. He had always envied the cooing readiness of the hero on the stage when anyone was in trouble. He wondered whether he would ever acquire that knack of pouring out a limpid stream of soothing words on such occasions. At present he could get no farther than a scowl and an almost offensive gruffness.

The happy thought struck him of consulting Psmith. It was his hour for pottering, so he pottered round to the Postage Department, where he found the old Etonian eyeing with disfavour a new satin tie which Bristow was wearing that morning for the first time.

'I say, Smith,' he said, 'I want to speak to you for a second.'

Psmith rose. Mike led the way to a quiet corner of the Telegrams Department.

'I tell you, Comrade Jackson,' said Psmith, 'I am hard pressed. The fight is beginning to be too much for me. After a grim struggle, after days of unremitting toil, I succeeded yesterday in inducing the man Bristow to abandon that rainbow waistcoat of his. Today I enter the building, blythe and buoyant, worn, of course, from the long struggle, but seeing with aching eyes the dawn of another, better era, and there is Comrade Bristow in a satin tie. It's hard, Comrade Jackson, it's hard, I tell you.'

'Look here, Smith,' said Mike, 'I wish you'd go round to the Cash and find out what's up with old Waller. He's got the hump about something. He's sitting there looking absolutely fed up with things. I hope there's nothing up. He's not a bad sort. It would be rot if anything rotten's happened.'

Psmith began to display a gentle interest.

'So other people have troubles as well as myself,' he murmured musingly. 'I had almost forgotten that. Comrade Waller's misfortunes cannot but be trivial compared with mine, but possibly it will be as well to ascertain their nature. I will reel round and make inquiries.'

'Good man,' said Mike. 'I'll wait here.'

Psmith departed, and returned, ten minutes later, looking more serious than when he had left.

'His kid's ill, poor chap,' he said briefly. 'Pretty badly too, from what I can gather. Pneumonia. Waller was up all night. He oughtn't to be here at all today. He doesn't know what he's doing half the time. He's absolutely fagged out. Look here, you'd better nip back and do as much of the work as you can. I shouldn't talk to him much if I were you. Buck along.'

Mike went. Mr Waller was still sitting staring out across the aisle. There was something more than a little gruesome in the sight of him. He wore a crushed, beaten look, as if all the life and fight had gone out of him. A customer came to the desk to cash a cheque. The cashier shovelled the money to him under the bars with the air of one whose mind is elsewhere. Mike could guess what he was feeling, and what he was thinking about. The fact that the snub-nosed Edward was, without exception, the most repulsive small boy he had ever met in this world, where repulsive small boys crowd and jostle one another, did not interfere with his appreciation of the cashier's state of mind. Mike's was essentially a sympathetic character. He had the gift of intuitive understanding, where people of whom he was fond were concerned. It was this which drew to him those who had intelligence enough to see beyond his sometimes rather forbidding manner, and to realize that his blunt speech was largely due to shyness. In spite of his prejudice against Edward, he could put himself into Mr Waller's place, and see the thing from his point of view.

Psmith's injunction to him not to talk much was unnecessary. Mike, as always, was rendered utterly dumb by the sight of suffering. He sat at his desk, occupying himself as best he could with the driblets of work which came to him.

Mr Waller's silence and absentness continued unchanged. The habit of years had made his work mechanical. Probably few of the customers who came to cash cheques suspected that there was anything the matter with the man who paid them their money. After all, most people look on the cashier of a bank as a sort of human slot-machine. You put in your cheque, and out comes money. It is no affair of yours whether life is treating the machine well or ill that day.

The hours dragged slowly by till five o'clock struck, and the cashier, putting on his coat and hat, passed silently out through the swing doors. He walked listlessly. He was evidently tired out.

Mike shut his ledger with a vicious bang, and went across to find
Psmith. He was glad the day was over.

20. Concerning a Cheque

Things never happen quite as one expects them to. Mike came to the office next morning prepared for a repetition of the previous day. He was amazed to find the cashier not merely cheerful, but even exuberantly cheerful. Edward, it appeared, had rallied in the afternoon, and, when his father had got home, had been out of danger. He was now going along excellently, and had stumped Ada, who was nursing him, with a question about the Thirty Years' War, only a few minutes before his father had left to catch his train. The cashier was overflowing with happiness and goodwill towards his species. He greeted customers with bright remarks on the weather, and snappy views on the leading events of the day: the former tinged with optimism, the latter full of a gentle spirit of toleration. His attitude towards the latest actions of His Majesty's Government was that of one who felt that, after all, there was probably some good even in the vilest of his fellow creatures, if one could only find it.

Altogether, the cloud had lifted from the Cash Department. All was joy, jollity, and song.

'The attitude of Comrade Waller,' said Psmith, on being informed of the change, 'is reassuring. I may now think of my own troubles. Comrade Bristow has blown into the office today in patent leather boots with white kid uppers, as I believe the technical term is. Add to that the fact that he is still wearing the satin tie, the waistcoat, and the ring, and you will understand why I have definitely decided this morning to abandon all hope of his reform. Henceforth my services, for what they are worth, are at the disposal of Comrade Bickersdyke. My time from now onward is his. He shall have the full educative value of my exclusive attention. I give Comrade Bristow up. Made straight for the corner flag, you understand,' he added, as Mr Rossiter emerged from his lair, 'and centred, and Sandy Turnbull headed a beautiful goal. I was just telling Jackson about the match against Blackburn Rovers,' he said to Mr Rossiter.

'Just so, just so. But get on with your work, Smith. We are a little behind-hand. I think perhaps it would be as well not to leave it just yet.'

'I will leap at it at once,' said Psmith cordially.

Mike went back to his department.

The day passed quickly. Mr Waller, in the intervals of work, talked a good deal, mostly of Edward, his doings, his sayings, and his prospects. The only thing that seemed to worry Mr Waller was the problem of how to employ his son's almost superhuman talents to the best advantage. Most of the goals towards which the average man strives struck him as too unambitious for the prodigy.

By the end of the day Mike had had enough of Edward. He never wished to hear the name again.

We do not claim originality for the statement that things never happen quite as one expects them to. We repeat it now because of its profound truth. The Edward's pneumonia episode having ended satisfactorily (or, rather, being apparently certain to end satisfactorily, for the invalid, though out of danger, was still in bed), Mike looked forward to a series of days unbroken by any but the minor troubles of life. For these he was prepared. What he did not expect was any big calamity.

At the beginning of the day there were no signs of it. The sky was blue and free from all suggestions of approaching thunderbolts. Mr Waller, still chirpy, had nothing but good news of Edward. Mike went for his morning stroll round the office feeling that things had settled down and had made up their mind to run smoothly.

When he got back, barely half an hour later, the storm had burst.

There was no one in the department at the moment of his arrival; but a few minutes later he saw Mr Waller come out of the manager's room, and make his way down the aisle.

It was his walk which first gave any hint that something was wrong. It was the same limp, crushed walk which Mike had seen when Edward's safety still hung in the balance.

As Mr Waller came nearer, Mike saw that the cashier's face was deadly pale.

Mr Waller caught sight of him and quickened his pace.

'Jackson,' he said.

Mike came forward.

'Do you remember —' he spoke slowly, and with an effort, 'do you remember a cheque coming through the day before yesterday for a hundred pounds, with Sir John Morrison's signature?'

'Yes. It came in the morning, rather late.'

Mike remembered the cheque perfectly well, owing to the amount. It was the only three-figure cheque which had come across the counter during the day. It had been presented just before the cashier had gone out to lunch. He recollected the man who had presented it, a tallish man with a beard. He had noticed him particularly because of the contrast between his manner and that of the cashier. The former had been so very cheery and breezy, the latter so dazed and silent.

'Why,' he said.

'It was a forgery,' muttered Mr Waller, sitting down heavily.

Mike could not take it in all at once. He was stunned. All he could understand was that a far worse thing had happened than anything he could have imagined.

'A forgery?' he said.

'A forgery. And a clumsy one. Oh it's hard. I should have seen it on any other day but that. I could not have missed it. They showed me the cheque in there just now. I could not believe that I had passed it. I don't remember doing it. My mind was far away. I don't remember the cheque or anything about it. Yet there it is.'

Once more Mike was tongue-tied. For the life of him he could not think of anything to say. Surely, he thought, he could find *something* in the shape of words to show his sympathy. But he could find nothing that would not sound horribly stilted and cold. He sat silent.

'Sir John is in there,' went on the cashier. 'He is furious. Mr Bickersdyke, too. They are both furious. I shall be dismissed. I shall lose my place. I shall be dismissed.' He was talking more to himself than to Mike. It was dreadful to see him sitting there, all limp and broken.

'I shall lose my place. Mr Bickersdyke has wanted to get rid of me for
a long time. He never liked me. I shall be dismissed. What can I do?
I'm an old man. I can't make another start. I am good for nothing.
Nobody will take an old man like me.'

His voice died away. There was a silence. Mike sat staring miserably in front of him.

Then, quite suddenly, an idea came to him. The whole pressure of the atmosphere seemed to lift. He saw a way out. It was a curious crooked way, but at that moment it stretched clear and broad before him. He felt lighthearted and excited, as if he were watching the development of some interesting play at the theatre.

He got up, smiling.

The cashier did not notice the movement. Somebody had come in to cash a cheque, and he was working mechanically.

Mike walked up the aisle to Mr Bickersdyke's room, and went in.

The manager was in his chair at the big table. Opposite him, facing slightly sideways, was a small, round, very red-faced man. Mr Bickersdyke was speaking as Mike entered.

'I can assure you, Sir John —' he was saying.

He looked up as the door opened.

'Well, Mr Jackson?'

Mike almost laughed. The situation was tickling him.

'Mr Waller has told me —' he began.

'I have already seen Mr Waller.'

'I know. He told me about the cheque. I came to explain.'

'Explain?'

'Yes. He didn't cash it at all.'

'I don't understand you, Mr Jackson.'
'I was at the counter when it was brought in,' said Mike. 'I cashed it.'

21. Psmith Makes Inquiries

Psmith, as was his habit of a morning when the fierce rush of his commercial duties had abated somewhat, was leaning gracefully against his desk, musing on many things, when he was aware that Bristow was standing before him.

Focusing his attention with some reluctance upon this blot on the horizon, he discovered that the exploiter of rainbow waistcoats and satin ties was addressing him.

'I say, Smithy,' said Bristow. He spoke in rather an awed voice.

'Say on, Comrade Bristow,' said Psmith graciously. 'You have our ear. You would seem to have something on your chest in addition to that Neapolitan ice garment which, I regret to see, you still flaunt. If it is one tithe as painful as that, you have my sympathy. Jerk it out, Comrade Bristow.'

'Jackson isn't half copping it from old Bick.'

'Isn't —? What exactly did you say?'

'He's getting it hot on the carpet.'

'You wish to indicate,' said Psmith, 'that there is some slight disturbance, some passing breeze between Comrades Jackson and Bickersdyke?'

Bristow chuckled.

'Breeze! Blooming hurricane, more like it. I was in Bick's room just now with a letter to sign, and I tell you, the fur was flying all over the bally shop. There was old Bick cursing for all he was worth, and a little red-faced buffer puffing out his cheeks in an armchair.'

'We all have our hobbies,' said Psmith.

'Jackson wasn't saying much. He jolly well hadn't a chance. Old Bick was shooting it out fourteen to the dozen.'

'I have been privileged,' said Psmith, 'to hear Comrade Bickersdyke speak both in his sanctum and in public. He has, as you suggest, a ready flow of speech. What, exactly was the cause of the turmoil?'

'I couldn't wait to hear. I was too jolly glad to get away. Old Bick looked at me as if he could eat me, snatched the letter out of my hand, signed it, and waved his hand at the door as a hint to hop it. Which I jolly well did. He had started jawing Jackson again before I was out of the room.'

'While applauding his hustle,' said Psmith, 'I fear that I must take official notice of this. Comrade Jackson is essentially a Sensitive Plant, highly strung, neurotic. I cannot have his nervous system jolted and disorganized in this manner, and his value as a confidential secretary and adviser impaired, even though it be only temporarily. I must look into this. I will go and see if the orgy is concluded. I will hear what Comrade Jackson has to say on the matter. I shall not act rashly, Comrade Bristow. If the man Bickersdyke is proved to have had good grounds for his outbreak, he shall escape uncensured. I may even look in on him and throw him a word of praise. But if I find, as I suspect, that he has wronged Comrade Jackson, I shall be forced to speak sharply to him.'

* * * * *

Mike had left the scene of battle by the time Psmith reached the Cash Department, and was sitting at his desk in a somewhat dazed condition, trying to clear his mind sufficiently to enable him to see exactly how matters stood as concerned himself. He felt confused and rattled. He had known, when he went to the manager's room to make his statement, that there would be trouble. But, then, trouble is such an elastic word. It embraces a hundred degrees of meaning. Mike had expected sentence of dismissal, and he had got it. So far he had nothing to complain of. But he had not expected it to come to him riding high on the crest of a great, frothing wave of verbal denunciation. Mr Bickersdyke, through constantly speaking in public, had developed the habit of fluent denunciation to a remarkable extent. He had thundered at Mike as if Mike had been his Majesty's Government or the Encroaching Alien, or something of that sort. And that kind of thing is a little overwhelming at short range. Mike's head was still spinning.

It continued to spin; but he never lost sight of the fact round which it revolved, namely, that he had been dismissed from the service of the bank. And for the first time he began to wonder what they would say about this at home.

Up till now the matter had seemed entirely a personal one. He had charged in to rescue the harassed cashier in precisely the same way as that in which he had dashed in to save him from Bill, the Stone-Flinging Scourge of Clapham Common. Mike's was one of those direct, honest minds which are apt to concentrate themselves on the crisis of the moment, and to leave the consequences out of the question entirely.

What would they say at home? That was the point.

Again, what could he do by way of earning a living? He did not know much about the City and its ways, but he knew enough to understand that summary dismissal from a bank is not the best recommendation one can put forward in applying for another job. And if he did not get another job in the City, what could he do? If it were only summer, he might get taken on somewhere as a cricket professional. Cricket was his line. He could earn his pay at that. But it was very far from being summer.

He had turned the problem over in his mind till his head ached, and had eaten in the process one-third of a wooden penholder, when Psmith arrived.

'It has reached me,' said Psmith, 'that you and Comrade Bickersdyke have been seen doing the Hackenschmidt-Gotch act on the floor. When my informant left, he tells me, Comrade B. had got a half-Nelson on you, and was biting pieces out of your ear. Is this so?'

Mike got up. Psmith was the man, he felt, to advise him in this crisis. Psmith's was the mind to grapple with his Hard Case.

'Look here, Smith,' he said, 'I want to speak to you. I'm in a bit of a hole, and perhaps you can tell me what to do. Let's go out and have a cup of coffee, shall we? I can't tell you about it here.'

'An admirable suggestion,' said Psmith. 'Things in the Postage Department are tolerably quiescent at present. Naturally I shall be missed, if I go out. But my absence will not spell irretrievable ruin, as it would at a period of greater commercial activity. Comrades Rossiter and Bristow have studied my methods. They know how I like things to be done. They are fully competent to conduct the business of the department in my absence. Let us, as you say, scud forth. We will go to a Mecca. Why so-called I do not know, nor, indeed, do I ever hope to know. There we may obtain, at a price, a passable cup of coffee, and you shall tell me your painful story.'

The Mecca, except for the curious aroma which pervades all Meccas, was deserted. Psmith, moving a box of dominoes on to the next table, sat down.

'Dominoes,' he said, 'is one of the few manly sports which have never had great attractions for me. A cousin of mine, who secured his chess blue at Oxford, would, they tell me, have represented his University in the dominoes match also, had he not unfortunately dislocated the radius bone of his bazooka while training for it. Except for him, there has been little dominoes talent in the Psmith family. Let us merely talk. What of this slight brass-rag-parting to which I alluded just now? Tell me all.'

He listened gravely while Mike related the incidents which had led up to his confession and the results of the same. At the conclusion of the narrative he sipped his coffee in silence for a moment.

'This habit of taking on to your shoulders the harvest of other people's bloomers,' he said meditatively, 'is growing upon you, Comrade Jackson. You must check it. It is like dram-drinking. You begin in a small way by breaking school rules to extract Comrade Jellicoe (perhaps the supremest of all the blitherers I have ever met) from a hole. If you had stopped there, all might have been well. But the thing, once started, fascinated you. Now you have landed yourself with a splash in the very centre of the Oxo in order to do a good turn to Comrade Waller. You must drop it, Comrade Jackson. When you were free and without ties, it did not so much matter. But now that you are confidential secretary and adviser to a Shropshire Psmith, the thing must stop. Your secretarial duties must be paramount. Nothing must be allowed to interfere with them. Yes. The thing must stop before it goes too far.'

'It seems to me,' said Mike, 'that it has gone too far. I've got the sack. I don't know how much farther you want it to go.'

Psmith stirred his coffee before replying.

'True,' he said, 'things look perhaps a shade rocky just now, but all is not yet lost. You must recollect that Comrade Bickersdyke spoke in the heat of the moment. That generous temperament was stirred to its depths. He did not pick his words. But calm will succeed storm, and we may be able to do something yet. I have some little influence with Comrade Bickersdyke. Wrongly, perhaps,' added Psmith modestly, 'he thinks somewhat highly of my judgement. If he sees that I am opposed to this step, he may possibly reconsider it. What Psmith thinks today, is his motto, I shall think tomorrow. However, we shall see.'

'I bet we shall!' said Mike ruefully.

'There is, moreover,' continued Psmith, 'another aspect to the affair. When you were being put through it, in Comrade Bickersdyke's inimitably breezy manner, Sir John What's-his-name was, I am given to understand, present. Naturally, to pacify the aggrieved bart., Comrade B. had to lay it on regardless of expense. In America, as possibly you are aware, there is a regular post of mistake-clerk, whose duty it is to receive in the neck anything that happens to be coming along when customers make complaints. He is hauled into the presence of the foaming customer, cursed, and sacked. The customer goes away appeased. The mistake-clerk, if the harangue has been unusually energetic, applies for a rise of salary. Now, possibly, in your case —'

'In my case,' interrupted Mike, 'there was none of that rot. Bickersdyke wasn't putting it on. He meant every word. Why, dash it all, you know yourself he'd be only too glad to sack me, just to get some of his own back with me.'

Psmith's eyes opened in pained surprise.

'Get some of his own back!' he repeated.

'Are you insinuating, Comrade Jackson, that my relations with Comrade Bickersdyke are not of the most pleasant and agreeable nature possible? How do these ideas get about? I yield to nobody in my respect for our manager. I may have had occasion from time to time to correct him in some trifling matter, but surely he is not the man to let such a thing rankle? No! I prefer to think that Comrade Bickersdyke regards me as his friend and well-wisher, and will lend a courteous ear to any proposal I see fit to make. I hope shortly to be able to prove this to you. I will discuss this little affair of the cheque with him at our ease at the club, and I shall be surprised if we do not come to some arrangement.'

'Look here, Smith,' said Mike earnestly, 'for goodness' sake don't go playing the goat. There's no earthly need for you to get lugged into this business. Don't you worry about me. I shall be all right.'

'I think,' said Psmith, 'that you will-when I have chatted with Comrade Bickersdyke.'

22. And Take Steps

On returning to the bank, Mike found Mr Waller in the grip of a peculiarly varied set of mixed feelings. Shortly after Mike's departure for the Mecca, the cashier had been summoned once more into the Presence, and had there been informed that, as apparently he had not been directly responsible for the gross piece of carelessness by which the bank had suffered so considerable a loss (here Sir John puffed out his cheeks like a meditative toad), the matter, as far as he was concerned, was at an end. On the other hand —! Here Mr Waller was hauled over the coals for Incredible Rashness in allowing a mere junior subordinate to handle important tasks like the paying out of money, and so on, till he felt raw all over. However, it was not dismissal. That was the great thing. And his principal sensation was one of relief.

Mingled with the relief were sympathy for Mike, gratitude to him for having given himself up so promptly, and a curiously dazed sensation, as if somebody had been hitting him on the head with a bolster.

All of which emotions, taken simultaneously, had the effect of rendering him completely dumb when he saw Mike. He felt that he did not know what to say to him. And as Mike, for his part, simply wanted to be let alone, and not compelled to talk, conversation was at something of a standstill in the Cash Department.

After five minutes, it occurred to Mr Waller that perhaps the best plan would be to interview Psmith. Psmith would know exactly how matters stood. He could not ask Mike point-blank whether he had been dismissed. But there was the probability that Psmith had been informed and would pass on the information.

Psmith received the cashier with a dignified kindliness.

'Oh, er, Smith,' said Mr Waller, 'I wanted just to ask you about Jackson.'

Psmith bowed his head gravely.

'Exactly,' he said. 'Comrade Jackson. I think I may say that you have come to the right man. Comrade Jackson has placed himself in my hands, and I am dealing with his case. A somewhat tricky business, but I shall see him through.'

'Has he —?' Mr Waller hesitated.

'You were saying?' said Psmith.

'Does Mr Bickersdyke intend to dismiss him?'

'At present,' admitted Psmith, 'there is some idea of that description floating-nebulously, as it were-in Comrade Bickersdyke's mind. Indeed, from what I gather from my client, the push was actually administered, in so many words. But tush! And possibly bah! we know what happens on these occasions, do we not? You and I are students of human nature, and we know that a man of Comrade Bickersdyke's warm-hearted type is apt to say in the heat of the moment a great deal more than he really means. Men of his impulsive character cannot help expressing themselves in times of stress with a certain generous strength which those who do not understand them are inclined to take a little too seriously. I shall have a chat with Comrade Bickersdyke at the conclusion of the day's work, and I have no doubt that we shall both laugh heartily over this little episode.'

Mr Waller pulled at his beard, with an expression on his face that seemed to suggest that he was not quite so confident on this point. He was about to put his doubts into words when Mr Rossiter appeared, and Psmith, murmuring something about duty, turned again to his ledger. The cashier drifted back to his own department.

It was one of Psmith's theories of Life, which he was accustomed to propound to Mike in the small hours of the morning with his feet on the mantelpiece, that the secret of success lay in taking advantage of one's occasional slices of luck, in seizing, as it were, the happy moment. When Mike, who had had the passage to write out ten times at Wrykyn on one occasion as an imposition, reminded him that Shakespeare had once said something about there being a tide in the affairs of men, which, taken at the flood, &c., Psmith had acknowledged with an easy grace that possibly Shakespeare *had* got on to it first, and that it was but one more proof of how often great minds thought alike.

Though waiving his claim to the copyright of the maxim, he nevertheless had a high opinion of it, and frequently acted upon it in the conduct of his own life.

Thus, when approaching the Senior Conservative Club at five o'clock with the idea of finding Mr Bickersdyke there, he observed his quarry entering the Turkish Baths which stand some twenty yards from the club's front door, he acted on his maxim, and decided, instead of waiting for the manager to finish his bath before approaching him on the subject of Mike, to corner him in the Baths themselves.

He gave Mr Bickersdyke five minutes' start. Then, reckoning that by that time he would probably have settled down, he pushed open the door and went in himself. And, having paid his money, and left his boots with the boy at the threshold, he was rewarded by the sight of the manager emerging from a box at the far end of the room, clad in the mottled towels which the bather, irrespective of his personal taste in dress, is obliged to wear in a Turkish bath.

Psmith made for the same box. Mr Bickersdyke's clothes lay at the head of one of the sofas, but nobody else had staked out a claim. Psmith took possession of the sofa next to the manager's. Then, humming lightly, he undressed, and made his way downstairs to the Hot Rooms. He rather fancied himself in towels. There was something about them which seemed to suit his figure. They gave him, he though, rather a *debonnaire* look. He paused for a moment before the looking-glass to examine himself, with approval, then pushed open the door of the Hot Rooms and went in.

23. Mr Bickersdyke Makes a Concession

Mr Bickersdyke was reclining in an easy-chair in the first room, staring before him in the boiled-fish manner customary in a Turkish Bath. Psmith dropped into the next seat with a cheery 'Good evening.' The manager started as if some firm hand had driven a bradawl into him. He looked at Psmith with what was intended to be a dignified stare. But dignity is hard to achieve in a couple of parti-coloured towels. The stare did not differ to any great extent from the conventional boiled-fish look, alluded to above.

Psmith settled himself comfortably in his chair. 'Fancy finding you here,' he said pleasantly. 'We seem always to be meeting. To me,' he added, with a reassuring smile, 'it is a great pleasure. A very great pleasure indeed. We see too little of each other during office hours. Not that one must grumble at that. Work before everything. You have your duties, I mine. It is merely unfortunate that those duties are not such as to enable us to toil side by side, encouraging each other with word and gesture. However, it is idle to repine. We must make the most of these chance meetings when the work of the day is over.'

Mr Bickersdyke heaved himself up from his chair and took another at the opposite end of the room. Psmith joined him.

'There's something pleasantly mysterious, to my mind,' said he chattily, 'in a Turkish Bath. It seems to take one out of the hurry and bustle of the everyday world. It is a quiet backwater in the rushing river of Life. I like to sit and think in a Turkish Bath. Except, of course, when I have a congenial companion to talk to. As now. To me —'

Mr Bickersdyke rose, and went into the next room.

'To me,' continued Psmith, again following, and seating himself beside the manager, 'there is, too, something eerie in these places. There is a certain sinister air about the attendants. They glide rather than walk. They say little. Who knows what they may be planning and plotting? That drip-drip again. It may be merely water, but how are we to know that it is not blood? It would be so easy to do away with a man in a Turkish Bath. Nobody has seen him come in. Nobody can trace him if he disappears. These are uncomfortable thoughts, Mr Bickersdyke.'

Mr Bickersdyke seemed to think them so. He rose again, and returned to the first room.

'I have made you restless,' said Psmith, in a voice of self-reproach, when he had settled himself once more by the manager's side. 'I am sorry. I will not pursue the subject. Indeed, I believe that my fears are unnecessary. Statistics show, I understand, that large numbers of men emerge in safety every year from Turkish Baths. There was another matter of which I wished to speak to you. It is a somewhat delicate matter, and I am only encouraged to mention it to you by the fact that you are so close a friend of my father's.'

Mr Bickersdyke had picked up an early edition of an evening paper, left on the table at his side by a previous bather, and was to all appearances engrossed in it. Psmith, however, not discouraged, proceeded to touch upon the matter of Mike.

'There was,' he said, 'some little friction, I hear, in the office today in connection with a cheque.' The evening paper hid the manager's expressive face, but from the fact that the hands holding it tightened their grip Psmith deduced that Mr Bickersdyke's attention was not wholly concentrated on the City news. Moreover, his toes wriggled. And when a man's toes wriggle, he is interested in what you are saying.

'All these petty breezes,' continued Psmith sympathetically, 'must be very trying to a man in your position, a man who wishes to be left alone in order to devote his entire thought to the niceties of the higher Finance. It is as if Napoleon, while planning out some intricate scheme of campaign, were to be called upon in the midst of his meditations to bully a private for not cleaning his buttons. Naturally, you were annoyed. Your giant brain, wrenched temporarily from its proper groove, expended its force in one tremendous reprimand of Comrade Jackson. It was as if one had diverted some terrific electric current which should have been controlling a vast system of machinery, and turned it on to annihilate a black-beetle. In the present case, of course, the result is as might have been expected. Comrade Jackson, not realizing the position

398

of affairs, went away with the absurd idea that all was over, that you meant all you said-briefly, that his number was up. I assured him that he was mistaken, but no! He persisted in declaring that all was over, that you had dismissed him from the bank.'

Mr Bickersdyke lowered the paper and glared bulbously at the old Etonian.

'Mr Jackson is perfectly right,' he snapped. 'Of course I dismissed him.'

'Yes, yes,' said Psmith, 'I have no doubt that at the moment you did work the rapid push. What I am endeavouring to point out is that Comrade Jackson is under the impression that the edict is permanent, that he can hope for no reprieve.'

'Nor can he.'

'You don't mean—'

'I mean what I say.'

'Ah, I quite understand,' said Psmith, as one who sees that he must make allowances. 'The incident is too recent. The storm has not yet had time to expend itself. You have not had leisure to think the matter over coolly. It is hard, of course, to be cool in a Turkish Bath. Your ganglions are still vibrating. Later, perhaps—'

'Once and for all,' growled Mr Bickersdyke, 'the thing is ended. Mr Jackson will leave the bank at the end of the month. We have no room for fools in the office.'

'You surprise me,' said Psmith. 'I should not have thought that the standard of intelligence in the bank was extremely high. With the exception of our two selves, I think that there are hardly any men of real intelligence on the staff. And comrade Jackson is improving every day. Being, as he is, under my constant supervision he is rapidly developing a stranglehold on his duties, which—'

'I have no wish to discuss the matter any further.'

'No, no. Quite so, quite so. Not another word. I am dumb.'

'There are limits you see, to the uses of impertinence, Mr Smith.'

Psmith started.

'You are not suggesting—! You do not mean that I—!'

'I have no more to say. I shall be glad if you will allow me to read my paper.'

Psmith waved a damp hand.

'I should be the last man,' he said stiffly, 'to force my conversation on another. I was under the impression that you enjoyed these little chats as keenly as I did. If I was wrong—'

He relapsed into a wounded silence. Mr Bickersdyke resumed his perusal of the evening paper, and presently, laying it down, rose and made his way to the room where muscular attendants were in waiting to perform that blend of Jiu-Jitsu and Catch-as-catch-can which is the most valuable and at the same time most painful part of a Turkish Bath.

It was not till he was resting on his sofa, swathed from head to foot in a sheet and smoking a cigarette, that he realized that Psmith was sharing his compartment.

He made the unpleasant discovery just as he had finished his first cigarette and lighted his second. He was blowing out the match when Psmith, accompanied by an attendant, appeared in the doorway, and proceeded to occupy the next sofa to himself. All that feeling of dreamy peace, which is the reward one receives for allowing oneself to be melted like wax and kneaded like bread, left him instantly. He felt hot and annoyed. To escape was out of the question. Once one has been scientifically wrapped up by the attendant and placed on one's sofa, one is a fixture. He lay scowling at the ceiling, resolved to combat all attempt at conversation with a stony silence.

Psmith, however, did not seem to desire conversation. He lay on his sofa motionless for a quarter of an hour, then reached out for a large book which lay on the table, and began to read.

When he did speak, he seemed to be speaking to himself. Every now and then he would murmur a few words, sometimes a single name. In spite of himself, Mr Bickersdyke found himself listening.

At first the murmurs conveyed nothing to him. Then suddenly a name caught his ear. Strowther was the name, and somehow it suggested something to him. He could not say precisely what. It seemed to touch some chord of memory. He knew no one of the name of Strowther. He was sure of that. And yet it was curiously familiar. An unusual name, too. He could not help feeling that at one time he must have known it quite well.

'Mr Strowther,' murmured Psmith, 'said that the hon. gentleman's remarks would have been nothing short of treason, if they had not been so obviously the mere babblings of an irresponsible lunatic. Cries of "Order, order," and a voice, "Sit down, fat-head!"'

For just one moment Mr Bickersdyke's memory poised motionless, like a hawk about to swoop. Then it darted at the mark. Everything came to him in a flash. The hands of the clock whizzed back. He was no longer Mr John Bickersdyke, manager of the London branch of the New Asiatic Bank, lying on a sofa in the Cumberland Street Turkish Baths. He was Jack Bickersdyke, clerk in the employ of Messrs Norton and Biggleswade, standing on a chair and shouting 'Order! order!' in the Masonic Room of the 'Red Lion' at Tulse Hill, while the members of the Tulse Hill Parliament, divided into two camps, yelled at one another, and young Tom Barlow, in his official capacity as Mister Speaker, waved his arms dumbly, and banged the table with his mallet in his efforts to restore calm.

He remembered the whole affair as if it had happened yesterday. It had been a speech of his own which had called forth the above expression of opinion from Strowther. He remembered Strowther now, a pale, spectacled clerk in Baxter and Abrahams, an inveterate upholder of the throne, the House of Lords and all constituted authority. Strowther had objected to the socialistic sentiments of his speech in connection with the Budget, and there had been a disturbance unparalleled even in the Tulse Hill Parliament, where disturbances were frequent and loud....

Psmith looked across at him with a bright smile. 'They report you verbatim,' he said. 'And rightly. A more able speech I have seldom read. I like the bit where you call the Royal Family "blood-suckers". Even then, it seems you knew how to express yourself fluently and well.'

Mr Bickersdyke sat up. The hands of the clock had moved again, and he was back in what Psmith had called the live, vivid present.

'What have you got there?' he demanded.

'It is a record,' said Psmith, 'of the meeting of an institution called the Tulse Hill Parliament. A bright, chatty little institution, too, if one may judge by these reports. You in particular, if I may say so, appear to have let yourself go with refreshing vim. Your political views have changed a great deal since those days, have they not? It is extremely interesting. A most fascinating study for political students. When I send these speeches of yours to the *Clarion* —'

Mr Bickersdyke bounded on his sofa.

'What!' he cried.

'I was saying,' said Psmith, 'that the *Clarion* will probably make a most interesting comparison between these speeches and those you have been making at Kenningford.'

'I — I — I forbid you to make any mention of these speeches.'

Psmith hesitated.

'It would be great fun seeing what the papers said,' he protested.

'Great fun!'

'It is true,' mused Psmith, 'that in a measure, it would dish you at the election. From what I saw of those light-hearted lads at Kenningford the other night, I should say they would be so amused that they would only just have enough strength left to stagger to the poll and vote for your opponent.'

Mr Bickersdyke broke out into a cold perspiration.

'I forbid you to send those speeches to the papers,' he cried.

Psmith reflected.

'You see,' he said at last, 'it is like this. The departure of Comrade Jackson, my confidential secretary and adviser, is certain to plunge me into a state of the deepest gloom. The only way I can see at present by which I can ensure even a momentary lightening of the inky cloud is the sending of these speeches to some bright paper like the *Clarion*. I feel certain that their comments would wring, at any rate, a sad, sweet smile from me. Possibly even a hearty laugh. I must, therefore, look on these very able speeches of yours in something of the light of an antidote. They will stand between me and black depression. Without them I am in the cart. With them I may possibly buoy myself up.'

Mr Bickersdyke shifted uneasily on his sofa. He glared at the floor. Then he eyed the ceiling as if it were a personal enemy of his. Finally he looked at Psmith. Psmith's eyes were closed in peaceful meditation.

'Very well,' said he at last. 'Jackson shall stop.'

Psmith came out of his thoughts with a start. 'You were observing —?' he said.

'I shall not dismiss Jackson,' said Mr Bickersdyke.

Psmith smiled winningly.

'Just as I had hoped,' he said. 'Your very justifiable anger melts before reflection. The storm subsides, and you are at leisure to examine the matter dispassionately. Doubts begin to creep in. Possibly, you say to yourself, I have been too hasty, too harsh. Justice must be tempered with mercy. I have caught Comrade Jackson bending, you add (still to yourself), but shall I press home my advantage too ruthlessly? No, you cry, I will abstain. And I applaud your action. I like to see this spirit of gentle toleration. It is bracing and comforting. As for these excellent speeches,' he added, 'I shall, of course, no longer have any need of their consolation. I can lay them aside. The sunlight can now enter and illumine my life through more ordinary channels. The cry goes round, "Psmith is himself again."'

Mr Bickersdyke said nothing. Unless a snort of fury may be counted as anything.

24. The Spirit of Unrest

During the following fortnight, two things happened which materially altered Mike's position in the bank.

The first was that Mr Bickersdyke was elected a member of Parliament. He got in by a small majority amidst scenes of disorder of a nature unusual even in Kenningford. Psmith, who went down on the polling-day to inspect the revels and came back with his hat smashed in, reported that, as far as he could see, the electors of Kenningford seemed to be in just that state of happy intoxication which might make them vote for Mr Bickersdyke by mistake. Also it had been discovered, on the eve of the poll, that the bank manager's opponent, in his youth, had been educated at a school in Germany, and had subsequently spent two years at Heidelberg University. These damaging revelations were having a marked effect on the warm-hearted patriots of Kenningford, who were now referring to the candidate in thick but earnest tones as 'the German Spy'.

'So that taking everything into consideration,' said Psmith, summing up, 'I fancy that Comrade Bickersdyke is home.'

And the papers next day proved that he was right.

'A hundred and fifty-seven,' said Psmith, as he read his paper at breakfast. 'Not what one would call a slashing victory. It is fortunate for Comrade Bickersdyke, I think, that I did not send those very able speeches of his to the *Clarion*'.

Till now Mike had been completely at a loss to understand why the manager had sent for him on the morning following the scene about the cheque, and informed him that he had reconsidered his decision to dismiss him. Mike could not help feeling that there was more in the matter than met the eye. Mr Bickersdyke had not spoken as if it gave him any pleasure to reprieve him. On the contrary, his manner was distinctly brusque. Mike was thoroughly puzzled. To Psmith's statement, that he had talked the matter over quietly with the manager and brought things to a satisfactory conclusion, he had paid little attention. But now he began to see light.

'Great Scott, Smith,' he said, 'did you tell him you'd send those speeches to the papers if he sacked me?'

Psmith looked at him through his eye-glass, and helped himself to another piece of toast.

'I am unable,' he said, 'to recall at this moment the exact terms of the very pleasant conversation I had with Comrade Bickersdyke on the occasion of our chance meeting in the Turkish Bath that afternoon; but, thinking things over quietly now that I have more leisure, I cannot help feeling that he may possibly have read some such intention into my words. You know how it is in these little chats, Comrade Jackson. One leaps to conclusions. Some casual word I happened to drop may have given him the idea you mention. At this distance of time it is impossible to say with any certainty. Suffice it that all has ended well. He *did* reconsider his resolve. I shall be only too happy if it turns out that the seed of the alteration in his views was sown by some careless word of mine. Perhaps we shall never know.'

Mike was beginning to mumble some awkward words of thanks, when Psmith resumed his discourse.

'Be that as it may, however,' he said, 'we cannot but perceive that Comrade Bickersdyke's election has altered our position to some extent. As you have pointed out, he may have been influenced in this recent affair by some chance remark of mine about those speeches. Now, however, they will cease to be of any value. Now that he is elected he has nothing to lose by their publication. I mention this by way of indicating that it is possible that, if another painful episode occurs, he may be more ruthless.'

'I see what you mean,' said Mike. 'If he catches me on the hop again, he'll simply go ahead and sack me.'

'That,' said Psmith, 'is more or less the position of affairs.'

The other event which altered Mike's life in the bank was his removal from Mr Waller's department to the Fixed Deposits. The work in the Fixed Deposits was less pleasant, and Mr Gregory, the head of the department was not of Mr Waller's type. Mr Gregory, before joining the home-staff of the New Asiatic Bank, had spent a number of years with a firm in the Far East, where he had acquired a liver and a habit of addressing those under him in a way that suggested the mate of a tramp steamer. Even on the days when his liver was not troubling him, he was truculent. And when, as usually happened, it did trouble him, he was a perfect fountain of abuse. Mike and he hated each other from the first. The work in the Fixed Deposits was not really difficult, when you got the hang of it, but there was a certain amount of confusion in it to a beginner; and Mike, in commercial matters, was as raw a beginner as ever began. In the two other departments through which he had passed, he had done tolerably well. As regarded his work in the Postage Department, stamping letters and taking them down to the post office was just about his form. It was the sort of work on which he could really get a grip. And in the Cash Department, Mr Waller's mild patience had helped him through. But with Mr Gregory it was different. Mike hated being shouted at. It confused him. And Mr Gregory invariably shouted. He always spoke as if he were competing against a high wind. With Mike he shouted more than usual. On his side, it must be admitted that Mike was something out of the common run of bank clerks. The whole system of banking was a horrid mystery to him. He did not understand why things were done, or how the various departments depended on and dove-tailed into one another. Each department seemed to him something separate and distinct. Why they were all in the same building at all he never really gathered. He knew that it could not be purely from motives of sociability, in order that the clerks might have each other's company during slack spells. That much he suspected, but beyond that he was vague.

It naturally followed that, after having grown, little by little, under Mr Waller's easy-going rule, to enjoy life in the bank, he now suffered a reaction. Within a day of his arrival in the Fixed Deposits he was loathing the place as earnestly as he had loathed it on the first morning.

Psmith, who had taken his place in the Cash Department, reported that Mr Waller was inconsolable at his loss.

'I do my best to cheer him up,' he said, 'and he smiles bravely every now and then. But when he thinks I am not looking, his head droops and that wistful expression comes into his face. The sunshine has gone out of his life.'

It had just come into Mike's, and, more than anything else, was making him restless and discontented. That is to say, it was now late spring: the sun shone cheerfully on the City; and cricket was in the air. And that was the trouble.

In the dark days, when everything was fog and slush, Mike had been contented enough to spend his mornings and afternoons in the bank, and go about with Psmith at night. Under such conditions, London is the best place in which to be, and the warmth and light of the bank were pleasant.

But now things had changed. The place had become a prison. With all the energy of one who had been born and bred in the country, Mike hated having to stay indoors on days when all the air was full of approaching summer. There were mornings when it was almost more than he could do to push open the swing doors, and go out of the fresh air into the stuffy atmosphere of the bank.

The days passed slowly, and the cricket season began. Instead of being a relief, this made matters worse. The little cricket he could get only made him want more. It was as if a starving man had been given a handful of wafer biscuits.

If the summer had been wet, he might have been less restless. But, as it happened, it was unusually fine. After a week of cold weather at the beginning of May, a hot spell set in. May passed in a blaze of sunshine. Large scores were made all over the country.

Mike's name had been down for the M.C.C. for some years, and he had become a member during his last season at Wrykyn. Once or twice a week he managed to get up to Lord's for half an hour's practice at the nets; and on Saturdays the bank had matches, in which he generally managed to knock the cover off rather ordinary club bowling. But it was not enough for him.

June came, and with it more sunshine. The atmosphere of the bank seemed more oppressive than ever.

25. At the Telephone

If one looks closely into those actions which are apparently due to sudden impulse, one generally finds that the sudden impulse was merely the last of a long series of events which led up to the action. Alone, it would not have been powerful enough to effect anything. But, coming after the way has been paved for it, it is irresistible. The hooligan who bonnets a policeman is apparently the victim of a sudden impulse. In reality, however, the bonneting is due to weeks of daily encounters with the constable, at each of which meetings the dislike for his helmet and the idea of smashing it in grow a little larger, till finally they blossom into the deed itself.

This was what happened in Mike's case. Day by day, through the summer, as the City grew hotter and stuffier, his hatred of the bank became more and more the thought that occupied his mind. It only needed a moderately strong temptation to make him break out and take the consequences.

Psmith noticed his restlessness and endeavoured to soothe it.

'All is not well,' he said, 'with Comrade Jackson, the Sunshine of the Home. I note a certain wanness of the cheek. The peach-bloom of your complexion is no longer up to sample. Your eye is wild; your merry laugh no longer rings through the bank, causing nervous customers to leap into the air with startled exclamations. You have the manner of one whose only friend on earth is a yellow dog, and who has lost the dog. Why is this, Comrade Jackson?'

They were talking in the flat at Clement's Inn. The night was hot. Through the open windows the roar of the Strand sounded faintly. Mike walked to the window and looked out.

'I'm sick of all this rot,' he said shortly.

Psmith shot an inquiring glance at him, but said nothing. This restlessness of Mike's was causing him a good deal of inconvenience, which he bore in patient silence, hoping for better times. With Mike obviously discontented and out of tune with all the world, there was but little amusement to be extracted from the evenings now. Mike did his best to be cheerful, but he could not shake off the caged feeling which made him restless.

'What rot it all is!' went on Mike, sitting down again. 'What's the good of it all? You go and sweat all day at a desk, day after day, for about twopence a year. And when you're about eighty-five, you retire. It isn't living at all. It's simply being a bally vegetable.'

'You aren't hankering, by any chance, to be a pirate of the Spanish main, or anything like that, are you?' inquired Psmith.

'And all this rot about going out East,' continued Mike. 'What's the good of going out East?'

'I gather from casual chit-chat in the office that one becomes something of a blood when one goes out East,' said Psmith. 'Have a dozen native clerks under you, all looking up to you as the Last Word in magnificence, and end by marrying the Governor's daughter.'

'End by getting some foul sort of fever, more likely, and being booted out as no further use to the bank.'

'You look on the gloomy side, Comrade Jackson. I seem to see you sitting in an armchair, fanned by devoted coolies, telling some Eastern potentate that you can give him five minutes. I understand that being in a bank in the Far East is one of the world's softest jobs. Millions of natives hang on your lightest word. Enthusiastic rajahs draw you aside and press jewels into your hand as a token of respect and esteem. When on an elephant's back you pass, somebody beats on a booming brass gong! The Banker of Bhong! Isn't your generous young heart stirred to any extent by the prospect? I am given to understand —'

'I've a jolly good mind to chuck up the whole thing and become a pro. I've got a birth qualification for Surrey. It's about the only thing I could do any good at.'

Psmith's manner became fatherly.

'*You're* all right,' he said. 'The hot weather has given you that tired feeling. What you want is a change of air. We will pop down together hand in hand this week-end to some seaside resort. You shall build sand castles, while I lie on the beach and read the paper. In the evening we will listen to the band, or stroll on the esplanade, not so much because we want to, as to give the natives a treat. Possibly, if the weather continues warm, we may even paddle. A vastly exhilarating pastime, I am led to believe, and so strengthening for the ankles. And on Monday morning we will return, bronzed and bursting with health, to our toil once more.'

'I'm going to bed,' said Mike, rising.

Psmith watched him lounge from the room, and shook his head sadly. All was not well with his confidential secretary and adviser.

The next day, which was a Thursday, found Mike no more reconciled to the prospect of spending from ten till five in the company of Mr Gregory and the ledgers. He was silent at breakfast, and Psmith, seeing that things were still wrong, abstained from conversation. Mike propped the *Sportsman* up against the hot-water jug, and read the cricket news. His county, captained by brother Joe, had, as he had learned already from yesterday's evening paper, beaten Sussex by five wickets at Brighton. Today they were due to play Middlesex at Lord's. Mike thought that he would try to get off early, and go and see some of the first day's play.

As events turned out, he got off a good deal earlier, and saw a good deal more of the first day's play than he had anticipated.

He had just finished the preliminary stages of the morning's work, which consisted mostly of washing his hands, changing his coat, and eating a section of a pen-holder, when William, the messenger, approached.

'You're wanted on the 'phone, Mr Jackson.'

The New Asiatic Bank, unlike the majority of London banks, was on the telephone, a fact which Psmith found a great convenience when securing seats at the theatre. Mike went to the box and took up the receiver.

'Hullo!' he said.

'Who's that?' said an agitated voice. 'Is that you, Mike? I'm Joe.'

'Hullo, Joe,' said Mike. 'What's up? I'm coming to see you this evening. I'm going to try and get off early.'

'Look here, Mike, are you busy at the bank just now?'

'Not at the moment. There's never anything much going on before eleven.'

'I mean, are you busy today? Could you possibly manage to get off and play for us against Middlesex?'

Mike nearly dropped the receiver.

'What?' he cried.

'There's been the dickens of a mix-up. We're one short, and you're our only hope. We can't possibly get another man in the time. We start in half an hour. Can you play?'

For the space of, perhaps, one minute, Mike thought.

'Well?' said Joe's voice.

The sudden vision of Lord's ground, all green and cool in the morning sunlight, was too much for Mike's resolution, sapped as it was by days of restlessness. The feeling surged over him that whatever happened afterwards, the joy of the match in perfect weather on a perfect wicket would make it worth while. What did it matter what happened afterwards?

'All right, Joe,' he said. 'I'll hop into a cab now, and go and get my things.'

'Good man,' said Joe, hugely relieved.

26. Breaking The News

Dashing away from the call-box, Mike nearly cannoned into Psmith, who was making his way pensively to the telephone with the object of ringing up the box office of the Haymarket Theatre.

'Sorry,' said Mike. 'Hullo, Smith.'

'Hullo indeed,' said Psmith, courteously. 'I rejoice, Comrade Jackson, to find you going about your commercial duties like a young bomb. How is it, people repeatedly ask me, that Comrade Jackson contrives to catch his employer's eye and win the friendly smile from the head of his department? My reply is that where others walk, Comrade Jackson runs. Where others stroll, Comrade Jackson legs it like a highly-trained mustang of the prairie. He does not loiter. He gets back to his department bathed in perspiration, in level time. He —'

'I say, Smith,' said Mike, 'you might do me a favour.'

'A thousand. Say on.'

'Just look in at the Fixed Deposits and tell old Gregory that I shan't be with him today, will you? I haven't time myself. I must rush!'

Psmith screwed his eyeglass into his eye, and examined Mike carefully.

'What exactly —?' be began.

'Tell the old ass I've popped off.'

'Just so, just so,' murmured Psmith, as one who assents to a thoroughly reasonable proposition. 'Tell him you have popped off. It shall be done. But it is within the bounds of possibility that Comrade Gregory may inquire further. Could you give me some inkling as to why you are popping?'

'My brother Joe has just rung me up from Lords. The county are playing Middlesex and they're one short. He wants me to roll up.'

Psmith shook his head sadly.

'I don't wish to interfere in any way,' he said, 'but I suppose you realize that, by acting thus, you are to some extent knocking the stuffing out of your chances of becoming manager of this bank? If you dash off now, I shouldn't count too much on that marrying the Governor's daughter scheme I sketched out for you last night. I doubt whether this is going to help you to hold the gorgeous East in fee, and all that sort of thing.'

'Oh, dash the gorgeous East.'

'By all means,' said Psmith obligingly. 'I just thought I'd mention it. I'll look in at Lord's this afternoon. I shall send my card up to you, and trust to your sympathetic cooperation to enable me to effect an entry into the pavilion on my face. My father is coming up to London today. I'll bring him along, too.'

'Right ho. Dash it, it's twenty to. So long. See you at Lord's.'

Psmith looked after his retreating form till it had vanished through the swing-door, and shrugged his shoulders resignedly, as if disclaiming all responsibility.

'He has gone without his hat,' he murmured. 'It seems to me that this is practically a case of running amok. And now to break the news to bereaved Comrade Gregory.'

He abandoned his intention of ringing up the Haymarket Theatre, and turning away from the call-box, walked meditatively down the aisle till he came to the Fixed Deposits Department, where the top of Mr Gregory's head was to be seen over the glass barrier, as he applied himself to his work.

Psmith, resting his elbows on the top of the barrier and holding his head between his hands, eyed the absorbed toiler for a moment in silence, then emitted a hollow groan.

Mr Gregory, who was ruling a line in a ledger-most of the work in the Fixed Deposits Department consisted of ruling lines in ledgers, sometimes in black ink, sometimes in red-started as if he had been stung, and made a complete mess of the ruled line. He lifted a fiery, bearded face, and met Psmith's eye, which shone with kindly sympathy.

He found words.

'What the dickens are you standing there for, mooing like a blanked cow?' he inquired.

'I was groaning,' explained Psmith with quiet dignity. 'And why was I groaning?' he continued. 'Because a shadow has fallen on the Fixed Deposits Department. Comrade Jackson, the Pride of the Office, has gone.'

Mr Gregory rose from his seat.

'I don't know who the dickens you are —' he began.

'I am Psmith,' said the old Etonian,

'Oh, you're Smith, are you?'

'With a preliminary P. Which, however, is not sounded.'

'And what's all this dashed nonsense about Jackson?'

'He is gone. Gone like the dew from the petal of a rose.'

'Gone! Where's he gone to?'

'Lord's.'

'What lord's?'

Psmith waved his hand gently.

'You misunderstand me. Comrade Jackson has not gone to mix with any member of our gay and thoughtless aristocracy. He has gone to Lord's cricket ground.'

Mr Gregory's beard bristled even more than was its wont.

'What!' he roared. 'Gone to watch a cricket match! Gone —!'

'Not to watch. To play. An urgent summons I need not say. Nothing but an urgent summons could have wrenched him from your very delightful society, I am sure.'

Mr Gregory glared.

'I don't want any of your impudence,' he said.

Psmith nodded gravely.

'We all have these curious likes and dislikes,' he said tolerantly. 'You do not like my impudence. Well, well, some people don't. And now, having broken the sad news, I will return to my own department.'

'Half a minute. You come with me and tell this yarn of yours to Mr Bickersdyke.'

'You think it would interest, amuse him? Perhaps you are right. Let us buttonhole Comrade Bickersdyke.'

Mr Bickersdyke was disengaged. The head of the Fixed Deposits Department stumped into the room. Psmith followed at a more leisurely pace.

'Allow me,' he said with a winning smile, as Mr Gregory opened his mouth to speak, 'to take this opportunity of congratulating you on your success at the election. A narrow but well-deserved victory.'

There was nothing cordial in the manager's manner.

'What do you want?' he said.

'Myself, nothing,' said Psmith. 'But I understand that Mr Gregory has some communication to make.'

'Tell Mr Bickersdyke that story of yours,' said Mr Gregory.

'Surely,' said Psmith reprovingly, 'this is no time for anecdotes. Mr Bickersdyke is busy. He —'

'Tell him what you told me about Jackson.'

Mr Bickersdyke looked up inquiringly.

'Jackson,' said Psmith, 'has been obliged to absent himself from work today owing to an urgent summons from his brother, who, I understand, has suffered a bereavement.'

'It's a lie,' roared Mr Gregory. 'You told me yourself he'd gone to play in a cricket match.'

'True. As I said, he received an urgent summons from his brother.'

'What about the bereavement, then?'

'The team was one short. His brother was very distressed about it. What could Comrade Jackson do? Could he refuse to help his brother when it was in his power? His generous nature is a byword. He did the only possible thing. He consented to play.'

Mr Bickersdyke spoke.

'Am I to understand,' he asked, with sinister calm, 'that Mr Jackson has left his work and gone off to play in a cricket match?'

'Something of that sort has, I believe, happened,' said Psmith. 'He knew, of course,' he added, bowing gracefully in Mr Gregory's direction, 'that he was leaving his work in thoroughly competent hands.'

'Thank you,' said Mr Bickersdyke. 'That will do. You will help Mr Gregory in his department for the time being, Mr Smith. I will arrange for somebody to take your place in your own department.'

'It will be a pleasure,' murmured Psmith.

'Show Mr Smith what he has to do, Mr Gregory,' said the manager.

They left the room.

'How curious, Comrade Gregory,' mused Psmith, as they went, 'are the workings of Fate! A moment back, and your life was a blank. Comrade Jackson, that prince of Fixed Depositors, had gone. How, you said to yourself despairingly, can his place be filled? Then the cloud broke, and the sun shone out again. *I* came to help you. What you lose on the swings, you make up on the roundabouts. Now show me what I have to do, and then let us make this department sizzle. You have drawn a good ticket, Comrade Gregory.'

27. At Lord's

Mike got to Lord's just as the umpires moved out into the field. He raced round to the pavilion. Joe met him on the stairs.

'It's all right,' he said. 'No hurry. We've won the toss. I've put you in fourth wicket.'

'Right ho,' said Mike. 'Glad we haven't to field just yet.'

'We oughtn't to have to field today if we don't chuck our wickets away.'

'Good wicket?'

'Like a billiard-table. I'm glad you were able to come. Have any difficulty in getting away?'

Joe Jackson's knowledge of the workings of a bank was of the slightest. He himself had never, since he left Oxford, been in a position where there were obstacles to getting off to play in first-class cricket. By profession he was agent to a sporting baronet whose hobby was the cricket of the county, and so, far from finding any difficulty in playing for the county, he was given to understand by his employer that that was his chief duty. It never occurred to him that Mike might find his bank less amenable in the matter of giving leave. His only fear, when he rang Mike up that morning, had been that this might be a particularly busy day at the New Asiatic Bank. If there was no special rush of work, he took it for granted that Mike would simply go to the manager, ask for leave to play in the match, and be given it with a beaming smile.

Mike did not answer the question, but asked one on his own account.

'How did you happen to be short?' he said.

'It was rotten luck. It was like this. We were altering our team after the Sussex match, to bring in Ballard, Keene, and Willis. They couldn't get down to Brighton, as the 'Varsity had a match, but there was nothing on for them in the last half of the week, so they'd promised to roll up.'

Ballard, Keene, and Willis were members of the Cambridge team, all very capable performers and much in demand by the county, when they could get away to play for it.

'Well?' said Mike.

'Well, we all came up by train from Brighton last night. But these three asses had arranged to motor down from Cambridge early today, and get here in time for the start. What happens? Why, Willis, who fancies himself as a chauffeur, undertakes to do the driving; and naturally, being an absolute rotter, goes and smashes up the whole concern just outside St Albans. The first thing I knew of it was when I got to Lord's at half past ten, and found a wire waiting for me to say that they were all three of them crocked, and couldn't possibly play. I tell you, it was a bit of a jar to get half an hour before the match started. Willis has sprained his ankle, apparently; Keene's damaged his wrist; and Ballard has smashed his collar-bone. I don't suppose they'll be able to play in the 'Varsity match. Rotten luck for Cambridge. Well, fortunately we'd had two reserve pros, with us at Brighton, who had come up to London with the team in case they might be wanted, so, with them, we were only one short. Then I thought of you. That's how it was.'

'I see,' said Mike. 'Who are the pros?'

'Davis and Brockley. Both bowlers. It weakens our batting a lot. Ballard or Willis might have got a stack of runs on this wicket. Still, we've got a certain amount of batting as it is. We oughtn't to do badly, if we're careful. You've been getting some practice, I suppose, this season?'

'In a sort of a way. Nets and so on. No matches of any importance.'

'Dash it, I wish you'd had a game or two in decent class cricket. Still, nets are better than nothing, I hope you'll be in form. We may want a pretty long knock from you, if things go wrong. These men seem to be settling down all right, thank goodness,' he added, looking out of the window at the county's first pair, Warrington and Mills, two professionals, who, as the result of ten minutes' play, had put up twenty.

'I'd better go and change,' said Mike, picking up his bag. 'You're in first wicket, I suppose?'

'Yes. And Reggie, second wicket.'

Reggie was another of Mike's brothers, not nearly so fine a player as Joe, but a sound bat, who generally made runs if allowed to stay in.

Mike changed, and went out into the little balcony at the top of the pavilion. He had it to himself. There were not many spectators in the pavilion at this early stage of the game.

There are few more restful places, if one wishes to think, than the upper balconies of Lord's pavilion. Mike, watching the game making its leisurely progress on the turf below, set himself seriously to review the situation in all its aspects. The exhilaration of bursting the bonds had begun to fade, and he found himself able to look into the matter of his desertion and weigh up the consequences. There was no doubt that he had cut the painter once and for all. Even a friendly-disposed management could hardly overlook what he had done. And the management of the New Asiatic Bank was the very reverse of friendly. Mr Bickersdyke, he knew, would jump at this chance of getting rid of him. He realized that he must look on his career in the bank as a closed book. It was definitely over, and he must now think about the future.

It was not a time for half-measures. He could not go home. He must carry the thing through, now that he had begun, and find something definite to do, to support himself.

There seemed only one opening for him. What could he do, he asked himself. Just one thing. He could play cricket. It was by his cricket that he must live. He would have to become a professional. Could he get taken on? That was the question. It was impossible that he should play for his own county on his residential qualification. He could not appear as a professional in the same team in which his brothers were playing as amateurs. He must stake all on his birth qualification for Surrey.

On the other hand, had he the credentials which Surrey would want? He had a school reputation. But was that enough? He could not help feeling that it might not be.

Thinking it over more tensely than he had ever thought over anything in his whole life, he saw clearly that everything depended on what sort of show he made in this match which was now in progress. It was his big chance. If he succeeded, all would be well. He did not care to think what his position would be if he did not succeed.

A distant appeal and a sound of clapping from the crowd broke in on his thoughts. Mills was out, caught at the wicket. The telegraph-board gave the total as forty-eight. Not sensational. The success of the team depended largely on what sort of a start the two professionals made.

The clapping broke out again as Joe made his way down the steps. Joe, as an All England player, was a favourite with the crowd.

Mike watched him play an over in his strong, graceful style: then it suddenly occurred to him that he would like to know how matters had gone at the bank in his absence.

He went down to the telephone, rang up the bank, and asked for Psmith.

Presently the familiar voice made itself heard.

'Hullo, Smith.'

'Hullo. Is that Comrade Jackson? How are things progressing?'

'Fairly well. We're in first. We've lost one wicket, and the fifty's just up. I say, what's happened at the bank?'

'I broke the news to Comrade Gregory. A charming personality. I feel that we shall be friends.'

'Was he sick?'

'In a measure, yes. Indeed, I may say he practically foamed at the mouth. I explained the situation, but he was not to be appeased. He jerked me into the presence of Comrade Bickersdyke, with whom I had a brief but entertaining chat. He had not a great deal to say, but he listened attentively to my narrative, and eventually told me off to take your place in the Fixed Deposits. That melancholy task I am now performing to the best of my ability. I find the work a little trying. There is too much ledger-lugging to be done for my simple tastes. I have been hauling ledgers from the safe all the morning. The cry is beginning to go round, "Psmith is willing, but can his physique stand the strain?" In the excitement of the moment just now I dropped a somewhat massive tome on to Comrade Gregory's foot, unfortunately, I understand, the foot in which he has of late been suffering twinges of gout. I passed the thing off with ready tact, but I cannot deny that there was a certain temporary coolness, which, indeed, is not yet past. These things, Comrade Jackson, are the whirlpools in the quiet stream of commercial life.'

'Have I got the sack?'

'No official pronouncement has been made to me as yet on the subject, but I think I should advise you, if you are offered another job in the course of the day, to accept it. I cannot say that you are precisely the pet of the management just at present. However, I have ideas for your future, which I will divulge when we meet. I propose to slide coyly from the office at about four o'clock. I am meeting my father at that hour. We shall come straight on to Lord's.'

'Right ho,' said Mike. 'I'll be looking out for you.'

'Is there any little message I can give Comrade Gregory from you?'

'You can give him my love, if you like.'

'It shall be done. Good-bye.'

'Good-bye.'

Mike replaced the receiver, and went up to his balcony again.

As soon as his eye fell on the telegraph-board he saw with a start that things had been moving rapidly in his brief absence. The numbers of the batsmen on the board were three and five.

'Great Scott!' he cried. 'Why, I'm in next. What on earth's been happening?'

He put on his pads hurriedly, expecting every moment that a wicket would fall and find him unprepared. But the batsmen were still together when he rose, ready for the fray, and went downstairs to get news.

He found his brother Reggie in the dressing-room.

'What's happened?' he said. 'How were you out?'

'L.b.w.,' said Reggie. 'Goodness knows how it happened. My eyesight must be going. I mistimed the thing altogether.'

'How was Warrington out?'

'Caught in the slips.'

'By Jove!' said Mike. 'This is pretty rocky. Three for sixty-one. We shall get mopped.'

'Unless you and Joe do something. There's no earthly need to get out. The wicket's as good as you want, and the bowling's nothing special. Well played, Joe!'

A beautiful glide to leg by the greatest of the Jacksons had rolled up against the pavilion rails. The fieldsmen changed across for the next over.

'If only Peters stops a bit —' began Mike, and broke off. Peters' off stump was lying at an angle of forty-five degrees.

'Well, he hasn't,' said Reggie grimly. 'Silly ass, why did he hit at that one? All he'd got to do was to stay in with Joe. Now it's up to you. Do try and do something, or we'll be out under the hundred.'

Mike waited till the outcoming batsman had turned in at the professionals' gate. Then he walked down the steps and out into the open, feeling more nervous than he had felt since that far-off day when he had first gone in to bat for Wrykyn against the M.C.C. He found his thoughts flying back to that occasion. Today, as then, everything seemed very distant and unreal. The spectators were miles away. He had often been to Lord's as a spectator, but the place seemed entirely unfamiliar now. He felt as if he were in a strange land.

He was conscious of Joe leaving the crease to meet him on his way. He smiled feebly. 'Buck up,' said Joe in that robust way of his which was so heartening. 'Nothing in the bowling, and the wicket like a shirt-front. Play just as if you were at the nets. And for goodness' sake don't try to score all your runs in the first over. Stick in, and we've got them.'

Mike smiled again more feebly than before, and made a weird gurgling noise in his throat.

It had been the Middlesex fast bowler who had destroyed Peters. Mike was not sorry. He did not object to fast bowling. He took guard, and looked round him, taking careful note of the positions of the slips.

As usual, once he was at the wicket the paralysed feeling left him. He became conscious again of his power. Dash it all, what was there to be afraid of? He was a jolly good bat, and he would jolly well show them that he was, too.

The fast bowler, with a preliminary bound, began his run. Mike settled himself into position, his whole soul concentrated on the ball. Everything else was wiped from his mind.

28. Psmith Arranges his Future

It was exactly four o'clock when Psmith, sliding unostentatiously from his stool, flicked divers pieces of dust from the leg of his trousers, and sidled towards the basement, where he was wont to keep his hat during business hours. He was aware that it would be a matter of some delicacy to leave the bank at that hour. There was a certain quantity of work still to be done in the Fixed Deposits Department-work in which, by rights, as Mike's understudy, he should have lent a sympathetic and helping hand. 'But what of that?' he mused, thoughtfully smoothing his hat with his knuckles. 'Comrade Gregory is a man who takes such an enthusiastic pleasure in his duties that he will go singing about the office when he discovers that he has got a double lot of work to do.'

With this comforting thought, he started on his perilous journey to the open air. As he walked delicately, not courting observation, he reminded himself of the hero of 'Pilgrim's Progress'. On all sides of him lay fearsome beasts, lying in wait to pounce upon him. At any moment Mr Gregory's hoarse roar might shatter the comparative stillness, or the sinister note of Mr Bickersdyke make itself heard.

'However,' said Psmith philosophically, 'these are Life's Trials, and must be borne patiently.'

A roundabout route, via the Postage and Inwards Bills Departments, took him to the swing-doors. It was here that the danger became acute. The doors were well within view of the Fixed Deposits Department, and Mr Gregory had an eye compared with which that of an eagle was more or less bleared.

Psmith sauntered to the door and pushed it open in a gingerly manner.

As he did so a bellow rang through the office, causing a timid customer, who had come in to arrange about an overdraft, to lose his nerve completely and postpone his business till the following afternoon.

Psmith looked up. Mr Gregory was leaning over the barrier which divided his lair from the outer world, and gesticulating violently.

'Where are you going,' roared the head of the Fixed Deposits.

Psmith did not reply. With a benevolent smile and a gesture intended to signify all would come right in the future, he slid through the swing-doors, and began to move down the street at a somewhat swifter pace than was his habit.

Once round the corner he slackened his speed.

'This can't go on,' he said to himself. 'This life of commerce is too great a strain. One is practically a hunted hare. Either the heads of my department must refrain from View Halloos when they observe me going for a stroll, or I abandon Commerce for some less exacting walk in life.'

He removed his hat, and allowed the cool breeze to play upon his forehead. The episode had been disturbing.

He was to meet his father at the Mansion House. As he reached that land-mark he saw with approval that punctuality was a virtue of which he had not the sole monopoly in the Smith family. His father was waiting for him at the tryst.

'Certainly, my boy,' said Mr Smith senior, all activity in a moment, when Psmith had suggested going to Lord's. 'Excellent. We must be getting on. We must not miss a moment of the match. Bless my soul: I haven't seen a first-class match this season. Where's a cab? Hi, cabby! No, that one's got some one in it. There's another. Hi! Here, lunatic! Are you blind? Good, he's seen us. That's right. Here he comes. Lord's Cricket Ground, cabby, as quick as you can. Jump in, Rupert, my boy, jump in.'

Psmith rarely jumped. He entered the cab with something of the stateliness of an old Roman Emperor boarding his chariot, and settled himself comfortably in his seat. Mr Smith dived in like a rabbit.

A vendor of newspapers came to the cab thrusting an evening paper into the interior. Psmith bought it.

'Let's see how they're getting on,' he said, opening the paper. 'Where are we? Lunch scores. Lord's. Aha! Comrade Jackson is in form.'

'Jackson?' said Mr Smith, 'is that the same youngster you brought home last summer? The batsman? Is he playing today?'

'He was not out thirty at lunch-time. He would appear to be making something of a stand with his brother Joe, who has made sixty-one up to the moment of going to press. It's possible he may still be in when we get there. In which case we shall not be able to slide into the pavilion.'

'A grand bat, that boy. I said so last summer. Better than any of his brothers. He's in the bank with you, isn't he?'

'He was this morning. I doubt, however, whether he can be said to be still in that position.'

'Eh? what? How's that?'

'There was some slight friction between him and the management. They wished him to be glued to his stool; he preferred to play for the county. I think we may say that Comrade Jackson has secured the Order of the Boot.'

'What? Do you mean to say —?'

Psmith related briefly the history of Mike's departure.

Mr Smith listened with interest.

'Well,' he said at last, 'hang me if I blame the boy. It's a sin cooping up a fellow who can bat like that in a bank. I should have done the same myself in his place.'

Psmith smoothed his waistcoat.

'Do you know, father,' he said, 'this bank business is far from being much of a catch. Indeed, I should describe it definitely as a bit off. I have given it a fair trial, and I now denounce it unhesitatingly as a shade too thick.'

'What? Are you getting tired of it?'

'Not precisely tired. But, after considerable reflection, I have come to the conclusion that my talents lie elsewhere. At lugging ledgers I am among the also-rans — a mere cipher. I have been wanting to speak to you about this for some time. If you have no objection, I should like to go to the Bar.'

'The Bar? Well —'

'I fancy I should make a pretty considerable hit as a barrister.'

Mr Smith reflected. The idea had not occurred to him before. Now that it was suggested, his always easily-fired imagination took hold of it readily. There was a good deal to be said for the Bar as a career. Psmith knew his father, and he knew that the thing was practically as good as settled. It was a new idea, and as such was bound to be favourably received.

'What I should do, if I were you,' he went on, as if he were advising a friend on some course of action certain to bring him profit and pleasure, 'is to take me away from the bank at once. Don't wait. There is no time like the present. Let me hand in my resignation tomorrow. The blow to the management, especially to Comrade Bickersdyke, will be a painful one, but it is the truest kindness to administer it swiftly. Let me resign tomorrow, and devote my time to quiet study. Then I can pop up to Cambridge next term, and all will be well.'

'I'll think it over —' began Mr Smith.

'Let us hustle,' urged Psmith. 'Let us Do It Now. It is the only way. Have I your leave to shoot in my resignation to Comrade Bickersdyke tomorrow morning?'

Mr Smith hesitated for a moment, then made up his mind.

'Very well,' he said. 'I really think it is a good idea. There are great opportunities open to a barrister. I wish we had thought of it before.'

'I am not altogether sorry that we did not,' said Psmith. 'I have enjoyed the chances my commercial life has given me of associating with such a man as Comrade Bickersdyke. In many ways a master-mind. But perhaps it is as well to close the chapter. How it happened it is hard to say, but somehow I fancy I did not precisely hit it off with Comrade Bickersdyke. With Psmith, the worker, he had no fault to find; but it seemed to me sometimes, during our festive evenings together at the club, that all was not well. From little, almost imperceptible signs I have suspected now and then that he would just as soon have been without my company. One cannot explain these things. It must have been some incompatibility of temperament. Perhaps he will manage to bear up at my departure. But here we are,' he added, as the cab drew up. 'I wonder if Comrade Jackson is still going strong.'

They passed through the turnstile, and caught sight of the telegraph-board.

'By Jove!' said Psmith, 'he is. I don't know if he's number three or number six. I expect he's number six. In which case he has got ninety-eight. We're just in time to see his century.'

29. And Mike's

For nearly two hours Mike had been experiencing the keenest pleasure that it had ever fallen to his lot to feel. From the moment he took his first ball till the luncheon interval he had suffered the acutest discomfort. His nervousness had left him to a great extent, but he had never really settled down. Sometimes by luck, and sometimes by skill, he had kept the ball out of his wicket; but he was scratching, and he knew it. Not for a single over had he been comfortable. On several occasions he had edged balls to leg and through the slips in quite an inferior manner, and it was seldom that he managed to hit with the centre of the bat.

Nobody is more alive to the fact that he is not playing up to his true form than the batsman. Even though his score mounted little by little into the twenties, Mike was miserable. If this was the best he could do on a perfect wicket, he felt there was not much hope for him as a professional.

The poorness of his play was accentuated by the brilliance of Joe's. Joe combined science and vigour to a remarkable degree. He laid on the wood with a graceful robustness which drew much cheering from the crowd. Beside him Mike was oppressed by that leaden sense of moral inferiority which weighs on a man who has turned up to dinner in ordinary clothes when everybody else has dressed. He felt awkward and conspicuously out of place.

Then came lunch-and after lunch a glorious change.

Volumes might be written on the cricket lunch and the influence it has on the run of the game; how it undoes one man, and sends another back to the fray like a giant refreshed; how it turns the brilliant fast bowler into the sluggish medium, and the nervous bat into the masterful smiter.

On Mike its effect was magical. He lunched wisely and well, chewing his food with the concentration of a thirty-three-bites a mouthful crank, and drinking dry ginger-ale. As he walked out with Joe after the interval he knew that a change had taken place in him. His nerve had come back, and with it his form.

It sometimes happens at cricket that when one feels particularly fit one gets snapped in the slips in the first over, or clean bowled by a full toss; but neither of these things happened to Mike. He stayed in, and began to score. Now there were no edgings through the slips and snicks to leg. He was meeting the ball in the centre of the bat, and meeting it vigorously. Two boundaries in successive balls off the fast bowler, hard, clean drives past extra-cover, put him at peace with all the world. He was on top. He had found himself.

Joe, at the other end, resumed his brilliant career. His century and
Mike's fifty arrived in the same over. The bowling began to grow loose.

Joe, having reached his century, slowed down somewhat, and Mike took up the running. The score rose rapidly.

A leg-theory bowler kept down the pace of the run-getting for a time, but the bowlers at the other end continued to give away runs. Mike's score passed from sixty to seventy, from seventy to eighty, from eighty to ninety. When the Smiths, father and son, came on to the ground the total was ninety-eight. Joe had made a hundred and thirty-three.

* * * * *

Mike reached his century just as Psmith and his father took their seats. A square cut off the slow bowler was just too wide for point to get to. By the time third man had sprinted across and returned the ball the batsmen had run two.

Mr Smith was enthusiastic.

'I tell you,' he said to Psmith, who was clapping in a gently encouraging manner, 'the boy's a wonderful bat. I said so when he was down with us. I remember telling him so myself. "I've seen your brothers play," I said, "and you're better than any of them." I remember it distinctly.

He'll be playing for England in another year or two. Fancy putting a cricketer like that into the City! It's a crime.'

'I gather,' said Psmith, 'that the family coffers had got a bit low. It was necessary for Comrade Jackson to do something by way of saving the Old Home.'

'He ought to be at the University. Look, he's got that man away to the boundary again. They'll never get him out.'

At six o'clock the partnership was broken, Joe running himself out in trying to snatch a single where no single was. He had made a hundred and eighty-nine.

Mike flung himself down on the turf with mixed feelings. He was sorry Joe was out, but he was very glad indeed of the chance of a rest. He was utterly fagged. A half-day match once a week is no training for first-class cricket. Joe, who had been playing all the season, was as tough as india-rubber, and trotted into the pavilion as fresh as if he had been having a brief spell at the nets. Mike, on the other hand, felt that he simply wanted to be dropped into a cold bath and left there indefinitely. There was only another half-hour's play, but he doubted if he could get through it.

He dragged himself up wearily as Joe's successor arrived at the wickets. He had crossed Joe before the latter's downfall, and it was his turn to take the bowling.

Something seemed to have gone out of him. He could not time the ball properly. The last ball of the over looked like a half-volley, and he hit out at it. But it was just short of a half-volley, and his stroke arrived too soon. The bowler, running in the direction of mid-on, brought off an easy c.-and-b.

Mike turned away towards the pavilion. He heard the gradually swelling applause in a sort of dream. It seemed to him hours before he reached the dressing-room.

He was sitting on a chair, wishing that somebody would come along and take off his pads, when Psmith's card was brought to him. A few moments later the old Etonian appeared in person.

'Hullo, Smith,' said Mike, 'By Jove! I'm done.'

'"How Little Willie Saved the Match,"' said Psmith. 'What you want is one of those gin and ginger-beers we hear so much about. Remove those pads, and let us flit downstairs in search of a couple. Well, Comrade Jackson, you have fought the good fight this day. My father sends his compliments. He is dining out, or he would have come up. He is going to look in at the flat latish.'

'How many did I get?' asked Mike. 'I was so jolly done I didn't think of looking.'

'A hundred and forty-eight of the best,' said Psmith. 'What will they say at the old homestead about this? Are you ready? Then let us test this fruity old ginger-beer of theirs.'

The two batsmen who had followed the big stand were apparently having a little stand all of their own. No more wickets fell before the drawing of stumps. Psmith waited for Mike while he changed, and carried him off in a cab to Simpson's, a restaurant which, as he justly observed, offered two great advantages, namely, that you need not dress, and, secondly, that you paid your half-crown, and were then at liberty to eat till you were helpless, if you felt so disposed, without extra charge.

Mike stopped short of this giddy height of mastication, but consumed enough to make him feel a great deal better. Psmith eyed his inroads on the menu with approval.

'There is nothing,' he said, 'like victualling up before an ordeal.'

'What's the ordeal?' said Mike.

'I propose to take you round to the club anon, where I trust we shall find Comrade Bickersdyke. We have much to say to one another.'

'Look here, I'm hanged —' began Mike.

'Yes, you must be there,' said Psmith. 'Your presence will serve to cheer Comrade B. up. Fate compels me to deal him a nasty blow, and he will want sympathy. I have got to break it to him that I am leaving the bank.'

'What, are you going to chuck it?'

418

Psmith inclined his head.

'The time,' he said, 'has come to part. It has served its turn. The startled whisper runs round the City. "Psmith has had sufficient."'

'What are you going to do?'

'I propose to enter the University of Cambridge, and there to study the intricacies of the Law, with a view to having a subsequent dash at becoming Lord Chancellor.'

'By Jove!' said Mike, 'you're lucky. I wish I were coming too.'

Psmith knocked the ash off his cigarette.

'Are you absolutely set on becoming a pro?' he asked.

'It depends on what you call set. It seems to me it's about all I can do.'

'I can offer you a not entirely scaly job,' said Smith, 'if you feel like taking it. In the course of conversation with my father during the match this afternoon, I gleaned the fact that he is anxious to secure your services as a species of agent. The vast Psmith estates, it seems, need a bright boy to keep an eye upon them. Are you prepared to accept the post?'

Mike stared.

'Me! Dash it all, how old do you think I am? I'm only nineteen.'

'I had suspected as much from the alabaster clearness of your unwrinkled brow. But my father does not wish you to enter upon your duties immediately. There would be a preliminary interval of three, possibly four, years at Cambridge, during which I presume, you would be learning divers facts concerning spuds, turmuts, and the like. At least,' said Psmith airily, 'I suppose so. Far be it from me to dictate the line of your researches.'

'Then I'm afraid it's off,' said Mike gloomily. 'My pater couldn't afford to send me to Cambridge.'

'That obstacle,' said Psmith, 'can be surmounted. You would, of course, accompany me to Cambridge, in the capacity, which you enjoy at the present moment, of my confidential secretary and adviser. Any expenses that might crop up would be defrayed from the Psmith family chest.'

Mike's eyes opened wide again.

'Do you mean,' he asked bluntly, 'that your pater would pay for me at the 'Varsity? No I say-dash it —I mean, I couldn't —'

'Do you suggest,' said Psmith, raising his eyebrows, 'that I should go to the University *without* a confidential secretary and adviser?'

'No, but I mean —' protested Mike.

'Then that's settled,' said Psmith. 'I knew you would not desert me in my hour of need, Comrade Jackson. "What will you do," asked my father, alarmed for my safety, "among these wild undergraduates? I fear for my Rupert." "Have no fear, father," I replied. "Comrade Jackson will be beside me." His face brightened immediately. "Comrade Jackson," he said, "is a man in whom I have the supremest confidence. If he is with you I shall sleep easy of nights." It was after that that the conversation drifted to the subject of agents.'

Psmith called for the bill and paid it in the affable manner of a monarch signing a charter. Mike sat silent, his mind in a whirl. He saw exactly what had happened. He could almost hear Psmith talking his father into agreeing with his scheme. He could think of nothing to say. As usually happened in any emotional crisis in his life, words absolutely deserted him. The thing was too big. Anything he could say would sound too feeble. When a friend has solved all your difficulties and smoothed out all the rough places which were looming in your path, you cannot thank him as if he had asked you to lunch. The occasion demanded some neat, polished speech; and neat, polished speeches were beyond Mike.

'I say, Psmith —' he began.

Psmith rose.

'Let us now,' he said, 'collect our hats and meander to the club, where, I have no doubt, we shall find Comrade Bickersdyke, all unconscious of impending misfortune, dreaming pleasantly over coffee and a cigar in the lower smoking-room.'

30. The Last Sad Farewells

As it happened, that was precisely what Mr Bickersdyke was doing. He was feeling thoroughly pleased with life. For nearly nine months Psmith had been to him a sort of spectre at the feast inspiring him with an ever-present feeling of discomfort which he had found impossible to shake off. And tonight he saw his way of getting rid of him.

At five minutes past four Mr Gregory, crimson and wrathful, had plunged into his room with a long statement of how Psmith, deputed to help in the life and thought of the Fixed Deposits Department, had left the building at four o'clock, when there was still another hour and a half's work to be done.

Moreover, Mr Gregory deposed, the errant one, seen sliding out of the swinging door, and summoned in a loud, clear voice to come back, had flatly disobeyed and had gone upon his ways 'Grinning at me,' said the aggrieved Mr Gregory, 'like a dashed ape.' A most unjust description of the sad, sweet smile which Psmith had bestowed upon him from the doorway.

Ever since that moment Mr Bickersdyke had felt that there was a silver lining to the cloud. Hitherto Psmith had left nothing to be desired in the manner in which he performed his work. His righteousness in the office had clothed him as in a suit of mail. But now he had slipped. To go off an hour and a half before the proper time, and to refuse to return when summoned by the head of his department-these were offences for which he could be dismissed without fuss. Mr Bickersdyke looked forward to tomorrow's interview with his employee.

Meanwhile, having enjoyed an excellent dinner, he was now, as Psmith had predicted, engaged with a cigar and a cup of coffee in the lower smoking-room of the Senior Conservative Club.

Psmith and Mike entered the room when he was about half through these luxuries.

Psmith's first action was to summon a waiter, and order a glass of neat brandy. 'Not for myself,' he explained to Mike. 'For Comrade Bickersdyke. He is about to sustain a nasty shock, and may need a restorative at a moment's notice. For all we know, his heart may not be strong. In any case, it is safest to have a pick-me-up handy.'

He paid the waiter, and advanced across the room, followed by Mike. In his hand, extended at arm's length, he bore the glass of brandy.

Mr Bickersdyke caught sight of the procession, and started. Psmith set the brandy down very carefully on the table, beside the manager's coffee cup, and, dropping into a chair, regarded him pityingly through his eyeglass. Mike, who felt embarrassed, took a seat some little way behind his companion. This was Psmith's affair, and he proposed to allow him to do the talking.

Mr Bickersdyke, except for a slight deepening of the colour of his complexion, gave no sign of having seen them. He puffed away at his cigar, his eyes fixed on the ceiling.

'An unpleasant task lies before us,' began Psmith in a low, sorrowful voice, 'and it must not be shirked. Have I your ear, Mr Bickersdyke?'

Addressed thus directly, the manager allowed his gaze to wander from the ceiling. He eyed Psmith for a moment like an elderly basilisk, then looked back at the ceiling again.

'I shall speak to you tomorrow,' he said.

Psmith heaved a heavy sigh.

'You will not see us tomorrow,' he said, pushing the brandy a little nearer.

Mr Bickersdyke's eyes left the ceiling once more.

'What do you mean?' he said.

'Drink this,' urged Psmith sympathetically, holding out the glass. 'Be brave,' he went on rapidly. 'Time softens the harshest blows. Shocks stun us for the moment, but we recover. Little by little we come to ourselves again. Life, which we had thought could hold no more pleasure for us, gradually shows itself not wholly grey.'

Mr Bickersdyke seemed about to make an observation at this point, but Psmith, with a wave of the hand, hurried on.

'We find that the sun still shines, the birds still sing. Things which used to entertain us resume their attraction. Gradually we emerge from the soup, and begin —'

'If you have anything to say to me,' said the manager, 'I should be glad if you would say it, and go.'

'You prefer me not to break the bad news gently?' said Psmith. 'Perhaps you are wise. In a word, then,' —he picked up the brandy and held it out to him —'Comrade Jackson and myself are leaving the bank.'

'I am aware of that,' said Mr Bickersdyke drily.

Psmith put down the glass.

'You have been told already?' he said. 'That accounts for your calm. The shock has expended its force on you, and can do no more. You are stunned. I am sorry, but it had to be. You will say that it is madness for us to offer our resignations, that our grip on the work of the bank made a prosperous career in Commerce certain for us. It may be so. But somehow we feel that our talents lie elsewhere. To Comrade Jackson the management of the Psmith estates seems the job on which he can get the rapid half-Nelson. For my own part, I feel that my long suit is the Bar. I am a poor, unready speaker, but I intend to acquire a knowledge of the Law which shall outweigh this defect. Before leaving you, I should like to say —I may speak for you as well as myself, Comrade Jackson —?'

Mike uttered his first contribution to the conversation —a gurgle-and relapsed into silence again.

'I should like to say,' continued Psmith, 'how much Comrade Jackson and I have enjoyed our stay in the bank. The insight it has given us into your masterly handling of the intricate mechanism of the office has been a treat we would not have missed. But our place is elsewhere.'

He rose. Mike followed his example with alacrity. It occurred to Mr Bickersdyke, as they turned to go, that he had not yet been able to get in a word about their dismissal. They were drifting away with all the honours of war.

'Come back,' he cried.

Psmith paused and shook his head sadly.

'This is unmanly, Comrade Bickersdyke,' he said. 'I had not expected this. That you should be dazed by the shock was natural. But that you should beg us to reconsider our resolve and return to the bank is unworthy of you. Be a man. Bite the bullet. The first keen pang will pass. Time will soften the feeling of bereavement. You must be brave. Come, Comrade Jackson.'

Mike responded to the call without hesitation.

'We will now,' said Psmith, leading the way to the door, 'push back to the flat. My father will be round there soon.' He looked over his shoulder. Mr Bickersdyke appeared to be wrapped in thought.

'A painful business,' sighed Psmith. 'The man seems quite broken up. It had to be, however. The bank was no place for us. An excellent career in many respects, but unsuitable for you and me. It is hard on Comrade Bickersdyke, especially as he took such trouble to get me into it, but I think we may say that we are well out of the place.'

Mike's mind roamed into the future. Cambridge first, and then an open-air life of the sort he had always dreamed of. The Problem of Life seemed to him to be solved. He looked on down the years, and he could see no troubles there of any kind whatsoever. Reason suggested that there were probably one or two knocking about somewhere, but this was no time to think of them. He examined the future, and found it good.

'I should jolly well think,' he said simply, 'that we might.'

The Prince and Betty

CHAPTER I

THE CABLE PROM MERVO

A pretty girl in a blue dress came out of the house, and began to walk slowly across the terrace to where Elsa Keith sat with Marvin Rossiter in the shade of the big sycamore. Elsa and Marvin had become engaged some few days before, and were generally to be found at this time sitting together in some shaded spot in the grounds of the Keith's Long Island home.

"What's troubling Betty, I wonder," said Elsa. "She looks worried."

Marvin turned his head.

"Is that your friend, Miss Silver?"

"That's Betty. We were at college together. I want you to like Betty."

"Then I will. When did she arrive?"

"Last night. She's here for a month. What's the matter, Betty? This is Marvin. I want you to like Marvin."

Betty Silver smiled. Her face, in repose, was rather wistful, but it lighted up when she smiled, and an unsuspected dimple came into being on her chin.

"Of course I shall," she said.

Her big gray eyes seemed to search Marvin's for an instant and Marvin had, almost subconsciously, a comfortable feeling that he had been tested and found worthy.

"What were you scowling at so ferociously, Betty?" asked Elsa.

"Was I scowling? I hope you didn't think it was at you. Oh, Elsa, I'm miserable! I shall have to leave this heavenly place."

"Betty!"

"At once. And I was meaning to have the most lovely time. See what has come!"

She held out some flimsy sheets of paper.

"A cable!" said Elsa.

"Great Scott! it looks like the scenario of a four-act play," said Marvin. "That's not all one cable, surely? Whoever sent it must be a millionaire."

"He is. It's from my stepfather. Read it out, Elsa. I want Mr. Rossiter to hear it. He may be able to tell me where Mervo is. Did you ever hear of Mervo, Mr. Rossiter?"

"Never. What is it?"

"It's a place where my stepfather is, and where I've got to go. I do call it hard. Go on, Elsa."

Elsa, who had been skimming the document with raised eyebrows, now read it out in its spacious entirety.

> On receipt of this come instantly Mervo without moment delay vital importance presence urgently required come wherever you are cancel engagements urgent necessity hustle have advised bank allow you draw any money you need expenses have booked stateroom *Mauretania* sailing Wednesday don't fail catch arrive Fishguard Monday train London sleep London catch first train Tuesday Dover now mind first train no taking root in London and spending a week shopping mid-day boat Dover Calais arrive Paris Tuesday evening Dine Paris catch train de luxe nine-fifteen Tuesday night for Marseilles have engaged sleeping coupe now mind Tuesday night no cutting loose around Paris stores you can do all that later on just now you want to get here right quick arrive Marseilles Wednesday morning boat Mervo Wednesday night will meet you Mervo now do you follow all that because if not cable at once and say which part of journey you don't understand now mind special points to be remembered firstly come instantly secondly no cutting loose around London Paris stores see.

"Well!" said Elsa, breathless.

"By George!" said Marvin. "He certainly seems to want you badly enough. He hasn't spared expense. He has put in about everything you could put into a cable."

"Except why he wants me," said Betty.

"Yes," said Elsa. "Why does he want you? And in such a desperate hurry, too!"

Marvin was re-reading the message.

"It isn't a mere invitation," he said. "There's no come-right-along-you'll-like-this-place-it's-fine about it. He seems to look on your company more as a necessity than a luxury. It's a sort of imperious C.Q.D."

"That's what makes it so strange. We have hardly met for years. Why, he didn't even know where I was. The cable was sent to the bank and forwarded on. And I don't know where he is!"

"Which brings us back," said Marvin, "to mysterious Mervo. Let us reason inductively. If you get to the place by taking a boat from Marseilles, it can't be far from the French coast. I should say at a venture that Mervo is an island in the Mediterranean. And a small island for if it had been a big one we should have heard of it."

"Marvin!" cried Elsa, her face beaming with proud affection. "How clever you are!"

"A mere gift," he said modestly. "I have been like that from a boy." He got up from his chair. "Isn't there an encyclopaedia in the library, Elsa?"

"Yes, but it's an old edition."

"It will probably touch on Mervo. I'll go and fetch it."

As he crossed the terrace, Elsa turned quickly to Betty.

"Well?" she said.

Betty smiled at her.

"He's a dear. Are you very happy, Elsa?"

Elsa's eyes danced. She drew in her breath softly. Betty looked at her in silence for a moment. The wistful expression was back on her face.

"Elsa," she said, suddenly. "What is it like? How does it feel, knowing that there's someone who is fonder of you than anything —?"

Elsa closed her eyes.

"It's like eating berries and cream in a new dress by moonlight on a summer night while somebody plays the violin far away in the distance so that you can just hear it," she said.

Her eyes opened again.

"And it's like coming along on a winter evening and seeing the windows lit up and knowing you've reached home."

Betty was clenching her hands, and breathing quickly.

"And it's like —"

"Elsa, don't! I can't bear it!"

"Betty! What's the matter?"

Betty smiled again, but painfully.

*"*It's stupid of me. I'm just jealous, that's all. I haven't got a Marvin, you see. You have."

"Well, there are plenty who would like to be your Marvin."

Betty's face grew cold.

"There are plenty who would like to be Benjamin Scobell's son-in-law," she said.

"Betty!" Elsa's voice was serious. "We've been friends for a good long time, so you'll let me say something, won't you? I think you're getting just the least bit hard. Now turn and rend me," she added good-humoredly.

"I'm not going to rend you," said Betty. "You're perfectly right. I am getting hard. How can I help it? Do you know how many men have asked me to marry them since I saw you last? Five."

"Betty!"

"And not one of them cared the slightest bit about me."

"But, Betty, dear, that's just what I mean. Why should you say that? How can you know?"

"How do I know? Well, I do know. Instinct, I suppose. The instinct of self-preservation which nature gives hunted animals. I can't think of a single man in the world-except your Marvin, of course-who wouldn't do anything for money." She stopped. "Well, yes, one."

Elsa leaned forward eagerly.

"Who, Betty?"

"You don't know him."

"But what's his name?"

Betty hesitated.

"Well, if I am on the witness-stand —Maude."

"Maude? I thought you said a man?"

"It's his name. John Maude."

"But, Betty! Why didn't you tell me before? This is tremendously interesting."

Betty laughed shortly.

"Not so very, really. I only met him two or three times, and I haven't seen him for years, and I don't suppose I shall ever see him again. He was a friend of Alice Beecher's brother, who was at Harvard. Alice took me over to meet her brother, and Mr. Maude was there. That's all."

Elsa was plainly disappointed.

"But how do you know, then —? What makes you think that he —?"

"Instinct, again, I suppose. I do know."

"And you've never met him since?"

Betty shook her head. Elsa relapsed into silence. She had a sense of pathos.

At the further end of the terrace Marvin Rossiter appeared, carrying a large volume.

"Here we are," he said. "Scared it up at the first attempt. Now then."

He sat down, and opened the book.

"You don't want to hear all about how Jason went there in search of the Golden Fleece, and how Ulysses is supposed to have taken it in on his round-trip? You want something more modern. Well, it's an island in the Mediterranean, as I said, and I'm surprised that you've never heard of it, Elsa, because it's celebrated in its way. It's the smallest independent state in the world. Smaller than Monaco, even. Here are some facts. Its population when this encyclopaedia was printed-there may be more now-was eleven thousand and sixteen. It was ruled over up to 1886 by a prince. But in that year the populace appear to have said to themselves, 'When in the course of human events....' Anyway, they fired the prince, and the place is now a republic. So that's where you're going, Miss Silver. I don't know if it's any consolation to you, but the island, according to this gentleman, is celebrated for the unspoilt beauty of its scenery. He also gives a list of the fish that can be caught there. It takes up about three lines."

"But what can my stepfather be doing there? I last heard of him in

London. Well, I suppose I shall have to go."

"I suppose you will," said Elsa mournfully. "But, oh, Betty, what a shame!"

CHAPTER II

MERVO AND ITS OWNER

"By heck!" cried Mr. Benjamin Scobell.

He wheeled round from the window, and transferred his gaze from the view to his sister Marion; losing by the action, for the view was a joy to the eye, which his sister Marion was not.

Mervo was looking its best under the hot morning sun. Mr. Scobell's villa stood near the summit of the only hill the island possessed, and from the window of the morning-room, where he had just finished breakfast, he had an uninterrupted view of valley, town, and harbor —a two-mile riot of green, gold and white, and beyond the white the blue satin of the Mediterranean. Mr. Scobell did not read poetry except that which advertised certain breakfast foods in which he was interested, or he might have been reminded of the Island of Flowers in Tennyson's "Voyage of Maeldive." Violets, pinks, crocuses, yellow and purple mesembryanthemum, lavender, myrtle, and rosemary... his two-mile view contained them all. The hillside below him was all aglow with the yellow fire of the mimosa. But his was not one of those emotional natures to which the meanest flower that blows can give thoughts that do often lie too deep for tears. A primrose by the river's brim a simple primrose was to him-or not so much a simple primrose, perhaps, as a basis for a possible Primrosina, the Soap that Really Cleans You.

He was a nasty little man to hold despotic sway over such a Paradise: a goblin in Fairyland. Somewhat below the middle height, he was lean of body and vulturine of face. He had a greedy mouth, a hooked nose, liquid green eyes and a sallow complexion. He was rarely seen without a half-smoked cigar between his lips. This at intervals he would relight, only to allow it to go out again; and when, after numerous fresh starts, it had dwindled beyond the limits of convenience, he would substitute another from the reserve supply that protruded from his vest-pocket.

* * * * *

How Benjamin Scobell had discovered the existence of Mervo is not known. It lay well outside the sphere of the ordinary financier. But Mr. Scobell took a pride in the versatility of his finance. It distinguished him from the uninspired who were content to concentrate themselves on steel, wheat and such-like things. It was Mr. Scobell's way to consider nothing as lying outside his sphere. In a financial sense he might have taken Terence's *Nihil humanum alienum* as his motto. He was interested in innumerable enterprises, great and small. He was the power behind a company which was endeavoring, without much success, to extract gold from the mountains of North Wales, and another which was trying, without any success at all, to do the same by sea water. He owned a model farm in Indiana, and a weekly paper in New York. He had financed patent medicines, patent foods, patent corks, patent corkscrews, patent devices of all kinds, some profitable, some the reverse.

Also-outside the ordinary gains of finance-he had expectations. He was the only male relative of his aunt, the celebrated Mrs. Jane Oakley, who lived in a cottage on Staten Island, and was reputed to spend five hundred dollars a year-some said less-out of her snug income of eighteen million. She was an unusual old lady in many ways, and, unfortunately, unusually full of deep-rooted prejudices. The fear lest he might inadvertently fall foul of these rarely ceased to haunt Mr. Scobell.

This man of many projects had descended upon Mervo like a stone on the surface of some quiet pool, bubbling over with modern enterprise in general and, in particular, with a scheme. Before his arrival, Mervo had been an island of dreams and slow movement and putting things off till to-morrow. The only really energetic thing it had ever done in its whole history had been to expel his late highness, Prince Charles, and change itself into a republic. And even that had been done with the minimum of fuss. The Prince was away at the time. Indeed, he had

427

been away for nearly three years, the pleasures of Paris, London and Vienna appealing to him more keenly than life among his subjects. Mervo, having thought the matter over during these years, decided that it had no further use for Prince Charles. Quite quietly, with none of that vulgar brawling which its neighbor, France, had found necessary in similar circumstances, it had struck his name off the pay-roll, and declared itself a republic. The royalist party, headed by General Poineau, had been distracted but impotent. The army, one hundred and fifteen strong, had gone solid for the new regime, and that had settled it. Mervo had then gone to sleep again. It was asleep when Mr. Scobell found it.

The financier's scheme was first revealed to M. d'Orby, the President of the Republic, a large, stout statesman with even more than the average Mervian instinct for slumber. He was asleep in a chair on the porch of his villa when Mr. Scobell paid his call, and it was not until the financier's secretary, who attended the seance in the capacity of interpreter, had rocked him vigorously from side to side for quite a minute that he displayed any signs of animation beyond a snore like the growling of distant thunder. When at length he opened his eyes, he perceived the nightmare-like form of Mr. Scobell standing before him, talking. The financier, impatient of delay, had begun to talk some moments before the great awakening.

"Sir," Mr. Scobell was saying, "I gotta proposition to which I'd like you to give your complete attention. Shake him some more, Crump. Sir, there's big money in it for all of us, if you and your crowd'll sit in. Money. *Lar' monnay*. No, that means change. What's money, Crump? *Arjong*? There's *arjong* in it, Squire. Get that? Oh, shucks! Hand it to him in French, Crump."

Mr. Secretary Crump translated. The President blinked, and intimated that he would hear more. Mr. Scobell relighted his cigar-stump, and proceeded.

"Say, you've heard of *Moosieer* Blonk? Ask the old skeesicks if he's ever heard of *Mersyaw* Blonk, Crump, the feller who started the gaming-tables at Monte Carlo."

Filtered through Mr. Crump, the question became intelligible to the President. He said he had heard of M. Blanc. Mr. Crump caught the reply and sent it on to Mr. Scobell, as the man on first base catches the ball and throws it to second.

Mr. Scobell relighted his cigar.

"Well, I'm in that line. I'm going to put this island on the map just like old Doctor Blonk put Monte Carlo. I've been studying up all about the old man, and I know just what he did and how he did it. Monte Carlo was just such another jerkwater little place as this is before he hit it. The government was down to its last bean and wondering where the Heck its next meal-ticket was coming from, when in blows Mr. Man, tucks up his shirt-sleeves, and starts the tables. And after that the place never looked back. You and your crowd gotta get together and pass a vote to give me a gambling concession here, same as they did him. Scobell's my name. Hand him that, Crump."

Mr. Crump obliged once more. A gleam of intelligence came into the President's dull eye. He nodded once or twice. He talked volubly in French to Mr. Crump, who responded in the same tongue.

"The idea seems to strike him, sir," said Mr. Crump.

"It ought to, if he isn't a clam," replied Mr. Scobell. He started to relight his cigar, but after scorching the tip of his nose, bowed to the inevitable and threw the relic away.

"See here," he said, having bitten the end off the next in order; "I've thought this thing out from soup to nuts. There's heaps of room for another Monte Carlo. Monte's a dandy place, but it's not perfect by a long way. To start with, it's hilly. You have to take the elevator to get to the Casino, and when you've gotten to the end of your roll and want to soak your pearl pin, where's the hock-shop? Half a mile away up the side of a mountain. It ain't right. In my Casino there's going to be a resident pawnbroker inside the building, just off the main entrance. That's only one of a heap of improvements. Another is that my Casino's scheduled to be a home from home, a place you can be real cosy in. You'll look around you, and the only thing you'll miss will be mother's face. Yes, sir, there's no need for a gambling Casino to look and feel and smell like the reading-room at the British Museum. Comfort, coziness and convenience. That's the ticket I'm running on. Slip that to the old gink, Crump."

A further outburst of the French language from Mr. Crump, supplemented on the part of the "old gink" by gesticulations, interrupted the proceedings.

"What's he saying now?" asked Mr. Scobell.

"He wants to know—"

"Don't tell. Let me guess. He wants to know what sort of a rake-off he and the other somnambulists will get-the darned old pirate! Is that it?"

Mr. Crump said that that was just it.

"That'll be all right," said Mr. Scobell. "Old man Blong's offer to the Prince of Monaco was five hundred thousand francs a year-that's somewhere around a hundred thousand dollars in real money-and half the profits made by the Casino. That's my offer, too. See how that hits him, Crump."

Mr. Crump investigated.

"He says he accepts gladly, on behalf of the Republic, sir," he announced.

M. d'Orby confirmed the statement by rising, dodging the cigar, and kissing Mr. Scobell on both cheeks.

"Cut it out," said the financier austerely, breaking out of the clinch. "We'll take the Apache Dance as read. Good-by, Squire. Glad it's settled. Now I can get busy."

He did. Workmen poured into Mervo, and in a very short time, dominating the town and reducing to insignificance the palace of the late Prince, once a passably imposing mansion, there rose beside the harbor a mammoth Casino of shining stone.

Imposing as was the exterior, it was on the interior that Mr. Scobell more particularly prided himself, and not without reason. Certainly, a man with money to lose could lose it here under the most charming conditions. It had been Mr. Scobell's object to avoid the cheerless grandeur of the rival institution down the coast. Instead of one large hall sprinkled with tables, each table had a room to itself, separated from its neighbor by sound-proof folding-doors. And as the building progressed, Mr. Scobell's active mind had soared above the original idea of domestic coziness to far greater heights of ingenuity. Each of the rooms was furnished and arranged in a different style. The note of individuality extended even to the *croupiers*. Thus, a man with money at his command could wander from the Dutch room, where, in the picturesque surroundings of a Dutch kitchen, *croupiers* in the costume of Holland ministered to his needs, to the Japanese room, where his coin would be raked in by quite passable imitations of the Samurai. If he had any left at this point, he was free to dispose of it under the auspices of near-Hindoos in the Indian room, of merry Swiss peasants in the Swiss room, or in other appropriately furnished apartments of red-shirted, Bret Harte miners, fur-clad Esquimaux, or languorous Spaniards. He could then, if a man of spirit, who did not know when he was beaten, collect the family jewels, and proceed down the main hall, accompanied by the strains of an excellent band, to the office of a gentlemanly pawnbroker, who spoke seven languages like a native and was prepared to advance money on reasonable security in all of them.

It was a colossal venture, but it suffered from the defect from which most big things suffer; it moved slowly. That it also moved steadily was to some extent a consolation to Mr. Scobell. Undoubtedly it would progress quicker and quicker, as time went on, until at length the Casino became a permanent gold mine. But at present it was being conducted at a loss. It was inevitable, but it irked Mr. Scobell. He paced the island and brooded. His mind dwelt incessantly on the problem. Ideas for promoting the prosperity of his nursling came to him at all hours-at meals, in the night watches, when he was shaving, walking, washing, reading, brushing his hair.

And now one had come to him as he stood looking at the view from the window of his morning-room, listening absently to his sister Marion as she read stray items of interest from the columns of the *New York Herald*, and had caused him to utter the exclamation recorded at the beginning of the chapter.

*****

"By Heck!" he said. "Read that again, Marion. I gottan idea."

Miss Scobell, deep in her paper, paid no attention. Few people would have taken her for the sister of the financier. She was his exact opposite in almost every way. He was small, jerky and aggressive; she, tall, deliberate and negative. She was one of those women whom nature seems to have produced with the object of attaching them to some man in a peculiar position of independent dependence, and who defy the imagination to picture them in any other condition whatsoever. One could not see Miss Scobell doing anything but pour out her brother's coffee, darn his socks, and sit placidly by while he talked. Yet it would have been untrue to describe her as dependent upon him. She had a detached mind. Though her whole life had been devoted to his comfort and though she admired him intensely, she never appeared to give his conversation any real attention. She listened to him much as she would have listened to a barking Pomeranian.

"Marion!" cried Mr. Scobell.

"A five-legged rabbit has been born in Carbondale, Southern Illinois," she announced.

Mr. Scobell cursed the five-legged rabbit.

"Never mind about your rabbits. I want to hear that piece you read before. The one about the Prince of Monaco. Will-you-listen, Marion!"

"The Prince of Monaco, dear? Yes. He has caught another fish or something of that sort, I think. Yes. A fish with 'telescope eyes,' the paper says. And very convenient too, I should imagine."

Mr. Scobell thumped the table.

"I've got it. I've found out what's the matter with this darned place. I see why the Casino hasn't struck its gait."

"*I* think it must be the *croupiers*, dear. I'm sure I never heard of *croupiers* in fancy costume before. It doesn't seem right. I'm sure people don't like those nasty Hindoos. I am quite nervous myself when I go into the Indian room. They look at me so oddly."

"Nonsense! That's the whole idea of the place, that it should be different. People are sick and tired of having their money gathered in by seedy-looking Dagoes in second-hand morning coats. We give 'em variety. It's not the Casino that's wrong: it's the darned island. What's the use of a republic to a place like this? I'm not saying that you don't want a republic for a live country that's got its way to make in the world; but for a little runt of a sawn-off, hobo, one-night stand like this you gotta have something picturesque, something that'll advertise the place, something that'll give a jolt to folks' curiosity, and make 'em talk! There's this Monaco gook. He snoops around in his yacht, digging up telescope-eyed fish, and people talk about it. 'Another darned fish,' they say. 'That's the 'steenth bite the Prince of Monaco has had this year.' It's like a soap advertisement. It works by suggestion. They get to thinking about the Prince and his pop-eyed fishes, and, first thing they know, they've packed their grips and come along to Monaco to have a peek at him. And when they're there, it's a safe bet they aren't going back again without trying to get a mess of easy money from the Bank. That's what this place wants. Whoever heard of this blamed Republic doing anything except eat and sleep? They used to have a prince here 'way back in eighty-something. Well, I'm going to have him working at the old stand again, right away."

Miss Scobell looked up from her paper, which she had been reading with absorbed interest throughout tins harangue.

"Dear?" she said enquiringly.

"I say I'm going to have him back again," said Mr. Scobell, a little damped. "I wish you would listen."

"I think you're quite right, dear. Who?"

"The Prince. Do listen, Marion. The Prince of this island, His Highness, the Prince of Mervo. I'm going to send for him and put him on the throne again."

"You can't, dear. He's dead."

"I know he's dead. You can't faze me on the history of this place. He died in ninety-one. But before he died he married an American girl, and there's a son, who's in America now, living with his uncle. It's the son I'm going to send for. I got it all from General Poineau. He's a royalist. He'll be tickled to pieces when Johnny comes marching home again. Old man Poineau told me all about it. The Prince married a girl called Westley, and then he was killed in an automobile accident, and his widow went back to America with the kid, to live with her brother. Poineau says he could lay his hand on him any time he pleased."

"I hope you won't do anything rash, dear," said his sister comfortably. "I'm sure we don't want any horrid revolution here, with people shooting and stabbing each other."

"Revolution?" cried Mr. Scobell. "Revolution! Well, I should say nix! Revolution nothing. I'm the man with the big stick in Mervo. Pretty near every adult on this island is dependent on my Casino for his weekly envelope, and what I say goes-without argument. I want a prince, so I gotta have a prince, and if any gazook makes a noise like a man with a grouch, he'll find himself fired."

Miss Scobell turned to her paper again.

"Very well, dear," she said. "Just as you please. I'm sure you know best."

"Sure!" said her brother. "You're a good guesser. I'll go and beat up old man Poineau right away."

CHAPTER III

JOHN

Ten days after Mr. Scobell's visit to General Poineau, John, Prince of Mervo, ignorant of the greatness so soon to be thrust upon him, was strolling thoughtfully along one of the main thoroughfares of that outpost of civilization, Jersey City. He was a big young man, tall and large of limb. His shoulders especially were of the massive type expressly designed by nature for driving wide gaps in the opposing line on the gridiron. He looked like one of nature's center-rushes, and had, indeed, played in that position for Harvard during two strenuous seasons. His face wore an expression of invincible good-humor. He had a wide, good-natured mouth, and a pair of friendly gray eyes. One felt that he liked his follow men and would be surprised and pained if they did not like him.

As he passed along the street, he looked a little anxious. Sherlock Holmes-and possibly even Doctor Watson-would have deduced that he had something on his conscience.

At the entrance to a large office building, he paused, and seemed to hesitate. Then, as if he had made up his mind to face an ordeal, he went in and pressed the button of the elevator.

Leaving the elevator at the third floor, he went down the passage, and pushed open a door on which was inscribed the legend, "Westley, Martin & Co."

A stout youth, walking across the office with his hands full of papers, stopped in astonishment.

"Hello, John Maude!" he cried.

The young man grinned.

"Say, where have you been? The old man's been as mad as a hornet since he found you had quit without leave. He was asking for you just now."

"I guess I'm up against it," admitted John cheerfully.

"Where did you go yesterday?"

John put the thing to him candidly, as man to man.

"See here, Spiller, suppose you got up one day and found it was a perfectly bully morning, and remembered that the Giants were playing the Athletics, and looked at your mail, and saw that someone had sent you a pass for the game —"

"Were you at the ball-game? You've got the nerve! Didn't you know there would be trouble?"

"Old man," said John frankly, "I could no more have turned down that pass — Oh, well, what's the use? It was just great. I suppose I'd better tackle the boss now. It's got to be done."

It was not a task to which many would have looked forward. Most of those who came into contact with Andrew Westley were afraid of him. He was a capable rather than a lovable man, and too self-controlled to be quite human. There was no recoil in him, no reaction after anger, as there would have been in a hotter-tempered man. He thought before he acted, but, when he acted, never yielded a step.

John, in all the years of their connection, had never been able to make anything of him. At first, he had been prepared to like him, as he liked nearly everybody. But Mr. Westley had discouraged all advances, and, as time went by, his nephew had come to look on him as something apart from the rest of the world, one of those things which no fellow could understand.

On Mr. Westley's side, there was something to be said in extenuation of his attitude. John reminded him of his father, and he had hated the late Prince of Mervo with a cold hatred that had for a time been the ruling passion of his life. He had loved his sister, and her married life had been one long torture to him, a torture rendered keener by the fact that he was powerless to protect either her happiness or her money. Her money was her own, to use as she pleased, and the use which pleased her most was to give it to her husband, who could always find a way of spending it. As to her happiness, that was equally out of his control. It was bound up in her Prince, who, unfortunately, was a bad custodian for it. At last, an automobile accident put an end to His Highness's hectic career (and, incidentally, to that of a blonde lady from the *Folies Bergeres*), and the Princess had returned to her brother's home, where, a year later, she died, leaving him in charge of her infant son.

Mr. Westley's desire from the first had been to eliminate as far as possible all memory of the late Prince. He gave John his sister's name, Maude, and brought him up as an American, in total ignorance of his father's identity. During all the years they had spent together, he had never mentioned the Prince's name.

He disliked John intensely. He fed him, clothed him, sent him to college, and gave him a place in his office, but he never for a moment relaxed his bleakness of front toward him. John was not unlike his father in appearance, though built on a larger scale, and, as time went on, little mannerisms, too, began to show themselves, that reminded Mr. Westley of the dead man, and killed any beginnings of affection.

John, for his part, had the philosophy which goes with perfect health. He fitted his uncle into the scheme of things, or, rather, set him outside them as an irreconcilable element, and went on his way enjoying life in his own good-humored fashion.

It was only lately, since he had joined the firm, that he had been conscious of any great strain. College had given him a glimpse of a larger life, and the office cramped him. He felt vaguely that there were bigger things in the world which he might be doing. His best friends, of whom he now saw little, were all men of adventure and enterprise, who had tried their hand at many things; men like Jimmy Pitt, who had done nearly everything that could be done before coming into an unexpected half-million; men like Rupert Smith, who had been at Harvard with him and was now a reporter on the *News*; men like Baker, Faraday, Williams-he could name half-a-dozen, all men who were *doing* something, who were out on the firing line.

He was not a man who worried. He had not that temperament. But sometimes he would wonder in rather a vague way whether he was not allowing life to slip by him a little too placidly. An occasional yearning for something larger would attack him. There seemed to be something in him that made for inaction. His soul was sleepy.

If he had been told of the identity of his father, it is possible that he might have understood. The Princes of Mervo had never taken readily to action and enterprise. For generations back, if they had varied at all, son from father, it had been in the color of hair or eyes, not in character — a weak, shiftless procession, with nothing to distinguish them from the common run of men except good looks and a talent for wasting money.

John was the first of the line who had in him the seeds of better things. The Westley blood and the bracing nature of his education had done much to counteract the Mervo strain. He did not know it, but the American in him was winning. The desire for action was growing steadily every day.

It had been Mervo that had sent him to the polo grounds on the previous day. That impulse had been purely Mervian. No prince of that island had ever resisted a temptation. But it was America that was sending him now to meet his uncle with a quiet unconcern as to the outcome of the interview. The spirit of adventure was in him. It was more than possible that Mr. Westley would sink the uncle in the employer and dismiss him as summarily as he would have dismissed any other clerk in similar circumstances. If so, he was prepared to welcome dismissal. Other men fought an unsheltered fight with the world, so why not he?

He moved towards the door of the inner office with a certain exhilaration.

As he approached, it flew open, disclosing Mr. Westley himself, a tall, thin man, at the sight of whom Spiller shot into his seat like a rabbit.

John went to meet him.

"Ah," said Mr. Westley; "come in here. I want to speak to you."

John followed him into the room.

"Sit down," said his uncle.

John waited while he dictated a letter. Neither spoke till the stenographer had left the room. John met the girl's eye as she passed. There was a compassionate look in it. John was popular with his fellow employes. His absence had been the cause of discussion and speculation among them, and the general verdict had been that there would be troublous times for him on the morrow.

When the door closed, Mr. Westley leaned back in his chair, and regarded his nephew steadily from under a pair of bushy gray eyebrows which lent a sort of hypnotic keenness to his gaze.

"You were at the ball-game yesterday?" he said.

The unexpectedness of the question startled John into a sharp laugh.

"Yes," he said, recovering himself.

"Without leave."

"It didn't seem worth while asking for leave."

"You mean that you relied so implicitly on our relationship to save you from the consequences?"

"No, I meant—"

"Well, we need not try and discover what you may have meant. What claim do you put forward for special consideration? Why should I treat you differently from any other member of the staff?"

John had a feeling that the interview was being taken at too rapid a pace. He felt confused.

"I don't want you to treat me differently," he said.

Mr. Westley did not reply. John saw that he had taken a check-book from its pigeonhole.

"I think we understand each other," said Mr. Westley. "There is no need for any discussion. I am writing you a check for ten thousand dollars—"

"Ten thousand dollars!"

"It happens to be your own. It was left to me in trust for you by your mother. By a miracle your father did not happen to spend it."

John caught the bitter note which the other could not keep out of his voice, and made one last attempt to probe this mystery. As a boy he had tried more than once before he realized that this was a forbidden topic.

"Who was my father?" he said.

Mr. Westley blotted the check carefully.

"Quite the worst blackguard I ever had the misfortune to know," he replied in an even tone. "Will you kindly give me a receipt for this? Then I need not detain you. You may return to the ball-game without any further delay. Possibly," he went on, "you may wonder why you have not received this money before. I persuaded your mother to let me use my discretion in choosing the time when it should be handed over to you. I decided to wait until, in my opinion, you had sense enough to use it properly. I do not think that time has arrived. I do not think it will ever arrive. But as we are parting company and shall, I hope, never meet again, you had better have it now."

John signed the receipt in silence.

"Thank you," said Mr. Westley. "Good-by."

At the door John hesitated. He had looked forward to this moment as one of excitement and adventure, but now that it had come it had left him in anything but an uplifted mood. He was naturally warm-hearted, and his uncle's cold anger hurt him. It was so different from anything sudden, so essentially not of the moment. He felt instinctively that it had been smoldering for a long time, and realized with a shock that his uncle had not been merely indifferent to him all these years, but had actually hated him. It was as if he had caught a glimpse of something ugly. He felt that this was the last scene of some long drawn-out tragedy.

Something made him turn impulsively back towards the desk.

"Uncle—" he cried.

He stopped. The hopelessness of attempting any step towards a better understanding overwhelmed him. Mr. Westley had begun to write. He must have seen John's movement, but he continued to write as if he were alone in the room.

John turned to the door again.

"Good-by," he said.

Mr. Westley did not look up.

CHAPTER IV

VIVE LE ROI!

When, an hour later, John landed in New York from the ferry, his mood had changed. The sun and the breeze had done their work. He looked on life once more with a cheerful and optimistic eye.

His first act, on landing, was to proceed to the office of the *News* and enquire for Rupert Smith. He felt that he had urgent need of a few minutes' conversation with him. Now that the painter had been definitely cut that bound him to the safe and conventional, and he had set out on his own account to lead the life adventurous, he was conscious of an absurd diffidence. New York looked different to him. It made him feel positively shy. A pressing need for a friendly native in this strange land manifested itself. Smith would have ideas and advice to bestow-he was notoriously prolific of both-and in this crisis both were highly necessary.

Smith, however, was not at the office. He had gone out, John was informed, earlier in the morning to cover a threatened strike somewhere down on the East Side. John did not go in search of him. The chance of finding him in that maze of mean streets was remote. He decided to go uptown, select a hotel, and lunch. To the need for lunch he attributed a certain sinking sensation of which he was becoming more and more aware, and which bore much too close a resemblance to dismay to be pleasant. The poet's statement that "the man who's square, his chances always are best; no circumstance can shoot a scare into the contents of his vest," is only true within limits. The squarest men, deposited suddenly in New York and faced with the prospect of earning his living there, is likely to quail for a moment. New York is not like other cities. London greets the stranger with a sleepy grunt. Paris giggles. New York howls. A gladiator, waiting in the center of the arena while the Colosseum officials fumbled with the bolts of the door behind which paced the noisy tiger he was to fight, must have had some of the emotions which John experienced during his first hour as a masterless man in Gotham.

A surface car carried him up Broadway. At Times Square the Astor Hotel loomed up on the left. It looked a pretty good hotel to John. He dismounted.

Half an hour later he decided that he was acclimated. He had secured a base of operations in the shape of a room on the seventh floor, his check was safely deposited in the hotel bank, and he was half-way through a lunch which had caused him already to look on New York not only as the finest city in the world, but also, on the whole, as the one city of all others in which a young man might make a fortune with the maximum of speed and the minimum of effort.

After lunch, having telegraphed his address to his uncle in case of mail, he took the latter's excellent advice and went to the polo grounds. Returning in time to dress, he dined at the hotel, after which he visited a near-by theater, and completed a pleasant and strenuous day at one of those friendly restaurants where the music is continuous and the waiters are apt to burst into song in the intervals of their other duties.

A second attempt to find Smith next morning failed, as the first had done. The staff of the News were out of bed and at work ridiculously early, and when John called up the office between eleven and twelve o'clock-nature's breakfast-hour —Smith was again down East, observing the movements of those who were about to strike or who had already struck.

It hardly seemed worth while starting to lay the bed plates of his fortune till he had consulted the expert. What would Rockefeller have done? He would, John felt certain, have gone to the ball-game.

He imitated the great financier.

* * * * *

It was while he was smoking a cigar after dinner that night, musing on the fortunes of the day's game and, in particular, on the almost criminal imbecility of the umpire, that he was dreamily aware that he was being "paged." A small boy in uniform was meandering through the room, chanting his name.

"Gent wants five minutes wit' you," announced the boy, intercepted.
"Hasn't got no card. Business, he says."

This disposed of the idea that Rupert Smith had discovered his retreat. John was puzzled. He could not think of another person in New York who knew of his presence at the Astor. But it was the unknown that he was in search of, and he decided to see the mysterious stranger.

"Send him along," he said.

The boy disappeared, and presently John observed him threading his way back among the tables, followed by a young man of extraordinary gravity of countenance, who was looking about him with an intent gaze through a pair of gold-rimmed spectacles.

John got up to meet him.

"My name is Maude," he said. "Won't you sit down? Have you had dinner?"

"Thank you, yes," said the spectacled young man.

"You'll have a cigar and coffee, then?"

"Thank you, yes."

The young man remained silent until the waiter had filled his cup.

"My name is Crump," he said. "I am Mr. Benjamin Scobell's private secretary."

"Yes?" said John. "Snug job?"

The other seemed to miss something in his voice.

"You have heard of Mr. Scobell?" he asked.

"Not to my knowledge," said John.

"Ah! you have lost touch very much with Mervo, of course."

John stared.

"Mervo?"

It sounded like some patent medicine.

"I have been instructed," said Mr. Crump solemnly, "to inform Your Highness that the Republic has been dissolved, and that your subjects offer you the throne of your ancestors."

John leaned back in his chair, and looked at the speaker in dumb amazement. The thought flashed across him that Mr. Crump had been perfectly correct in saying that he had dined.

His attitude appeared to astound Mr. Crump. He goggled through his spectacles at John, who was reminded of some rare fish.

"You are John Maude? You said you were."

"I'm John Maude right enough. We're solid on that point."

"And your mother was the only sister of Mr. Andrew Westley?"

"You're right there, too."

"Then there is no mistake. I say the Republic —" He paused, as if struck with an idea. "Don't you know?" he said. "Your father —"

John became suddenly interested.

"If you've got anything to tell me about my father, go right ahead. You'll be the only man I've ever met who has said a word about him. Who the deuce was he, anyway?"

Mr. Crump's face cleared.

"I understand. I had not expected this. You have been kept in ignorance. Your father, Mr. Maude, was the late Prince Charles of Mervo."

It was not easy to astonish John, but this announcement did so. He dropped his cigar in a shower of gray ash on to his trousers, and retrieved it almost mechanically, his wide-open eyes fixed on the other's face.

"What!" he cried.

Mr. Crump nodded gravely.

"You are Prince John of Mervo, and I am here —" he got into his stride as he reached the familiar phrase —"to inform Your Highness that the Republic has been dissolved, and that your subjects offer you the throne of your ancestors."

A horrid doubt seized John.

"You're stringing me. One of those Indians at the *News*, Rupert Smith, or someone, has put you up to this."

Mr. Crump appeared wounded.

"If Your Highness would glance at these documents — This is a copy of the register of the church in which your mother and father were married."

John glanced at the document. It was perfectly lucid.

"Then-then it's true!" he said.

"Perfectly true, Your Highness. And I am here to inform —"

"But where the deuce is Mervo? I never heard of the place."

"It is an island principality in the Mediterranean, Your High —"

"For goodness' sake, old man, don't keep calling me 'Your Highness.' It may be fun to you, but it makes me feel a perfect ass. Let me get into the thing gradually."

Mr. Crump felt in his pocket.

"Mr. Scobell," he said, producing a roll of bills, "entrusted me with money to defray any expenses —"

More than any words, this spectacle removed any lingering doubt which John might have had as to the possibility of this being some intricate practical joke.

"Are these for me?" he said.

Mr. Crump passed them across to him.

"There are a thousand dollars here," he said. "I am also instructed to say that you are at liberty to draw further against Mr. Scobell's account at the Wall Street office of the European and Asiatic Bank."

The name Scobell had been recurring like a *leit-motif* in Mr. Crump's conversation. This suddenly came home to John.

"Before we go any further," he said, "let's get one thing clear. Who is this Mr. Scobell? How does he get mixed up in this?"

"He is the proprietor of the Casino at Mervo."

"He seems to be one of those generous, open-handed fellows. Nothing of the tight wad about him."

"He is deeply interested in Your High-in your return."

John laid the roll of bills beside his coffee cup, and relighted his cigar.

"That's mighty good of him," he said. "It strikes me, old man, that I am not absolutely up-to-date as regards the internal affairs of this important little kingdom of mine. How would it be if you were to put me next to one or two facts? Start at the beginning and go right on."

When Mr. Crump had finished a condensed history of Mervo and Mervian politics, John smoked in silence for some minutes.

"Life, Crump," he said at last, "is certainly speeding up as far as I am concerned. Up till now nothing in particular has ever happened to me. A couple of days ago I lost my job, was given ten thousand dollars that I didn't know existed, and now you tell me I'm a prince. Well, well! These are stirring times. When do we start for the old homestead?"

"Mr. Scobell was exceedingly anxious that we should return by Saturday's boat."

"Saturday? What, to-morrow?"

"Perhaps it is too soon. You will not be able to settle your affairs?"

"I guess I can settle my affairs all right. I've only got to pack a grip and tip the bell hops. And as Scobell seems to be financing this show, perhaps it's up to me to step lively if he wants it. But it's a pity. I was just beginning to like this place. There is generally something doing along the White Way after twilight, Crump."

The gravity of Mr. Scobell's secretary broke up unexpectedly into a slow, wide smile. His eyes behind their glasses gleamed with a wistful light.

"Gee!" he murmured.

John looked at him, amazed.

"Crump," he cried. "Crump, I believe you're a sport!"

Mr. Crump seemed completely to have forgotten his responsible position as secretary to a millionaire and special messenger to a prince. He smirked.

"I'd have liked a day or two in the old burg," he said softly. "I haven't been to Rector's since Ponto was a pup."

John reached across the table and seized the secretary's hand.

"Crump," he said, "you *are* a sport. This is no time for delay.

If we are to liven up this great city, we must get busy right away.

Grab your hat, and come along. One doesn't become a prince every day.

The occasion wants celebrating. Are you with me, Crump, old scout?"

"Sure thing," said the envoy ecstatically.

* * * * *

At eight o'clock on the following morning, two young men, hatless and a little rumpled, but obviously cheerful, entered the Astor Hotel, demanding breakfast.

A bell boy who met them was addressed by the larger of the two, and asked his name.

"Desmond Ryan," he replied.

The young man patted him on his shoulder.

"I appoint you, Desmond Ryan," he said, "Grand Hereditary Bell Hop to the Court of Mervo."

Thus did Prince John formally enter into his kingdom.

CHAPTER V

MR. SCOBELL HAS ANOTHER IDEA

Owing to collaboration between Fate and Mr. Scobell, John's state entry into Mervo was an interesting blend between a pageant and a vaudeville sketch. The pageant idea was Mr. Scobell's. Fate supplied the vaudeville.

The reception at the quay, when the little steamer that plied between Marseilles and the island principality gave up its precious freight, was not on quite so impressive a scale as might have been given to the monarch of a more powerful kingdom; but John was not disappointed. During the voyage from New York, in the intervals of seasickness-for he was a poor sailor-Mr. Crump had supplied him with certain facts about Mervo, one of which was that its adult population numbered just under thirteen thousand, and this had prepared him for any shortcomings in the way of popular demonstration.

As a matter of fact, Mr. Scobell was exceedingly pleased with the scale of the reception, which to his mind amounted practically to pomp. The Palace Guard, forty strong, lined the quay. Besides these, there were four officers, a band, and sixteen mounted carbineers. The rest of the army was dotted along the streets. In addition to the military, there was a gathering of a hundred and fifty civilians, mainly drawn from fishing circles. The majority of these remained stolidly silent throughout, but three, more emotional, cheered vigorously as a young man was seen to step on to the gangway, carrying a grip, and make for the shore. General Poineau, a white-haired warrior with a fierce mustache, strode forward and saluted. The Palace Guards presented arms. The band struck up the Mervian national anthem. General Poineau, lowering his hand, put on a pair of *pince-nez* and began to unroll an address of welcome.

It was then seen that the young man was Mr. Crump. General Poineau removed his glasses and gave an impatient twirl to his mustache. Mr. Scobell, who for possibly the first time in his career was not smoking (though, as was afterward made manifest, he had the materials on his person), bustled to the front.

"Where's his nibs, Crump?" he enquired.

The secretary's reply was swept away in a flood of melody. To the band Mr. Crump's face was strange. They had no reason to suppose that he was not Prince John, and they acted accordingly. With a rattle of drums they burst once more into their spirited rendering of the national anthem.

Mr. Scobell sawed the air with his arms, but was powerless to dam the flood.

"His Highness is shaving, sir!" bawled Mr. Crump, depositing his grip on the quay and making a trumpet of his hands.

"Shaving!"

"Yes, sir. I told him he ought to come along, but His Highness said he wasn't going to land looking like a tramp comedian."

By this time General Poineau had explained matters to the band and they checked the national anthem abruptly in the middle of a bar, with the exception of the cornet player, who continued gallantly by himself till a feeling of loneliness brought the truth home to him. An awkward stage wait followed, which lasted until John was seen crossing the deck, when there were more cheers, and General Poineau, resuming his *pince-nez*, brought out the address of welcome again.

At this point Mr. Scobell made his presence felt.

"Glad to meet you, Prince," he said, coming forward. "Scobell's my name. Shake hands with General Poineau. No, that's wrong. I guess he kisses your hand, don't he?"

"I'll swing on him if he does," said John, cheerfully.

Mr. Scobell eyed him doubtfully. His Highness did not appear to him to be treating the inaugural ceremony with that reserved dignity which we like to see in princes on these occasions. Mr. Scobell was a business man. He wanted his money's worth. His idea of a Prince of Mervo was something statuesquely aloof, something-he could not express it exactly-on the lines of the illustrations in the Zenda stories in the magazines-about eight feet high and shinily magnificent, something that would give the place a tone. That was what he had had in his mind when he sent for John. He did not want a cheerful young man in a soft hat and a flannel suit who looked as if at any moment he might burst into a college yell.

General Poineau, meanwhile, had embarked on the address of welcome.
John regarded him thoughtfully.

"I can see," he said to Mr. Scobell, "that the gentleman is making a good speech, but what is he saying? That is what gets past me."

"He is welcoming Your Highness," said Mr. Crump, the linguist, "in the name of the people of Mervo."

"Who, I notice, have had the bully good sense to stay in bed. I guess they knew that the Boy Orator would do all that was necessary. He hasn't said anything about a bite of breakfast, has he? Has his address happened to work around to the subject of shredded wheat and shirred eggs yet? That's the part that's going to make a hit with me."

"There'll be breakfast at my villa, Your Highness," said Mr. Scobell.
"My automobile is waiting along there."

The General reached his peroration, worked his way through it, and finished with a military clash of heels and a salute. The band rattled off the national anthem once more.

"Now, what?" said John, turning to Mr. Scobell. "Breakfast?"

"I guess you'd better say a few words to them, Your Highness; they'll expect it."

"But I can't speak the language, and they can't understand English. The thing'll be a stand-off."

"Crump will hand it to 'em. Here, Crump."

"Sir?"

"Line up and shoot His Highness's remarks into 'em."

"Yes, sir."

"It's all very well for you, Crump," said John. "You probably enjoy this sort of thing. I don't. I haven't felt such a fool since I sang 'The Maiden's Prayer' on Tremont Street when I was joining the frat. Are you ready? No, it's no good. I don't know what to say."

"Tell 'em you're tickled to death," advised Mr. Scobell anxiously.

John smiled in a friendly manner at the populace. Then he coughed. "Gentlemen," he said — "and more particularly the sport on my left who has just spoken his piece whose name I can't remember —I thank you for the warm welcome you have given me. If it is any satisfaction to you to know that it has made me feel like thirty cents, you may have that satisfaction. Thirty is a liberal estimate."

"'His Highness is overwhelmed by your loyal welcome. He thanks you warmly,'" translated Mr. Crump, tactfully.

"I feel that we shall get along nicely together," continued John. "If you are chumps enough to turn out of your comfortable beds at this time of the morning simply to see me, you can't be very hard to please. We shall hit it off fine."

Mr. Crump: "His Highness hopes and believes that he will always continue to command the affection of his people."

"I —" John paused. "That's the lot," he said. "The flow of inspiration has ceased. The magic fire has gone out. Break it to 'em, Crump. For me, breakfast."

During the early portion of the ride Mr. Scobell was silent and thoughtful. John's speech had impressed him neither as oratory nor as an index to his frame of mind. He had not interrupted him, because he knew that none of those present could understand what was being said, and that Mr. Crump was to be relied on as an editor. But he had not enjoyed it. He did not take the people of Mervo seriously himself, but in the Prince such an attitude struck him as unbecoming. Then he cheered up. After all, John had given evidence of having a certain amount of what he would have called "get-up" in him. For the purposes for which he needed him, a tendency to make light of things was not amiss. It was essentially as a performing prince that he had engaged John. He wanted him to do unusual things, which would make people talk-aeroplaning was one that occurred to him. Perhaps a prince who took a serious view of his position would try to raise the people's minds and start reforms and generally be a nuisance. John could, at any rate, be relied upon not to do that.

His face cleared.

"Have a good cigar, Prince?" he said, cordially, inserting two fingers in his vest-pocket.

"Sure, Mike," said His Highness affably.

Breakfast over, Mr. Scobell replaced the remains of his cigar between his lips, and turned to business.

"Eh, Prince?" he said.

"Yes!"

"I want you, Prince," said Mr. Scobell, "to help boom this place. That's where you come in."

"Sure," said John.

"As to ruling and all that," continued Mr. Scobell, "there isn't any to do. The place runs itself. Some guy gave it a shove a thousand years ago, and it's been rolling along ever since. What I want you to do is the picturesque stunts. Get a yacht and catch rare fishes. Whoop it up. Entertain swell guys when they come here. Have a Court-see what I mean? —same as over in England. Go around in aeroplanes and that style of thing. Don't worry about money. That'll be all right. You draw your steady hundred thousand a year and a good chunk more besides, when we begin to get a move on, so the dough proposition doesn't need to scare you any."

"Do I, by George!" said John. "It seems to me that I've fallen into a pretty soft thing here. There'll be a joker in the deck somewhere, I guess. There always is in these good things. But I don't see it yet. You can count me in all right."

"Good boy," said Mr. Scobell. "And now you'll be wanting to get to the Palace. I'll have them bring the automobile round."

The council of state broke up.

Having seen John off in the car, the financier proceeded to his sister's sitting-room. Miss Scobell had breakfasted apart that morning, by request, her brother giving her to understand that matters of state, unsuited to the ear of a third party, must be discussed at the meal. She was reading her *New York Herald*.

"Well," said Mr. Scobell, "he's come."

"Yes, dear?"

"And just the sort I want. Saw the idea of the thing right away, and is ready to go the limit. No nonsense about him."

"Is he nice-looking, Bennie?"

"Sure. All these Mervo princes have been good-lookers, I hear, and this one must be near the top of the list. You'll like him, Marion. All the girls will be crazy about him in a week."

Miss Scobell turned a page.

"Is he married?"

Her brother started.

"Married? I never thought of that. But no, I guess he's not. He'd have mentioned it. He's not the sort to hush up a thing like that. I —"

He stopped short. His green eyes gleamed excitedly.

"Marion!" he cried. "*Marion!*"

"Well, dear?"

"Listen. Gee, this thing is going to be the biggest ever. I gotta new idea. It just came to me. Your saying that put it into my head. Do you know what I'm going to do? I'm going to cable over to Betty to come right along here, and I'm going to have her marry this prince guy. Yes, sir!"

For once Miss Scobell showed signs that her brother's conversation really interested her. She laid down her paper, and stared at him.

"Betty!"

"Sure, Betty. Why not? She's a pretty girl. Clever too. The Prince'll be lucky to get such a wife, for all his darned ancestors away back to the flood."

"But suppose Betty does not like him?"

"Like him? She's gotta like him. Say, can't you make your mind soar, or won't you? Can't you see that a thing like this has gotta be fixed different from a marriage between-between a ribbon-counter clerk and the girl who takes the money at a twenty-five-cent hash restaurant in Flatbush? This is a royal alliance. Do you suppose that when a European princess is introduced to the prince she's going to marry, they let her say: 'Nothing doing. I don't like the shape of his nose'?"

He gave a spirited imitation of a European princess objecting to the shape of her selected husband's nose.

"It isn't very romantic, Bennie," sighed Miss Scobell. She was a confirmed reader of the more sentimental class of fiction, and this business-like treatment of love's young dream jarred upon her.

"It's founding a dynasty. Isn't that romantic enough for you? You make me tired, Marion."

Miss Scobell sighed again.

"Very well, dear. I suppose you know best. But perhaps the Prince won't like Betty."

Mr. Scobell gave a snort of disgust.

"Marion," he said, "you've got a mind like a chunk of wet dough. Can't you understand that the Prince is just as much in my employment as the man who scrubs the Casino steps? I'm hiring him to be Prince of Mervo, and his first job as Prince of Mervo will be to marry Betty. I'd like to see him kick!" He began to pace the room. "By Heck, it's going to make this place boom to beat the band. It'll be the biggest kind of advertisement. Restoration of Royalty at Mervo. That'll make them take notice by itself. Then, biff! right on top of that, Royal Romance-Prince Weds American Girl-Love at First Sight-Picturesque Wedding! Gee, we'll wipe Monte Carlo clean off the map. We'll have 'em licked to a splinter. We-It's the greatest scheme on earth."

"I have no doubt you are right, Bennie," said Miss Scobell, "but —" her voice became dreamy again —"it's not very romantic."

"Oh, shucks!" said the schemer impatiently. "Here, where's a cable form?"

CHAPTER VI

YOUNG ADAM CUPID

On a red sandstone rock at the edge of the water, where the island curved sharply out into the sea, Prince John of Mervo sat and brooded on first causes. For nearly an hour and a half he had been engaged in an earnest attempt to trace to its source the acute fit of depression which had come-apparently from nowhere-to poison his existence that morning.

It was his seventh day on the island, and he could remember every incident of his brief reign. The only thing that eluded him was the recollection of the exact point when the shadow of discontent had begun to spread itself over his mind. Looking back, it seemed to him that he had done nothing during that week but enjoy each new aspect of his position as it was introduced to his notice. Yet here he was, sitting on a lonely rock, consumed with an unquenchable restlessness, a kind of trapped sensation. Exactly when and exactly how Fate, that king of gold-brick men, had cheated him he could not say; but he knew, with a certainty that defied argument, that there had been sharp practise, and that in an unguarded moment he had been induced to part with something of infinite value in exchange for a gilded fraud.

The mystery baffled him. He sent his mind back to the first definite entry of Mervo into the foreground of his life. He had come up from his stateroom on to the deck of the little steamer, and there in the pearl-gray of the morning was the island, gradually taking definite shape as the pink mists shredded away before the rays of the rising sun. As the ship rounded the point where the lighthouse still flashed a needless warning from its cluster of jagged rocks, he had had his first view of the town, nestling at the foot of the hill, gleaming white against the green, with the gold-domed Casino towering in its midst. In all Southern Europe there was no view to match it for quiet beauty. For all his thews and sinews there was poetry in John, and the sight had stirred him like wine.

It was not then that depression had begun, nor was it during the reception at the quay.

The days that had followed had been peaceful and amusing. He could not detect in any one of them a sign of the approaching shadow. They had been lazy days. His duties had been much more simple than he had anticipated. He had not known, before he tried it, that it was possible to be a prince with so small an expenditure of mental energy. As Mr. Scobell had hinted, to all intents and purposes he was a mere ornament. His work began at eleven in the morning, and finished as a rule at about a quarter after. At the hour named a report of the happenings of the previous day was brought to him. When he had read it the state asked no more of him until the next morning.

The report was made up of such items as "A fisherman named Lesieur called Carbineer Ferrier a fool in the market-place at eleven minutes after two this afternoon; he has not been arrested, but is being watched," and generally gave John a few minutes of mild enjoyment. Certainly he could not recollect that it had ever depressed him.

No, it had been something else that had worked the mischief and in another moment the thing stood revealed, beyond all question of doubt. What had unsettled him was that unexpected meeting with Betty Silver last night at the Casino.

He had been sitting at the Dutch table. He generally visited the Casino after dinner. The light and movement of the place interested him. As a rule, he merely strolled through the rooms, watching the play; but last night he had slipped into a vacant seat. He had only just settled himself when he was aware of a girl standing beside him. He got up.

"Would you care —?" he had begun, and then he saw her face.

It had all happened in an instant. Some chord in him, numbed till then, had begun to throb. It was as if he had awakened from a dream, or returned to consciousness after being stunned. There was something in the sight of her, standing there so cool and neat and composed, so typically American, a sort of goddess of America, in the heat and stir of the Casino, that struck him like a blow.

How long was it since he had seen her last? Not more than a couple of years. It seemed centuries. It all came back to him. It was during his last winter at Harvard that they had met. A college friend of hers had been the sister of a college friend of his. They had met several times, but he could not recollect having taken any particular notice of her then, beyond recognizing that she was certainly pretty. The world had been full of pretty American girls then. But now —

He looked at her. And, as he looked, he heard America calling to him. Mervo, by the appeal of its novelty, had caused him to forget. But now, quite suddenly, he knew that he was homesick-and it astonished him, the readiness with which he had permitted Mr. Crump to lead him away into bondage. It seemed incredible that he had not foreseen what must happen.

Love comes to some gently, imperceptibly, creeping in as the tide, through unsuspected creeks and inlets, creeps on a sleeping man, until he wakes to find himself surrounded. But to others it comes as a wave, breaking on them, beating them down, whirling them away.

It was so with John. In that instant when their eyes met the miracle must have happened. It seemed to him, as he recalled the scene now, that he had loved her before he had had time to frame his first remark. It amazed him that he could ever have been blind to the fact that he loved her, she was so obviously the only girl in the world.

"You-you don't remember me," he stammered.

She was flushing a little under his stare, but her eyes were shining.

"I remember you very well, Mr. Maude," she said with a smile. "I thought I knew your shoulders before you turned round. What are you doing here?"

"I —"

There was a hush. The *croupier* had set the ball rolling. A wizened little man and two ladies of determined aspect were looking up disapprovingly. John realized that he was the only person in the room not silent. It was impossible to tell her the story of the change in his fortunes in the middle of this crowd. He stopped, and the moment passed.

The ball dropped with a rattle. The tension relaxed.

"Won't you take this seat?" said John.

"No, thank you. I'm not playing. I only just stopped to look on. My aunt is in one of the rooms, and I want to make her come home. I'm tired."

"Have you —?"

He caught the eye of the wizened man, and stopped again.

"Have you been in Mervo long?" he said, as the ball fell.

"I only arrived this morning. It seems lovely. I must explore to-morrow."

She was beginning to move off.

"Er —" John coughed to remove what seemed to him a deposit of sawdust and unshelled nuts in his throat. "Er-may I —will you let me show you —" prolonged struggle with the nuts and sawdust; then rapidly —"some of the places to-morrow?"

He had hardly spoken the words when it was borne in upon him that he was a vulgar, pushing bounder, presuming on a dead and buried acquaintanceship to force his company on a girl who naturally did not want it, and who would now proceed to snub him as he deserved. He quailed. Though he had not had time to collect and examine and label his feelings, he was sufficiently in touch with them to know that a snub from her would be the most terrible thing that could possibly happen to him.

She did not snub him. Indeed, if he had been in a state of mind coherent enough to allow him to observe, he might have detected in her eyes and her voice signs of pleasure.

"I should like it very much," she said.

John made his big effort. He attacked the nuts and sawdust which had come back and settled down again in company with a large lump of some unidentified material, as if he were bucking center. They broke before him as, long ago, the Yale line had done, and his voice rang out as if through a megaphone, to the unconcealed disgust of the neighboring gamesters.

"If you go along the path at the foot of the hill," he bellowed rapidly, "and follow it down to the sea, you get a little bay full of red sandstone rocks-you can't miss it-and there's a fine view of the island from there. I'd like awfully well to show that to you. It's great."

She nodded.

"Then shall we meet there?" she said. "When?"

John was in no mood to postpone the event.

"As early as ever you like," he roared.

"At about ten, then. Good-night, Mr. Maude."

* * * * *

John had reached the bay at half-past eight, and had been on guard there ever since. It was now past ten, but still there were no signs of Betty. His depression increased. He told himself that she had forgotten. Then, that she had remembered, but had changed her mind. Then, that she had never meant to come at all. He could not decide which of the three theories was the most distressing.

His mood became morbidly introspective. He was weighed down by a sense of his own unworthiness. He submitted himself to a thorough examination, and the conclusion to which he came was that, as an aspirant to the regard, of a girl like Betty, he did not score a single point. No wonder she had ignored the appointment.

A cold sweat broke out on him. This was the snub! She had not administered it in the Casino simply in order that, by being delayed, its force might be the more overwhelming.

He looked at his watch again, and the world grew black. It was twelve minutes after ten.

John, in his time, had thought and read a good deal about love. Ever since he had grown up, he had wanted to fall in love. He had imagined love as a perpetual exhilaration, something that flooded life with a golden glow as if by the pressing of a button or the pulling of a switch, and automatically removed from it everything mean and hard and uncomfortable; a something that made a man feel grand and god-like, looking down (benevolently, of course) on his fellow men as from some lofty mountain.

That it should make him feel a worm-like humility had not entered his calculations. He was beginning to see something of the possibilities of love. His tentative excursions into the unknown emotion, while at college, had never really deceived him; even at the time a sort of second self had looked on and sneered at the poor imitation.

This was different. This had nothing to do with moonlight and soft music. It was raw and hard. It hurt. It was a thing sharp and jagged, tearing at the roots of his soul.

He turned his head, and looked up the path for the hundredth time, and this time he sprang to his feet. Between the pines on the hillside his eye had caught the flutter of a white dress.

CHAPTER VII

MR. SCOBELL IS FRANK

Much may happen in these rapid times in the course of an hour and a half. While John was keeping his vigil on the sandstone rock, Betty was having an interview with Mr. Scobell which was to produce far-reaching results, and which, incidentally, was to leave her angrier and more at war with the whole of her world than she could remember to have been in the entire course of her life.

The interview began, shortly after breakfast, in a gentle and tactful manner, with Aunt Marion at the helm. But Mr. Scobell was not the man to stand by silently while persons were being tactful. At the end of the second minute he had plunged through his sister's mild monologue like a rhinoceros through a cobweb, and had stated definitely, with an economy of words, the exact part which Betty was to play in Mervian affairs.

"You say you want to know why you were cabled for. I'll tell you. There's no use talking for half a day before you get to the point. I guess you've heard that there's a prince here instead of a republic now? Well, that's where you come in."

"Do you mean—?" she hesitated.

"Yes, I do," said Mr. Scobell. There was a touch of doggedness in his voice. He was not going to stand any nonsense, by Heck, but there was no doubt that Betty's wide-open eyes were not very easy to meet. He went on rapidly. "Cut out any fool notions about romance." Miss Scobell, who was knitting a sock, checked her needles for a moment in order to sigh. Her brother eyed her morosely, then resumed his remarks. "This is a matter of state. That's it. You gotta cut out fool notions and act for good of state. You gotta look at it in the proper spirit. Great honor-see what I mean? Princess and all that. Chance of a lifetime-dynasty-you gotta look at it that way."

Miss Scobell heaved another sigh, and dropped a stitch.

"For the love of Mike," said her brother, irritably, "don't snort like that, Marion."

"Very well, dear."

Betty had not taken her eyes off him from his first word. An unbiased observer would have said that she made a pretty picture, standing there, in her white dress, but in the matter of pictures, still life was evidently what Mr. Scobell preferred for his gaze never wandered from the cigar stump which he had removed from his mouth in order to knock off the ash.

Betty continued to regard him steadfastly. The shock of his words had to some extent numbed her. At this moment she was merely thinking, quite dispassionately, what a singularly nasty little man he looked, and wondering-not for the first time-what strange quality, invisible to everybody else, it had been in him that had made her mother his adoring slave during the whole of their married life.

Then her mind began to work actively once more. She was a Western girl, and an insistence on freedom was the first article in her creed. A great rush of anger filled her, that this man should set himself up to dictate to her.

"Do you mean that you want me to marry this Prince?" she said.

"That's right."

"I won't do anything of the sort."

"Pshaw! Don't be foolish. You make me tired."

Betty's eye shone mutinously. Her cheeks were flushed, and her slim, boyish figure quivered. Her chin, always determined, became a silent Declaration of Independence.

"I won't," she said.

Aunt Marion, suspending operations on the sock, went on with tact at the point where her brother's interruption had forced her to leave off.

"I'm sure he's a very nice young man. I have not seen him, but everybody says so. You like him, Bennie, don't you?"

"Sure, I like him. He's a corker. Wait till you see him, Betty. Nobody's asking you to marry him before lunch. You'll have plenty of time to get acquainted. It beats me what you're kicking at. You give me a pain in the neck. Be reasonable."

Betty sought for arguments to clinch her refusal.

"It's ridiculous," she said. "You talk as if you had just to wave your hand. Why should your prince want to marry a girl he has never seen?"

"He will," said Mr. Scobell confidently.

"How do you know?"

"Because I know he's a sensible young skeesicks. That's how. See here, Betty, you've gotten hold of wrong ideas about this place. You don't understand the position of affairs. Your aunt didn't till I put her wise."

"He bit my head off, my dear," murmured Miss Scobell, knitting placidly.

"You're thinking that Mervo is an ordinary state, and that the Prince is one of those independent, all-wool, off-with-his-darned-head rulers like you read about in the best sellers. Well, you've got another guess coming. If you want to know who's the big noise here, it's me-me! This Prince guy is my hired man. See? Who sent for him? I did. Who put him on the throne? I did. Who pays him his salary? I do, from the profits of the Casino. Now do you understand? He knows his job. He knows which side his bread's buttered. When I tell him about this marriage, do you know what he'll say? He'll say 'Thank you, sir!' That's how things are in this island."

Betty shuddered. Her face was white with humiliation. She half-raised her hands with an impulsive movement to hide it.

"I won't. I won't. I won't!" she gasped.

Mr. Scobell was pacing the room in an ecstasy of triumphant rhetoric.

"There's another thing," he said, swinging round suddenly and causing his sister to drop another stitch. "Maybe you think he's some kind of a Dago, this guy? Maybe that's what's biting you. Let me tell you that he's an American-pretty near as much an American as you are yourself."

Betty stared at him.

"An American!"

"Don't believe it, eh? Well, let me tell you that his mother was born and raised in Jersey, and that he has lived all his life in the States. He's no little runt of a Dago. No, sir. He's a Harvard man, six-foot high and weighs two hundred pounds. That's the sort of man he is. I guess that's not American enough for you, maybe? No?"

"You do shout so, Bennie!" murmured Miss Scobell. "I'm sure there's no need."

Betty uttered a cry. Something had told her who he was, this Harvard man who had sold himself. That species of sixth sense which lies undeveloped at the back of our minds during the ordinary happenings of life wakes sometimes in moments of keen emotion. At its highest, it is prophecy; at its lowest, a vague presentiment. It woke in Betty now. There was no particular reason why she should have connected her stepfather's words with John. The term he had used was an elastic one. Among the visitors to the island there were probably several Harvard men. But somehow she knew.

"Who is he?" she cried. "What was his name before he-when he —?"

"His name?" said Mr. Scobell. "John Maude. Maude was his mother's name. She was a Miss Westley. Here, where are you going?"

Betty was walking slowly toward the door. Something in her face checked Mr. Scobell.

"I want to think," she said quietly. "I'm going out."

* * * * *

In days of old, in the age of legend, omens warned heroes of impending doom. But to-day the gods have grown weary, and we rush unsuspecting on our fate. No owl hooted, no thunder rolled from the blue sky as John went up the path to meet the white dress that gleamed between the trees.

His heart was singing within him. She had come. She had not forgotten, or changed her mind, or willfully abandoned him. His mood lightened swiftly. Humility vanished. He was not such an outcast, after all. He was someone. He was the man Betty Silver had come to meet.

But with the sight of her face came reaction.

Her face was pale and cold and hard. She did not speak or smile. As she drew near she looked at him, and there was that in her look which set a chill wind blowing through the world and cast a veil across the sun.

And in this bleak world they stood silent and motionless while eons rolled by.

Betty was the first to speak.

"I'm late," she said.

John searched in his brain for words, and came empty away. He shook his head dumbly.

"Shall we sit down?" said Betty.

John indicated silently the sandstone rock on which he had been communing with himself.

They sat down. A sense of being preposterously and indecently big obsessed John. There seemed no end to him. Wherever he looked, there were hands and feet and legs. He was a vast blot on the face of the earth. He glanced out of the corner of his eye at Betty. She was gazing out to sea.

He dived into his brain again. It was absurd! There must be something to say.

And then he realized that a worse thing had befallen. He had no voice. It had gone. He knew that, try he never so hard to speak, he would not be able to utter a word. A nightmare feeling of unreality came upon him. Had he ever spoken? Had he ever done anything but sit dumbly on that rock, looking at those sea gulls out in the water?

He shot another swift glance at Betty, and a thrill went through him.

There were tears in her eyes.

The next moment-the action was almost automatic-his left hand was clasping her right, and he was moving along the rock to her side.

She snatched her hand away.

His brain, ransacked for the third time, yielded a single word.

"Betty!"

She got up quickly.

In the confused state of his mind, John found it necessary if he were to speak at all, to say the essential thing in the shortest possible way. Polished periods are not for the man who is feeling deeply.

He blurted out, huskily, "I love you!" and finding that this was all that he could say, was silent.

Even to himself the words, as he spoke them, sounded bald and meaningless. To Betty, shaken by her encounter with Mr. Scobell, they sounded artificial, as if he were forcing himself to repeat a lesson. They jarred upon her.

"Don't!" she said sharply. "Oh, don't!"

Her voice stabbed him. It could not have stirred him more if she had uttered a cry of physical pain.

"Don't! I know. I've been told."

"Been told?"

She went on quickly.

"I know all about it. My stepfather has just told me. He said-he said you were his —" she choked —"his hired man; that he paid you to stay here and advertise the Casino. Oh, it's too horrible! That it should be you! You, who have been-you can't understand what you-have been to me-ever since we met; you couldn't understand. I can't tell you —a sort of help-something-something that —I can't put it into words. Only it used to help me just to think of you. It was almost impersonal. I didn't mind if I never saw you again. I didn't expect ever to see you again. It was just being able to think of you. It helped-you were something I could trust. Something strong-solid." She laughed bitterly. "I suppose I made a hero of you. Girls are fools. But it helped me to feel that there was one man alive who-who put his honor above money —"

She broke off. John stood motionless, staring at the ground. For the first time in his easy-going life he knew shame. Even now he had not grasped to the full the purport of her words. The scales were falling from his eyes, but as yet he saw but dimly.

She began to speak again, in a low, monotonous voice, almost as if she were talking to herself. She was looking past him, at the gulls that swooped and skimmed above the glittering water.

"I'm so tired of money-money-money. Everything's money. Isn't there a man in the world who won't sell himself? I thought that you —I suppose I'm stupid. It's business, I suppose. One expects too much."

She looked at him wearily.

"Good-by," she said. "I'm going."

He did not move.

She turned, and went slowly up the path. Still he made no movement. A spell seemed to be on him. His eyes never left her as she passed into the shadow of the trees. For a moment her white dress stood out clearly. She had stopped. With his whole soul he prayed that she would look back. But she moved on once more, and was gone. And suddenly a strange weakness came upon John. He trembled. The hillside flickered before his eyes for an instant, and he clutched at the sandstone rock to steady himself.

Then his brain cleared, and he found himself thinking swiftly. He could not let her go like this. He must overtake her. He must stop her. He must speak to her. He must say-he did not know what it was that he would say-anything, so that he spoke to her again.

He raced up the path, calling her name. No answer came to his cries. Above him lay the hillside, dozing in the noonday sun; below, the Mediterranean, sleek and blue, without a ripple. He stood alone in a land of silence and sleep.

CHAPTER VIII

AN ULTIMATUM FROM THE THRONE

At half-past twelve that morning business took Mr. Benjamin Scobell to the royal Palace. He was not a man who believed in letting the grass grow under his feet. He prided himself on his briskness of attack. Every now and then Mr. Crump, searching the newspapers, would discover and hand to him a paragraph alluding to his "hustling methods." When this happened, he would preserve the clipping and carry it about in his vest-pocket with his cigars till time and friction wore it away. He liked to think of himself as swift and sudden-the Human Thunderbolt.

In this matter of the royal alliance, it was his intention to have at it and clear it up at once. Having put his views clearly before Betty, he now proposed to lay them with equal clarity before the Prince. There was no sense in putting the thing off. The sooner all parties concerned understood the position of affairs, the sooner the business would be settled.

That Betty had not received his information with joy did not distress him. He had a poor opinion of the feminine intelligence. Girls got their minds full of nonsense from reading novels and seeing plays-like Betty. Betty objected to those who were wiser than herself providing a perfectly good prince for her to marry. Some fool notion of romance, of course. Not that he was angry. He did not blame her any more than the surgeon blames a patient for the possession of an unsuitable appendix. There was no animus in the matter. Her mind was suffering from foolish ideas, and he was the surgeon whose task it was to operate upon it. That was all. One had to expect foolishness in women. It was their nature. The only thing to do was to tie a rope to them and let them run around till they were tired of it, then pull them in. He saw his way to managing Betty.

Nor did he anticipate trouble with John. He had taken an estimate of John's character, and it did not seem to him likely that it contained unsuspected depths. He set John down, as he had told Betty, as a young man acute enough to know when he had a good job and sufficiently sensible to make concessions in order to retain it. Betty, after the manner of woman, might make a fuss before yielding to the inevitable, but from level-headed John he looked for placid acquiescence.

His mood, as the automobile whirred its way down the hill toward the town, was sunny. He looked on life benevolently and found it good. The view appealed to him more than it had managed to do on other days. As a rule, he was the man of blood and iron who had no time for admiring scenery, but to-day he vouchsafed it a not unkindly glance. It was certainly a dandy little place, this island of his. A vineyard on the right caught his eye. He made a mental note to uproot it and run up a hotel in its place. Further down the hill, he selected a site for a villa, where the mimosa blazed, and another where at present there were a number of utterly useless violets. A certain practical element was apt, perhaps, to color Mr. Scobell's half-hours with nature.

The sight of the steamboat leaving the harbor on its journey to Marseilles gave him another idea. Now that Mervo was a going concern, a real live proposition, it was high time that it should have an adequate service of boats. The present system of one a day was absurd. He made a note to look into the matter. These people wanted waking up.

Arriving at the Palace, he was informed that His Highness had gone out shortly after breakfast, and had not returned. The majordomo gave the information with a tinkle of disapproval in his voice. Before taking up his duties at Mervo, he had held a similar position in the household of a German prince, where rigid ceremonial obtained, and John's cheerful disregard of the formalities frankly shocked him. To take the present case for instance: When His Highness of Swartzheim had felt inclined to enjoy the air of a morning, it had been a domestic event full of stir and pomp. He had not merely crammed a soft hat over his eyes and strolled out with his hands in his pockets, but without a word to his household staff as to where he was going or when he might be expected to return.

Mr. Scobell received the news equably, and directed his chauffeur to return to the villa. He could not have done better, for, on his arrival, he was met with the information that His Highness had called to see him shortly after he had left, and was now waiting in the morning-room.

The sound of footsteps came to Mr. Scobell's ears as he approached the room. His Highness appeared to be pacing the floor like a caged animal at the luncheon hour. The resemblance was heightened by the expression in the royal eye as His Highness swung round at the opening of the door and faced the financier.

"Why, say, Prince," said Mr. Scobell, "this is lucky. I been looking for you. I just been to the Palace, and the main guy there told me you had gone out."

"I did. And I met your stepdaughter."

Mr. Scobell was astonished. Fate was certainly smoothing his way if it arranged meetings between Betty and the Prince before he had time to do it himself. There might be no need for the iron hand after all.

"You did?" he said. "Say, how the Heck did you come to do that? What did you know about Betty?"

"Miss Silver and I had met before, in America, when I was in college."

Mr. Scobell slapped his thigh joyously.

"Gee, it's all working out like a fiction story in the magazines!"

"Is it?" said John. "How? And, for the matter of that, what?"

Mr. Scobell answered question with question. "Say, Prince, you and Betty were pretty good friends in the old days, I guess?"

John looked at him coldly.

"We won't discuss that, if you don't mind," he said.

His tone annoyed Mr. Scobell. Off came the velvet glove, and the iron hand displayed itself. His green eyes glowed dully and the tip of his nose wriggled, as was its habit in times of emotion.

"Is that so?" he cried, regarding John with disfavor. "Well, I guess! Won't discuss it! You gotta discuss it, Your Royal Texas League Highness! You want making a head shorter, my bucko. You —"

John's demeanor had become so dangerous that he broke off abruptly, and with an unostentatious movement, as of a man strolling carelessly about his private sanctum, put himself within easy reach of the door handle.

He then became satirical.

"Maybe Your Serene, Imperial Two-by-Fourness would care to suggest a subject we can discuss?"

John took a step forward.

"Yes, I will," he said between his teeth. "You were talking to Miss Silver about me this morning. She told me one or two of the things you said, and they opened my eyes. Until I heard them, I had not quite understood my position. I do now. You said, among other things, that I was your hired man."

"It wasn't intended for you to hear," said Mr. Scobell, slightly mollified, "and Betty shouldn't oughter have handed it to you. I don't wonder you feel raw. I wouldn't say that sort of thing to a guy's face. Sure, no. Tact's my middle name. But, since you have heard it, well —!"

"Don't apologize. You were quite right. I was a fool not to see it before. No description could have been fairer. You might have said much more. You might have added that I was nothing more than a steerer for a gambling hell."

"Oh, come, Prince!"

There was a knock at the door. A footman entered, bearing, with a detached air, as if he disclaimed all responsibility, a letter on a silver tray.

Mr. Scobell slit the envelope, and began to read. As he did so his eyes grew round, and his mouth slowly opened till his cigar stump, after hanging for a moment from his lower lip, dropped off like an exhausted bivalve and rolled along the carpet.

"Prince," he gasped, "she's gone. Betty!"

"Gone! What do you mean?"

"She's beaten it. She's half-way to Marseilles by now. Gee, and I saw the darned boat going out!"

"She's gone!"

"This is from her. Listen what she says:

> "*By the time you read this I shall be gone. I am going back to America as quickly as I can. I am giving this to a boy to take to you directly the boat has started. Please do not try to bring me back. I would sooner die than marry the Prince.*"

John started violently.

"What!" he cried.

Mr. Scobell nodded sympathy.

"That's what she says. She sure has it in bad for you. What does she mean? Seeing you and she are old friends —"

"I don't understand. Why does she say that to you? Why should she think that you knew that I had asked her to marry me?"

"Eh?" cried Mr. Scobell. "You asked her to marry you? And she turned you down! Prince, this beats the band. Say, you and I must get together and do something. The girl's mad. See here, you aren't wise to what's been happening. I been fixing this thing up. I fetched you over here, and then I fetched Betty, and I was going to have you two marry. I told Betty all about it this morning."

John cut through his explanations with a sudden sharp cry. A blinding blaze of understanding had flashed upon him. It was as if he had been groping his way in a dark cavern and had stumbled unexpectedly into brilliant sunlight. He understood everything now. Every word that Betty had spoken, every gesture that she had made, had become amazingly clear. He saw now why she had shrunk back from him, why her eyes had worn that look. He dared not face the picture of himself as he must have appeared in those eyes, the man whom Mr. Benjamin Scobell's Casino was paying to marry her, the hired man earning his wages by speaking words of love.

A feeling of physical sickness came over him. He held to the table for support as he had held to the sandstone rock. And then came rage, rage such as he had never felt before, rage that he had not thought himself capable of feeling. It swept over him in a wave, pouring through his veins and blinding him, and he clung to the table till his knuckles whitened under the strain, for he knew that he was very near to murder.

A minute passed. He walked to the window, and stood there, looking out. Vaguely he heard Mr. Scobell's voice at his back, talking on, but the words had no meaning for him.

He had begun to think with a curious coolness. His detachment surprised him. It was one of those rare moments in a man's life when, from the outside, through a breach in that wall of excuses and self-deception which he has been at such pains to build, he looks at himself impartially.

The sight that John saw through the wall was not comforting. It was not a heroic soul that, stripped of its defenses, shivered beneath the scrutiny. In another mood he would have mended the breach, excusing and extenuating, but not now. He looked at himself without pity, and saw himself weak, slothful, devoid of all that was clean and fine, and a bitter contempt filled him.

Outside the window, a blaze of color, Mervo smiled up at him, and suddenly he found himself loathing its exotic beauty. He felt stifled. This was no place for a man. A vision of clean winds and wide spaces came to him.

And just then, at the foot of the hill, the dome of the Casino caught the sun, and flashed out in a blaze of gold.

He swung round and faced Mr. Scobell. He had made up his mind.

The financier was still talking.

"So that's how it stands, Prince," he was saying, "and it's up to us to get busy."

John looked at him.

"I intend to," he said.

"Good boy!" said the financier.

"To begin with, I shall run you out of this place, Mr. Scobell."

The other gasped.

"There is going to be a cleaning-up," John went on. "I've thought it out. There will be no more gambling in Mervo."

"You're crazy with the heat!" gasped Mr. Scobell. "Abolish gambling? You can't."

"I can. That concession of yours isn't worth the paper it's written on. The Republic gave it to you. The Republic's finished. If you want to conduct a Casino in Mervo, there's only one man who can give you permission, and that's myself. The acts of the Republic are not binding on me. For a week you have been gambling on this island without a concession and now it's going to stop. Do you understand?"

"But, Prince, talk sense." Mr. Scobell's voice was almost tearful. "It's you who don't understand. Do, for the love of Mike, come down off the roof and talk sense. Do you suppose that these guys here will stand for this? Not on your life. Not for a minute. See here. I'm not blaming you. I know you don't know what you're saying. But listen here. You must cut out this kind of thing. You mustn't get these ideas in your head. You stick to your job, and don't butt in on other folks'. Do you know how long you'd stay Prince of this joint if you started in to monkey with my Casino? Just about long enough to let you pack a collar-stud and a toothbrush into your grip. And after that there wouldn't be any more Prince, sonnie. You stick to your job and I'll stick to mine. You're a mighty good Prince for all that's required of you. You're ornamental, and you've got get-up in you. You just keep right on being a good boy, and don't start trying stunts off your own beat, and you'll do fine. Don't forget that I'm the big noise here. I'm old Grayback from 'way back in Mervo. See! I've only to twiddle my fingers and there'll be a revolution and you for the Down-and-Out Club. Don't you forget it, sonnie."

John shrugged his shoulders.

"I've said all I have to say. You've had your notice to quit. After to-night the Casino is closed."

"But don't I tell you the people won't stand for it?"

"That's for them to decide. They may have some self-respect."

"They'll fire you!"

"Very well. That will prove that they have not."

"Prince, talk sense! You can't mean that you'll throw away a hundred thousand dollars a year as if it was dirt!"

"It is dirt when it's made that way. We needn't discuss it any more."

"But, Prince!"

"It's finished."

"But, say —!"

John had left the room.

He had been gone several minutes before the financier recovered full possession of his faculties.

When he did, his remarks were brief and to the point.

"Bug-house!" he gasped. "Abso-lutely bug-house!"

CHAPTER IX

MERVO CHANGES ITS CONSTITUTION

Humor, if one looks into it, is principally a matter of retrospect. In after years John was wont to look back with amusement on the revolution which ejected him from the throne of his ancestors. But at the time its mirthfulness did not appeal to him. He was in a frenzy of restlessness. He wanted Betty. He wanted to see her and explain. Explanations could not restore him to the place he had held in her mind, but at least they would show her that he was not the thing he had appeared.

Mervo had become a prison. He ached for America. But, before he could go, this matter of the Casino must be settled. It was obvious that it could only be settled in one way. He did not credit his subjects with the high-mindedness that puts ideals first and money after. That military and civilians alike would rally to a man round Mr. Scobell and the Casino he was well aware. But this did not affect his determination to remain till the last. If he went now, he would be like a boy who makes a runaway ring at the doorbell. Until he should receive formal notice of dismissal, he must stay, although every day had forty-eight hours and every hour twice its complement of weary minutes.

So he waited, chafing, while Mervo examined the situation, turned it over in its mind, discussed it, slept upon it, discussed it again, and displayed generally that ponderous leisureliness which is the Mervian's birthright.

Indeed, the earliest demonstration was not Mervian at all. It came from the visitors to the island, and consisted of a deputation of four, headed by the wizened little man, who had frowned at John in the Dutch room on the occasion of his meeting with Betty, and a stolid individual with a bald forehead and a walrus mustache.

The tone of the deputation was, from the first, querulous. The wizened man had constituted himself spokesman. He introduced the party-the walrus as Colonel Finch, the others as Herr von Mandelbaum and Mr. Archer-Cleeve. His own name was Pugh, and the whole party, like the other visitors whom they represented, had, it seemed, come to Mervo, at great trouble and expense, to patronize the tables, only to find these suddenly, without a word of warning, withdrawn from their patronage. And what the deputation wished to know was, What did it all mean?

"We were amazed, sir-Your Highness," said Mr. Pugh. "We could not-we cannot-understand it. The entire thing is a baffling mystery to us. We asked the soldiers at the door. They referred us to Mr. Scobell. We asked Mr. Scobell. He referred us to you. And now we have come, as the representatives of our fellow visitors to this island, to ask Your Highness what it means!"

"Have a cigar," said John, extending the box. Mr. Pugh waved aside the preferred gift impatiently. Not so Herr von Mandelbaum, who slid forward after the manner of one in quest of second base and retired with his prize to the rear of the little army once more.

Mr. Archer-Cleeve, a young man with carefully parted fair hair and the expression of a strayed sheep, contributed a remark.

"No, but I say, by Jove, you know, I mean really, you know, what?"

That was Mr. Archer-Cleeve upon the situation.

"We have not come here for cigars," said Mr. Pugh. "We have come here, Your Highness, for an explanation."

"Of what?" said John.

Mr. Pugh made an impatient gesture.

"Do you question my right to rule this massive country as I think best, Mr. Pugh?"

"It is a high-handed proceeding," said the wizened little man.

The walrus spoke for the first time.

"What say?" he murmured huskily.

"I said," repeated Mr. Pugh, raising his voice, "that it was a high-handed proceeding, Colonel."

The walrus nodded heavily, in assent, with closed eyes.

"Yah," said Herr von Mandelbaum through the smoke.

John looked at the spokesman.

"You are from England, Mr. Pugh?"

"Yes, sir. I am a British citizen."

"Suppose some enterprising person began to run a gambling hell in Piccadilly, would the authorities look on and smile?"

"That is an entirely different matter, sir. You are quibbling. In England gambling is forbidden by law."

"So it is in Mervo, Mr. Pugh."

"Tchah!"

"What say?" said the walrus.

"I said 'Tchah!' Colonel."

"Why?" said the walrus.

"Because His Highness quibbled."

The walrus nodded approvingly.

"His Highness did nothing of the sort," said John. "Gambling is forbidden in Mervo for the same reason that it is forbidden in England, because it demoralizes the people."

"This is absurd, sir. Gambling has been permitted in Mervo for nearly a year."

"But not by me, Mr. Pugh. The Republic certainly granted Mr. Scobell a concession. But, when I came to the throne, it became necessary for him to get a concession from me. I refused it. Hence the closed doors."

Mr. Archer-Cleeve once more. "But—" He paused. "Forgotten what I was going to say," he said to the room at large.

Herr von Mandelbaum made some remark at the back of his throat, but was ignored.

John spoke again.

"If you were a prince, Mr. Pugh, would you find it pleasant to be in the pay of a gambling hell?"

"That is neither here nor—"

"On the contrary, it is, very much. I happen to have some self-respect. I've only just found it out, it's true, but it's there all right. I don't want to be a prince-take it from me, it's a much overrated profession-but if I've got to be one, I'll specialize. I won't combine it with being a bunco steerer on the side. As long as I am on the throne, this high-toned crap-shooting will continue a back number."

"What say?" said the walrus.

"I said that, while I am on the throne here, people who feel it necessary to chant 'Come, little seven!' must do it elsewhere."

"I don't understand you," said Mr. Pugh. "Your remarks are absolutely unintelligible."

"Never mind. My actions speak for themselves. It doesn't matter how I describe it-what it comes to is that the Casino is closed. You can follow that? Mervo is no longer running wide open. The lid is on."

"Then let me tell you, sir—" Mr. Pugh brought a bony fist down with a thump on the table—"that you are playing with fire. Understand me, sir, we are not here to threaten. We are a peaceful deputation of visitors. But I have observed your people, sir. I have watched them narrowly. And let me tell you that you are walking on a volcano. Already there are signs of grave discontent."

"Already!" cried John. "Already's good. I guess they call it going some in this infernal country if they can keep awake long enough to take action within a year after a thing has happened. I don't know if you have any influence with the populace, Mr. Pugh-you seem a pretty warm and important sort of person-but, if you have, do please ask them as a favor to me to get a move on. It's no good saying that I'm walking on a volcano. I'm from Missouri. I want to be shown. Let's see this volcano. Bring it out and make it trot around."

"You may jest —"

"Who's jesting? I'm not. It's a mighty serious thing for me. I want to get away. The only thing that's keeping me in this forsaken place is this delay. These people are obviously going to fire me sooner or later. Why on earth can't they do it at once?"

"What say?" said the walrus.

"You may well ask, Colonel," said Mr. Pugh, staring amazed at John.

"His Highness appears completely to have lost his senses."

The walrus looked at John as if expecting some demonstration of practical insanity, but, finding him outwardly calm, closed his eyes and nodded heavily again.

"I must say, don't you know," said Mr. Archer-Cleeve, "it beats me, what?"

The entire deputation seemed to consider that John's last speech needed footnotes.

John was in no mood to supply them. His patience was exhausted.

"I guess we'll call this conference finished," he said. "You've been told all you came to find out, —my reason for closing the Casino. If it doesn't strike you as a satisfactory reason, that's up to you. Do what you like about it. The one thing you may take as a solid fact-and you can spread it around the town as much as ever you please-is that it is closed, and is not going to be reopened while I'm ruler here."

The deputation then withdrew, reluctantly.

* * * * *

On the following morning there came a note from Mr. Scobell. It was brief. "Come on down before the shooting begins," it ran. John tore it up.

It was on the same evening that definite hostilities may be said to have begun.

Between the Palace and the market-place there was a narrow street of flagged stone, which was busy during the early part of the day but deserted after sundown. Along this street, at about seven o'clock, John was strolling with a cigarette, when he was aware of a man crouching, with his back toward him. So absorbed was the man in something which he was writing on the stones that he did not hear John's approach, and the latter, coming up from behind was enabled to see over his shoulder. In large letters of chalk he read the words: *"Conspuez le Prince."*

John's knowledge of French was not profound, but he could understand this, and it annoyed him.

As he looked, the man, squatting on his heels, bent forward to touch up one of the letters. If he had been deliberately posing, he could not have assumed a more convenient attitude.

John had been a footballer before he was a prince. The temptation was too much for him. He drew back his foot —

There was a howl and a thud, and John resumed his stroll. The first gun from Fort Sumter had been fired.

* * * * *

Early next morning a window at the rear of the palace was broken by a stone, and toward noon one of the soldiers on guard in front of the Casino was narrowly missed by an anonymous orange. For Mervo this was practically equivalent to the attack on the Bastille, and John, when the report of the atrocities was brought to him, became hopeful.

But the effort seemed temporarily to have exhausted the fury of the mob. The rest of that day and the whole of the next passed without sensation.

After breakfast on the following morning Mr. Crump paid a visit to the Palace. John was glad to see him. The staff of the Palace were loyal, but considered as cheery companions, they were handicapped by the fact that they spoke no English, while John spoke no French.

Mr. Crump was the bearer of another note from Mr. Scobell. This time John tore it up unread, and, turning to the secretary, invited him to sit down and make himself at home.

Sipping a cocktail and smoking one of John's cigars, Mr. Crump became confidential.

"This is a queer business," he said. "Old Ben is chewing pieces out of the furniture up there. He's mad clean through. He's losing money all the while the people are making up their minds about this thing, and it beats him why they're so slow."

"It beats me, too. I don't believe these hook-worm victims ever turned my father out. Or, if they did, somebody must have injected radium into them first. I'll give them another couple of days, and, if they haven't fixed it by then, I'll go, and leave them to do what they like about it."

"Go! Do you want to go?"

"Of course I want to go! Do you think I like stringing along in this musical comedy island? I'm crazy to get back to America. I don't blame you, Crump, because it was not your fault, but, by George! if I had known what you were letting me in for when you carried me off here, I'd have called up the police reserves. Hello! What's this?"

He rose to his feet as the sound of agitated voices came from the other side of the door. The next moment it flew open, revealing General Poineau and an assorted group of footmen and other domestics. Excitement seemed to be in the air.

General Poineau rushed forward into the room, and flung his arms above his head. Then he dropped them to his side, and shrugged his shoulders, finishing in an attitude reminiscent of Plate 6 ("Despair") in "The Home Reciter."

"*Mon Prince!*" he moaned.

A perfect avalanche of French burst from the group outside the door.

"Crump!" cried John. "Stand by me, Crump! Get busy! This is where you make your big play. Never mind the chorus gentlemen in the passage. Concentrate yourself on Poineau. What's he talking about? I believe he's come to tell me the people have wakened up. Offer him a cocktail. What's the French for corpse-reviver? Get busy, Crump."

The general had begun to speak rapidly, with a wealth of gestures. It astonished John that Mr. Crump could follow the harangue as apparently he did.

"Well?" said John.

Mr. Crump looked grave.

"He says there is a large mob in the market-place. They are talking —"

"They would be!"

"—of moving in force on the Palace. The Palace Guards have gone over to the people. General Poineau urges you to disguise yourself and escape while there is time. You will be safe at his villa till the excitement subsides, when you can be smuggled over to France during the night —"

"Not for mine," said John, shaking his head. "It's mighty good of you, General, and I appreciate it, but I can't wait till night. The boat leaves for Marseilles in another hour. I'll catch that. I can manage it comfortably. I'll go up and pack my grip. Crump, entertain the General while I'm gone, will you? I won't be a moment."

But as he left the room there came through the open window the mutter of a crowd. He stopped. General Poineau whipped out his sword, and brought it to the salute. John patted him on the shoulder.

"You're a sport, General," he said, "but we sha'n't want it. Come along, Crump. Come and help me address the multitude."

The window of the room looked out on to a square. There was a small balcony with a stone parapet. As John stepped out, a howl of rage burst from the mob.

John walked on to the balcony, and stood looking down on them, resting his arms on the parapet. The howl was repeated, and from somewhere at the back of the crowd came the sharp crack of a rifle, and a shot, the first and last of the campaign, clipped a strip of flannel from the collar of his coat and splashed against the wall.

A broad smile spread over his face.

If he had studied for a year, he could not have hit on a swifter or more effective method of quieting the mob. There was something so engaging and friendly in his smile that the howling died away and fists that has been shaken unclenched themselves and fell. There was an expectant silence in the square.

John beckoned to Crump, who came on to the balcony with some reluctance, being mistrustful of the unseen sportsman with the rifle.

"Tell 'em it's all right, Crump, and that there's no call for any fuss.
From their manner I gather that I am no longer needed on this throne.
Ask them if that's right?"

A small man, who appeared to be in command of the crowd, stepped forward as the secretary finished speaking, and shouted some words which drew a murmur of approval from his followers.

"He wants to know," interpreted Mr. Crump, "if you will allow the
Casino to open again."

"Tell him no, but add that I shall be tickled to death to abdicate, if that's what they want. Speed them up, old man. Tell them to make up their minds on the jump, because I want to catch that boat. Don't let them get to discussing it, or they'll stand there talking till sunset. Yes or no. That's the idea."

There was a moment's surprised silence when Mr. Crump had spoken. The Mervian mind was unused to being hustled in this way. Then a voice shouted, as it were tentatively, *"Vive la Republique!"* and at once the cry was taken up on all sides.

John beamed down on them.

"That's right," he said. "Bully! I knew you could get a move on as quick as anyone else, if you gave your minds to it. This is what I call something like a revolution. It's a model to every country in the world. But I guess we must close down the entertainment now, or I shall be missing the boat. Will you tell them, Crump, that any citizen who cares for a drink and a cigar will find it in the Palace. Tell the household staff to stand by to pull corks. It's dry work revolutionizing. And now I really must be going. I've run it mighty fine. Slip one of these fellows down there half a dollar and send him to fetch a cab. I must step lively."

* * * * *

Five minutes later the revolutionists, obviously embarrassed and ill at ease, were sheepishly gulping down their refreshment beneath the stony eye of the majordomo and his assistants, while upstairs in the state bedroom the deposed Prince was whistling "Dixie" and packing the royal pajamas into a suitcase.

CHAPTER X

MRS. OAKLEY

Betty, when she stepped on board the boat for Marseilles, had had no definite plan of action. She had been caught up and swept away by an over-mastering desire for escape that left no room in her mind for thoughts of the morrow. It was not till the train was roaring its way across southern France that she found herself sufficiently composed to review her position and make plans.

She would not go back. She could not. The words she had used in her letter to Mr. Scobell were no melodramatic rhetoric. They were a plain and literal statement of the truth. Death would be infinitely preferable to life at Mervo on her stepfather's conditions.

But, that settled, what then? What was she to do? The gods are businesslike. They sell; they do not give. And for what they sell they demand a heavy price. We may buy life of them in many ways: with our honor, our health, our independence, our happiness, with our brains or with our hands. But somehow or other, in whatever currency we may choose to pay it, the price must be paid.

Betty faced the problem. What had she? What could she give? Her independence? That, certainly. She saw now what a mockery that fancied independence had been. She had come and gone as she pleased, her path smoothed by her stepfather's money, and she had been accustomed to consider herself free. She had learned wisdom now, and could understand that it was only by sacrificing such artificial independence that she could win through to freedom. The world was a market, and the only independent people in it were those who had a market value.

What was her market value? What could she do? She looked back at her life, and saw that she had dabbled. She had a little of most things-enough of nothing. She could sketch a little, play a little, sing a little, write a little. Also-and, as she remembered it, she felt for the first time a tremor of hope-she could use a typewriter reasonably well. That one accomplishment stood out in the welter of her thoughts, solid and comforting, like a rock in a quicksand. It was something definite, something marketable, something of value for which persons paid.

The tremor of hope did not comfort her long. Her mood was critical, and she saw that in this, her one accomplishment, she was, as in everything else, an amateur. She could not compete against professionals. She closed her eyes, and had a momentary vision of those professionals, keen of face, leathern of finger, rattling out myriads of words at a dizzy speed. And, at that, all her courage suddenly broke; she drooped forlornly, and, hiding her face on the cushioned arm-rest, she began to cry.

Tears are the Turkish bath of the soul. Nature never intended woman to pass dry-eyed through crises of emotion. A casual stranger, meeting Betty on her way to the boat, might have thought that she looked a little worried,—nothing more. The same stranger, if he had happened to enter the compartment at this juncture, would have set her down at sight as broken-hearted beyond recovery. Yet such is the magic of tears that it was at this very moment that Betty was beginning to be conscious of a distinct change for the better. Her heart still ached, and to think of John even for an instant was to feel the knife turning in the wound, but her brain was clear; the panic fear had gone, and she faced the future resolutely once more. For she had just remembered the existence of Mrs. Oakley.

* * * * *

Only once in her life had Betty met her stepfather's celebrated aunt, and the meeting had taken place nearly twelve years ago. The figure that remained in her memory was of a pale-eyed, grenadier-like old lady, almost entirely surrounded by clocks. It was these clocks that had impressed her most. She was too young to be awed by the knowledge that the tall old woman who stared at her just like a sandy cat she had once possessed was one of the three richest women in the whole wide world. She only remembered thinking that the finger which emerged from the plaid shawl and prodded her cheek was unpleasantly bony. But the clocks had absorbed her. It was as if all the clocks in the world had been gathered together into that one room. There had been big clocks, with almost human faces; small, perky clocks; clocks of strange shape; and one dingy, medium-sized clock in particular which had made her cry out with delight. Her visit had chanced to begin shortly before eleven in the morning, and she had not been in the room ten minutes before there was a whirring, and the majority of the clocks began to announce the hour, each after its own fashion-some with a slow bloom, some with a rapid, bell-like sound. But the medium-sized clock, unexpectedly belying its appearance of being nothing of particular importance, had performed its task in a way quite distinct from the others. It had suddenly produced from its interior a shabby little gold man with a trumpet, who had blown eleven little blasts before sliding backward into his house and shutting the door after him. Betty had waited in rapt silence till he finished, and had then shouted eagerly for more.

Just as the beginner at golf may effect a drive surpassing that of the expert, so may a child unconsciously eclipse the practised courtier. There was no soft side to Mrs. Oakley's character, as thousands of suave would-be borrowers had discovered in their time, but there was a soft spot. To general praise of her collection of clocks she was impervious; it was unique, and she did not require you to tell her so, but exhibit admiration for the clock with the little trumpeter, and she melted. It was the one oasis of sentiment in the Sahara of her mental outlook, the grain of radium in the pitchblende. Years ago it had stood in a little New England farmhouse, and a child had clapped her hands and shouted, even as Betty had done, when the golden man slid from his hiding-place. Much water had flowed beneath the bridge since those days. Many things had happened to the child. But she still kept her old love for the trumpeter. The world knew nothing of this. The world, if it had known, would have been delighted to stand before the clock and admire it volubly, by the day. But it had no inkling of the trumpeter's importance, and, when it came to visit Mrs. Oakley, was apt to waste its time showering compliments on the obvious beauties of the queens of the collection.

But Betty, ignoring these, jumped up and down before the dingy clock, demanding further trumpetings, and, turning to Mrs. Oakley, as one possessing influence, she was aware of a curious, intent look in the old lady's eyes.

"Do you like that clock, my dear?" said Mrs. Oakley.

"Yes! Oh, yes!"

"Perhaps you shall have it some day, honey."

Betty was probably the only person who had been admitted to that room who would not, on the strength of this remark, have steered the conversation gently to the subject of a small loan. Instead, she ran to the old lady, and kissed her. And, as to what had happened after that, memory was vague. There had been some talk, she remembered, of a dollar to buy candy, but it had come to nothing, and now that she had grown older and had read the frequent paragraphs and anecdotes that appeared in the papers about her stepfather's aunt, she could understand why. She knew now what everybody knew of Mrs. Oakley-her history, her eccentricities, and the miserliness of which the papers spoke with a satirical lightness that seemed somehow but a thin disguise for what was almost admiration.

Mrs. Oakley was one of two children, a son and a daughter, of a Vermont farmer. Of her early life no records remain. Her public history begins when she was twenty-two and came to New York. After two years' struggling, she found a position in the firm of one Redgrave. Those who knew her then speak of her as a tall, handsome girl, hard and intensely ambitious. From contemporary accounts she seems to have out-Nietzsched Nietzsche. Nietzsche's vision stopped short at the superman. Jane Scobell was a superwoman. She had all the titanic selfishness and indifference to the comfort of others which marks the superman, and, in addition, undeniable good looks and a knowledge of the weaknesses of men. Poor Mr. Redgrave had not had a chance from the start. She married him within a year. Two years later, catching the bulls in an unguarded moment, Mr. Redgrave despoiled them of a trifle over three million dollars, and died the same day of an apoplectic stroke caused by the excitement of victory. His widow, after a tour in Europe, returned to the United States and visited Pittsburg. Any sociologist will support the statement that it is difficult, almost impossible, for an attractive widow, visiting Pittsburg, not to marry a millionaire, even if she is not particularly anxious to do so. If such an act is the primary object of her visit, the thing becomes a certainty. Groping through the smoke, Jane Redgrave seized and carried off no less a quarry than Alexander Baynes Oakley, a widower, whose income was one of the seven wonders of the world. In the fullness of time he, too, died, and Jane Oakley was left with the sole control of two vast fortunes.

She did not marry again, though it was rumored that it took three secretaries, working nine hours a day, to cope with the written proposals, and that butler after butler contracted clergyman's sore throat through denying admittance to amorous callers. In the ten years after Alexander Baynes' death, every impecunious aristocrat in the civilized world must have made his dash for the matrimonial pole. But her pale eyes looked them over, and dismissed them.

During those early years she was tempted once or twice to speculation. A failure in a cotton deal not only cured her of this taste, but seems to have marked the point in her career when her thoughts began to turn to parsimony. Until then she had lived in some state, but now, gradually at first, then swiftly, she began to cut down her expenses. Now we find her in an apartment in West Central Park, next in a Washington Square hotel, then in a Harlem flat, and finally-her last, fixed abiding-place —in a small cottage on Staten Island.

It was a curious life that she led, this woman who could have bought kingdoms if she had willed it. A Swedish maid-of-all-work was her only companion. By day she would walk in her little garden, or dust, arrange and wind up her clocks. At night, she would knit, or read one of the frequent reports that arrived at the cottage from charity workers on the East Side. Those were her two hobbies, and her only extravagances-clocks and charity.

Her charity had its limitations. In actual money she expended little. She was a theoretical philanthropist. She lent her influence, her time, and her advice, but seldom her bank balance. Arrange an entertainment for the delectation of the poor, and you would find her on the platform, but her name would not be on the list of subscribers to the funds. She would deliver a lecture on thrift to an audience of factory girls, and she would give them a practical example of what she preached.

Yet, with all its limitations, her charity was partly genuine. Her mind was like a country in the grip of civil war. One-half of her sincerely pitied the poor, burned at any story of oppression, and cried "Give!" but the other cried "Halt!" and held her back, and between the two she fell.

* * * * *

It was to this somewhat unpromising haven of refuge that Betty's mind now turned in her trouble. She did not expect great things. She could not have said exactly what she did expect. But, at least, the cottage on Staten Island offered a resting-place on her journey, even if it could not be the journey's end. Her mad dash from Mervo ceased to be objectless. It led somewhere.

CHAPTER XI

A LETTER OF INTRODUCTION

New York, revisited, had much the same effect on Betty as it had had on John during his first morning of independence. As the liner came up the bay, and the great buildings stood out against the clear blue of the sky, she felt afraid and lonely. That terror which is said to attack immigrants on their first sight of the New York sky-line came to her, as she leaned on the rail, and with it a feeling of utter misery. By a continual effort during the voyage she had kept her thoughts from turning to John, but now he rose up insistently before her, and she realized all that had gone out of her life.

She rebelled against the mad cruelty of the fate which had brought them together again. It seemed to her now that she must always have loved him, but it had been such a vague, gentle thing, this love, before that last meeting-hardly more than a pleasant accompaniment to her life, something to think about in idle moments, a help and a support when things were running crosswise. She had been so satisfied with it, so content to keep him a mere memory. It seemed so needless and wanton to destroy her illusion.

Of love as a wild-beast passion, tearing and torturing quite ordinary persons like herself, she had always been a little sceptical. The great love poems of the world, when she read them, had always left her with the feeling that their authors were of different clay from herself and had no common meeting ground with her. She had seen her friends fall in love, as they called it, and it had been very pretty and charming, but as far removed from the frenzies of the poets as an amateur's snapshot of Niagara from the cataract itself. Elsa Keith, for instance, was obviously very fond and proud of Marvin, but she seemed perfectly placid about it. She loved, but she could still spare half an hour for the discussion of a new frock. Her soul did not appear to have been revolutionized in any way.

Gradually Betty had come to the conclusion that love, in the full sense of the word, was one of the things that did not happen. And now, as if to punish her presumption, it had leaped from hiding and seized her.

There was nothing exaggerated or unintelligible in the poets now. They ceased to be inhabitants of another world, swayed by curiously complex emotions. They were her brothers-ordinary men with ordinary feelings and a strange gift for expressing them. She knew now that it was possible to hate the man you loved and to love the man you hated, to ache for the sight of someone even while you fled from him.

It did not take her long to pass the Customs. A small grip constituted her entire baggage. Having left this in the keeping of the amiable proprietor of a near-by delicatessen store, she made her way to the ferry.

Her first enquiry brought her to the cottage. Mrs. Oakley was a celebrity on Staten Island. At the door she paused for a moment, then knocked.

The Swede servant, she who had been there at her former visit, twelve years ago, received her stolidly. Mrs. Oakley was dusting her clocks.

"Ask her if she can see me," said Betty. "I'm —" great step-niece sounded too ridiculous — "I'm her niece," she said.

The handmaid went and returned, stolid as ever. "Ay tal her vat yu say about niece, and she say she not knowing any niece," she announced.

Betty amended the description, and presently the Swede returned once more, and motioned her to enter.

Like so many scenes of childhood, the room of the clocks was sharply stamped on Betty's memory, and, as she came into it now, it seemed to her that nothing had changed. There were the clocks, all round the walls, of every shape and size, the big clocks with the human faces and the small, perky clocks. There was the dingy, medium-sized clock that held the trumpeter. And there, looking at her with just the old sandy-cat expression in her pale eyes, was Mrs. Oakley.

Even the possession of an income of eighteen million dollars and a unique collection of clocks cannot place a woman above the making of the obvious remark.

"How you have grown!" said Mrs. Oakley.

The words seemed to melt the chill that had gathered around Betty's heart. She had been prepared to enter into long explanations, and the knowledge that these would not be required was very comforting.

"Do you remember me?" she exclaimed.

"You are the little girl who clapped her hands at the trumpeter, but you are not little now."

"I'm not so very big," said Betty, smiling. She felt curiously at home, and pity for the loneliness of this strange old woman caused her to forget her own troubles.

"You look pretty when you smile," said Mrs. Oakley thoughtfully. She continued to look closely at her. "You are in trouble," she said.

Betty met her eyes frankly.

"Yes," she said.

The old woman bent her head over a Sevres china clock, and stroked it tenderly with her feather duster.

"Why did you run away?" she asked without looking up.

Betty had a feeling that the ground was being cut from beneath her feet. She had expected to have to explain who she was and why she had come, and behold, both were unnecessary. It was uncanny. And then the obvious explanation occurred to her.

"Did my stepfather cable?" she asked.

Mrs. Oakley laid down the feather duster and, opening a drawer, produced some sheets of paper-to the initiated eye plainly one of Mr. Scobell's lengthy messages.

"A wickedly extravagant cable," she said, frowning at it. "He could have expressed himself perfectly well at a quarter of the expense."

Betty began to read. The dimple on her chin appeared for a moment as she did so. The tone of the message was so obsequious. There was no trace of the old peremptory note in it. The words "dearest aunt" occurred no fewer than six times in the course of the essay, its author being apparently reckless of the fact that it was costing him half a dollar a time. Mrs. Oakley had been quite right in her criticism. The gist of the cable was, "*Betty has run away to America dearest aunt ridiculous is sure to visit you please dearest aunt do not encourage her.*" The rest was pure padding.

Mrs. Oakley watched her with a glowering eye. "If Bennie Scobell," she soliloquized, "imagines that he can dictate to me —" She ceased, leaving an impressive hiatus. Unhappy Mr. Scobell, convicted of dictation even after three dollars' worth of "dearest aunt!"

Betty handed back the cable. Her chin, emblem of war, was tilted and advanced.

"I'll tell you why I ran away, Aunt," she said.

Mrs. Oakley listened to her story in silence. Betty did not relate it at great length, for with every word she spoke, the thought of John stabbed her afresh. She omitted much that has been told in this chronicle. But she disclosed the essential fact, that Napoleonic Mr. Scobell had tried to force her into a marriage with a man she did not-she hesitated at the word-did not respect, she concluded.

Mrs. Oakley regarded her inscrutably for a while before replying.

"Respect!" she said at last. "I have never met a man in my life whom I could respect. Harpies! Every one of them! Every one of them! Every one of them!"

She was muttering to herself. It is possible that her thoughts were back with those persevering young aristocrats of her second widowhood. Certainly, if she had sometimes displayed a touch of the pirate in her dealings with man, man, it must be said in fairness, had not always shown his best side to her.

"Respect!" she muttered again. "Did you like him, this Prince of yours?"

Betty's eyes filled. She made no reply.

"Well, never mind," said Mrs. Oakley. "Don't cry, child! I'm not going to press you. You must have hated him or else loved him very much, or you would never have run away.... Dictate to me!" she broke off, half-aloud, her mind evidently once more on Mr. Scobell's unfortunate cable.

Betty could bear it no longer.

"I loved him!" she cried. "I loved him!"

She was shaking with dry sobs. She felt the old woman's eyes upon her, but she could not stop.

A sudden whirr cut through the silence. One of the large clocks near the door was beginning to strike the hour. Instantly the rest began to do the same, till the room was full of the noise. And above the din there sounded sharp and clear the note of the little trumpet.

The noise died away with metallic echoings.

"Honey!"

It was a changed voice that spoke. Betty looked up, and saw that the eyes that met hers were very soft. She moved quickly to the old woman's side.

"Honey, I'm going to tell you something about myself that nobody dreams of. Betty, when I was your age, *I* ran away from a man because I loved him. It was just a little village tragedy, my dear. I think he was fond of me, but father was poor and her folks were the great people of the place, and he married her. And I ran away, like you, and went to New York."

Betty pressed her hand. It was trembling.

"I'm so sorry," she whispered.

"I went to New York because I wanted to kill my heart. And I killed it. There's only one way. Work! Work! Work!" She was sitting bolt upright, and the soft look had gone out of her eyes. They were hard and fiery under the drawn brows. "Work! Ah, I worked! I never rested. For two years. Two whole years. It fought back at me. It tore me to bits. But I wouldn't stop. I worked on, I killed it."

She stopped, quivering. Betty was cold with a nameless dismay. She felt as if she were standing in the dark on the brink of an abyss.

The old woman began to speak again.

"Child, it's the same with you. Your heart's tearing you. Don't let it! It will get worse and worse if you are afraid of it. Fight it! Kill it! Work!"

She stopped again, clenching and unclenching her fingers, as if she were strangling some living thing. There was silence for a long moment.

"What can you do?" she asked suddenly.

Her voice was calm and unemotional again. The abruptness of the transition from passion to the practical took Betty aback. She could not speak.

"There must be something," continued Mrs. Oakley. "When I was your age I had taught myself bookkeeping, shorthand, and typewriting. What can you do? Can you use a typewriter?"

Blessed word!

"Yes," said Betty promptly.

"Well?"

"Not very well?"

"H'm. Well, I expect you will do it well enough for Mr. Renshaw-on my recommendation. I'll give you a letter to him. He is the editor of a small weekly paper. I don't know how much he will offer you, but take it and *work!* You'll find him pleasant. I have met him at charity organization meetings on the East Side. He's useful at the entertainments-does conjuring tricks-stupid, but they seem to amuse people. You'll find him pleasant. There."

She had been writing the letter of introduction during the course of these remarks. At the last word she blotted it, and placed it in an envelope.

"That's the address," she said. "J. Brabazon Renshaw, Office of *Peaceful Moments*. Take it to him now. Good-by."

It was as if she were ashamed of her late display of emotion. She spoke abruptly, and her pale eyes were expressionless. Betty thanked her and turned to go.

"Tell me how you get on," said Mrs. Oakley.

"Yes," said Betty.

"And *work*. Keep on working!"

There was a momentary return of her former manner as she spoke the words, and Betty wavered. She longed to say something comforting, something that would show that she understood.

Mrs. Oakley had taken up the feather duster again.

"Steena will show you out," she said curtly. And Betty was aware of the stolid Swede in the doorway. The interview was plainly at an end.

"Good-by, Aunt," she said, "and thank you ever so much—for everything."

CHAPTER XII

"PEACEFUL MOMENTS"

The man in the street did not appear to know it, but a great crisis was imminent in New York journalism.

Everything seemed much as usual in the city. The cars ran blithely on Broadway. Newsboys shouted their mystic slogan, "Wuxtry!" with undiminished vim. Society thronged Fifth Avenue without a furrow on its brow. At a thousand street corners a thousand policemen preserved their air of massive superiority to the things of this world. Of all the four million not one showed the least sign of perturbation.

Nevertheless, the crisis was at hand. Mr. J. Brabazon Renshaw, Editor-in-chief of *Peaceful Moments*, was about to leave his post and start on a three-months' vacation.

Peaceful Moments, as its name (an inspiration of Mr. Renshaw's own) was designed to imply, was a journal of the home. It was the sort of paper which the father of the family is expected to take back with him from the office and read aloud to the chicks before bedtime under the shade of the rubber plant.

Circumstances had left the development of the paper almost entirely to Mr. Renshaw. Its contents were varied. There was a "Moments in the Nursery" page, conducted by Luella Granville Waterman and devoted mainly to anecdotes of the family canary, by Jane (aged six), and similar works of the younger set. There was a "Moments of Meditation" page, conducted by the Reverend Edwin T. Philpotts; a "Moments among the Masters" page, consisting of assorted chunks looted from the literature of the past, when foreheads were bulged and thoughts profound, by Mr. Renshaw himself; one or two other special pages; a short story; answers to correspondents on domestic matters; and a "Moments of Mirth" page, conducted by one B. Henderson Asher—a very painful affair.

The proprietor of this admirable journal was that Napoleon of finance, Mr. Benjamin Scobell.

That this should have been so is but one proof of the many-sidedness of that great man.

Mr. Scobell had founded *Peaceful Moments* at an early stage in his career, and it was only at very rare intervals nowadays that he recollected that he still owned it. He had so many irons in the fire now that he had no time to waste his brain tissues thinking about a paper like *Peaceful Moments*. It was one of his failures. It certainly paid its way and brought him a small sum each year, but to him it was a failure, a bombshell that had fizzled.

He had intended to do big things with *Peaceful Moments*. He had meant to start a new epoch in the literature of Manhattan.

"I gottan idea," he had said to Miss Scobell. "All this yellow journalism-red blood and all that-folks are tired of it. They want something milder. Wholesome, see what I mean? There's money in it. Guys make a roll too big to lift by selling soft drinks, don't they? Well, I'm going to run a soft-drink paper. See?"

The enterprise had started well. To begin with, he had found the ideal editor. He had met Mr. Renshaw at a down-East gathering presided over by Mrs. Oakley, and his Napoleonic eye had seen in J. Brabazon the seeds of domestic greatness. Before they parted, he had come to terms with him. Nor had the latter failed to justify his intuition. He made an admirable editor. It was not Mr. Renshaw's fault that the new paper had failed to electrify America. It was the public on whom the responsibility for the failure must be laid. They spoiled the whole thing. Certain of the faithful subscribed, it is true, and continued to subscribe, but the great heart of the public remained untouched. The great heart of the public declined to be interested in the meditations of Mr. Philpotts and the humor of Mr. B. Henderson Asher, and continued to spend its money along the bad old channels. The thing began to bore Mr. Scobell. He left the conduct of the journal more and more to Mr. Renshaw, until finally-it was just after the idea for extracting gold from sea water had struck him-he put the whole business definitely out of his mind. (His actual words were that he never wanted to see or hear of the darned thing again, inasmuch as it gave him a pain in the neck.) Mr. Renshaw was given a free hand as to the editing, and all matters of finance connected with the enterprise were placed in the hands of Mr. Scobell's solicitors, who had instructions to sell the journal, if, as its owner crisply put it, they could find any chump who was enough of a darned chump to give real money for it. Up to the present the great army of chumps had fallen short of this ideal standard of darned chumphood.

Ever since this parting of the ways, Mr. Renshaw had been in his element. Under his guidance *Peaceful Moments* had reached a level of domesticity which made other so-called domestic journals look like sporting supplements. But at last the work had told upon him. Whether it was the effort of digging into the literature of the past every week, or the strain of reading B. Henderson Asher's "Moments of Mirth" is uncertain. At any rate, his labors had ended in wrecking his health to such an extent that the doctor had ordered him three months' complete rest, in the woods or mountains, whichever he preferred; and, being a farseeing man, who went to the root of things, had absolutely declined to consent to Mr. Renshaw's suggestion that he keep in touch with the paper during his vacation. He was adamant. He had seen copies of *Peaceful Moments* once or twice, and refused to permit a man in Mr. Renshaw's state of health to come in contact with Luella Granville Waterman's "Moments in the Nursery" and B. Henderson Asher's "Moments of Mirth."

"You must forget that such a paper exists," he said. "You must dismiss the whole thing from your mind, live in the open, and develop some flesh and muscle."

Mr. Renshaw had bowed before the sentence, howbeit gloomily, and now, on the morning of Betty's departure from Mrs. Oakley's house with the letter of introduction, was giving his final instructions to his temporary successor.

This temporary successor in the editorship was none other than John's friend, Rupert Smith, late of the *News*.

Smith, on leaving Harvard, had been attracted by newspaper work, and had found his first billet on a Western journal of the type whose society column consists of such items as "Jim Thompson was to town yesterday with a bunch of other cheap skates. We take this opportunity of once more informing Jim that he is a liar and a skunk," and whose editor works with a pistol on his desk and another in his hip-pocket. Graduating from this, he had proceeded to a reporter's post on a daily paper in Kentucky, where there were blood feuds and other Southern devices for preventing life from becoming dull. All this was good, but even while he enjoyed these experiences, New York, the magnet, had been tugging at him, and at last, after two eventful years on the Kentucky paper, he had come East, and eventually won through to the staff of the *News*.

His presence in the office of *Peaceful Moments* was due to the uncomfortable habit of most of the New York daily papers of cutting down their staff of reporters during the summer. The dismissed had, to sustain them, the knowledge that they would return, like the swallows, anon, and be received back into their old places; but in the meantime they suffered the inconvenience of having to support themselves as best they could. Smith, when, in the company of half-a-dozen others, he had had to leave the *News*, had heard of the vacant post of assistant editor on *Peaceful Moments*, and had applied for and received it. Whereby he was more fortunate than some of his late colleagues; though, as the character of his new work unrolled itself before him, he was frequently doubtful on that point. For the atmosphere of *Peaceful Moments*, however wholesome, was certainly not exciting, and his happened to be essentially a nature that needed the stimulus of excitement. Even in Park Row, the denizens of which street are rarely slaves to the conventional and safe, he had a well-established reputation in this matter. Others of his acquaintances welcomed excitement when it came to them in the course of the day's work, but it was Smith's practise to go in search of it. He was a young man of spirit and resource.

His appearance, to those who did not know him, hardly suggested this. He was very tall and thin, with a dark, solemn face. He was a purist in the matter of clothes, and even in times of storm and stress presented an immaculate appearance to the world. In his left eye, attached to a cord, he wore a monocle.

Through this, at the present moment, he was gazing benevolently at Mr. Renshaw, as the latter fussed about the office in the throes of departure. To the editor's rapid fire of advice and warning he listened with the pleased and indulgent air of a father whose infant son frisks before him. Mr. Renshaw interested him. To Smith's mind Mr. Renshaw, put him in any show you pleased, would alone have been worth the price of admission.

"Well," chirruped the holiday-maker—he was a little man with a long neck, and he always chirruped—"Well, I think that is all, Mr. Smith. Oh, ah, yes! The stenographer. You will need a new stenographer."

The *Peaceful Moments* stenographer had resigned her position three days before, in order to get married.

"Unquestionably, Comrade Renshaw," said Smith. "A blonde."

Mr. Renshaw looked annoyed.

"I have told you before, Mr. Smith, I object to your addressing me as Comrade. It is not-it is not-er-fitting."

Smith waved a deprecating hand.

"Say no more," he said. "I will correct the habit. I have been studying the principles of Socialism somewhat deeply of late, and I came to the conclusion that I must join the cause. It looked good to me. You work for the equal distribution of property, and start in by swiping all you can and sitting on it. A noble scheme. Me for it. But I am interrupting you."

Mr. Renshaw had to pause for a moment to reorganize his ideas.

"I think-ah, yes. I think it would be best perhaps to wait for a day or two in case Mrs. Oakley should recommend someone. I mentioned the vacancy in the office to her, and she said she would give the matter her attention. I should prefer, if possible, to give the place to her nominee. She—"

"—has eighteen million a year," said Smith. "I understand. Scatter seeds of kindness."

Mr. Renshaw looked at him sharply. Smith's face was solemn and thoughtful.

"Nothing of the kind," the editor said, after a pause. "I should prefer Mrs. Oakley's nominee because Mrs. Oakley is a shrewd, practical woman who-er-who-who, in fact—"

"Just so," said Smith, eying him gravely through the monocle. "Entirely."

The scrutiny irritated Mr. Renshaw.

"Do put that thing away, Mr. Smith," he said.

"That thing?"

"Yes, that ridiculous glass. Put it away."

"Instantly," said Smith, replacing the monocle in his vest-pocket. "You object to it? Well, well, many people do. We all have these curious likes and dislikes. It is these clashings of personal taste which constitute what we call life. Yes. You were saying?"

Mr. Renshaw wrinkled his forehead.

"I have forgotten what I intended to say," he said querulously. "You have driven it out of my head."

Smith clicked his tongue sympathetically. Mr. Renshaw looked at his watch.

"Dear me," he said, "I must be going. I shall miss my train. But I think I have covered the ground quite thoroughly. You understand everything?"

"Absolutely," said Smith. "I look on myself as some engineer controlling a machine with a light hand on the throttle. Or like some faithful hound whose master—"

"Ah! There is just one thing. Mrs. Julia Burdett Parslow is a little inclined to be unpunctual with her 'Moments with Budding Girlhood.' If this should happen while I am away, just write her a letter, quite a pleasant letter, you understand, pointing out the necessity of being in good time. She must realize that we are a machine."

"Exactly," murmured Smith.

"The machinery of the paper cannot run smoothly unless contributors are in good time with their copy."

"Precisely," said Smith. "They are the janitors of the literary world. Let them turn off the steam heat, and where are we? If Mrs. Julia Burdett Parslow is not up to time with the hot air, how shall our 'Girlhood' escape being nipped in the bud?"

"And there is just one other thing. I wish you would correct a slight tendency I have noticed lately in Mr. Asher to be just a trifle-well, not precisely risky, but perhaps a shade broad in his humor."

"Young blood!" sighed Smith. "Young blood!"

"Mr. Asher is a very sensible man, and he will understand. Well, that is all, I think. Now, I really must be going. Good-by, Mr. Smith."

"Good-by."

At the door Mr. Renshaw paused with the air of an exile bidding farewell to his native land, sighed and trotted out.

Smith put his feet upon the table, flicked a speck of dust from his coat-sleeve, and resumed his task of reading the proofs of Luella Granville Waterman's "Moments in the Nursery."

* * * * *

He had not been working long, when Pugsy Maloney, the office boy, entered.

"Say!" said Pugsy.

"Say on, Comrade Maloney."

"Dere's a loidy out dere wit a letter for Mr. Renshaw."

"Have you acquainted her with the fact that Mr. Renshaw has passed to other climes?"

"Huh?"

"Have you, in the course of your conversation with this lady, mentioned that Mr. Renshaw has beaten it?"

"Sure, I did. And she says can she see you?"

Smith removed his feet from the table.

"Certainly," he said. "Who am I that I should deny people these little treats? Ask her to come in, Comrade Maloney."

CHAPTER XIII

BETTY MAKES A FRIEND

Betty had appealed to Master Maloney's esthetic sense of beauty directly she appeared before him. It was with regret, therefore, rather than with the usual calm triumph of the office boy, that he informed her that the editor was not in. Also, seeing that she was evidently perturbed by the information, he had gone out of his way to suggest that she lay her business, whatever it might be, before Mr. Renshaw's temporary successor.

Smith received her with Old-World courtesy.

"Will you sit down?" he said. "Not to wait for Comrade Renshaw, of course. He will not be back for another three months. Perhaps I can help you. I am acting editor. The work is not light," he added gratuitously. "Sometimes the cry goes round New York, 'Can Smith get through it all? Will his strength support his unquenchable spirit?' But I stagger on. I do not repine. What was it that you wished to see Comrade Renshaw about?"

He swung his monocle lightly by its cord. For the first time since she had entered the office Betty was rather glad that Mr. Renshaw was away. Conscious of her defects as a stenographer she had been looking forward somewhat apprehensively to the interview with her prospective employer. But this long, solemn youth put her at her ease. His manner suggested in some indefinable way that the whole thing was a sort of round game.

"I came about the typewriting," she said.

Smith looked at her with interest.

"Are you the nominee?"

"I beg your pardon?"

"Do you come from Mrs. Oakley?"

"Yes."

"Then all is well. The decks have been cleared against your coming. Consider yourself engaged as our official typist. By the way, *can* you type?"

Betty laughed. This was certainly not the awkward interview she had been picturing in her mind.

"Yes," she said, "but I'm afraid I'm not very good at it."

"Never mind," said Smith. "I'm not very good at editing. Yet here I am. I foresee that we shall make an ideal team. Together, we will toil early and late till we whoop up this domestic journal into a shining model of what a domestic journal should be. What that is, at present, I do not exactly know. Excursion trains will be run from the Middle West to see this domestic journal. Visitors from Oshkosh will do it before going on to Grant's tomb. What exactly is your name?"

Betty hesitated. Yes, perhaps it would be better. "Brown," she said.

"Mine is Smith. The smiling child in the outer office is Pugsy Maloney, one of our most prominent citizens. Homely in appearance, perhaps, but one of us. You will get to like Comrade Maloney. And now, to touch on a painful subject-work. Would you care to start in now, or have you any other engagements? Perhaps you wish to see the sights of this beautiful little city before beginning? You would prefer to start in now? Excellent. You could not have come at a more suitable time, for I was on the very point of sallying out to purchase about twenty-five cents' worth of lunch. We editors, Comrade Brown, find that our tissues need constant restoration, such is the strenuous nature of our duties. You will find one or two letters on that table. Good-by, then, for the present."

He picked up his hat, smoothed it carefully and with a courtly inclination of his head, left the room.

Betty sat down, and began to think. So she was really earning her own living! It was a stimulating thought. She felt a little bewildered. She had imagined something so different.

Mrs. Oakley had certainly said that *Peaceful Moments* was a small paper, but despite that, her imagination had conjured up visions of bustle and activity, and a peremptory, overdriven editor, snapping out words of command. Smith, with his careful speech and general air of calm detachment from the noisy side of life, created an atmosphere of restfulness. If this was a sample of life in the office, she thought, the paper had been well named. She felt soothed and almost happy.

Interesting and exciting things, New York things, began to happen at once. To her, meditating, there entered Pugsy Maloney, the guardian of the gate of this shrine of Peace, a nonchalant youth of about fifteen, with a freckled, mask-like face, the expression of which never varied, bearing in his arms a cat. The cat was struggling violently, but he appeared quite unconscious of it. Its existence did not seem to occur to him.

"Say!" said Pugsy.

Betty was fond of cats.

"Oh, don't hurt her!" she cried anxiously.

Master Maloney eyed the cat as if he were seeing it for the first time.

"I wasn't hoitin' her," he said, without emotion. "Dere was two fresh kids in the street sickin' a dawg on to her. And I comes up and says, 'G'wan! What do youse t'ink youse doin', fussin' de poor dumb animal?' An' one of de guys, he says, 'G'wan! Who do youse t'ink youse is?' An' I says, 'I'm de guy what's goin' to swat youse on de coco, smarty, if youse don't quit fussin' de poor dumb animal.' So wit' dat he makes a break at swattin' me one, but I swats him one, an' I swats de odder feller one, an' den I swats dem bote some more, an' I gits de kitty, an' I brings her in here, cos I t'inks maybe youse'll look after her. I can't be boddered myself. Cats is foolishness."

And, having finished this Homeric narrative, Master Maloney fixed an expressionless eye on the ceiling, and was silent.

"How splendid of you, Pugsy!" cried Betty. "She might have been killed, poor thing."

"She had it pretty fierce," admitted Master Maloney, gazing dispassionately at the rescued animal, which had escaped from his clutch and taken up a strong position on an upper shelf of the bookcase.

"Will you go out and get her some milk, Pugsy? She's probably starving. Here's a quarter. Will you keep the change?"

"Sure thing," assented Master Maloney.

He strolled slowly out, while Betty, mounting a chair, proceeded to chirrup and snap her fingers in the effort to establish the foundations of an *entente cordiale* with the cat.

By the time Pugsy returned, carrying a five-cent bottle of milk, the animal had vacated the shelf, and was sitting on the table, polishing her face. The milk having been poured into the lid of a tobacco tin, in lieu of a saucer, she suspended her operations and adjourned for refreshments, Pugsy, having no immediate duties on hand, concentrated himself on the cat.

"Say!" he said.

"Well?"

"Dat kitty. Pipe de leather collar she's wearin'."

Betty had noticed earlier in the proceedings that a narrow leather collar encircled the animal's neck.

"Guess I know where dat kitty belongs. Dey all has dose collars. I guess she's one of Bat Jarvis's kitties. He's got twenty-t'ree of dem, and dey all has dose collars."

"Bat Jarvis?"

"Sure."

"Who is he?"

Pugsy looked at her incredulously.

"Say! Ain't youse never heard of Bat Jarvis? He's —he's Bat Jarvis."

"Do you know him?"

"Sure, I knows him."

"Does he live near here?"

"Sure, he lives near here."

"Then I think the best thing for you to do is to run round and tell him that I am taking care of his cat, and that he had better come and fetch it. I must be getting on with my work, or I shall never finish it."

She settled down to type the letters Smith had indicated. She attacked her task cautiously. She was one of those typists who are at their best when they do not have to hurry.

She was putting the finishing touches to the last of the batch, when there was a shuffling of feet in the outer room, followed by a knock on the door. The next moment there entered a short, burly young man, around whom there hung, like an aroma, an indescribable air of toughness, partly due, perhaps, to the fact that he wore his hair in a well-oiled fringe almost down to his eyebrows, thus presenting the appearance of having no forehead at all. His eyes were small and set close together. His mouth was wide, his jaw prominent. Not, in short, the sort of man you would have picked out on sight as a model citizen. He blinked furtively, as his eyes met Betty's, and looked round the room. His face lighted up as he saw the cat.

"Say!" he said, stepping forward, and touching the cat's collar. "Ma'am, mine!"

"Are you Mr. Jarvis?" asked Betty.

The visitor nodded, not without a touch of complacency, as of a monarch abandoning his incognito.

For Mr. Jarvis was a celebrity.

By profession he was a dealer in animals, birds, and snakes. He had a fancier's shop on Groome Street, in the heart of the Bowery. This was on the ground floor. His living abode was in the upper story of that house, and it was there that he kept the twenty-three cats whose necks were adorned with leather collars.

But it was not the fact that he possessed twenty-three cats with leather collars that had made Mr. Jarvis a celebrity. A man may win a local reputation, if only for eccentricity, by such means. Mr. Jarvis' reputation was far from being purely local. Broadway knew him, and the Tenderloin. Tammany Hall knew him. Long Island City knew him. For Bat Jarvis was the leader of the famous Groome Street Gang, the largest and most influential of the four big gangs of the East Side.

To Betty, so little does the world often know of its greatest men, he was merely a decidedly repellent-looking young man in unbecoming clothes. But his evident affection for the cat gave her a feeling of fellowship toward him. She beamed upon him, and Mr. Jarvis, who was wont to face the glare of rivals without flinching, avoided her eye and shuffled with embarrassment.

"I'm so glad she's safe!" said Betty. "There were two boys teasing her in the street. I've been giving her some milk."

Mr. Jarvis nodded, with his eyes on the floor.

There was a pause. Then he looked up, and, fixing his gaze some three feet above her head, spoke.

"Say!" he said, and paused again. Betty waited expectantly.

He relaxed into silence again, apparently thinking.

"Say!" he said. "Ma'am, obliged. Fond of de kit. I am."

"She's a dear," said Betty, tickling the cat under the ear.

"Ma'am," went on Mr. Jarvis, pursuing his theme, "obliged. Sha'n't fergit it. Any time you're in bad, glad to be of service. Bat Jarvis. Groome Street. Anybody'll show youse where I live."

He paused, and shuffled his feet; then, tucking the cat more firmly under his arm, left the room. Betty heard him shuffling downstairs.

He had hardly gone, when the door opened again, and Smith came in.

"So you have had company while I was away?" he said. "Who was the grandee with the cat? An old childhood's friend? Was he trying to sell the animal to us?"

"That was Mr. Bat Jarvis," said Betty.

Smith looked interested.

"Bat! What was he doing here?"

Betty related the story of the cat. Smith nodded thoughtfully.

"Well," he said, "I don't know that Comrade Jarvis is precisely the sort of friend I would go out of my way to select. Still, you never know what might happen. He might come in useful. And now, let us concentrate ourselves tensely on this very entertaining little journal of ours, and see if we cannot stagger humanity with it."

CHAPTER XIV

A CHANGE OF POLICY

The feeling of tranquillity which had come to Betty on her first acquaintance with *Peaceful Moments* seemed to deepen as the days went by, and with each day she found the sharp pain at her heart less vehement. It was still there, but it was dulled. The novelty of her life and surroundings kept it in check. New York is an egotist. It will suffer no divided attention. "Look at me!" says the voice of the city imperiously, and its children obey. It snatches their thoughts from their inner griefs, and concentrates them on the pageant that rolls unceasingly from one end of the island to the other. One may despair in New York, but it is difficult to brood on the past; for New York is the City of the Present, the City of Things that are Going On.

To Betty everything was new and strange. Her previous acquaintance with the metropolis had not been extensive. Mr. Scobell's home-or, rather, the house which he owned in America-was on the outskirts of Philadelphia, and it was there that she had lived when she was not paying visits. Occasionally, during horse-show week, or at some other time of festivity, she had spent a few days with friends who lived in Madison or upper Fifth Avenue, but beyond that, New York was a closed book to her.

It would have been a miracle in the circumstances, if John and Mervo and the whole of the events since the arrival of the great cable had not to some extent become a little dream-like. When she was alone at night, and had leisure to think, the dream became a reality once more; but in her hours of work, or what passed for work in the office of *Peaceful Moments*, and in the hours she spent walking about the streets and observing the ways of this new world of hers, it faded. Everything was so bright and busy! Every moment had its fresh interest.

And, above all, there was the sense of adventure. She was twenty-four; she had health and an imagination; and almost unconsciously she was stimulated by the thrill of being for the first time in her life genuinely at large. The child's love of hiding dies hard in us. To Betty, to walk abroad in New York in the midst of hurrying crowds, just Betty Brown-one of four million and no longer the beautiful Miss Silver of the society column, was to taste the romance of disguise, or invisibility.

During office hours she came near to complete contentment. To an expert stenographer the amount of work to be done would have seemed ridiculously small, but Betty, who liked plenty of time for a task, generally managed to make it last comfortably through the day.

This was partly owing to the fact that her editor, when not actually at work himself, was accustomed to engage her in conversation, and to keep her so engaged until the entrance of Pugsy Maloney heralded the arrival of some caller.

Betty liked Smith. His odd ways, his conversation, and his extreme solicitude for his clothes amused her. She found his outlook on life refreshing. Smith was an optimist. Whatever cataclysm might occur, he never doubted for a moment that he would be comfortably on the summit of the debris when all was over. He amazed Betty with his stories of his reportorial adventures. He told them for the most part as humorous stories at his own expense, but the fact remained that in a considerable proportion of them he had only escaped a sudden and violent death by adroitness or pure good luck. His conversation opened up a new world to Betty. She began to see that in America, and especially in New York, anything may happen to anybody. She looked on Smith with new eyes.

"But surely all this," she said one morning, after he had come to the end of the story of a highly delicate piece of interviewing work in connection with some Cumberland Mountains feudists, "surely all this—" She looked round the room.

"Domesticity?" suggested Smith.

"Yes," said Betty. "Surely it all seems rather tame to you?"

Smith sighed.

475

"Comrade Brown," he said, "you have touched the spot with an unerring finger."

Since Mr. Renshaw's departure, the flatness of life had come home to Smith with renewed emphasis. Before, there had always been the quiet entertainment of watching the editor at work, but now he was feeling restless. Like John at Mervo, he was practically nothing but an ornament. *Peaceful Moments*, like Mervo, had been set rolling and had continued to roll on almost automatically. The staff of regular contributors sent in their various pages. There was nothing for the man in charge to do. Mr. Renshaw had been one of those men who have a genius for being as busy over nothing as if it were some colossal work, but Smith had not that gift. He liked something that he could grip and that gripped him. He was becoming desperately bored. He felt like a marooned sailor on a barren rock of domesticity.

A visitor who called at the office at this time did nothing to remove this sensation of being outside everything that made life worth living. Betty, returning to the office one afternoon, found Smith in the doorway, just parting from a thickset young man. There was a rather gloomy expression on the thickset young man's face.

Smith, too, she noted, when they were back in the inner office, seemed to have something on his mind. He was strangely silent.

"Comrade Brown," he said at last, "I wish this little journal of ours had a sporting page."

Betty laughed.

"Less ribaldry," protested Smith pained. "This is a sad affair. You saw the man I was talking to? That was Kid Brady. I used to know him when I was out West. He wants to fight anyone in the country at a hundred and thirty-three pounds. We all have our hobbies. That is Comrade Brady's."

"Is he a boxer?"

"He would like to be. Out West, nobody could touch him. He's in the championship class. But he has been pottering about New York for a month without being able to get a fight. If we had a sporting page on *Peaceful Moments* we could do him some good, but I don't see how we can write him up," said Smith, picking up a copy of the paper, and regarding it gloomily, "in 'Moments in the Nursery' or 'Moments with Budding Girlhood.'"

He put up his eyeglass, and stared at the offending journal with the air of a vegetarian who has found a caterpillar in his salad. Incredulity, dismay, and disgust fought for precedence in his expression.

"B. Henderson Asher," he said severely, "ought to be in some sort of a home. Cain killed Abel for telling him that story."

He turned to another page, and scrutinized it with deepening gloom.

"Is Luella Granville Waterman by any chance a friend of yours, Comrade Brown? No? I am glad. For it seems to me that for sheer, concentrated piffle, she is in a class by herself."

He read on for a few moments in silence, then looked up and fixed Betty with his monocle. There was righteous wrath in his eyes.

"And people," he said, "are paying money for this! *Money!* Even now they are sitting down and writing checks for a year's subscription. It isn't right! It's a skin game. I am assisting in a carefully planned skin game!"

"But perhaps they like it," suggested Betty.

Smith shook his head.

"It is kind of you to try and soothe my conscience, but it is useless. I see my position too clearly. Think of it, Comrade Brown! Thousands of poor, doddering, half-witted creatures in Brooklyn and Flatbush, who ought not really to have control of their own money at all, are getting buncoed out of whatever it is per annum in exchange for-how shall I put it in a forcible yet refined and gentlemanly manner? —for cat's meat of this description. Why, selling gold bricks is honest compared with it. And I am temporarily responsible for the black business!"

He extended a lean hand with melodramatic suddenness toward Betty. The unexpectedness of the movement caused her to start back in her chair with a little exclamation of surprise. Smith nodded with a kind of mournful satisfaction.

"Exactly!" he said. "As I expected! You shrink from me. You avoid my polluted hand. How could it be otherwise? A conscientious green-goods man would do the same." He rose from his seat. "Your attitude," he said, "confirms me in a decision that has been in my mind for some days. I will no longer calmly accept this terrible position. I will try to make amends. While I am in charge, I will give our public something worth reading. All these Watermans and Ashers and Parslows must go!"

"Go!"

"Go!" repeated Smith firmly. "I have been thinking it over for days. You cannot look me in the face, Comrade Brown, and say that there is a single feature which would not be better away. I mean in the paper, not in my face. Every one of these punk pages must disappear. Letters must be despatched at once, informing Julia Burdett Parslow and the others, and in particular B. Henderson Asher, who, on brief acquaintance, strikes me as an ideal candidate for a lethal chamber-that, unless they cease their contributions instantly, we shall call up the police reserves. Then we can begin to move."

Betty, like most of his acquaintances, seldom knew whether Smith was talking seriously or not. She decided to assume, till he should dismiss the idea, that he meant what he said.

"But you can't!" she exclaimed.

"With your kind cooperation, nothing easier. You supply the mechanical work. I will compose the letters. First, B. Henderson Asher. 'Dear Sir'—"

"But —" she fell back on her original remark —"but you can't. What will Mr. Renshaw say when he comes back?"

"Sufficient unto the day. I have a suspicion that he will be the first to approve. His vacation will have made him see things differently-purified him, as it were. His conscience will be alive once more."

"But —"

"Why should we worry ourselves because the end of this venture is wrapped in obscurity? Why, Columbus didn't know where he was going to when he set out. All he knew was some highly interesting fact about an egg. What that was, I do not at the moment recall, but I understand it acted on Columbus like a tonic. We are the Columbuses of the journalistic world. Full steam ahead, and see what happens. If Comrade Renshaw is not pleased, why, I shall have been a martyr to a good cause. It is a far, far better thing that I do than I have ever done, so to speak. Why should I allow possible inconvenience to myself to stand in the way of the happiness which we propose to inject into those Brooklyn and Flatbush homes? Are you ready then, once more? 'Dear Sir —'"

Betty gave in.

When the letters were finished, she made one more objection.

"They are certain to call here and make a fuss," she said, "Mr. Asher and the rest."

"You think they will not bear the blow with manly fortitude?"

"I certainly do. And I think it's hard on them, too. Suppose they depend for a living on what they make from *Peaceful Moments?*"

"They don't," said Smith reassuringly. "I've looked into that. Have no pity for them. They are amateurs-degraded creatures of substance who take the cocktails out of the mouths of deserving professionals. B. Henderson Asher, for instance, is largely interested in gents' haberdashery. And so with the others. We touch their pride, perhaps, but not their purses."

Betty's soft heart was distinctly relieved by the information.

"I see," she said. "But suppose they do call, what will you do? It will be very unpleasant."

Smith pondered.

"True," he said. "True. I think you are right there. My nervous system is so delicately attuned that anything in the shape of a brawl would reduce it to a frazzle. I think that, for this occasion only, we will promote Comrade Maloney to the post of editor. He is a stern, hard, rugged man who does not care how unpopular he is. Yes, I think that would be best."

He signed the letters with a firm hand, "per pro P. Maloney, editor."

Then he lit a cigarette, and leaned back in his chair.

"An excellent morning's work," he said. "Already I begin to feel the dawnings of a new self-respect."

Betty, thinking the thing over, a little dazed by the rapidity of Smith's method of action, had found a fresh flaw in the scheme.

"If you send Mr. Asher and the others away, how are you going to bring the paper out at all? You can't write it all yourself."

Smith looked at her with benevolent admiration.

"She thinks of everything," he murmured. "That busy brain is never still. No, Comrade Brown, I do not propose to write the whole paper myself. I do not shirk work when it gets me in a corner and I can't side-step, but there are limits. I propose to apply to a few of my late companions of Park Row, bright boys who will be delighted to come across with red-hot stuff for a moderate fee."

"And the proprietor of the paper? Won't he make any objection?"

Smith shook his head with a touch of reproof.

"You seem determined to try to look on the dark side. Do you insinuate that we are not acting in the proprietor's best interests? When he gets his check for the receipts, after I have handled the paper awhile, he will go singing about the streets. His beaming smile will be a byword. Visitors will be shown it as one of the sights. His only doubt will be whether to send his money to the bank or keep it in tubs and roll in it. And anyway," he added, "he's in Europe somewhere, and never sees the paper, sensible man."

He scratched a speck of dust off his coat-sleeve with his finger nail.

"This is a big thing," he resumed. "Wait till you see the first number of the new series. My idea is that *Peaceful Moments* shall become a pretty warm proposition. Its tone shall be such that the public will wonder why we do not print it on asbestos. We shall comment on all the live events of the week-murders, Wall Street scandals, glove fights, and the like, in a manner which will make our readers' spines thrill. Above all, we shall be the guardians of the people's rights. We shall be a spot light, showing up the dark places and bringing into prominence those who would endeavor in any way to put the people in Dutch. We shall detect the wrongdoer, and hand him such a series of resentful wallops that he will abandon his little games and become a model citizen. In this way we shall produce a bright, readable little sheet which will make our city sit up and take notice. I think so. I think so. And now I must be hustling about and seeing our new contributors. There is no time to waste."

CHAPTER XV

THE HONEYED WORD

The offices of Peaceful Moments were in a large building in a street off Madison Avenue. They consisted of a sort of outer lair, where Pugsy Maloney spent his time reading tales of life on the prairies and heading off undesirable visitors; a small room, into which desirable but premature visitors were loosed, to wait their turn for admission into the Presence; and a larger room beyond, which was the editorial sanctum.

Smith, returning from luncheon on the day following his announcement of the great change, found both Betty and Pugsy waiting in the outer lair, evidently with news of import.

"Mr. Smith," began Betty.

"Dey're in dere," said Master Maloney with his customary terseness.

"Who, exactly?" asked Smith.

"De whole bunch of dem."

Smith inspected Pugsy through his eyeglass. "Can you give me any particulars?" he asked patiently. "You are well-meaning, but vague, Comrade Maloney. Who are in there?"

"About 'steen of dem!" said Pugsy.

"Mr. Asher," said Betty, "and Mr. Philpotts, and all the rest of them." She struggled for a moment, but, unable to resist the temptation, added, "I told you so."

A faint smile appeared upon Smith's face.

"Dey just butted in," said Master Maloney, resuming his narrative. "I was sittin' here, readin' me book, when de foist of de guys blows in. 'Boy,' says he, 'is de editor in?' 'Nope,' I says. 'I'll go in and wait,' says he. 'Nuttin' doin',' says I. 'Nix on de goin'-in act.' I might as well have saved me breat! In he butts. In about t'ree minutes along comes another gazebo. 'Boy,' says he, 'is de editor in?' 'Nope,' I says. 'I'll wait,' says he, lightin' out for de door, and in he butts. Wit' dat I sees de proposition's too fierce for muh. I can't keep dese big husky guys out if dey bucks center like dat. So when de rest of de bunch comes along, I don't try to give dem de trun down. I says, 'Well, gent,' I says, 'it's up to youse. De editor ain't in, but, if you feels lonesome, push t'roo. Dere's plenty dere to keep youse company. I can't be boddered!'"

"And what more could you have said?" agreed Smith approvingly. "Tell me, did these gentlemen appear to be gay and light-hearted, or did they seem to be looking for someone with a hatchet?"

"Dey was hoppin' mad, de whole bunch of dem."

"Dreadfully," attested Betty.

"As I suspected," said Smith, "but we must not repine. These trifling contretemps are the penalties we pay for our high journalistic aims. I fancy that with the aid of the diplomatic smile and the honeyed word I may manage to win out. Will you come and give me your moral support, Comrade Brown?"

He opened the door of the inner room for Betty, and followed her in.

Master Maloney's statement that "about 'steen" visitors had arrived proved to be a little exaggerated. There were five men in the room.

As Smith entered, every eye was turned upon him. To an outside spectator he would have seemed rather like a very well-dressed Daniel introduced into a den of singularly irritable lions. Five pairs of eyes were smoldering with a long-nursed resentment. Five brows were corrugated with wrathful lines. Such, however, was the simple majesty of Smith's demeanor that for a moment there was dead silence. Not a word was spoken as he paced, wrapped in thought, to the editorial chair. Stillness brooded over the room as he carefully dusted that piece of furniture, and, having done so to his satisfaction, hitched up the knees of his trousers and sank gracefully into a sitting position.

This accomplished, he looked up and started. He gazed round the room.

479

"Ha! I am observed!" he murmured.

The words broke the spell. Instantly the five visitors burst simultaneously into speech.

"Are you the acting editor of this paper?"

"I wish to have a word with you, sir."

"Mr. Maloney, I presume?"

"Pardon me!"

"I should like a few moments' conversation."

The start was good and even, but the gentleman who said "Pardon me!" necessarily finished first, with the rest nowhere.

Smith turned to him, bowed, and fixed him with a benevolent gaze through his eyeglass.

"Are you Mr. Maloney, may I ask?" enquired the favored one.

The others paused for the reply. Smith shook his head. "My name is Smith."

"Where is Mr. Maloney?"

Smith looked across at Betty, who had seated herself in her place by the typewriter.

"Where did you tell me Mr. Maloney had gone to, Miss Brown? Ah, well, never mind. Is there anything *I* can do for you, gentlemen? I am on the editorial staff of this paper."

"Then, maybe," said a small, round gentleman who, so far, had done only chorus work, "you can tell me what all this means? My name is Waterman, sir. I am here on behalf of my wife, whose name you doubtless know."

"Correct me if I am wrong," said Smith, "but I should say it, also, was Waterman."

"Luella Granville Waterman, sir!" said the little man proudly. "My wife," he went on, "has received this extraordinary communication from a man signing himself P. Maloney. We are both at a loss to make head or tail of it."

"It seems reasonably clear to me," said Smith, reading the letter.

"It's an outrage. My wife has been a contributor to this journal since its foundation. We are both intimate friends of Mr. Renshaw, to whom my wife's work has always given complete satisfaction. And now, without the slightest warning, comes this peremptory dismissal from P. Maloney. Who is P. Maloney? Where is Mr. Renshaw?"

The chorus burst forth. It seemed that that was what they all wanted to know. Who was P. Maloney? Where was Mr. Renshaw?

"I am the Reverend Edwin T. Philpott, sir," said a cadaverous-looking man with light blue eyes and a melancholy face. "I have contributed 'Moments of Meditation' to this journal for some considerable time."

Smith nodded.

"I know, yours has always seemed to me work which the world will not willingly let die."

The Reverend Edwin's frosty face thawed into a bleak smile.

"And yet," continued Smith, "I gather that P. Maloney, on the other hand, actually wishes to hurry on its decease. Strange!"

A man in a serge suit, who had been lurking behind Betty, bobbed into the open.

"Where's this fellow Maloney? P. Maloney. That's the man we want to see. I've been working for this paper without a break, except when I had the grip, for four years, and now up comes this Maloney fellow, if you please, and tells me in so many words that the paper's got no use for me."

"These are life's tragedies," sighed Smith.

"What does he mean by it? That's what I want to know. And that's what these gentlemen want to know. See here —"

"I am addressing —" said Smith.

"Asher's my name. B. Henderson Asher. I write 'Moments of Mirth.'"

A look almost of excitement came into Smith's face, such a look as a visitor to a foreign land might wear when confronted with some great national monument. He stood up and shook Mr. Asher reverently by the hand.

"Gentlemen," he said, reseating himself, "this is a painful case. The circumstances, as you will admit when you have heard all, are peculiar. You have asked me where Mr. Renshaw is. I don't know."

"You don't know!" exclaimed Mr. Asher.

"Nobody knows. With luck you may find a black cat in a coal cellar on a moonless night, but not Mr. Renshaw. Shortly after I joined this journal, he started out on a vacation, by his doctor's orders, and left no address. No letters were to be forwarded. He was to enjoy complete rest. Who can say where he is now? Possibly racing down some rugged slope in the Rockies with two grizzlies and a wildcat in earnest pursuit. Possibly in the midst of Florida Everglades, making a noise like a piece of meat in order to snare alligators. Who can tell?"

Silent consternation prevailed among his audience.

"Then, do you mean to say," demanded Mr. Asher, "that this fellow Maloney's the boss here, and that what he says goes?"

Smith bowed.

"Exactly. A man of intensely masterful character, he will brook no opposition. I am powerless to sway him. Suggestions from myself as to the conduct of the paper would infuriate him. He believes that radical changes are necessary in the policy of *Peaceful Moments*, and he will carry them through if it snows. Doubtless he would gladly consider your work if it fitted in with his ideas. A rapid-fire impression of a glove fight, a spine-shaking word picture of a railway smash, or something on those lines, would be welcomed. But —"

"I have never heard of such a thing," said Mr. Waterman indignantly.

"In this life," said Smith, shaking his head, "we must be prepared for every emergency. We must distinguish between the unusual and the impossible. It is unusual for the acting editor of a weekly paper to revolutionize its existing policy, and you have rashly ordered your life on the assumption that it is impossible. You are unprepared. The thing comes on you as a surprise. The cry goes round New York, 'Comrades Asher, Waterman, Philpotts, and others have been taken unawares. They cannot cope with the situation.'"

"But what is to be done?" cried Mr. Asher.

"Nothing, I fear, except to wait. It may be that when Mr. Renshaw, having dodged the bears and eluded the wildcat, returns to his post, he will decide not to continue the paper on the lines at present mapped out. He should be back in about ten weeks."

"Ten weeks!"

"Till then, the only thing to do is to wait. You may rely on me to keep a watchful eye on your interests. When your thoughts tend to take a gloomy turn say to yourselves, 'All is well. Smith is keeping a watchful eye on our interests.'"

"All the same, I should like to see this P. Maloney," said Mr. Asher.

"I shouldn't," said Smith. "I speak in your best interests. P. Maloney is a man of the fiercest passions. He cannot brook interference. If you should argue with him, there is no knowing what might not happen. He would be the first to regret any violent action, when once he had cooled off, but — Of course, if you wish it I could arrange a meeting. No? I think you are wise. And now, gentlemen, as I have a good deal of work to get through —

"All very disturbing to the man of culture and refinement," said Smith, as the door closed behind the last of the malcontents. "But I think that we may now consider the line clear. I see no further obstacle in our path. I fear I have made Comrade Maloney perhaps a shade unpopular with our late contributors, but these things must be. We must clench our teeth and face them manfully. He suffers in an excellent cause."

CHAPTER XVI

TWO VISITORS TO THE OFFICE

There was once an editor of a paper in the Far West who was sitting at his desk, musing pleasantly on life, when a bullet crashed through the window and imbedded itself in the wall at the back of his head. A happy smile lighted up the editor's face. "Ah!" he said complacently, "I knew that personal column of ours would make a hit!"

What the bullet was to the Far West editor, the visit of Mr. Martin Parker to the offices of *Peaceful Moments* was to Smith.

It occurred shortly after the publication of the second number of the new series, and was directly due to Betty's first and only suggestion for the welfare of the paper.

If the first number of the series had not staggered humanity, it had at least caused a certain amount of comment. The warm weather had begun, and there was nothing much going on in New York. The papers were consequently free to take notice of the change in the policy of *Peaceful Moments*. Through the agency of Smith's newspaper friends, it received some very satisfactory free advertisement, and the sudden increase in the sales enabled Smith to bear up with fortitude against the numerous letters of complaint from old subscribers who did not know what was good for them. Visions of a large new public which should replace these Brooklyn and Flatbush ingrates filled his mind.

The sporting section of the paper pleased him most. The personality of Kid Brady bulked large in it. A photograph of the ambitious pugilist, looking moody and important in an attitude of self-defense, filled half a page, and under the photograph was the legend, "Jimmy Garvin must meet this boy." Jimmy was the present holder of the light-weight title. He had won it a year before, and since then had confined himself to smoking cigars as long as walking sticks and appearing nightly in a vaudeville sketch entitled, "A Fight for Honor." His reminiscences were being published in a Sunday paper. It was this that gave Smith the idea of publishing Kid Brady's autobiography in *Peaceful Moments*, an idea which won the Kid's whole-hearted gratitude. Like most pugilists he had a passion for bursting into print. Print is the fighter's accolade. It signifies that he has arrived. He was grateful to Smith, too, for not editing his contributions. Jimmy Garvin groaned under the supervision of a member of the staff of his Sunday paper, who deleted his best passages and altered the rest into Addisonian English. The readers of *Peaceful Moments* got their Brady raw.

"Comrade Brady," said Smith meditatively to Betty one morning, "has a singularly pure and pleasing style. It is bound to appeal powerfully to the many-headed. Listen to this. Our hero is fighting one Benson in the latter's home town, San Francisco, and the audience is rooting hard for the native son. Here is Comrade Brady on the subject: 'I looked around that house, and I seen I hadn't a friend in it. And then the gong goes, and I says to myself how I has one friend, my old mother down in Illinois, and I goes in and mixes it, and then I seen Benson losing his goat, so I gives him a half-scissor hook, and in the next round I picks up a sleep-producer from the floor and hands it to him, and he takes the count.' That is what the public wants. Crisp, lucid, and to the point. If that does not get him a fight with some eminent person, nothing will."

He leaned back in his chair.

"What we really need now," he said thoughtfully, "is a good, honest, muck-raking series. That's the thing to put a paper on the map. The worst of it is that everything seems to have been done. Have you by any chance a second 'Frenzied Finance' at the back of your mind? Or proofs that nut sundaes are composed principally of ptomaine and outlying portions of the American workingman? It would be the making of us."

Now it happened that in the course of her rambles through the city Betty had lost herself one morning in the slums. The experience had impressed itself on her mind with an extraordinary vividness. Her lot had always been cast in pleasant places, and she had never before been brought into close touch with this side of life. The sight of actual raw misery had come home to her with an added force from that circumstance. Wandering on, she had reached a street which eclipsed in cheerlessness even its squalid neighbors. All the smells and noises of the East Side seemed to be penned up here in a sort of canyon. The masses of dirty clothes hanging from the fire-escapes increased the atmosphere of depression. Groups of ragged children covered the roadway.

It was these that had stamped the scene so indelibly on her memory. She loved children, and these seemed so draggled and uncared-for.

Smith's words gave her an idea.

"Do you know Broster Street, Mr. Smith?" she asked.

"Down on the East Side? Yes, I went there once to get a story, one red-hot night in August, when I was on the *News*. The Ice Company had been putting up their prices, and trouble was expected down there. I was sent to cover it."

He did not add that he had spent a week's salary that night, buying ice and distributing it among the denizens of Broster Street.

"It's an awful place," said Betty, her eyes filling with tears. "Those poor children!"

Smith nodded.

"Some of those tenement houses are fierce," he said thoughtfully. Like Betty, he found himself with a singularly clear recollection of his one visit to Broster Street. "But you can't do anything."

"Why not?" cried Betty. "Oh, why not? Surely you couldn't have a better subject for your series? It's wicked. People only want to be told about them to make them better. Why can't we draw attention to them?"

"It's been done already. Not about Broster Street, but about other tenements. Tenements as a subject are played out. The public isn't interested in them. Besides, it wouldn't be any use. You can't tree the man who is really responsible, unless you can spend thousands scaring up evidence. The land belongs in the first place to some corporation or other. They lease it to a lessee. When there's a fuss, they say they aren't responsible, it's up to the lessee. And he, bright boy, lies so low you can't find out who it is."

"But we could try," urged Betty.

Smith looked at her curiously. The cause was plainly one that lay near to her heart. Her face was flushed and eager. He wavered, and, having wavered, he did what no practical man should do. He allowed sentiment to interfere with business. He knew that a series of articles on Broster Street would probably be so much dead weight on the paper, something to be skipped by the average reader, but he put the thought aside.

"Very well," he said. "If you care to turn in a few crisp remarks on the subject, I'll print them."

Betty's first instalment was ready on the following morning. It was a curious composition. A critic might have classed it with Kid Brady's reminiscences, for there was a complete absence of literary style. It was just a wail of pity, and a cry of indignation, straight from the heart and split up into paragraphs.

Smith read it with interest, and sent it off to the printer unaltered.

"Have another ready for next week, Comrade Brown," he said. "It's a long shot, but this might turn out to be just what we need."

And when, two days after the publication of the number containing the article, Mr. Martin Parker called at the office, he felt that the long shot had won out.

He was holding forth on life in general to Betty shortly before the luncheon hour when Pugsy Maloney entered bearing a card.

"Martin Parker?" said Smith, taking it. "I don't know him. We make new friends daily."

"He's a guy wit' a tall-shaped hat," volunteered Master Maloney, "an' he's wearing a dude suit an' shiny shoes."

"Comrade Parker," said Smith approvingly, "has evidently not been blind to the importance of a visit to *Peaceful Moments*. He has dressed himself in his best. He has felt, rightly, that this is no occasion for the flannel suit and the old straw hat. I would not have it otherwise. It is the right spirit. Show the guy in. We will give him audience."

Pugsy withdrew.

Mr. Martin Parker proved to be a man who might have been any age between thirty-five and forty-five. He had a dark face and a black mustache. As Pugsy had stated, in effect, he wore a morning coat, trousers with a crease which brought a smile of kindly approval to Smith's face, and patent-leather shoes of pronounced shininess.

"I want to see the editor," he said.

"Will you take a seat?" said Smith.

He pushed a chair toward the visitor, who seated himself with the care inspired by a perfect trouser crease. There was a momentary silence while he selected a spot on the table on which to place his hat.

"I have come about a private matter," he said, looking meaningly at Betty, who got up and began to move toward the door. Smith nodded to her, and she went out.

"Say," said Mr. Parker, "hasn't something happened to this paper these last few weeks? It used not to take such an interest in things, used it?"

"You are very right," responded Smith. "Comrade Renshaw's methods were good in their way. I have no quarrel with Comrade Renshaw. But he did not lead public thought. He catered exclusively to children with water on the brain and men and women with solid ivory skulls. I feel that there are other and larger publics. I cannot content myself with ladling out a weekly dole of predigested mental breakfast food. I —"

"Then you, I guess," said Mr. Parker, "are responsible for this Broster Street thing?"

"At any rate, I approve of it and put it in the paper. If any husky guy, as Comrade Maloney would put it, is anxious to aim a swift kick at the author of that article, he can aim it at me."

"I see," said Mr. Parker. He paused. "It said 'Number one' in the paper. Does that mean there are going to be more of them?"

"There is no flaw in your reasoning. There are to be several more."

Mr. Parker looked at the door. It was closed. He bent forward.

"See here," he said, "I'm going to talk straight, if you'll let me."

"Assuredly, Comrade Parker. There must be no secrets, no restraint between us. I would not have you go away and say to yourself, 'Did I make my meaning clear? Was I too elusive?'"

Mr. Parker scratched the floor with the point of a gleaming shoe. He seemed to be searching for words.

"Say on," urged Smith. "Have you come to point out some flaw in that article? Does it fall short in any way of your standard for such work?"

Mr. Parker came to the point.

"If I were you," he said, "I should quit it. I shouldn't go on with those articles."

"Why?" enquired Smith.

"Because," said Mr. Parker.

He looked at Smith, and smiled slowly, an ingratiating smile. Smith did not respond.

"I do not completely gather your meaning," he said. "I fear I must ask you to hand it to me with still more breezy frankness. Do you speak from purely friendly motives? Are you advising me to discontinue the series because you fear that it will damage the literary reputation of the paper? Do you speak solely as a literary connoisseur? Or are there other reasons?"

Mr. Parker leaned forward.

"The gentleman whom I represent —"

"Then this is no matter of your own personal taste? There is another?"

"See here, I'm representing a gentleman who shall be nameless, and I've come on his behalf to tip you off to quit this game. These articles of yours are liable to cause him inconvenience."

"Financial? Do you mean that he may possibly have to spend some of his spare doubloons in making Broster Street fit to live in?"

"It's not so much the money. It's the publicity. There are reasons why he would prefer not to have it made too public that he's the owner of the tenements down there."

"Well, he knows what to do. If he makes Broster Street fit for a not-too-fastidious pig to live in —"

Mr. Parker coughed. A tentative cough, suggesting that the situation was now about to enter upon a more delicate phase.

"Now, see here, sir," he said, "I'm going to be frank. I'm going to put my cards on the table, and see if we can't fix something up. Now, see here. We don't want any unpleasantness. You aren't in this business for your health, eh? You've got your living to make, same as everybody else, I guess. Well, this is how it stands. To a certain extent, I don't mind owning, since we're being frank with one another, you've got us-that's to say, this gentleman I'm speaking of-in a cleft stick. Frankly, that Broster Street story of yours has attracted attention—I saw it myself in two Sunday papers-and if there's going to be any more of them-Well, now, here's a square proposition. How much do you want to stop those articles? That's straight. I've been frank with you, and I want you to be frank with me. What's your figure? Name it, and if you don't want the earth I guess we needn't quarrel."

He looked expectantly at Smith. Smith, gazing sadly at him through his monocle, spoke quietly, with the restrained dignity of some old Roman senator dealing with the enemies of the Republic.

"Comrade Parker," he said, "I fear that you have allowed your intercourse with this worldly city to undermine your moral sense. It is useless to dangle rich bribes before the editorial eyes. *Peaceful Moments* cannot be muzzled. You doubtless mean well, according to your somewhat murky lights, but we are not for sale, except at fifteen cents weekly. From the hills of Maine to the Everglades of Florida, from Portland, Oregon, to Melonsquashville, Tennessee, one sentence is in every man's mouth. And what is that sentence? I give you three guesses. You give it up? It is this: '*Peaceful Moments* cannot be muzzled!'"

Mr. Parker rose.

"Nothing doing, then?" he said.

"Nothing."

Mr. Parker picked up his hat.

"See here," he said, a grating note in his voice, hitherto smooth and conciliatory, "I've no time to fool away talking to you. I've given you your chance. Those stories are going to be stopped. And if you've any sense in you at all, you'll stop them yourself before you get hurt. That's all I've got to say, and that goes."

He went out, closing the door behind him with a bang that added emphasis to his words.

"All very painful and disturbing," murmured Smith. "Comrade Brown!" he called.

Betty came in.

"Did our late visitor bite a piece out of you on his way out? He was in the mood to do something of the sort."

"He seemed angry," said Betty.

"He *was* angry," said Smith. "Do you know what has happened, Comrade Brown? With your very first contribution to the paper you have hit the bull's-eye. You have done the state some service. Friend Parker came as the representative of the owner of those Broster Street houses. He wanted to buy us off. We've got them scared, or he wouldn't have shown his hand with such refreshing candor. Have you any engagements at present?"

"I was just going out to lunch, if you could spare me."

485

"Not alone. This lunch is on the office. As editor of this journal I will entertain you, if you will allow me, to a magnificent banquet. *Peaceful Moments* is grateful to you. *Peaceful Moments,*" he added, with the contented look the Far West editor must have worn as the bullet came through the window, "is, owing to you, going some now."

* * * * *

When they returned from lunch, and reentered the outer office, Pugsy Maloney, raising his eyes for a moment from his book, met them with the information that another caller had arrived and was waiting in the inner room.

"Dere's a guy in dere waitin' to see youse," he said, jerking his head towards the door.

"Yet another guy? This is our busy day. Did he give a name?"

"Says his name's Maude," said Master Maloney, turning a page.

"Maude!" cried Betty, falling back.

Smith beamed.

"Old John Maude!" he said. "Great! I've been wondering what on earth he's been doing with himself all this time. Good-old John! You'll like him," he said, turning, and stopped abruptly, for he was speaking to the empty air. Betty had disappeared.

"Where's Miss Brown, Pugsy?" he said. "Where did she go?"

Pugsy vouchsafed another jerk of the head, in the direction of the outer door.

"She's beaten it," he said. "I seen her make a break for de stairs. Guess she's forgotten to remember somet'ing," he added indifferently, turning once more to his romance of prairie life. "Goils is bone-heads."

CHAPTER XVII

THE MAN AT THE ASTOR

Refraining from discussing with Master Maloney the alleged bone-headedness of girls, Smith went through into the inner room, and found John sitting in the editorial chair, glancing through the latest number of *Peaceful Moments*.

"Why, John, friend of my youth," he said, "where have you been hiding all this time? I called you up at your office weeks ago, and an acid voice informed me that you were no longer there. Have you been fired?"

"Yes," said John. "Why aren't you on the *News* any more? Nobody seemed to know where you were, till I met Faraday this morning, who told me you were here."

Smith was conscious of an impression that in some subtle way John had changed since their last meeting. For a moment he could not have said what had given him this impression. Then it flashed upon him. Before, John had always been, like Mrs. Fezziwig in "The Christmas Carol," one vast substantial smile. He had beamed cheerfully on what to him was evidently the best of all possible worlds. Now, however, it would seem that doubts had occurred to him as to the universal perfection of things. His face was graver. His eyes and his mouth alike gave evidence of disturbing happenings.

In the matter of confidences, Smith was not a believer in spade-work. If they were offered to him, he was invariably sympathetic, but he never dug for them. That John had something on his mind was obvious, but he intended to allow him, if he wished to reveal it, to select his own time for the revelation.

John, for his part, had no intention of sharing this particular trouble even with Smith. It was too new and intimate for discussion.

It was only since his return to New York that the futility of his quest had really come home to him. In the belief of having at last escaped from Mervo he had been inclined to overlook obstacles. It had seemed to him, while he waited for his late subjects to dismiss him, that, once he could move, all would be simple. New York had dispelled that idea. Logically, he saw with perfect clearness, there was no reason why he and Betty should ever meet again.

To retain a spark of hope beneath this knowledge was not easy and John, having been in New York now for nearly three weeks without any encouragement from the fates, was near the breaking point. A gray apathy had succeeded the frenzied restlessness of the first few days. The necessity for some kind of work that would to some extent occupy his mind was borne in upon him, and the thought of Smith had followed naturally. If anybody could supply distraction, it would be Smith. Faraday, another of the temporary exiles from the *News*, whom he had met by chance in Washington Square, had informed him of Smith's new position and of the renaissance of *Peaceful Moments*, and he had hurried to the office to present himself as an unskilled but willing volunteer to the cause. Inspection of the current number of the paper had convinced him that the *Peaceful Moments* atmosphere, if it could not cure, would at least relieve.

"Faraday told me all about what you had done to this paper," he said.
"I came to see if you would let me in on it. I want work."

"Excellent!" said Smith. "Consider yourself one of us."
"I've never done any newspaper work, of course, but—"
"Never!" cried Smith. "Is it so long since the deaf old college days that you forget the *Gridiron*?"

In their last year at Harvard, Smith and John, assisted by others of a congenial spirit, had published a small but lively magazine devoted to college topics, with such success-from one point of view-that on the appearance of the third number it was suppressed by the authorities.

"You were the life and soul of the *Gridiron*," went on Smith. "You shall be the life and soul of *Peaceful Moments*. You have special qualifications for the post. A young man once called at the office of a certain newspaper, and asked for a job. 'Have you any specialty?' enquired the editor. 'Yes,' replied the bright boy, 'I am rather good at invective.' 'Any particular kind of invective?' queried the man up top. 'No,' replied our hero, 'just general invective.' Such is your case, my son. You have a genius for general invective. You are the man *Peaceful Moments* has been waiting for."

"If you think so—"

"I do think so. Let us consider it settled. And now, tell me, what do you think of our little journal?"

"Well-aren't you asking for trouble? Isn't the proprietor—?"

Smith waved his hand airily.

"Dismiss him from your mind," he said. "He is a gentleman of the name of Benjamin Scobell, who—"

"Benjamin Scobell!"

"Who lives in Europe and never sees the paper. I happen to know that he is anxious to get rid of it. His solicitors have instructions to accept any reasonable offer. If only I could close in on a small roll, I would buy it myself, for by the time we have finished our improvements, it will be a sound investment for the young speculator. Have you read the Broster Street story? It has hit somebody already. Already some unknown individual is grasping the lemon in his unwilling fingers. And-to remove any diffidence you may still have about lending your sympathetic aid-that was written by no hardened professional, but by our stenographer. She'll be in soon, and I'll introduce you. You'll like her. I do not despair, later on, of securing an epoch-making contribution from Comrade Maloney."

As he spoke, that bulwark of the paper entered in person, bearing an envelope.

"Ah, Comrade Maloney," said Smith. "Is that your contribution? What is the subject? 'Mustangs I have Met?'"

"A kid brought dis," said Pugsy. "Dere ain't no answer."

Smith read the letter with raised eyebrows.

"We shall have to get another stenographer," he said. "The gifted author of our Broster Street series has quit."

"Oh!" said John, not interested.

"Quit at a moment's notice and without explanation. I can't understand it."

"I guess she had some reason," said John, absently. He was inclined to be absent during these days. His mind was always stealing away to occupy itself with the problem of the discovery of Betty. The motives that might have led a stenographer to resign her position had no interest for him.

Smith shrugged his shoulders.

"Oh, Woman, Woman!" he said resignedly.

"She says she will send in some more Broster Street stuff, though, which is a comfort. But I'm sorry she's quit. You would have liked her."

"Yes?" said John.

At this moment there came from the outer office a piercing squeal. It penetrated into the editorial sanctum, losing only a small part of its strength on the way. Smith looked up with patient sadness.

"If Comrade Maloney," he said, "is going to take to singing during business hours, I fear this journal must put up its shutters. Concentrated thought will be out of the question."

He moved to the door and flung it open as a second squeal rent the air, and found Master Maloney writhing in the grip of a tough-looking person in patched trousers and a stained sweater. His left ear was firmly grasped between the stranger's finger and thumb.

The tough person released Pugsy, and, having eyed Smith keenly for a moment, made a dash for the stairs, leaving the guardian of the gate rubbing his ear resentfully.

"He blows in," said Master Maloney, aggrieved, "an' asks is de editor in. I tells him no, an' he nips me by the ear when I tries to stop him buttin' t'roo."

"Comrade Maloney," said Smith, "you are a martyr. What would Horatius have done if somebody had nipped him by the ear when he was holding the bridge? It might have made all the difference. Did the gentleman state his business?"

"Nope. Just tried to butt t'roo."

"One of these strong, silent men. The world is full of us. These are the perils of the journalistic life. You will be safer and happier when you are a cowboy, Comrade Maloney."

Smith was thoughtful as he returned to the inner room.

"Things are warming up, John," he said. "The sport who has just left evidently came just to get a sight of me. Otherwise, why should he tear himself away without stopping for a chat. I suppose he was sent to mark me down for whichever gang Comrade Parker is employing."

"What do you mean?" said John. "All this gets past me. Who is Parker?"

Smith related the events leading up to Mr. Parker's visit, and described what had happened on that occasion.

"So, before you throw in your lot with this journal," he concluded, "it would be well to think the matter over. You must weigh the pros and cons. Is your passion for literature such that you do not mind being put out of business with a black-jack for the cause? Will the knowledge that a low-browed gentleman is waiting round the corner for you stimulate or hinder you in your work? There's no doubt now that we are up against a tough crowd."

"By Jove!" said John. "I hadn't a notion it was like that."

"You feel, then, that on the whole —"

"I feel that on the whole this is just the business I've been hunting for. You couldn't keep me out of it now with an ax."

Smith looked at him curiously, but refrained from enquiries. That there must be something at the back of this craving for adventure and excitement, he knew. The easy-going John he had known of old would certainly not have deserted the danger zone, but he would not have welcomed entry to it so keenly. It was plain that he was hungry for work that would keep him from thought. Smith was eminently a patient young man, and though the problem of what upheaval had happened to change John to such an extent interested him greatly, he was prepared to wait for explanations.

Of the imminence of the danger he was perfectly aware. He had known from the first that Mr. Parker's concluding words were not an empty threat. His experience as a reporter had given him the knowledge that is only given in its entirety to police and newspaper men: that there are two New Yorks-one, a modern, well-policed city, through which one may walk from end to end without encountering adventure; the other, a city as full of sinister intrigue, of whisperings and conspiracies, of battle, murder, and sudden death in dark byways, as any town of mediaeval Italy. Given certain conditions, anything may happen in New York. And Smith realized that these conditions now prevailed in his own case. He had come into conflict with New York's underworld. Circumstances had placed him below the surface, where only his wits could help him.

He would have been prepared to see the thing through by himself, but there was no doubt that John as an ally would be a distinct comfort.

Nevertheless, he felt compelled to give his friend a last chance of withdrawing.

"You know," he said, "there is really no reason why you should —"

"But I'm going to," interrupted John. "That's all there is to it. What's going to happen, anyway? I don't know anything about these gangs. I thought they spent all their time shooting each other up."

"Not all, unfortunately, Comrade John. They are always charmed to take on a small job like this on the side."

"And what does it come to? Do we have an entire gang camping on our trail in a solid mass, or only one or two toughs?"

"Merely a section, I should imagine. Comrade Parker would go to the main boss of the gang-Bat Jarvis, if it was the Groome Street gang, or Spider Reilly and Dude Dawson if he wanted the Three Points or the Table Hill lot. The boss would chat over the matter with his own special partners, and they would fix it up among themselves. The rest of the gang would probably know nothing about it. The fewer in the game, you see, the fewer to divide the Parker dollars. So what we have to do is to keep a lookout for a dozen or so aristocrats of that dignified deportment which comes from constant association with the main boss, and, if we can elude these, all will be well."

* * * * *

It was by Smith's suggestion that the editorial staff of *Peaceful Moments* dined that night at the Astor roof-garden.

"The tired brain," he said, "needs to recuperate. To feed on such a night as this in some low-down hostelry on the level of the street, with German waiters breathing heavily down the back of one's neck and two fiddles and a piano hitting up ragtime about three feet from one's tympanum, would be false economy. Here, fanned by cool breezes and surrounded by passably fair women and brave men, one may do a certain amount of tissue-restoring. Moreover, there is little danger up here of being slugged by our moth-eaten acquaintance of this afternoon. We shall probably find him waiting for us at the main entrance with a black-jack, but till then —"

He turned with gentle grace to his soup. It was a warm night, and the roof-garden was full. From where they sat they could see the million twinkling lights of the city. John, watching them, as he smoked a cigarette at the conclusion of the meal, had fallen into a dream. He came to himself with a start, to find Smith in conversation with a waiter.

"Yes, my name is Smith," he was saying.

The waiter retired to one of the tables and spoke to a young man sitting there. John, recollected having seen this solitary diner looking in their direction once or twice during dinner, but the fact had not impressed him.

"What's the matter?" he asked.

"The man at that table sent over to ask if my name was Smith. It was. He is now coming along to chat in person. I wonder why. I don't know him from Adam."

The stranger was threading his way between the tables.

"Can I have a word with you, Mr. Smith?" he said. The waiter brought a chair and he seated himself.

"By the way," said Smith, "my friend, Mr. Maude. Your own name will doubtless come up in the course of general chitchat over the coffee-cups."

"Not on your tintype it won't," said the stranger decidedly. "It won't be needed. Is Mr. Maude on your paper? That's all right, then. I can go ahead."

He turned to Smith.

"It's about that Broster Street thing."

"More fame!" murmured Smith. "We certainly are making a hit with the great public over Broster Street."

"Well, you understand certain parties have got it in against you?"

"A charming conversationalist, one Comrade Parker, hinted at something of the sort in a recent conversation. We shall endeavor, however, to look after ourselves."

"You'll need to. The man behind is a big bug."

"Who is he?"

The stranger shrugged his shoulders.

"Search me. You wouldn't expect him to give that away."

"Then on what system have you estimated the size of the gentleman's bug-hood? What makes you think that he's a big bug?"

"By the number of dollars he was ready to put up to have you put through."

Smith's eyes gleamed for an instant, but he spoke as coolly as ever.

"Oh!" he said. "And which gang has he hired?"

"I couldn't say. He-his agent, that is-came to Bat Jarvis. Bat for some reason turned the job down."

"He did? Why?"

"Search me. Nobody knows. But just as soon as he heard who it was he was being asked to lay for, he turned it down cold. Said none of his fellows was going to put a finger on anyone who had anything to do with your paper. I don't know what you've been doing to Bat, but he sure is the long-lost brother to you."

"A powerful argument in favor of kindness to animals!" said Smith. "One of his celebrated stud of cats came into the possession of our stenographer. What did she do? Instead of having the animal made into a nourishing soup, she restored it to its bereaved owner. Observe the sequel. We are very much obliged to Comrade Jarvis."

"He sent me along," went on the stranger, "to tell you to watch out, because one of the other gangs was dead sure to take on the job. And he said you were to know that he wasn't mixed up in it. Well, that's all. I'll be pushing along. I've a date. Glad to have met you, Mr. Maude. Good-night."

For a few moments after he had gone, Smith and John sat smoking in silence.

"What's the time?" asked Smith suddenly. "If it's not too late-Hello, here comes our friend once more."

The stranger came up to the table, a light overcoat over his dress clothes. From the pocket of this he produced a watch.

"Force of habit," he said apologetically, handing it to John. "You'll pardon me. Good-night again."

CHAPTER XVIII

THE HIGHFIELD

John looked after him, open-mouthed. The events of the evening had been a revelation to him. He had not realized the ramifications of New York's underworld. That members of the gangs should appear in gorgeous raiment in the Astor roof-garden was a surprise. "And now," said Smith, "that our friend has so sportingly returned your watch, take a look at it and see the time. Nine? Excellent. We shall do it comfortably."

"What's that?" asked John.

"Our visit to the Highfield. A young friend of mine who is fighting there to-night sent me tickets a few days ago. In your perusal of *Peaceful Moments* you may have chanced to see mention of one Kid Brady. He is the man. I was intending to go in any case, but an idea has just struck me that we might combine pleasure with business. Has it occurred to you that these black-jack specialists may drop in on us at the office? And, if so, that Comrade Maloney's statement that we are not in may be insufficient to keep them out? Comrade Brady would be an invaluable assistant. And as we are his pugilistic sponsors, without whom he would not have got this fight at all, I think we may say that he will do any little thing we may ask of him."

It was certainly true that, from the moment the paper had taken up his cause, Kid Brady's star had been in the ascendant. The sporting pages of the big dailies had begun to notice him, until finally the management of the Highfield Club had signed him on for a ten-round bout with a certain Cyclone Dick Fisher.

"He should," continued Smith, "if equipped in any degree with the finer feelings, be bubbling over with gratitude toward us. At any rate, it is worth investigating."

* * * * *

Far away from the comfortable glare of Broadway, in a place of disheveled houses and insufficient street-lamps, there stands the old warehouse which modern enterprise has converted into the Highfield Athletic and Gymnastic Club. The imagination, stimulated by the title, conjures up picture-covered walls, padded chairs, and seas of white shirt front. The Highfield differs in some respects from this fancy picture. Indeed, it would be hard to find a respect in which it does not differ. But these names are so misleading! The title under which the Highfield used to be known till a few years back was "Swifty Bob's." It was a good, honest title. You knew what to export, and if you attended seances at Swifty Bob's you left your gold watch and your little savings at home. But a wave of anti-pugilistic feeling swept over the New York authorities. Promoters of boxing contests found themselves, to their acute disgust, raided by the police. The industry began to languish. Persons avoided places where at any moment the festivities might be marred by an inrush of large men in blue uniforms, armed with locust sticks.

And then some big-brained person suggested the club idea, which stands alone as an example of American dry humor. At once there were no boxing contests in New York; Swifty Bob and his fellows would have been shocked at the idea of such a thing. All that happened now was exhibition sparring bouts between members of the club. It is true that next day the papers very tactlessly reported the friendly exhibition spar as if it had been quite a serious affair, but that was not the fault of Swifty Bob.

Kid Brady, the chosen of *Peaceful Moments*, was billed for a "ten-round exhibition contest," to be the main event of the evening's entertainment.

* * * * *

A long journey on the subway took them to the neighborhood, and after considerable wandering they arrived at their destination.

Smith's tickets were for a ring-side box, a species of sheep pen of unpolished wood, with four hard chairs in it. The interior of the Highfield Athletic and Gymnastic Club was severely free from anything in the shape of luxury and ornament. Along the four walls were raised benches in tiers. On these were seated as tough-looking a collection of citizens as one might wish to see. On chairs at the ringside were the reporters with tickers at their sides. In the center of the room, brilliantly lighted by half-a-dozen electric chandeliers, was the ring.

There were preliminary bouts before the main event. A burly gentleman in shirt-sleeves entered the ring, followed by two slim youths in fighting costume and a massive person in a red jersey, blue serge trousers, and yellow braces, who chewed gum with an abstracted air throughout the proceedings.

The burly gentleman gave tongue in a voice that cleft the air like a cannon ball.

"Ex-hibit-i-on four-round bout between Patsy Milligan and Tommy
Goodley, members of this club. Patsy on my right, Tommy on my left.
Gentlemen will kindly stop smokin'."

The audience did nothing of the sort. Possibly they did not apply the description to themselves. Possibly they considered the appeal a mere formula. Somewhere in the background a gong sounded, and Patsy, from the right, stepped briskly forward to meet Tommy, approaching from the left.

The contest was short but energetic. At intervals the combatants would cling affectionately to one another, and on these occasions the red-jerseyed man, still chewing gum and still wearing the same air of being lost in abstract thought, would split up the mass by the simple method of ploughing his way between the pair. Toward the end of the first round Thomas, eluding a left swing, put Patrick neatly to the floor, where the latter remained for the necessary ten seconds.

The remaining preliminaries proved disappointing. So much so that in the last of the series a soured sportsman on one of the benches near the roof began in satirical mood to whistle the "Merry Widow Waltz." It was here that the red-jerseyed thinker for the first and last time came out of his meditative trance. He leaned over the ropes, and spoke, without heat, but firmly:

"If that guy whistling back up yonder thinks he can do better than these boys, he can come right down into the ring."

The whistling ceased.

There was a distinct air of relief when the last preliminary was finished and preparations for the main bout began. It did not commence at once. There were formalities to be gone through, introductions and the like. The burly gentleman reappeared from nowhere, ushering into the ring a sheepishly grinning youth in a flannel suit.

"In-ter-*doo*-cin' Young Leary," he bellowed impressively, "a noo member of this club, who will box some good boy here in September."

He walked to the other side of the ring and repeated the remark. A raucous welcome was accorded to the new member.

Two other notable performers were introduced in a similar manner, and then the building became suddenly full of noise, for a tall youth in a bath robe, attended by a little army of assistants, had entered the ring. One of the army carried a bright green bucket, on which were painted in white letters the words "Cyclone Dick Fisher." A moment later there was another, though a far less, uproar, as Kid Brady, his pleasant face wearing a self-conscious smirk, ducked under the ropes and sat down in the opposite corner.

"Ex-hib-it-i-on ten-round bout," thundered the burly gentleman, "between Cyclone Dick Fisher —"

Loud applause. Mr. Fisher was one of the famous, a fighter with a reputation from New York to San Francisco. He was generally considered the most likely man to give the hitherto invincible Jimmy Garvin a hard battle for the light-weight championship.

"Oh, you Dick!" roared the crowd.

Mr. Fisher bowed benevolently.

"—and Kid Brady, member of this—"

There was noticeably less applause for the Kid. He was an unknown. A few of those present had heard of his victories in the West, but these were but a small section of the crowd. When the faint applause had ceased, Smith rose to his feet.

"Oh, you Kid!" he observed encouragingly. "I should not like Comrade Brady," he said, reseating himself, "to think that he has no friend but his poor old mother, as occurred on a previous occasion."

The burly gentleman, followed by the two armies of assistants, dropped down from the ring, and the gong sounded.

Mr. Fisher sprang from his corner as if somebody had touched a spring. He seemed to be of the opinion that if you are a cyclone, it is never too soon to begin behaving like one. He danced round the Kid with an india-rubber agility. The *Peaceful Moments* representative exhibited more stolidity. Except for the fact that he was in fighting attitude, with one gloved hand moving slowly in the neighborhood of his stocky chest, and the other pawing the air on a line with his square jaw, one would have said that he did not realize the position of affairs. He wore the friendly smile of the good-natured guest who is led forward by his hostess to join in some game to amuse the children.

Suddenly his opponent's long left shot out. The Kid, who had been strolling forward, received it under the chin, and continued to stroll forward as if nothing of note had happened. He gave the impression of being aware that Mr. Fisher had committed a breach of good taste and of being resolved to pass it off with ready tact.

The Cyclone, having executed a backward leap, a forward leap, and a feint, landed heavily with both hands. The Kid's genial smile did not even quiver, but he continued to move forward. His opponent's left flashed out again, but this time, instead of ignoring the matter, the Kid replied with a heavy right swing, and Mr. Fisher leaping back, found himself against the ropes. By the time he had got out of that uncongenial position, two more of the Kid's swings had found their mark. Mr. Fisher, somewhat perturbed, scuttled out into the middle of the ring, the Kid following in his self-contained, stolid way.

The Cyclone now became still more cyclonic. He had a left arm which seemed to open out in joints like a telescope. Several times when the Kid appeared well out of distance there was a thud as a brown glove ripped in over his guard and jerked his head back. But always he kept boring in, delivering an occasional right to the body with the pleased smile of an infant destroying a Noah's ark with a tack-hammer. Despite these efforts, however, he was plainly getting all the worst of it. Energetic Mr. Fisher, relying on his long left, was putting in three blows to his one. When the gong sounded, ending the first round, the house was practically solid for the Cyclone. Whoops and yells rose from everywhere. The building rang with shouts of, "Oh, you Dick!"

Smith turned sadly to John.

"It seems to me," he said, "that this merry meeting looks like doing Comrade Brady no good. I should not be surprised at any moment to see his head bounce off on to the floor."

Rounds two and three were a repetition of round one. The Cyclone raged almost unchecked about the ring. In one lightning rally in the third he brought his right across squarely on to the Kid's jaw. It was a blow which should have knocked any boxer out. The Kid merely staggered slightly, and returned to business still smiling.

With the opening of round four there came a subtle change. The Cyclone's fury was expending itself. That long left shot out less sharply. Instead of being knocked back by it, the *Peaceful Moments* champion now took the hits in his stride, and came shuffling in with his damaging body-blows. There were cheers and "Oh, you Dick's!" at the sound of the gong, but there was an appealing note in them this time. The gallant sportsmen whose connection with boxing was confined to watching other men fight and betting on what they considered a certainty, and who would have expired promptly if anyone had tapped them sharply on their well-filled vests, were beginning to fear that they might lose their money after all.

In the fifth round the thing became a certainty. Like the month of March, the Cyclone, who had come in like a lion, was going out like a lamb. A slight decrease in the pleasantness of the Kid's smile was noticeable. His expression began to resemble more nearly the gloomy importance of the *Peaceful Moments* photographs. Yells of agony from panic-stricken speculators around the ring began to smite the rafters. The Cyclone, now but a gentle breeze, clutched repeatedly, hanging on like a leech till removed by the red-jerseyed referee.

Suddenly a grisly silence fell upon the house. For the Kid, battered, but obviously content, was standing in the middle of the ring, while on the ropes the Cyclone, drooping like a wet sock, was sliding slowly to the floor.

"*Peaceful Moments* wins," said Smith. "An omen, I fancy, Comrade John."

Penetrating into the Kid's dressing-room some moments later, the editorial staff found the winner of the ten-round exhibition bout between members of the club seated on a chair having his right leg rubbed by a shock-headed man in a sweater, who had been one of his seconds during the conflict. The Kid beamed as they entered.

"Gents," he said, "come right in. Mighty glad to see you."

"It is a relief to me, Comrade Brady," said Smith, "to find that you can see us. I had expected to find that Comrade Fisher's purposeful wallops had completely closed your star-likes."

"Sure, I never felt them. He's a good, quick boy, is Dick, but," continued the Kid with powerful imagery "he couldn't hit a hole in a block of ice-cream, not if he was to use a coke-hammer."

"And yet at one period in the proceedings," said Smith, "I fancied that your head would come unglued at the neck. But the fear was merely transient. When you began to get going, why, then I felt like some watcher of the skies when a new planet swims into his ken, or like stout Cortez when with eagle eyes he stared at the Pacific."

The Kid blinked.

"How's that?" he enquired.

"And why did I feel like that, Comrade Brady? I will tell you. Because my faith in you was justified. Because there before me stood the ideal fighting editor of *Peaceful Moments*. It is not a post that any weakling can fill. Mere charm of manner cannot qualify a man for the position. No one can hold down the job simply by having a kind heart or being good at comic songs. No. We want a man of thews and sinews, a man who would rather be hit on the head with a half-brick than not. And you, Comrade Brady, are such a man."

The shock-headed man, who during this conversation had been concentrating himself on his subject's left leg now announced that he guessed that would about do, and having advised the Kid not to stop and pick daisies, but to get into his clothes at once before he caught a chill, bade the company goodnight and retired.

Smith shut the door.

"Comrade Brady," he said, "you know those articles about the tenements we've been having in the paper?"

"Sure. I read 'em. They're to the good. It was about time some strong josher came and put it across 'em."

"So we thought. Comrade Parker, however, totally disagreed with us."

"Parker?"

"That's what I'm coming to," said Smith. "The day before yesterday a man named Parker called at the office and tried to buy us off."

"You gave him the hook, I guess?" queried the interested Kid.

"To such an extent, Comrade Brady," said Smith, "that he left breathing threatenings and slaughter. And it is for that reason that we have ventured to call upon you. We're pretty sure by this time that Comrade Parker has put one of the gangs on to us."

"You don't say!" exclaimed the Kid. "Gee! They're tough propositions, those gangs."

"So we've come along to you. We can look after ourselves out of the office, but what we want is someone to help in case they try to rush us there. In brief, a fighting editor. At all costs we must have privacy. No writer can prune and polish his sentences to his satisfaction if he is compelled constantly to break off in order to eject boisterous toughs. We therefore offer you the job of sitting in the outer room and intercepting these bravoes before they can reach us. The salary we leave to you. There are doubloons and to spare in the old oak chest. Take what you need and put the rest-if any-back. How does the offer strike you, Comrade Brady?"

"Gents," said the Kid, "it's this way."

He slipped into his coat, and resumed.

"Now that I've made good by licking Dick, they'll be giving me a chance of a big fight. Maybe with Jimmy Garvin. Well, if that happens, see what I mean? I'll have to be going away somewhere and getting into training. I shouldn't be able to come and sit with you. But, if you gents feel like it, I'd be mighty glad to come in till I'm wanted to go into training camp."

"Great," said Smith. "And touching salary —"

"Shucks!" said the Kid with emphasis. "Nix on the salary thing. I wouldn't take a dime. If it hadn't 'a' been for you, I'd have been waiting still for a chance of lining up in the championship class. That's good enough for me. Any old thing you want me to do, I'll do it, and glad to."

"Comrade Brady," said Smith warmly, "you are, if I may say so, the goods. You are, beyond a doubt, supremely the stuff. We three, then, hand-in-hand, will face the foe, and if the foe has good, sound sense, he will keep right away. You appear to be ready. Shall we meander forth?"

The building was empty and the lights were out when they emerged from the dressing-room. They had to grope their way in darkness. It was raining when they reached the street, and the only signs of life were a moist policeman and the distant glare of saloon lights down the road.

They turned off to the left, and, after walking some hundred yards, found themselves in a blind alley.

"Hello!" said John. "Where have we come to?"

Smith sighed.

"In my trusting way," he said, "I had imagined that either you or Comrade Brady was in charge of this expedition and taking me by a known route to the nearest subway station. I did not think to ask. I placed myself, without hesitation, wholly in your hands."

"I thought the Kid knew the way," said John.

"I was just taggin' along with you gents," protested the light-weight. "I thought you was taking me right. This is the first time I been up here."

"Next time we three go on a little jaunt anywhere," said Smith resignedly, "it would be as well to take a map and a corps of guides with us. Otherwise we shall start for Broadway and finish up at Minneapolis."

They emerged from the blind alley and stood in the dark street, looking doubtfully up and down it.

"Aha!" said Smith suddenly. "I perceive a native. Several natives, in fact. Quite a little covey of them. We will put our case before them, concealing nothing, and rely on their advice to take us to our goal."

A little knot of men was approaching from the left. In the darkness it was impossible to say how many of them were there. Smith stepped forward, the Kid at his side.

"Excuse me, sir," he said to the leader, "but if you can spare me a moment of your valuable time —"

There was a sudden shuffle of feet on the pavement, a quick movement on the part of the Kid, a chunky sound as of wood striking wood, and the man Smith had been addressing fell to the ground in a heap.

As he fell, something dropped from his hand on to the pavement with a bump and a rattle. Stooping swiftly, the Kid picked it up, and handed it to Smith. His fingers closed upon it. It was a short, wicked-looking little bludgeon, the black-jack of the New York tough.

"Get busy," advised the Kid briefly.

CHAPTER XIX

THE FIRST BATTLE

The promptitude and despatch with which the Kid had attended to the gentleman with the black-jack had not been without its effect on the followers of the stricken one. Physical courage is not an outstanding quality of the New York gangsman. His personal preference is for retreat when it is a question of unpleasantness with a stranger. And, in any case, even when warring among themselves, the gangs exhibit a lively distaste for the hard knocks of hand-to-hand fighting. Their chosen method of battling is to lie down on the ground and shoot.

The Kid's rapid work on the present occasion created a good deal of confusion. There was no doubt that much had been hoped for from speedy attack. Also, the generalship of the expedition had been in the hands of the fallen warrior. His removal from the sphere of active influence had left the party without a head. And, to add to their discomfiture, they could not account for the Kid. Smith they knew, and John was to be accounted for, but who was this stranger with the square shoulders and the uppercut that landed like a cannon ball? Something approaching a panic prevailed among the gang.

It was not lessened by the behavior of the intended victims. John was the first to join issue. He had been a few paces behind the others during the black-jack incident, but, dark as it was, he had seen enough to show him that the occasion was, as Smith would have said, one for the shrewd blow rather than the prolonged parley. With a shout, he made a football rush into the confused mass of the enemy. A moment later Smith and the Kid followed, and there raged over the body of the fallen leader a battle of Homeric type.

It was not a long affair. The rules and conditions governing the encounter offended the delicate sensibilities of the gang. Like artists who feel themselves trammeled by distasteful conventions, they were damped and could not do themselves justice. Their forte was long-range fighting with pistols. With that they felt en rapport. But this vulgar brawling in the darkness with muscular opponents who hit hard and often with the clenched fist was distasteful to them. They could not develop any enthusiasm for it. They carried pistols, but it was too dark and the combatants were too entangled to allow them to use these.

There was but one thing to be done. Reluctant as they might be to abandon their fallen leader, it must be done. Already they were suffering grievously from John, the black-jack, and the lightning blows of the Kid. For a moment they hung, wavering, then stampeded in half-a-dozen different directions, melting into the night whence they had come.

John, full of zeal, pursued one fugitive some fifty yards down the street, but his quarry, exhibiting a rare turn of speed, easily outstripped him.

He came back, panting, to find Smith and the Kid examining the fallen leader of the departed ones with the aid of a match, which went out just as John arrived.

The Kid struck another. The head of it fell off and dropped upon the up-turned face. The victim stirred, shook himself, sat up, and began to mutter something in a foggy voice.

"He's still woozy," said the Kid.

"Still-what exactly, Comrade Brady?"

"In the air," explained the Kid. "Bats in the belfry. Dizzy. See what I mean? It's often like that when a feller puts one in with a bit of weight behind it just where that one landed. Gee! I remember when I fought Martin Kelly; I was only starting to learn the game then. Martin and me was mixing it good and hard all over the ring, when suddenly he puts over a stiff one right on the point. What do you think I done? Fall down and take the count? Not on your life. I just turns round and walks straight out of the ring to my dressing-room. Willie Harvey, who was seconding me, comes tearing in after me, and finds me getting into my clothes. 'What's doing, Kid?' he asks. 'I'm going fishin', Willie,' I says. 'It's a lovely day.' 'You've lost the fight,' he

497

says. 'Fight?' says I. 'What fight?' See what I mean? I hadn't a notion of what had happened. It was half an hour and more before I could remember a thing."

During this reminiscence, the man on the ground had contrived to clear his mind of the mistiness induced by the Kid's upper cut. The first sign he showed of returning intelligence was a sudden dash for safety up the road. But he had not gone five yards when he sat down limply.

The Kid was inspired to further reminiscence.

"Guess he's feeling pretty poor," he said. "It's no good him trying to run for a while after he's put his chin in the way of a real live one. I remember when Joe Peterson put me out, way back when I was new to the game-it was the same year I fought Martin Kelly. He had an awful punch, had old Joe, and he put me down and out in the eighth round. After the fight they found me on the fire-escape outside my dressing-room. 'Come in, Kid,' says they. 'It's all right, chaps,' I says, 'I'm dying.' Like that. 'It's all right, chaps, I'm dying.' Same with this guy. See what I mean?"

They formed a group about the fallen black-jack expert.

"Pardon us," said Smith courteously, "for breaking in upon your reverie, but if you could spare us a moment of your valuable time, there are one or two things which we would like to know."

"Sure thing," agreed the Kid.

"In the first place," continued Smith, "would it be betraying professional secrets if you told us which particular bevy of energetic cutthroats it is to which you are attached?"

"Gent," explained the Kid, "wants to know what's your gang."

The man on the ground muttered something that to Smith and John was unintelligible.

"It would be a charity," said the former, "if some philanthropist would give this fellow elocution lessons. Can you interpret, Comrade Brady?"

"Says it's the Three Points," said the Kid.

"The Three Points? That's Spider Reilly's lot. Perhaps this *is* Spider Reilly?"

"Nope," said the Kid. "I know the Spider. This ain't him. This is some other mutt."

"Which other mutt in particular?" asked Smith. "Try and find out, Comrade Brady. You seem to be able to understand what he says. To me, personally, his remarks sound like the output of a gramophone with a hot potato in its mouth."

"Says he's Jack Repetto," announced the interpreter.

There was another interruption at this moment. The bashful Mr. Repetto, plainly a man who was not happy in the society of strangers, made another attempt to withdraw. Reaching out a pair of lean hands, he pulled the Kid's legs from under him with a swift jerk, and, wriggling to his feet, started off again down the road. Once more, however, desire outran performance. He got as far as the nearest street-lamp, but no further. The giddiness seemed to overcome him again, for he grasped the lamp-post, and, sliding slowly to the ground, sat there motionless.

The Kid, whose fall had jolted and bruised him, was inclined to be wrathful and vindictive. He was the first of the three to reach the elusive Mr. Repetto, and if that worthy had happened to be standing instead of sitting it might have gone hard with him. But the Kid was not the man to attack a fallen foe. He contented himself with brushing the dust off his person and addressing a richly abusive flow of remarks to Mr. Repetto.

Under the rays of the lamp it was possible to discern more closely the features of the black-jack exponent. There was a subtle but noticeable resemblance to those of Mr. Bat Jarvis. Apparently the latter's oiled forelock, worn low over the forehead, was more a concession to the general fashion prevailing in gang circles than an expression of personal taste. Mr. Repetto had it, too. In his case it was almost white, for the fallen warrior was an albino. His eyes, which were closed, had white lashes and were set as near together as Nature had been able to manage without actually running them into one another. His underlip protruded and drooped. Looking at him, one felt instinctively that no judging committee of a beauty contest would hesitate a moment before him.

It soon became apparent that the light of the lamp, though bestowing the doubtful privilege of a clearer view of Mr. Repetto's face, held certain disadvantages. Scarcely had the staff of *Peaceful Moments* reached the faint yellow pool of light, in the center of which Mr. Repetto reclined, than, with a suddenness which caused them to leap into the air, there sounded from the darkness down the road the crack-crack-crack of a revolver. Instantly from the opposite direction came other shots. Three bullets cut grooves in the roadway almost at John's feet. The Kid gave a sudden howl. Smith's hat, suddenly imbued with life, sprang into the air and vanished, whirling into the night.

The thought did not come to them consciously at the moment, there being little time to think, but it was evident as soon as, diving out of the circle of light into the sheltering darkness, they crouched down and waited for the next move, that a somewhat skilful ambush had been effected. The other members of the gang, who had fled with such remarkable speed, had by no means been eliminated altogether from the game. While the questioning of Mr. Repetto had been in progress, they had crept back, unperceived except by Mr. Repetto himself. It being too dark for successful shooting, it had become Mr. Repetto's task to lure his captors into the light, which he had accomplished with considerable skill.

For some minutes the battle halted. There was dead silence. The circle of light was empty now. Mr. Repetto had vanished. A tentative shot from nowhere ripped through the air close to where Smith lay flattened on the pavement. And then the pavement began to vibrate and give out a curious resonant sound. Somewhere-it might be near or far —a policeman had heard the shots, and was signaling for help to other policemen along the line by beating on the flagstones with his night stick. The noise grew, filling the still air. From somewhere down the road sounded the ring of running feet.

"De cops!" cried a voice. "Beat it!"

Next moment the night was full of clatter. The gang was "beating it."

Smith rose to his feet and felt his wet and muddy clothes ruefully.

The rescue party was coming up at the gallop.

"What's doing?" asked a voice.

"Nothing now," said the disgusted voice of the Kid from the shadows. "They've beaten it."

The circle of lamplight became as if by mutual consent a general rendezvous. Three gray-clad policemen, tough, clean-shaven men with keen eyes and square jaws, stood there, revolvers in one hand, night sticks in the other. Smith, hatless and muddy, joined them. John and the Kid, the latter bleeding freely from his left ear, the lobe of which had been chipped by a bullet, were the last to arrive.

"What's been the rough-house?" inquired one of the policemen, mildly interested.

"Do you know a sport of the name of Repetto?" enquired Smith.

"Jack Repetto? Sure."

"He belongs to the Three Points," said another intelligent officer, as one naming some fashionable club.

"When next you see him," said Smith, "I should be obliged if you would use your authority to make him buy me a new hat. I could do with another pair of trousers, too, but I will not press the trousers. A new hat is, however, essential. Mine has a six-inch hole in it."

"Shot at you, did they?" said one of the policemen, as who should say, "Tut, tut!"

"Shot at us!" burst out the ruffled Kid. "What do you think's been happening? Think an aeroplane ran into my ear and took half of it off? Think the noise was somebody opening bottles of pop? Think those guys that sneaked off down the road was just training for a Marathon?"

"Comrade Brady," said Smith, "touches the spot. He —"

"Say, are you Kid Brady?" enquired one of the officers. For the first time the constabulary had begun to display real animation.

"Reckoned I'd seen you somewhere!" said another. "You licked Cyclone Dick all right, Kid, I hear."

"And who but a bone-head thought he wouldn't?" demanded the third warmly. "He could whip a dozen Cyclone Dicks in the same evening with his eyes shut."

"He's the next champeen," admitted the first speaker.

"If he juts it over Jimmy Garvin," argued the second.

"Jimmy Garvin!" cried the third. "He can whip twenty Jimmy Garvins with his feet tied. I tell you —"

"I am loath," observed Smith, "to interrupt this very impressive brain barbecue, but, trivial as it may seem to you, to me there is a certain interest in this other little matter of my ruined hat. I know that it may strike you as hypersensitive of us to protest against being riddled with bullets, but —"

"Well, what's been doin'?" inquired the Force. It was a nuisance, this perpetual harping on trifles when the deep question of the light-weight championship of the world was under discussion, but the sooner it was attended to, the sooner it would be over.

John undertook to explain.

"The Three Points laid for us," he said. "This man, Jack Repetto, was bossing the crowd. The Kid put one over on to Jack Repetto's chin, and we were asking him a few questions when the rest came back, and started shooting. Then we got to cover quick, and you came up and they beat it."

"That," said Smith, nodding, "is a very fair *precis* of the evening's events. We should like you, if you will be so good, to corral this Comrade Repetto, and see that he buys me a new hat."

"We'll round Jack up," said one of the policemen indulgently.

"Do it nicely," urged Smith. "Don't go hurting his feelings."

The second policeman gave it as his opinion that Jack was getting too gay. The third policeman conceded this. Jack, he said, had shown signs for some time past of asking for it in the neck. It was an error on Jack's part, he gave his hearers to understand, to assume that the lid was completely off the great city of New York.

"Too blamed fresh he's gettin'," the trio agreed. They seemed to think it was too bad of Jack.

"The wrath of the Law," said Smith, "is very terrible. We will leave the matter, then, in your hands. In the meantime, we should be glad if you would direct us to the nearest subway station. Just at the moment, the cheerful lights of the Great White Way are what I seem chiefly to need."

* * * * *

So ended the opening engagement of the campaign, in a satisfactory but far from decisive victory for the *Peaceful Moments*' army.

"The victory," said Smith, "was not bloodless. Comrade Brady's ear, my hat-these are not slight casualties. On the other hand, the elimination of Comrade Repetto is pleasant. I know few men whom I would not rather meet on a lonely road than Comrade Repetto. He is one of nature's black-jackers. Probably the thing crept upon him slowly. He started, possibly, in a merely tentative way by slugging one of the family circle. His aunt, let us say, or his small brother. But, once started, he is unable to resist the craving. The thing grips him like dram-drinking. He black-jacks now not because he really wants to, but because he cannot help himself. There's something singularly consoling in the thought that Comrade Repetto will no longer be among those present."

"There are others," said John.

"As you justly remark," said Smith, "there are others. I am glad we have secured Comrade Brady's services. We may need them."

CHAPTER XX

BETTY AT LARGE

It was not till Betty found herself many blocks distant from the office of *Peaceful Moments* that she checked her headlong flight. She had run down the stairs and out into the street blindly, filled only with that passion for escape which had swept her away from Mervo. Not till she had dived into the human river of Broadway and reached Times Square did she feel secure. Then, with less haste, she walked on to the park, and sat down on a bench, to think.

Inevitably she had placed her own construction on John's sudden appearance in New York and at the spot where only one person in any way connected with Mervo knew her to be. She did not know that Smith and he were friends, and did not, therefore, suspect that the former and not herself might be the object of his visit. Nor had any word reached her of what had happened at Mervo after her departure. She had taken it for granted that things had continued as she had left them; and the only possible explanation to her of John's presence in New York was that, acting under orders from Mr. Scobell, he had come to try and bring her back.

She shuddered as she conjured up the scene that must have taken place if Pugsy had not mentioned his name and she had gone on into the inner room. In itself the thought that, after what she had said that morning on the island, after she had forced on him, stripping it of the uttermost rag of disguise, the realization of how his position appeared to her, he should have come, under orders, to bring her back, was well-nigh unendurable. But to have met him, to have seen the man she loved plunging still deeper into shame, would have been pain beyond bearing. Better a thousand times than that this panic flight into the iron wilderness of New York.

It was cool and soothing in the park. The roar of the city was hushed. It was pleasant to sit there and watch the squirrels playing on the green slopes or scampering up into the branches through which one could see the gleam of water. Her thoughts became less chaotic. The peace of the summer afternoon stole upon her.

It did not take her long to make up her mind that the door of *Peaceful Moments* was closed to her. John, not finding her, might go away, but he would return. Reluctantly, she abandoned the paper. Her heart was heavy when she had formed the decision. She had been as happy at *Peaceful Moments* as it was possible for her to be now. She would miss Smith and the leisurely work and the feeling of being one of a team, working in a good cause. And that, brought Broster Street back to her mind, and she thought of the children. No, she could not abandon them. She had started the tenement articles, and she would go on with them. But she must do it without ever venturing into the dangerous neighborhood of the office.

A squirrel ran up and sat begging for a nut. Betty searched in the grass in the hope of finding one, but came upon nothing but shells. The squirrel bounded away, with a disdainful flick of the tail.

Betty laughed.

"You think of nothing but food. You ought to be ashamed to be so greedy."

And then it came to her suddenly that it was no trifle, this same problem of food.

The warm, green park seemed to grow chill and gray. Once again she must deal with life's material side.

Her case was at the same time better and worse than it had been on that other occasion when she had faced the future in the French train; better, because then New York had been to her something vague and terrifying, while now it was her city; worse, because she could no longer seek help from Mrs. Oakley.

That Mrs. Oakley had given John the information which had enabled him to discover her hiding-place, Betty felt certain. By what other possible means could he have found it? Why Mrs. Oakley, whom she had considered an ally, should have done so, she did not know. She attributed it to a change of mind, a reconsideration of the case when uninfluenced by sentiment.

And yet it seemed strange. Perhaps John had gone to her and the sight of him had won the old lady over to his side. It might be so. At any rate, it meant that the cottage on Staten Island, like the office of *Peaceful Moments*, was closed to her. She must look elsewhere for help, or trust entirely to herself.

She sat on, thinking, with grave, troubled eyes, while the shadows lengthened and the birds rustled sleepily in the branches overhead.

* * * * *

Among the good qualities, none too numerous, of Mr. Bat Jarvis, of Groome Street in the Bowery, early rising was not included. It was his habit to retire to rest at an advanced hour, and to balance accounts by lying abed on the following morning. This idiosyncrasy of his was well known in the neighborhood and respected, and it was generally bold to be both bad taste and unsafe to visit Bat's shop until near the fashionable hour for luncheon, when the great one, shirt-sleeved and smoking a short pipe, would appear in the doorway, looking out upon the world and giving it to understand that he was now open to be approached by deserving acquaintances.

When, therefore, at ten o'clock in the morning his slumbers were cut short by a sharp rapping at the front door, his first impression was that he had been dreaming. When, after a brief interval, the noise was resumed, he rose in his might and, knuckling the sleep from his eyes, went down, tight-lipped, to interview this person.

He had got as far as a preliminary "Say!" when speech was wiped from his lips as with a sponge, and he stood gaping and ashamed, for the murderer of sleep and untimely knocker on front doors was Betty.

Mr. Jarvis had not forgotten Betty. His meeting with her at the office of *Peaceful Moments* had marked an epoch in his life. Never before had anyone quite like her crossed his path, and at that moment romance had come to him. His was essentially a respectful admiration. He was content-indeed, he preferred to worship from afar. Of his own initiative he would never have met her again. In her presence, with those gray eyes of hers looking at him, tremors ran down his spine, and his conscience, usually a battered and downtrodden wreck, became fiercely aggressive. She filled him with novel emotions, and whether these were pleasant or painful was more than he could say. He had not the gift of analysis where his feelings were concerned. To himself he put it, broadly, that she made him feel like a nickel with a hole in it. But that was not entirely satisfactory. There were other and pleasanter emotions mixed in with this humility. The thought of her made him feel, for instance, vaguely chivalrous. He wanted to do risky and useful things for her. Thus, if any fresh guy should endeavor to get gay with her, it would, he felt, be a privilege to fix that same guy. If she should be in bad, he would be more than ready to get busy on her behalf.

But he had never expected to meet her again, certainly not on his own doorstep at ten in the morning. To Bat ten in the morning was included with the small hours.

Betty smiled at him, a little anxiously. She had no suspicion that she played star to Mr. Jarvis' moth in the latter's life, and, as she eyed him, standing there on the doorstep, her excuse for coming to him began to seem terribly flimsy. Not being aware that he was in reality a tough Bayard, keenly desirous of obeying her lightest word, she had staked her all on the chance of his remembering the cat episode and being grateful on account of it; and in the cold light of the morning this idea, born in the watches of the night, when things tend to lose their proportion, struck her as less happy than she had fancied. Suppose he had forgotten all about it! Suppose he should be violent! For a moment her heart sank. He certainly was not a pleasing and encouraging sight, as he stood there blinking at her. No man looks his best immediately on rising from bed, and Bat, even at his best, was not a hero of romance. His forelock drooped dankly over his brow; there was stubble on his chin; his eyes were red, like a dog's. He did not look like the Fairy Prince who was to save her in her trouble.

"I —I hope you remember me, Mr. Jarvis," she faltered. "Your cat. I —"

He nodded speechlessly. Hideous things happened to his face. He was really trying to smile pleasantly, but it seemed a scowl to Betty, and her voice died away.

Mr. Jarvis spoke.

"Ma'am-sure! —step 'nside."

Betty followed him into the shop. There were birds in cages on the walls, and, patroling the floor, a great company of cats, each with its leather collar. One rubbed itself against Betty's skirt. She picked it up, and began to stroke it. And, looking over its head at Mr. Jarvis, she was aware that he was beaming sheepishly.

His eyes darted away the instant they met hers, but Betty had seen enough to show her that she had mistaken nervousness for truculence. Immediately, she was at her ease, and womanlike, had begun to control the situation. She made conversation pleasantly, praising the cats, admiring the birds, touching lightly on the general subject of domestic pets, until her woman's sixth sense told her that her host's panic had passed, and that she might now proceed to discuss business.

"I hope you don't mind my coming to you, Mr. Jarvis," she said. "You know you told me to if ever I were in trouble, so I've taken you at your word. You don't mind?"

Mr. Jarvis gulped, and searched for words.

"Glad," he said at last.

"I've left *Peaceful Moments*. You know I used to be stenographer there."

She was surprised and gratified to see a look of consternation spread itself across Mr. Jarvis' face. It was a hopeful sign that he should take her cause to heart to such an extent.

But Mr. Jarvis' consternation was not due wholly to solicitude for her. His thoughts at that moment, put, after having been expurgated, into speech, might have been summed up in the line: "Of all sad words of tongue or pen the saddest are these, 'It might have been'!"

"Ain't youse woikin' dere no more? Is dat right?" he gasped. "Gee! I wisht I'd 'a' known it sooner. Why, a guy come to me and wants to give me half a ton of the long green to go to dat poiper what youse was woikin' on and fix de guy what's runnin' it. An' I truns him down 'cos I don't want you to be frown out of your job. Say, why youse quit woikin' dere?" His eyes narrowed as an idea struck him. "Say," he went on, "you ain't bin fired? Has de boss give youse de trun-down? 'Cos if he has, say de woid and I'll fix him for youse, loidy. An' it won't set you back a nickel," he concluded handsomely.

"No, no," cried Betty, horrified. "Mr. Smith has been very kind to me.
I left of my own free will."

Mr. Jarvis looked disappointed. His demeanor was like that of some mediaeval knight called back on the eve of starting out to battle with the Paynim for the honor of his lady.

"What was that you said about the man who came to you and offered you money?" asked Betty.

Her mind had flashed back to Mr. Parker's visit, and her heart was beating quickly.

"Sure! He come to me all right an' wants de guy on de poiper fixed. An'
I truns him down."

"Oh! You won't dream of doing anything to hurt Mr. Smith, will you, Mr.
Jarvis?" said Betty anxiously.

"Not if you say so, loidy."

"And your-friends? You won't let them do anything?"

"Nope."

Betty breathed freely again. Her knowledge of the East Side was small, and that there might be those there who acted independently of Mr. Jarvis, disdainful of his influence, did not occur to her. She returned to her own affairs, satisfied that danger no longer threatened.

"Mr. Jarvis, I wonder if you can help me. I want to find some work to do," she said.

"Woik?"

"I have to earn my living, you see, and I'm afraid I don't know how to begin."

Mr. Jarvis pondered. "What sort of woik?"

"Any sort," said Betty valiantly. "I don't care what it is."

Mr. Jarvis knitted his brows in thought. He was not used to being an employment agency. But Betty was Betty, and even at the cost of a headache he must think of something.

At the end of five minutes inspiration came to him.

"Say," he said, "what do youse call de guy dat sits an' takes de money at an eatin'-joint? Cashier? Well, say, could youse be dat?"

"It would be just the thing. Do you know a place?"

"Sure. Just around de corner. I'll take you dere."

Betty waited while he put on his coat, and they started out. Betty chatted as they walked, but Mr. Jarvis, who appeared a little self-conscious beneath the unconcealed interest of the neighbors, was silent. At intervals he would turn and glare ferociously at the heads that popped out of windows or protruded from doorways. Fame has its penalties, and most of the population of that portion of the Bowery had turned out to see their most prominent citizen so romantically employed as a squire of dames.

After a short walk Bat halted the expedition before a dingy restaurant. The glass window bore in battered letters the name, Fontelli.

"Dis is de joint," he said.

Inside the restaurant a dreamy-eyed Italian sat gazing at vacancy and twirling a pointed mustache. In a far corner a solitary customer was finishing a late breakfast.

Signor Fontelli, for the sad-eyed exile was he, sprang to his feet at the sight of Mr. Jarvis' well-known figure. An ingratiating, but nervous, smile came into view behind the pointed mustache.

"Hey, Tony," said Mr. Jarvis, coming at once to the point, "I want you to know dis loidy. She's going to be cashier at dis joint."

Signor Fontelli looked at Betty and shook his head. He smiled deprecatingly. His manner seemed to indicate that, while she met with the approval of Fontelli, the slave of her sex, to Fontelli, the employer, she appealed in vain. He gave his mustache a sorrowful twirl.

"Ah, no," he sighed. "Not da cashier do I need. I take-a myself da money."

Mr. Jarvis looked at him coldly. He continued to look at him coldly. His lower jaw began slowly to protrude, and his forehead retreated further behind its zareba of forelock.

There was a pause. The signor was plainly embarrassed.

"Dis loidy," repeated Mr. Jarvis, "is cashier at dis joint at six per —" He paused. "Does dat go?" he added smoothly.

Certainly there was magnetism about Mr. Jarvis. With a minimum of words he produced remarkable results. Something seemed to happen suddenly to Signor Fontelli's spine. He wilted like a tired flower. A gesture, in which were blended resignation, humility, and a desire to be at peace with all men, particularly Mr. Jarvis, completed his capitulation.

Mr. Jarvis waited while Betty was instructed in her simple duties, then drew her aside.

"Say," he remarked confidentially, "youse'll be all right here. Six per ain't all de dough dere is in de woild, but, bein' cashier, see, you can swipe a whole heap more whenever you feel like it. And if Tony registers a kick, I'll come around and talk to him-see? Dat's right. Good-morning, loidy."

And, having delivered these admirable hints to young cashiers in a hurry to get rich, Mr. Jarvis ducked his head in a species of bow, declined to be thanked, and shuffled out into the street, leaving Betty to open her new career by taking thirty-seven cents from the late breakfaster.

CHAPTER XXI

CHANGES IN THE STAFF

Three days had elapsed since the battle which had opened the campaign, and there had been no further movement on the part of the enemy. Smith was puzzled. A strange quiet seemed to be brooding over the other camp. He could not believe that a single defeat had crushed the foe, but it was hard to think of any other explanation.

It was Pugsy Maloney who, on the fourth morning, brought to the office the inner history of the truce. His version was brief and unadorned, as was the way with his narratives. Such things as first causes and piquant details he avoided, as tending to prolong the telling excessively, thus keeping him from the perusal of his cowboy stories. He gave the thing out merely as an item of general interest, a bubble on the surface of the life of a great city. He did not know how nearly interested were his employers in any matter touching that gang which is known as the Three Points.

Pugsy said: "Dere's been fuss'n going on down where I live. Dude Dawson's mad at Spider Reilly, and now de Table Hills is layin' for de T'ree Points, to soak it to 'em. Dat's right."

He then retired to his outer fastness, yielding further details jerkily and with the distrait air of one whose mind is elsewhere.

Skilfully extracted and pieced together, these details formed themselves into the following typical narrative of East Side life.

There were four really important gangs in New York at this time. There were other less important institutions besides, but these were little more than mere friendly gatherings of old boyhood chums for purposes of mutual companionship. They might grow into formidable organizations in time, but for the moment the amount of ice which good judges declared them to cut was but small. They would "stick up" an occasional wayfarer for his "cush," and they carried "canisters" and sometimes fired them off, but these things do not signify the cutting of ice. In matters political there were only four gangs which counted, the East Side, the Groome Street, the Three Points and the Table Hill. Greatest of these, by virtue of their numbers, were the East Side and the Groome Street, the latter presided over at the time of this story by Mr. Bat Jarvis. These two were colossal, and, though they might fight each other, were immune from attack at the hands of the rest.

But between the other gangs, and especially between the Table Hill and the Three Points, which were much of a size, warfare raged as frequently as among the Republics of South America. There had always been bad blood between the Table Hill and the Three Points. Little events, trifling in themselves, had always occurred to shatter friendly relations just when there seemed a chance of their being formed. Thus, just as the Table Hillites were beginning to forgive the Three Points for shooting the redoubtable Paul Horgan down at Coney Island, a Three Pointer injudiciously wiped out a Table Hillite near Canal Street. He pleaded self-defense, and in any case it was probably mere thoughtlessness, but nevertheless the Table Hillites were ruffled.

That had been a month or so back. During that month things had been simmering down, and peace was just preparing to brood when there occurred the incident alluded to by Pugsy, the regrettable falling out between Dude Dawson and Spider Reilly.

To be as brief as possible, Dude Dawson had gone to spend a happy evening at a dancing saloon named Shamrock Hall, near Groome Street. Now, Shamrock Hall belonged to a Mr. Maginnis, a friend of Bat Jarvis, and was under the direct protection of that celebrity. It was, therefore, sacred ground, and Mr. Dawson visited it in a purely private and peaceful capacity. The last thing he intended was to spoil the harmony of the evening.

Alas for the best intentions! Two-stepping clumsily round the room-for he was a poor, though enthusiastic, dancer-Dude Dawson collided with and upset a certain Reddy Davis and his partner. Reddy Davis was a member of the Three Points, and his temper was the temper of a red-headed man. He "slugged" Mr. Dawson. Mr. Dawson, more skilful at the fray than at the dance, joined battle willingly, and they were absorbed in a stirring combat, when an interruption occurred. In the far corner of the room, surrounded by admiring friends, sat Spider Reilly, monarch of the Three Points. He had noticed that there was a slight disturbance at the other side of the hall, but had given it little attention till the dancing ceasing suddenly and the floor emptying itself of its crowd, he had a plain view of Mr. Dawson and Mr. Davis squaring up at each other for the second round.

We must assume that Mr. Reilly was not thinking of what he did, for his action was contrary to all rules of gang etiquette. In the street it would have been perfectly legitimate, even praiseworthy, but in a dance-hall under the protection of a neutral power it was unpardonable.

What he did was to produce his revolver, and shoot the unsuspecting Mr. Dawson in the leg. Having done which, he left hurriedly, fearing the wrath of Bat Jarvis.

Mr. Dawson, meanwhile, was attended to and helped home. Willing informants gave him the name of his aggressor, and before morning the Table Hill camp was in a ferment. Shooting broke out in three places, though there were no casualties.

When the day dawned there existed between the two gangs a state of war more bitter than any in their record, for this time it was chieftain who had assaulted chieftain, Royal blood had been spilt.

Such was the explanation of the lull in the campaign against *Peaceful Moments*. The new war had taken the mind of Spider Reilly and his warriors off the paper and its affairs for the moment, much as the unexpected appearance of a mad bull would make a man forget that he had come out snipe-shooting.

At present there had been no pitched battle. As was usual between the gangs, war had broken out in a somewhat tentative fashion at first. There had been skirmishes by the wayside, but nothing more. The two armies were sparring for an opening.

* * * * *

Smith was distinctly relieved at the respite, for necessitating careful thought. This was the defection of Kid Brady.

The Kid's easy defeat of Cyclone Dick Fisher had naturally created a sensation in sporting circles. He had become famous in a night. It was not with surprise, therefore, that Smith received from his fighting editor the information that he had been matched against one Eddie Wood, whose fame outshone even that of the late Cyclone.

The Kid, a white man to the core, exhibited quite a feudal loyalty to the paper which had raised him from the ruck and placed him on the road to eminence.

"Say the word," he said, "and I'll call it off. If you feel you need me around here, Mr. Smith, say so, and I'll side-step Eddie."

"Comrade Brady," said Smith with enthusiasm, "I have had occasion before to call you sport. I do so again. But I'm not going to stand in your way. If you eliminate this Comrade Wood, they will have to give you a chance against Jimmy Garvin, won't they?"

"I guess that's right," said the Kid. "Eddie stayed nineteen rounds against Jimmy, and, if I can put him away, it gets me clear into line with Jim, and he'll have to meet me."

"Then go in and win, Comrade Brady. We shall miss you. It will be as if a ray of sunshine had been removed from the office. But you mustn't throw a chance away."

"I'll train at White Plains," said the Kid, "so I'll be pretty near in case I'm wanted."

"Oh, we shall be all right," said Smith, "and if you win, we'll bring out a special number. Good luck, Comrade Brady, and many thanks for your help."

* * * * *

John, when he arrived at the office and learned the news, was for relying on their own unaided efforts.

"And, anyway," he said, "I don't see who else there is to help us. You could tell the police, I suppose," he went on doubtfully.

Smith shook his head.

"The New York policeman, Comrade John, is, like all great men, somewhat peculiar. If you go to a New York policeman and exhibit a black eye, he is more likely to express admiration for the handiwork of the citizen responsible for the same than sympathy. No; since coming to this city I have developed a habit of taking care of myself, or employing private help. I do not want allies who will merely shake their heads at Comrade Reilly and his merry men, however sternly. I want someone who, if necessary, will soak it to them good."

"Sure," said John. "But who is there now the Kid's gone?"

"Who else but Comrade Jarvis?" said Smith.

"Jarvis? Bat Jarvis?"

"The same. I fancy that we shall find, on enquiry, that we are ace high with him. At any rate, there is no harm in sounding him. It is true that he may have forgotten, or it may be that it is to Comrade Brown alone that he is —"

"Who's Brown?" asked John.

"Our late stenographer," explained Smith. "A Miss Brown. She entertained Comrade Jarvis' cat, if you remember. I wonder what has become of her. She has sent in three more corking efforts on the subject of Broster Street, but she gives no address. I wish I knew where she was. I'd have liked for you to meet her."

CHAPTER XXII

A GATHERING OF CAT SPECIALISTS

"It will probably be necessary," said Smith, as they set out for Groome Street, "to allude to you, Comrade John, in the course of this interview, as one of our most eminent living cat-fanciers. You have never met Comrade Jarvis, I believe? Well, he is a gentleman with just about enough forehead to prevent his front hair getting inextricably blended with his eyebrows, and he owns twenty-three cats, each with a leather collar round its neck. It is, I fancy, the cat note which we shall have to strike to-day. If only Comrade Brown were with us, we could appeal to his finer feelings. But he has seen me only once and you never, and I should not care to bet that he will feel the least particle of dismay at the idea of our occiputs getting all mussed up with a black-jack. But when I inform him that you are an English cat-fancier, and that in your island home you have seventy-four fine cats, mostly Angoras, that will be a different matter. I shall be surprised if he does not fall on your neck."

They found Mr. Jarvis in his fancier's shop, engaged in the intellectual occupation of greasing a cat's paws with butter. He looked up as they entered, and then resumed his task.

"Comrade Jarvis," said Smith, "we meet again. You remember me?"

"Nope," said Mr. Jarvis promptly.

Smith was not discouraged.

"Ah!" he said tolerantly, "the fierce rush of New York life! How it wipes from the retina to-day the image impressed on it but yesterday. Is it not so, Comrade Jarvis?"

The cat-expert concentrated himself on his patient's paws without replying.

"A fine animal," said Smith, adjusting his monocle. "To what particular family of the *Felis Domestica* does that belong? In color it resembles a Neapolitan ice more than anything."

Mr. Jarvis' manner became unfriendly.

"Say, what do youse want? That's straight, ain't it? If youse want to buy a boid or a snake, why don't youse say so?"

"I stand corrected," said Smith; "I should have remembered that time is money. I called in here partly in the hope that, though you only met me once-on the stairs of my office, you might retain pleasant recollections of me, but principally in order that I might make two very eminent cat-fanciers acquainted. This," he said, with a wave of his hand in the direction of John, "is Comrade Maude, possibly the best known of English cat-fanciers. Comrade Maude's stud of Angoras is celebrated wherever the English language is spoken."

Mr. Jarvis's expression changed. He rose, and, having inspected John with silent admiration for a while, extended a well-buttered hand towards him. Smith looked on benevolently.

"What Comrade Maude does not know about cats," he said, "is not knowledge. His information on Angoras alone would fill a volume."

"Say" —Mr. Jarvis was evidently touching on a point which had weighed deeply upon him— "why's catnip called catnip?"

John looked at Smith helplessly. It sounded like a riddle, but it was obvious that Mr. Jarvis's motive in putting the question was not frivolous. He really wished to know.

"The word, as Comrade Maude was just about to observe," said Smith, "is a corruption of catmint. Why it should be so corrupted I do not know. But what of that? The subject is too deep to be gone fully into at the moment. I should recommend you to read Mr. Maude's little brochure on the matter. Passing lightly on from that —"

"Did youse ever have a cat dat ate bettles?" enquired Mr. Jarvis.

"There was a time when many of Comrade Maude's *Felidae* supported life almost entirely on beetles."

"Did they git thin?"

John felt it was time, if he were to preserve his reputation, to assert himself.

"No," he replied firmly.

Mr. Jarvis looked astonished.

"English beetles," said Smith, "don't make cats thin. Passing lightly —"

"I had a cat oncst," said Mr. Jarvis, ignoring the remark and sticking to his point, "dat ate beetles and got thin and used to tie itself inter knots."

"A versatile animal," agreed Smith.

"Say," Mr. Jarvis went on, now plainly on a subject near to his heart, "dem beetles is fierce. Sure! Can't keep de cats off of eatin' dem, I can't. First t'ing you know dey've swallowed dem, and den dey gits thin and ties theirselves into knots."

"You should put them into strait-waistcoats," said Smith. "Passing, however, lightly —"

"Say, ever have a cross-eyed cat?"

"Comrade Maude's cats," said Smith, "have happily been almost entirely free from strabismus."

"Dey's lucky, cross-eyed cats is. You has a cross-eyed cat, and not'in' don't never go wrong. But, say, was dere ever a cat wit' one blue and one yaller one in your bunch? Gee! it's fierce when it's like dat. It's a skidoo, is a cat wit' one blue eye and one yaller one. Puts you in bad, surest t'ing you know. Oncst a guy give me a cat like dat, and first t'ing you know I'm in bad all round. It wasn't till I give him away to de cop on de corner and gets me one dat's cross-eyed dat I lifts de skidoo off of me."

"And what happened to the cop?" enquired Smith, interested.

"Oh, he got in bad, sure enough," said Mr. Jarvis without emotion. "One of de boys what he'd pinched and had sent up the road once lays for him and puts one over on him wit a blackjack. Sure. Dat's what comes of havin' a cat wit' one blue and one yaller one."

Mr. Jarvis relapsed into silence. He seemed to be meditating on the inscrutable workings of Fate. Smith took advantage of the pause to leave the cat topic and touch on matters of more vital import.

"Tense and exhilarating as is this discussion of the optical peculiarities of cats," he said, "there is another matter on which, if you will permit me, I should like to touch. I would hesitate to bore you with my own private troubles, but this is a matter which concerns Comrade Maude as well as myself, and I can see that your regard for Comrade Maude is almost an obsession."

"How's that?"

"I can see," said Smith, "that Comrade Maude is a man to whom you give the glad hand."

Mr. Jarvis regarded John with respectful affection.

"Sure! He's to the good, Mr. Maude is."

"Exactly," said Smith. "To resume, then. The fact is, Comrade Jarvis, we are much persecuted by scoundrels. How sad it is in this world! We look to every side. We look to north, east, south, and west, and what do we see? Mainly scoundrels. I fancy you have heard a little about our troubles before this. In fact, I gather that the same scoundrels actually approached you with a view to engaging your services to do us up, but that you very handsomely refused the contract. We are the staff of *Peaceful Moments*."

"*Peaceful Moments*," said Mr. Jarvis. "Sure, dat's right. A guy comes to me and says he wants you put through it, but I gives him de trundown."

"So I was informed," said Smith. "Well, failing you, they went to a gentleman of the name of Reilly —"

"Spider Reilly?"

"Exactly. Spider Reilly, the lessee and manager of the Three Points gang."

Mr. Jarvis frowned.

"Dose T'ree Points, dey're to de bad. Dey're fresh."

"It is too true, Comrade Jarvis."

"Say," went on Mr. Jarvis, waxing wrathful at the recollection, "what do youse t'ink dem fresh stiffs done de odder night? Started some rough woik in me own dance-joint."

"Shamrock Hall?" said Smith. "I heard about it."

"Dat's right, Shamrock Hall. Got gay, dey did, wit' some of the Table Hillers. Say, I got it in for dem gazebos, sure I have. Surest t'ing you know."

Smith beamed approval.

"That," he said, "is the right spirit. Nothing could be more admirable. We are bound together by our common desire to check the ever-growing spirit of freshness among the members of the Three Points. Add to that the fact that we are united by a sympathetic knowledge of the manners and customs of cats, and especially that Comrade Maude, England's greatest fancier, is our mutual friend, and what more do we want? Nothing."

"Mr. Maude's to de good," assented Mr. Jarvis, eying John once more in friendly fashion.

"We are all to the good," said Smith. "Now, the thing I wished to ask you is this. The office of the paper was, until this morning, securely guarded by Comrade Brady, whose name will be familiar to you."

"De Kid?"

"On the bull's-eye, as usual. Kid Brady, the coming light-weight champion of the world. Well, he has unfortunately been compelled to leave us, and the way into the office is consequently clear to any sand-bag specialist who cares to wander in. So what I came to ask was, will you take Comrade Brady's place for a few days?"

"How's that?"

"Will you come in and sit in the office for the next day or so and help hold the fort? I may mention that there is money attached to the job. We will pay for your services."

Mr. Jarvis reflected but a brief moment.

"Why, sure," he said. "Me fer dat."

"Excellent, Comrade Jarvis. Nothing could be better. We will see you to-morrow, then. I rather fancy that the gay band of Three Pointers who will undoubtedly visit the offices of *Peaceful Moments* in the next few days is scheduled to run up against the surprise of their lives."

"Sure t'ing. I'll bring me canister."

"Do," said Smith. "In certain circumstances one canister is worth a flood of rhetoric. Till to-morrow, then, Comrade Jarvis. I am very much obliged to you."

* * * * *

"Not at all a bad hour's work," he said complacently, as they turned out of Groome Street. "A vote of thanks to you, John, for your invaluable assistance."

"I didn't do much," said John, with a grin.

"Apparently, no. In reality, yes. Your manner was exactly right. Reserved, yet not haughty. Just what an eminent cat-fancier's manner should be. I could see that you made a pronounced hit with Comrade Jarvis. By the way, as he is going to show up at the office to-morrow, perhaps it would be as well if you were to look up a few facts bearing on the feline world. There is no knowing what thirst for information a night's rest may not give Comrade Jarvis. I do not presume to dictate, but if you were to make yourself a thorough master of the subject of catnip, for instance, it might quite possibly come in useful."

CHAPTER XXIII

THE RETIREMENT OF SMITH

The first member of the staff of *Peaceful Moments* to arrive at the office on the following morning was Master Maloney. This sounds like the beginning of a "Plod and Punctuality," or "How Great Fortunes have been Made" story, but, as a matter of fact, Master Maloney, like Mr. Bat Jarvis, was no early bird. Larks who rose in his neighborhood, rose alone. He did not get up with them. He was supposed to be at the office at nine o'clock. It was a point of honor with him, a sort of daily declaration of independence, never to put in an appearance before nine-thirty. On this particular morning he was punctual to the minute, or half an hour late, whichever way you choose to look at it.

He had only whistled a few bars of "My Little Irish Rose," and had barely got into the first page of his story of life on the prairie, when Kid Brady appeared. The Kid had come to pay a farewell visit. He had not yet begun training, and he was making the best of the short time before such comforts should be forbidden by smoking a big black cigar. Master Maloney eyed him admiringly. The Kid, unknown to that gentleman himself, was Pugsy's ideal. He came from the Plains, and had, indeed, once actually been a cowboy; he was a coming champion; and he could smoke big black cigars. There was no trace of his official well-what-is-it-now? air about Pugsy as he laid down his book and prepared to converse.

"Say, Mr. Smith around anywhere, Pugsy?" asked the Kid.

"Naw, Mr. Brady. He ain't came yet," replied Master Maloney respectfully.

"Late, ain't he?"

"Sure! He generally blows in before I do."

"Wonder what's keepin' him?"

As he spoke, John appeared. "Hello, Kid," he said. "Come to say good-by?"

"Yep," said the Kid. "Seen Mr. Smith around anywhere, Mr. Maude?"

"Hasn't he come yet? I guess he'll be here soon. Hello, who's this?"

A small boy was standing at the door, holding a note.

"Mr. Maude?" he said. "Cop at Jefferson Market give me dis fer you."

"What!" He took the letter, and gave the boy a dime. "Why, it's from Smith. Great Scott!"

It was apparent that the Kid was politely endeavoring to veil his curiosity. Master Maloney had no such delicacy.

"What's in de letter, boss?" he enquired.

"The letter," said John slowly, "is from Mr. Smith. And it says that he was sentenced this morning to thirty days on the Island for resisting the police."

"He's de guy!" admitted Master Maloney approvingly.

"What's that?" said the Kid. "Mr. Smith been slugging cops! What's he been doin' that for?"

"I must go and find out at once. It beats me."

It did not take John long to reach Jefferson Market, and by the judicious expenditure of a few dollars he was enabled to obtain an interview with Smith in a back room.

The editor of *Peaceful Moments* was seated on a bench, looking remarkably disheveled. There was a bruise on his forehead, just where the hair began. He was, however, cheerful.

"Ah, John," he said. "You got my note all right, then?" John looked at him, concerned.

"What on earth does it all mean?"

Smith heaved a regretful sigh.

"I fear," he said, "I have made precisely the blamed fool of myself that Comrade Parker hoped I would."

"Parker!"

Smith nodded.

"I may be misjudging him, but I seem to see the hand of Comrade Parker in this. We had a raid at my house last night, John. We were pulled."

"What on earth —?"

"Somebody-if it was not Comrade Parker it was some other citizen dripping with public spirit-tipped the police off that certain sports were running a pool-room in the house where I live."

On his departure from the *News*, Smith, from motives of economy, had moved from his hotel in Washington Square and taken a furnished room on Fourteenth Street.

"There actually was a pool-room there," he went on, "so possibly I am wronging Comrade Parker in thinking that this was a scheme of his for getting me out of the way. At any rate, somebody gave the tip, and at about three o'clock this morning I was aroused from a dreamless slumber by quite a considerable hammering at my door. There, standing on the mat, were two policemen. Very cordially the honest fellows invited me to go with them. A conveyance, it seemed, waited in the street without. I disclaimed all connection with the bad gambling persons below, but they replied that they were cleaning up the house, and, if I wished to make any remarks, I had better make them to the magistrate. This seemed reasonable. I said I would put on some clothes and come along. They demurred. They said they couldn't wait about while I put on clothes. I pointed out that sky-blue pajamas with old-rose frogs were not the costume in which the editor of a great New York weekly paper should be seen abroad in one of the world's greatest cities, but they assured me-more by their manner than their words-that my misgivings were groundless, so I yielded. These men, I told myself, have lived longer in New York than I. They know what is done, and what is not done. I will bow to their views. So I was starting to go with them like a lamb, when one of them gave me a shove in the ribs with his night stick. And it was here that I fancy I may have committed a slight error of policy."

He smiled dreamily for a moment, then went on.

"I admit that the old Berserk blood of the Smiths boiled at that juncture. I picked up a sleep-producer from the floor, as Comrade Brady would say, and handed it to the big-stick merchant. He went down like a sack of coal over the bookcase, and at that moment I rather fancy the other gentleman must have got busy with his club. At any rate, somebody suddenly loosed off some fifty thousand dollars' worth of fireworks, and the next thing I knew was that the curtain had risen for the next act on me, discovered sitting in a prison cell, with an out-size in lumps on my forehead."

He sighed again.

"What *Peaceful Moments* really needs," he said, "is a *sitz-redacteur*. A *sitz-redacteur*, John, is a gentleman employed by German newspapers with a taste for *lese-majeste* to go to prison whenever required in place of the real editor. The real editor hints in his bright and snappy editorial, for instance, that the Kaiser's mustache gives him bad dreams. The police force swoops down in a body on the office of the journal, and are met by the *sitz-redacteur*, who goes with them cheerfully, allowing the editor to remain and sketch out plans for his next week's article on the Crown Prince. We need a *sitz-redacteur* on *Peaceful Moments* almost as much as a fighting editor. Not now, of course. This has finished the thing. You'll have to close down the paper now."

"Close it down!" cried John. "You bet I won't."

"My dear old son," said Smith seriously, "what earthly reason have you for going on with it? You only came in to help me, and I am no more. I am gone like some beautiful flower that withers in the night. Where's the sense of getting yourself beaten up then? Quit!"

John shook his head.

"I wouldn't quit now if you paid me."

"But —"

A policeman appeared at the door.

"Say, pal," he remarked to John, "you'll have to be fading away soon, I guess. Give you three minutes more. Say it quick."

He retired. Smith looked at John.

"You won't quit?" he said.

"No."

Smith smiled.

"You're an all-wool sport, John," he said. "I don't suppose you know how to spell quit. Well, then, if you are determined to stand by the ship like Comrade Casabianca, I'll tell you an idea that came to me in the watches of the night. If ever you want to get ideas, John, you spend a night in one of these cells. They flock to you. I suppose I did more profound thinking last night than I've ever done in my life. Well, here's the idea. Act on it or not, as you please. I was thinking over the whole business from soup to nuts, and it struck me that the queerest part of it all is that whoever owns these Broster Street tenements should care a Canadian dime whether we find out who he is or not."

"Well, there's the publicity," began John.

"Tush!" said Smith. "And possibly bah! Do you suppose that the sort of man who runs Broster Street is likely to care a darn about publicity? What does it matter to him if the papers soak it to him for about two days? He knows they'll drop him and go on to something else on the third, and he knows he's broken no law. No, there's something more in this business than that. Don't think that this bright boy wants to hush us up simply because he is a sensitive plant who can't bear to think that people should be cross with him. He has got some private reason for wanting to lie low."

"Well, but what difference —?"

"Comrade, I'll tell you. It makes this difference: that the rents are almost certainly collected by some confidential person belonging to his own crowd, not by an ordinary collector. In other words, the collector knows the name of the man he's collecting for. But for this little misfortune of mine, I was going to suggest that we waylay that collector, administer the Third Degree, and ask him who his boss is."

John uttered an exclamation.

"You're right! I'll do it."

"You think you can? Alone?"

"Sure! Don't you worry. I'll—"

The door opened and the policeman reappeared.

"Time's up. Slide, sonny."

John said good-by to Smith, and went out. He had a last glimpse of his late editor, a sad smile on his face, telling the policeman what was apparently a humorous story. Complete good will seemed to exist between them. John consoled himself as he went away with the reflection that Smith's was a temperament that would probably find a bright side even to a thirty-days' visit to Blackwell's Island.

He walked thoughtfully back to the office. There was something lonely, and yet wonderfully exhilarating, in the realization that he was now alone and in sole charge of the campaign. It braced him. For the first time in several weeks he felt positively light-hearted.

CHAPTER XXIV

THE CAMPAIGN QUICKENS

Mr. Jarvis was as good as his word. Early in the afternoon he made his appearance at the office of *Peaceful Moments*, his forelock more than usually well oiled in honor of the occasion, and his right coat-pocket bulging in a manner that betrayed to the initiated eye the presence of his trusty "canister." With him, in addition, he brought a long, thin young man who wore under his brown tweed coat a blue-and-red striped sweater. Whether he brought him as an ally in case of need or merely as a kindred soul with whom he might commune during his vigil, did not appear.

Pugsy, startled out of his wonted calm by the arrival of this distinguished company, gazed after the pair, as they passed into the inner office, with protruding eyes.

John greeted the allies warmly, and explained Smith's absence. Mr. Jarvis listened to the story with interest, and introduced his colleague.

"T'ought I'd let him chase along. Long Otto's his monaker."

"Sure!" said John. "The more the merrier. Take a seat. You'll find cigars over there. You won't mind my not talking for the moment? There's a wad of work to clear up."

This was an overstatement. He was comparatively free of work, press day having only just gone by; but he was keenly anxious to avoid conversation on the subject of cats, of his ignorance of which Mr. Jarvis's appearance had suddenly reminded him. He took up an old proof sheet and began to glance through it, frowning thoughtfully.

Mr. Jarvis regarded the paraphernalia of literature on the table with interest. So did Long Otto, who, however, being a man of silent habit, made no comment. Throughout the seance and the events which followed it he confined himself to an occasional grunt. He seemed to lack other modes of expression.

"Is dis where youse writes up pieces fer de poiper?" enquired Mr. Jarvis.

"This is the spot," said John. "On busy mornings you could hear our brains buzzing in Madison Square Garden. Oh, one moment."

He rose and went into the outer office.

"Pugsy," he said, "do you know Broster Street?"

"Sure."

"Could you find out for me exactly when the man comes round collecting the rents?"

"Surest t'ing you know. I knows a kid what knows anodder kid what lives dere."

"Then go and do it now. And, after you've found out, you can take the rest of the day off."

"Me fer dat," said Master Maloney with enthusiasm. "I'll take me goil to de Bronx Zoo."

"Your girl? I didn't know you'd got a girl, Pugsy. I always imagined you as one of those strong, stern, blood-and-iron men who despised girls. Who is she?"

"Aw, she's a kid," said Pugsy. "Her pa runs a delicatessen shop down our street. She ain't a bad mutt," added the ardent swain. "I'm her steady."

"Well, mind you send me a card for the wedding. And if two dollars would be a help—"

"Sure t'ing. T'anks, boss. You're all right."

It had occurred to John that the less time Pugsy spent in the outer office during the next few days, the better. The lull in the warfare could not last much longer, and at any moment a visit from Spider Reilly and his adherents might be expected. Their probable first move in such an event would be to knock Master Maloney on the head to prevent his giving warning of their approach.

Events proved that he had not been mistaken. He had not been back in the inner office for more than a quarter of an hour when there came from without the sound of stealthy movements.

514

The handle of the door began to revolve slowly and quietly. The next moment three figures tumbled into the room.

It was evident that they had not expected to find the door unlocked, and the absence of resistance when they applied their weight had surprising effects. Two of the three did not pause in their career till they cannoned against the table. The third checked himself by holding the handle.

John got up coolly.

"Come right in," he said. "What can we do for you?" It had been too dark on the other occasion of his meeting with the Three Pointers to take note of their faces, though he fancied that he had seen the man holding the door-handle before. The others were strangers. They were all exceedingly unprepossessing in appearance.

There was a pause. The three marauders had become aware of the presence of Mr. Jarvis and his colleague, and the meeting was causing them embarrassment, which may have been due in part to the fact that both had produced and were toying meditatively with ugly-looking pistols.

Mr. Jarvis spoke.

"Well," he said, "what's doin'?"

The man to whom the question was directly addressed appeared to have some difficulty in finding a reply. He shuffled his feet, and looked at the floor. His two companions seemed equally at a loss.

"Goin' to start anything?" enquired Mr. Jarvis, casually.

The humor of the situation suddenly tickled John. The embarrassment of the uninvited guests was ludicrous.

"You've just dropped in for a quiet chat, is that it?" he said. "Well, we're all delighted to see you. The cigars are on the table. Draw up your chairs."

Mr. Jarvis opposed the motion. He drew slow circles in the air with his revolver.

"Say! Youse had best beat it. See?"

Long Otto grunted sympathy with the advice.

"And youse had best go back to Spider Reilly," continued Mr. Jarvis, "and tell him there ain't nothin' doing in the way of rough-house wit' dis gent here. And you can tell de Spider," went on Bat with growing ferocity, "dat next time he gits fresh and starts in to shootin' up my dance-joint, I'll bite de head off'n him. See? Dat goes. If he t'inks his little two-by-four crowd can git way wit' de Groome Street, he's got anodder guess comin'. An' don't fergit dis gent here and me is friends, and anyone dat starts anyt'ing wit' dis gent is going to find trouble. Does dat go? Beat it."

He jerked his shoulder in the direction of the door.

The delegation then withdrew.

"Thanks," said John. "I'm much obliged to you both. You're certainly there with the goods as fighting editors. I don't know what I should have done without you."

"Aw, Chee!" said Mr. Jarvis, handsomely dismissing the matter. Long
Otto kicked the leg of a table, and grunted.

Pugsy Maloney's report on the following morning was entirely satisfactory. Rents were collected in Broster Street on Thursdays. Nothing could have been more convenient, for that very day happened to be Thursday.

"I rubbered around," said Pugsy, "an' done de sleut' act, an' it's this way. Dere's a feller blows in every T'ursday 'bout six o'clock, an' den it's up to de folks to dig down inter deir jeans for de stuff, or out dey goes before supper. I got dat from my kid frien' what knows a kid what lives dere. An' say, he has it pretty fierce, dat kid. De kid what lives dere. He's a wop kid, an Italian, an' he's in bad 'cos his pa comes over from Italy to woik on de subway."

"I don't see why that puts him in bad," said John wonderingly. "You don't construct your stories well, Pugsy. You start at the end, then go back to any part which happens to appeal to you at the moment, and eventually wind up at the beginning. Why is this kid in bad because his father has come to work on the subway?"

"Why, sure, because his pa got fired an' swatted de foreman one on de coco, an' dey gives him t'oity days. So de kid's all alone, an' no one to pay de rent."

"I see," said John. "Well, come along with me and introduce me, and I'll look after that."

At half-past five John closed the office for the day, and, armed with a big stick and conducted by Master Maloney, made his way to Broster Street. To reach it, it was necessary to pass through a section of the enemy's country, but the perilous passage was safely negotiated. The expedition reached its unsavory goal intact.

The wop kid inhabited a small room at the very top of a building half-way down the street. He was out when John and Pugsy arrived.

It was not an abode of luxury, the tenement; they had to feel their way up the stairs in almost pitch darkness. Most of the doors were shut, but one on the second floor was ajar. Through the opening John had a glimpse of a number of women sitting on up-turned boxes. The floor was covered with little heaps of linen. All the women were sewing. Stumbling in the darkness, John almost fell against the door. None of the women looked up at the noise. In Broster Street time was evidently money.

On the top floor Pugsy halted before the open door of an empty room. The architect in this case had apparently given rein to a passion for originality, for he had constructed the apartment without a window of any sort whatsoever. The entire stock of air used by the occupants came through a small opening over the door.

It was a warm day, and John recoiled hastily.

"Is this the kid's room?" he said. "I guess the corridor's good enough for me to wait in. What the owner of this place wants," he went on reflectively, "is scalping. Well, we'll do it in the paper if we can't in any other way. Is this your kid?"

A small boy had appeared. He seemed surprised to see visitors. Pugsy undertook to do the honors. Pugsy, as interpreter, was energetic, but not wholly successful. He appeared to have a fixed idea that the Italian language was one easily mastered by the simple method of saying "da" instead of "the," and adding a final "a" to any word that seemed to him to need one.

"Say, kid," he began, "has da rent-a-man come yet-a?"

The black eyes of the wop kid clouded. He gesticulated, and said something in his native language.

"He hasn't got next," reported Master Maloney. "He can't git on to me curves. Dese wop kids is all bone-heads. Say, kid, look-a here." He walked to the door, rapped on it smartly, and, assuming a look of extreme ferocity, stretched out his hand and thundered: "Unbelt-a! Slip-a me da stuff!"

The wop kid's puzzlement in the face of this address became pathetic.

"This," said John, deeply interested, "is getting exciting. Don't give in, Pugsy. I guess the trouble is that your too perfect Italian accent is making the kid homesick."

Master Maloney made a gesture of disgust.

"I'm t'roo. Dese Dagoes makes me tired. Dey don't know enough to go upstairs to take de elevated. Beat it, you mutt," he observed with moody displeasure, accompanying the words with a gesture which conveyed its own meaning. The wop kid, plainly glad to get away, slipped down the stairs like a shadow.

Pugsy shrugged his shoulders.

"Boss," he said resignedly, "it's up to youse."

John reflected.

"It's all right," he said. "Of course, if the collector had been here, the kid wouldn't be. All I've got to do is to wait."

He peered over the banisters into the darkness below.

516

"Not that it's not enough," he said; "for of all the poisonous places I ever met this is the worst. I wish whoever built it had thought to put in a few windows. His idea of ventilation was apparently to leave a hole about the size of a lima bean and let the thing go at that."

"I guess there's a door on to de roof somewhere," suggested Pugsy. "At de joint where I lives dere is."

His surmise proved correct. At the end of the passage a ladder, nailed against the wall, ended in a large square opening, through which was visible, if not "that narrow strip of blue which prisoners call the sky," at any rate a tall brick chimney and a clothesline covered with garments that waved lazily in the breeze.

John stood beneath it, looking up.

"Well," he said, "this isn't much, but it's better than nothing. I suppose the architect of this place was one of those fellows who don't begin to appreciate air till it's thick enough to scoop chunks out with a spoon. It's an acquired taste, I guess, like Limburger cheese. And now, Pugsy, old scout, you had better beat it. There may be a rough-house here any minute now."

Pugsy looked up, indignant.

"Beat it?"

"While your shoe-leather's good," said John firmly. "This is no place for a minister's son. Take it from me."

"I want to stop and pipe de fun," objected Master Maloney.

"What fun?"

"I guess you ain't here to play ball," surmised Pugsy shrewdly, eying the big stick.

"Never mind why I'm here," said John. "Beat it. I'll tell you all about it to-morrow."

Master Maloney prepared reluctantly to depart. As he did so there was a sound of well-shod feet on the stairs, and a man in a snuff-colored suit, wearing a brown Homburg hat and carrying a small notebook in one hand, walked briskly up the stairs. His whole appearance proclaimed him to be the long-expected collector of rents.

CHAPTER XXV

CORNERED

He did not see John for a moment, and had reached the door of the room when he became aware of a presence. He turned in surprise. He was a smallish, pale-faced man with protruding eyes and teeth which gave him a certain resemblance to a rabbit.

"Hello!" he said.

"Welcome to our city," said John, stepping unostentatiously between him and the stairs.

Master Maloney, who had taken advantage of the interruption to edge back into the center of things, now appeared to consider the question of his departure permanently shelved. He sidled to a corner of the landing, and sat down on an empty soap box with the air of a dramatic critic at the opening night of a new play. The scene looked good to him. It promised interesting developments. He was an earnest student of the drama, as exhibited in the theaters of the East Side, and few had ever applauded the hero of "Escaped from Sing Sing," or hissed the villain of "Nellie, the Beautiful Cloak-model" with more fervor. He liked his drama to have plenty of action, and to his practised eye this one promised well. There was a set expression on John's face which suggested great things.

His pleasure was abruptly quenched. John, placing a firm hand on his collar, led him to the top of the stairs and pushed him down.

"Beat it," he said.

The rent-collector watched these things with a puzzled eye. He now turned to John.

"Say, seen anything of the wops that live here?" he enquired. "My name's Gooch. I've come to take the rent."

John nodded.

"I don't think there's much chance of your seeing them to-night," he said. "The father, I hear, is in prison. You won't get any rent out of him."

"Then it's outside for theirs," said Mr. Gooch definitely.

"What about the kid?" said John. "Where's he to go?"

"That's up to him. Nothing to do with me. I'm only acting under orders from up top."

"Whose orders?" enquired John.

"The gent who owns this joint."

"Who is he?"

Suspicion crept into the protruding eyes of the rent-collector.

"Say!" he demanded. "Who are you anyway, and what do you think you're doing here? That's what I'd like to know. What do you want with the name of the owner of this place? What business is it of yours?"

"I'm a newspaper man."

"I guessed you were," said Mr. Gooch with triumph. "You can't bluff me. Well, it's no good, sonny. I've nothing for you. You'd better chase off and try something else."

He became more friendly.

"Say, though," he said, "I just guessed you were from some paper. I wish I could give you a story, but I can't. I guess it's this *Peaceful Moments* business that's been and put your editor on to this joint, ain't it? Say, though, that's a queer thing, that paper. Why, only a few weeks ago it used to be a sort of take-home-and-read-to-the-kids affair. A friend of mine used to buy it regular. And then suddenly it comes out with a regular whoop, and starts knocking these tenements and boosting Kid Brady, and all that. It gets past me. All I know is that it's begun to get this place talked about. Why, you see for yourself how it is. Here is your editor sending you down to get a story about it. But, say, those *Peaceful Moments* guys are taking big risks. I tell you straight they are, and I know. I happen to be wise to a thing or two about what's going on on the other side, and I tell you there's going to be something doing if they don't

518

cut it out quick. Mr. Qem, the fellow who owns this place isn't the man to sit still and smile. He's going to get busy. Say, what paper do you come from?"

"*Peaceful Moments*," said John.

For a moment the inwardness of the information did not seem to come home to Mr. Gooch. Then it hit him. He spun round. John was standing squarely between him and the stairs.

"Hey, what's all this?" demanded Mr. Gooch nervously. The light was dim in the passage, but it was sufficiently light to enable him to see John's face, and it did not reassure him.

"I'll soon tell you," said John. "First, however, let's get this business of the kid's rent settled. Take it out of this and give me the receipt."

He pulled out a bill.

"Curse his rent," said Mr. Gooch. "Let me pass."

"Soon," said John. "Business before pleasure. How much does the kid have to pay for the privilege of suffocating in this infernal place? As much as that? Well, give me a receipt, and then we can get on to more important things."

"Let me pass."

"Receipt," said John laconically.

Mr. Gooch looked at the big stick, then scribbled a few words in his notebook and tore out the page. John thanked him.

"I will see that it reaches him," he said. "And now will you kindly tell me the name of the man for whom you collected that money?"

"Let me pass," bellowed Mr. Gooch. "I'll bring an action against you for assault and battery. Playing a fool game like this! Get away from those stairs."

"There has been no assault and battery-yet," said John. "Well, are you going to tell me?"

Mr. Gooch shuffled restlessly. John leaned against the banisters.

"As you said a moment ago," he observed, "the staff of *Peaceful Moments* is taking big risks. I knew it before you told me. I have had practical demonstration of the fact. And that is why this Broster Street thing has got to be finished quick. We can't afford to wait. So I am going to have you tell me this man's name right now."

"Help!" yelled Mr. Gooch.

The noise died away, echoing against the walls. No answering cry came from below. Custom had staled the piquancy of such cries in Broster Street. If anybody heard it, nobody thought the matter worth investigation.

"If you do that again," said John, "I'll break you in half. Now then! I can't wait much longer. Get busy!"

He looked huge and sinister to Mr. Gooch, standing there in the uncertain light; it was very lonely on that top floor and the rest of the world seemed infinitely far away. Mr. Gooch wavered. He was loyal to his employer, but he was still more loyal to Mr. Gooch.

"Well?" said John.

There was a clatter on the stairs of one running swiftly, and Pugsy Maloney burst into view. For the first time since John had known him, Pugsy was openly excited.

"Say, boss," he cried, "dey's coming!"

"What? Who?"

"Why, dem. I seen dem T'ree Pointers-Spider Reilly an'—"

He broke off with a yelp of surprise. Mr. Gooch had seized his opportunity, and had made his dash for safety. With a rush he dived past John, nearly upsetting Pugsy, who stood in his path, and sprang down the stairs. Once he tripped, but recovered himself, and in another instant only the faint sound of his hurrying footsteps reached them.

519

John had made a movement as if to follow, but the full meaning of Pugsy's words came upon him and he stopped.

"Spider Reilly?" he said.

"I guess it was Spider Reilly," said Pugsy, excitedly. "Dey called him Spider. I guess dey piped youse comin' in here. Gee! it's pretty fierce, boss, dis! What youse goin' to do?"

"Where did you see them, Pugsy?"

"On the street just outside. Dere was a bunch of dem spielin' togedder, and I hears dem say you was in here. Dere ain't no ways out but de front, so dey ain't hurryin'. Dey just reckon to pike along upstairs, peekin' inter each room till dey find you. An' dere's a bunch of dem goin' to wait on de street in case youse beat it past down de stairs while de odder guys is rubberin' for youse. Gee, ain't dis de limit!"

John stood thinking. His mind was working rapidly. Suddenly he smiled.

"It's all right, Pugsy," he said. "It looks bad, but I see a way out. I'm going up that ladder there and through the trapdoor on to the roof. I shall be all right there. If they find me, they can only get at me one at a time. And, while I'm there, here's what I want you to do."

"Shall I go for de cops, boss?"

"No, not the cops. Do you know where Dude Dawson lives?"

The light of intelligence began to shine in Master Maloney's face. His eye glistened with approval. This was strategy of the right sort.

"I can ask around," he said. "I'll soon find him all right."

"Do, and as quick as you can. And when you've found him tell him that his old chum, Spider Reilly, is here, with the rest of his crowd. And now I'd better be getting up on to my perch. Off you go, Pugsy, my son, and don't take a week about it. Good-by."

Pugsy vanished, and John, going to the ladder, climbed out on to the roof with his big stick. He looked about him. The examination was satisfactory. The trapdoor appeared to be the only means of access to the roof, and between this roof and that of the next building there was a broad gulf. The position was practically impregnable. Only one thing could undo him, and that was, if the enemy should mount to the next roof and shoot from there. And even then he would have cover in the shape of the chimney. It was a pity that the trap opened downward, for he had no means of securing it and was obliged to allow it to hang open. But, except for that, his position could hardly have been stronger.

As yet there was no sound of the enemy's approach. Evidently, as Pugsy had said, they were conducting the search, room by room, in a thorough and leisurely way. He listened with his ear close to the open trapdoor, but could hear nothing.

A startled exclamation directly behind him brought him to his feet in a flash, every muscle tense. He whirled his stick above his head as he turned, ready to strike, then let it fall with a clatter. For there, a bare yard away, stood Betty.

CHAPTER XXVI

JOURNEY'S END

The capacity of the human brain for surprise, like that of the human body for pain, is limited. For a single instant a sense of utter unreality struck John like a physical blow. The world flickered before his eyes and the air seemed full of strange noises. Then, quite suddenly, these things passed, and he found himself looking at her with a total absence of astonishment, mildly amused in some remote corner of his brain at his own calm. It was absurd, he told himself, that he should be feeling as if he had known of her presence there all the time. Yet it was so. If this were a dream, he could not be taking the miracle more as a matter of course. Joy at the sight of her he felt, keen and almost painful, but no surprise. The shock had stunned his sense of wonder.

She was wearing a calico apron over her dress, an apron that had evidently been designed for a large woman. Swathed in its folds, she suggested a child playing at being grown up. Her sleeves were rolled back to the elbow, and her slim arms dripped with water. Strands of brown hair were blowing loose in the evening breeze. To John she had never seemed so bewitchingly pretty. He stared at her till the pallor of her face gave way to a warm red glow.

As they stood there, speechless, there came from the other side of the chimney, softly at first, then swelling, the sound of a child's voice, raised in a tentative wail. Betty started violently. The next moment she was gone, and from the unseen parts beyond the chimney came the noise of splashing water.

And at the same instant, through the trap, came a trampling of feet and the sound of whispering. The enemy had reached the top floor.

John was conscious of a remarkable exhilaration. He felt insanely light-hearted. He laughed aloud at the thought that until then he had completely forgotten the very existence of these earnest seekers after his downfall. He threw back his head and shouted. There was something so ridiculous in their assumption that they mattered to a man who had found Betty again.

He thrust his head down through the trap, to see what was going on. The dark passage was full of indistinct forms, gathered together in puzzled groups. The mystery of the vanished object of their pursuit was being discussed in hoarse whispers.

Suddenly there was an excited shout, then a rush of feet. John drew back his head, and waited, gripping his stick.

Voices called to each other in the passage below.

"De roof!"

"On top de roof!"

"He's beaten it for de roof!"

Feet shuffled on the stone floor. The voices ceased abruptly. And then, like a jack-in-the-box, there popped through the trap a head and shoulders.

The new arrival was a young man with a shock of red hair, a broken nose, and a mouth from which force or the passage of time had removed three front teeth. He held on to the edge of the trap, and stared up at John.

John beamed down at him, and shifted his grip on the stick.

"Who's here?" he cried. "Historic picture. 'Old Dr. Cook discovers the
North Pole.'"

The red-headed young man blinked. The strong light of the open air was trying to his eyes. "Youse had best come down," he observed coldly. "We've got youse."

"And," continued John, unmoved, "is instantly handed a gum-drop by his faithful Eskimo."

As he spoke, he brought the stick down on the knuckles which disfigured the edges of the trap. The intruder uttered a howl and dropped out of sight. In the passage below there were whisperings and mutterings, growing gradually louder till something resembling coherent conversation came to John's ears, as he knelt by the trap making meditative billiard shots with the stick at a small pebble.

"Aw g'wan! Don't be a quitter."

"Who's a quitter?"

"Youse a quitter. Get on top de roof. He can't hoit youse."

"De guy's gotten a big stick."

John nodded appreciatively.

"I and Theodore," he murmured.

A somewhat baffled silence on the part of the attacking force was followed by further conversation.

"Gee! Some guy's got to go up."

Murmur of assent from the audience.

A voice, in inspired tones: "Let Sam do it."

The suggestion made a hit. There was no doubt about that. It was a success from the start. Quite a little chorus of voices expressed sincere approval of the very happy solution to what had seemed an insoluble problem. John, listening from above, failed to detect in the choir of glad voices one that might belong to Sam himself. Probably gratification had rendered the chosen one dumb.

"Yes, let Sam do it," cried the unseen chorus. The first speaker, unnecessarily, perhaps-for the motion had been carried almost unanimously-but possibly with the idea of convincing the one member of the party in whose bosom doubts might conceivably be harbored, went on to adduce reasons.

"Sam bein' a coon," he argued, "ain't goin' to git hoit by no stick.
Youse can't hoit a coon by soakin' him on de coco, can you, Sam?"

John waited with some interest for the reply, but it did not come.
Possibly Sam did not wish to generalize on insufficient experience.

"We can but try," said John softly, turning the stick round in his fingers.

A report like a cannon sounded in the passage below. It was merely a revolver shot, but in the confined space it was deafening. The bullet sang up into the sky.

"Never hit me," said John cheerfully.

The noise was succeeded by a shuffling of feet. John grasped his stick more firmly. This was evidently the real attack. The revolver shot had been a mere demonstration of artillery to cover the infantry's advance.

Sure enough, the next moment a woolly head popped through the opening, and a pair of rolling eyes gleamed up at him.

"Why, Sam!" he said cordially, "this is great. Now for our interesting experiment. My idea is that you *can* hurt a coon's head with a stick if you hit it hard enough. Keep quite still. Now. What, are you coming up? Sam, I hate to do it, but—"

A yell rang out. John's theory had been tested and proved correct.

By this time the affair had begun to attract spectators. The noise of the revolver had proved a fine advertisement. The roof of the house next door began to fill up. Only a few of the occupants could get a clear view of the proceedings, for the chimney intervened. There was considerable speculation as to what was passing in the Three Points camp. John was the popular favorite. The early comers had seen his interview with Sam, and were relating it with gusto to their friends. Their attitude toward John was that of a group of men watching a dog at a rat hole. They looked to him to provide entertainment for them, but they realized that the first move must be with the attackers. They were fair-minded men, and they did not expect John to make any aggressive move.

Their indignation, when the proceedings began to grow slow, was directed entirely at the dilatory Three Pointers. They hooted the Three Pointers. They urged them to go home and tuck themselves up in bed. The spectators were mostly Irishmen, and it offended them to see what should have been a spirited fight so grossly bungled.

"G'wan away home, ye quitters!" roared one.

A second member of the audience alluded to them as "stiffs."

It was evident that the besieging army was beginning to grow a little unpopular. More action was needed if they were to retain the esteem of Broster Street.

Suddenly there came another and a longer explosion from below, and more bullets wasted themselves on air. John sighed.

"You make me tired," he said.

The Irish neighbors expressed the same sentiment in different and more forcible words. There was no doubt about it-as warriors, the Three Pointers were failing to give satisfaction.

A voice from the passage called to John.

"Say!"

"Well?" said John.

"Are youse comin' down off out of dat roof?"

"Would you mind repeating that remark?"

"Are youse goin' to quit off out of dat roof?"

"Go away and learn some grammar," said John severely.

"Hey!"

"Well?"

"Are youse —?"

"No, my son," said John, "since you ask it, I am not. I like being up here. How is Sam?"

There was silence below. The time began to pass slowly. The Irishmen on the other roof, now definitely abandoning hope of further entertainment, proceeded with hoots of derision to climb down one by one into the recesses of their own house.

And then from the street far below there came a fusillade of shots and a babel of shouts and counter-shouts. The roof of the house next door filled again with a magical swiftness, and the low wall facing the street became black with the backs of those craning over. There appeared to be great doings in the street.

John smiled comfortably.

In the army of the corridor confusion had arisen. A scout, clattering upstairs, had brought the news of the Table Hillites' advent, and there was doubt as to the proper course to pursue. Certain voices urged going down to help the main body. Others pointed out that this would mean abandoning the siege of the roof. The scout who had brought the news was eloquent in favor of the first course.

"Gee!" he cried, "don't I keep tellin' youse dat de Table Hills is here? Sure, dere's a whole bunch of dem, and unless youse come on down dey'll bite de hull head off of us lot. Leave dat stiff on de roof. Let Sam wait here wit' his canister, and den he can't get down, 'cos Sam'll pump him full of lead while he's beatin' it t'roo de trapdoor. Sure!"

John nodded reflectively.

"There is certainly something in that," he murmured. "I guess the grand rescue scene in the third act has sprung a leak. This will want thinking over."

In the street the disturbance had now become terrible. Both sides were hard at it, and the Irishmen on the roof, rewarded at last for their long vigil, were yelling encouragement promiscuously and whooping with the unfettered ecstasy of men who are getting the treat of their lives without having paid a penny for it.

The behavior of the New York policeman in affairs of this kind is based on principles of the soundest practical wisdom. The unthinking man would rush in and attempt to crush the combat in its earliest and fiercest stages. The New York policeman, knowing the importance of his safety, and the insignificance of the gangsman's, permits the opposing forces to hammer each other into a certain distaste for battle, and then, when both sides have begun to have enough of it, rushes in himself and clubs everything in sight. It is an admirable process in its results, but it is sure rather than swift.

Proceedings in the affair below had not yet reached the police-interference stage. The noise, what with the shots and yells from the street and the ear-piercing approval of the roof audience, was just working up to a climax.

John rose. He was tired of kneeling by the trap, and there was no likelihood of Sam making another attempt to climb through. He got up and stretched himself.

And then he saw that Betty was standing beside him, holding with each hand a small and-by Broster Street standards-uncannily clean child. The children were scared and whimpering, and she stooped to soothe them. Then she turned to John, her eyes wide with anxiety.

"Are you hurt?" she cried. "What has been happening? Are you hurt?"

John's heart leaped at the anxious break in her voice.

"It's all right," he said soothingly. "It's absolutely all right. Everything's over."

As if to give him the lie, the noise in the street swelled to a crescendo of yells and shots.

"What's that?" cried Betty, starting.

"I fancy," said John, "the police must be taking a hand. It's all right. There's a little trouble down below there between two of the gangs. It won't last long now."

"Who were those men?"

"My friends in the passage?" he said lightly. "Those were some of the Three Points gang. We were holding the concluding exercise of a rather lively campaign that's been —"

Betty leaned weakly against the chimney. There was silence now in the street. Only the distant rumble of an elevated train broke the stillness. She drew her hands from the children's grasp, and covered her face. As she lowered them again, John saw that the blood had left her cheeks. She was white and shaking. He moved forward impulsively.

"Betty!"

She tottered, reaching blindly for the chimney for support, and without further words he gathered her into his arms as if she had been the child she looked, and held her there, clutching her to him fiercely, kissing the brown hair that brushed against his face, and soothing her with vague murmurings.

Her breath came in broken gasps. She laughed hysterically.

"I thought they were killing you-killing you-and I couldn't leave my babies-they were so frightened, poor little mites —I thought they were killing you."

"Betty!"

Her arms about his neck tightened their grip convulsively, forcing his head down until his face rested against hers. And so they stood, rigid, while the two children stared with round eyes and whimpered unheeded.

Her grip relaxed. Her hands dropped slowly to her side. She leaned back against the circle of his arms, and looked up at him —a strange look, full of a sweet humility.

"I thought I was strong," she said quietly. "I'm weak-but I don't care."

He looked at her with glowing eyes, not understanding, but content that the journey was ended, that she was there, in his arms, speaking to him.

"I always loved you, dear," she went on. "You knew that, didn't you? But I thought I was strong enough to give you up for-for a principle-but I was wrong. I can't do without you —I knew it just now when I saw —" She stopped, and shuddered. "I can't do without you," she repented.

She felt the muscles of his arms quiver, and pressed more closely against them. They were strong arms, protecting arms, restful to lean against at the journey's end.

CHAPTER XXVII

A LEMON

That bulwark of *Peaceful Moments*, Pugsy Maloney, was rather the man of action than the man of tact. Otherwise, when, a moment later, he thrust his head up through the trap, he would have withdrawn delicately, and not split the silence with a raucous "Hey!" which acted on John and Betty like an electric shock.

John glowered at him. Betty was pink, but composed. Pugsy climbed leisurely on to the roof, and surveyed the group.

"Why, hello!" he said, as he saw Betty more closely.

"Well, Pugsy," said Betty. "How are you?"

John turned in surprise.

"Do you know Pugsy?"

Betty looked at him, puzzled.

"Why, of course I do."

"Sure," said Pugsy. "Miss Brown was stenographer on de poiper till she beat it."

"Miss Brown!"

There was utter bewilderment in John's face.

"I changed my name when I went to *Peaceful Moments*."

"Then are you—did you —?"

"Yes, I wrote those articles. That's how I happen to be here now. I come down every day and help look after the babies. Poor little souls, there seems to be nobody else here who has time to do it. It's dreadful. Some of them—you wouldn't believe —I don't think they could ever have had a real bath in their lives."

"Baths is foolishness," commented Master Maloney austerely, eying the scoured infants with a touch of disfavor.

John was reminded of a second mystery that needed solution.

"How on earth did you get up here, Pugsy?" he asked. "How did you get past Sam?"

"Sam? I didn't see no Sam. Who's Sam?"

"One of those fellows. A coon. They left him on guard with a gun, so that I shouldn't get down."

"Ah, I met a coon beating it down de stairs. I guess dat was him. I guess he got cold feet."

"Then there's nothing to stop us from getting down."

"Nope. Dat's right. Dere ain't a T'ree Pointer wit'in a mile. De cops have been loadin' dem into de patrol-wagon by de dozen."

John turned to Betty.

"We'll go and have dinner somewhere. You haven't begun to explain things yet."

Betty shook her head with a smile.

"I haven't got time to go out to dinners," she said. "I'm a working-girl. I'm cashier at Fontelli's Italian Restaurant. I shall be on duty in another half-hour."

John was aghast.

"You!"

"It's a very good situation," said Betty demurely. "Six dollars a week and what I steal. I haven't stolen anything yet, and I think Mr. Jarvis is a little disappointed in me. But of course I haven't settled down properly."

"Jarvis? Bat Jarvis?"

"Yes. He has been very good to me. He got me this place, and has looked after me all the time."

"I'll buy him a thousand cats," said John fervently. "But, Betty, you mustn't go there any more. You must quit. You —"

"If *Peaceful Moments* would reengage me?" said Betty.

She spoke lightly, but her face was serious.

"Dear," she said quickly, "I can't be away from you now, while there's danger. I couldn't bear it. Will you let me come?"

He hesitated.

"You will. You must." Her manner changed again. "That's settled, then. Pugsy, I'm coming back to the paper. Are you glad?"

"Sure t'ing," said Pugsy. "You're to de good."

"And now," she went on, "I must give these babies back to their mothers, and then I'll come with you."

She lowered herself through the trap, and John handed the children down to her. Pugsy looked on, smoking a thoughtful cigarette.

John drew a deep breath. Pugsy, removing the cigarette from his mouth, delivered himself of a stately word of praise.

"She's a boid," he said.

"Pugsy," said John, feeling in his pocket, and producing a roll of bills, "a dollar a word is our rate for contributions like that."

* * * * *

John pushed back his chair slightly, stretched out his legs, and lighted a cigarette, watching Betty fondly through the smoke. The resources of the Knickerbocker Hotel had proved equal to supplying the staff of *Peaceful Moments* with an excellent dinner, and John had stoutly declined to give or listen to any explanations until the coffee arrived.

"Thousands of promising careers," he said, "have been ruined by the fatal practise of talking seriously at dinner. But now we might begin."

Betty looked at him across the table with shining eyes. It was good to be together again.

"My explanations won't take long," she said. "I ran away from you. And, when you found me, I ran away again."

"But I didn't find you," objected John. "That was my trouble."

"But my aunt told you I was at *Peaceful Moments*!"

"On the contrary, I didn't even know you had an aunt."

"Well, she's not exactly that. She's my stepfather's aunt-Mrs. Oakley. I was certain you had gone straight to her, and that she had told you where I was."

"The Mrs. Oakley? The-er-philanthropist?"

"Don't laugh at her," said Betty quickly. "She was so good to me!"

"She passes," said John decidedly.

"And now," said Betty, "it's your turn."

John lighted another cigarette.

"My story," he said, "is rather longer. When they threw me out of Mervo —"

"What!"

"I'm afraid you don't keep abreast of European history," he said. "Haven't you heard of the great revolution in Mervo and the overthrow of the dynasty? Bloodless, but invigorating. The populace rose against me as one man-except good old General Poineau. He was for me, and Crump was neutral, but apart from them my subjects were unanimous. There's a republic again in Mervo now."

"But why? What had you done?"

"Well, I abolished the gaming-tables. But, more probably," he went on quickly, "they saw what a perfect dub I was in every —"

She interrupted him.

"Do you mean to say that, just because of me —?"

"Well," he said awkwardly, "as a matter of fact what you said did make me think over my position, and, of course, directly I thought over it-oh, well, anyway, I closed down gambling in Mervo, and then—"

"John!"

He was aware of a small hand creeping round the table under cover of the cloth. He pressed it swiftly, and, looking round, caught the eye of a hovering waiter, who swooped like a respectful hawk.

"Did you want anything, sir?"

"I've got it, thanks," said John.

The waiter moved away.

"Well, directly they had fired me, I came over here. I don't know what I expected to do. I suppose I thought I might find you by chance. I pretty soon saw how hopeless it was, and it struck me that, if I didn't get some work to do mighty quick, I shouldn't be much good to anyone except the alienists."

"Dear!"

The waiter stared, but John's eyes stopped him in mid-swoop.

"Then I found Smith —"

"Where is Mr. Smith?"

"In prison," said John with a chuckle.

"In prison!"

"He resisted and assaulted the police. I'll tell you about it later. Well, Smith told me of the alterations in *Peaceful Moments*, and I saw that it was just the thing for me. And it has occupied my mind quite some. To think of you being the writer of those Broster Street articles! You certainly have started something, Betty! Goodness knows where it will end. I hoped to have brought off a coup this afternoon, but the arrival of Sam and his friends just spoiled it."

"This afternoon? Yes, why were you there? What were you doing?"

"I was interviewing the collector of rents and trying to dig his employer's name out of him. It was Smith's idea. Smith's theory was that the owner of the tenements must have some special private reason for lying low, and that he would employ some special fellow, whom he could trust, as a rent-collector. And I'm pretty certain he was right. I cornered the collector, a little, rabbit-faced man named Gooch, and I believe he was on the point of-What's the matter?"

Betty's forehead was wrinkled. Her eyes wore a far-away expression.

"I'm trying to remember something. I seem to know the name, Gooch. And I seem to associate it with a little, rabbit-faced man. And-quick, tell me some more about him. He's just hovering about on the edge of my memory. Quick! Push him in!"

John threw his mind back to the interview in the dark passage, trying to reconstruct it.

"He's small," he said slowly. "His eyes protrude-so do his teeth-He-he-yes, I remember now-he has a curious red mark —"

"On his right cheek," said Betty triumphantly.

"By Jove!" cried John. "You've got him?"

"I remember him perfectly. He was —" She stopped with a little gasp.

"Yes?"

"John, he was one of my stepfather's secretaries," she said.

They looked at each other in silence.

"It can't be," said John at length.

"It can. It is. He must be. He has scores of interests everywhere. He prides himself on it. It's the most natural thing."

John shook his head doubtfully.

"But why all the fuss? Your stepfather isn't the man to mind public opinion —"

"But don't you see? It's as Mr. Smith said. The private reason. It's as clear as daylight. Naturally he would do anything rather than be found out. Don't you see? Because of Mrs. Oakley."

"Because of Mrs. Oakley?"

"You don't know her as I do. She is a curious mixture. She's double-natured. You called her the philanthropist just now. Well, she would be one, if-if she could bear to part with money. Yes, I know it sounds ridiculous. But it's so. She is mean about money, but she honestly hates to hear of anybody treating poor people badly. If my stepfather were really the owner of those tenements, and she should find it out, she would have nothing more to do with him. It's true. I know her."

The smile passed away from John's face.

"By George!" he said. "It certainly begins to hang together."

"I know I'm right."

"I think you are."

He sat meditating for a moment.

"Well?" he said at last.

"What do you mean?"

"I mean, what are we to do? Do we go on with this?"

"Go on with it? I don't understand."

"I mean-well, it has become rather a family matter, you see. Do you feel as-warlike against Mr. Scobell as you did against an unknown lessee?"

Betty's eyes sparkled.

"I don't think I should feel any different if-if it was you," she said. "I've been spending days and days in those houses, John dear, and I've seen such utter squalor and misery, where there needn't be any at all if only the owner would do his duty, and-and —"

She stopped. Her eyes were misty.

"Thumbs down, in fact," said John, nodding. "I'm with you."

As he spoke, two men came down the broad staircase into the grill-room. Betty's back was towards them, but John saw them, and stared.

"What are you looking at?" asked Betty.

"Will you count ten before looking round?"

"What is it?"

"Your stepfather has just come in."

"What!"

"He's sitting at the other side of the room, directly behind you. Count ten!"

But Betty had twisted round in her chair.

"Where? Where?"

"Just where you're looking. Don't let him see you."

"I don't — Oh!"

"Got him?"

He leaned back in his chair.

"The plot thickens, eh?" he said. "What is Mr. Scobell doing in New York, I wonder, if he has not come to keep an eye on his interests?"

Betty had whipped round again. Her face was white with excitement.

"It's true," she whispered. "I was right. Do you see who that is with him? The man?"

"Do you know him? He's a stranger to me."

"It's Mr. Parker," said Betty.

John drew in his breath sharply.

"Are you sure?"

"Positive."

John laughed quietly. He thought for a moment, then beckoned to the hovering waiter.

"What are you going to do?" asked Betty.

"Bring me a small lemon," said John.

"Lemon squash, sir?"

"Not a lemon squash. A plain lemon. The fruit of that name. The common or garden citron, which is sharp to the taste and not pleasant to have handed to one. Also a piece of note paper, a little tissue paper, and an envelope.

"What are you going to do?" asked Betty again.

John beamed.

"Did you ever read the Sherlock Holmes story entitled 'The Five Orange Pips'? Well, when a man in that story received a mysterious envelope containing five orange pips, it was a sign that he was due to get his. It was all over, as far as he was concerned, except 'phoning for the undertaker. I propose to treat Mr. Scobell better than that. He shall have a whole lemon."

The waiter returned. John wrapped up the lemon carefully, wrote on the note paper the words, "To B. Scobell, Esq., Property Owner, Broster Street, from Prince John of *Peaceful Moments*, this gift," and enclosed it in the envelope.

"Do you see that gentleman at the table by the pillar?" he said. "Give him these. Just say a gentleman sent them."

The waiter smiled doubtfully. John added a two-dollar bill to the collection in his hand.

"You needn't give him that," he said.

The waiter smiled again, but this time not doubtfully.

"And now," said John as the messenger ambled off, "perhaps it would be just as well if we retired."

CHAPTER XXVIII

THE FINAL ATTEMPT

Proof that his shot had not missed its mark was supplied to John immediately upon his arrival at the office on the following morning, when he was met by Pugsy Maloney with the information that a gentleman had called to see him.

"With or without a black-jack?" enquired John. "Did he give any name?"

"Sure. Parker's his name. He blew in oncst before when Mr. Smith was here. I loosed him into de odder room."

John walked through. The man he had seen with Mr. Scobell at the Knickerbocker was standing at the window.

"Mr. Parker?"

The other turned, as the door opened, and looked at him keenly.

"Are you Mr. Maude?"

"I am," said John.

"I guess you don't need to be told what I've come about?"

"No."

"See here," said Mr. Parker. "I don't know how you've found things out, but you've done it, and we're through. We quit."

"I'm glad of that," said John. "Would you mind informing Spider Reilly of that fact? It will make life pleasanter for all of us."

"Mr. Scobell sent me along here to ask you to come and talk over this thing with him. He's at the Knickerbocker. I've a cab waiting outside. Can you come along?"

"I'd rather he came here."

"And I bet he'd rather come here than be where he is. That little surprise packet of yours last night put him down and out. Gave him a stroke of some sort. He's in bed now, with half-a-dozen doctors working on him."

John thought for a moment.

"Oh," he said slowly, "if it's that–very well."

He could not help feeling a touch of remorse. He had no reason to be fond of Mr. Scobell, but he was sorry that this should have happened.

They went out on the street. A taximeter cab was standing by the sidewalk. They got in. Neither spoke. John was thoughtful and preoccupied. Mr. Parker, too, appeared to be absorbed in his own thoughts. He sat with folded arms and lowered head.

The cab buzzed up Fifth Avenue. Suddenly something, half-seen through the window, brought John to himself with a jerk. It was the great white mass of the Plaza Hotel. The next moment he saw that they were abreast of the park, and for the first time an icy wave of suspicion swept over him.

"Here, what's this?" he cried. "Where are you taking me?"

Mr. Parker's right hand came swiftly out of ambush, and something gleamed in the sun.

"Don't move," said Mr. Parker. The hard nozzle of a pistol pressed against John's chest. "Keep that hand still."

John dropped his hand. Mr. Parker leaned back, with the pistol resting easily on his knee. The cab began to move more quickly.

John's mind was in a whirl. His chief emotion was not fear, but disgust that he should have allowed himself to be trapped, with such absurd ease. He blushed for himself. Mr. Parker's face was expressionless, but who could say what tumults of silent laughter were not going on inside him? John bit his lip.

"Well?" he said at last.

Mr. Parker did not reply.

"Well?" said John again. "What's the next move?"

It flashed across his mind that, unless driven to it by an attack, his captor would do nothing for the moment without running grave risks himself. To shoot now would be to attract attention. The cab would be overtaken at once by bicycle police, and stopped. There would be no escape. No, nothing could happen till they reached open country. At least he would have time to think this matter over in all its bearings.

Mr. Parker ignored the question. He was sitting in the same attitude of watchfulness, the revolver resting on his knee. He seemed mistrustful of John's right hand, which was hanging limply at his side. It was from this quarter that he appeared to expect attack. The cab was bowling easily up the broad street, past rows and rows of high houses each looking exactly the same as the last. Occasionally, to the right, through a break in the line of buildings, a glimpse of the river could be seen.

A faint hope occurred to John that, by talking, he might put the other off his guard for just that instant which was all he asked. He exerted himself to find material for conversation.

"Tell me," he said, "what you said about Mr. Scobell, was that true? About his being ill in bed?"

Mr. Parker did not answer, but a wintry smile flittered across his face.

"It was not?" said John. "Well, I'm glad of that. I don't wish Mr. Scobell any harm."

Mr. Parker looked at him doubtfully.

"Say, why are you in this game at all?" he said. "What made you butt in?"

"One must do something," said John. "It's interesting work."

"If you'll quit —"

John shook his head.

"I own it's a tempting proposition, things being as they are, but I won't give up yet. You never know what may happen."

"Well, you can make a mighty near guess this trip."

"You can't do a thing yet, that's sure," said John confidently. "If you shot me now, the cab would be stopped, and you would be lynched by the populace. I seem to see them tearing you limb from limb. 'She loves me!' Off comes an arm. 'She loves me not!' A leg joins the little heap on the ground. That is what would happen, Mr. Parker."

The other shrugged his shoulders, and relapsed into silence once more.

"What are you going to do with me, Mr. Parker?" asked John.

Mr. Parker did not reply.

* * * * *

The cab moved swiftly on. Now they had reached the open country. An occasional wooden shack was passed, but that was all. At any moment, John felt, the climax of the drama might be reached, and he got ready. His muscles stiffened for a spring. There was little chance of its being effective, but at least it would be good to put up some kind of a fight. And he had a faint hope that the suddenness of his movement might upset the other's aim. He was bound to be hit somewhere. That was certain. But quickness might save him to some extent. He braced his leg against the back of the cab. And, as he did so, its smooth speed changed to a series of jarring jumps, each more emphatic than the last. It slowed down, then came to a halt. There was a thud, as the chauffeur jumped down. John heard him fumbling in the tool box. Presently the body of the machine was raised slightly as he got to work with the jack. John's muscles relaxed. He leaned back. Surely something could be made of this new development.

But the hand that held the revolver never wavered. He paused, irresolute. And at the moment somebody spoke in the road outside.

"Had a breakdown?" enquired the voice.

John recognized it. It was the voice of Kid Brady.

* * * * *

The Kid, as he had stated that he intended to do, had begun his training for his match with Eddie Wood at White Plains. It was his practise to open a course of training with a little gentle road-work, and it was while jogging along the highway a couple of miles from his training camp, in company with the two thick-necked gentlemen who acted as his sparring partners, that he had come upon the broken-down taxicab.

If this had happened after his training had begun in real earnest, he would have averted his eyes from the spectacle, however alluring, and continued on his way without a pause. But now, as he had not yet settled down to genuine hard work, he felt justified in turning aside and looking into the matter. The fact that the chauffeur, who seemed to be a taciturn man, lacking the conversational graces, manifestly objected to an audience, deterred him not at all. One cannot have everything in this world, and the Kid and his attendant thick-necks were content to watch the process of mending the tire, without demanding the additional joy of sparkling small talk from the man in charge of the operations.

"Guy's had a breakdown, sure," said the first of the thick-necks.

"Surest thing you know," agreed his colleague.

"Seems to me the tire's punctured," said the Kid.

All three concentrated their gaze on the machine.

"Kid's right," said thick-neck number one. "Guy's been an' bust a tire."

"Surest thing you know," said thick-neck number two.

They observed the perspiring chauffeur in silence for a while.

"Wonder how he did that, now?" speculated the Kid.

"Ran over a nail, I guess," said thick-neck number one.

"Surest thing you know," said the other, who, while perhaps somewhat deficient in the matter of original thought, was a most useful fellow to have by one —a sort of Boswell.

"Did you run over a nail?" the Kid enquired of the chauffeur.

The chauffeur worked on, unheeding.

"This is his busy day," said the first thick-neck, with satire. "Guy's too full of work to talk to us."

"Deaf, shouldn't wonder," surmised the Kid. "Say, wonder what's he doing with a taxi so far out of the city."

"Some guy tells him to drive him out here, I guess. Say, it'll cost him something, too. He'll have to strip off a few from his roll to pay for this."

John glanced at Mr. Parker, quivering with excitement. It was his last chance. Would the Kid think to look inside the cab, or would he move on? Could he risk a shout?

Mr. Parker leaned forward, and thrust the muzzle of the pistol against his body. The possibilities of the situation had evidently not been lost upon him.

"Keep quiet," he whispered.

Outside, the conversation had begun again, and the Kid had made his decision.

"Pretty rich guy inside," he said, following up his companion's train of thought. "I'm going to rubber through the window."

John met Mr. Parker's eye, and smiled.

There came the sound of the Kid's feet grating on the road, as he turned, and, as he heard it, Mr. Parker for the first time lost his head. With a vague idea of screening John, he half-rose. The pistol wavered. It was the chance John had prayed for. His left hand shot out, grasped the other's wrist, and gave it a sharp wrench. The pistol went off with a deafening report, the

532

bullet passing through the back of the cab, then fell to the floor, as the fingers lost their hold. And the next moment John's right fist, darting upward, crashed home.

The effect was instantaneous. John had risen from his seat as he delivered the blow, and it got the full benefit of his weight. Mr. Parker literally crumpled up. His head jerked, then fell limply forward. John pushed him on to the seat as he slid toward the floor.

The interested face of the Kid appeared at the window. Behind him could be seen portions of the faces of the two thick-necks.

"Hello, Kid," said John. "I heard your voice. I hoped you might look in for a chat."

The Kid stared, amazed.

"What's doin'?" he queried.

"A good deal. I'll explain later. First, will you kindly knock that chauffeur down and sit on his head?"

"De guy's beat it," volunteered the first thick-neck.

"Surest thing you know," said the other.

"What's been doin'?" asked the Kid. "What are you going to do with this guy?"

John inspected the prostrate Mr. Parker, who had begun to stir slightly.

"I guess we'll leave him here," he said. "I've had all of his company that I need for to-day. Show me the nearest station, Kid. I must be getting back to New York. I'll tell you all about it as we go. A walk will do me good. Riding in a taxi is pleasant, but, believe me, you can have too much of it."

CHAPTER XXIX

A REPRESENTATIVE GATHERING

When John returned to the office, he found that his absence had been causing Betty an anxious hour's waiting. She had been informed by Pugsy that he had gone out in the company of Mr. Parker, and she felt uneasy. She turned white at his story of the ride, but he minimized the dangers.

"I don't think he ever meant to shoot. I think he was going to shut me up somewhere out there, and keep me till I promised to be good."

"Do you think my stepfather told him to do it?"

"I doubt it. I fancy Parker is a man who acts a good deal on his own inspirations. But we'll ask him, when he calls to-day."

"Is he going to call?"

"I have an idea he will," said John. "I sent him a note just now, asking if he could manage a visit."

It was unfortunate, in the light of subsequent events, that Mr. Jarvis should have seen fit to bring with him to the office that afternoon two of his collection of cats, and that Long Otto, who, as before, accompanied him, should have been fired by his example to the extent of introducing a large yellow dog. For before the afternoon was ended, space in the office was destined to be at premium.

Mr. Jarvis, when he had recovered from the surprise of seeing Betty and learning that she had returned to her old situation, explained:

"T'ought I'd bring de kits along," he said. "Dey starts fuss'n' wit' each odder yesterday, so I brings dem along."

John inspected the menagerie without resentment.

"Sure!" he said. "They add a kind of peaceful touch to the scene."

The atmosphere was, indeed, one of peace. The dog, after an inquisitive journey round the room, lay down and went to sleep. The cats settled themselves comfortably, one on each of Mr. Jarvis' knees. Long Otto, surveying the ceiling with his customary glassy stare, smoked a long cigar. And Bat, scratching one of the cats under the ear, began to entertain John with some reminiscences of fits and kittens.

But the peace did not last. Ten minutes had barely elapsed when the dog, sitting up with a start, uttered a whine. The door burst open and a little man dashed in. He was brown in the face, and had evidently been living recently in the open air. Behind him was a crowd of uncertain numbers. They were all strangers to John.

"Yes?" he said.

The little man glared speechlessly at the occupants of the room. The two Bowery boys rose awkwardly. The cats fell to the floor.

The rest of the party had entered. Betty recognized the Reverend Edwin T. Philpotts and Mr. B. Henderson Asher.

"My name is Renshaw," said the little man, having found speech.

"What can I do for you?" asked John.

The question appeared to astound the other.

"What can you —! Of all —!"

"Mr. Renshaw is the editor of *Peaceful Moments*," she said. "Mr. Smith was only acting for him."

Mr. Renshaw caught the name.

"Yes. Mr. Smith. I want to see Mr. Smith. Where is he?"

"In prison," said John.

"In prison!"

John nodded.

"A good many things have happened since you left for your vacation. Smith assaulted a policeman, and is now on Blackwell's Island."

Mr. Renshaw gasped. Mr. B. Henderson Asher stared, and stumbled over the cat.

"And who are you?" asked the editor.

"My name is Maude. I —"

He broke off, to turn his attention to Mr. Jarvis and Mr. Asher, between whom unpleasantness seemed to have arisen. Mr. Jarvis, holding a cat in his arms, was scowling at Mr. Asher, who had backed away and appeared apprehensive.

"What is the trouble?" asked John.

"Dis guy here wit' two left feet," said Bat querulously, "treads on de kit."

Mr. Renshaw, eying Bat and the silent Otto with disgust, intervened.

"Who are these persons?" he enquired.

"Poison yourself," rejoined Bat, justly incensed. "Who's de little squirt, Mr. Maude?"

John waved his hands.

"Gentlemen, gentlemen," he said, "why descend to mere personalities? I ought to have introduced you. This is Mr. Renshaw, our editor. These, Mr. Renshaw, are Bat Jarvis and Long Otto, our acting fighting editors, vice Kid Brady, absent on unavoidable business."

The name stung Mr. Renshaw to indignation, as Smith's had done.

"Brady!" he shrilled. "I insist that you give me a full explanation. I go away by my doctor's orders for a vacation, leaving Mr. Smith to conduct the paper on certain clearly defined lines. By mere chance, while on my vacation, I saw a copy of the paper. It had been ruined."

"Ruined?" said John. "On the contrary. The circulation has been going up every week."

"Who is this person, Brady? With Mr. Philpotts I have been going carefully over the numbers which have been issued since my departure —"

"An intellectual treat," murmured John.

"—and in each there is a picture of this young man in a costume which I will not particularize —"

"There is hardly enough of it to particularize."

"—together with a page of disgusting autobiographical matter."

John held up his hand.

"I protest," he said. "We court criticism, but this is mere abuse. I appeal to these gentlemen to say whether this, for instance, is not bright and interesting."

He picked up the current number of *Peaceful Moments*, and turned to the Kid's page.

"This," he said, "describes a certain ten-round unpleasantness with one Mexican Joe. 'Joe comes up for the second round and he gives me a nasty look, but I thinks of my mother and swats him one in the lower ribs. He gives me another nasty look. "All right, Kid," he says; "now I'll knock you up into the gallery." And with that he cuts loose with a right swing, but I falls into the clinch, and then —'"

"Pah!" exclaimed Mr. Renshaw.

"Go on, boss," urged Mr. Jarvis approvingly. "It's to de good, dat stuff."

"There!" said John triumphantly. "You heard? Mr. Jarvis, one of the most firmly established critics east of Fifth Avenue stamps Kid Brady's reminiscences with the hall-mark of his approval."

"I falls fer de Kid every time," assented Mr. Jarvis.

"Sure! You know a good thing when you see one. Why," he went on warmly, "there is stuff in these reminiscences which would stir the blood of a jellyfish. Let me quote you another passage, to show that they are not only enthralling, but helpful as well. Let me see, where is it? Ah, I have it. 'A bully good way of putting a guy out of business is this. You don't want to use it in the ring, because rightly speaking it's a foul, but you will find it mighty useful if any thick-neck comes up to you in the street and tries to start anything. It's this way. While he's setting himself for a punch, just place the tips of the fingers of your left hand on the right side of the chest. Then bring down the heel of your left hand. There isn't a guy living that could stand up against that. The fingers give you a leverage to beat the band. The guy doubles up, and you upper-cut him with your right, and out he goes.' Now, I bet you never knew that before, Mr. Philpotts. Try it on your parishioners."

"*Peaceful Moments*," said Mr. Renshaw irately, "is no medium for exploiting low prize-fighters."

"Low prize-fighters! No, no! The Kid is as decent a little chap as you'd meet anywhere. And right up in the championship class, too! He's matched against Eddie Wood at this very moment. And Mr. Waterman will support me in my statement that a victory over Eddie Wood means that he gets a cast-iron claim to meet Jimmy Garvin for the championship."

"It is abominable," burst forth Mr. Renshaw. "It is disgraceful. The paper is ruined."

"You keep saying that. It really isn't so. The returns are excellent. Prosperity beams on us like a sun. The proprietor is more than satisfied."

"Indeed!" said Mr. Renshaw sardonically.

"Sure," said John.

Mr. Renshaw laughed an acid laugh.

"You may not know it," he said, "but Mr. Scobell is in New York at this very moment. We arrived together yesterday on the *Mauretania*. I was spending my vacation in England when I happened to see the copy of the paper. I instantly communicated with Mr. Scobell, who was at Mervo, an island in the Mediterranean —"

"I seem to know the name —"

" —and received in reply a long cable desiring me to return to New York immediately. I sailed on the *Mauretania*, and found that he was one of the passengers. He was extremely agitated, let me tell you. So that your impudent assertion that the proprietor is pleased —"

John raised his eyebrows.

"I don't quite understand," he said. "From what you say, one would almost imagine that you thought Mr. Scobell was the proprietor of this paper."

Mr. Renshaw stared. Everyone stared, except Mr. Jarvis, who, since the readings from the Kid's reminiscences had ceased, had lost interest in the proceedings, and was now entertaining the cats with a ball of paper tied to a string.

"Thought that Mr. Scobell —?" repeated Mr. Renshaw. "Who is, if he is not?"

"I am," said John.

There was a moment's absolute silence.

"You!" cried Mr. Renshaw.

"You!" exclaimed Mr. Waterman, Mr. Asher, and the Reverend Edwin T. Philpotts.

"Sure thing," said John.

Mr. Renshaw groped for a chair, and sat down.

"Am I going mad?" he demanded feebly. "Do I understand you to say that you own this paper?"

"I do."

"Since when?"

"Roughly speaking, about three days."

Among his audience (still excepting Mr. Jarvis, who was tickling one of the cats and whistling a plaintive melody) there was a tendency toward awkward silence. To start assailing a seeming nonentity and then to discover he is the proprietor of the paper to which you wish to contribute is like kicking an apparently empty hat and finding your rich uncle inside it. Mr. Renshaw in particular was disturbed. Editorships of the kind to which he aspired are not easy to get. If he were to be removed from *Peaceful Moments* he would find it hard to place himself anywhere else. Editors, like manuscripts, are rejected from want of space.

"I had a little money to invest," continued John. "And it seemed to me that I couldn't do better than put it into *Peaceful Moments*. If it did nothing else, it would give me a free hand in pursuing a policy in which I was interested. Smith told me that Mr. Scobell's representatives had instructions to accept any offer, so I made an offer, and they jumped at it."

Pugsy Maloney entered, bearing a card.

"Ask him to wait just one moment," said John, reading it.

He turned to Mr. Renshaw.

"Mr. Renshaw," he said, "if you took hold of the paper again, helped by these other gentlemen, do you think you could gather in our old subscribers and generally make the thing a live proposition on the old lines? Because, if so, I should be glad if you would start in with the next number. I am through with the present policy. At least, I hope to be in a few minutes. Do you think you can undertake that?"

Mr. Renshaw, with a sigh of relief, intimated that he could.

"Good," said John. "And now I'm afraid I must ask you to go. A rather private and delicate interview is in the offing. Bat, I'm very much obliged to you and Otto for your help. I don't know what we should have done without it."

"Aw, Chee!" said Mr. Jarvis.

"Then good-by for the present."

"Good-by, boss. Good-by, loidy."

Long Otto pulled his forelock, and, accompanied by the cats and the dog, they left the room.

When Mr. Renshaw and the others had followed them, John rang the bell for Pugsy.

"Ask Mr. Scobell to step in," he said.

The man of many enterprises entered. His appearance had deteriorated since John had last met him. He had the air of one who has been caught in the machinery. His face was even sallower than of yore, and there was no gleam in his dull green eyes.

He started at the sight of Betty, but he was evidently too absorbed in the business in hand to be surprised at seeing her. He sank into a chair, and stared gloomily at John.

"Well?" he said.

"Well?" said John.

"This," observed Mr. Scobell simply, "is hell." He drew a cigar stump mechanically from his vest pocket and lighted it.

"What are you going to do about it?" he asked.

"What are you?" said John. "It's up to you."

Mr. Scobell gazed heavily into vacancy.

"Ever since I started in to monkey with that darned Mervo," he said sadly, "there ain't a thing gone right. I haven't been able to turn around without bumping into myself. Everything I touch turns to mud. I guess I can still breathe, but I'm not betting on that lasting long. Of all the darned hoodoos that island was the worst. Say, I gotta close down that Casino. What do you know about that! Sure thing. The old lady won't stand for it. I had a letter from her." He turned to Betty. "You got her all worked up, Betty. I'm not blaming you. It's just my jinx. She took it into her head I'd been treating you mean, and she kicked at the Casino. I gotta close it down or nix on the heir thing. That was enough for me. I'm going to turn it into a hotel."

He relighted his cigar.

"And now, just as I got her smoothed down, along comes this darned tenement business. Say, Prince, for the love of Mike cut it out. If those houses are as bad as you say they are, and the old lady finds out that I own them, it'll be Katie bar the door for me. She wouldn't stand for it for a moment. I guess I didn't treat you good, Prince, but let's forget it. Ease up on this rough stuff. I'll do anything you want."

Betty spoke.

"We only want you to make the houses fit to live in," she said. "I don't believe you know what they're like."

"Why, no. I left Parker in charge. It was up to him to do what was wanted. Say, Prince, I want to talk to you about that guy, Parker. I understand he's been rather rough with you and your crowd. That wasn't my doing. I didn't know anything about it till he told me. It's the darned Wild West strain in him coming out. He used to do those sort of things out there, and he's forgotten his manners. I pay him well, and I guess he thinks that's the way it's up to him to earn it. You mustn't mind Parker."

"Oh, well! So long as he means well—!" said John. "I've no grudge against Parker. I've settled with him."

"Well, then, what about this Broster Street thing? You want me to fix some improvements, is that it?"

"That's it."

"Why, say, I'll do that. Sure. And then you'll quit handing out the newspaper stories? That goes. I'll start right in."

He rose.

"That's taken a heap off my mind," he said.

"There's just one other thing," said John. "Have you by any chance such a thing as a stepfather's blessing on you?"

"Eh?"

John took Betty's hand.

"We've come round to your views, Mr. Scobell," he said. "That scheme of yours for our future looks good to us."

Mr. Scobell bit through his cigar in his emotion.

"Now, why the Heck," he moaned, "couldn't you have had the sense to do that before, and save all this trouble?"

CHAPTER XXX

CONCLUSION

Smith drew thoughtfully at his cigar, and shifted himself more comfortably into his chair. It was long since he had visited the West, and he had found all the old magic in the still, scented darkness of the prairie night. He gave a little sigh of content. When John, a year before, had announced his intention of buying this ranch, and, as it seemed to Smith, burying himself alive a thousand miles from anywhere, he had disapproved. He had pointed out that John was not doing what Fate expected of him. A miracle, in the shape of a six-figure wedding present from Mrs. Oakley, who had never been known before, in the memory of man, to give away a millionth of that sum, had happened to him. Fate, argued Smith, plainly intended him to stay in New York and spend his money in a civilized way.

John had had only one reply, but it was clinching.

"Betty likes the idea," he said, and Smith ceased to argue.

Now, as he sat smoking on the porch on the first night of his inaugural visit to the ranch, a conviction was creeping over him that John had chosen wisely.

A door opened behind him. Betty came out on to the porch, and dropped into a chair close to where John's cigar glowed redly in the darkness. They sat there without speaking. The stirring of unseen cattle in the corral made a soothing accompaniment to thought.

"It is very pleasant for an old jail bird like myself," said Smith at last, "to sit here at my ease. I wish all our absent friends could be with us to-night. Or perhaps not quite all. Let us say, Comrade Parker here, Comrades Brady and Maloney over there by you, and our old friend Renshaw sharing the floor with B. Henderson Asher, Bat Jarvis, and the cats. By the way, I was round at Broster Street before I left New York. There is certainly an improvement. Millionaires now stop there instead of going on to the Plaza. Are you asleep, John?"

"No."

"Excellent. I also saw Comrade Brady before I left. He has definitely got on his match with Jimmy Garvin."

"Good. He'll win."

"The papers seem to think so. *Peaceful Moments*, however, I am sorry to say, is silent on the subject. It was not like this in the good old days. How is the paper going now, John? Are the receipts satisfactory?"

"Pretty fair. Renshaw is rather a marvel in his way. He seems to have roped in nearly all the old subscribers. They eat out of his hand."

Smith stretched himself.

"These," he said, "are the moments in life to which we look back with that wistful pleasure. This peaceful scene, John, will remain with me when I have forgotten that such a man as Spider Reilly ever existed. These are the real Peaceful Moments."

He closed his eyes. The cigar dropped from his fingers. There was a long silence.

"Mr. Smith," said Betty.

There was no answer.

"He's asleep," said John. "He had a long journey to-day."

Betty drew her chair closer. From somewhere out in the darkness, from the direction of the men's quarters, came the soft tinkle of a guitar and a voice droning a Mexican love-song.

Her hand stole out and found his. They began to talk in whispers.

Psmith, Journalist

CHAPTER I

"COSY MOMENTS"

The man in the street would not have known it, but a great crisis was imminent in New York journalism.

Everything seemed much as usual in the city. The cars ran blithely on Broadway. Newsboys shouted "Wux-try!" into the ears of nervous pedestrians with their usual Caruso-like vim. Society passed up and down Fifth Avenue in its automobiles, and was there a furrow of anxiety upon Society's brow? None. At a thousand street corners a thousand policemen preserved their air of massive superiority to the things of this world. Not one of them showed the least sign of perturbation. Nevertheless, the crisis was at hand. Mr. J. Fillken Wilberfloss, editor-in-chief of *Cosy Moments*, was about to leave his post and start on a ten weeks' holiday.

In New York one may find every class of paper which the imagination can conceive. Every grade of society is catered for. If an Esquimau came to New York, the first thing he would find on the bookstalls in all probability would be the *Blubber Magazine*, or some similar production written by Esquimaux for Esquimaux. Everybody reads in New York, and reads all the time. The New Yorker peruses his favourite paper while he is being jammed into a crowded compartment on the subway or leaping like an antelope into a moving Street car.

There was thus a public for *Cosy Moments*. *Cosy Moments*, as its name (an inspiration of Mr. Wilberfloss's own) is designed to imply, is a journal for the home. It is the sort of paper which the father of the family is expected to take home with him from his office and read aloud to the chicks before bed-time. It was founded by its proprietor, Mr. Benjamin White, as an antidote to yellow journalism. One is forced to admit that up to the present yellow journalism seems to be competing against it with a certain measure of success. Headlines are still of as generous a size as heretofore, and there is no tendency on the part of editors to scamp the details of the last murder-case.

Nevertheless, *Cosy Moments* thrives. It has its public.

Its contents are mildly interesting, if you like that sort of thing. There is a "Moments in the Nursery" page, conducted by Luella Granville Waterman, to which parents are invited to contribute the bright speeches of their offspring, and which bristles with little stories about the nursery canary, by Jane (aged six), and other works of rising young authors. There is a "Moments of Meditation" page, conducted by the Reverend Edwin T. Philpotts; a "Moments Among the Masters" page, consisting of assorted chunks looted from the literature of the past, when foreheads were bulgy and thoughts profound, by Mr. Wilberfloss himself; one or two other pages; a short story; answers to correspondents on domestic matters; and a "Moments of Mirth" page, conducted by an alleged humorist of the name of B. Henderson Asher, which is about the most painful production ever served up to a confiding public.

The guiding spirit of *Cosy Moments* was Mr. Wilberfloss. Circumstances had left the development of the paper mainly to him. For the past twelve months the proprietor had been away in Europe, taking the waters at Carlsbad, and the sole control of *Cosy Moments* had passed into the hands of Mr. Wilberfloss. Nor had he proved unworthy of the trust or unequal to the duties. In that year *Cosy Moments* had reached the highest possible level of domesticity. Anything not calculated to appeal to the home had been rigidly excluded. And as a result the circulation had increased steadily. Two extra pages had been added, "Moments Among the Shoppers" and "Moments with Society." And the advertisements had grown in volume. But the work had told upon the Editor. Work of that sort carries its penalties with it. Success means absorption, and absorption spells softening of the brain.

Whether it was the strain of digging into the literature of the past every week, or the effort of reading B. Henderson Asher's "Moments of Mirth" is uncertain. At any rate, his duties, combined with the heat of a New York summer, had sapped Mr. Wilberfloss's health to such an extent that the doctor had ordered him ten weeks' complete rest in the mountains. This Mr. Wilberfloss could, perhaps, have endured, if this had been all. There are worse places than the mountains of America in which to spend ten weeks of the tail-end of summer, when the sun has ceased to grill and the mosquitoes have relaxed their exertions. But it was not all. The doctor, a far-seeing man who went down to first causes, had absolutely declined to consent to Mr. Wilberfloss's suggestion that he should keep in touch with the paper during his vacation. He was adamant. He had seen copies of *Cosy Moments* once or twice, and he refused to permit a man in the editor's state of health to come in contact with Luella Granville Waterman's "Moments in the Nursery" and B. Henderson Asher's "Moments of Mirth." The medicine-man put his foot down firmly.

"You must not see so much as the cover of the paper for ten weeks," he said. "And I'm not so sure that it shouldn't be longer. You must forget that such a paper exists. You must dismiss the whole thing from your mind, live in the open, and develop a little flesh and muscle."

To Mr. Wilberfloss the sentence was almost equivalent to penal servitude. It was with tears in his voice that he was giving his final instructions to his sub-editor, in whose charge the paper would be left during his absence. He had taken a long time doing this. For two days he had been fussing in and out of the office, to the discontent of its inmates, more especially Billy Windsor, the sub-editor, who was now listening moodily to the last harangue of the series, with the air of one whose heart is not in the subject. Billy Windsor was a tall, wiry, loose-jointed young man, with unkempt hair and the general demeanour of a caged eagle. Looking at him, one could picture him astride of a bronco, rounding up cattle, or cooking his dinner at a camp-fire. Somehow he did not seem to fit into the *Cosy Moments* atmosphere.

"Well, I think that that is all, Mr. Windsor," chirruped the editor. He was a little man with a long neck and large *pince-nez*, and he always chirruped. "You understand the general lines on which I think the paper should be conducted?" The sub-editor nodded. Mr. Wilberfloss made him tired. Sometimes he made him more tired than at other times. At the present moment he filled him with an aching weariness. The editor meant well, and was full of zeal, but he had a habit of covering and recovering the ground. He possessed the art of saying the same obvious thing in a number of different ways to a degree which is found usually only in politicians. If Mr. Wilberfloss had been a politician, he would have been one of those dealers in glittering generalities who used to be fashionable in American politics.

"There is just one thing," he continued "Mrs. Julia Burdett Parslow is a little inclined — I may have mentioned this before —"

"You did," said the sub-editor.

Mr. Wilberfloss chirruped on, unchecked.

"A little inclined to be late with her 'Moments with Budding Girlhood'. If this should happen while I am away, just write her a letter, quite a pleasant letter, you understand, pointing out the necessity of being in good time. The machinery of a weekly paper, of course, cannot run smoothly unless contributors are in good time with their copy. She is a very sensible woman, and she will understand, I am sure, if you point it out to her."

The sub-editor nodded.

"And there is just one other thing. I wish you would correct a slight tendency I have noticed lately in Mr. Asher to be just a trifle-well, not precisely *risky*, but perhaps a shade *broad* in his humour."

"His what?" said Billy Windsor.

"Mr. Asher is a very sensible man, and he will be the first to acknowledge that his sense of humour has led him just a little beyond the bounds. You understand? Well, that is all, I think. Now I must really be going, or I shall miss my train. Good-bye, Mr. Windsor."

"Good-bye," said the sub-editor thankfully.

At the door Mr. Wilberfloss paused with the air of an exile bidding farewell to his native land, sighed, and trotted out.

Billy Windsor put his feet upon the table, and with a deep scowl resumed his task of reading the proofs of Luella Granville Waterman's "Moments in the Nursery."

CHAPTER II

BILLY WINDSOR

Billy Windsor had started life twenty-five years before this story opens on his father's ranch in Wyoming. From there he had gone to a local paper of the type whose Society column consists of such items as "Pawnee Jim Williams was to town yesterday with a bunch of other cheap skates. We take this opportunity of once more informing Jim that he is a liar and a skunk," and whose editor works with a revolver on his desk and another in his hip-pocket. Graduating from this, he had proceeded to a reporter's post on a daily paper in a Kentucky town, where there were blood feuds and other Southern devices for preventing life from becoming dull. All this time New York, the magnet, had been tugging at him. All reporters dream of reaching New York. At last, after four years on the Kentucky paper, he had come East, minus the lobe of one ear and plus a long scar that ran diagonally across his left shoulder, and had worked without much success as a free-lance. He was tough and ready for anything that might come his way, but these things are a great deal a matter of luck. The cub-reporter cannot make a name for himself unless he is favoured by fortune. Things had not come Billy Windsor's way. His work had been confined to turning in reports of fires and small street accidents, which the various papers to which he supplied them cut down to a couple of inches.

Billy had been in a bad way when he had happened upon the sub-editorship of *Cosy Moments*. He despised the work with all his heart, and the salary was infinitesimal. But it was regular, and for a while Billy felt that a regular salary was the greatest thing on earth. But he still dreamed of winning through to a post on one of the big New York dailies, where there was something doing and a man would have a chance of showing what was in him.

The unfortunate thing, however, was that *Cosy Moments* took up his time so completely. He had no chance of attracting the notice of big editors by his present work, and he had no leisure for doing any other.

All of which may go to explain why his normal aspect was that of a caged eagle.

To him, brooding over the outpourings of Luella Granville Waterman, there entered Pugsy Maloney, the office-boy, bearing a struggling cat.

"Say!" said Pugsy.

He was a nonchalant youth, with a freckled, mask-like face, the expression of which never varied. He appeared unconscious of the cat. Its existence did not seem to occur to him.

"Well?" said Billy, looking up. "Hello, what have you got there?"

Master Maloney eyed the cat, as if he were seeing it for the first time.

"It's a kitty what I got in de street," he said.

"Don't hurt the poor brute. Put her down."

Master Maloney obediently dropped the cat, which sprang nimbly on to an upper shelf of the book-case.

"I wasn't hoitin' her," he said, without emotion. "Dere was two fellers in de street sickin' a dawg on to her. An' I comes up an' says, 'G'wan! What do youse t'ink you're doin', fussin' de poor dumb animal?' An' one of de guys, he says, 'G'wan! Who do youse t'ink youse is?' An' I says, 'I'm de guy what's goin' to swat youse one on de coco if youse don't quit fussin' de poor dumb animal.' So wit dat he makes a break at swattin' me one, but I swats him one, an' I swats de odder feller one, an' den I swats dem bote some more, an' I gets de kitty, an' I brings her in here, cos I t'inks maybe youse'll look after her."

And having finished this Homeric narrative, Master Maloney fixed an expressionless eye on the ceiling, and was silent.

Billy Windsor, like most men of the plains, combined the toughest of muscle with the softest of hearts. He was always ready at any moment to become the champion of the oppressed on the slightest provocation. His alliance with Pugsy Maloney had begun on the occasion when he had rescued that youth from the clutches of a large negro, who, probably from the soundest of motives, was endeavouring to slay him. Billy had not inquired into the rights and wrongs of the matter: he had merely sailed in and rescued the office-boy. And Pugsy, though he had made no verbal comment on the affair, had shown in many ways that he was not ungrateful.

"Bully for you, Pugsy!" he cried. "You're a little sport. Here"—he produced a dollar-bill—"go out and get some milk for the poor brute. She's probably starving. Keep the change."

"Sure thing," assented Master Maloney. He strolled slowly out, while Billy Windsor, mounting a chair, proceeded to chirrup and snap his fingers in the effort to establish the foundations of an *entente cordiale* with the rescued cat.

By the time that Pugsy returned, carrying a five-cent bottle of milk, the animal had vacated the book-shelf, and was sitting on the table, washing her face. The milk having been poured into the lid of a tobacco-tin, in lieu of a saucer, she suspended her operations and adjourned for refreshments. Billy, business being business, turned again to Luella Granville Waterman, but Pugsy, having no immediate duties on hand, concentrated himself on the cat.

"Say!" he said.

"Well?"

"Dat kitty."

"What about her?"

"Pipe de leather collar she's wearing."

Billy had noticed earlier in the proceedings that a narrow leather collar encircled the cat's neck. He had not paid any particular attention to it. "What about it?" he said.

"Guess I know where dat kitty belongs. Dey all have dose collars. I guess she's one of Bat Jarvis's kitties. He's got a lot of dem for fair, and every one wit one of dem collars round deir neck."

"Who's Bat Jarvis? Do you mean the gang-leader?"

"Sure. He's a cousin of mine," said Master Maloney with pride.

"Is he?" said Billy. "Nice sort of fellow to have in the family. So you think that's his cat?"

"Sure. He's got twenty-t'ree of dem, and dey all has dose collars."

"Are you on speaking terms with the gentleman?"

"Huh?"

"Do you know Bat Jarvis to speak to?"

"Sure. He's me cousin."

"Well, tell him I've got the cat, and that if he wants it he'd better come round to my place. You know where I live?"

"Sure."

"Fancy you being a cousin of Bat's, Pugsy. Why did you never tell us? Are you going to join the gang some day?"

"Nope. Nothin' doin'. I'm goin' to be a cow-boy."

"Good for you. Well, you tell him when you see him. And now, my lad, out you get, because if I'm interrupted any more I shan't get through to-night."

"Sure," said Master Maloney, retiring.

"Oh, and Pugsy . . ."

"Huh?"

"Go out and get a good big basket. I shall want one to carry this animal home in."

"Sure," said Master Maloney.

CHAPTER III

AT "THE GARDENIA"

"It would ill beseem me, Comrade Jackson," said Psmith, thoughtfully sipping his coffee, "to run down the metropolis of a great and friendly nation, but candour compels me to state that New York is in some respects a singularly blighted town."

"What's the matter with it?" asked Mike.

"Too decorous, Comrade Jackson. I came over here principally, it is true, to be at your side, should you be in any way persecuted by scoundrels. But at the same time I confess that at the back of my mind there lurked a hope that stirring adventures might come my way. I had heard so much of the place. Report had it that an earnest seeker after amusement might have a tolerably spacious rag in this modern Byzantium. I thought that a few weeks here might restore that keen edge to my nervous system which the languor of the past term had in a measure blunted. I wished my visit to be a tonic rather than a sedative. I anticipated that on my return the cry would go round Cambridge, 'Psmith has been to New York. He is full of oats. For he on honey-dew hath fed, and drunk the milk of Paradise. He is hot stuff. Rah!' But what do we find?"

He paused, and lit a cigarette.

"What do we find?" he asked again.

"I don't know," said Mike. "What?"

"A very judicious query, Comrade Jackson. What, indeed? We find a town very like London. A quiet, self-respecting town, admirable to the apostle of social reform, but disappointing to one who, like myself, arrives with a brush and a little bucket of red paint, all eager for a treat. I have been here a week, and I have not seen a single citizen clubbed by a policeman. No negroes dance cake-walks in the street. No cow-boy has let off his revolver at random in Broadway. The cables flash the message across the ocean, 'Psmith is losing his illusions.'"

Mike had come to America with a team of the M.C.C. which was touring the cricket-playing section of the United States. Psmith had accompanied him in a private capacity. It was the end of their first year at Cambridge, and Mike, with a century against Oxford to his credit, had been one of the first to be invited to join the tour. Psmith, who had played cricket in a rather desultory way at the University, had not risen to these heights. He had merely taken the opportunity of Mike's visit to the other side to accompany him. Cambridge had proved pleasant to Psmith, but a trifle quiet. He had welcomed the chance of getting a change of scene.

So far the visit had failed to satisfy him. Mike, whose tastes in pleasure were simple, was delighted with everything. The cricket so far had been rather of the picnic order, but it was very pleasant; and there was no limit to the hospitality with which the visitors were treated. It was this more than anything which had caused Psmith's grave disapproval of things American. He was not a member of the team, so that the advantages of the hospitality did not reach him. He had all the disadvantages. He saw far too little of Mike. When he wished to consult his confidential secretary and adviser on some aspect of Life, that invaluable official was generally absent at dinner with the rest of the team. To-night was one of the rare occasions when Mike could get away. Psmith was becoming bored. New York is a better city than London to be alone in, but it is never pleasant to be alone in any big city.

As they sat discussing New York's shortcomings over their coffee, a young man passed them, carrying a basket, and seated himself at the next table. He was a tall, loose-jointed young man, with unkempt hair.

A waiter made an ingratiating gesture towards the basket, but the young man stopped him. "Not on your life, sonny," he said. "This stays right here." He placed it carefully on the floor beside his chair, and proceeded to order dinner.

Psmith watched him thoughtfully.

547

"I have a suspicion, Comrade Jackson," he said, "that this will prove to be a somewhat stout fellow. If possible, we will engage him in conversation. I wonder what he's got in the basket. I must get my Sherlock Holmes system to work. What is the most likely thing for a man to have in a basket? You would reply, in your unthinking way, 'sandwiches.' Error. A man with a basketful of sandwiches does not need to dine at restaurants. We must try again."

The young man at the next table had ordered a jug of milk to be accompanied by a saucer. These having arrived, he proceeded to lift the basket on to his lap, pour the milk into the saucer, and remove the lid from the basket. Instantly, with a yell which made the young man's table the centre of interest to all the diners, a large grey cat shot up like a rocket, and darted across the room. Psmith watched with silent interest.

It is hard to astonish the waiters at a New York restaurant, but when the cat performed this feat there was a squeal of surprise all round the room. Waiters rushed to and fro, futile but energetic. The cat, having secured a strong strategic position on the top of a large oil-painting which hung on the far wall, was expressing loud disapproval of the efforts of one of the waiters to drive it from its post with a walking-stick. The young man, seeing these manoeuvres, uttered a wrathful shout, and rushed to the rescue.

"Comrade Jackson," said Psmith, rising, "we must be in this."

When they arrived on the scene of hostilities, the young man had just possessed himself of the walking-stick, and was deep in a complex argument with the head-waiter on the ethics of the matter. The head-waiter, a stout impassive German, had taken his stand on a point of etiquette. "Id is," he said, "to bring gats into der grill-room vorbidden. No gendleman would gats into der grill-room bring. Der gendleman —"

The young man meanwhile was making enticing sounds, to which the cat was maintaining an attitude of reserved hostility. He turned furiously on the head-waiter.

"For goodness' sake," he cried, "can't you see the poor brute's scared stiff? Why don't you clear your gang of German comedians away, and give her a chance to come down?"

"Der gendleman —" argued the head-waiter.

Psmith stepped forward and touched him on the arm.

"May I have a word with you in private?"

"Zo?"

Psmith drew him away.

"You don't know who that is?" he whispered, nodding towards the young man.

"No gendleman he is," asserted the head-waiter. "Der gendleman would not der gat into —"

Psmith shook his head pityingly.

"These petty matters of etiquette are not for his Grace-but, hush, he wishes to preserve his incognito."

"Ingognito?"

"You understand. You are a man of the world, Comrade-may I call you Freddie? You understand, Comrade Freddie, that in a man in his Grace's position a few little eccentricities may be pardoned. You follow me, Frederick?"

The head-waiter's eye rested upon the young man with a new interest and respect.

"He is noble?" he inquired with awe.

"He is here strictly incognito, you understand," said Psmith warningly. The head-waiter nodded.

The young man meanwhile had broken down the cat's reserve, and was now standing with her in his arms, apparently anxious to fight all-comers in her defence. The head-waiter approached deferentially.

"Der gendleman," he said, indicating Psmith, who beamed in a friendly manner through his eye-glass, "haf everything exblained. All will now quite satisfactory be."

The young man looked inquiringly at Psmith, who winked encouragingly. The head-waiter bowed.

"Let me present Comrade Jackson," said Psmith, "the pet of our English Smart Set. I am Psmith, one of the Shropshire Psmiths. This is a great moment. Shall we be moving back? We were about to order a second instalment of coffee, to correct the effects of a fatiguing day. Perhaps you would care to join us?"

"Sure," said the alleged duke.

"This," said Psmith, when they were seated, and the head-waiter had ceased to hover, "is a great meeting. I was complaining with some acerbity to Comrade Jackson, before you introduced your very interesting performing-animal speciality, that things in New York were too quiet, too decorous. I have an inkling, Comrade —"

"Windsor's my name."

"I have an inkling, Comrade Windsor, that we see eye to eye on the subject."

"I guess that's right. I was raised in the plains, and I lived in Kentucky a while. There's more doing there in a day than there is here in a month. Say, how did you fix it with the old man?"

"With Comrade Freddie? I have a certain amount of influence with him. He is content to order his movements in the main by my judgment. I assured him that all would be well, and he yielded." Psmith gazed with interest at the cat, which was lapping milk from the saucer. "Are you training that animal for a show of some kind, Comrade Windsor, or is it a domestic pet?"

"I've adopted her. The office-boy on our paper got her away from a dog this morning, and gave her to me."

"Your paper?"

"*Cosy Moments*," said Billy Windsor, with a touch of shame.

"*Cosy Moments*?" said Psmith reflectively. "I regret that the bright little sheet has not come my way up to the present. I must seize an early opportunity of perusing it."

"Don't you do it."

"You've no paternal pride in the little journal?"

"It's bad enough to hurt," said Billy Windsor disgustedly. "If you really want to see it, come along with me to my place, and I'll show you a copy."

"It will be a pleasure," said Psmith. "Comrade Jackson, have you any previous engagement for to-night?"

"I'm not doing anything," said Mike.

"Then let us stagger forth with Comrade Windsor. While he is loading up that basket, we will be collecting our hats. . . . I am not half sure, Comrade Jackson," he added, as they walked out, "that Comrade Windsor may not prove to be the genial spirit for whom I have been searching. If you could give me your undivided company, I should ask no more. But with you constantly away, mingling with the gay throng, it is imperative that I have some solid man to accompany me in my ramblings hither and thither. It is possible that Comrade Windsor may possess the qualifications necessary for the post. But here he comes. Let us foregather with him and observe him in private life before arriving at any premature decision."

CHAPTER IV

BAT JARVIS

Billy Windsor lived in a single room on East Fourteenth Street. Space in New York is valuable, and the average bachelor's apartments consist of one room with a bathroom opening off it. During the daytime this one room loses all traces of being used for sleeping purposes at night. Billy Windsor's room was very much like a public-school study. Along one wall ran a settee. At night this became a bed; but in the daytime it was a settee and nothing but a settee. There was no space for a great deal of furniture. There was one rocking-chair, two ordinary chairs, a table, a book-stand, a typewriter-nobody uses pens in New York-and on the walls a mixed collection of photographs, drawings, knives, and skins, relics of their owner's prairie days. Over the door was the head of a young bear.

Billy's first act on arriving in this sanctum was to release the cat, which, having moved restlessly about for some moments, finally came to the conclusion that there was no means of getting out, and settled itself on a corner of the settee. Psmith, sinking gracefully down beside it, stretched out his legs and lit a cigarette. Mike took one of the ordinary chairs; and Billy Windsor, planting himself in the rocker, began to rock rhythmically to and fro, a performance which he kept up untiringly all the time.

"A peaceful scene," observed Psmith. "Three great minds, keen, alert, restless during business hours, relax. All is calm and pleasant chit-chat. You have snug quarters up here, Comrade Windsor. I hold that there is nothing like one's own roof-tree. It is a great treat to one who, like myself, is located in one of these vast caravanserai-to be exact, the Astor-to pass a few moments in the quiet privacy of an apartment such as this."

"It's beastly expensive at the Astor," said Mike.

"The place has that drawback also. Anon, Comrade Jackson, I think we will hunt around for some such cubby-hole as this, built for two. Our nervous systems must be conserved."

"On Fourth Avenue," said Billy Windsor, "you can get quite good flats very cheap. Furnished, too. You should move there. It's not much of a neighbourhood. I don't know if you mind that?"

"Far from it, Comrade Windsor. It is my aim to see New York in all its phases. If a certain amount of harmless revelry can be whacked out of Fourth Avenue, we must dash there with the vim of highly-trained smell-dogs. Are you with me, Comrade Jackson?"

"All right," said Mike.

"And now, Comrade Windsor, it would be a pleasure to me to peruse that little journal of which you spoke. I have had so few opportunities of getting into touch with the literature of this great country."

Billy Windsor stretched out an arm and pulled a bundle of papers from the book-stand. He tossed them on to the settee by Psmith's side.

"There you are," he said, "if you really feel like it. Don't say I didn't warn you. If you've got the nerve, read on."

Psmith had picked up one of the papers when there came a shuffling of feet in the passage outside, followed by a knock upon the door. The next moment there appeared in the doorway a short, stout young man. There was an indescribable air of toughness about him, partly due to the fact that he wore his hair in a well-oiled fringe almost down to his eyebrows, which gave him the appearance of having no forehead at all. His eyes were small and set close together. His mouth was wide, his jaw prominent. Not, in short, the sort of man you would have picked out on sight as a model citizen.

His entrance was marked by a curious sibilant sound, which, on acquaintance, proved to be a whistled tune. During the interview which followed, except when he was speaking, the visitor whistled softly and unceasingly.

"Mr. Windsor?" he said to the company at large.

Psmith waved a hand towards the rocking-chair. "That," he said, "is Comrade Windsor. To your right is Comrade Jackson, England's favourite son. I am Psmith."

The visitor blinked furtively, and whistled another tune. As he looked round the room, his eye fell on the cat. His face lit up.

"Say!" he said, stepping forward, and touching the cat's collar, "mine, mister."

"Are you Bat Jarvis?" asked Windsor with interest.

"Sure," said the visitor, not without a touch of complacency, as of a monarch abandoning his incognito.

For Mr. Jarvis was a celebrity.

By profession he was a dealer in animals, birds, and snakes. He had a fancier's shop in Groome street, in the heart of the Bowery. This was on the ground-floor. His living abode was in the upper story of that house, and it was there that he kept the twenty-three cats whose necks were adorned with leather collars, and whose numbers had so recently been reduced to twenty-two. But it was not the fact that he possessed twenty-three cats with leather collars that made Mr. Jarvis a celebrity.

A man may win a purely local reputation, if only for eccentricity, by such means. But Mr. Jarvis's reputation was far from being purely local. Broadway knew him, and the Tenderloin. Tammany Hall knew him. Long Island City knew him. In the underworld of New York his name was a by-word. For Bat Jarvis was the leader of the famous Groome Street Gang, the most noted of all New York's collections of Apaches. More, he was the founder and originator of it. And, curiously enough, it had come into being from motives of sheer benevolence. In Groome Street in those days there had been a dance-hall, named the Shamrock and presided over by one Maginnis, an Irishman and a friend of Bat's. At the Shamrock nightly dances were given and well attended by the youth of the neighbourhood at ten cents a head. All might have been well, had it not been for certain other youths of the neighbourhood who did not dance and so had to seek other means of getting rid of their surplus energy. It was the practice of these light-hearted sportsmen to pay their ten cents for admittance, and once in, to make hay. And this habit, Mr. Maginnis found, was having a marked effect on his earnings. For genuine lovers of the dance fought shy of a place where at any moment Philistines might burst in and break heads and furniture. In this crisis the proprietor thought of his friend Bat Jarvis. Bat at that time had a solid reputation as a man of his hands. It is true that, as his detractors pointed out, he had killed no one—a defect which he had subsequently corrected; but his admirers based his claim to respect on his many meritorious performances with fists and with the black-jack. And Mr. Maginnis for one held him in the very highest esteem. To Bat accordingly he went, and laid his painful case before him. He offered him a handsome salary to be on hand at the nightly dances and check undue revelry by his own robust methods. Bat had accepted the offer. He had gone to Shamrock Hall; and with him, faithful adherents, had gone such stalwarts as Long Otto, Red Logan, Tommy Jefferson, and Pete Brodie. Shamrock Hall became a place of joy and order; and-more important still-the nucleus of the Groome Street Gang had been formed. The work progressed. Off-shoots of the main gang sprang up here and there about the East Side. Small thieves, pickpockets and the like, flocked to Mr. Jarvis as their tribal leader and protector and he protected them. For he, with his followers, were of use to the politicians. The New York gangs, and especially the Groome Street Gang, have brought to a fine art the gentle practice of "repeating"; which, broadly speaking, is the art of voting a number of different times at different polling-stations on election days. A man who can vote, say, ten times in a single day for you, and who controls a great number of followers who are also prepared, if they like you, to vote ten times in a single day for you, is worth cultivating. So the politicians passed the word to the police, and the police left the Groome Street Gang unmolested and they waxed fat and flourished.

Such was Bat Jarvis.

* * * * *

"Pipe de collar," said Mr. Jarvis, touching the cat's neck. "Mine, mister."

"Pugsy said it must be," said Billy Windsor. "We found two fellows setting a dog on to it, so we took it in for safety."

Mr. Jarvis nodded approval.

"There's a basket here, if you want it," said Billy.

"Nope. Here, kit."

Mr. Jarvis stooped, and, still whistling softly, lifted the cat. He looked round the company, met Psmith's eye-glass, was transfixed by it for a moment, and finally turned again to Billy Windsor.

"Say!" he said, and paused. "Obliged," he added.

He shifted the cat on to his left arm, and extended his right hand to Billy.

"Shake!" he said.

Billy did so.

Mr. Jarvis continued to stand and whistle for a few moments more.

"Say!" he said at length, fixing his roving gaze once more upon Billy. "Obliged. Fond of de kit, I am."

Psmith nodded approvingly.

"And rightly," he said. "Rightly, Comrade Jarvis. She is not unworthy of your affection. A most companionable animal, full of the highest spirits. Her knockabout act in the restaurant would have satisfied the most jaded critic. No diner-out can afford to be without such a cat. Such a cat spells death to boredom."

Mr. Jarvis eyed him fixedly, as if pondering over his remarks. Then he turned to Billy again.

"Say!" he said. "Any time you're in bad. Glad to be of service. You know the address. Groome Street. Bat Jarvis. Good night. Obliged."

He paused and whistled a few more bars, then nodded to Psmith and Mike, and left the room. They heard him shuffling downstairs.

"A blithe spirit," said Psmith. "Not garrulous, perhaps, but what of that? I am a man of few words myself. Comrade Jarvis's massive silences appeal to me. He seems to have taken a fancy to you, Comrade Windsor."

Billy Windsor laughed.

"I don't know that he's just the sort of side-partner I'd go out of my way to choose, from what I've heard about him. Still, if one got mixed up with any of that East-Side crowd, he would be a mighty useful friend to have. I guess there's no harm done by getting him grateful."

"Assuredly not," said Psmith. "We should not despise the humblest. And now, Comrade Windsor," he said, taking up the paper again, "let me concentrate myself tensely on this very entertaining little journal of yours. Comrade Jackson, here is one for you. For sound, clear-headed criticism," he added to Billy, "Comrade Jackson's name is a by-word in our English literary salons. His opinion will be both of interest and of profit to you, Comrade Windsor."

CHAPTER V

PLANNING IMPROVEMENTS

"By the way," said Psmith, "what is your exact position on this paper? Practically, we know well, you are its back-bone, its life-blood; but what is your technical position? When your proprietor is congratulating himself on having secured the ideal man for your job, what precise job does he congratulate himself on having secured the ideal man for?"

"I'm sub-editor."

"Merely sub? You deserve a more responsible post than that, Comrade Windsor. Where is your proprietor? I must buttonhole him and point out to him what a wealth of talent he is allowing to waste itself. You must have scope."

"He's in Europe. At Carlsbad, or somewhere. He never comes near the paper. He just sits tight and draws the profits. He lets the editor look after things. Just at present I'm acting as editor."

"Ah! then at last you have your big chance. You are free, untrammelled."

"You bet I'm not," said Billy Windsor. "Guess again. There's no room for developing free untrammelled ideas on this paper. When you've looked at it, you'll see that each page is run by some one. I'm simply the fellow who minds the shop."

Psmith clicked his tongue sympathetically. "It is like setting a gifted French chef to wash up dishes," he said. "A man of your undoubted powers, Comrade Windsor, should have more scope. That is the cry, 'more scope!' I must look into this matter. When I gaze at your broad, bulging forehead, when I see the clear light of intelligence in your eyes, and hear the grey matter splashing restlessly about in your cerebellum, I say to myself without hesitation, 'Comrade Windsor must have more scope.'" He looked at Mike, who was turning over the leaves of his copy of *Cosy Moments* in a sort of dull despair. "Well, Comrade Jackson, and what is your verdict?"

Mike looked at Billy Windsor. He wished to be polite, yet he could find nothing polite to say. Billy interpreted the look.

"Go on," he said. "Say it. It can't be worse than what I think."

"I expect some people would like it awfully," said Mike.

"They must, or they wouldn't buy it. I've never met any of them yet, though."

Psmith was deep in Luella Granville Waterman's "Moments in the Nursery." He turned to Billy Windsor.

"Luella Granville Waterman," he said, "is not by any chance your *nom-de-plume*, Comrade Windsor?"

"Not on your life. Don't think it."

"I am glad," said Psmith courteously. "For, speaking as man to man, I must confess that for sheer, concentrated bilge she gets away with the biscuit with almost insolent ease. Luella Granville Waterman must go."

"How do you mean?"

"She must go," repeated Psmith firmly. "Your first act, now that you have swiped the editorial chair, must be to sack her."

"But, say, I can't. The editor thinks a heap of her stuff."

"We cannot help his troubles. We must act for the good of the paper. Moreover, you said, I think, that he was away?"

"So he is. But he'll come back."

"Sufficient unto the day, Comrade Windsor. I have a suspicion that he will be the first to approve your action. His holiday will have cleared his brain. Make a note of improvement number one-the sacking of Luella Granville Waterman."

"I guess it'll be followed pretty quick by improvement number two-the sacking of William Windsor. I can't go monkeying about with the paper that way."

Psmith reflected for a moment.

"Has this job of yours any special attractions for you, Comrade Windsor?"

"I guess not."

"As I suspected. You yearn for scope. What exactly are your ambitions?"

"I want to get a job on one of the big dailies. I don't see how I'm going to fix it, though, at the present rate."

Psmith rose, and tapped him earnestly on the chest.

"Comrade Windsor, you have touched the spot. You are wasting the golden hours of your youth. You must move. You must hustle. You must make Windsor of *Cosy Moments* a name to conjure with. You must boost this sheet up till New York rings with your exploits. On the present lines that is impossible. You must strike out a line for yourself. You must show the world that even *Cosy Moments* cannot keep a good man down."

He resumed his seat.

"How do you mean?" said Billy Windsor.

Psmith turned to Mike.

"Comrade Jackson, if you were editing this paper, is there a single feature you would willingly retain?"

"I don't think there is," said Mike. "It's all pretty bad rot."

"My opinion in a nutshell," said Psmith, approvingly. "Comrade Jackson," he explained, turning to Billy, "has a secure reputation on the other side for the keenness and lucidity of his views upon literature. You may safely build upon him. In England when Comrade Jackson says 'Turn' we all turn. Now, my views on the matter are as follows. *Cosy Moments*, in my opinion (worthless, were it not backed by such a virtuoso as Comrade Jackson), needs more snap, more go. All these putrid pages must disappear. Letters must be despatched to-morrow morning, informing Luella Granville Waterman and the others (and in particular B. Henderson Asher, who from a cursory glance strikes me as an ideal candidate for a lethal chamber) that, unless they cease their contributions instantly, you will be compelled to place yourself under police protection. After that we can begin to move."

Billy Windsor sat and rocked himself in his chair without replying. He was trying to assimilate this idea. So far the grandeur of it had dazed him. It was too spacious, too revolutionary. Could it be done? It would undoubtedly mean the sack when Mr. J. Fillken Wilberfloss returned and found the apple of his eye torn asunder and, so to speak, deprived of its choicest pips. On the other hand . . . His brow suddenly cleared. After all, what was the sack? One crowded hour of glorious life is worth an age without a name, and he would have no name as long as he clung to his present position. The editor would be away ten weeks. He would have ten weeks in which to try himself out. Hope leaped within him. In ten weeks he could change *Cosy Moments* into a real live paper. He wondered that the idea had not occurred to him before. The trifling fact that the despised journal was the property of Mr. Benjamin White, and that he had no right whatever to tinker with it without that gentleman's approval, may have occurred to him, but, if it did, it occurred so momentarily that he did not notice it. In these crises one cannot think of everything.

"I'm on," he said, briefly.

Psmith smiled approvingly.

"That," he said, "is the right spirit. You will, I fancy, have little cause to regret your decision. Fortunately, if I may say so, I happen to have a certain amount of leisure just now. It is at your disposal. I have had little experience of journalistic work, but I foresee that I shall be a quick learner. I will become your sub-editor, without salary."

"Bully for you," said Billy Windsor.

"Comrade Jackson," continued Psmith, "is unhappily more fettered. The exigencies of his cricket tour will compel him constantly to be gadding about, now to Philadelphia, now to Saskatchewan, anon to Onehorseville, Ga. His services, therefore, cannot be relied upon continuously. From him, accordingly, we shall expect little but moral support. An occasional congratulatory telegram. Now and then a bright smile of approval. The bulk of the work will devolve upon our two selves."

"Let it devolve," said Billy Windsor, enthusiastically.

"Assuredly," said Psmith. "And now to decide upon our main scheme. You, of course, are the editor, and my suggestions are merely suggestions, subject to your approval. But, briefly, my idea is that *Cosy Moments* should become red-hot stuff. I could wish its tone to be such that the public will wonder why we do not print it on asbestos. We must chronicle all the live events of the day, murders, fires, and the like in a manner which will make our readers' spines thrill. Above all, we must be the guardians of the People's rights. We must be a search-light, showing up the dark spot in the souls of those who would endeavour in any way to do the PEOPLE in the eye. We must detect the wrong-doer, and deliver him such a series of resentful buffs that he will abandon his little games and become a model citizen. The details of the campaign we must think out after, but I fancy that, if we follow those main lines, we shall produce a bright, readable little sheet which will in a measure make this city sit up and take notice. Are you with me, Comrade Windsor?"

"Surest thing you know," said Billy with fervour.

CHAPTER VI

THE TENEMENTS

To alter the scheme of a weekly from cover to cover is not a task that is completed without work. The dismissal of *Cosy Moments'* entire staff of contributors left a gap in the paper which had to be filled, and owing to the nearness of press day there was no time to fill it before the issue of the next number. The editorial staff had to be satisfied with heading every page with the words "Look out! Look out!! Look out!!! See foot of page!!!!" printing in the space at the bottom the legend, "Next Week! See Editorial!" and compiling in conjunction a snappy editorial, setting forth the proposed changes. This was largely the work of Psmith.

"Comrade Jackson," he said to Mike, as they set forth one evening in search of their new flat, "I fancy I have found my metier. Commerce, many considered, was the line I should take; and doubtless, had I stuck to that walk in life, I should soon have become a financial magnate. But something seemed to whisper to me, even in the midst of my triumphs in the New Asiatic Bank, that there were other fields. For the moment it seems to me that I have found the job for which nature specially designed me. At last I have Scope. And without Scope, where are we? Wedged tightly in among the ribstons. There are some very fine passages in that editorial. The last paragraph, beginning '*Cosy Moments* cannot be muzzled,' in particular. I like it. It strikes the right note. It should stir the blood of a free and independent people till they sit in platoons on the doorstep of our office, waiting for the next number to appear."

"How about that next number?" asked Mike. "Are you and Windsor going to fill the whole paper yourselves?"

"By no means. It seems that Comrade Windsor knows certain stout fellows, reporters on other papers, who will be delighted to weigh in with stuff for a moderate fee."

"How about Luella What's-her-name and the others? How have they taken it?"

"Up to the present we have no means of ascertaining. The letters giving them the miss-in-baulk in no uncertain voice were only despatched yesterday. But it cannot affect us how they writhe beneath the blow. There is no reprieve."

Mike roared with laughter.

"It's the rummiest business I ever struck," he said. "I'm jolly glad it's not my paper. It's pretty lucky for you two lunatics that the proprietor's in Europe."

Psmith regarded him with pained surprise.

"I do not understand you, Comrade Jackson. Do you insinuate that we are not acting in the proprietor's best interests? When he sees the receipts, after we have handled the paper for a while, he will go singing about his hotel. His beaming smile will be a by-word in Carlsbad. Visitors will be shown it as one of the sights. His only doubt will be whether to send his money to the bank or keep it in tubs and roll in it. We are on to a big thing, Comrade Jackson. Wait till you see our first number."

"And how about the editor? I should think that first number would bring him back foaming at the mouth."

"I have ascertained from Comrade Windsor that there is nothing to fear from that quarter. By a singular stroke of good fortune Comrade Wilberfloss-his name is Wilberfloss-has been ordered complete rest during his holiday. The kindly medico, realising the fearful strain inflicted by reading *Cosy Moments* in its old form, specifically mentioned that the paper was to be withheld from him until he returned."

"And when he does return, what are you going to do?"

"By that time, doubtless, the paper will be in so flourishing a state that he will confess how wrong his own methods were and adopt ours without a murmur. In the meantime, Comrade Jackson, I would call your attention to the fact that we seem to have lost our way. In the exhilaration of this little chat, our footsteps have wandered. Where we are, goodness only knows. I can only say that I shouldn't care to have to live here."

"There's a name up on the other side of that lamp-post."

"Let us wend in that direction. Ah, Pleasant Street? I fancy that the master-mind who chose that name must have had the rudiments of a sense of humour."

It was indeed a repellent neighbourhood in which they had arrived. The New York slum stands in a class of its own. It is unique. The height of the houses and the narrowness of the streets seem to condense its unpleasantness. All the smells and noises, which are many and varied, are penned up in a sort of canyon, and gain in vehemence from the fact. The masses of dirty clothes hanging from the fire-escapes increase the depression. Nowhere in the city does one realise so fully the disadvantages of a lack of space. New York, being an island, has had no room to spread. It is a town of human sardines. In the poorer quarters the congestion is unbelievable.

Psmith and Mike picked their way through the groups of ragged children who covered the roadway. There seemed to be thousands of them.

"Poor kids!" said Mike. "It must be awful living in a hole like this."

Psmith said nothing. He was looking thoughtful. He glanced up at the grimy buildings on each side. On the lower floors one could see into dark, bare rooms. These were the star apartments of the tenement-houses, for they opened on to the street, and so got a little light and air. The imagination jibbed at the thought of the back rooms.

"I wonder who owns these places," said Psmith. "It seems to me that there's what you might call room for improvement. It wouldn't be a scaly idea to turn that *Cosy Moments* search-light we were talking about on to them."

They walked on a few steps.

"Look here," said Psmith, stopping. "This place makes me sick. I'm going in to have a look round. I expect some muscular householder will resent the intrusion and boot us out, but we'll risk it."

Followed by Mike, he turned in at one of the doors. A group of men
leaning against the opposite wall looked at them without curiosity.
Probably they took them for reporters hunting for a story.
Reporters were the only tolerably well-dressed visitors Pleasant
Street ever entertained.

It was almost pitch dark on the stairs. They had to feel their way up. Most of the doors were shut but one on the second floor was ajar. Through the opening they had a glimpse of a number of women sitting round on boxes. The floor was covered with little heaps of linen. All the women were sewing. Mike, stumbling in the darkness, almost fell against the door. None of the women looked up at the noise. Time was evidently money in Pleasant Street.

On the fourth floor there was an open door. The room was empty. It was a good representative Pleasant Street back room. The architect in this case had given rein to a passion for originality. He had constructed the room without a window of any sort whatsoever. There was a square opening in the door. Through this, it was to be presumed, the entire stock of air used by the occupants was supposed to come.

They stumbled downstairs again and out into the street. By contrast with the conditions indoors the street seemed spacious and breezy.

"This," said Psmith, as they walked on, "is where *Cosy Moments* gets busy at a singularly early date."

"What are you going to do?" asked Mike.

"I propose, Comrade Jackson," said Psmith, "if Comrade Windsor is agreeable, to make things as warm for the owner of this place as I jolly well know how. What he wants, of course," he proceeded in the tone of a family doctor prescribing for a patient, "is disembowelling. I

557

fancy, however, that a mawkishly sentimental legislature will prevent our performing that national service. We must endeavour to do what we can by means of kindly criticism in the paper. And now, having settled that important point, let us try and get out of this place of wrath, and find Fourth Avenue."

CHAPTER VII

VISITORS AT THE OFFICE

On the following morning Mike had to leave with the team for Philadelphia. Psmith came down to the ferry to see him off, and hung about moodily until the time of departure.

"It is saddening me to a great extent, Comrade Jackson," he said, "this perpetual parting of the ways. When I think of the happy moments we have spent hand-in-hand across the seas, it fills me with a certain melancholy to have you flitting off in this manner without me. Yet there is another side to the picture. To me there is something singularly impressive in our unhesitating reply to the calls of Duty. Your Duty summons you to Philadelphia, to knock the cover off the local bowling. Mine retains me here, to play my part in the great work of making New York sit up. By the time you return, with a century or two, I trust, in your bag, the good work should, I fancy, be getting something of a move on. I will complete the arrangements with regard to the flat."

After leaving Pleasant Street they had found Fourth Avenue by a devious route, and had opened negotiations for a large flat near Thirtieth Street. It was immediately above a saloon, which was something of a drawback, but the landlord had assured them that the voices of the revellers did not penetrate to it.

* * * * *

When the ferry-boat had borne Mike off across the river, Psmith turned to stroll to the office of *Cosy Moments*. The day was fine, and on the whole, despite Mike's desertion, he felt pleased with life. Psmith's was a nature which required a certain amount of stimulus in the way of gentle excitement; and it seemed to him that the conduct of the remodelled *Cosy Moments* might supply this. He liked Billy Windsor, and looked forward to a not unenjoyable time till Mike should return.

The offices of *Cosy Moments* were in a large building in the street off Madison Avenue. They consisted of a sort of outer lair, where Pugsy Maloney spent his time reading tales of life in the prairies and heading off undesirable visitors; a small room, which would have belonged to the stenographer if *Cosy Moments* had possessed one; and a larger room beyond, which was the editorial sanctum.

As Psmith passed through the front door, Pugsy Maloney rose.

"Say!" said Master Maloney.

"Say on, Comrade Maloney," said Psmith.

"Dey're in dere."

"Who, precisely?"

"A whole bunch of dem."

Psmith inspected Master Maloney through his eye-glass. "Can you give me any particulars?" he asked patiently. "You are well-meaning, but vague, Comrade Maloney. Who are in there?"

"De whole bunch of dem. Dere's Mr. Asher and the Rev. Philpotts and a gazebo what calls himself Waterman and about 'steen more of dem."

A faint smile appeared upon Psmith's face.

"And is Comrade Windsor in there, too, in the middle of them?"

"Nope. Mr. Windsor's out to lunch."

"Comrade Windsor knows his business. Why did you let them in?"

"Sure, dey just butted in," said Master Maloney complainingly. "I was sittin' here, readin' me book, when de foist of de guys blew in. 'Boy,' says he, 'is de editor in?' 'Nope,' I says. 'I'll go in an' wait,' says he. 'Nuttin' doin',' says I. 'Nix on de goin' in act.' I might as well have saved me breat'. In he butts, and he's in der now. Well, in about t'ree minutes along comes another gazebo. 'Boy,' says he, 'is de editor in?' 'Nope,' I says. 'I'll wait,' says he lightin' out for de door. Wit dat I sees de proposition's too fierce for muh. I can't keep dese big husky guys out if dey's for buttin' in. So when de rest of de bunch comes along, I don't try to give dem de t'run down. I says, 'Well, gents,' I says, 'it's up to youse. De editor ain't in, but if youse wants to join de giddy t'rong, push t'roo inter de inner room. I can't be boddered.'"

"And what more *could* you have said?" agreed Psmith approvingly. "Tell me, Comrade Maloney, what was the general average aspect of these determined spirits?"

"Huh?"

"Did they seem to you to be gay, lighthearted? Did they carol snatches of song as they went? Or did they appear to be looking for some one with a hatchet?"

"Dey was hoppin'-mad, de whole bunch of dem."

"As I suspected. But we must not repine, Comrade Maloney. These trifling contretemps are the penalties we pay for our high journalistic aims. I will interview these merchants. I fancy that with the aid of the Diplomatic Smile and the Honeyed Word I may manage to pull through. It is as well, perhaps, that Comrade Windsor is out. The situation calls for the handling of a man of delicate culture and nice tact. Comrade Windsor would probably have endeavoured to clear the room with a chair. If he should arrive during the seance, Comrade Maloney, be so good as to inform him of the state of affairs, and tell him not to come in. Give him my compliments, and tell him to go out and watch the snowdrops growing in Madison Square Garden."

"Sure," said Master Maloney.

Then Psmith, having smoothed the nap of his hat and flicked a speck of dust from his coat-sleeve, walked to the door of the inner room and went in.

CHAPTER VIII

THE HONEYED WORD

Master Maloney's statement that "about 'steen visitors" had arrived in addition to Messrs. Asher, Waterman, and the Rev. Philpotts proved to have been due to a great extent to a somewhat feverish imagination. There were only five men in the room.

As Psmith entered, every eye was turned upon him. To an outside spectator he would have seemed rather like a very well-dressed Daniel introduced into a den of singularly irritable lions. Five pairs of eyes were smouldering with a long-nursed resentment. Five brows were corrugated with wrathful lines. Such, however, was the simple majesty of Psmith's demeanour that for a moment there was dead silence. Not a word was spoken as he paced, wrapped in thought, to the editorial chair. Stillness brooded over the room as he carefully dusted that piece of furniture, and, having done so to his satisfaction, hitched up the knees of his trousers and sank gracefully into a sitting position.

This accomplished, he looked up and started. He gazed round the room.

"Ha! I am observed!" he murmured.

The words broke the spell. Instantly, the five visitors burst simultaneously into speech.

"Are you the acting editor of this paper?"

"I wish to have a word with you, sir."

"Mr. Windsor, I presume?"

"Pardon me!"

"I should like a few moments' conversation."

The start was good and even; but the gentleman who said "Pardon me!" necessarily finished first with the rest nowhere.

Psmith turned to him, bowed, and fixed him with a benevolent gaze through his eye-glass.

"Are you Mr. Windsor, sir, may I ask?" inquired the favoured one.

The others paused for the reply.

"Alas! no," said Psmith with manly regret.

"Then who are you?"

"I am Psmith."

There was a pause.

"Where is Mr. Windsor?"

"He is, I fancy, champing about forty cents' worth of lunch at some neighbouring hostelry."

"When will he return?"

"Anon. But how much anon I fear I cannot say."

The visitors looked at each other.

"This is exceedingly annoying," said the man who had said "Pardon me!" "I came for the express purpose of seeing Mr. Windsor."

"So did I," chimed in the rest. "Same here. So did I."

Psmith bowed courteously.

"Comrade Windsor's loss is my gain. Is there anything I can do for you?"

"Are you on the editorial staff of this paper?"

"I am acting sub-editor. The work is not light," added Psmith gratuitously. "Sometimes the cry goes round, 'Can Psmith get through it all? Will his strength support his unquenchable spirit?' But I stagger on. I do not repine."

"Then maybe you can tell me what all this means?" said a small round gentleman who so far had done only chorus work.

"If it is in my power to do so, it shall be done, Comrade —I have not the pleasure of your name."

"My name is Waterman, sir. I am here on behalf of my wife, whose name you doubtless know."

"Correct me if I am wrong," said Psmith, "but I should say it, also, was Waterman."

"Luella Granville Waterman, sir," said the little man proudly. Psmith removed his eye-glass, polished it, and replaced it in his eye. He felt that he must run no risk of not seeing clearly the husband of one who, in his opinion, stood alone in literary circles as a purveyor of sheer bilge.

"My wife," continued the little man, producing an envelope and handing it to Psmith, "has received this extraordinary communication from a man signing himself W. Windsor. We are both at a loss to make head or tail of it."

Psmith was reading the letter.

"It seems reasonably clear to me," he said.

"It is an outrage. My wife has been a contributor to this journal from its foundation. Her work has given every satisfaction to Mr. Wilberfloss. And now, without the slightest warning, comes this peremptory dismissal from W. Windsor. Who is W. Windsor? Where is Mr. Wilberfloss?"

The chorus burst forth. It seemed that that was what they all wanted to know: Who was W. Windsor? Where was Mr. Wilberfloss?

"I am the Reverend Edwin T. Philpotts, sir," said a cadaverous-looking man with pale blue eyes and a melancholy face. "I have contributed 'Moments of Meditation' to this journal for a very considerable period of time."

"I have read your page with the keenest interest," said Psmith. "I may be wrong, but yours seems to me work which the world will not willingly let die."

The Reverend Edwin's frosty face thawed into a bleak smile.

"And yet," continued Psmith, "I gather that Comrade Windsor, on the other hand, actually wishes to hurry on its decease. It is these strange contradictions, these clashings of personal taste, which make up what we call life. Here we have, on the one hand—"

A man with a face like a walnut, who had hitherto lurked almost unseen behind a stout person in a serge suit, bobbed into the open, and spoke his piece.

"Where's this fellow Windsor? W. Windsor. That's the man we want to see. I've been working for this paper without a break, except when I had the mumps, for four years, and I've reason to know that my page was as widely read and appreciated as any in New York. And now up comes this Windsor fellow, if you please, and tells me in so many words the paper's got no use for me."

"These are life's tragedies," murmured Psmith.

"What's he mean by it? That's what I want to know. And that's what these gentlemen want to know-See here—"

"I am addressing—?" said Psmith.

"Asher's my name. B. Henderson Asher. I write 'Moments of Mirth.'"

A look almost of excitement came into Psmith's face, such a look as a visitor to a foreign land might wear when confronted with some great national monument. That he should be privileged to look upon the author of "Moments of Mirth" in the flesh, face to face, was almost too much.

"Comrade Asher," he said reverently, "may I shake your hand?"

The other extended his hand with some suspicion.

"Your 'Moments of Mirth,'" said Psmith, shaking it, "have frequently reconciled me to the toothache."

He reseated himself.

"Gentlemen," he said, "this is a painful case. The circumstances, as you will readily admit when you have heard all, are peculiar. You have asked me where Mr. Wilberfloss is. I do not know."

"You don't know!" exclaimed Mr. Waterman.

"I don't know. You don't know. They," said Psmith, indicating the rest with a wave of the hand, "don't know. Nobody knows. His locality is as hard to ascertain as that of a black cat in a coal-cellar on a moonless night. Shortly before I joined this journal, Mr. Wilberfloss, by his doctor's orders, started out on a holiday, leaving no address. No letters were to be forwarded. He was to enjoy complete rest. Where is he now? Who shall say? Possibly legging it down some rugged slope in the Rockies, with two bears and a wild cat in earnest pursuit. Possibly in the midst of some Florida everglade, making a noise like a piece of meat in order to snare crocodiles. Possibly in Canada, baiting moose-traps. We have no data."

Silent consternation prevailed among the audience. Finally the Rev. Edwin T. Philpotts was struck with an idea.

"Where is Mr. White?" he asked.
The point was well received.
"Yes, where's Mr. Benjamin White?" chorused the rest.
Psmith shook his head.
"In Europe. I cannot say more."
The audience's consternation deepened.
"Then, do you mean to say," demanded Mr. Asher, "that this fellow Windsor's the boss here, that what he says goes?"

Psmith bowed.
"With your customary clear-headedness, Comrade Asher, you have got home on the bull's-eye first pop. Comrade Windsor is indeed the boss. A man of intensely masterful character, he will brook no opposition. I am powerless to sway him. Suggestions from myself as to the conduct of the paper would infuriate him. He believes that radical changes are necessary in the programme of *Cosy Moments*, and he means to put them through if it snows. Doubtless he would gladly consider your work if it fitted in with his ideas. A snappy account of a glove-fight, a spine-shaking word-picture of a railway smash, or something on those lines, would be welcomed. But —"

"I have never heard of such a thing," said Mr. Waterman indignantly.
Psmith sighed.
"Some time ago," he said, "—how long it seems! —I remember saying to a young friend of mine of the name of Spiller, 'Comrade Spiller, never confuse the unusual with the impossible.' It is my guiding rule in life. It is unusual for the substitute-editor of a weekly paper to do a Captain Kidd act and take entire command of the journal on his own account; but is it impossible? Alas no. Comrade Windsor has done it. That is where you, Comrade Asher, and you, gentlemen, have landed yourselves squarely in the broth. You have confused the unusual with the impossible."

"But what is to be done?" cried Mr. Asher.
"I fear that there is nothing to be done, except wait. The present *régime* is but an experiment. It may be that when Comrade Wilberfloss, having dodged the bears and eluded the wild cat, returns to his post at the helm of this journal, he may decide not to continue on the lines at present mapped out. He should be back in about ten weeks."

"Ten weeks!"
"I fancy that was to be the duration of his holiday. Till then my advice to you gentlemen is to wait. You may rely on me to keep a watchful eye upon your interests. When your thoughts tend to take a gloomy turn, say to yourselves, 'All is well. Psmith is keeping a watchful eye upon our interests.'"

"All the same, I should like to see this W. Windsor," said Mr. Asher.

Psmith shook his head.
"I shouldn't," he said. "I speak in your best interests. Comrade Windsor is a man of the fiercest passions. He cannot brook interference. Were you to question the wisdom of his plans,

there is no knowing what might not happen. He would be the first to regret any violent action, when once he had cooled off, but would that be any consolation to his victim? I think not. Of course, if you wish it, I could arrange a meeting—"

Mr. Asher said no, he thought it didn't matter.

"I guess I can wait," he said.

"That," said Psmith approvingly, "is the right spirit. Wait. That is the watch-word. And now," he added, rising, "I wonder if a bit of lunch somewhere might not be a good thing? We have had an interesting but fatiguing little chat. Our tissues require restoring. If you gentlemen would care to join me—"

Ten minutes later the company was seated in complete harmony round a table at the Knickerbocker. Psmith, with the dignified bonhomie of a seigneur of the old school, was ordering the wine; while B. Henderson Asher, brimming over with good-humour, was relating to an attentive circle an anecdote which should have appeared in his next instalment of "Moments of Mirth."

CHAPTER IX

FULL STEAM AHEAD

When Psmith returned to the office, he found Billy Windsor in the doorway, just parting from a thick-set young man, who seemed to be expressing his gratitude to the editor for some good turn. He was shaking him warmly by the hand.

Psmith stood aside to let him pass.

"An old college chum, Comrade Windsor?" he asked.

"That was Kid Brady."

"The name is unfamiliar to me. Another contributor?"

"He's from my part of the country-Wyoming. He wants to fight any one in the world at a hundred and thirty-three pounds."

"We all have our hobbies. Comrade Brady appears to have selected a somewhat exciting one. He would find stamp-collecting less exacting."

"It hasn't given him much excitement so far, poor chap," said Billy Windsor. "He's in the championship class, and here he has been pottering about New York for a month without being able to get a fight. It's always the way in this rotten East," continued Billy, warming up as was his custom when discussing a case of oppression and injustice. "It's all graft here. You've got to let half a dozen brutes dip into every dollar you earn, or you don't get a chance. If the kid had a manager, he'd get all the fights he wanted. And the manager would get nearly all the money. I've told him that we will back him up."

"You have hit it, Comrade Windsor," said Psmith with enthusiasm. "*Cosy Moments* shall be Comrade Brady's manager. We will give him a much-needed boost up in our columns. A sporting section is what the paper requires more than anything."

"If things go on as they've started, what it will require still more will be a fighting-editor. Pugsy tells me you had visitors while I was out."

"A few," said Psmith. "One or two very entertaining fellows. Comrades Asher, Philpotts, and others. I have just been giving them a bite of lunch at the Knickerbocker."

"Lunch!"

"A most pleasant little lunch. We are now as brothers. I fear I have made you perhaps a shade unpopular with our late contributors; but these things must be. We must clench our teeth and face them manfully. If I were you, I think I should not drop in at the house of Comrade Asher and the rest to take pot-luck for some little time to come. In order to soothe the squad I was compelled to curse you to some extent."

"Don't mind me."

"I think I may say I didn't."

"Say, look here, you must charge up the price of that lunch to the office. Necessary expenses, you know."

"I could not dream of doing such a thing, Comrade Windsor. The whole affair was a great treat to me. I have few pleasures. Comrade Asher alone was worth the money. I found his society intensely interesting. I have always believed in the Darwinian theory. Comrade Asher confirmed my views."

They went into the inner office. Psmith removed his hat and coat.

"And now once more to work," he said. "Psmith the *flaneur* of Fifth
Avenue ceases to exist. In his place we find Psmith the hard-headed
sub-editor. Be so good as to indicate a job of work for me,
Comrade Windsor. I am champing at my bit."

Billy Windsor sat down, and lit his pipe.

565

"What we want most," he said thoughtfully, "is some big topic. That's the only way to get a paper going. Look at *Everybody's Magazine*. They didn't amount to a row of beans till Lawson started his 'Frenzied Finance' articles. Directly they began, the whole country was squealing for copies. *Everybody's* put up their price from ten to fifteen cents, and now they lead the field."

"The country must squeal for *Cosy Moments*," said Psmith firmly. "I fancy I have a scheme which may not prove wholly scaly. Wandering yesterday with Comrade Jackson in a search for Fourth Avenue, I happened upon a spot called Pleasant Street. Do you know it?"

Billy Windsor nodded.

"I went down there once or twice when I was a reporter. It's a beastly place."

"It is a singularly beastly place. We went into one of the houses."

"They're pretty bad."

"Who owns them?"

"I don't know. Probably some millionaire. Those tenement houses are about as paying an investment as you can have."

"Hasn't anybody ever tried to do anything about them?"

"Not so far as I know. It's pretty difficult to get at these fellows, you see. But they're fierce, aren't they, those houses!"

"What," asked Psmith, "is the precise difficulty of getting at these merchants?"

"Well, it's this way. There are all sorts of laws about the places, but any one who wants can get round them as easy as falling off a log. The law says a tenement house is a building occupied by more than two families. Well, when there's a fuss, all the man has to do is to clear out all the families but two. Then, when the inspector fellow comes along, and says, let's say, 'Where's your running water on each floor? That's what the law says you've got to have, and here are these people having to go downstairs and out of doors to fetch their water supplies,' the landlord simply replies, 'Nothing doing. This isn't a tenement house at all. There are only two families here.' And when the fuss has blown over, back come the rest of the crowd, and things go on the same as before."

"I see," said Psmith. "A very cheery scheme."

"Then there's another thing. You can't get hold of the man who's really responsible, unless you're prepared to spend thousands ferreting out evidence. The land belongs in the first place to some corporation or other. They lease it to a lessee. When there's a fuss, they say they aren't responsible, it's up to the lessee. And he lies so low that you can't find out who he is. It's all just like the East. Everything in the East is as crooked as Pearl Street. If you want a square deal, you've got to come out Wyoming way."

"The main problem, then," said Psmith, "appears to be the discovery of the lessee, lad? Surely a powerful organ like *Cosy Moments*, with its vast ramifications, could bring off a thing like that?"

"I doubt it. We'll try, anyway. There's no knowing but what we may have luck."

"Precisely," said Psmith. "Full steam ahead, and trust to luck. The chances are that, if we go on long enough, we shall eventually arrive somewhere. After all, Columbus didn't know that America existed when he set out. All he knew was some highly interesting fact about an egg. What that was, I do not at the moment recall, but it bucked Columbus up like a tonic. It made him fizz ahead like a two-year-old. The facts which will nerve us to effort are two. In the first place, we know that there must be some one at the bottom of the business. Secondly, as there appears to be no law of libel whatsoever in this great and free country, we shall be enabled to haul up our slacks with a considerable absence of restraint."

"Sure," said Billy Windsor. "Which of us is going to write the first article?"

"You may leave it to me, Comrade Windsor. I am no hardened old journalist, I fear, but I have certain qualifications for the post. A young man once called at the office of a certain newspaper, and asked for a job. 'Have you any special line?' asked the editor. 'Yes,' said the bright lad, 'I am rather good at invective.' 'Any special kind of invective?' queried the man up top. 'No,' replied our hero, 'just general invective.' Such is my own case, Comrade Windsor. I am a very fair purveyor of good, general invective. And as my visit to Pleasant Street is of such recent date, I am tolerably full of my subject. Taking full advantage of the benevolent laws of this country governing libel, I fancy I will produce a screed which will make this anonymous lessee feel as if he had inadvertently seated himself upon a tin-tack. Give me pen and paper, Comrade Windsor, instruct Comrade Maloney to suspend his whistling till such time as I am better able to listen to it; and I think we have got a success."

CHAPTER X

GOING SOME

There was once an editor of a paper in the Far West who was sitting at his desk, musing pleasantly of life, when a bullet crashed through the window and embedded itself in the wall at the back of his head. A happy smile lit up the editor's face. "Ah," he said complacently, "I knew that Personal column of ours was going to be a success!"

What the bullet was to the Far West editor, the visit of Mr. Francis Parker to the offices of *Cosy Moments* was to Billy Windsor.

It occurred in the third week of the new *régime* of the paper. *Cosy Moments*, under its new management, had bounded ahead like a motor-car when the throttle is opened. Incessant work had been the order of the day. Billy Windsor's hair had become more dishevelled than ever, and even Psmith had at moments lost a certain amount of his dignified calm. Sandwiched in between the painful case of Kid Brady and the matter of the tenements, which formed the star items of the paper's contents, was a mass of bright reading dealing with the events of the day. Billy Windsor's newspaper friends had turned in some fine, snappy stuff in their best Yellow Journal manner, relating to the more stirring happenings in the city. Psmith, who had constituted himself guardian of the literary and dramatic interests of the paper, had employed his gift of general invective to considerable effect, as was shown by a conversation between Master Maloney and a visitor one morning, heard through the open door.

"I wish to see the editor of this paper," said the visitor.

"Editor not in," said Master Maloney, untruthfully.

"Ha! Then when he returns I wish you to give him a message."

"Sure."

"I am Aubrey Bodkin, of the National Theatre. Give him my compliments, and tell him that Mr. Bodkin does not lightly forget."

An unsolicited testimonial which caused Psmith the keenest satisfaction.

The section of the paper devoted to Kid Brady was attractive to all those with sporting blood in them. Each week there appeared in the same place on the same page a portrait of the Kid, looking moody and important, in an attitude of self-defence, and under the portrait the legend, "Jimmy Garvin must meet this boy." Jimmy was the present holder of the light-weight title. He had won it a year before, and since then had confined himself to smoking cigars as long as walking-sticks and appearing nightly as the star in a music-hall sketch entitled "A Fight for Honour." His reminiscences were appearing weekly in a Sunday paper. It was this that gave Psmith the idea of publishing Kid Brady's autobiography in *Cosy Moments*, an idea which made the Kid his devoted adherent from then on. Like most pugilists, the Kid had a passion for bursting into print, and his life had been saddened up to the present by the refusal of the press to publish his reminiscences. To appear in print is the fighter's accolade. It signifies that he has arrived. Psmith extended the hospitality of page four of *Cosy Moments* to Kid Brady, and the latter leaped at the chance. He was grateful to Psmith for not editing his contributions. Other pugilists, contributing to other papers, groaned under the supervision of a member of the staff who cut out their best passages and altered the rest into Addisonian English. The readers of *Cosy Moments* got Kid Brady raw.

"Comrade Brady," said Psmith to Billy, "has a singularly pure and pleasing style. It is bound to appeal powerfully to the many-headed. Listen to this bit. Our hero is fighting Battling Jack Benson in that eminent artist's native town of Louisville, and the citizens have given their native son the Approving Hand, while receiving Comrade Brady with chilly silence. Here is the Kid on the subject: 'I looked around that house, and I seen I hadn't a friend in it. And then the gong goes, and I says to myself how I has one friend, my poor old mother way out in

Wyoming, and I goes in and mixes it, and then I seen Benson losing his goat, so I ups with an awful half-scissor hook to the plexus, and in the next round I seen Benson has a chunk of yellow, and I gets in with a hay-maker and I picks up another sleep-producer from the floor and hands it him, and he takes the count all right.'. . Crisp, lucid, and to the point. That is what the public wants. If this does not bring Comrade Garvin up to the scratch, nothing will."

But the feature of the paper was the "Tenement" series. It was late summer now, and there was nothing much going on in New York. The public was consequently free to take notice. The sale of *Cosy Moments* proceeded briskly. As Psmith had predicted, the change of policy had the effect of improving the sales to a marked extent. Letters of complaint from old subscribers poured into the office daily. But, as Billy Windsor complacently remarked, they had paid their subscriptions, so that the money was safe whether they read the paper or not. And, meanwhile, a large new public had sprung up and was growing every week. Advertisements came trooping in. *Cosy Moments*, in short, was passing through an era of prosperity undreamed of in its history.

"Young blood," said Psmith nonchalantly, "young blood. That is the secret. A paper must keep up to date, or it falls behind its competitors in the race. Comrade Wilberfloss's methods were possibly sound, but too limited and archaic. They lacked ginger. We of the younger generation have our fingers more firmly on the public pulse. We read off the public's unspoken wishes as if by intuition. We know the game from A to Z."

At this moment Master Maloney entered, bearing in his hand a card.

"'Francis Parker'?" said Billy, taking it. "Don't know him."

"Nor I," said Psmith. "We make new friends daily."

"He's a guy with a tall-shaped hat," volunteered Master Maloney, "an' he's wearin' a dude suit an' shiny shoes."

"Comrade Parker," said Psmith approvingly, "has evidently not been blind to the importance of a visit to *Cosy Moments*. He has dressed himself in his best. He has felt, rightly, that this is no occasion for the old straw hat and the baggy flannels. I would not have it otherwise. It is the right spirit. Shall we give him audience, Comrade Windsor?"

"I wonder what he wants."

"That," said Psmith, "we shall ascertain more clearly after a personal interview. Comrade Maloney, show the gentleman in. We can give him three and a quarter minutes."

Pugsy withdrew.

Mr. Francis Parker proved to be a man who might have been any age between twenty-five and thirty-five. He had a smooth, clean-shaven face, and a cat-like way of moving. As Pugsy had stated in effect, he wore a tail-coat, trousers with a crease which brought a smile of kindly approval to Psmith's face, and patent-leather boots of pronounced shininess. Gloves and a tall hat, which he carried, completed an impressive picture.

He moved softly into the room.

"I wished to see the editor."

Psmith waved a hand towards Billy.

"The treat has not been denied you," he said. "Before you is Comrade Windsor, the Wyoming cracker-jack. He is our editor. I myself—I am Psmith-though but a subordinate, may also claim the title in a measure. Technically, I am but a sub-editor; but such is the mutual esteem in which Comrade Windsor and I hold each other that we may practically be said to be inseparable. We have no secrets from each other. You may address us both impartially. Will you sit for a space?"

He pushed a chair towards the visitor, who seated himself with the care inspired by a perfect trouser-crease. There was a momentary silence while he selected a spot on the table on which to place his hat.

"The style of the paper has changed greatly, has it not, during the past few weeks?" he said. "I have never been, shall I say, a constant reader of *Cosy Moments*, and I may be wrong. But is not its interest in current affairs a recent development?"

569

"You are very right," responded Psmith. "Comrade Windsor, a man of alert and restless temperament, felt that a change was essential if *Cosy Moments* was to lead public thought. Comrade Wilberfloss's methods were good in their way. I have no quarrel with Comrade Wilberfloss. But he did not lead public thought. He catered exclusively for children with water on the brain, and men and women with solid ivory skulls. Comrade Windsor, with a broader view, feels that there are other and larger publics. He refuses to content himself with ladling out a weekly dole of mental predigested breakfast food. He provides meat. He —"

"Then-excuse me —" said Mr. Parker, turning to Billy, "You, I take it, are responsible for this very vigorous attack on the tenement-house owners?"

"You can take it I am," said Billy.

Psmith interposed.

"We are both responsible, Comrade Parker. If any husky guy, as I fancy Master Maloney would phrase it, is anxious to aim a swift kick at the man behind those articles, he must distribute it evenly between Comrade Windsor and myself."

"I see." Mr. Parker paused. "They are-er-very outspoken articles," he added.

"Warm stuff," agreed Psmith. "Distinctly warm stuff."

"May I speak frankly?" said Mr. Parker.

"Assuredly, Comrade Parker. There must be no secrets, no restraint between us. We would not have you go away and say to yourself, 'Did I make my meaning clear? Was I too elusive?' Say on."

"I am speaking in your best interests."

"Who would doubt it, Comrade Parker. Nothing has buoyed us up more strongly during the hours of doubt through which we have passed than the knowledge that you wish us well."

Billy Windsor suddenly became militant. There was a feline smoothness about the visitor which had been jarring upon him ever since he first spoke. Billy was of the plains, the home of blunt speech, where you looked your man in the eye and said it quick. Mr. Parker was too bland for human consumption. He offended Billy's honest soul.

"See here," cried he, leaning forward, "what's it all about? Let's have it. If you've anything to say about those articles, say it right out. Never mind our best interests. We can look after them. Let's have what's worrying you."

Psmith waved a deprecating hand.

"Do not let us be abrupt on this happy occasion. To me it is enough simply to sit and chat with Comrade Parker, irrespective of the trend of his conversation. Still, as time is money, and this is our busy day, possibly it might be as well, sir, if you unburdened yourself as soon as convenient. Have you come to point out some flaw in those articles? Do they fall short in any way of your standard for such work?"

Mr. Parker's smooth face did not change its expression, but he came to the point.

"I should not go on with them if I were you," he said.

"Why?" demanded Billy.

"There are reasons why you should not," said Mr. Parker.

"And there are reasons why we should."

"Less powerful ones."

There proceeded from Billy a noise not describable in words. It was partly a snort, partly a growl. It resembled more than anything else the preliminary sniffing snarl a bull-dog emits before he joins battle. Billy's cow-boy blood was up. He was rapidly approaching the state of mind in which the men of the plains, finding speech unequal to the expression of their thoughts, reach for their guns.

Psmith intervened.

"We do not completely gather your meaning, Comrade Parker. I fear we must ask you to hand it to us with still more breezy frankness. Do you speak from purely friendly motives? Are you advising us to discontinue the articles merely because you fear that they will damage our literary reputation? Or are there other reasons why you feel that they should cease? Do you speak solely as a literary connoisseur? Is it the style or the subject-matter of which you disapprove?"

Mr. Parker leaned forward.

"The gentleman whom I represent —"

"Then this is no matter of your own personal taste? You are an emissary?"

"These articles are causing a certain inconvenience to the gentleman whom I represent. Or, rather, he feels that, if continued, they may do so."

"You mean," broke in Billy explosively, "that if we kick up enough fuss to make somebody start a commission to inquire into this rotten business, your friend who owns the private Hades we're trying to get improved, will have to get busy and lose some of his money by making the houses fit to live in? Is that it?"

"It is not so much the money, Mr. Windsor, though, of course, the expense would be considerable. My employer is a wealthy man."

"I bet he is," said Billy disgustedly. "I've no doubt he makes a mighty good pile out of Pleasant Street."

"It is not so much the money," repeated Mr. Parker, "as the publicity involved. I speak quite frankly. There are reasons why my employer would prefer not to come before the public just now as the owner of the Pleasant Street property. I need not go into those reasons. It is sufficient to say that they are strong ones."

"Well, he knows what to do, I guess. The moment he starts in to make those houses decent, the articles stop. It's up to him."

Psmith nodded.

"Comrade Windsor is correct. He has hit the mark and rung the bell. No conscientious judge would withhold from Comrade Windsor a cigar or a cocoanut, according as his private preference might dictate. That is the matter in a nutshell. Remove the reason for those very scholarly articles, and they cease."

Mr. Parker shook his head.

"I fear that is not feasible. The expense of reconstructing the houses makes that impossible."

"Then there's no use in talking," said Billy. "The articles will go on."

Mr. Parker coughed. A tentative cough, suggesting that the situation was now about to enter upon a more delicate phase. Billy and Psmith waited for him to begin. From their point of view the discussion was over. If it was to be reopened on fresh lines, it was for their visitor to effect that reopening.

"Now, I'm going to be frank, gentlemen," said he, as who should say, "We are all friends here. Let us be hearty." "I'm going to put my cards on the table, and see if we can't fix something up. Now, see here: We don't want unpleasantness. You aren't in this business for your healths, eh? You've got your living to make, just like everybody else, I guess. Well, see here. This is how it stands. To a certain extant, I don't mind admitting, seeing that we're being frank with one another, you two gentlemen have got us-that's to say, my employer-in a cleft stick. Frankly, those articles are beginning to attract attention, and if they go on there's going to be a lot of inconvenience for my employer. That's clear, I reckon. Well, now, here's a square proposition. How much do you want to stop those articles? That's straight. I've been frank with you, and I want you to be frank with me. What's your figure? Name it, and, if it's not too high, I guess we needn't quarrel."

He looked expectantly at Billy. Billy's eyes were bulging. He struggled for speech. He had got as far as "Say!" when Psmith interrupted him. Psmith, gazing sadly at Mr. Parker through his monocle, spoke quietly, with the restrained dignity of some old Roman senator dealing with the enemies of the Republic.

"Comrade Parker," he said, "I fear that you have allowed constant communication with the conscienceless commercialism of this worldly city to undermine your moral sense. It is useless to dangle rich bribes before our eyes. *Cosy Moments* cannot be muzzled. You doubtless mean well, according to your-if I may say so-somewhat murky lights, but we are not for sale, except

571

at ten cents weekly. From the hills of Maine to the Everglades of Florida, from Sandy Hook to San Francisco, from Portland, Oregon, to Melonsquashville, Tennessee, one sentence is in every man's mouth. And what is that sentence? I give you three guesses. You give it up? It is this: '*Cosy Moments* cannot be muzzled!'"

Mr. Parker rose.

"There's nothing more to be done then," he said.

"Nothing," agreed Psmith, "except to make a noise like a hoop and roll away."

"And do it quick," yelled Billy, exploding like a fire-cracker.

Psmith bowed.

"Speed," he admitted, "would be no bad thing. Frankly-if I may borrow the expression-your square proposition has wounded us. I am a man of powerful self-restraint, one of those strong, silent men, and I can curb my emotions. But I fear that Comrade Windsor's generous temperament may at any moment prompt him to start throwing ink-pots. And in Wyoming his deadly aim with the ink-pot won him among the admiring cowboys the sobriquet of Crack-Shot Cuthbert. As man to man, Comrade Parker, I should advise you to bound swiftly away."

"I'm going," said Mr. Parker, picking up his hat. "And I'll give you a piece of advice, too. Those articles are going to be stopped, and if you've any sense between you, you'll stop them yourselves before you get hurt. That's all I've got to say, and that goes."

He went out, closing the door behind him with a bang that added emphasis to his words.

"To men of nicely poised nervous organisation such as ourselves, Comrade Windsor," said Psmith, smoothing his waistcoat thoughtfully, "these scenes are acutely painful. We wince before them. Our ganglions quiver like cinematographs. Gradually recovering command of ourselves, we review the situation. Did our visitor's final remarks convey anything definite to you? Were they the mere casual badinage of a parting guest, or was there something solid behind them?"

Billy Windsor was looking serious.

"I guess he meant it all right. He's evidently working for somebody pretty big, and that sort of man would have a pull with all kinds of Thugs. We shall have to watch out. Now that they find we can't be bought, they'll try the other way. They mean business sure enough. But, by George, let 'em! We're up against a big thing, and I'm going to see it through if they put every gang in New York on to us."

"Precisely, Comrade Windsor. *Cosy Moments*, as I have had occasion to observe before, cannot be muzzled."

"That's right," said Billy Windsor. "And," he added, with the contented look the Far West editor must have worn as the bullet came through the window, "we must have got them scared, or they wouldn't have shown their hand that way. I guess we're making a hit. *Cosy Moments* is going some now."

CHAPTER XI

THE MAN AT THE ASTOR

The duties of Master Pugsy Maloney at the offices of *Cosy Moments* were not heavy; and he was accustomed to occupy his large store of leisure by reading narratives dealing with life in the prairies, which he acquired at a neighbouring shop at cut rates in consideration of their being shop-soiled. It was while he was engrossed in one of these, on the morning following the visit of Mr. Parker, that the seedy-looking man made his appearance. He walked in from the street, and stood before Master Maloney.

"Hey, kid," he said.

Pugsy looked up with some hauteur. He resented being addressed as "kid" by perfect strangers.

"Editor in, Tommy?" inquired the man.

Pugsy by this time had taken a thorough dislike to him. To be called "kid" was bad. The subtle insult of "Tommy" was still worse.

"Nope," he said curtly, fixing his eyes again on his book. A movement on the part of the visitor attracted his attention. The seedy man was making for the door of the inner room. Pugsy instantly ceased to be the student and became the man of action. He sprang from his seat and wriggled in between the man and the door.

"Youse can't butt in dere," he said authoritatively. "Chase yerself."

The man eyed him with displeasure.

"Fresh kid!" he observed disapprovingly.

"Fade away," urged Master Maloney.

The visitor's reply was to extend a hand and grasp Pugsy's left ear between a long finger and thumb. Since time began, small boys in every country have had but one answer for this action. Pugsy made it. He emitted a piercing squeal in which pain, fear, and resentment strove for supremacy.

The noise penetrated into the editorial sanctum, losing only a small part of its strength on the way. Psmith, who was at work on a review of a book of poetry, looked up with patient sadness.

"If Comrade Maloney," he said, "is going to take to singing as well as whistling, I fear this journal must put up its shutters. Concentrated thought will be out of the question."

A second squeal rent the air. Billy Windsor jumped up.

"Somebody must be hurting the kid," he exclaimed.

He hurried to the door and flung it open. Psmith followed at a more leisurely pace. The seedy man, caught in the act, released Master Maloney, who stood rubbing his ear with resentment written on every feature.

On such occasions as this Billy was a man of few words. He made a dive for the seedy man; but the latter, who during the preceding moment had been eyeing the two editors as if he were committing their appearance to memory, sprang back, and was off down the stairs with the agility of a Marathon runner.

"He blows in," said Master Maloney, aggrieved, "and asks is de editor dere. I tells him no, 'cos youse said youse wasn't, and he nips me by the ear when I gets busy to stop him gettin' t'roo."

"Comrade Maloney," said Psmith, "you are a martyr. What would Horatius have done if somebody had nipped him by the ear when he was holding the bridge? The story does not consider the possibility. Yet it might have made all the difference. Did the gentleman state his business?"

"Nope. Just tried to butt t'roo."

"Another of these strong silent men. The world is full of us. These are the perils of the journalistic life. You will be safer and happier when you are rounding up cows on your mustang."

"I wonder what he wanted," said Billy, when they were back again in the inner room.

573

"Who can say, Comrade Windsor? Possibly our autographs. Possibly five minutes' chat on general subjects."

"I don't like the look of him," said Billy.

"Whereas what Comrade Maloney objected to was the feel of him. In what respect did his look jar upon you? His clothes were poorly cut, but such things, I know, leave you unmoved."

"It seems to me," said Billy thoughtfully, "as if he came just to get a sight of us."

"And he got it. Ah, Providence is good to the poor."

"Whoever's behind those tenements isn't going to stick at any odd trifle. We must watch out. That man was probably sent to mark us down for one of the gangs. Now they'll know what we look like, and they can get after us."

"These are the drawbacks to being public men, Comrade Windsor. We must bear them manfully, without wincing."

Billy turned again to his work.

"I'm not going to wince," he said, "so's you could notice it with a microscope. What I'm going to do is to buy a good big stick. And I'd advise you to do the same."

* * * * *

It was by Psmith's suggestion that the editorial staff of *Cosy Moments* dined that night in the roof-garden at the top of the Astor Hotel.

"The tired brain," he said, "needs to recuperate. To feed on such a night as this in some low-down hostelry on the level of the street, with German waiters breathing heavily down the back of one's neck and two fiddles and a piano whacking out 'Beautiful Eyes' about three feet from one's tympanum, would be false economy. Here, fanned by cool breezes and surrounded by fair women and brave men, one may do a bit of tissue-restoring. Moreover, there is little danger up here of being slugged by our moth-eaten acquaintance of this morning. A man with trousers like his would not be allowed in. We shall probably find him waiting for us at the main entrance with a sand-bag, when we leave, but, till then —"

He turned with gentle grace to his soup.

It was a warm night, and the roof-garden was full. From where they sat they could see the million twinkling lights of the city. Towards the end of the meal, Psmith's gaze concentrated itself on the advertisement of a certain brand of ginger-ale in Times Square. It is a mass of electric light arranged in the shape of a great bottle, and at regular intervals there proceed from the bottle's mouth flashes of flame representing ginger-ale. The thing began to exercise a hypnotic effect on Psmith. He came to himself with a start, to find Billy Windsor in conversation with a waiter.

"Yes, my name's Windsor," Billy was saying.

The waiter bowed and retired to one of the tables where a young man in evening clothes was seated. Psmith recollected having seen this solitary diner looking in their direction once or twice during dinner, but the fact had not impressed him.

"What is happening, Comrade Windsor?" he inquired. "I was musing with a certain tenseness at the moment, and the rush of events has left me behind."

"Man at that table wanted to know if my name was Windsor," said Billy.

"Ah?" said Psmith, interested; "and was it?"

"Here he comes. I wonder what he wants. I don't know the man from Adam."

The stranger was threading his way between the tables.

"Can I have a word with you, Mr. Windsor?" he said.

Billy looked at him curiously. Recent events had made him wary of strangers.

"Won't you sit down?" he said.

A waiter was bringing a chair. The young man seated himself.

"By the way," added Billy; "my friend, Mr. Smith."

"Pleased to meet you," said the other.

"I don't know your name," Billy hesitated.

"Never mind about my name," said the stranger. "It won't be needed. Is Mr. Smith on your paper? Excuse my asking."

Psmith bowed. "That's all right, then. I can go ahead." He bent forward.

"Neither of you gentlemen are hard of hearing, eh?"

"In the old prairie days," said Psmith, "Comrade Windsor was known to the Indians as Boola-Ba-Na-Gosh, which, as you doubtless know, signifies Big-Chief-Who-Can-Hear-A-Fly-Clear-Its-Throat. I too can hear as well as the next man. Why?"

"That's all right, then. I don't want to have to shout it. There's some things it's better not to yell."

He turned to Billy, who had been looking at him all the while with a combination of interest and suspicion. The man might or might not be friendly. In the meantime, there was no harm in being on one's guard. Billy's experience as a cub-reporter had given him the knowledge that is only given in its entirety to police and newspaper men: that there are two New Yorks. One is a modern, well-policed city, through which one may walk from end to end without encountering adventure. The other is a city as full of sinister intrigue, of whisperings and conspiracies, of battle, murder, and sudden death in dark by-ways, as any town of mediaeval Italy. Given certain conditions, anything may happen to any one in New York. And Billy realised that these conditions now prevailed in his own case. He had come into conflict with New York's underworld. Circumstances had placed him below the surface, where only his wits could help him.

"It's about that tenement business," said the stranger.

Billy bristled. "Well, what about it?" he demanded truculently.

The stranger raised a long and curiously delicately shaped hand. "Don't bite at me," he said. "This isn't my funeral. I've no kick coming. I'm a friend."

"Yet you don't tell us your name."

"Never mind my name. If you were in my line of business, you wouldn't be so durned stuck on this name thing. Call me Smith, if you like."

"You could select no nobler pseudonym," said Psmith cordially.

"Eh? Oh, I see. Well, make it Brown, then. Anything you please. It don't signify. See here, let's get back. About this tenement thing. You understand certain parties have got it in against you?"

"A charming conversationalist, one Comrade Parker, hinted at something of the sort," said Psmith, "in a recent interview. *Cosy Moments*, however, cannot be muzzled."

"Well?" said Billy.

"You're up against a big proposition."

"We can look after ourselves."

"Gum! you'll need to. The man behind is a big bug."

Billy leaned forward eagerly.

"Who is he?"

The other shrugged his shoulders.

"I don't know. You wouldn't expect a man like that to give himself away."

"Then how do you know he's a big bug?"

"Precisely," said Psmith. "On what system have you estimated the size of the gentleman's bughood?"

The stranger lit a cigar.

"By the number of dollars he was ready to put up to have you done in."

575

Billy's eyes snapped.

"Oh?" he said. "And which gang has he given the job to?"

"I wish I could tell you. He-his agent, that is-came to Bat Jarvis."

"The cat-expert?" said Psmith. "A man of singularly winsome personality."

"Bat turned the job down."

"Why was that?" inquired Billy.

"He said he needed the money as much as the next man, but when he found out who he was supposed to lay for, he gave his job the frozen face. Said you were a friend of his and none of his fellows were going to put a finger on you. I don't know what you've been doing to Bat, but he's certainly Willie the Long-Lost Brother with you."

"A powerful argument in favour of kindness to animals!" said Psmith. "Comrade Windsor came into possession of one of Comrade Jarvis's celebrated stud of cats. What did he do? Instead of having the animal made into a nourishing soup, he restored it to its bereaved owner. Observe the sequel. He is now as a prize tortoiseshell to Comrade Jarvis."

"So Bat wouldn't stand for it?" said Billy.

"Not on his life. Turned it down without a blink. And he sent me along to find you and tell you so."

"We are much obliged to Comrade Jarvis," said Psmith.

"He told me to tell you to watch out, because another gang is dead sure to take on the job. But he said you were to know he wasn't mixed up in it. He also said that any time you were in bad, he'd do his best for you. You've certainly made the biggest kind of hit with Bat. I haven't seen him so worked up over a thing in years. Well, that's all, I reckon. Guess I'll be pushing along. I've a date to keep. Glad to have met you. Glad to have met you, Mr. Smith. Pardon me, you have an insect on your coat."

He flicked at Psmith's coat with a quick movement. Psmith thanked him gravely.

"Good night," concluded the stranger, moving off. For a few moments after he had gone, Psmith and Billy sat smoking in silence. They had plenty to think about.

"How's the time going?" asked Billy at length. Psmith felt for his watch, and looked at Billy with some sadness.

"I am sorry to say, Comrade Windsor—"

"Hullo," said Billy, "here's that man coming back again."

The stranger came up to their table, wearing a light overcoat over his dress clothes. From the pocket of this he produced a gold watch.

"Force of habit," he said apologetically, handing it to Psmith.
"You'll pardon me. Good night, gentlemen, again."

CHAPTER XII

A RED TAXIMETER

The Astor Hotel faces on to Times Square. A few paces to the right of the main entrance the Times Building towers to the sky; and at the foot of this the stream of traffic breaks, forming two channels. To the right of the building is Seventh Avenue, quiet, dark, and dull. To the left is Broadway, the Great White Way, the longest, straightest, brightest, wickedest street in the world.

Psmith and Billy, having left the Astor, started to walk down Broadway to Billy's lodgings in Fourteenth Street. The usual crowd was drifting slowly up and down in the glare of the white lights.

They had reached Herald Square, when a voice behind them exclaimed, "Why, it's Mr. Windsor!"

They wheeled round. A flashily dressed man was standing with outstetched hand.

"I saw you come out of the Astor," he said cheerily. "I said to myself, 'I know that man.' Darned if I could put a name to you, though. So I just followed you along, and right here it came to me."

"It did, did it?" said Billy politely.

"It did, sir. I've never set eyes on you before, but I've seen so many photographs of you that I reckon we're old friends. I know your father very well, Mr. Windsor. He showed me the photographs. You may have heard him speak of me-Jack Lake? How is the old man? Seen him lately?"

"Not for some time. He was well when he last wrote."

"Good for him. He would be. Tough as a plank, old Joe Windsor. We always called him Joe."

"You'd have known him down in Missouri, of course?" said Billy.

"That's right. In Missouri. We were side-partners for years. Now, see here, Mr. Windsor, it's early yet. Won't you and your friend come along with me and have a smoke and a chat? I live right here in Thirty-Third Street. I'd be right glad for you to come."

"I don't doubt it," said Billy, "but I'm afraid you'll have to excuse us."

"In a hurry, are you?"

"Not in the least."

"Then come right along."

"No, thanks."

"Say, why not? It's only a step."

"Because we don't want to. Good night."

He turned, and started to walk away. The other stood for a moment, staring; then crossed the road.

Psmith broke the silence.

"Correct me if I am wrong, Comrade Windsor," he said tentatively, "but were you not a trifle-shall we say abrupt? —with the old family friend?"

Billy Windsor laughed.

"If my father's name was Joseph," he said, "instead of being William, the same as mine, and if he'd ever been in Missouri in his life, which he hasn't, and if I'd been photographed since I was a kid, which I haven't been, I might have gone along. As it was, I thought it better not to."

"These are deep waters, Comrade Windsor. Do you mean to intimate —?"

"If they can't do any better than that, we shan't have much to worry us. What do they take us for, I wonder? Farmers? Playing off a comic-supplement bluff like that on us!"

There was honest indignation in Billy's voice.

"You think, then, that if we had accepted Comrade Lake's invitation, and gone along for a smoke and a chat, the chat would not have been of the pleasantest nature?"

"We should have been put out of business."

"I have heard so much," said Psmith, thoughtfully, "of the lavish hospitality of the American."

"Taxi, sir?"

A red taximeter cab was crawling down the road at their side. Billy shook his head.

"Not that a taxi would be an unsound scheme," said Psmith.

"Not that particular one, if you don't mind."

"Something about it that offends your aesthetic taste?" queried Psmith sympathetically.

"Something about it makes my aesthetic taste kick like a mule," said Billy.

"Ah, we highly strung literary men do have these curious prejudices. We cannot help it. We are the slaves of our temperaments. Let us walk, then. After all, the night is fine, and we are young and strong."

They had reached Twenty-Third Street when Billy stopped. "I don't know about walking," he said. "Suppose we take the Elevated?"

"Anything you wish, Comrade Windsor. I am in your hands."

They cut across into Sixth Avenue, and walked up the stairs to the station of the Elevated Railway. A train was just coming in.

"Has it escaped your notice, Comrade Windsor," said Psmith after a pause, "that, so far from speeding to your lodgings, we are going in precisely the opposite direction? We are in an up-town train."

"I noticed it," said Billy briefly.

"Are we going anywhere in particular?"

"This train goes as far as Hundred and Tenth Street. We'll go up to there."

"And then?"

"And then we'll come back."

"And after that, I suppose, we'll make a trip to Philadelphia, or Chicago, or somewhere? Well, well, I am in your hands, Comrade Windsor. The night is yet young. Take me where you will. It is only five cents a go, and we have money in our purses. We are two young men out for reckless dissipation. By all means let us have it."

At Hundred and Tenth Street they left the train, went down the stairs, and crossed the street. Half-way across Billy stopped.

"What now, Comrade Windsor?" inquired Psmith patiently. "Have you thought of some new form of entertainment?"

Billy was making for a spot some few yards down the road. Looking in that direction, Psmith saw his objective. In the shadow of the Elevated there was standing a taximeter cab.

"Taxi, sir?" said the driver, as they approached.

"We are giving you a great deal of trouble," said Billy. "You must be losing money over this job. All this while you might be getting fares down-town."

"These meetings, however," urged Psmith, "are very pleasant."

"I can save you worrying," said Billy. "My address is 84 East Fourteenth Street. We are going back there now."

"Search me," said the driver, "I don't know what you're talking about."

"I thought perhaps you did," replied Billy. "Good night."

"These things are very disturbing," said Psmith, when they were in the train. "Dignity is impossible when one is compelled to be the Hunted Fawn. When did you begin to suspect that yonder merchant was doing the sleuth-hound act?"

"When I saw him in Broadway having a heart-to-heart talk with our friend from Missouri."

"He must be something of an expert at the game to have kept on our track."

"Not on your life. It's as easy as falling off a log. There are only certain places where you can get off an Elevated train. All he'd got to do was to get there before the train, and wait. I didn't expect to dodge him by taking the Elevated. I just wanted to make certain of his game."

The train pulled up at the Fourteenth Street station. In the roadway at the foot of the opposite staircase was a red taximeter cab.

CHAPTER XIII

REVIEWING THE SITUATION

Arriving at the bed-sitting-room, Billy proceeded to occupy the rocking-chair, and, as was his wont, began to rock himself rhythmically to and fro. Psmith seated himself gracefully on the couch-bed. There was a silence.

The events of the evening had been a revelation to Psmith. He had not realised before the extent of the ramifications of New York's underworld. That members of the gangs should crop up in the Astor roof-garden and in gorgeous raiment in the middle of Broadway was a surprise. When Billy Windsor had mentioned the gangs, he had formed a mental picture of low-browed hooligans, keeping carefully to their own quarter of the town. This picture had been correct, as far as it went, but it had not gone far enough. The bulk of the gangs of New York are of the hooligan class, and are rarely met with outside their natural boundaries. But each gang has its more prosperous members; gentlemen, who, like the man of the Astor roof-garden, support life by more delicate and genteel methods than the rest. The main body rely for their incomes, except at election-time, on such primitive feats as robbing intoxicated pedestrians. The aristocracy of the gangs soar higher.

It was a considerable time before Billy spoke.

"Say," he said, "this thing wants talking over."

"By all means, Comrade Windsor."

"It's this way. There's no doubt now that we're up against a mighty big proposition."

"Something of the sort would seem to be the case."

"It's like this. I'm going to see this through. It isn't only that I want to do a bit of good to the poor cusses in those tenements, though I'd do it for that alone. But, as far as I'm concerned, there's something to it besides that. If we win out, I'm going to get a job out of one of the big dailies. It'll give me just the chance I need. See what I mean? Well, it's different with you. I don't see that it's up to you to run the risk of getting yourself put out of business with a black-jack, and maybe shot. Once you get mixed up with the gangs there's no saying what's going to be doing. Well, I don't see why you shouldn't quit. All this has got nothing to do with you. You're over here on a vacation. You haven't got to make a living this side. You want to go about and have a good time, instead of getting mixed up with —"

He broke off.

"Well, that's what I wanted to say, anyway," he concluded.

Psmith looked at him reproachfully.

"Are you trying to *sack* me, Comrade Windsor?"

"How's that?"

"In various treatises on 'How to Succeed in Literature,'" said Psmith sadly, "which I have read from time to time, I have always found it stated that what the novice chiefly needed was an editor who believed in him. In you, Comrade Windsor, I fancied that I had found such an editor."

"What's all this about?" demanded Billy. "I'm making no kick about your work."

"I gathered from your remarks that you were anxious to receive my resignation."

"Well, I told you why. I didn't want you be black-jacked."

"Was that the only reason?"

"Sure."

"Then all is well," said Psmith, relieved. "For the moment I fancied that my literary talents had been weighed in the balance and adjudged below par. If that is all-why, these are the mere everyday risks of the young journalist's life. Without them we should be dull and dissatisfied. Our work would lose its fire. Men such as ourselves, Comrade Windsor, need a certain stimulus, a certain fillip, if they are to keep up their high standards. The knowledge that a low-browed gentleman is waiting round the corner with a sand-bag poised in air will just supply that stimulus. Also that fillip. It will give our output precisely the edge it requires."

"Then you'll stay in this thing? You'll stick to the work?"

"Like a conscientious leech, Comrade Windsor."

"Bully for you," said Billy.

It was not Psmith's habit, when he felt deeply on any subject, to exhibit his feelings; and this matter of the tenements had hit him harder than any one who did not know him intimately would have imagined. Mike would have understood him, but Billy Windsor was too recent an acquaintance. Psmith was one of those people who are content to accept most of the happenings of life in an airy spirit of tolerance. Life had been more or less of a game with him up till now. In his previous encounters with those with whom fate had brought him in contact there had been little at stake. The prize of victory had been merely a comfortable feeling of having had the best of a battle of wits; the penalty of defeat nothing worse than the discomfort of having failed to score. But this tenement business was different. Here he had touched the realities. There was something worth fighting for. His lot had been cast in pleasant places, and the sight of actual raw misery had come home to him with an added force from that circumstance. He was fully aware of the risks that he must run. The words of the man at the Astor, and still more the episodes of the family friend from Missouri and the taximeter cab, had shown him that this thing was on a different plane from anything that had happened to him before. It was a fight without the gloves, and to a finish at that. But he meant to see it through. Somehow or other those tenement houses had got to be cleaned up. If it meant trouble, as it undoubtedly did, that trouble would have to be faced.

"Now that Comrade Jarvis," he said, "showing a spirit of forbearance which, I am bound to say, does him credit, has declined the congenial task of fracturing our occiputs, who should you say, Comrade Windsor, would be the chosen substitute?"

Billy shook his head. "Now that Bat has turned up the job, it might be any one of three gangs. There are four main gangs, you know. Bat's is the biggest. But the smallest of them's large enough to put us away, if we give them the chance."

"I don't quite grasp the nice points of this matter. Do you mean that we have an entire gang on our trail in one solid mass, or will it be merely a section?"

"Well, a section, I guess, if it comes to that. Parker, or whoever fixed this thing up, would go to the main boss of the gang. If it was the Three Points, he'd go to Spider Reilly. If it was the Table Hill lot, he'd look up Dude Dawson. And so on."

"And what then?"

"And then the boss would talk it over with his own special partners. Every gang-leader has about a dozen of them. A sort of Inner Circle. They'd fix it up among themselves. The rest of the gang wouldn't know anything about it. The fewer in the game, you see, the fewer to split up the dollars."

"I see. Then things are not so black. All we have to do is to look out for about a dozen hooligans with a natural dignity in their bearing, the result of intimacy with the main boss. Carefully eluding these aristocrats, we shall win through. I fancy, Comrade Windsor, that all may yet be well. What steps do you propose to take by way of self-defence?"

"Keep out in the middle of the street, and not go off the Broadway after dark. You're pretty safe on Broadway. There's too much light for them there."

"Now that our sleuth-hound friend in the taximeter has ascertained your address, shall you change it?"

"It wouldn't do any good. They'd soon find where I'd gone to. How about yours?"

"I fancy I shall be tolerably all right. A particularly massive policeman is on duty at my very doors. So much for our private lives. But what of the day-time? Suppose these sandbag-specialists drop in at the office during business hours. Will Comrade Maloney's frank and manly statement that we are not in be sufficient to keep them out? I doubt it. All unused to the nice conventions of polite society, these rugged persons will charge through. In such circumstances good work will be hard to achieve. Your literary man must have complete quiet if he is to give the public of his best. But stay. An idea!"

"Well?"

"Comrade Brady. The Peerless Kid. The man *Cosy Moments* is running for the light-weight championship. We are his pugilistic sponsors. You may say that it is entirely owing to our efforts that he has obtained this match with-who exactly is the gentleman Comrade Brady fights at the Highfield Club on Friday night?"

"Cyclone Al. Wolmann, isn't it?"

"You are right. As I was saying, but for us the privilege of smiting Comrade Cyclone Al. Wolmann under the fifth rib on Friday night would almost certainly have been denied to him."

It almost seemed as if he were right. From the moment the paper had taken up his cause, Kid Brady's star had undoubtedly been in the ascendant. People began to talk about him as a likely man. Edgren, in the *Evening World*, had a paragraph about his chances for the light-weight title. Tad, in the *Journal*, drew a picture of him. Finally, the management of the Highfield Club had signed him for a ten-round bout with Mr. Wolmann. There were, therefore, reasons why *Cosy Moments* should feel a claim on the Kid's services.

"He should," continued Psmith, "if equipped in any degree with finer feelings, be bubbling over with gratitude towards us. 'But for *Cosy Moments*,' he should be saying to himself, 'where should I be? Among the also-rans.' I imagine that he will do any little thing we care to ask of him. I suggest that we approach Comrade Brady, explain the facts of the case, and offer him at a comfortable salary the post of fighting-editor of *Cosy Moments*. His duties will be to sit in the room opening out of ours, girded as to the loins and full of martial spirit, and apply some of those half-scissor hooks of his to the persons of any who overcome the opposition of Comrade Maloney. We, meanwhile, will enjoy that leisure and freedom from interruption which is so essential to the artist."

"It's not a bad idea," said Billy.

"It is about the soundest idea," said Psmith, "that has ever been struck. One of your newspaper friends shall supply us with tickets, and Friday night shall see us at the Highfield."

CHAPTER XIV

THE HIGHFIELD

Far up at the other end of the island, on the banks of the Harlem River, there stands the old warehouse which modern progress has converted into the Highfield Athletic and Gymnastic Club. The imagination, stimulated by the title, conjures up a sort of National Sporting Club, with pictures on the walls, padding on the chairs, and a sea of white shirt-fronts from roof to floor. But the Highfield differs in some respects from this fancy picture. Indeed, it would be hard to find a respect in which it does not differ. But these names are so misleading. The title under which the Highfield used to be known till a few years back was "Swifty Bob's." It was a good, honest title. You knew what to expect; and if you attended *séances* at Swifty Bob's you left your gold watch and your little savings at home. But a wave of anti-pugilistic feeling swept over the New York authorities. Promoters of boxing contests found themselves, to their acute disgust, raided by the police. The industry began to languish. People avoided places where at any moment the festivities might be marred by an inrush of large men in blue uniforms armed with locust-sticks.

And then some big-brained person suggested the club idea, which stands alone as an example of American dry humour. There are now no boxing contests in New York. Swifty Bob and his fellows would be shocked at the idea of such a thing. All that happens now is exhibition sparring bouts between members of the club. It is true that next day the papers very tactlessly report the friendly exhibition spar as if it had been quite a serious affair, but that is not the fault of Swifty Bob.

Kid Brady, the chosen of *Cosy Moments*, was billed for a "ten-round exhibition contest," to be the main event of the evening's entertainment. No decisions are permitted at these clubs. Unless a regrettable accident occurs, and one of the sparrers is knocked out, the verdict is left to the newspapers next day. It is not uncommon to find a man win easily in the *World*, draw in the *American*, and be badly beaten in the *Evening Mail*. The system leads to a certain amount of confusion, but it has the merit of offering consolation to a much-smitten warrior.

The best method of getting to the Highfield is by the Subway. To see the Subway in its most characteristic mood one must travel on it during the rush-hour, when its patrons are packed into the carriages in one solid jam by muscular guards and policemen, shoving in a manner reminiscent of a Rugby football scrum. When Psmith and Billy entered it on the Friday evening, it was comparatively empty. All the seats were occupied, but only a few of the straps and hardly any of the space reserved by law for the conductor alone.

Conversation on the Subway is impossible. The ingenious gentlemen who constructed it started with the object of making it noisy. Not ordinarily noisy, like a ton of coal falling on to a sheet of tin, but really noisy. So they fashioned the pillars of thin steel, and the sleepers of thin wood, and loosened all the nuts, and now a Subway train in motion suggests a prolonged dynamite explosion blended with the voice of some great cataract.

Psmith, forced into temporary silence by this combination of noises, started to make up for lost time on arriving in the street once more.

"A thoroughly unpleasant neighbourhood," he said, critically surveying the dark streets. "I fear me, Comrade Windsor, that we have been somewhat rash in venturing as far into the middle west as this. If ever there was a blighted locality where low-browed desperadoes might be expected to spring with whoops of joy from every corner, this blighted locality is that blighted locality. But we must carry on. In which direction, should you say, does this arena lie?"

It had begun to rain as they left Billy's lodgings. Psmith turned up the collar of his Burberry.

"We suffer much in the cause of Literature," he said. "Let us inquire of this genial soul if he knows where the Highfield is."

The pedestrian referred to proved to be going there himself. They went on together, Psmith courteously offering views on the weather and forecasts of the success of Kid Brady in the approaching contest.

Rattling on, he was alluding to the prominent part *Cosy Moments* had played in the affair, when a rough thrust from Windsor's elbow brought home to him his indiscretion.

He stopped suddenly, wishing he had not said as much. Their connection with that militant journal was not a thing even to be suggested to casual acquaintances, especially in such a particularly ill-lighted neighbourhood as that through which they were now passing.

Their companion, however, who seemed to be a man of small speech, made no comment. Psmith deftly turned the conversation back to the subject of the weather, and was deep in a comparison of the respective climates of England and the United States, when they turned a corner and found themselves opposite a gloomy, barn-like building, over the door of which it was just possible to decipher in the darkness the words "Highfield Athletic and Gymnastic Club."

The tickets which Billy Windsor had obtained from his newspaper friend were for one of the boxes. These proved to be sort of sheep-pens of unpolished wood, each with four hard chairs in it. The interior of the Highfield Athletic and Gymnastic Club was severely free from anything in the shape of luxury and ornament. Along the four walls were raised benches in tiers. On these were seated as tough-looking a collection of citizens as one might wish to see. On chairs at the ring-side were the reporters, with tickers at their sides, by means of which they tapped details of each round through to their down-town offices, where write-up reporters were waiting to read off and elaborate the messages. In the centre of the room, brilliantly lighted by half a dozen electric chandeliers, was the ring.

There were preliminary bouts before the main event. A burly gentleman in shirt-sleeves entered the ring, followed by two slim youths in fighting costume and a massive person in a red jersey, blue serge trousers, and yellow braces, who chewed gum with an abstracted air throughout the proceedings.

The burly gentleman gave tongue in a voice that cleft the air like a cannon-ball.

"Ex-hib-it-i-on four-round bout between Patsy Milligan and Tommy
Goodley, members of this club. Patsy on my right, Tommy on my left.
Gentlemen will kindly stop smokin'."

The audience did nothing of the sort. Possibly they did not apply the description to themselves. Possibly they considered the appeal a mere formula. Somewhere in the background a gong sounded, and Patsy, from the right, stepped briskly forward to meet Tommy, approaching from the left.

The contest was short but energetic. At intervals the combatants would cling affectionately to one another, and on these occasions the red-jerseyed man, still chewing gum and still wearing the same air of being lost in abstract thought, would split up the mass by the simple method of ploughing his way between the pair. Towards the end of the first round Thomas, eluding a left swing, put Patrick neatly to the floor, where the latter remained for the necessary ten seconds.

The remaining preliminaries proved disappointing. So much so that in the last of the series a soured sportsman on one of the benches near the roof began in satirical mood to whistle the "Merry Widow Waltz." It was here that the red-jerseyed thinker for the first and last time came out of his meditative trance. He leaned over the ropes, and spoke-without heat, but firmly.

"If that guy whistling back up yonder thinks he can do better than these boys, he can come right down into the ring."

The whistling ceased.

There was a distinct air of relief when the last preliminary was finished and preparations for the main bout began. It did not commence at once. There were formalities to be gone through, introductions and the like. The burly gentleman reappeared from nowhere, ushering into the ring a sheepishly-grinning youth in a flannel suit.

"In-ter-*doo*-cin' Young Leary," he bellowed impressively, "a noo member of this chub, who will box some good boy here in September."

He walked to the other side of the ring and repeated the remark. A raucous welcome was accorded to the new member.

Two other notable performers were introduced in a similar manner, and then the building became suddenly full of noise, for a tall youth in a bath-robe, attended by a little army of assistants, had entered the ring. One of the army carried a bright green bucket, on which were painted in white letters the words "Cyclone Al. Wolmann." A moment later there was another, though a far lesser, uproar, as Kid Brady, his pleasant face wearing a self-conscious smirk, ducked under the ropes and sat down in the opposite corner.

"Ex-hib-it-i-on ten-round bout," thundered the burly gentleman, "between Cyclone. Al. Wolmann —"

Loud applause. Mr. Wolmann was one of the famous, a fighter with a reputation from New York to San Francisco. He was generally considered the most likely man to give the hitherto invincible Jimmy Garvin a hard battle for the light-weight championship.

"Oh, you Al.!" roared the crowd.

Mr. Wolmann bowed benevolently.

" —and Kid Brady, members of this —"

There was noticeably less applause for the Kid. He was an unknown. A few of those present had heard of his victories in the West, but these were but a small section of the crowd. When the faint applause had ceased, Psmith rose to his feet.

"Oh, you Kid!" he observed encouragingly.

"I should not like Comrade Brady," he said, reseating himself, "to think that he has no friend but his poor old mother, as, you will recollect, occurred on a previous occasion."

The burly gentleman, followed by the two armies of assistants, dropped down from the ring, and the gong sounded.

Mr. Wolmann sprang from his corner as if somebody had touched a spring. He seemed to be of the opinion that if you are a cyclone, it is never too soon to begin behaving like one. He danced round the Kid with an india-rubber agility. The *Cosy Moments* representative exhibited more stolidity. Except for the fact that he was in fighting attitude, with one gloved hand moving slowly in the neighbourhood of his stocky chest, and the other pawing the air on a line with his square jaw, one would have said that he did not realise the position of affairs. He wore the friendly smile of the good-natured guest who is led forward by his hostess to join in some round game.

Suddenly his opponent's long left shot out. The Kid, who had been strolling forward, received it under the chin, and continued to stroll forward as if nothing of note had happened. He gave the impression of being aware that Mr. Wolmann had committed a breach of good taste and of being resolved to pass it off with ready tact.

The Cyclone, having executed a backward leap, a forward leap, and a feint, landed heavily with both hands. The Kid's genial smile did not even quiver, but he continued to move forward. His opponent's left flashed out again, but this time, instead of ignoring the matter, the Kid replied with a heavy right swing; and Mr. Wolmann, leaping back, found himself against the ropes. By the time he had got out of that uncongenial position, two more of the Kid's swings had found their mark. Mr. Wolmann, somewhat perturbed, scuttered out into the middle of the ring, the Kid following in his self-contained, solid way.

The Cyclone now became still more cyclonic. He had a left arm which seemed to open out in joints like a telescope. Several times when the Kid appeared well out of distance there was a thud as a brown glove ripped in over his guard and jerked his head back. But always he kept boring in, delivering an occasional right to the body with the pleased smile of an infant destroying a Noah's Ark with a tack-hammer. Despite these efforts, however, he was plainly getting all the worst of it. Energetic Mr. Wolmann, relying on his long left, was putting in three blows to his one. When the gong sounded, ending the first round, the house was practically solid for the Cyclone. Whoops and yells rose from everywhere. The building rang with shouts of, "Oh, you Al.!"

Psmith turned sadly to Billy.

"It seems to me, Comrade Windsor," he said, "that this merry meeting looks like doing Comrade Brady no good. I should not be surprised at any moment to see his head bounce off on to the floor."

"Wait," said Billy. "He'll win yet."

"You think so?"

"Sure. He comes from Wyoming," said Billy with simple confidence.

Rounds two and three were a repetition of round one. The Cyclone raged almost unchecked about the ring. In one lightning rally in the third he brought his right across squarely on to the Kid's jaw. It was a blow which should have knocked any boxer out. The Kid merely staggered slightly and returned to business, still smiling.

"See!" roared Billy enthusiastically in Psmith's ear, above the uproar. "He doesn't mind it! He likes it! He comes from Wyoming!"

With the opening of round four there came a subtle change. The Cyclone's fury was expending itself. That long left shot out less sharply. Instead of being knocked back by it, the *Cosy Moments* champion now took the hits in his stride, and came shuffling in with his damaging body-blows. There were cheers and "Oh, you Al.'s!" at the sound of the gong, but there was an appealing note in them this time. The gallant sportsmen whose connection with boxing was confined to watching other men fight, and betting on what they considered a certainty, and who would have expired promptly if any one had tapped them sharply on their well-filled waistcoats, were beginning to fear that they might lose their money after all.

In the fifth round the thing became a certainty. Like the month of March, the Cyclone, who had come in like a lion, was going out like a lamb. A slight decrease in the pleasantness of the Kid's smile was noticeable. His expression began to resemble more nearly the gloomy importance of the *Cosy Moments* photographs. Yells of agony from panic-stricken speculators around the ring began to smite the rafters. The Cyclone, now but a gentle breeze, clutched repeatedly, hanging on like a leech till removed by the red-jerseyed referee.

Suddenly a grisly silence fell upon the house. It was broken by a cow-boy yell from Billy Windsor. For the Kid, battered, but obviously content, was standing in the middle of the ring, while on the ropes the Cyclone, drooping like a wet sock, was sliding slowly to the floor.

"*Cosy Moments* wins," said Psmith. "An omen, I fancy, Comrade Windsor."

CHAPTER XV

AN ADDITION TO THE STAFF

Penetrating into the Kid's dressing-room some moments later, the editorial staff found the winner of the ten-round exhibition bout between members of the club seated on a chair, having his right leg rubbed by a shock-headed man in a sweater, who had been one of his seconds during the conflict. The Kid beamed as they entered.

"Gents," he said, "come right in. Mighty glad to see you."

"It is a relief to me, Comrade Brady," said Psmith, "to find that you can see us. I had expected to find that Comrade Wolmann's purposeful buffs had completely closed your star-likes."

"Sure, I never felt them. He's a good quick boy, is Al., but," continued the Kid with powerful imagery, "he couldn't hit a hole in a block of ice-cream, not if he was to use a hammer."

"And yet at one period in the proceedings, Comrade Brady," said Psmith, "I fancied that your head would come unglued at the neck. But the fear was merely transient. When you began to administer those—am I correct in saying? —half-scissor hooks to the body, why, then I felt like some watcher of the skies when a new planet swims into his ken; or like stout Cortez when with eagle eyes he stared at the Pacific."

The Kid blinked.

"How's that?" he inquired.

"And why did I feel like that, Comrade Brady? I will tell you. Because my faith in you was justified. Because there before me stood the ideal fighting-editor of *Cosy Moments*. It is not a post that any weakling can fill. There charm of manner cannot qualify a man for the position. No one can hold down the job simply by having a kind heart or being good at farmyard imitations. No. We want a man of thews and sinews, a man who would rather be hit on the head with a half-brick than not. And you, Comrade Brady, are such a man."

The Kid turned appealingly to Billy.

"Say, this gets past me, Mr. Windsor. Put me wise."

"Can we have a couple of words with you alone, Kid?" said Billy.

"We want to talk over something with you."

"Sure. Sit down, gents. Jack'll be through in a minute."

Jack, who during this conversation had been concentrating himself on his subject's left leg, now announced that he guessed that would about do, and having advised the Kid not to stop and pick daisies, but to get into his clothes at once before he caught a chill, bade the company good night and retired.

Billy shut the door.

"Kid," he said, "you know those articles about the tenements we've been having in the paper?"

"Sure. I read 'em. They're to the good."

Psmith bowed.

"You stimulate us, Comrade Brady. This is praise from Sir Hubert
Stanley."

"It was about time some strong josher came and put it across to 'em," added the Kid.

"So we thought. Comrade Parker, however, totally disagreed with us."

"Parker?"

"That's what I'm coming to," said Billy. "The day before yesterday a man named Parker called at the office and tried to buy us off."

Billy's voice grew indignant at the recollection.

"You gave him the hook, I guess?" queried the interested Kid.

"To such an extent, Comrade Brady," said Psmith, "that he left breathing threatenings and slaughter. And it is for that reason that we have ventured to call upon you."

"It's this way," said Billy. "We're pretty sure by this time that whoever the man is this fellow Parker's working for has put one of the gangs on to us."

"You don't say!" exclaimed the Kid. "Gum! Mr. Windsor, they're tough propositions, those gangs."

"We've been followed in the streets, and once they put up a bluff to get us where they could do us in. So we've come along to you. We can look after ourselves out of the office, you see, but what we want is some one to help in case they try to rush us there."

"In brief, a fighting-editor," said Psmith. "At all costs we must have privacy. No writer can prune and polish his sentences to his satisfaction if he is compelled constantly to break off in order to eject boisterous hooligans. We therefore offer you the job of sitting in the outer room and intercepting these bravoes before they can reach us. The salary we leave to you. There are doubloons and to spare in the old oak chest. Take what you need and put the rest-if any-back. How does the offer strike you, Comrade Brady?"

"We don't want to get you in under false pretences, Kid," said Billy. "Of course, they may not come anywhere near the office. But still, if they did, there would be something doing. What do you feel about it?"

"Gents," said the Kid, "it's this way."

He stepped into his coat, and resumed.

"Now that I've made good by getting the decision over Al., they'll be giving me a chance of a big fight. Maybe with Jimmy Garvin. Well, if that happens, see what I mean? I'll have to be going away somewhere and getting into training. I shouldn't be able to come and sit with you. But, if you gents feel like it, I'd be mighty glad to come in till I'm wanted to go into training-camp."

"Great," said Billy; "that would suit us all the way up. If you'd do that, Kid, we'd be tickled to death."

"And touching salary —" put in Psmith.

"Shucks!" said the Kid with emphasis. "Nix on the salary thing. I wouldn't take a dime. If it hadn't a-been for you gents, I'd have been waiting still for a chance of lining up in the championship class. That's good enough for me. Any old thing you gents want me to do, I'll do it. And glad, too."

"Comrade Brady," said Psmith warmly, "you are, if I may say so, the goods. You are, beyond a doubt, supremely the stuff. We three, then, hand-in-hand, will face the foe; and if the foe has good, sound sense, he will keep right away. You appear to be ready. Shall we meander forth?"

The building was empty and the lights were out when they emerged from the dressing-room. They had to grope their way in darkness. It was still raining when they reached the street, and the only signs of life were a moist policeman and the distant glare of public-house lights down the road.

They turned off to the left, and, after walking some hundred yards, found themselves in a blind alley.

"Hullo!" said Billy. "Where have we come to?"

Psmith sighed.

"In my trusting way," he said, "I had imagined that either you or Comrade Brady was in charge of this expedition and taking me by a known route to the nearest Subway station. I did not think to ask. I placed myself, without hesitation, wholly in your hands."

"I thought the Kid knew the way," said Billy.

"I was just taggin' along with you gents," protested the light-weight, "I thought you was taking me right. This is the first time I been up here."

"Next time we three go on a little jaunt anywhere," said Psmith resignedly, "it would be as well to take a map and a corps of guides with us. Otherwise we shall start for Broadway and finish up at Minneapolis."

They emerged from the blind alley and stood in the dark street, looking doubtfully up and down it.

"Aha!" said Psmith suddenly, "I perceive a native. Several natives, in fact. Quite a little covey of them. We will put our case before them, concealing nothing, and rely on their advice to take us to our goal."

A little knot of men was approaching from the left. In the darkness it was impossible to say how many of them there were. Psmith stepped forward, the Kid at his side.

"Excuse me, sir," he said to the leader, "but if you can spare me a moment of your valuable time —"

There was a sudden shuffle of feet on the pavement, a quick movement on the part of the Kid, a chunky sound as of wood striking wood, and the man Psmith had been addressing fell to the ground in a heap.

As he fell, something dropped from his hand on to the pavement with a bump and a rattle. Stooping swiftly, the Kid picked it up, and handed it to Psmith. His fingers closed upon it. It was a short, wicked-looking little bludgeon, the black-jack of the New York tough.

"Get busy," advised the Kid briefly.

CHAPTER XVI

THE FIRST BATTLE

The promptitude and despatch with which the Kid had attended to the gentleman with the black-jack had not been without its effect on the followers of the stricken one. Physical courage is not an outstanding quality of the New York hooligan. His personal preference is for retreat when it is a question of unpleasantness with a stranger. And, in any case, even when warring among themselves, the gangs exhibit a lively distaste for the hard knocks of hand-to-hand fighting. Their chosen method of battling is to lie down on the ground and shoot. This is more suited to their physique, which is rarely great. The gangsman, as a rule, is stunted and slight of build.

The Kid's rapid work on the present occasion created a good deal of confusion. There was no doubt that much had been hoped for from speedy attack. Also, the generalship of the expedition had been in the hands of the fallen warrior. His removal from the sphere of active influence had left the party without a head. And, to add to their discomfiture, they could not account for the Kid. Psmith they knew, and Billy Windsor they knew, but who was this stranger with the square shoulders and the upper-cut that landed like a cannon-ball? Something approaching a panic prevailed among the gang.

It was not lessened by the behaviour of the intended victims. Billy Windsor, armed with the big stick which he had bought after the visit of Mr. Parker, was the first to join issue. He had been a few paces behind the others during the black-jack incident; but, dark as it was, he had seen enough to show him that the occasion was, as Psmith would have said, one for the Shrewd Blow rather than the Prolonged Parley. With a whoop of the purest Wyoming brand, he sprang forward into the confused mass of the enemy. A moment later Psmith and the Kid followed, and there raged over the body of the fallen leader a battle of Homeric type.

It was not a long affair. The rules and conditions governing the encounter offended the delicate sensibilities of the gang. Like artists who feel themselves trammelled by distasteful conventions, they were damped and could not do themselves justice. Their forte was long-range fighting with pistols. With that they felt *en rapport*. But this vulgar brawling in the darkness with muscular opponents who hit hard and often with sticks and hands was distasteful to them. They could not develop any enthusiasm for it. They carried pistols, but it was too dark and the combatants were too entangled to allow them to use these. Besides, this was not the dear, homely old Bowery, where a gentleman may fire a pistol without exciting vulgar comment. It was up-town, where curious crowds might collect at the first shot.

There was but one thing to be done. Reluctant as they might be to abandon their fallen leader, they must tear themselves away. Already they were suffering grievously from the stick, the black-jack, and the lightning blows of the Kid. For a moment they hung, wavering; then stampeded in half a dozen different directions, melting into the night whence they had come.

Billy, full of zeal, pursued one fugitive some fifty yards down the street, but his quarry, exhibiting a rare turn of speed, easily outstripped him.

He came back, panting, to find Psmith and the Kid examining the fallen leader of the departed ones with the aid of a match, which went out just as Billy arrived.

"It is our friend of the earlier part of the evening, Comrade Windsor," said Psmith. "The merchant with whom we hob-nobbed on our way to the Highfield. In a moment of imprudence I mentioned *Cosy Moments*. I fancy that this was his first intimation that we were in the offing. His visit to the Highfield was paid, I think, purely from sport-loving motives. He was not on our trail. He came merely to see if Comrade Brady was proficient with his hands. Subsequent events must have justified our fighting editor in his eyes. It seems to be a moot point whether he will ever recover consciousness."

"Mighty good thing if he doesn't," said Billy uncharitably.

"From one point of view, Comrade Windsor, yes. Such an event would undoubtedly be an excellent thing for the public good. But from our point of view, it would be as well if he were to sit up and take notice. We could ascertain from him who he is and which particular collection of horny-handeds he represents. Light another match, Comrade Brady."

The Kid did so. The head of it fell off and dropped upon the up-turned face. The hooligan stirred, shook himself, sat up, and began to mutter something in a foggy voice.

"He's still woozy," said the Kid.

"Still-what exactly, Comrade Brady?"

"In the air," explained the Kid. "Bats in the belfry. Dizzy. See what I mean? It's often like that when a feller puts one in with a bit of weight behind it just where that one landed. Gum! I remember when I fought Martin Kelly; I was only starting to learn the game then. Martin and me was mixing it good and hard all over the ring, when suddenly he puts over a stiff one right on the point. What do you think I done? Fall down and take the count? Not on your life. I just turns round and walks straight out of the ring to my dressing-room. Willie Harvey, who was seconding me, comes tearing in after me, and finds me getting into my clothes. 'What's doing, Kid?' he asks. 'I'm going fishin', Willie,' I says. 'It's a lovely day.' 'You've lost the fight,' he says. 'Fight?' says I. 'What fight?' See what I mean? I hadn't a notion of what had happened. It was a half an hour and more before I could remember a thing."

During this reminiscence, the man on the ground had contrived to clear his mind of the mistiness induced by the Kid's upper-cut. The first sign he showed of returning intelligence was a sudden dash for safety up the road. But he had not gone five yards when he sat down limply.

The Kid was inspired to further reminiscence. "Guess he's feeling pretty poor," he said. "It's no good him trying to run for a while after he's put his chin in the way of a real live one. I remember when Joe Peterson put me out, way back when I was new to the game-it was the same year I fought Martin Kelly. He had an awful punch, had old Joe, and he put me down and out in the eighth round. After the fight they found me on the fire-escape outside my dressing-room. 'Come in, Kid,' says they. 'It's all right, chaps,' I says, 'I'm dying.' Like that. 'It's all right, chaps, I'm dying.' Same with this guy. See what I mean?"

They formed a group about the fallen black-jack expert.

"Pardon us," said Psmith courteously, "for breaking in upon your reverie; but, if you could spare us a moment of your valuable time, there are one or two things which we should like to know."

"Sure thing," agreed the Kid.

"In the first place," continued Psmith, "would it be betraying professional secrets if you told us which particular bevy of energetic sandbaggers it is to which you are attached?"

"Gent," explained the Kid, "wants to know what's your gang."

The man on the ground muttered something that to Psmith and Billy was unintelligible.

"It would be a charity," said the former, "if some philanthropist would give this blighter elocution lessons. Can you interpret, Comrade Brady?"

"Says it's the Three Points," said the Kid.

"The Three Points? Let me see, is that Dude Dawson, Comrade Windsor, or the other gentleman?"

"It's Spider Reilly. Dude Dawson runs the Table Hill crowd."

"Perhaps this *is* Spider Reilly?"

"Nope," said the Kid. "I know the Spider. This ain't him. This is some other mutt."

"Which other mutt in particular?" asked Psmith. "Try and find out, Comrade Brady. You seem to be able to understand what he says. To me, personally, his remarks sound like the output of a gramophone with a hot potato in its mouth."

"Says he's Jack Repetto," announced the interpreter.

There was another interruption at this moment. The bashful Mr. Repetto, plainly a man who was not happy in the society of strangers, made another attempt to withdraw. Reaching out a pair of lean hands, he pulled the Kid's legs from under him with a swift jerk, and, wriggling to his feet, started off again down the road. Once more, however, desire outran performance. He got as far as the nearest street-lamp, but no farther. The giddiness seemed to overcome him again, for he grasped the lamp-post, and, sliding slowly to the ground, sat there motionless.

The Kid, whose fall had jolted and bruised him, was inclined to be wrathful and vindictive. He was the first of the three to reach the elusive Mr. Repetto, and if that worthy had happened to be standing instead of sitting it might have gone hard with him. But the Kid was not the man to attack a fallen foe. He contented himself with brushing the dust off his person and addressing a richly abusive flow of remarks to Mr. Repetto.

Under the rays of the lamp it was possible to discern more closely the features of the black-jack exponent. There was a subtle but noticeable resemblance to those of Mr. Bat Jarvis. Apparently the latter's oiled forelock, worn low over the forehead, was more a concession to the general fashion prevailing in gang circles than an expression of personal taste. Mr. Repetto had it, too. In his case it was almost white, for the fallen warrior was an albino. His eyes, which were closed, had white lashes and were set as near together as Nature had been able to manage without actually running them into one another. His under-lip protruded and drooped. Looking at him, one felt instinctively that no judging committee of a beauty contest would hesitate a moment before him.

It soon became apparent that the light of the lamp, though bestowing the doubtful privilege of a clearer view of Mr. Repetto's face, held certain disadvantages. Scarcely had the staff of *Cosy Moments* reached the faint yellow pool of light, in the centre of which Mr. Repetto reclined, than, with a suddenness which caused them to leap into the air, there sounded from the darkness down the road the *crack-crack-crack* of a revolver. Instantly from the opposite direction came other shots. Three bullets flicked grooves in the roadway almost at Billy's feet. The Kid gave a sudden howl. Psmith's hat, suddenly imbued with life, sprang into the air and vanished, whirling into the night.

The thought did not come to them consciously at the moment, there being little time to think, but it was evident as soon as, diving out of the circle of light into the sheltering darkness, they crouched down and waited for the next move, that a somewhat skilful ambush had been effected. The other members of the gang, who had fled with such remarkable speed, had by no means been eliminated altogether from the game. While the questioning of Mr. Repetto had been in progress, they had crept back, unperceived except by Mr. Repetto himself. It being too dark for successful shooting, it had become Mr. Repetto's task to lure his captors into the light, which he had accomplished with considerable skill.

For some minutes the battle halted. There was dead silence. The circle of light was empty now. Mr. Repetto had vanished. A tentative shot from nowhere ripped through the air close to where Psmith lay flattened on the pavement. And then the pavement began to vibrate and give out a curious resonant sound. To Psmith it conveyed nothing, but to the opposing army it meant much. They knew it for what it was. Somewhere-it might be near or far —a policeman had heard the shots, and was signalling for help to other policemen along the line by beating on the flag-stones with his night-stick, the New York constable's substitute for the London police-whistle.

The noise grew, filling the still air. From somewhere down the road sounded the ring of running feet.

"De cops!" cried a voice. "Beat it!"

Next moment the night was full of clatter. The gang was "beating it."

Psmith rose to his feet and dusted his clothes ruefully. For the first time he realised the horrors of war. His hat had gone for ever. His trousers could never be the same again after their close acquaintance with the pavement.

The rescue party was coming up at the gallop.

The New York policeman may lack the quiet dignity of his London rival, but he is a hustler.

"What's doing?"

"Nothing now," said the disgusted voice of Billy Windsor from the shadows. "They've beaten it."

The circle of lamplight became as if by mutual consent a general rendezvous. Three grey-clad policemen, tough, clean-shaven men with keen eyes and square jaws, stood there, revolver in one hand, night-stick in the other. Psmith, hatless and dusty, joined them. Billy Windsor and the Kid, the latter bleeding freely from his left ear, the lobe of which had been chipped by a bullet, were the last to arrive.

"What's bin the rough house?" inquired one of the policemen, mildly interested.

"Do you know a sportsman of the name of Repetto?" inquired Psmith.

"Jack Repetto! Sure."

"He belongs to the Three Points," said another intelligent officer, as one naming some fashionable club.

"When next you see him," said Psmith, "I should be obliged if you would use your authority to make him buy me a new hat. I could do with another pair of trousers, too; but I will not press the trousers. A new hat, is, however, essential. Mine has a six-inch hole in it."

"Shot at you, did they?" said one of the policemen, as who should say, "Dash the lads, they're always up to some of their larks."

"Shot at us!" burst out the ruffled Kid. "What do you think's bin happening? Think an aeroplane ran into my ear and took half of it off? Think the noise was somebody opening bottles of pop? Think those guys that sneaked off down the road was just training for a Marathon?"

"Comrade Brady," said Psmith, "touches the spot. He —"

"Say, are you Kid Brady?" inquired one of the officers. For the first time the constabulary had begun to display any real animation.

"Reckoned I'd seen you somewhere!" said another. "You licked
Cyclone Al. all right, Kid, I hear."

"And who but a bone-head thought he wouldn't?" demanded the third warmly. "He could whip a dozen Cyclone Al.'s in the same evening with his eyes shut."

"He's the next champeen," admitted the first speaker.

"If he puts it over Jimmy Garvin," argued the second.

"Jimmy Garvin!" cried the third. "He can whip twenty Jimmy Garvins with his feet tied. I tell you —"

"I am loath," observed Psmith, "to interrupt this very impressive brain-barbecue, but, trivial as it may seem to you, to me there is a certain interest in this other little matter of my ruined hat. I know that it may strike you as hypersensitive of us to protest against being riddled with bullets, but —"

"Well, what's bin doin'?" inquired the Force. It was a nuisance, this perpetual harping on trifles when the deep question of the light-weight Championship of the World was under discussion, but the sooner it was attended to, the sooner it would be over.

Billy Windsor undertook to explain.

"The Three Points laid for us," he said. "Jack Repetto was bossing the crowd. I don't know who the rest were. The Kid put one over on to Jack Repetto's chin, and we were asking him a few questions when the rest came back, and started into shooting. Then we got to cover quick, and you came up and they beat it."

"That," said Psmith, nodding, "is a very fair *précis* of the evening's events. We should like you, if you will be so good, to corral this Comrade Repetto, and see that he buys me a new hat."

"We'll round Jack up," said one of the policemen indulgently.

"Do it nicely," urged Psmith. "Don't go hurting his feelings."

The second policeman gave it as his opinion that Jack was getting too gay. The third policeman conceded this. Jack, he said, had shown signs for some time past of asking for it in the neck. It was an error on Jack's part, he gave his hearers to understand, to assume that the lid was completely off the great city of New York.

"Too blamed fresh he's gettin'," the trio agreed. They could not have been more disapproving if they had been prefects at Haileybury and Mr. Repetto a first-termer who had been detected in the act of wearing his cap on the back of his head.

They seemed to think it was too bad of Jack.

"The wrath of the Law," said Psmith, "is very terrible. We will leave the matter, then, in your hands. In the meantime, we should be glad if you would direct us to the nearest Subway station. Just at the moment, the cheerful lights of the Great White Way are what I seem to chiefly need."

CHAPTER XVII

GUERILLA WARFARE

Thus ended the opening engagement of the campaign, seemingly in a victory for the *Cosy Moments* army. Billy Windsor, however, shook his head.

"We've got mighty little out of it," he said.

"The victory," said Psmith, "was not bloodless. Comrade Brady's ear, my hat-these are not slight casualties. On the other hand, surely we are one up? Surely we have gained ground? The elimination of Comrade Repetto from the scheme of things in itself is something. I know few men I would not rather meet in a lonely road than Comrade Repetto. He is one of Nature's sand-baggers. Probably the thing crept upon him slowly. He started, possibly, in a merely tentative way by slugging one of the family circle. His nurse, let us say, or his young brother. But, once started, he is unable to resist the craving. The thing grips him like dram-drinking. He sandbags now not because he really wants to, but because he cannot help himself. To me there is something consoling in the thought that Comrade Repetto will no longer be among those present."

"What makes you think that?"

"I should imagine that a benevolent Law will put him away in his little cell for at least a brief spell."

"Not on your life," said Billy. "He'll prove an alibi."

Psmith's eyeglass dropped out of his eye. He replaced it, and gazed, astonished, at Billy.

"An alibi? When three keen-eyed men actually caught him at it?"

"He can find thirty toughs to swear he was five miles away."

"And get the court to believe it?" said Psmith.

"Sure," said Billy disgustedly. "You don't catch them hurting a gangsman unless they're pushed against the wall. The politicians don't want the gangs in gaol, especially as the Aldermanic elections will be on in a few weeks. Did you ever hear of Monk Eastman?"

"I fancy not, Comrade Windsor. If I did, the name has escaped me. Who was this cleric?"

"He was the first boss of the East Side gang, before Kid Twist took it on."

"Yes?"

"He was arrested dozens of times, but he always got off. Do you know what he said once, when they pulled him for thugging a fellow out in New Jersey?"

"I fear not, Comrade Windsor. Tell me all."

"He said, 'You're arresting me, huh? Say, you want to look where you're goin'; I cut some ice in this town. I made half the big politicians in New York!' That was what he said."

"His small-talk," said Psmith, "seems to have been bright and well-expressed. What happened then? Was he restored to his friends and his relations?"

"Sure, he was. What do you think? Well, Jack Repetto isn't Monk Eastman, but he's in with Spider Reilly, and the Spider's in with the men behind. Jack'll get off."

"It looks to me, Comrade Windsor," said Psmith thoughtfully, "as if my stay in this great city were going to cost me a small fortune in hats."

Billy's prophecy proved absolutely correct. The police were as good as their word. In due season they rounded up the impulsive Mr. Repetto, and he was haled before a magistrate. And then, what a beautiful exhibition of brotherly love and auld-lang-syne camaraderie was witnessed! One by one, smirking sheepishly, but giving out their evidence with unshaken earnestness, eleven greasy, wandering-eyed youths mounted the witness-stand and affirmed on oath that at the time mentioned dear old Jack had been making merry in their company in a genial and law-abiding fashion, many, many blocks below the scene of the regrettable assault. The magistrate discharged the prisoner, and the prisoner, meeting Billy and Psmith in the street outside, leered triumphantly at them.

Billy stepped up to him. "You may have wriggled out of this," he said furiously, "but if you don't get a move on and quit looking at me like that, I'll knock you over the Singer Building. Hump yourself."

Mr. Repetto humped himself.

So was victory turned into defeat, and Billy's jaw became squarer and his eye more full of the light of battle than ever. And there was need of a square jaw and a battle-lit eye, for now began a period of guerilla warfare such as no New York paper had ever had to fight against.

It was Wheeler, the gaunt manager of the business side of the journal, who first brought it to the notice of the editorial staff. Wheeler was a man for whom in business hours nothing existed but his job; and his job was to look after the distribution of the paper. As to the contents of the paper he was absolutely ignorant. He had been with *Cosy Moments* from its start, but he had never read a line of it. He handled it as if it were so much soap. The scholarly writings of Mr. Wilberfloss, the mirth-provoking sallies of Mr. B. Henderson Asher, the tender outpourings of Louella Granville Waterman-all these were things outside his ken. He was a distributor, and he distributed.

A few days after the restoration of Mr. Repetto to East Side Society, Mr. Wheeler came into the editorial room with information and desire for information.

He endeavoured to satisfy the latter first.

"What's doing, anyway?" he asked. He then proceeded to his information. "Some one's got it in against the paper, sure," he said. "I don't know what it's all about. I ha'n't never read the thing. Don't see what any one could have against a paper with a name like *Cosy Moments*, anyway. The way things have been going last few days, seems it might be the organ of a blamed mining-camp what the boys have took a dislike to."

"What's been happening?" asked Billy with gleaming eyes.

"Why, nothing in the world to fuss about, only our carriers can't go out without being beaten up by gangs of toughs. Pat Harrigan's in the hospital now. Just been looking in on him. Pat's a feller who likes to fight. Rather fight he would than see a ball-game. But this was too much for him. Know what happened? Why, see here, just like this it was. Pat goes out with his cart. Passing through a low-down street on his way up-town he's held up by a bunch of toughs. He shows fight. Half a dozen of them attend to him, while the rest gets clean away with every copy of the paper there was in the cart. When the cop comes along, there's Pat in pieces on the ground and nobody in sight but a Dago chewing gum. Cop asks the Dago what's been doing, and the Dago says he's only just come round the corner and ha'n't seen nothing of anybody. What I want to know is, what's it all about? Who's got it in for us and why?"

Mr. Wheeler leaned back in his chair, while Billy, his hair rumpled more than ever and his eyes glowing, explained the situation. Mr. Wheeler listened absolutely unmoved, and, when the narrative had come to an end, gave it as his opinion that the editorial staff had sand. That was his sole comment. "It's up to you," he said, rising. "You know your business. Say, though, some one had better get busy right quick and do something to stop these guys rough-housing like this. If we get a few more carriers beat up the way Pat was, there'll be a strike. It's not as if they were all Irishmen. The most of them are Dagoes and such, and they don't want any more fight than they can get by beating their wives and kicking kids off the sidewalk. I'll do my best to get this paper distributed right and it's a shame if it ain't, because it's going big just now-but it's up to you. Good day, gents."

He went out. Psmith looked at Billy.

"As Comrade Wheeler remarks," he said, "it is up to us. What do you propose to do about it? This is a move of the enemy which I have not anticipated. I had fancied that their operations would be confined exclusively to our two selves. If they are going to strew the street with our carriers, we are somewhat in the soup."

596

Billy said nothing. He was chewing the stem of an unlighted pipe. Psmith went on.

"It means, of course, that we must buck up to a certain extent. If the campaign is to be a long one, they have us where the hair is crisp. We cannot stand the strain. *Cosy Moments* cannot be muzzled, but it can undoubtedly be choked. What we want to do is to find out the name of the man behind the tenements as soon as ever we can and publish it; and, then, if we perish, fall yelling the name."

Billy admitted the soundness of this scheme, but wished to know how it was to be done.

"Comrade Windsor," said Psmith. "I have been thinking this thing over, and it seems to me that we are on the wrong track, or rather we aren't on any track at all; we are simply marking time. What we want to do is to go out and hustle round till we stir up something. Our line up to the present has been to sit at home and scream vigorously in the hope of some stout fellow hearing and rushing to help. In other words, we've been saying in the paper what an out-size in scugs the merchant must be who owns those tenements, in the hope that somebody else will agree with us and be sufficiently interested to get to work and find out who the blighter is. That's all wrong. What we must do now, Comrade Windsor, is put on our hats, such hats as Comrade Repetto has left us, and sally forth as sleuth-hounds on our own account."

"Yes, but how?" demanded Billy. "That's all right in theory, but how's it going to work in practice? The only thing that can corner the man is a commission."

"Far from it, Comrade Windsor. The job may be worked more simply. I don't know how often the rents are collected in these places, but I should say at a venture once a week. My idea is to hang negligently round till the rent-collector arrives, and when he has loomed up on the horizon, buttonhole him and ask him quite politely, as man to man, whether he is collecting those rents for himself or for somebody else, and if somebody else, who that somebody else is. Simple, I fancy? Yet brainy. Do you take me, Comrade Windsor?"

Billy sat up, excited. "I believe you've hit it."

Psmith shot his cuffs modestly.

CHAPTER XVIII

AN EPISODE BY THE WAY

It was Pugsy Maloney who, on the following morning, brought to the office the gist of what is related in this chapter. Pugsy's version was, however, brief and unadorned, as was the way with his narratives. Such things as first causes and piquant details he avoided, as tending to prolong the telling excessively, thus keeping him from perusal of his cowboy stories. The way Pugsy put it was as follows. He gave the thing out merely as an item of general interest, a bubble on the surface of the life of a great city. He did not know how nearly interested were his employers in any matter touching that gang which is known as the Three Points. Pugsy said: "Dere's trouble down where I live. Dude Dawson's mad at Spider Reilly, an' now de Table Hills are layin' for de T'ree Points. Sure." He had then retired to his outer fastness, yielding further details jerkily and with the distrait air of one whose mind is elsewhere.

Skilfully extracted and pieced together, these details formed themselves into the following typical narrative of East Side life in New York.

The really important gangs of New York are four. There are other less important institutions, but these are little more than mere friendly gatherings of old boyhood chums for purposes of mutual companionship. In time they may grow, as did Bat Jarvis's coterie, into formidable organisations, for the soil is undoubtedly propitious to such growth. But at present the amount of ice which good judges declare them to cut is but small. They "stick up" an occasional wayfarer for his "cush," and they carry "canisters" and sometimes fire them off, but these things do not signify the cutting of ice. In matters political there are only four gangs which count, the East Side, the Groome Street, the Three Points, and the Table Hill. Greatest of these by virtue of their numbers are the East Side and the Groome Street, the latter presided over at the time of this story by Mr. Bat Jarvis. These two are colossal, and, though they may fight each other, are immune from attack at the hands of lesser gangs. But between the other gangs, and especially between the Table Hill and the Three Points, which are much of a size, warfare rages as briskly as among the republics of South America. There has always been bad blood between the Table Hill and the Three Points, and until they wipe each other out after the manner of the Kilkenny cats, it is probable that there always will be. Little events, trifling in themselves, have always occurred to shatter friendly relations just when there has seemed a chance of their being formed. Thus, just as the Table Hillites were beginning to forgive the Three Points for shooting the redoubtable Paul Horgan down at Coney Island, a Three Pointer injudiciously wiped out another of the rival gang near Canal Street. He pleaded self-defence, and in any case it was probably mere thoughtlessness, but nevertheless the Table Hillites were ruffled.

That had been a month or so back. During that month things had been simmering down, and peace was just preparing to brood when there occurred the incident to which Pugsy had alluded, the regrettable falling out of Dude Dawson and Spider Reilly at Mr. Maginnis's dancing saloon, Shamrock Hall, the same which Bat Jarvis had been called in to protect in the days before the Groome Street gang began to be.

Shamrock Hall, being under the eyes of the great Bat, was, of course, forbidden ground; and it was with no intention of spoiling the harmony of the evening that Mr. Dawson had looked in. He was there in a purely private and peaceful character.

As he sat smoking, sipping, and observing the revels, there settled at the next table Mr. Robert ("Nigger") Coston, an eminent member of the Three Points.

There being temporary peace between the two gangs, the great men exchanged a not unfriendly nod and, after a short pause, a word or two. Mr. Coston, alluding to an Italian who had just pirouetted past, remarked that there sure was some class to the way that wop hit it up. Mr. Dawson said Yup, there sure was. You would have said that all Nature smiled.

Alas! The next moment the sky was covered with black clouds and the storm broke. For Mr. Dawson, continuing in this vein of criticism, rather injudiciously gave it as his opinion that one of the lady dancers had two left feet.

For a moment Mr. Coston did not see which lady was alluded to.

"De goil in de pink skoit," said Mr. Dawson, facilitating the other's search by pointing with a much-chewed cigarette. It was at this moment that Nature's smile was shut off as if by a tap. For the lady in the pink skirt had been in receipt of Mr. Coston's respectful devotion for the past eight days.

From this point onwards the march of events was rapid.

Mr. Coston, rising, asked Mr. Dawson who he thought he, Mr. Dawson, was.

Mr. Dawson, extinguishing his cigarette and placing it behind his ear, replied that he was the fellow who could bite his, Mr. Coston's, head off.

Mr. Coston said: "Huh?"

Mr. Dawson said: "Sure."

Mr. Coston called Mr. Dawson a pie-faced rubber-necked four-flusher.

Mr. Dawson called Mr. Coston a coon.

And that was where the trouble really started.

It was secretly a great grief to Mr. Coston that his skin was of so swarthy a hue. To be permitted to address Mr. Coston face to face by his nickname was a sign of the closest friendship, to which only Spider Reilly, Jack Repetto, and one or two more of the gang could aspire. Others spoke of him as Nigger, or, more briefly, Nig-strictly behind his back. For Mr. Coston had a wide reputation as a fighter, and his particular mode of battling was to descend on his antagonist and bite him. Into this action he flung himself with the passionate abandonment of the artist. When he bit he bit. He did not nibble.

If a friend had called Mr. Coston "Nig" he would have been running grave risks. A stranger, and a leader of a rival gang, who addressed him as "coon" was more than asking for trouble. He was pleading for it.

Great men seldom waste time. Mr. Coston, leaning towards Mr. Dawson, promptly bit him on the cheek. Mr. Dawson bounded from his seat. Such was the excitement of the moment that, instead of drawing his "canister," he forgot that he had one on his person, and, seizing a mug which had held beer, bounced it vigorously on Mr. Coston's skull, which, being of solid wood, merely gave out a resonant note and remained unbroken.

So far the honours were comparatively even, with perhaps a slight balance in favour of Mr. Coston. But now occurred an incident which turned the scale, and made war between the gangs inevitable. In the far corner of the room, surrounded by a crowd of admiring friends, sat Spider Reilly, monarch of the Three Points. He had noticed that there was a slight disturbance at the other side of the hall, but had given it little attention till, the dancing ceasing suddenly and the floor emptying itself of its crowd, he had a plain view of Mr. Dawson and Mr. Coston squaring up at each other for the second round. We must assume that Mr. Reilly was not thinking what he did, for his action was contrary to all rules of gang-etiquette. In the street it would have been perfectly legitimate, even praiseworthy, but in a dance-hall belonging to a neutral power it was unpardonable.

What he did was to produce his "canister" and pick off the unsuspecting Mr. Dawson just as that exquisite was preparing to get in some more good work with the beer-mug. The leader of the Table Hillites fell with a crash, shot through the leg; and Spider Reilly, together with Mr. Coston and others of the Three Points, sped through the doorway for safety, fearing the wrath of Bat Jarvis, who, it was known, would countenance no such episodes at the dance-hall which he had undertaken to protect.

Mr. Dawson, meanwhile, was attended to and helped home. Willing informants gave him the name of his aggressor, and before morning the Table Hill camp was in ferment. Shooting broke out in three places, though there were no casualties. When the day dawned there existed between the two gangs a state of war more bitter than any in their record; for this time it was no question of obscure nonentities. Chieftain had assaulted chieftain; royal blood had been spilt.

* * * * *

"Comrade Windsor," said Psmith, when Master Maloney had spoken his last word, "we must take careful note of this little matter. I rather fancy that sooner or later we may be able to turn it to our profit. I am sorry for Dude Dawson, anyhow. Though I have never met him, I have a sort of instinctive respect for him. A man such as he would feel a bullet through his trouser-leg more than one of common clay who cared little how his clothes looked."

CHAPTER XIX

IN PLEASANT STREET

Careful inquiries, conducted incognito by Master Maloney among the denizens of Pleasant Street, brought the information that rents in the tenements were collected not weekly but monthly, a fact which must undoubtedly cause a troublesome hitch in the campaign. Rent-day, announced Pugsy, fell on the last day of the month.

"I rubbered around," he said, "and did de sleut' act, and I finds t'ings out. Dere's a feller comes round 'bout supper time dat day, an' den it's up to de fam'lies what lives in de tenements to dig down into deir jeans fer de stuff, or out dey goes dat same night."

"Evidently a hustler, our nameless friend," said Psmith.

"I got dat from a kid what knows anuder kid what lives dere," explained Master Maloney. "Say," he proceeded confidentially, "dat kid's in bad, sure he is. Dat second kid, de one what lives dere. He's a wop kid, an —"

"A what, Comrade Maloney?"

"A wop. A Dago. Why, don't you get next? Why, an Italian. Sure, dat's right. Well, dis kid, he is sure to de bad, 'cos his father come over from Italy to work on de Subway."

"I don't see why that puts him in bad," said Billy Windsor wonderingly.

"Nor I," agreed Psmith. "Your narratives, Comrade Maloney, always seem to me to suffer from a certain lack of construction. You start at the end, and then you go back to any portion of the story which happens to appeal to you at the moment, eventually winding up at the beginning. Why should the fact that this stripling's father has come over from Italy to work on the Subway be a misfortune?"

"Why, sure, because he got fired an' went an' swatted de foreman one on de coco, an' de magistrate gives him t'oity days."

"And then, Comrade Maloney? This thing is beginning to get clearer. You are like Sherlock Holmes. After you've explained a thing from start to finish-or, as you prefer to do, from finish to start-it becomes quite simple."

"Why, den dis kid's in bad for fair, 'cos der ain't nobody to pungle de bones."

"Pungle de what, Comrade Maloney?"

"De bones. De stuff. Dat's right. De dollars. He's all alone, dis kid, so when de rent-guy blows in, who's to slip him over de simoleons? It'll be outside for his, quick."

Billy warmed up at this tale of distress in his usual way. "Somebody ought to do something. It's a vile shame the kid being turned out like that."

"We will see to it, Comrade Windsor. *Cosy Moments* shall step in. We will combine business with pleasure, paying the stripling's rent and corralling the rent-collector at the same time. What is today? How long before the end of the month? Another week! A murrain on it, Comrade Windsor. Two murrains. This delay may undo us."

But the days went by without any further movement on the part of the enemy. A strange quiet seemed to be brooding over the other camp. As a matter of fact, the sudden outbreak of active hostilities with the Table Hill contingent had had the effect of taking the minds of Spider Reilly and his warriors off *Cosy Moments* and its affairs, much as the unexpected appearance of a mad bull would make a man forget that he had come out butterfly-hunting. Psmith and Billy could wait; they were not likely to take the offensive; but the Table Hillites demanded instant attention.

War had broken out, as was usual between the gangs, in a somewhat tentative fashion at first sight. There had been sniping and skirmishes by the wayside, but as yet no pitched battle. The two armies were sparring for an opening.

* * * * *

The end of the week arrived, and Psmith and Billy, conducted by Master Maloney, made their way to Pleasant Street. To get there it was necessary to pass through a section of the enemy's country; but the perilous passage was safely negotiated. The expedition reached its unsavoury goal intact.

The wop kid, whose name, it appeared, was Giuseppe Orloni, inhabited a small room at the very top of the building next to the one Psmith and Mike had visited on their first appearance in Pleasant Street. He was out when the party, led by Pugsy up dark stairs, arrived; and, on returning, seemed both surprised and alarmed to see visitors. Pugsy undertook to do the honours. Pugsy as interpreter was energetic but not wholly successful. He appeared to have a fixed idea that the Italian language was one easily mastered by the simple method of saying "da" instead of "the," and tacking on a final "a" to any word that seemed to him to need one.

"Say, kid," he began, "has da rent-a-man come yet-a?"

The black eyes of the wop kid clouded. He gesticulated, and said something in his native language.

"He hasn't got next," reported Master Maloney. "He can't git on to me curves. Dese wop kids is all boneheads. Say, kid, look-a here." He walked out of the room and closed the door; then, rapping on it smartly from the outside, re-entered and, assuming a look of extreme ferocity, stretched out his hand and thundered: "Unbelt-a! Slip-a me da stuff!"

The wop kid's puzzlement became pathetic.

"This," said Psmith, deeply interested, "is getting about as tense as anything I ever struck. Don't give in, Comrade Maloney. Who knows but that you may yet win through? I fancy the trouble is that your too perfect Italian accent is making the youth home-sick. Once more to the breach, Comrade Maloney."

Master Maloney made a gesture of disgust. "I'm t'roo. Dese Dagoes makes me tired. Dey don't know enough to go upstairs to take de Elevated. Beat it, you mutt," he observed with moody displeasure to the wop kid, accompanying the words with a gesture which conveyed its own meaning. The wop kid, plainly glad to get away, slipped out of the door like a shadow.

Pugsy shrugged his shoulders.

"Gents," he said resignedly, "it's up to youse."

"I fancy," said Psmith, "that this is one of those moments when it is necessary for me to unlimber my Sherlock Holmes system. As thus. If the rent collector *had* been here, it is certain, I think, that Comrade Spaghetti, or whatever you said his name was, wouldn't have been. That is to say, if the rent collector had called and found no money waiting for him, surely Comrade Spaghetti would have been out in the cold night instead of under his own roof-tree. Do you follow me, Comrade Maloney?"

"That's right," said Billy Windsor. "Of course."

"Elementary, my dear Watson, elementary," murmured Psmith.

"So all we have to do is to sit here and wait."

"All?" said Psmith sadly. "Surely it is enough. For of all the scaly localities I have struck this seems to me the scaliest. The architect of this Stately Home of America seems to have had a positive hatred for windows. His idea of ventilation was to leave a hole in the wall about the size of a lima bean and let the thing go at that. If our friend does not arrive shortly, I shall pull down the roof. Why, gadzooks! Not to mention stap my vitals! Isn't that a trap-door up there? Make a long-arm, Comrade Windsor."

Billy got on a chair and pulled the bolt. The trap-door opened downwards. It fell, disclosing a square of deep blue sky.

"Gum!" he said. "Fancy living in this atmosphere when you don't have to. Fancy these fellows keeping that shut all the time."

"I expect it is an acquired taste," said Psmith, "like Limburger cheese. They don't begin to appreciate air till it is thick enough to scoop chunks out of with a spoon. Then they get up on their hind legs and inflate their chests and say, 'This is fine! This beats ozone hollow!'

Leave it open, Comrade Windsor. And now, as to the problem of dispensing with Comrade Maloney's services?"

"Sure," said Billy. "Beat it, Pugsy, my lad."

Pugsy looked up, indignant.

"Beat it?" he queried.

"While your shoe leather's good," said Billy. "This is no place for a minister's son. There may be a rough house in here any minute, and you would be in the way."

"I want to stop and pipe de fun," objected Master Maloney.

"Never mind. Cut off. We'll tell you all about it to-morrow."

Master Maloney prepared reluctantly to depart. As he did so there was a sound of a well-shod foot on the stairs, and a man in a snuff-coloured suit, wearing a brown Homburg hat and carrying a small notebook in one hand, walked briskly into the room. It was not necessary for Psmith to get his Sherlock Holmes system to work. His whole appearance proclaimed the new-comer to be the long-expected collector of rents.

CHAPTER XX

CORNERED

He stood in the doorway looking with some surprise at the group inside. He was a smallish, pale-faced man with protruding eyes and teeth which gave him a certain resemblance to a rabbit.

"Hello," he said.

"Welcome to New York," said Psmith.

Master Maloney, who had taken advantage of the interruption to edge farther into the room, now appeared to consider the question of his departure permanently shelved. He sidled to a corner and sat down on an empty soap-box with the air of a dramatic critic at the opening night of a new play. The scene looked good to him. It promised interesting developments. Master Maloney was an earnest student of the drama, as exhibited in the theatres of the East Side, and few had ever applauded the hero of "Escaped from Sing-Sing," or hissed the villain of "Nellie, the Beautiful Cloak-Model" with more fervour than he. He liked his drama to have plenty of action, and to his practised eye this one promised well. Psmith he looked upon as a quite amiable lunatic, from whom little was to be expected; but there was a set expression on Billy Windsor's face which suggested great things.

His pleasure was abruptly quenched. Billy Windsor, placing a firm hand on his collar, led him to the door and pushed him out, closing the door behind him.

The rent collector watched these things with a puzzled eye. He now turned to Psmith.

"Say, seen anything of the wops that live here?" he inquired.

"I am addressing —?" said Psmith courteously.

"My name's Gooch."

Psmith bowed.

"Touching these wops, Comrade Gooch," he said, "I fear there is little chance of your seeing them to-night, unless you wait some considerable time. With one of them-the son and heir of the family, I should say-we have just been having a highly interesting and informative chat. Comrade Maloney, who has just left us, acted as interpreter. The father, I am told, is in the dungeon below the castle moat for a brief spell for punching his foreman in the eye. The result? The rent is not forthcoming."

"Then it's outside for theirs," said Mr. Gooch definitely.

"It's a big shame," broke in Billy, "turning the kid out. Where's he to go?"

"That's up to him. Nothing to do with me. I'm only acting under orders from up top."

"Whose orders, Comrade Gooch?" inquired Psmith.

"The gent who owns this joint."

"Who is he?" said Billy.

Suspicion crept into the protruding eyes of the rent collector. He waxed wroth. "Say!" he demanded. "Who are you two guys, anyway, and what do you think you're doing here? That's what I'd like to know. What do you want with the name of the owner of this place? What business is it of yours?"

"The fact is, Comrade Gooch, we are newspaper men."

"I guessed you were," said Mr. Gooch with triumph. "You can't bluff me. Well, it's no good, boys. I've nothing for you. You'd better chase off and try something else."

He became more friendly.

"Say, though," he said, "I just guessed you were from some paper. I wish I could give you a story, but I can't. I guess it's this *Cosy Moments* business that's been and put your editor on to this joint, ain't it? Say, though, that's a queer thing, that paper. Why, only a few weeks ago it used to be a sort of take-home-and-read-to-the-kids affair. A friend of mine used to buy it regular. And then suddenly it comes out with a regular whoop, and started knocking these tenements and boosting Kid Brady, and all that. I can't understand it. All I know is that it's begun to get this place talked about. Why, you see for yourselves how it is. Here is your editor sending you down to get a story about it. But, say, those *Cosy Moments* guys are taking big risks. I tell you straight they are, and that goes. I happen to know a thing or two about what's going on on the other side, and I tell you there's going to be something doing if they don't cut it out quick. Mr. —" he stopped and chuckled, "Mr. Jones isn't the man to sit still and smile. He's going to get busy. Say, what paper do you boys come from?"

"*Cosy Moments*, Comrade Gooch," Psmith replied. "Immediately behind you, between you and the door, is Comrade Windsor, our editor. I am Psmith. I sub-edit."

For a moment the inwardness of the information did not seem to come home to Mr. Gooch. Then it hit him. He spun round. Billy Windsor was standing with his back against the door and a more than nasty look on his face.

"What's all this?" demanded Mr. Gooch.

"I will explain all," said Psmith soothingly. "In the first place, however, this matter of Comrade Spaghetti's rent. Sooner than see that friend of my boyhood slung out to do the wandering-child-in-the-snow act, I will brass up for him."

"Confound his rent. Let me out."

"Business before pleasure. How much is it? Twelve dollars? For the privilege of suffocating in this compact little Black Hole? By my halidom, Comrade Gooch, that gentleman whose name you are so shortly to tell us has a very fair idea of how to charge! But who am I that I should criticise? Here are the simoleons, as our young friend, Comrade Maloney, would call them. Push me over a receipt."

"Let me out."

"Anon, gossip, anon.—Shakespeare. First, the receipt."

Mr. Gooch scribbled a few words in his notebook and tore out the page. Psmith thanked him.

"I will see that it reaches Comrade Spaghetti," he said. "And now to a more important matter. Don't put away that notebook. Turn to a clean page, moisten your pencil, and write as follows. Are you ready? By the way, what is your Christian name? . . . Gooch, Gooch, this is no way to speak! Well, if you are sensitive on the point, we will waive the Christian name. It is my duty to tell you, however, that I suspect it to be Percy. Let us push on. Are you ready, once more? Pencil moistened? Very well, then. 'I'—comma—'being of sound mind and body'—comma—'and a bright little chap altogether'—comma-Why, you're not writing."

"Let me out," bellowed Mr. Gooch. "I'll summon you for assault and battery. Playing a fool game like this! Get away from that door."

"There has been no assault and battery yet, Comrade Gooch, but who shall predict how long so happy a state of things will last? Do not be deceived by our gay and smiling faces, Comrade Gooch. We mean business. Let me put the whole position of affairs before you; and I am sure a man of your perception will see that there is only one thing to be done."

He dusted the only chair in the room with infinite care and sat down. Billy Windsor, who had not spoken a word or moved an inch since the beginning of the interview, continued to stand and be silent. Mr. Gooch shuffled restlessly in the middle of the room.

"As you justly observed a moment ago," said Psmith, "the staff of *Cosy Moments* is taking big risks. We do not rely on your unsupported word for that. We have had practical demonstration of the fact from one J. Repetto, who tried some few nights ago to put us out of business. Well, it struck us both that we had better get hold of the name of the blighter who runs these tenements as quickly as possible, before Comrade Repetto's next night out. That is what we should like you to give us, Comrade Gooch. And we should like it in writing. And, on second thoughts, in ink. I have one of those patent non-leakable fountain pens in my pocket. The Old Journalist's Best Friend. Most of the ink has come out and is permeating the lining of my coat, but I think there is still sufficient for our needs. Remind me later, Comrade Gooch, to continue on the subject of fountain pens. I have much to say on the theme. Meanwhile, however, business, business. That is the cry."

He produced a pen and an old letter, the last page of which was blank, and began to write.

"How does this strike you?" he said. " 'I' —(I have left a blank for the Christian name: you can write it in yourself later) —'I, blank Gooch, being a collector of rents in Pleasant Street, New York, do hereby swear' —hush, Comrade Gooch, there is no need to do it yet —'that the name of the owner of the Pleasant Street tenements, who is responsible for the perfectly foul conditions there, is—' And that is where you come in, Comrade Gooch. That is where we need your specialised knowledge. Who is he?"

Billy Windsor reached out and grabbed the rent collector by the collar. Having done this, he proceeded to shake him.

Billy was muscular, and his heart was so much in the business that Mr. Gooch behaved as if he had been caught in a high wind. It is probable that in another moment the desired information might have been shaken out of him, but before this could happen there was a banging at the door, followed by the entrance of Master Maloney. For the first time since Psmith had known him, Pugsy was openly excited.

"Say," he began, "youse had better beat it quick, you had. Dey's coming!"

"And now go back to the beginning, Comrade Maloney," said Psmith patiently, "which in the exuberance of the moment you have skipped. Who are coming?"

"Why, dem. De guys."

Psmith shook his head.

"Your habit of omitting essentials, Comrade Maloney, is going to undo you one of these days. When you get to that ranch of yours, you will probably start out to gallop after the cattle without remembering to mount your mustang. There are four million guys in New York. Which section is it that is coming?"

"Gum! I don't know how many dere is ob dem. I seen Spider Reilly an' Jack Repetto an'—"

"Say no more," said Psmith. "If Comrade Repetto is there, that is enough for me. I am going to get on the roof and pull it up after me."

Billy released Mr. Gooch, who fell, puffing, on to the low bed, which stood in one corner of the room.

"They must have spotted us as we were coming here," he said, "and followed us. Where did you see them, Pugsy?"

"On de Street just outside. Dere was a bunch of dem talkin' togedder, and I hears dem say you was in here. One of dem seen you come in, an dere ain't no ways out but de front, so dey ain't hurryin'! Dey just reckon to pike along upstairs, lookin' into each room till dey finds you. An dere's a bunch of dem goin' to wait on de Street in case youse beat it past down de stairs while de udder guys is rubberin' for youse. Say, gents, it's pretty fierce, dis proposition. What are youse goin' to do?"

Mr. Gooch, from the bed, laughed unpleasantly.

"I guess you ain't the only assault-and-battery artists in the business," he said. "Looks to me as if some one else was going to get shaken up some."

Billy looked at Psmith.

"Well?" he said. "What shall we do? Go down and try and rush through?"

Psmith shook his head.

"Not so, Comrade Windsor, but about as much otherwise as you can jolly well imagine."

"Well, what then?"

"We will stay here. Or rather we will hop nimbly up on to the roof through that skylight. Once there, we may engage these varlets on fairly equal terms. They can only get through one at a time. And while they are doing it I will give my celebrated imitation of Horatius. We had better be moving. Our luggage, fortunately, is small. Merely Comrade Gooch. If you will get through the skylight, I will pass him up to you."

Mr. Gooch, with much verbal embroidery, stated that he would not go. Psmith acted promptly. Gripping the struggling rent collector round the waist, and ignoring his frantic kicks as mere errors in taste, he lifted him to the trap-door, whence the head, shoulders and arms of

Billy Windsor protruded into the room. Billy collected the collector, and then Psmith turned to Pugsy.

"Comrade Maloney."

"Huh?"

"Have I your ear?"

"Huh?"

"Are you listening till you feel that your ears are the size of footballs? Then drink this in. For weeks you have been praying for a chance to show your devotion to the great cause; or if you haven't, you ought to have been. That chance has come. You alone can save us. In a sense, of course, we do not need to be saved. They will find it hard to get at us, I fancy, on the roof. But it ill befits the dignity of the editorial staff of a great New York weekly to roost like pigeons for any length of time; and consequently it is up to you."

"Shall I go for de cops, Mr. Smith?"

"No, Comrade Maloney, I thank you. I have seen the cops in action, and they did not impress me. We do not want allies who will merely shake their heads at Comrade Repetto and the others, however sternly. We want some one who will swoop down upon these merry roisterers, and, as it were, soak to them good. Do you know where Dude Dawson lives?"

The light of intelligence began to shine in Master Maloney's face. His eye glistened with respectful approval. This was strategy of the right sort.

"Dude Dawson? Nope. But I can ask around."

"Do so, Comrade Maloney. And when found, tell him that his old college chum, Spider Reilly, is here. He will not be able to come himself, I fear, but he can send representatives."

"Sure."

"That's all, then. Go downstairs with a gay and jaunty air, as if you had no connection with the old firm at all. Whistle a few lively bars. Make careless gestures. Thus shall you win through. And now it would be no bad idea, I fancy, for me to join the rest of the brains of the paper up aloft. Off you go, Comrade Maloney. And, in passing, don't take a week about it. Leg it with all the speed you possess."

Pugsy vanished, and Psmith closed the door behind him. Inspection revealed the fact that it possessed no lock. As a barrier it was useless. He left it ajar, and, jumping up, gripped the edge of the opening in the roof and pulled himself through.

Billy Windsor was seated comfortably on Mr. Gooch's chest a few feet away. By his side was his big stick. Psmith possessed himself of this, and looked about him. The examination was satisfactory. The trap-door appeared to be the only means of access to the roof, and between their roof and that of the next house there was a broad gulf.

"Practically impregnable," he murmured. "Only one thing can dish us, Comrade Windsor; and that is if they have the sense to get on to the roof next door and start shooting. Even in that case, however, we have cover in the shape of the chimneys. I think we may fairly say that all is well. How are you getting along? Has the patient responded at all?"

"Not yet," said Billy. "But he's going to."

"He will be in your charge. I must devote myself exclusively to guarding the bridge. It is a pity that the trap has not got a bolt this side. If it had, the thing would be a perfect picnic. As it is, we must leave it open. But we mustn't expect everything."

Billy was about to speak, but Psmith suddenly held up his hand warningly. From the room below came a sound of feet.

For a moment the silence was tense. Then from Mr. Gooch's lips there escaped a screech.

"This way! They're up —"

The words were cut short as Billy banged his hand over the speaker's mouth. But the thing was done.

"On top de roof," cried a voice. "Dey've beaten it for de roof."

The chair rasped over the floor. Feet shuffled. And then, like a jack-in-the-box, there popped through the opening a head and shoulders.

CHAPTER XXI

THE BATTLE OF PLEASANT STREET

The new arrival was a young man with a shock of red hair, an ingrowing Roman nose, and a mouth from which force or the passage of time had removed three front teeth. He held on to the edges of the trap with his hands, and stared in a glassy manner into Psmith's face, which was within a foot of his own.

There was a momentary pause, broken by an oath from Mr. Gooch, who was still undergoing treatment in the background.

"Aha!" said Psmith genially. "Historic picture. 'Doctor Cook discovers the North Pole.'"

The red-headed young man blinked. The strong light of the open air was trying to his eyes.

"Youse had better come down," he observed coldly. "We've got youse."

"And," continued Psmith, unmoved, "is instantly handed a gum-drop by his faithful Esquimaux."

As he spoke, he brought the stick down on the knuckles which disfigured the edges of the trap. The intruder uttered a howl and dropped out of sight. In the room below there were whisperings and mutterings, growing gradually louder till something resembling coherent conversation came to Psmith's ears, as he knelt by the trap making meditative billiard-shots with the stick at a small pebble.

"Aw g'wan! Don't be a quitter!"

"Who's a quitter?"

"Youse is a quitter. Get on top de roof. He can't hoit youse."

"De guy's gotten a big stick." Psmith nodded appreciatively. "I and Roosevelt," he murmured.

A somewhat baffled silence on the part of the attacking force was followed by further conversation.

"Gum! some guy's got to go up." Murmur of assent from the audience.

A voice, in inspired tones: "Let Sam do it!"

This suggestion made a hit. There was no doubt about that. It was a success from the start. Quite a little chorus of voices expressed sincere approval of the very happy solution to what had seemed an insoluble problem. Psmith, listening from above, failed to detect in the choir of glad voices one that might belong to Sam himself. Probably gratification had rendered the chosen one dumb.

"Yes, let Sam do it!" cried the unseen chorus. The first speaker, unnecessarily, perhaps-for the motion had been carried almost unanimously-but possibly with the idea of convincing the one member of the party in whose bosom doubts might conceivably be harboured, went on to adduce reasons.

"Sam bein' a coon," he argued, "ain't goin' to git hoit by no stick. Youse can't hoit a coon by soakin' him on de coco, can you, Sam?"

Psmith waited with some interest for the reply, but it did not come. Possibly Sam did not wish to generalise on insufficient experience.

"*Solvitur ambulando*," said Psmith softly, turning the stick round in his fingers. "Comrade Windsor!"

"Hullo?"

"Is it possible to hurt a coloured gentleman by hitting him on the head with a stick?"

"If you hit him hard enough."

"I knew there was some way out of the difficulty," said Psmith with satisfaction. "How are you getting on up at your end of the table, Comrade Windsor?"

"Fine."

"Any result yet?"

"Not at present."

"Don't give up."

"Not me."

"The right spirit, Comrade Win—"

A report like a cannon in the room below interrupted him. It was merely a revolver shot, but in the confined space it was deafening. The bullet sang up into the sky.

"Never hit me!" said Psmith with dignified triumph.

The noise was succeeded by a shuffling of feet. Psmith grasped his stick more firmly. This was evidently the real attack. The revolver shot had been a mere demonstration of artillery to cover the infantry's advance.

Sure enough, the next moment a woolly head popped through the opening, and a pair of rolling eyes gleamed up at the old Etonian.

"Why, Sam!" said Psmith cordially, "this is well met! I remember *you*. Yes, indeed, I do. Wasn't you the feller with the open umbereller that I met one rainy morning on the Av-en-ue? What, are you coming up? Sam, I hate to do it, but—"

A yell rang out.

"What was that?" asked Billy Windsor over his shoulder.

"Your statement, Comrade Windsor, has been tested and proved correct."

By this time the affair had begun to draw a "gate." The noise of the revolver had proved a fine advertisement. The roof of the house next door began to fill up. Only a few of the occupants could get a clear view of the proceedings, for a large chimney-stack intervened. There was considerable speculation as to what was passing between Billy Windsor and Mr. Gooch. Psmith's share in the entertainment was more obvious. The early comers had seen his interview with Sam, and were relating it with gusto to their friends. Their attitude towards Psmith was that of a group of men watching a terrier at a rat-hole. They looked to him to provide entertainment for them, but they realised that the first move must be with the attackers. They were fair-minded men, and they did not expect Psmith to make any aggressive move.

Their indignation, when the proceedings began to grow slow, was directed entirely at the dilatory Three Pointers. With an aggrieved air, akin to that of a crowd at a cricket match when batsmen are playing for a draw, they began to "barrack." They hooted the Three Pointers. They begged them to go home and tuck themselves up in bed. The men on the roof were mostly Irishmen, and it offended them to see what should have been a spirited fight so grossly bungled.

"G'wan away home, ye quitters!" roared one.

"Call yersilves the Three Points, do ye? An' would ye know what *I* call ye? The Young Ladies' Seminary!" bellowed another with withering scorn.

A third member of the audience alluded to them as "stiffs."

"I fear, Comrade Windsor," said Psmith, "that our blithe friends below are beginning to grow a little unpopular with the many-headed. They must be up and doing if they wish to retain the esteem of Pleasant Street. Aha!"

Another and a longer explosion from below, and more bullets wasted themselves on air. Psmith sighed.

"They make me tired," he said. "This is no time for a *feu de joie*. Action! That is the cry. Action! Get busy, you blighters!"

The Irish neighbours expressed the same sentiment in different and more forcible words. There was no doubt about it-as warriors, the Three Pointers had failed to give satisfaction.

A voice from the room called up to Psmith.

"Say!"

"You have our ear," said Psmith.

"What's that?"

"I said you had our ear."

"Are youse stiffs comin' down off out of dat roof?"

"Would you mind repeating that remark?"

"Are youse guys goin' to quit off out of dat roof?"

"Your grammar is perfectly beastly," said Psmith severely.

"Hey!"

"Well?"

"Are youse guys —?"

"No, my lad," said Psmith, "since you ask, we are not. And why? Because the air up here is refreshing, the view pleasant, and we are expecting at any moment an important communication from Comrade Gooch."

"We're goin' to wait here till youse come down."

"If you wish it," said Psmith courteously, "by all means do. Who am I that I should dictate your movements? The most I aspire to is to check them when they take an upward direction."

There was silence below. The time began to pass slowly. The Irishmen on the other roof, now definitely abandoning hope of further entertainment, proceeded with hoots of scorn to climb down one by one into the recesses of their own house.

Suddenly from the street far below there came a fusillade of shots and a babel of shouts and counter-shouts. The roof of the house next door, which had been emptying itself slowly and reluctantly, filled again with a magical swiftness, and the low wall facing into the street became black with the backs of those craning over.

"What's that?" inquired Billy.

"I rather fancy," said Psmith, "that our allies of the Table Hill contingent must have arrived. I sent Comrade Maloney to explain matters to Dude Dawson, and it seems as if that golden-hearted sportsman had responded. There appear to be great doings in the street."

In the room below confusion had arisen. A scout, clattering upstairs, had brought the news of the Table Hillites' advent, and there was doubt as to the proper course to pursue. Certain voices urged going down to help the main body. Others pointed out that that would mean abandoning the siege of the roof. The scout who had brought the news was eloquent in favour of the first course.

"Gum!" he cried, "don't I keep tellin' youse dat de Table Hills is here? Sure, dere's a whole bunch of dem, and unless youse come on down dey'll bite de hull head off of us lot. Leave those stiffs on de roof. Let Sam wait here with his canister, and den dey can't get down, 'cos Sam'll pump dem full of lead while dey're beatin' it t'roo de trap-door. Sure."

Psmith nodded reflectively.

"There is certainly something in what the bright boy says," he murmured. "It seems to me the grand rescue scene in the third act has sprung a leak. This will want thinking over."

In the street the disturbance had now become terrific. Both sides were hard at it, and the Irishmen on the roof, rewarded at last for their long vigil, were yelling encouragement promiscuously and whooping with the unfettered ecstasy of men who are getting the treat of their lives without having paid a penny for it.

The behaviour of the New York policeman in affairs of this kind is based on principles of the soundest practical wisdom. The unthinking man would rush in and attempt to crush the combat in its earliest and fiercest stages. The New York policeman, knowing the importance of his own safety, and the insignificance of the gangsman's, permits the opposing forces to hammer each other into a certain distaste for battle, and then, when both sides have begun to have enough of it, rushes in himself and clubs everything in sight. It is an admirable process in its results, but it is sure rather than swift.

Proceedings in the affair below had not yet reached the police interference stage. The noise, what with the shots and yells from the street and the ear-piercing approval of the roof-audience, was just working up to a climax.

Psmith rose. He was tired of kneeling by the trap, and there was no likelihood of Sam making another attempt to climb through. He walked towards Billy.

As he did so, Billy got up and turned to him. His eyes were gleaming with excitement. His whole attitude was triumphant. In his hand he waved a strip of paper.

"I've got it," he cried.

"Excellent, Comrade Windsor," said Psmith. "Surely we must win through now. All we have to do is to get off this roof, and fate cannot touch us. Are two mammoth minds such as ours unequal to such a feat? It can hardly be. Let us ponder."

"Why not go down through the trap? They've all gone to the street."

Psmith shook his head.

"All," he replied, "save Sam. Sam was the subject of my late successful experiment, when I proved that coloured gentlemen's heads could be hurt with a stick. He is now waiting below, armed with a pistol, ready-even anxious-to pick us off as we climb through the trap. How would it be to drop Comrade Gooch through first, and so draw his fire? Comrade Gooch, I am sure, would be delighted to do a little thing like that for old friends of our standing or-but what's that!"

"What's the matter?"

"Is that a ladder that I see before me, its handle to my hand? It is! Comrade Windsor, we win through. *Cosy Moments'* editorial staff may be tree'd, but it cannot be put out of business. Comrade Windsor, take the other end of that ladder and follow me."

The ladder was lying against the farther wall. It was long, more than long enough for the purpose for which it was needed. Psmith and Billy rested it on the coping, and pushed it till the other end reached across the gulf to the roof of the house next door, Mr. Gooch eyeing them in silence the while.

Psmith turned to him.

"Comrade Gooch," he said, "do nothing to apprise our friend Sam of these proceedings. I speak in your best interests. Sam is in no mood to make nice distinctions between friend and foe. If you bring him up here, he will probably mistake you for a member of the staff of *Cosy Moments*, and loose off in your direction without waiting for explanations. I think you had better come with us. I will go first, Comrade Windsor, so that if the ladder breaks, the paper will lose merely a sub-editor, not an editor."

He went down on all-fours, and in this attitude wormed his way across to the opposite roof, whose occupants, engrossed in the fight in the street, in which the police had now joined, had their backs turned and did not observe him. Mr. Gooch, pallid and obviously ill-attuned to such feats, followed him; and finally Billy Windsor reached the other side.

"Neat," said Psmith complacently. "Uncommonly neat. Comrade Gooch reminded me of the untamed chamois of the Alps, leaping from crag to crag."

In the street there was now comparative silence. The police, with their clubs, had knocked the last remnant of fight out of the combatants. Shooting had definitely ceased.

"I think," said Psmith, "that we might now descend. If you have no other engagements, Comrade Windsor, I will take you to the Knickerbocker, and buy you a square meal. I would ask for the pleasure of your company also, Comrade Gooch, were it not that matters of private moment, relating to the policy of the paper, must be discussed at the table. Some other day, perhaps. We are infinitely obliged to you for your sympathetic co-operation in this little matter. And now good-bye. Comrade Windsor, let us debouch."

CHAPTER XXII

CONCERNING MR. WARING

Psmith pushed back his chair slightly, stretched out his legs, and lit a cigarette. The resources of the Knickerbocker Hotel had proved equal to supplying the fatigued staff of *Cosy Moments* with an excellent dinner, and Psmith had stoutly declined to talk business until the coffee arrived. This had been hard on Billy, who was bursting with his news. Beyond a hint that it was sensational he had not been permitted to go.

"More bright young careers than I care to think of," said Psmith, "have been ruined by the fatal practice of talking shop at dinner. But now that we are through, Comrade Windsor, by all means let us have it. What's the name which Comrade Gooch so eagerly divulged?"

Billy leaned forward excitedly.

"Stewart Waring," he whispered.

"Stewart who?" asked Psmith.

Billy stared.

"Great Scott, man!" he said, "haven't you heard of Stewart Waring?"

"The name seems vaguely familiar, like Isinglass or Post-toasties. I seem to know it, but it conveys nothing to me."

"Don't you ever read the papers?"

"I toy with my *American* of a morning, but my interest is confined mainly to the sporting page which reminds me that Comrade Brady has been matched against one Eddie Wood a month from to-day. Gratifying as it is to find one of the staff getting on in life, I fear this will cause us a certain amount of inconvenience. Comrade Brady will have to leave the office temporarily in order to go into training, and what shall we do then for a fighting editor? However, possibly we may not need one now. *Cosy Moments* should be able shortly to give its message to the world and ease up for a while. Which brings us back to the point. Who is Stewart Waring?"

"Stewart Waring is running for City Alderman. He's one of the biggest men in New York!"

"Do you mean in girth? If so, he seems to have selected the right career for himself."

"He's one of the bosses. He used to be Commissioner of Buildings for the city."

"Commissioner of Buildings? What exactly did that let him in for?"

"It let him in for a lot of graft."

"How was that?"

"Oh, he took it off the contractors. Shut his eyes and held out his hands when they ran up rotten buildings that a strong breeze would have knocked down, and places like that Pleasant Street hole without any ventilation."

"Why did he throw up the job?" inquired Psmith. "It seems to me that it was among the World's Softest. Certain drawbacks to it, perhaps, to the man with the Hair-Trigger Conscience; but I gather that Comrade Waring did not line up in that class. What was his trouble?"

"His trouble," said Billy, "was that he stood in with a contractor who was putting up a music-hall, and the contractor put it up with material about as strong as a heap of meringues, and it collapsed on the third night and killed half the audience."

"And then?"

"The papers raised a howl, and they got after the contractor, and the contractor gave Waring away. It killed him for the time being."

"I should have thought it would have had that excellent result permanently," said Psmith thoughtfully. "Do you mean to say he got back again after that?"

"He had to quit being Commissioner, of course, and leave the town for a time; but affairs move so fast here that a thing like that blows over. He made a bit of a pile out of the job, and could afford to lie low for a year or two."

"How long ago was that?"

"Five years. People don't remember a thing here that happened five years back unless they're reminded of it."

Psmith lit another cigarette.

"We will remind them," he said.

Billy nodded.

"Of course," he said, "one or two of the papers against him in this Aldermanic Election business tried to bring the thing up, but they didn't cut any ice. The other papers said it was a shame, hounding a man who was sorry for the past and who was trying to make good now; so they dropped it. Everybody thought that Waring was on the level now. He's been shooting off a lot of hot air lately about philanthropy and so on. Not that he has actually done a thing-not so much as given a supper to a dozen news-boys; but he's talked, and talk gets over if you keep it up long enough."

Psmith nodded adhesion to this dictum.

"So that naturally he wants to keep it dark about these tenements. It'll smash him at the election when it gets known."

"Why is he so set on becoming an Alderman," inquired Psmith.

"There's a lot of graft to being an Alderman," explained Billy.

"I see. No wonder the poor gentleman was so energetic in his methods. What is our move now, Comrade Windsor?"

Billy stared.

"Why, publish the name, of course."

"But before then? How are we going to ensure the safety of our evidence? We stand or fall entirely by that slip of paper, because we've got the beggar's name in the writing of his own collector, and that's proof positive."

"That's all right," said Billy, patting his breast-pocket. "Nobody's going to get it from me."

Psmith dipped his hand into his trouser-pocket.

"Comrade Windsor," he said, producing a piece of paper, "how do we go?"

He leaned back in his chair, surveying Billy blandly through his eye-glass. Billy's eyes were goggling. He looked from Psmith to the paper and from the paper to Psmith.

"What-what the —?" he stammered. "Why, it's it!"

Psmith nodded.

"How on earth did you get it?"

Psmith knocked the ash off his cigarette.

"Comrade Windsor," he said, "I do not wish to cavil or carp or rub it in in any way. I will merely remark that you pretty nearly landed us in the soup, and pass on to more congenial topics. Didn't you know we were followed to this place?"

"Followed!"

"By a merchant in what Comrade Maloney would call a tall-shaped hat. I spotted him at an early date, somewhere down by Twenty-ninth Street. When we dived into Sixth Avenue for a space at Thirty-third Street, did he dive, too? He did. And when we turned into Forty-second Street, there he was. I tell you, Comrade Windsor, leeches were aloof, and burrs non-adhesive compared with that tall-shaped-hatted blighter."

"Yes?"

"Do you remember, as you came to the entrance of this place, somebody knocking against you?"

"Yes, there was a pretty big crush in the entrance."

"There was; but not so big as all that. There was plenty of room for this merchant to pass if he had wished. Instead of which he butted into you. I happened to be waiting for just that, so

I managed to attach myself to his wrist with some vim and give it a fairly hefty wrench. The paper was inside his hand."

Billy was leaning forward with a pale face.

"Jove!" he muttered.

"That about sums it up," said Psmith.

Billy snatched the paper from the table and extended it towards him.

"Here," he said feverishly, "you take it. Gum, I never thought I was such a mutt! I'm not fit to take charge of a toothpick. Fancy me not being on the watch for something of that sort. I guess I was so tickled with myself at the thought of having got the thing, that it never struck me they might try for it. But I'm through. No more for me. You're the man in charge now."

Psmith shook his head.

"These stately compliments," he said, "do my old heart good, but I fancy I know a better plan. It happened that I chanced to have my eye on the blighter in the tall-shaped hat, and so was enabled to land him among the ribstones; but who knows but that in the crowd on Broadway there may not lurk other, unidentified blighters in equally tall-shaped hats, one of whom may work the same sleight-of-hand speciality on me? It was not that you were not capable of taking care of that paper: it was simply that you didn't happen to spot the man. Now observe me closely, for what follows is an exhibition of Brain."

He paid the bill, and they went out into the entrance-hall of the hotel. Psmith, sitting down at a table, placed the paper in an envelope and addressed it to himself at the address of *Cosy Moments*. After which, he stamped the envelope and dropped it into the letter-box at the back of the hall.

"And now, Comrade Windsor," he said, "let us stroll gently homewards down the Great White Way. What matter though it be fairly stiff with low-browed bravoes in tall-shaped hats? They cannot harm us. From me, if they search me thoroughly, they may scoop a matter of eleven dollars, a watch, two stamps, and a packet of chewing-gum. Whether they would do any better with you I do not know. At any rate, they wouldn't get that paper; and that's the main thing."

"You're a genius," said Billy Windsor.

"You think so?" said Psmith diffidently. "Well, well, perhaps you are right, perhaps you are right. Did you notice the hired ruffian in the flannel suit who just passed? He wore a baffled look, I fancy. And hark! Wasn't that a muttered 'Failed!' I heard? Or was it the breeze moaning in the tree-tops? To-night is a cold, disappointing night for Hired Ruffians, Comrade Windsor."

CHAPTER XXIII

REDUCTIONS IN THE STAFF

The first member of the staff of *Cosy Moments* to arrive at the office on the following morning was Master Maloney. This sounds like the beginning of a "Plod and Punctuality," or "How Great Fortunes have been Made" story; but, as a matter of fact, Master Maloney was no early bird. Larks who rose in his neighbourhood, rose alone. He did not get up with them. He was supposed to be at the office at nine o'clock. It was a point of honour with him, a sort of daily declaration of independence, never to put in an appearance before nine-thirty. On this particular morning he was punctual to the minute, or half an hour late, whichever way you choose to look at it.

He had only whistled a few bars of "My Little Irish Rose," and had barely got into the first page of his story of life on the prairie when Kid Brady appeared. The Kid, as was his habit when not in training, was smoking a big black cigar. Master Maloney eyed him admiringly. The Kid, unknown to that gentleman himself, was Pugsy's ideal. He came from the Plains; and had, indeed, once actually been a cowboy; he was a coming champion; and he could smoke black cigars. It was, therefore, without his usual well-what-is-it-now? air that Pugsy laid down his book, and prepared to converse.

"Say, Mr. Smith or Mr. Windsor about, Pugsy?" asked the Kid.

"Naw, Mr. Brady, they ain't came yet," replied Master Maloney respectfully.

"Late, ain't they?"

"Sure. Mr. Windsor generally blows in before I do."

"Wonder what's keepin' them."

"P'raps, dey've bin put out of business," suggested Pugsy nonchalantly.

"How's that?"

Pugsy related the events of the previous day, relaxing something of his austere calm as he did so. When he came to the part where the Table Hill allies swooped down on the unsuspecting Three Pointers, he was almost animated.

"Say," said the Kid approvingly, "that Smith guy's got more grey matter under his thatch than you'd think to look at him. I —"

"Comrade Brady," said a voice in the doorway, "you do me proud."

"Why, say," said the Kid, turning, "I guess the laugh's on me. I didn't see you, Mr. Smith. Pugsy's been tellin' me how you sent him for the Table Hills yesterday. That was cute. It was mighty smart. But say, those guys are goin' some, ain't they now! Seems as if they was dead set on puttin' you out of business."

"Their manner yesterday, Comrade Brady, certainly suggested the presence of some sketchy outline of such an ideal in their minds. One Sam, in particular, an ebony-hued sportsman, threw himself into the task with great vim. I rather fancy he is waiting for us with his revolver to this moment. But why worry? Here we are, safe and sound, and Comrade Windsor may be expected to arrive at any moment. I see, Comrade Brady, that you have been matched against one Eddie Wood."

"It's about that I wanted to see you, Mr. Smith. Say, now that things have been and brushed up so, what with these gang guys layin' for you the way they're doin', I guess you'll be needin' me around here. Isn't that right? Say the word and I'll call off this Eddie Wood fight."

"Comrade Brady," said Psmith with some enthusiasm, "I call that a sporting offer. I'm very much obliged. But we mustn't stand in your way. If you eliminate this Comrade Wood, they will have to give you a chance against Jimmy Garvin, won't they?"

"I guess that's right, sir," said the Kid. "Eddie stayed nineteen rounds against Jimmy, and if I can put him away, it gets me into line with Jimmy, and he can't side-step me."

"Then go in and win, Comrade Brady. We shall miss you. It will be as if a ray of sunshine had been removed from the office. But you mustn't throw a chance away. We shall be all right, I think."

"I'll train at White Plains," said the Kid. "That ain't far from here, so I'll be pretty near in case I'm wanted. Hullo, who's here?"

He pointed to the door. A small boy was standing there, holding a note.

"Mr. Smith?"

"Sir to you," said Psmith courteously.

"P. Smith?"

"The same. This is your lucky day."

"Cop at Jefferson Market give me dis to take to youse."

"A cop in Jefferson Market?" repeated Psmith. "I did not know I had friends among the constabulary there. Why, it's from Comrade Windsor." He opened the envelope and read the letter. "Thanks," he said, giving the boy a quarter-dollar.

It was apparent the Kid was politely endeavouring to veil his curiosity. Master Maloney had no such scruples.

"What's in de letter, boss?" he inquired.

"The letter, Comrade Maloney, is from our Mr. Windsor, and relates in terse language the following facts, that our editor last night hit a policeman in the eye, and that he was sentenced this morning to thirty days on Blackwell's Island."

"He's de guy!" admitted Master Maloney approvingly.

"What's that?" said the Kid. "Mr. Windsor bin punchin' cops! What's he bin doin' that for?"

"He gives no clue. I must go and find out. Could you help Comrade Maloney mind the shop for a few moments while I push round to Jefferson Market and make inquiries?"

"Sure. But say, fancy Mr. Windsor cuttin' loose that way!" said the Kid admiringly.

The Jefferson Market Police Court is a little way down town, near Washington Square. It did not take Psmith long to reach it, and by the judicious expenditure of a few dollars he was enabled to obtain an interview with Billy in a back room.

The chief editor of *Cosy Moments* was seated on a bench, looking upon the world through a pair of much blackened eyes. His general appearance was dishevelled. He had the air of a man who has been caught in the machinery.

"Hullo, Smith," he said. "You got my note all right then?"

Psmith looked at him, concerned.

"Comrade Windsor," he said, "what on earth has been happening to you?"

"Oh, that's all right," said Billy. "That's nothing."

"Nothing! You look as if you had been run over by a motor-car."

"The cops did that," said Billy, without any apparent resentment. "They always turn nasty if you put up a fight. I was a fool to do it, I suppose, but I got so mad. They knew perfectly well that I had nothing to do with any pool-room downstairs."

Psmith's eye-glass dropped from his eye.

"Pool-room, Comrade Windsor?"

"Yes. The house where I live was raided late last night. It seems that some gamblers have been running a pool-room on the ground floor. Why the cops should have thought I had anything to do with it, when I was sleeping peacefully upstairs, is more than I can understand. Anyway, at about three in the morning there was the dickens of a banging at my door. I got up to see what was doing, and found a couple of Policemen there. They told me to come along with them to the station. I asked what on earth for. I might have known it was no use arguing with a New York cop. They said they had been tipped off that there was a pool-room being run in the house, and that they were cleaning up the house, and if I wanted to say anything I'd better say it to the magistrate. I said, all right, I'd put on some clothes and come with them. They said they couldn't wait about while I put on clothes. I said I wasn't going to travel about New York in pyjamas, and started to get into my shirt. One of them gave me a shove in the ribs with his night-stick, and told me to come along quick. And that made me so mad I hit out." A chuckle escaped Billy. "He wasn't expecting it, and I got him fair. He went down over the bookcase. The other cop took a swipe at me with his club, but by that time I was so mad I'd have taken on Jim Jeffries, if he had shown up and got in my way. I just sailed in, and was beginning to make the man think that he had stumbled on Stanley Ketchel or Kid Brady or a dynamite explosion by mistake, when the other fellow loosed himself from the bookcase, and they started in on me together, and there was a general rough house, in the middle of which somebody seemed to let off about fifty thousand dollars' worth of fireworks all in a bunch; and I didn't remember anything more till I found myself in a cell, pretty nearly knocked to pieces. That's my little life-history. I guess I was a fool to cut loose that way, but I was so mad I didn't stop to think."

Psmith sighed.

"You have told me your painful story," he said. "Now hear mine. After parting with you last night, I went meditatively back to my Fourth Avenue address, and, with a courtly good night to the large policeman who, as I have mentioned in previous conversations, is stationed almost at my very door, I passed on into my room, and had soon sunk into a dreamless slumber. At about three o'clock in the morning I was aroused by a somewhat hefty banging on the door."

"What!"

"A banging at the door," repeated Psmith. "There, standing on the mat, were three policemen. From their remarks I gathered that certain bright spirits had been running a gambling establishment in the lower regions of the building-where, I think I told you, there is a saloon-and the Law was now about to clean up the place. Very cordially the honest fellows invited me to go with them. A conveyance, it seemed, waited in the street without. I pointed out, even as you appear to have done, that sea-green pyjamas with old rose frogs were not the costume in which a Shropshire Psmith should be seen abroad in one of the world's greatest cities; but they assured me-more by their manner than their words-that my misgivings were out of place, so I yielded. These men, I told myself, have lived longer in New York than I. They know what is done and what is not done. I will bow to their views. So I went with them, and after a very pleasant and cosy little ride in the patrol waggon, arrived at the police station. This morning I chatted a while with the courteous magistrate, convinced him by means of arguments and by silent evidence of my open, honest face and unwavering eye that I was not a professional gambler, and came away without a stain on my character."

Billy Windsor listened to this narrative with growing interest.

"Gum! it's them!" he cried.

"As Comrade Maloney would say," said Psmith, "meaning what, Comrade Windsor?"

"Why, the fellows who are after that paper. They tipped the police off about the pool-rooms, knowing that we should be hauled off without having time to take anything with us. I'll bet anything you like they have been in and searched our rooms by now."

"As regards yours, Comrade Windsor, I cannot say. But it is an undoubted fact that mine, which I revisited before going to the office, in order to correct what seemed to me even on reflection certain drawbacks to my costume, looks as if two cyclones and a threshing machine had passed through it."

"They've searched it?"

"With a fine-toothed comb. Not one of my objects of vertu but has been displaced."

Billy Windsor slapped his knee.

617

"It was lucky you thought of sending that paper by post," he said. "We should have been done if you hadn't. But, say," he went on miserably, "this is awful. Things are just warming up for the final burst, and I'm out of it all."

"For thirty days," sighed Psmith. "What *Cosy Moments* really needs is a *sitz-redacteur*."

"A what?"

"A *sitz-redacteur*, Comrade Windsor, is a gentleman employed by German newspapers with a taste for *lèse majesté* to go to prison whenever required in place of the real editor. The real editor hints in his bright and snappy editorial, for instance, that the Kaiser's moustache reminds him of a bad dream. The police force swoops down en masse on the office of the journal, and are met by the *sitz-redacteur*, who goes with them peaceably, allowing the editor to remain and sketch out plans for his next week's article on the Crown Prince. We need a *sitz-redacteur* on *Cosy Moments* almost as much as a fighting editor; and we have neither."

"The Kid has had to leave then?"

"He wants to go into training at once. He very sportingly offered to cancel his match, but of course that would never do. Unless you consider Comrade Maloney equal to the job, I must look around me for some one else. I shall be too fully occupied with purely literary matters to be able to deal with chance callers. But I have a scheme."

"What's that?"

"It seems to me that we are allowing much excellent material to lie unused in the shape of Comrade Jarvis."

"Bat Jarvis."

"The same. The cat-specialist to whom you endeared yourself somewhat earlier in the proceedings by befriending one of his wandering animals. Little deeds of kindness, little acts of love, as you have doubtless heard, help, etc. Should we not give Comrade Jarvis an opportunity of proving the correctness of this statement? I think so. Shortly after you-if you will forgive me for touching on a painful subject-have been haled to your dungeon, I will push round to Comrade Jarvis's address, and sound him on the subject. Unfortunately, his affection is confined, I fancy, to you. Whether he will consent to put himself out on my behalf remains to be seen. However, there is no harm in trying. If nothing else comes of the visit, I shall at least have had the opportunity of chatting with one of our most prominent citizens."

A policeman appeared at the door.

"Say, pal," he remarked to Psmith, "you'll have to be fading away soon, I guess. Give you three minutes more. Say it quick."

He retired. Billy leaned forward to Psmith.

"I guess they won't give me much chance," he whispered, "but if you see me around in the next day or two, don't be surprised."

"I fail to follow you, Comrade Windsor."

"Men have escaped from Blackwell's Island before now. Not many, it's true; but it has been done."

Psmith shook his head.

"I shouldn't," he said. "They're bound to catch you, and then you will be immersed in the soup beyond hope of recovery. I shouldn't wonder if they put you in your little cell for a year or so."

"I don't care," said Billy stoutly. "I'd give a year later on to be round and about now."

"I shouldn't," urged Psmith. "All will be well with the paper. You have left a good man at the helm."

"I guess I shan't get a chance, but I'll try it if I do."

The door opened and the policeman reappeared.

"Time's up, I reckon."

"Well, good-bye, Comrade Windsor," said Psmith regretfully. "Abstain from undue worrying. It's a walk-over from now on, and there's no earthly need for you to be around the office.

Once, I admit, this could not have been said. But now things have simplified themselves. Have no fear. This act is going to be a scream from start to finish."

CHAPTER XXIV

A GATHERING OF CAT-SPECIALISTS

Master Maloney raised his eyes for a moment from his book as Psmith re-entered the office.

"Dere's a guy in dere waitin' ter see youse," he said briefly, jerking his head in the direction of the inner room.

"A guy waiting to see me, Comrade Maloney? With or without a sand-bag?"

"Says his name's Jackson," said Master Maloney, turning a page.

Psmith moved quickly to the door of the inner room.

"Why, Comrade Jackson," he said, with the air of a father welcoming home the prodigal son, "this is the maddest, merriest day of all the glad New Year. Where did you come from?"

Mike, looking very brown and in excellent condition, put down the paper he was reading.

"Hullo, Psmith," he said. "I got back this morning. We're playing a game over in Brooklyn to-morrow."

"No engagements of any importance to-day?"

"Not a thing. Why?"

"Because I propose to take you to visit Comrade Jarvis, whom you will doubtless remember."

"Jarvis?" said Mike, puzzled. "I don't remember any Jarvis."

"Let your mind wander back a little through the jungle of the past. Do you recollect paying a visit to Comrade Windsor's room —"

"By the way, where is Windsor?"

"In prison. Well, on that evening —"

"In prison?"

"For thirty days. For slugging a policeman. More of this, however, anon. Let us return to that evening. Don't you remember a certain gentleman with just about enough forehead to keep his front hair from getting all tangled up with his eye-brows?"

"Oh, the cat chap? *I* know."

"As you very justly observe, Comrade Jackson, the cat chap. For going straight to the mark and seizing on the salient point of a situation, I know of no one who can last two minutes against you. Comrade Jarvis may have other sides to his character-possibly many-but it is as a cat chap that I wish to approach him to-day."

"What's the idea? What are you going to see him for?"

"We," corrected Psmith. "I will explain all at a little luncheon at which I trust that you will be my guest. Already, such is the stress of this journalistic life, I hear my tissues crying out imperatively to be restored. An oyster and a glass of milk somewhere round the corner, Comrade Jackson? I think so, I think so."

* * * * *

"I was reading *Cosy Moments* in there," said Mike, as they lunched. "You certainly seem to have bucked it up rather. Kid Brady's reminiscences are hot stuff."

"Somewhat sizzling, Comrade Jackson," admitted Psmith. "They have, however, unfortunately cost us a fighting editor."

"How's that?"

"Such is the boost we have given Comrade Brady, that he is now never without a match. He has had to leave us to-day to go to White Plains to train for an encounter with a certain Mr. Wood, a four-ounce-glove juggler of established fame."

"I expect you need a fighting editor, don't you?"

"He is indispensable, Comrade Jackson, indispensable."

"No rotting. Has anybody cut up rough about the stuff you've printed?"

"Cut up rough? Gadzooks! I need merely say that one critical reader put a bullet through my hat—"

"Rot! Not really?"

"While others kept me tree'd on top of a roof for the space of nearly an hour. Assuredly they have cut up rough, Comrade Jackson."

"Great Scott! Tell us."

Psmith briefly recounted the adventures of the past few weeks.

"But, man," said Mike, when he had finished "why on earth don't you call in the police?"

"We have mentioned the matter to certain of the force. They appeared tolerably interested, but showed no tendency to leap excitedly to our assistance. The New York policeman, Comrade Jackson, like all great men, is somewhat peculiar. If you go to a New York policeman and exhibit a black eye, he will examine it and express some admiration for the abilities of the citizen responsible for the same. If you press the matter, he becomes bored, and says, 'Ain't youse satisfied with what youse got? G'wan!' His advice in such cases is good, and should be followed. No; since coming to this city I have developed a habit of taking care of myself, or employing private help. That is why I should like you, if you will, to come with me to call upon Comrade Jarvis. He is a person of considerable influence among that section of the populace which is endeavouring to smash in our occiputs. Indeed, I know of nobody who cuts a greater quantity of ice. If I can only enlist Comrade Jarvis's assistance, all will be well. If you are through with your refreshment, shall we be moving in his direction? By the way, it will probably be necessary in the course of our interview to allude to you as one of our most eminent living cat-fanciers. You do not object? Remember that you have in your English home seventy-four fine cats, mostly Angoras. Are you on to that? Then let us be going. Comrade Maloney has given me the address. It is a goodish step down on the East side. I should like to take a taxi, but it might seem ostentatious. Let us walk."

* * * * *

They found Mr. Jarvis in his Groome Street fancier's shop, engaged in the intellectual occupation of greasing a cat's paws with butter. He looked up as they entered, and began to breathe a melody with a certain coyness.

"Comrade Jarvis," said Psmith, "we meet again. You remember me?"

"Nope," said Mr. Jarvis, pausing for a moment in the middle of a bar, and then taking up the air where he had left off. Psmith was not discouraged.

"Ah," he said tolerantly, "the fierce rush of New York life. How it wipes from the retina of to-day the image impressed on it but yesterday. Are you with me, Comrade Jarvis?"

The cat-expert concentrated himself on the cat's paws without replying.

"A fine animal," said Psmith, adjusting his eyeglass. "To which particular family of the Felis Domestica does that belong? In colour it resembles a Neapolitan ice more than anything."

Mr. Jarvis's manner became unfriendly.

"Say, what do youse want? That's straight ain't it? If youse want to buy a boid or a snake why don't youse say so?"

"I stand corrected," said Psmith. "I should have remembered that time is money. I called in here partly on the strength of being a colleague and side-partner of Comrade Windsor—"

"Mr. Windsor! De gent what caught my cat?"

"The same-and partly in order that I might make two very eminent cat-fanciers acquainted. This," he said, with a wave of his hand in the direction of the silently protesting Mike, "is Comrade Jackson, possibly the best known of our English cat-fanciers. Comrade Jackson's stud of Angoras is celebrated wherever the King's English is spoken, and in Hoxton."

Mr. Jarvis rose, and, having inspected Mike with silent admiration for a while, extended a well-buttered hand towards him. Psmith looked on benevolently.

"What Comrade Jackson does not know about cats," he said, "is not knowledge. His information on Angoras alone would fill a volume."

"Say," —Mr. Jarvis was evidently touching on a point which had weighed deeply upon him — "why's catnip called catnip?"

Mike looked at Psmith helplessly. It sounded like a riddle, but it was obvious that Mr. Jarvis's motive in putting the question was not frivolous. He really wished to know.

"The word, as Comrade Jackson was just about to observe," said Psmith, "is a corruption of cat-mint. Why it should be so corrupted I do not know. But what of that? The subject is too deep to be gone fully into at the moment. I should recommend you to read Comrade Jackson's little brochure on the matter. Passing lightly on from that —"

"Did youse ever have a cat dat ate beetles?" inquired Mr. Jarvis.

"There was a time when many of Comrade Jackson's felidae supported life almost entirely on beetles."

"Did they git thin?"

Mike felt that it was time, if he was to preserve his reputation, to assert himself.

"No," he replied firmly.

Mr. Jarvis looked astonished.

"English beetles," said Psmith, "don't make cats thin. Passing lightly —"

"I had a cat oncest," said Mr. Jarvis, ignoring the remark and sticking to his point, "dat ate beetles and got thin and used to tie itself into knots."

"A versatile animal," agreed Psmith.

"Say," Mr. Jarvis went on, now plainly on a subject near to his heart, "dem beetles is fierce. Sure. Can't keep de cats off of eatin' dem, I can't. First t'ing you know dey've swallowed dem, and den dey gits thin and ties theirselves into knots."

"You should put them into strait-waistcoats," said Psmith.

"Passing, however, lightly —"

"Say, ever have a cross-eyed cat?"

"Comrade Jackson's cats," said Psmith, "have happily been almost free from strabismus."

"Dey's lucky, cross-eyed cats is. You has a cross-eyed cat, and not'in' don't never go wrong. But, say, was dere ever a cat wit one blue eye and one yaller one in your bunch? Gum, it's fierce when it's like dat. It's a real skiddoo, is a cat wit one blue eye and one yaller one. Puts you in bad, surest t'ing you know. Oncest a guy give me a cat like dat, and first t'ing you know I'm in bad all round. It wasn't till I give him away to de cop on de corner and gets me one dat's cross-eyed dat I lifts de skiddoo off of me."

"And what happened to the cop?" inquired Psmith, interested.

"Oh, he got in bad, sure enough," said Mr. Jarvis without emotion. "One of de boys what he'd pinched and had sent to de Island once lays for him and puts one over him wit a black-jack. Sure. Dat's what comes of havin' a cat wit one blue eye and one yaller one."

Mr. Jarvis relapsed into silence. He seemed to be meditating on the inscrutable workings of Fate. Psmith took advantage of the pause to leave the cat topic and touch on matter of more vital import.

"Tense and exhilarating as is this discussion of the optical peculiarities of cats," he said, "there is another matter on which, if you will permit me, I should like to touch. I would hesitate to bore you with my own private troubles, but this is a matter which concerns Comrade Windsor as well as myself, and I know that your regard for Comrade Windsor is almost an obsession."

"How's that?"

"I should say," said Psmith, "that Comrade Windsor is a man to whom you give the glad hand."

"Sure. He's to the good, Mr. Windsor is. He caught me cat."

"He did. By the way, was that the one that used to tie itself into knots?"

"Nope. Dat was anudder."

"Ah! However, to resume. The fact is, Comrade Jarvis, we are much persecuted by scoundrels. How sad it is in this world! We look to every side. We look north, east, south, and west, and what do we see? Mainly scoundrels. I fancy you have heard a little about our troubles before this. In fact, I gather that the same scoundrels actually approached you with a view to engaging your services to do us in, but that you very handsomely refused the contract."

"Sure," said Mr. Jarvis, dimly comprehending.

"A guy comes to me and says he wants you and Mr. Windsor put through it, but I gives him de t'run down. 'Nuttin' done,' I says. 'Mr. Windsor caught me cat.'"

"So I was informed," said Psmith. "Well, failing you, they went to a gentleman of the name of Reilly."

"Spider Reilly?"

"You have hit it, Comrade Jarvis. Spider Reilly, the lessee and manager of the Three Points gang."

"Dose T'ree Points, dey're to de bad. Dey're fresh."

"It is too true, Comrade Jarvis."

"Say," went on Mr. Jarvis, waxing wrathful at the recollection, "what do youse t'ink dem fresh stiffs done de udder night. Started some rough woik in me own dance-joint."

"Shamrock Hall?" said Psmith.

"Dat's right. Shamrock Hall. Got gay, dey did, wit some of de Table Hillers. Say, I got it in for dem gazebos, sure I have. Surest t'ing you know."

Psmith beamed approval.

"That," he said, "is the right spirit. Nothing could be more admirable. We are bound together by our common desire to check the ever-growing spirit of freshness among the members of the Three Points. Add to that the fact that we are united by a sympathetic knowledge of the manners and customs of cats, and especially that Comrade Jackson, England's greatest fancier, is our mutual friend, and what more do we want? Nothing."

"Mr. Jackson's to de good," assented Mr. Jarvis, eyeing Mike in friendly fashion.

"We are all to de good," said Psmith. "Now the thing I wished to ask you is this. The office of the paper on which I work was until this morning securely guarded by Comrade Brady, whose name will be familiar to you."

"De Kid?"

"On the bull's-eye, as usual, Comrade Jarvis. Kid Brady, the coming light-weight champion of the world. Well, he has unfortunately been compelled to leave us, and the way into the office is consequently clear to any sand-bag specialist who cares to wander in. Matters connected with the paper have become so poignant during the last few days that an inrush of these same specialists is almost a certainty, unless—and this is where you come in."

"Me?"

"Will you take Comrade Brady's place for a few days?"

"How's that?"

"Will you come in and sit in the office for the next day or so and help hold the fort? I may mention that there is money attached to the job. We will pay for your services. How do we go, Comrade Jarvis?"

Mr. Jarvis reflected but a brief moment.

"Why, sure," he said. "Me fer dat. When do I start?"

"Excellent, Comrade Jarvis. Nothing could be better. I am obliged. I rather fancy that the gay band of Three Pointers who will undoubtedly visit the offices of *Cosy Moments* in the next few days, probably to-morrow, are due to run up against the surprise of their lives. Could you be there at ten to-morrow morning?"

"Sure t'ing. I'll bring me canister."

"I should," said Psmith. "In certain circumstances one canister is worth a flood of rhetoric. Till to-morrow, then, Comrade Jarvis. I am very much obliged to you."

* * * * *

"Not at all a bad hour's work," said Psmith complacently, as they turned out of Groome Street. "A vote of thanks to you, Comrade Jackson, for your invaluable assistance."

"It strikes me I didn't do much," said Mike with a grin.

"Apparently, no. In reality, yes. Your manner was exactly right. Reserved, yet not haughty. Just what an eminent cat-fancier's manner should be. I could see that you made a pronounced hit with Comrade Jarvis. By the way, if you are going to show up at the office to-morrow, perhaps it would be as well if you were to look up a few facts bearing on the feline world. There is no knowing what thirst for information a night's rest may not give Comrade Jarvis. I do not presume to dictate, but if you were to make yourself a thorough master of the subject of catnip, for instance, it might quite possibly come in useful."

CHAPTER XXV

TRAPPED

Mr. Jarvis was as good as his word. On the following morning, at ten o'clock to the minute, he made his appearance at the office of *Cosy Moments*, his fore-lock more than usually well oiled in honour of the occasion, and his right coat-pocket bulging in a manner that betrayed to the initiated eye the presence of the faithful "canister." With him, in addition to his revolver, he brought a long, thin young man who wore under his brown tweed coat a blue-and-red striped jersey. Whether he brought him as an ally in case of need or merely as a kindred soul with whom he might commune during his vigil, was not ascertained.

Pugsy, startled out of his wonted calm by the arrival of this distinguished company, observed the pair, as they passed through into the inner office, with protruding eyes, and sat speechless for a full five minutes. Psmith received the new-corners in the editorial sanctum with courteous warmth. Mr. Jarvis introduced his colleague.

"Thought I'd bring him along. Long Otto's his monaker."

"You did very rightly, Comrade Jarvis," Psmith assured him. "Your unerring instinct did not play you false when it told you that Comrade Otto would be as welcome as the flowers in May. With Comrade Otto I fancy we shall make a combination which will require a certain amount of tackling."

Mr. Jarvis confirmed this view. Long Otto, he affirmed, was no rube, but a scrapper from Biffville-on-the-Slosh. The hardiest hooligan would shrink from introducing rough-house proceedings into a room graced by the combined presence of Long Otto and himself.

"Then," said Psmith, "I can go about my professional duties with a light heart. I may possibly sing a bar or two. You will find cigars in that box. If you and Comrade Otto will select one apiece and group yourselves tastefully about the room in chairs, I will start in to hit up a slightly spicy editorial on the coming election."

Mr. Jarvis regarded the paraphernalia of literature on the table with interest. So did Long Otto, who, however, being a man of silent habit, made no comment. Throughout the seance and the events which followed it he confined himself to an occasional grunt. He seemed to lack other modes of expression. A charming chap, however.

"Is dis where youse writes up pieces fer de paper?" inquired Mr. Jarvis, eyeing the table.

"It is," said Psmith. "In Comrade Windsor's pre-dungeon days he was wont to sit where I am sitting now, while I bivouacked over there at the smaller table. On busy mornings you could hear our brains buzzing in Madison Square Garden. But wait! A thought strikes me."

He called for Pugsy.

"Comrade Maloney," he said, "if the Editorial Staff of this paper were to give you a day off, could you employ it to profit?"

"Surest t'ing you know," replied Pugsy with some fervour. "I'd take me goil to de Bronx Zoo."

"Your girl?" said Psmith inquiringly. "I had heard no inkling of this, Comrade Maloney. I had always imagined you one of those strong, rugged, blood-and-iron men who were above the softer emotions. Who is she?"

"Aw, she's a kid," said Pugsy. "Her pa runs a delicatessen shop down our street. She ain't a bad mutt," added the ardent swain. "I'm her steady."

"See that I have a card for the wedding, Comrade Maloney," said Psmith, "and in the meantime take her to the Bronx, as you suggest."

"Won't youse be wantin' me to-day?"

"Not to-day. You need a holiday. Unflagging toil is sapping your physique. Go up and watch the animals, and remember me very kindly to the Peruvian Llama, whom friends have sometimes told me I resemble in appearance. And if two dollars would in any way add to the gaiety of the jaunt . . ."

"Sure t'ing. T'anks, boss."

"It occurred to me," said Psmith, when he had gone, "that the probable first move of any enterprising Three Pointer who invaded this office would be to knock Comrade Maloney on the head to prevent his announcing him. Comrade Maloney's services are too valuable to allow him to be exposed to unnecessary perils. Any visitors who call must find their way in for themselves. And now to work. Work, the what's-its-name of the thingummy and the thing-um-a-bob of the what d'you-call-it."

For about a quarter of an hour the only sound that broke the silence of the room was the scratching of Psmith's pen and the musical expectoration of Messrs. Otto and Jarvis. Finally Psmith leaned back in his chair with a satisfied expression, and spoke.

"While, as of course you know, Comrade Jarvis," he said, "there is no agony like the agony of literary composition, such toil has its compensations. The editorial I have just completed contains its measure of balm. Comrade Otto will bear me out in my statement that there is a subtle joy in the manufacture of the well-formed phrase. Am I not right, Comrade Otto?"

The long one gazed appealingly at Mr. Jarvis, who spoke for him.

"He's a bit shy on handin' out woids, is Otto," he said.

Psmith nodded.

"I understand. I am a man of few words myself. All great men are like that. Von Moltke, Comrade Otto, and myself. But what are words? Action is the thing. That is the cry. Action. If that is Comrade Otto's forte, so much the better, for I fancy that action rather than words is what we may be needing in the space of about a quarter of a minute. At least, if the footsteps I hear without are, as I suspect, those of our friends of the Three Points."

Jarvis and Long Otto turned towards the door. Psmith was right. Some one was moving stealthily in the outer office. Judging from the sound, more than one person.

"It is just as well," said Psmith softly, "that Comrade Maloney is not at his customary post. Now, in about a quarter of a minute, as I said–Aha!"

The handle of the door began to revolve slowly and quietly. The next moment three figures tumbled into the room. It was evident that they had not expected to find the door unlocked, and the absence of resistance when they applied their weight had had surprising effects. Two of the three did not pause in their career till they cannoned against the table. The third, who was holding the handle, was more fortunate.

Psmith rose with a kindly smile to welcome his guests.

"Why, surely!" he said in a pleased voice. "I thought I knew the face. Comrade Repetto, this is a treat. Have you come bringing me a new hat?"

The white-haired leader's face, as he spoke, was within a few inches of his own. Psmith's observant eye noted that the bruise still lingered on the chin where Kid Brady's upper-cut had landed at their previous meeting.

"I cannot offer you all seats," he went on, "unless you care to dispose yourselves upon the tables. I wonder if you know my friend, Mr. Bat Jarvis? And my friend, Mr. L. Otto? Let us all get acquainted on this merry occasion."

The three invaders had been aware of the presence of the great Bat and his colleague for some moments, and the meeting seemed to be causing them embarrassment. This may have been due to the fact that both Mr. Jarvis and Mr. Otto had produced and were toying meditatively with distinctly ugly-looking pistols.

Mr. Jarvis spoke.

"Well," he said, "what's doin'?"

Mr. Repetto, to whom the remark was directly addressed, appeared to have some difficulty in finding a reply. He shuffled his feet, and looked at the floor. His two companions seemed equally at a loss.

"Goin' to start any rough stuff?" inquired Mr. Jarvis casually.

"The cigars are on the table," said Psmith hospitably. "Draw up your chairs, and let's all be jolly. I will open the proceedings with a song."

In a rich baritone, with his eyeglass fixed the while on Mr. Repetto, he proceeded to relieve himself of the first verse of "I only know I love thee."

"Chorus, please," he added, as he finished. "Come along, Comrade Repetto. Why this shrinking coyness? Fling out your chest, and cut loose."

But Mr. Repetto's eye was fastened on Mr. Jarvis's revolver. The sight apparently had the effect of quenching his desire for song.

"'Lov' muh, ahnd ther world is-ah-mine!'" concluded Psmith.

He looked round the assembled company.

"Comrade Otto," he observed, "will now recite that pathetic little poem 'Baby's Sock is now a Blue-bag.' Pray, gentlemen, silence for Comrade Otto."

He looked inquiringly at the long youth, who remained mute. Psmith clicked his tongue regretfully.

"Comrade Jarvis," he said, "I fear that as a smoking-concert this is not going to be a success. I understand, however. Comrade Repetto and his colleagues have come here on business, and nothing will make them forget it. Typical New York men of affairs, they close their minds to all influences that might lure them from their business. Let us get on, then. What did you wish to see me about, Comrade Repetto?"

Mr. Repetto's reply was unintelligible.

Mr. Jarvis made a suggestion.

"Youse had better beat it," he said.

Long Otto grunted sympathy with this advice.

"And youse had better go back to Spider Reilly," continued Mr. Jarvis, "and tell him that there's nothin' doin' in the way of rough house wit dis gent here." He indicated Psmith, who bowed. "And you can tell de Spider," went on Bat with growing ferocity, "dat next time he gits gay and starts in to shoot guys in me dance-joint I'll bite de head off'n him. See? Does dat go? If he t'inks his little two-by-four gang can put it across de Groome Street, he can try. Dat's right. An' don't fergit dis gent here and me is pals, and any one dat starts anyt'ing wit dis gent is going to have to git busy wit me. Does dat go?"

Psmith coughed, and shot his cuffs.

"I do not know," he said, in the manner of a chairman addressing a meeting, "that I have anything to add to the very well-expressed remarks of my friend, Comrade Jarvis. He has, in my opinion, covered the ground very thoroughly and satisfactorily. It now only remains for me to pass a vote of thanks to Comrade Jarvis and to declare this meeting at an end."

"Beat it," said Mr. Jarvis, pointing to the door.

The delegation then withdrew.

"I am very much obliged," said Psmith, "for your courtly assistance, Comrade Jarvis. But for you I do not care to think with what a splash I might not have been immersed in the gumbo. Thank you, Comrade Jarvis. And you, Comrade Otto."

"Aw chee!" said Mr. Jarvis, handsomely dismissing the matter. Mr. Otto kicked the leg of the table, and grunted.

* * * * *

For half an hour after the departure of the Three Pointers Psmith chatted amiably to his two assistants on matters of general interest. The exchange of ideas was somewhat one-sided, though Mr. Jarvis had one or two striking items of information to impart, notably some hints on the treatment of fits in kittens.

At the end of this period the conversation was once more interrupted by the sound of movements in the outer office.

"If dat's dose stiffs come back —" began Mr. Jarvis, reaching for his revolver.

"Stay your hand, Comrade Jarvis," said as a sharp knock sounded on the door. "I do not think it can be our late friends. Comrade Repetto's knowledge of the usages of polite society is too limited, I fancy, to prompt him to knock on doors. Come in."

The door opened. It was not Mr. Repetto or his colleagues, but another old friend. No other, in fact, than Mr. Francis Parker, he who had come as an embassy from the man up top in the very beginning of affairs, and had departed, wrathful, mouthing declarations of war. As on his previous visit, he wore the dude suit, the shiny shoes, and the tall-shaped hat.

"Welcome, Comrade Parker," said Psmith. "It is too long since we met. Comrade Jarvis I think you know. If I am right, that is to say, in supposing that it was you who approached him at an earlier stage in the proceedings with a view to engaging his sympathetic aid in the great work of putting Comrade Windsor and myself out of business. The gentleman on your left is Comrade Otto."

Mr. Parker was looking at Bat in bewilderment. It was plain that he had not expected to find Psmith entertaining such company.

"Did you come purely for friendly chit-chat, Comrade Parker," inquired Psmith, "or was there, woven into the social motives of your call, a desire to talk business of any kind?"

"My business is private. I didn't expect a crowd."

"Especially of ancient friends such as Comrade Jarvis. Well, well, you are breaking up a most interesting little symposium. Comrade Jarvis, I think I shall be forced to postpone our very entertaining discussion of fits in kittens till a more opportune moment. Meanwhile, as Comrade Parker wishes to talk over some private business —"

Bat Jarvis rose.

"I'll beat it," he said.

"Reluctantly, I hope, Comrade Jarvis. As reluctantly as I hint that I would be alone. If I might drop in some time at your private residence?"

"Sure," said Mr. Jarvis warmly.

"Excellent. Well, for the present, good-bye. And many thanks for your invaluable co-operation."

"Aw chee!" said Mr. Jarvis.

"And now, Comrade Parker," said Psmith, when the door had closed, "let her rip. What can I do for you?"

"You seem to be all to the merry with Bat Jarvis," observed Mr. Parker.

"The phrase exactly expresses it, Comrade Parker. I am as a tortoiseshell kitten to him. But, touching your business?"

Mr. Parker was silent for a moment.

"See here," he said at last, "aren't you going to be good? Say, what's the use of keeping on at this fool game? Why not quit it before you get hurt?"

Psmith smoothed his waistcoat reflectively.

"I may be wrong, Comrade Parker," he said, "but it seems to me that the chances of my getting hurt are not so great as you appear to imagine. The person who is in danger of getting hurt seems to me to be the gentleman whose name is on that paper which is now in my possession."

"Where is it?" demanded Mr. Parker quickly.

Psmith eyed him benevolently.

"If you will pardon the expression, Comrade Parker," he said,

"'Aha!' Meaning that I propose to keep that information to myself."

Mr. Parker shrugged his shoulders.

"You know your own business, I guess."

Psmith nodded.

"You are absolutely correct, Comrade Parker. I do. Now that *Cosy Moments* has our excellent friend Comrade Jarvis on its side, are you not to a certain extent among the Blenheim Oranges? I think so. I think so."

As he spoke there was a rap at the door. A small boy entered. In his hand was a scrap of paper.

"Guy asks me give dis to gazebo named Smiff," he said.

"There are many gazebos of that name, my lad. One of whom I am which, as Artemus Ward was wont to observe. Possibly the missive is for me."

He took the paper. It was dated from an address on the East Side.

"Dear Smith," it ran. "Come here as quick as you can, and bring some money. Explain when I see you."

It was signed "W. W."

So Billy Windsor had fulfilled his promise. He had escaped.

A feeling of regret for the futility of the thing was Psmith's first emotion. Billy could be of no possible help in the campaign at its present point. All the work that remained to be done could easily be carried through without his assistance. And by breaking out from the Island he had committed an offence which was bound to carry with it serious penalties. For the first time since his connection with *Cosy Moments* began Psmith was really disturbed.

He turned to Mr. Parker.

"Comrade Parker," he said, "I regret to state that this office is now closing for the day. But for this, I should be delighted to sit chatting with you. As it is —"

"Very well," said Mr. Parker. "Then you mean to go on with this business?"

"Though it snows, Comrade Parker."

They went out into the street, Psmith thoughtful and hardly realising the other's presence. By the side of the pavement a few yards down the road a taximeter-cab was standing. Psmith hailed it.

Mr. Parker was still beside him. It occurred to Psmith that it would not do to let him hear the address Billy Windsor had given in his note.

"Turn and go on down the street," he said to the driver.

He had taken his seat and was closing the door, when it was snatched from his grasp and Mr. Parker darted on to the seat opposite. The next moment the cab had started up the street instead of down and the hard muzzle of a revolver was pressing against Psmith's waistcoat.

"Now what?" said Mr. Parker smoothly, leaning back with the pistol resting easily on his knee.

CHAPTER XXVI

A FRIEND IN NEED

"The point is well taken," said Psmith thoughtfully.

"You think so?" said Mr. Parker.

"I am convinced of it."

"Good. But don't move. Put that hand back where it was."

"You think of everything, Comrade Parker."

He dropped his hand on to the seat, and remained silent for a few moments. The taxi-cab was buzzing along up Fifth Avenue now. Looking towards the window, Psmith saw that they were nearing the park. The great white mass of the Plaza Hotel showed up on the left.

"Did you ever stop at the Plaza, Comrade Parker?"

"No," said Mr. Parker shortly.

"Don't bite at me, Comrade Parker. Why be brusque on so joyous an occasion? Better men than us have stopped at the Plaza. Ah, the Park! How fresh the leaves, Comrade Parker, how green the herbage! Fling your eye at yonder grassy knoll."

He raised his hand to point. Instantly the revolver was against his waistcoat, making an unwelcome crease in that immaculate garment.

"I told you to keep that hand where it was."

"You did, Comrade Parker, you did. The fault," said Psmith handsomely, "was entirely mine. Carried away by my love of nature, I forgot. It shall not occur again."

"It had better not," said Mr. Parker unpleasantly. "If it does, I'll blow a hole through you."

Psmith raised his eyebrows.

"That, Comrade Parker," he said, "is where you make your error. You would no more shoot me in the heart of the metropolis than, I trust, you would wear a made-up tie with evening dress. Your skin, however unhealthy to the eye of the casual observer, is doubtless precious to yourself, and you are not the man I take you for if you would risk it purely for the momentary pleasure of plugging me with a revolver. The cry goes round criminal circles in New York, 'Comrade Parker is not such a fool as he looks.' Think for a moment what would happen. The shot would ring out, and instantly bicycle-policemen would be pursuing this taxi-cab with the purposeful speed of greyhounds trying to win the Waterloo Cup. You would be headed off and stopped. Ha! What is this? Psmith, the People's Pet, weltering in his gore? Death to the assassin! I fear nothing could save you from the fury of the mob, Comrade Parker. I seem to see them meditatively plucking you limb from limb. 'She loves me!' Off comes an arm. 'She loves me not.' A leg joins the little heap of limbs on the ground. That is how it would be. And what would you have left out of it? Merely, as I say, the momentary pleasure of potting me. And it isn't as if such a feat could give you the thrill of successful marksmanship. Anybody could hit a man with a pistol at an inch and a quarter. I fear you have not thought this matter out with sufficient care, Comrade Parker. You said to yourself, 'Happy thought, I will kidnap Psmith!' and all your friends said, 'Parker is the man with the big brain!' But now, while it is true that I can't get out, you are moaning, 'What on earth shall I do with him, now that I have got him?'"

"You think so, do you?"

"I am convinced of it. Your face is contorted with the anguish of mental stress. Let this be a lesson to you, Comrade Parker, never to embark on any enterprise of which you do not see the end."

"I guess I see the end of this all right."

"You have the advantage of me then, Comrade Parker. It seems to me that we have nothing before us but to go on riding about New York till you feel that my society begins to pall."

"You figure you're clever, I guess."

"There are few brighter brains in this city, Comrade Parker. But why this sudden tribute?"

"You reckon you've thought it all out, eh?"

"There may be a flaw in my reasoning, but I confess I do not at the moment see where it lies. Have you detected one?"

"I guess so."

"Ah! And what is it?"

"You seem to think New York's the only place on the map."

"Meaning what, Comrade Parker?"

"It might be a fool trick to shoot you in the city as you say, but, you see, we aren't due to stay in the city. This cab is moving on."

"Like John Brown's soul," said Psmith, nodding. "I see. Then you propose to make quite a little tour in this cab?"

"You've got it."

"And when we are out in the open country, where there are no witnesses, things may begin to move."

"That's it."

"Then," said Psmith heartily, "till that moment arrives what we must do is to entertain each other with conversation. You can take no step of any sort for a full half-hour, possibly more, so let us give ourselves up to the merriment of the passing instant. Are you good at riddles, Comrade Parker? How much wood would a wood-chuck chuck, assuming for purposes of argument that it was in the power of a wood-chuck to chuck wood?"

Mr. Parker did not attempt to solve this problem. He was sitting in the same attitude of watchfulness, the revolver resting on his knee. He seemed mistrustful of Psmith's right hand, which was hanging limply at his side. It was from this quarter that he seemed to expect attack. The cab was bowling easily up the broad street, past rows on rows of high houses, all looking exactly the same. Occasionally, to the right, through a break in the line of buildings, a glimpse of the river could be seen.

Psmith resumed the conversation.

"You are not interested in wood-chucks, Comrade Parker? Well, well, many people are not. A passion for the flora and fauna of our forests is innate rather than acquired. Let us talk of something else. Tell me about your home-life, Comrade Parker. Are you married? Are there any little Parkers running about the house? When you return from this very pleasant excursion will baby voices crow gleefully, 'Fahzer's come home'?"

Mr. Parker said nothing.

"I see," said Psmith with ready sympathy. "I understand. Say no more. You are unmarried. She wouldn't have you. Alas, Comrade Parker! However, thus it is! We look around us, and what do we see? A solid phalanx of the girls we have loved and lost. Tell me about her, Comrade Parker. Was it your face or your manners at which she drew the line?"

Mr. Parker leaned forward with a scowl. Psmith did not move, but his right hand, as it hung, closed. Another moment and Mr. Parker's chin would be in just the right position for a swift upper-cut...

This fact appeared suddenly to dawn on Mr. Parker himself. He drew back quickly, and half raised the revolver. Psmith's hand resumed its normal attitude.

"Leaving more painful topics," said Psmith, "let us turn to another point. That note which the grubby stripling brought to me at the office purported to come from Comrade Windsor, and stated that he had escaped from Blackwell's Island, and was awaiting my arrival at some address in the Bowery. Would you mind telling me, purely to satisfy my curiosity, if that note was genuine? I have never made a close study of Comrade Windsor's handwriting, and in an unguarded moment I may have assumed too much."

Mr. Parker permitted himself a smile.

"I guess you aren't so clever after all," he said. "The note was a fake all right."

"And you had this cab waiting for me on the chance?"

Mr. Parker nodded.

"Sherlock Holmes was right," said Psmith regretfully. "You may remember that he advised Doctor Watson never to take the first cab, or the second. He should have gone further, and urged him not to take cabs at all. Walking is far healthier."

"You'll find it so," said Mr. Parker.

Psmith eyed him curiously.

"What *are* you going to do with me, Comrade Parker?" he asked.

Mr. Parker did not reply. Psmith's eye turned again to the window. They had covered much ground since last he had looked at the view. They were off Manhattan Island now, and the houses were beginning to thin out. Soon, travelling at their present rate, they must come into the open country. Psmith relapsed into silence. It was necessary for him to think. He had been talking in the hope of getting the other off his guard; but Mr. Parker was evidently too keenly on the look-out. The hand that held the revolver never wavered. The muzzle, pointing in an upward direction, was aimed at Psmith's waist. There was no doubt that a move on his part would be fatal. If the pistol went off, it must hit him. If it had been pointed at his head in the orthodox way he might have risked a sudden blow to knock it aside, but in the present circumstances that would be useless. There was nothing to do but wait.

The cab moved swiftly on. Now they had reached the open country. An occasional wooden shack was passed, but that was all. At any moment the climax of the drama might be reached. Psmith's muscles stiffened for a spring. There was little chance of its being effective, but at least it would be better to put up some kind of a fight. And he had a faint hope that the suddenness of his movement might upset the other's aim. He was bound to be hit somewhere. That was certain. But quickness might save him to some extent.

He braced his leg against the back of the cab. In another moment he would have sprung; but just then the smooth speed of the cab changed to a series of jarring bumps, each more emphatic than the last. It slowed down, then came to a halt. One of the tyres had burst.

There was a thud, as the chauffeur jumped down. They heard him fumbling in the tool-box. Presently the body of the machine was raised slightly as he got to work with the jack.

It was about a minute later that somebody in the road outside spoke.

"Had a breakdown?" inquired the voice. Psmith recognised it. It was the voice of Kid Brady.

CHAPTER XXVII

PSMITH CONCLUDES HIS RIDE

The Kid, as he had stated to Psmith at their last interview that he intended to do, had begun his training for his match with Eddie Wood, at White Plains, a village distant but a few miles from New York. It was his practice to open a course of training with a little gentle road-work; and it was while jogging along the highway a couple of miles from his training-camp, in company with the two thick-necked gentlemen who acted as his sparring-partners, that he had come upon the broken-down taxi-cab.

If this had happened after his training had begun in real earnest, he would have averted his eyes from the spectacle, however alluring, and continued on his way without a pause. But now, as he had not yet settled down to genuine hard work, he felt justified in turning aside and looking into the matter. The fact that the chauffeur, who seemed to be a taciturn man, lacking the conversational graces, manifestly objected to an audience, deterred him not at all. One cannot have everything in this world, and the Kid and his attendant thick-necks were content to watch the process of mending the tyre, without demanding the additional joy of sparkling small-talk from the man in charge of the operations.

"Guy's had a breakdown, sure," said the first of the thick-necks.

"Surest thing you know," agreed his colleague.

"Seems to me the tyre's punctured," said the Kid.

All three concentrated their gaze on the machine

"Kid's right," said thick-neck number one. "Guy's been an' bust a tyre."

"Surest thing you know," said thick-neck number two.

They observed the perspiring chauffeur in silence for a while.

"Wonder how he did that, now?" speculated the Kid.

"Guy ran over a nail, I guess," said thick-neck number one.

"Surest thing you know," said the other, who, while perhaps somewhat lacking in the matter of original thought, was a most useful fellow to have by one. A sort of Boswell.

"Did you run over a nail?" the Kid inquired of the chauffeur.

The chauffeur ignored the question.

"This is his busy day," said the first thick-neck with satire. "Guy's too full of work to talk to us."

"Deaf, shouldn't wonder," surmised the Kid.

"Say, wonder what he's doin' with a taxi so far out of the city."

"Some guy tells him to drive him out here, I guess. Say, it'll cost him something, too. He'll have to strip off a few from his roll to pay for this."

Psmith, in the interior of the cab, glanced at Mr. Parker.

"You heard, Comrade Parker? He is right, I fancy. The bill—"

Mr. Parker dug viciously at him with the revolver.

"Keep quiet," he whispered, "or you'll get hurt."

Psmith suspended his remarks.

Outside, the conversation had begun again.

"Pretty rich guy inside," said the Kid, following up his companion's train of thought. "I'm goin' to rubber in at the window."

Psmith, meeting Mr. Parker's eye, smiled pleasantly. There was no answering smile on the other's face.

There came the sound of the Kid's feet grating on the road as he turned; and as he heard it Mr. Parker, that eminent tactician, for the first time lost his head. With a vague idea of screening Psmith from the eyes of the man in the road he half rose. For an instant the muzzle of the pistol ceased to point at Psmith's waistcoat. It was the very chance Psmith had been waiting for. His left hand shot out, grasped the other's wrist, and gave it a sharp wrench. The revolver went off with a deafening report, the bullet passing through the back of the cab; then fell to the floor, as the fingers lost their hold. The next moment Psmith's right fist, darting upwards, took Mr. Parker neatly under the angle of the jaw.

The effect was instantaneous. Psmith had risen from his seat as he delivered the blow, and it consequently got the full benefit of his weight, which was not small. Mr. Parker literally crumpled up. His head jerked back, then fell limply on his chest. He would have slipped to the floor had not Psmith pushed him on to the seat.

The interested face of the Kid appeared at the window. Behind him could be seen portions of the faces of the two thick-necks.

"Ah, Comrade Brady!" said Psmith genially. "I heard your voice, and was hoping you might look in for a chat."

"What's doin', Mr. Smith?" queried the excited Kid.

"Much, Comrade Brady, much. I will tell you all anon. Meanwhile, however, kindly knock that chauffeur down and sit on his head. He's a bad person."

"De guy's beat it," volunteered the first thick-neck.

"Surest thing you know," said the other.

"What's been doin', Mr. Smith?" asked the Kid.

"I'll tell you about it as we go, Comrade Brady," said Psmith, stepping into the road. "Riding in a taxi is pleasant provided it is not overdone. For the moment I have had sufficient. A bit of walking will do me good."

"What are you going to do with this guy, Mr. Smith?" asked the Kid, pointing to Parker, who had begun to stir slightly.

Psmith inspected the stricken one gravely.

"I have no use for him, Comrade Brady," he said. "Our ride together gave me as much of his society as I desire for to-day. Unless you or either of your friends are collecting Parkers, I propose that we leave him where he is. We may as well take the gun, however. In my opinion, Comrade Parker is not the proper man to have such a weapon. He is too prone to go firing it off in any direction at a moment's notice, causing inconvenience to all." He groped on the floor of the cab for the revolver. "Now, Comrade Brady," he said, straightening himself up, "I am at your disposal. Shall we be pushing on?"

* * * * *

It was late in the evening when Psmith returned to the metropolis, after a pleasant afternoon at the Brady training-camp. The Kid, having heard the details of the ride, offered once more to abandon his match with Eddie Wood, but Psmith would not hear of it. He was fairly satisfied that the opposition had fired their last shot, and that their next move would be to endeavour to come to terms. They could not hope to catch him off his guard a second time, and, as far as hired assault and battery were concerned, he was as safe in New York, now that Bat Jarvis had declared himself on his side, as he would have been in the middle of a desert. What Bat said was law on the East Side. No hooligan, however eager to make money, would dare to act against a *protégé* of the Groome Street leader.

The only flaw in Psmith's contentment was the absence of Billy Windsor. On this night of all nights the editorial staff of *Cosy Moments* should have been together to celebrate the successful outcome of their campaign. Psmith dined alone, his enjoyment of the rather special dinner which he felt justified in ordering in honour of the occasion somewhat diminished by the thought of Billy's hard case. He had seen Mr William Collier in *The Man from Mexico*, and that had given him an understanding of what a term of imprisonment on Blackwell's Island meant. Billy, during these lean days, must be supporting life on bread, bean soup, and water. Psmith, toying with the hors d'oeuvre, was somewhat saddened by the thought.

* * * * *

All was quiet at the office on the following day. Bat Jarvis, again accompanied by the faithful Otto, took up his position in the inner room, prepared to repel all invaders; but none arrived. No sounds broke the peace of the outer office except the whistling of Master Maloney.

Things were almost dull when the telephone bell rang. Psmith took down the receiver.

"Hullo?" he said.

"I'm Parker," said a moody voice.

Psmith uttered a cry of welcome.

"Why, Comrade Parker, this is splendid! How goes it? Did you get back all right yesterday? I was sorry to have to tear myself away, but I had other engagements. But why use the telephone? Why not come here in person? You know how welcome you are. Hire a taxi-cab and come right round."

Mr. Parker made no reply to the invitation.

"Mr. Waring would like to see you."

"Who, Comrade Parker?"

"Mr. Stewart Waring."

"The celebrated tenement house-owner?"

Silence from the other end of the wire. "Well," said Psmith, "what step does he propose to take towards it?"

"He tells me to say that he will be in his office at twelve o'clock to-morrow morning. His office is in the Morton Building, Nassau Street."

Psmith clicked his tongue regretfully.

"Then I do not see how we can meet," he said. "I shall be here."

"He wishes to see you at his office."

"I am sorry, Comrade Parker. It is impossible. I am very busy just now, as you may know, preparing the next number, the one in which we publish the name of the owner of the Pleasant Street Tenements. Otherwise, I should be delighted. Perhaps later, when the rush of work has diminished somewhat."

"Am I to tell Mr. Waring that you refuse?"

"If you are seeing him at any time and feel at a loss for something to say, perhaps you might mention it. Is there anything else I can do for you, Comrade Parker?"

"See here —"

"Nothing? Then good-bye. Look in when you're this way."

He hung up the receiver.

As he did so, he was aware of Master Maloney standing beside the table.

"Yes, Comrade Maloney?"

"Telegram," said Pugsy. "For Mr. Windsor."

Psmith ripped open the envelope.

The message ran:

"Returning to-day. Will be at office to-morrow morning," and it was signed "Wilberfloss."

"See who's here!" said Psmith softly.

CHAPTER XXVIII

STANDING ROOM ONLY

In the light of subsequent events it was perhaps the least bit unfortunate that Mr. Jarvis should have seen fit to bring with him to the office of *Cosy Moments* on the following morning two of his celebrated squad of cats, and that Long Otto, who, as usual, accompanied him, should have been fired by his example to the extent of introducing a large and rather boisterous yellow dog. They were not to be blamed, of course. They could not know that before the morning was over space in the office would be at a premium. Still, it was unfortunate.

Mr. Jarvis was slightly apologetic.

"T'ought I'd bring de kits along," he said. "Dey started in scrappin' yesterday when I was here, so to-day I says I'll keep my eye on dem."

Psmith inspected the menagerie without resentment.

"Assuredly, Comrade Jarvis," he said. "They add a pleasantly cosy and domestic touch to the scene. The only possible criticism I can find to make has to do with their probable brawling with the dog."

"Oh, dey won't scrap wit de dawg. Dey knows him."

"But is he aware of that? He looks to me a somewhat impulsive animal. Well, well, the matter's in your hands. If you will undertake to look after the refereeing of any pogrom that may arise, I say no more."

Mr. Jarvis's statement as to the friendly relations between the animals proved to be correct. The dog made no attempt to annihilate the cats. After an inquisitive journey round the room he lay down and went to sleep, and an era of peace set in. The cats had settled themselves comfortably, one on each of Mr. Jarvis's knees, and Long Otto, surveying the ceiling with his customary glassy stare, smoked a long cigar in silence. Bat breathed a tune, and scratched one of the cats under the ear. It was a soothing scene.

But it did not last. Ten minutes had barely elapsed when the yellow dog, sitting up with a start, uttered a whine. In the outer office could be heard a stir and movement. The next moment the door burst open and a little man dashed in. He had a peeled nose and showed other evidences of having been living in the open air. Behind him was a crowd of uncertain numbers. Psmith recognised the leaders of this crowd. They were the Reverend Edwin T. Philpotts and Mr. B. Henderson Asher.

"Why, Comrade Asher," he said, "this is indeed a Moment of Mirth. I have been wondering for weeks where you could have got to. And Comrade Philpotts! Am I wrong in saying that this is the maddest, merriest day of all the glad New Year?"

The rest of the crowd had entered the room.

"Comrade Waterman, too!" cried Psmith. "Why we have all met before. Except—"

He glanced inquiringly at the little man with the peeled nose.

"My name is Wilberfloss," said the other with austerity. "Will you be so good as to tell me where Mr. Windsor is?"

A murmur of approval from his followers.

"In one moment," said Psmith. "First, however, let me introduce two important members of our staff. On your right, Mr. Bat Jarvis. On your left, Mr. Long Otto. Both of Groome Street."

The two Bowery boys rose awkwardly. The cats fell in an avalanche to the floor. Long Otto, in his haste, trod on the dog, which began barking, a process which it kept up almost without a pause during the rest of the interview.

"Mr. Wilberfloss," said Psmith in an aside to Bat, "is widely known as a cat fancier in Brooklyn circles."

"Honest?" said Mr. Jarvis. He tapped Mr. Wilberfloss in friendly fashion on the chest. "Say," he asked, "did youse ever have a cat wit one blue and one yellow eye?"

Mr. Wilberfloss side-stepped and turned once more to Psmith, who was offering B. Henderson Asher a cigarette.

"Who are you?" he demanded.

"Who am *I*?" repeated Psmith in an astonished tone.

"Who are you?"

"I am Psmith," said the old Etonian reverently. "There is a preliminary P before the name. This, however, is silent. Like the tomb. Compare such words as ptarmigan, psalm, and phthisis."

"These gentlemen tell me you're acting editor. Who appointed you?"

Psmith reflected.

"It is rather a nice point," he said. "It might be claimed that I appointed myself. You may say, however, that Comrade Windsor appointed me."

"Ah! And where is Mr. Windsor?"

"In prison," said Psmith sorrowfully.

"In prison!"

Psmith nodded.

"It is too true. Such is the generous impulsiveness of Comrade Windsor's nature that he hit a policeman, was promptly gathered in, and is now serving a sentence of thirty days on Blackwell's Island."

Mr. Wilberfloss looked at Mr. Philpotts. Mr. Asher looked at Mr. Wilberfloss. Mr. Waterman started, and stumbled over a cat.

"I never heard of such a thing," said Mr. Wilberfloss.

A faint, sad smile played across Psmith's face.

"Do you remember, Comrade Waterman—I fancy it was to you that I made the remark—my commenting at our previous interview on the rashness of confusing the unusual with the improbable? Here we see Comrade Wilberfloss, big-brained though he is, falling into error."

"I shall dismiss Mr. Windsor immediately," said the big-brained one.

"From Blackwell's Island?" said Psmith. "I am sure you will earn his gratitude if you do. They live on bean soup there. Bean soup and bread, and not much of either."

He broke off, to turn his attention to Mr. Jarvis and Mr. Waterman, between whom bad blood seemed to have arisen. Mr. Jarvis, holding a cat in his arms, was glowering at Mr. Waterman, who had backed away and seemed nervous.

"What is the trouble, Comrade Jarvis?"

"Dat guy dere wit two left feet," said Bat querulously, "goes and treads on de kit. I—"

"I assure you it was a pure accident. The animal—"

Mr. Wilberfloss, eyeing Bat and the silent Otto with disgust, intervened.

"Who are these persons, Mr. Smith?" he inquired.

"Poisson yourself," rejoined Bat, justly incensed. "Who's de little guy wit de peeled breezer, Mr. Smith?"

Psmith waved his hands.

"Gentlemen, gentlemen," he said, "let us not descend to mere personalities. I thought I had introduced you. This, Comrade Jarvis, is Mr. Wilberfloss, the editor of this journal. These, Comrade Wilberfloss-Zam-buk would put your nose right in a day-are, respectively, Bat Jarvis and Long Otto, our acting fighting-editors, vice Kid Brady, absent on unavoidable business."

"Kid Brady!" shrilled Mr. Wilberfloss. "I insist that you give me a full explanation of this matter. I go away by my doctor's orders for ten weeks, leaving Mr. Windsor to conduct the paper on certain well-defined lines. I return yesterday, and, getting into communication with Mr. Philpotts, what do I find? Why, that in my absence the paper has been ruined."

"Ruined?" said Psmith. "On the contrary. Examine the returns, and you will see that the circulation has gone up every week. *Cosy Moments* was never so prosperous and flourishing.

Comrade Otto, do you think you could use your personal influence with that dog to induce it to suspend its barking for a while? It is musical, but renders conversation difficult."

Long Otto raised a massive boot and aimed it at the animal, which, dodging with a yelp, cannoned against the second cat and had its nose scratched. Piercing shrieks cleft the air.

"I demand an explanation," roared Mr. Wilberfloss above the din.

"I think, Comrade Otto," said Psmith, "it would make things a little easier if you removed that dog."

He opened the door. The dog shot out. They could hear it being ejected from the outer office by Master Maloney. When there was silence, Psmith turned courteously to the editor.

"You were saying, Comrade Wilberfloss?"

"Who is this person Brady? With Mr. Philpotts I have been going carefully over the numbers which have been issued since my departure —"

"An intellectual treat," murmured Psmith.

"—and in each there is a picture of this young man in a costume which I will not particularise —"

"There is hardly enough of it to particularise."

"—together with a page of disgusting autobiographical matter."

Psmith held up his hand.

"I protest," he said. "We court criticism, but this is mere abuse. I appeal to these gentlemen to say whether this, for instance, is not bright and interesting."

He picked up the current number of *Cosy Moments*, and turned to the Kid's page.

"This," he said. "Describing a certain ten-round unpleasantness with one Mexican Joe. 'Joe comes up for the second round and he gives me a nasty look, but I thinks of my mother and swats him one in the lower ribs. He hollers foul, but nix on that. Referee says, "Fight on." Joe gives me another nasty look. "All right, Kid," he says; "now I'll knock you up into the gallery." And with that he cuts loose with a right swing, but I falls into the clinch, and then —-!' "

"Bah!" exclaimed Mr. Wilberfloss.

"Go on, boss," urged Mr. Jarvis approvingly. "It's to de good, dat stuff."

"There!" said Psmith triumphantly. "You heard? Comrade Jarvis, one of the most firmly established critics east of Fifth Avenue, stamps Kid Brady's reminiscences with the hall-mark of his approval."

"I falls fer de Kid every time," assented Mr. Jarvis.

"Assuredly, Comrade Jarvis. You know a good thing when you see one. Why," he went on warmly, "there is stuff in these reminiscences which would stir the blood of a jelly-fish. Let me quote you another passage to show that they are not only enthralling, but helpful as well. Let me see, where is it? Ah, I have it. 'A bully good way of putting a guy out of business is this. You don't want to use it in the ring, because by Queensberry Rules it's a foul; but you will find it mighty useful if any thick-neck comes up to you in the street and tries to start anything. It's this way. While he's setting himself for a punch, just place the tips of the fingers of your left hand on the right side of his chest. Then bring down the heel of your left hand. There isn't a guy living that could stand up against that. The fingers give you a leverage to beat the band. The guy doubles up, and you upper-cut him with your right, and out he goes.' Now, I bet you never knew that before, Comrade Philpotts. Try it on your parishioners."

"*Cosy Moments*," said Mr. Wilberfloss irately, "is no medium for exploiting low prize-fighters."

"Low prize-fighters! Comrade Wilberfloss, you have been misinformed. The Kid is as decent a little chap as you'd meet anywhere. You do not seem to appreciate the philanthropic motives of the paper in adopting Comrade Brady's cause. Think of it, Comrade Wilberfloss. There was that unfortunate stripling with only two pleasures in life, to love his mother and to knock the heads off other youths whose weight coincided with his own; and misfortune, until we took him up, had barred him almost completely from the second pastime. Our editorial heart was melted. We adopted Comrade Brady. And look at him now! Matched against Eddie Wood! And Comrade Waterman will support me in my statement that a victory over Eddie Wood means that he gets a legitimate claim to meet Jimmy Garvin for the championship."

"It is abominable," burst forth Mr. Wilberfloss. "It is disgraceful. I never heard of such a thing. The paper is ruined."

"You keep reverting to that statement, Comrade Wilberfloss. Can nothing reassure you? The returns are excellent. Prosperity beams on us like a sun. The proprietor is more than satisfied."

"The proprietor?" gasped Mr. Wilberfloss. "Does *he* know how you have treated the paper?"

"He is cognisant of our every move."

"And he approves?"

"He more than approves."

Mr. Wilberfloss snorted.

"I don't believe it," he said.

The assembled ex-contributors backed up this statement with a united murmur. B. Henderson Asher snorted satirically.

"They don't believe it," sighed Psmith. "Nevertheless, it is true."

"It is not true," thundered Mr. Wilberfloss, hopping to avoid a perambulating cat. "Nothing will convince me of it. Mr. Benjamin White is not a maniac."

"I trust not," said Psmith. "I sincerely trust not. I have every reason to believe in his complete sanity. What makes you fancy that there is even a possibility of his being-er —?"

"Nobody but a lunatic would approve of seeing his paper ruined."

"Again!" said Psmith. "I fear that the notion that this journal is ruined has become an obsession with you, Comrade Wilberfloss. Once again I assure you that it is more than prosperous."

"If," said Mr. Wilberfloss, "you imagine that I intend to take your word in this matter, you are mistaken. I shall cable Mr. White to-day, and inquire whether these alterations in the paper meet with his approval."

"I shouldn't, Comrade Wilberfloss. Cables are expensive, and in these hard times a penny saved is a penny earned. Why worry Comrade White? He is so far away, so out of touch with our New York literary life. I think it is practically a certainty that he has not the slightest inkling of any changes in the paper."

Mr. Wilberfloss uttered a cry of triumph.

"I knew it," he said, "I knew it. I knew you would give up when it came to the point, and you were driven into a corner. Now, perhaps, you will admit that Mr. White has given no sanction for the alterations in the paper?"

A puzzled look crept into Psmith's face.

"I think, Comrade Wilberfloss," he said, "we are talking at cross-purposes. You keep harping on Comrade White and his views and tastes. One would almost imagine that you fancied that Comrade White was the proprietor of this paper."

Mr. Wilberfloss stared. B. Henderson Asher stared. Every one stared, except Mr. Jarvis, who, since the readings from the Kid's reminiscences had ceased, had lost interest in the discussion, and was now entertaining the cats with a ball of paper tied to a string.

"Fancied that Mr. White . . .?" repeated Mr. Wilberfloss. "I don't follow you. Who is, if he isn't?"

Psmith removed his monocle, polished it thoughtfully, and put it back in its place.

"I am," he said.

CHAPTER XXIX

THE KNOCK-OUT FOR MR. WARING

"You!" cried Mr. Wilberfloss.

"The same," said Psmith.

"You!" exclaimed Messrs. Waterman, Asher, and the Reverend Edwin Philpotts.

"On the spot!" said Psmith.

Mr. Wilberfloss groped for a chair and sat down.

"Am I going mad?" he demanded feebly.

"Not so, Comrade Wilberfloss," said Psmith encouragingly. "All is well. The cry goes round New York, 'Comrade Wilberfloss is to the good. He does not gibber.'"

"Do I understand you to say that you own this paper?"

"I do."

"Since when?"

"Roughly speaking, about a month."

Among his audience (still excepting Mr. Jarvis, who was tickling one of the cats and whistling a plaintive melody) there was a tendency toward awkward silence. To start bally-ragging a seeming nonentity and then to discover he is the proprietor of the paper to which you wish to contribute is like kicking an apparently empty hat and finding your rich uncle inside it. Mr. Wilberfloss in particular was disturbed. Editorships of the kind which he aspired to are not easy to get. If he were to be removed from *Cosy Moments* he would find it hard to place himself anywhere else. Editors, like manuscripts, are rejected from want of space.

"Very early in my connection with this journal," said Psmith, "I saw that I was on to a good thing. I had long been convinced that about the nearest approach to the perfect job in this world, where good jobs are so hard to acquire, was to own a paper. All you had to do, once you had secured your paper, was to sit back and watch the other fellows work, and from time to time forward big cheques to the bank. Nothing could be more nicely attuned to the tastes of a Shropshire Psmith. The glimpses I was enabled to get of the workings of this little journal gave me the impression that Comrade White was not attached with any paternal fervour to *Cosy Moments*. He regarded it, I deduced, not so much as a life-work as in the light of an investment. I assumed that Comrade White had his price, and wrote to my father, who was visiting Carlsbad at the moment, to ascertain what that price might be. He cabled it to me. It was reasonable. Now it so happens that an uncle of mine some years ago left me a considerable number of simoleons, and though I shall not be legally entitled actually to close in on the opulence for a matter of nine months or so, I anticipated that my father would have no objection to staking me to the necessary amount on the security of my little bit of money. My father has spent some time of late hurling me at various professions, and we had agreed some time ago that the Law was to be my long suit. Paper-owning, however, may be combined with being Lord Chancellor, and I knew he would have no objection to my being a Napoleon of the Press on this side. So we closed with Comrade White, and —"

There was a knock at the door, and Master Maloney entered with a card.

"Guy's waiting outside," he said.

"Mr. Stewart Waring," read Psmith. "Comrade Maloney, do you know what Mahomet did when the mountain would not come to him?"

"Search me," said the office-boy indifferently.

"He went to the mountain. It was a wise thing to do. As a general rule in life you can't beat it. Remember that, Comrade Maloney."

"Sure," said Pugsy. "Shall I send the guy in?"

"Surest thing you know, Comrade Maloney."

He turned to the assembled company.

"Gentlemen," he said, "you know how I hate to have to send you away, but would you mind withdrawing in good order? A somewhat delicate and private interview is in the offing. Comrade Jarvis, we will meet anon. Your services to the paper have been greatly appreciated. If I might drop in some afternoon and inspect the remainder of your zoo —?"

"Any time you're down Groome Street way. Glad."

"I will make a point of it. Comrade Wilberfloss, would you mind remaining? As editor of this journal, you should be present. If the rest of you would look in about this time to-morrow — Show Mr. Waring in, Comrade Maloney."

He took a seat.

"We are now, Comrade Wilberfloss," he said, "at a crisis in the affairs of this journal, but I fancy we shall win through."

The door opened, and Pugsy announced Mr. Waring.

The owner of the Pleasant Street Tenements was of what is usually called commanding presence. He was tall and broad, and more than a little stout. His face was clean-shaven and curiously expressionless. Bushy eyebrows topped a pair of cold grey eyes. He walked into the room with the air of one who is not wont to apologise for existing. There are some men who seem to fill any room in which they may be. Mr. Waring was one of these.

He set his hat down on the table without speaking. After which he looked at Mr. Wilberfloss, who shrank a little beneath his gaze.

Psmith had risen to greet him.

"Won't you sit down?" he said.

"I prefer to stand."

"Just as you wish. This is Liberty Hall."

Mr. Waring again glanced at Mr. Wilberfloss.

"What I have to say is private," he said.

"All is well," said Psmith reassuringly. "It is no stranger that you see before you, no mere irresponsible lounger who has butted in by chance. That is Comrade J. Fillken Wilberfloss, the editor of this journal."

"The editor? I understood —"

"I know what you would say. You have Comrade Windsor in your mind. He was merely acting as editor while the chief was away hunting sand-eels in the jungles of Texas. In his absence Comrade Windsor and I did our best to keep the old journal booming along, but it lacked the master-hand. But now all is well: Comrade Wilberfloss is once more doing stunts at the old stand. You may speak as freely before him as you would before well, let us say Comrade Parker."

"Who are you, then, if this gentleman is the editor?"

"I am the proprietor."

"I understood that a Mr. White was the proprietor."

"Not so," said Psmith. "There was a time when that was the case, but not now. Things move so swiftly in New York journalistic matters that a man may well be excused for not keeping abreast of the times, especially one who, like yourself, is interested in politics and house-ownership rather than in literature. Are you sure you won't sit down?"

Mr. Waring brought his hand down with a bang on the table, causing Mr. Wilberfloss to leap a clear two inches from his chair.

"What are you doing it for?" he demanded explosively. "I tell you, you had better quit it. It isn't healthy."

Psmith shook his head.

"You are merely stating in other-and, if I may say so, inferior-words what Comrade Parker said to us. I did not object to giving up valuable time to listen to Comrade Parker. He is a fascinating conversationalist, and it was a privilege to hob-nob with him. But if you are merely intending to cover the ground covered by him, I fear I must remind you that this is one of our busy days. Have you no new light to fling upon the subject?"

Mr. Waring wiped his forehead. He was playing a lost game, and he was not the sort of man who plays lost games well. The Waring type is dangerous when it is winning, but it is apt to crumple up against strong defence.

His next words proved his demoralisation.

"I'll sue you for libel," said he.

Psmith looked at him admiringly.

"Say no more," he said, "for you will never beat that. For pure richness and whimsical humour it stands alone. During the past seven weeks you have been endeavouring in your cheery fashion to blot the editorial staff of this paper off the face of the earth in a variety of ingenious and entertaining ways; and now you propose to sue us for libel! I wish Comrade Windsor could have heard you say that. It would have hit him right."

Mr. Waring accepted the invitation he had refused before. He sat down.

"What are you going to do?" he said.

It was the white flag. The fight had gone out of him.

Psmith leaned back in his chair.

"I'll tell you," he said. "I've thought the whole thing out. The right plan would be to put the complete kybosh (if I may use the expression) on your chances of becoming an alderman. On the other hand, I have been studying the papers of late, and it seems to me that it doesn't much matter who gets elected. Of course the opposition papers may have allowed their zeal to run away with them, but even assuming that to be the case, the other candidates appear to be a pretty fair contingent of blighters. If I were a native of New York, perhaps I might take a more fervid interest in the matter, but as I am merely passing through your beautiful little city, it doesn't seem to me to make any very substantial difference who gets in. To be absolutely candid, my view of the thing is this. If the People are chumps enough to elect you, then they deserve you. I hope I don't hurt your feelings in any way. I am merely stating my own individual opinion."

Mr. Waring made no remark.

"The only thing that really interests me," resumed Psmith, "is the matter of these tenements. I shall shortly be leaving this country to resume the strangle-hold on Learning which I relinquished at the beginning of the Long Vacation. If I were to depart without bringing off improvements down Pleasant Street way, I shouldn't be able to enjoy my meals. The startled cry would go round Cambridge: 'Something is the matter with Psmith. He is off his feed. He should try Blenkinsop's Balm for the Bilious.' But no balm would do me any good. I should simply droop and fade slowly away like a neglected lily. And you wouldn't like that, Comrade Wilberfloss, would you?"

Mr. Wilberfloss, thus suddenly pulled into the conversation, again leaped in his seat.

"What I propose to do," continued Psmith, without waiting for an answer, "is to touch you for the good round sum of five thousand and three dollars."

Mr. Waring half rose.

"Five thousand dollars!"

"Five thousand and three dollars," said Psmith. "It may possibly have escaped your memory, but a certain minion of yours, one J. Repetto, utterly ruined a practically new hat of mine. If you think that I can afford to come to New York and scatter hats about as if they were mere dross, you are making the culminating error of a misspent life. Three dollars are what I need for a new one. The balance of your cheque, the five thousand, I propose to apply to making those tenements fit for a tolerably fastidious pig to live in."

"Five thousand!" cried Mr. Waring. "It's monstrous."

"It isn't," said Psmith. "It's more or less of a minimum. I have made inquiries. So out with the good old cheque-book, and let's all be jolly."

"I have no cheque-book with me."

"*I* have," said Psmith, producing one from a drawer. "Cross out the name of my bank, substitute yours, and fate cannot touch us."

Mr. Waring hesitated for a moment, then capitulated. Psmith watched, as he wrote, with an indulgent and fatherly eye.

"Finished?" he said. "Comrade Maloney."

"Youse hollering fer me?" asked that youth, appearing at the door.

"Bet your life I am, Comrade Maloney. Have you ever seen an untamed mustang of the prairie?"

"Nope. But I've read about dem."

"Well, run like one down to Wall Street with this cheque, and pay it in to my account at the International Bank."

Pugsy disappeared.

"Cheques," said Psmith, "have been known to be stopped. Who knows but what, on reflection, you might not have changed your mind?"

"What guarantee have I," asked Mr. Waring, "that these attacks on me in your paper will stop?"

"If you like," said Psmith, "I will write you a note to that effect. But it will not be necessary. I propose, with Comrade Wilberfloss's assistance, to restore *Cosy Moments* to its old style. Some days ago the editor of Comrade Windsor's late daily paper called up on the telephone and asked to speak to him. I explained the painful circumstances, and, later, went round and hob-nobbed with the great man. A very pleasant fellow. He asks to re-engage Comrade Windsor's services at a pretty sizeable salary, so, as far as our prison expert is concerned, all may be said to be well. He has got where he wanted. *Cosy Moments* may therefore ease up a bit. If, at about the beginning of next month, you should hear a deafening squeal of joy ring through this city, it will be the infants of New York and their parents receiving the news that *Cosy Moments* stands where it did. May I count on your services, Comrade Wilberfloss? Excellent. I see I may. Then perhaps you would not mind passing the word round among Comrades Asher, Waterman, and the rest of the squad, and telling them to burnish their brains and be ready to wade in at a moment's notice. I fear you will have a pretty tough job roping in the old subscribers again, but it can be done. I look to you, Comrade Wilberfloss. Are you on?"

Mr. Wilberfloss, wriggling in his chair, intimated that he was.

CONCLUSION

IT was a drizzly November evening. The streets of Cambridge were a compound of mud, mist, and melancholy. But in Psmith's rooms the fire burned brightly, the kettle droned, and all, as the proprietor had just observed, was joy, jollity, and song. Psmith, in pyjamas and a college blazer, was lying on the sofa. Mike, who had been playing football, was reclining in a comatose state in an arm-chair by the fire.

"How pleasant it would be," said Psmith dreamily, "if all our friends on the other side of the Atlantic could share this very peaceful moment with us! Or perhaps not quite all. Let us say, Comrade Windsor in the chair over there, Comrades Brady and Maloney on the table, and our old pal Wilberfloss sharing the floor with B. Henderson Asher, Bat Jarvis, and the cats. By the way, I think it would be a graceful act if you were to write to Comrade Jarvis from time to time telling him how your Angoras are getting on. He regards you as the World's Most Prominent Citizen. A line from you every now and then would sweeten the lad's existence."

Mike stirred sleepily in his chair.

"What?" he said drowsily.

"Never mind, Comrade Jackson. Let us pass lightly on. I am filled with a strange content to-night. I may be wrong, but it seems to me that all is singularly to de good, as Comrade Maloney would put it. Advices from Comrade Windsor inform me that that prince of blighters, Waring, was rejected by an intelligent electorate. Those keen, clear-sighted citizens refused to vote for him to an extent that you could notice without a microscope. Still, he has one consolation. He owns what, when the improvements are completed, will be the finest and most commodious tenement houses in New York. Millionaires will stop at them instead of going to the Plaza. Are you asleep, Comrade Jackson?"

"Um-m," said Mike.

"That is excellent. You could not be better employed. Keep listening. Comrade Windsor also stated-as indeed did the sporting papers-that Comrade Brady put it all over friend Eddie Wood, administering the sleep-producer in the eighth round. My authorities are silent as to whether or not the lethal blow was a half-scissor hook, but I presume such to have been the case. The Kid is now definitely matched against Comrade Garvin for the championship, and the experts seem to think that he should win. He is a stout fellow, is Comrade Brady, and I hope he wins through. He will probably come to England later on. When he does, we must show him round. I don't think you ever met him, did you, Comrade Jackson?"

"Ur-r," said Mike.

"Say no more," said Psmith. "I take you."

He reached out for a cigarette.

"These," he said, comfortably, "are the moments in life to which we look back with that wistful pleasure. What of my boyhood at Eton? Do I remember with the keenest joy the brain-tourneys in the old form-room, and the bally rot which used to take place on the Fourth of June? No. Burned deeply into my memory is a certain hot bath I took after one of the foulest cross-country runs that ever occurred outside Dante's Inferno. So with the present moment. This peaceful scene, Comrade Jackson, will remain with me when I have forgotten that such a person as Comrade Repetto ever existed. These are the real *Cosy Moments*. And while on that subject you will be glad to hear that the little sheet is going strong. The man Wilberfloss is a marvel in his way. He appears to have gathered in the majority of the old subscribers again. Hopping mad but a brief while ago, they now eat out of his hand. You've really no notion what a feeling of quiet pride it gives you owning a paper. I try not to show it, but I seem to myself to be looking down on the world from some lofty peak. Yesterday night, when I was looking down from the peak without a cap and gown, a proctor slid up. To-day I had to dig down into my jeans for a matter of two plunks. But what of it? Life must inevitably be dotted with these minor tragedies. I do not repine. The whisper goes round, 'Psmith bites the bullet, and wears a brave smile.' Comrade Jackson —"

A snore came from the chair.

Psmith sighed. But he did not repine. He bit the bullet. His eyes closed.

Five minutes later a slight snore came from the sofa, too.

The man behind *Cosy Moments* slept.

CPSIA information can be obtained
at www.ICGtesting.com
Printed in the USA
BVHW032250161122
652180BV00011B/83